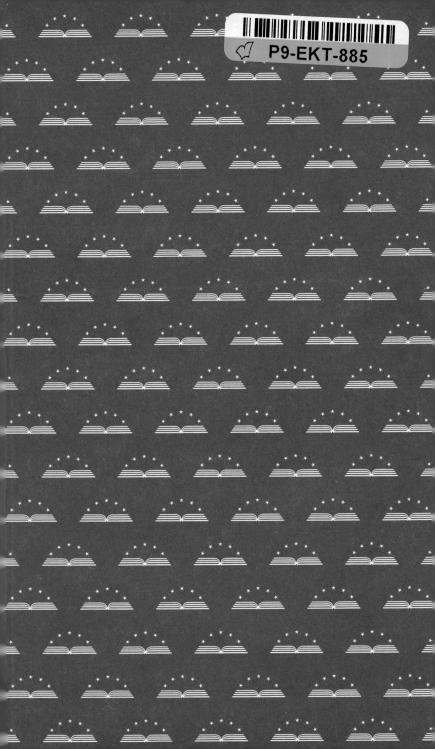

SHERWOOD ANDERSON

SHERWOOD ANDERSON

COLLECTED STORIES

Charles Baxter, *editor*

THE LIBRARY OF AMERICA

The paper used in this publication meets the
minimum requirements of the American National Standard for
Information Sciences—Permanence of Paper for Printed
Library Materials, ANSI Z39.48—1984.

Distributed to the trade in the United States
by Penguin Group (USA) Inc.
and in Canada by Penguin Books Canada Ltd.

Library of Congress Control Number: 2012935174
ISBN 978-1-59853-204-3

———

First Printing
The Library of America—235

Manufactured in the United States of America

Contents

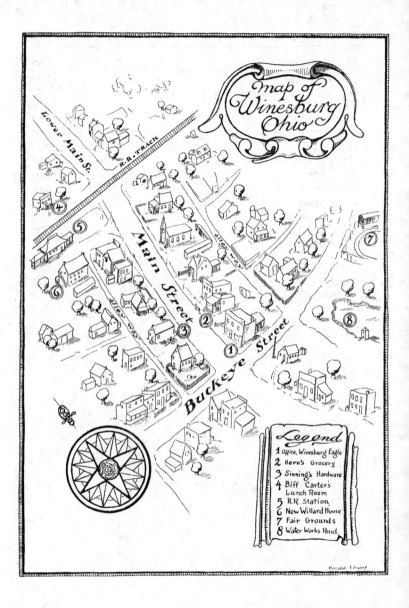

Map of
Winesburg
Ohio

Lower Main St.

R.R. Track

Main Street

Buckeye Street

Legend
1 Office, Winesburg Eagle
2 Hern's Grocery
3 Sinning's Hardware
4 Biff Carter's Lunch Room
5 R.R. Station
6 New Willard House
7 Fair Grounds
8 Water Works Pond

WINESBURG, OHIO

A GROUP OF TALES OF
OHIO SMALL TOWN LIFE

THE TALES AND THE PERSONS

The Book of the Grotesque

THE writer, an old man with a white mustache, had some difficulty in getting into bed. The windows of the house in which he lived were high and he wanted to look at the trees when he awoke in the morning. A carpenter came to fix the bed so that it would be on a level with the window.

Quite a fuss was made about the matter. The carpenter, who had been a soldier in the Civil War, came into the writer's room and sat down to talk of building a platform for the purpose of raising the bed. The writer had cigars lying about and the carpenter smoked.

For a time the two men talked of the raising of the bed and then they talked of other things. The soldier got on the subject of the war. The writer, in fact, led him to that subject. The carpenter had once been a prisoner in Andersonville prison and had lost a brother. The brother had died of starvation, and whenever the carpenter got upon that subject he cried. He, like the old writer, had a white mustache, and when he cried he puckered up his lips and the mustache bobbed up and down. The weeping old man with the cigar in his mouth was ludicrous. The plan the writer had for the raising of his bed was forgotten and later the carpenter did it in his own way and the writer, who was past sixty, had to help himself with a chair when he went to bed at night.

In his bed the writer rolled over on his side and lay quite still. For years he had been beset with notions concerning his heart. He was a hard smoker and his heart fluttered. The idea had got into his mind that he would some time die unexpectedly and always when he got into bed he thought of that. It did not alarm him. The effect in fact was quite a special thing and not easily explained. It made him more alive, there in bed, than at any other time. Perfectly still he lay and his body was old and not of much use any more, but something inside him was altogether young. He was like a pregnant woman, only that the thing inside him was not a baby but a youth. No, it wasn't a youth, it was a woman, young, and wearing a coat of mail like a knight. It is absurd, you see, to try to tell what was inside the

old writer as he lay on his high bed and listened to the fluttering of his heart. The thing to get at is what the writer, or the
young thing within the writer, was thinking about.

The old writer, like all of the people in the world, had got,
during his long life, a great many notions in his head. He had
once been quite handsome and a number of women had been
in love with him. And then, of course, he had known people,
many people, known them in a peculiarly intimate way that
was different from the way in which you and I know people. At
least that is what the writer thought and the thought pleased
him. Why quarrel with an old man concerning his thoughts?

In the bed the writer had a dream that was not a dream. As
he grew somewhat sleepy but was still conscious, figures began
to appear before his eyes. He imagined the young indescribable thing within himself was driving a long procession of figures before his eyes.

You see the interest in all this lies in the figures that went
before the eyes of the writer. They were all grotesques. All of
the men and women the writer had ever known had become
grotesques.

The grotesques were not all horrible. Some were amusing,
some almost beautiful, and one, a woman all drawn out of
shape, hurt the old man by her grotesqueness. When she passed
he made a noise like a small dog whimpering. Had you come
into the room you might have supposed the old man had unpleasant dreams or perhaps indigestion.

For an hour the procession of grotesques passed before the
eyes of the old man, and then, although it was a painful thing
to do, he crept out of bed and began to write. Some one of the
grotesques had made a deep impression on his mind and he
wanted to describe it.

At his desk the writer worked for an hour. In the end he
wrote a book which he called "The Book of the Grotesque." It
was never published, but I saw it once and it made an indelible
impression on my mind. The book had one central thought
that is very strange and has always remained with me. By remembering it I have been able to understand many people and
things that I was never able to understand before. The thought
was involved but a simple statement of it would be something
like this:

That in the beginning when the world was young there were a great many thoughts but no such thing as a truth. Man made the truths himself and each truth was a composite of a great many vague thoughts. All about in the world were the truths and they were all beautiful.

The old man had listed hundreds of the truths in his book. I will not try to tell you of all of them. There was the truth of virginity and the truth of passion, the truth of wealth and of poverty, of thrift and of profligacy, of carefulness and abandon. Hundreds and hundreds were the truths and they were all beautiful.

And then the people came along. Each as he appeared snatched up one of the truths and some who were quite strong snatched up a dozen of them.

It was the truths that made the people grotesques. The old man had quite an elaborate theory concerning the matter. It was his notion that the moment one of the people took one of the truths to himself, called it his truth, and tried to live his life by it, he became a grotesque and the truth he embraced became a falsehood.

You can see for yourself how the old man, who had spent all of his life writing and was filled with words, would write hundreds of pages concerning this matter. The subject would become so big in his mind that he himself would be in danger of becoming a grotesque. He didn't, I suppose, for the same reason that he never published the book. It was the young thing inside him that saved the old man.

Concerning the old carpenter who fixed the bed for the writer, I only mentioned him because he, like many of what are called very common people, became the nearest thing to what is understandable and lovable of all the grotesques in the writer's book.

WINESBURG, OHIO

Hands

UPON the half decayed veranda of a small frame house that stood near the edge of a ravine near the town of Winesburg, Ohio, a fat little old man walked nervously up and down. Across a long field that had been seeded for clover but that had produced only a dense crop of yellow mustard weeds, he could see the public highway along which went a wagon filled with berry pickers returning from the fields. The berry pickers, youths and maidens, laughed and shouted boisterously. A boy clad in a blue shirt leaped from the wagon and attempted to drag after him one of the maidens who screamed and protested shrilly. The feet of the boy in the road kicked up a cloud of dust that floated across the face of the departing sun. Over the long field came a thin girlish voice. "Oh, you Wing Biddlebaum, comb your hair, it's falling into your eyes," commanded the voice to the man, who was bald and whose nervous little hands fiddled about the bare white forehead as though arranging a mass of tangled locks.

Wing Biddlebaum, forever frightened and beset by a ghostly band of doubts, did not think of himself as in any way a part of the life of the town where he had lived for twenty years. Among all the people of Winesburg but one had come close to him. With George Willard, son of Tom Willard, the proprietor of the new Willard House, he had formed something like a friendship. George Willard was the reporter on the *Winesburg Eagle* and sometimes in the evenings he walked out along the highway to Wing Biddlebaum's house. Now as the old man walked up and down on the veranda, his hands moving nervously about, he was hoping that George Willard would come and spend the evening with him. After the wagon containing the berry pickers had passed, he went across the field through the tall mustard weeds and climbing a rail fence peered anxiously along the road to the town. For a moment he stood thus, rubbing his hands together and looking up and down the

9

road, and then, fear overcoming him, ran back to walk again
upon the porch on his own house.

In the presence of George Willard, Wing Biddlebaum, who
for twenty years had been the town mystery, lost something of
his timidity, and his shadowy personality, submerged in a sea of
doubts, came forth to look at the world. With the young reporter at his side, he ventured in the light of day into Main
Street or strode up and down on the rickety front porch of his
own house, talking excitedly. The voice that had been low and
trembling became shrill and loud. The bent figure straightened. With a kind of wriggle, like a fish returned to the brook
by the fisherman, Biddlebaum the silent began to talk, striving
to put into words the ideas that had been accumulated by his
mind during long years of silence.

Wing Biddlebaum talked much with his hands. The slender
expressive fingers, forever active, forever striving to conceal
themselves in his pockets or behind his back, came forth and
became the piston rods of his machinery of expression.

The story of Wing Biddlebaum is a story of hands. Their
restless activity, like unto the beating of the wings of an imprisoned bird, had given him his name. Some obscure poet of the
town had thought of it. The hands alarmed their owner. He
wanted to keep them hidden away and looked with amazement at the quiet inexpressive hands of other men who worked
beside him in the fields, or passed, driving sleepy teams on
country roads.

When he talked to George Willard, Wing Biddlebaum closed
his fists and beat with them upon a table or on the walls of his
house. The action made him more comfortable. If the desire
to talk came to him when the two were walking in the fields,
he sought out a stump or the top board of a fence and with his
hands pounding busily talked with renewed ease.

The story of Wing Biddlebaum's hands is worth a book in
itself. Sympathetically set forth it would tap many strange, beautiful qualities in obscure men. It is a job for a poet. In
Winesburg the hands had attracted attention merely because
of their activity. With them Wing Biddlebaum had picked as
high as a hundred and forty quarts of strawberries in a day.
They became his distinguishing feature, the source of his fame.

Also they made more grotesque an already grotesque and elusive individuality. Winesburg was proud of the hands of Wing Biddlebaum in the same spirit in which it was proud of Banker White's new stone house and Wesley Moyer's bay stallion, Tony Tip, that had won the two-fifteen trot at the fall races in Cleveland.

As for George Willard, he had many times wanted to ask about the hands. At times an almost overwhelming curiosity had taken hold of him. He felt that there must be a reason for their strange activity and their inclination to keep hidden away and only a growing respect for Wing Biddlebaum kept him from blurting out the questions that were often in his mind.

Once he had been on the point of asking. The two were walking in the fields on a summer afternoon and had stopped to sit upon a grassy bank. All afternoon Wing Biddlebaum had talked as one inspired. By a fence he had stopped and beating like a giant woodpecker upon the top board had shouted at George Willard, condemning his tendency to be too much influenced by the people about him. "You are destroying yourself," he cried. "You have the inclination to be alone and to dream and you are afraid of dreams. You want to be like others in town here. You hear them talk and you try to imitate them."

On the grassy bank Wing Biddlebaum had tried again to drive his point home. His voice became soft and reminiscent, and with a sigh of contentment he launched into a long rambling talk, speaking as one lost in a dream.

Out of the dream Wing Biddlebaum made a picture for George Willard. In the picture men lived again in a kind of pastoral golden age. Across a green open country came clean-limbed young men, some afoot, some mounted upon horses. In crowds the young men came to gather about the feet of an old man who sat beneath a tree in a tiny garden and who talked to them.

Wing Biddlebaum became wholly inspired. For once he forgot the hands. Slowly they stole forth and lay upon George Willard's shoulders. Something new and bold came into the voice that talked. "You must try to forget all you have learned," said the old man. "You must begin to dream. From this time on you must shut your ears to the roaring of the voices."

Pausing in his speech, Wing Biddlebaum looked long and earnestly at George Willard. His eyes glowed. Again he raised the hands to caress the boy and then a look of horror swept over his face.

With a convulsive movement of his body, Wing Biddlebaum sprang to his feet and thrust his hands deep into his trousers pockets. Tears came to his eyes. "I must be getting along home. I can talk no more with you," he said nervously.

Without looking back, the old man had hurried down the hillside and across a meadow, leaving George Willard perplexed and frightened upon the grassy slope. With a shiver of dread the boy arose and went along the road toward town. "I'll not ask him about his hands," he thought, touched by the memory of the terror he had seen in the man's eyes. "There's something wrong, but I don't want to know what it is. His hands have something to do with his fear of me and of everyone."

And George Willard was right. Let us look briefly into the story of the hands. Perhaps our talking of them will arouse the poet who will tell the hidden wonder story of the influence for which the hands were but fluttering pennants of promise.

In his youth Wing Biddlebaum had been a school teacher in a town in Pennsylvania. He was not then known as Wing Biddlebaum, but went by the less euphonic name of Adolph Myers. As Adolph Myers he was much loved by the boys of his school.

Adolph Myers was meant by nature to be a teacher of youth. He was one of those rare, little-understood men who rule by a power so gentle that it passes as a lovable weakness. In their feeling for the boys under their charge such men are not unlike the finer sort of women in their love of men.

And yet that is but crudely stated. It needs the poet there. With the boys of his school, Adolph Myers had walked in the evening or had sat talking until dusk upon the schoolhouse steps lost in a kind of dream. Here and there went his hands, caressing the shoulders of the boys, playing about the tousled heads. As he talked his voice became soft and musical. There was a caress in that also. In a way the voice and the hands, the stroking of the shoulders and the touching of the hair was a part of the schoolmaster's effort to carry a dream into the young minds. By the caress that was in his fingers he expressed himself. He was one of those men in whom the force that creates life is diffused, not centralized. Under the caress of his hands doubt and disbelief went out of the minds of the boys and they began also to dream.

And then the tragedy. A half-witted boy of the school became enamored of the young master. In his bed at night he imagined unspeakable things and in the morning went forth to tell his dreams as facts. Strange, hideous accusations fell from his loose-hung lips. Through the Pennsylvania town went a shiver. Hidden, shadowy doubts that had been in men's minds concerning Adolph Myers were galvanized into beliefs.

The tragedy did not linger. Trembling lads were jerked out of bed and questioned. "He put his arms about me," said one. "His fingers were always playing in my hair," said another.

One afternoon a man of the town, Henry Bradford, who kept a saloon, came to the schoolhouse door. Calling Adolph Myers into the school yard he began to beat him with his fists. As his hard knuckles beat down into the frightened face of the schoolmaster, his wrath became more and more terrible. Screaming with dismay, the children ran here and there like disturbed insects. "I'll teach you to put your hands on my boy, you beast," roared the saloon keeper, who, tired of beating the master, had begun to kick him about the yard.

Adolph Myers was driven from the Pennsylvania town in the night. With lanterns in their hands a dozen men came to the door of the house where he lived alone and commanded that he dress and come forth. It was raining and one of the men had a rope in his hands. They had intended to hang the schoolmaster, but something in his figure, so small, white, and pitiful, touched their hearts and they let him escape. As he ran away into the darkness they repented of their weakness and ran after him, swearing and throwing sticks and great balls of soft mud at the figure that screamed and ran faster and faster into the darkness.

For twenty years Adolph Myers had lived alone in Winesburg. He was but forty but looked sixty-five. The name of Biddlebaum he got from a box of goods seen at a freight station as he hurried through an eastern Ohio town. He had an aunt in Winesburg, a black-toothed old woman who raised chickens, and with her he lived until she died. He had been ill for a year after the experience in Pennsylvania, and after his recovery worked as a day laborer in the fields, going timidly about and striving to conceal his hands. Although he did not understand what had happened he felt that the hands must be to blame. Again and again the fathers of the boys had talked of the hands. "Keep your hands to yourself," the saloon keeper had roared, dancing with fury in the schoolhouse yard.

Upon the veranda of his house by the ravine, Wing Biddlebaum continued to walk up and down until the sun had disappeared and the road beyond the field was lost in the grey shadows. Going into his house he cut slices of bread and spread honey upon them. When the rumble of the evening train that took away the express cars loaded with the day's harvest of berries had passed and restored the silence of the summer night, he went again to walk upon the veranda. In the darkness he could not see the hands and they became quiet. Although he still hungered for the presence of the boy, who was the medium through which he expressed his love of man, the hunger became again a part of his loneliness and his waiting. Lighting a lamp, Wing Biddlebaum washed the few dishes soiled by his simple meal and, setting up a folding cot by the screen door that led to the porch, prepared to undress for the night. A few stray white bread crumbs lay on the cleanly washed floor by the table; putting the lamp upon a low stool he began to pick up the crumbs, carrying them to his mouth one by one with unbelievable rapidity. In the dense blotch of light beneath the table, the kneeling figure looked like a priest engaged in some service of his church. The nervous expressive fingers, flashing in and out of the light, might well have been mistaken for the fingers of the devotee going swiftly through decade after decade of his rosary.

Paper Pills

HE was an old man with a white beard and huge nose and hands. Long before the time during which we will know him, he was a doctor and drove a jaded white horse from house to house through the streets of Winesburg. Later he married a girl who had money. She had been left a large fertile farm when her father died. The girl was quiet, tall, and dark, and to many people she seemed very beautiful. Everyone in Winesburg wondered why she married the doctor. Within a year after the marriage she died.

The knuckles of the doctor's hand were extraordinarily large. When the hands were closed they looked like clusters of unpainted wooden balls as large as walnuts fastened together by steel rods. He smoked a cob pipe and after his wife's death sat all day in his empty office close by a window that was covered with cobwebs. He never opened the window. Once on a hot day in August he tried but found it stuck fast and after that he forgot all about it.

Winesburg had forgotten the old man, but in Doctor Reefy there were the seeds of something very fine. Alone in his musty office in the Heffner Block above the Paris Dry Goods Company's Store, he worked ceaselessly, building up something that he himself destroyed. Little pyramids of truth he erected and after erecting knocked them down again that he might have the truths to erect other pyramids.

Doctor Reefy was a tall man who had worn one suit of clothes for ten years. It was frayed at the sleeves and little holes had appeared at the knees and elbows. In the office he wore also a linen duster with huge pockets into which he continually stuffed scraps of paper. After some weeks the scraps of paper became little hard round balls, and when the pockets were filled he dumped them out upon the floor. For ten years he had but one friend, another old man named John Spaniard who owned a tree nursery. Sometimes, in a playful mood, old Doctor Reefy took from his pockets a handful of the paper balls and threw them at the nursery man. "That is to confound you, you blithering old sentimentalist," he cried, shaking with laughter.

The story of Doctor Reefy and his courtship of the tall dark girl who became his wife and left her money to him is a very curious story. It is delicious, like the twisted little apples that grow in the orchards of Winesburg. In the fall one walks in the orchards and the ground is hard with frost underfoot. The apples have been taken from the trees by the pickers. They have been put in barrels and shipped to the cities where they will be eaten in apartments that are filled with books, magazines, furniture, and people. On the trees are only a few gnarled apples that the pickers have rejected. They look like the knuckles of Doctor Reefy's hands. One nibbles at them and they are delicious. Into a little round place at the side of the apple has been gathered all of its sweetness. One runs from tree to tree over the frosted ground picking the gnarled, twisted apples and filling his pockets with them. Only the few know the sweetness of the twisted apples.

The girl and Doctor Reefy began their courtship on a summer afternoon. He was forty-five then and already he had begun the practice of filling his pockets with the scraps of paper that became hard balls and were thrown away. The habit had been formed as he sat in his buggy behind the jaded grey horse and went slowly along country roads. On the papers were written thoughts, ends of thoughts, beginnings of thoughts.

One by one the mind of Doctor Reefy had made the thoughts. Out of many of them he formed a truth that arose gigantic in his mind. The truth clouded the world. It became terrible and then faded away and the little thoughts began again.

The tall dark girl came to see Doctor Reefy because she was in the family way and had become frightened. She was in that condition because of a series of circumstances also curious.

The death of her father and mother and the rich acres of land that had come down to her had set a train of suitors on her heels. For two years she saw suitors almost every evening. Except two they were all alike. They talked to her of passion and there was a strained eager quality in their voices and in their eyes when they looked at her. The two who were different were much unlike each other. One of them, a slender young man with white hands, the son of a jeweler in Winesburg, talked continually of virginity. When he was with her he was never off the subject. The other, a black-haired boy with large ears, said nothing at all but always managed to get her into the darkness where he began to kiss her.

For a time the tall dark girl thought she would marry the jeweler's son. For hours she sat in silence listening as he talked to her and then she began to be afraid of something. Beneath his talk of virginity she began to think there was a lust greater than in all the others. At times it seemed to her that as he talked he was holding her body in his hands. She imagined him turning it slowly about in the white hands and staring at it. At night she dreamed that he had bitten into her body and that his jaws were dripping. She had the dream three times, then she became in the family way to the one who said nothing at all but who in the moment of his passion actually did bite her shoulder so that for days the marks of his teeth showed.

After the tall dark girl came to know Doctor Reefy it seemed to her that she never wanted to leave him again. She went into his office one morning and without her saying anything he seemed to know what had happened to her.

In the office of the doctor there was a woman, the wife of the man who kept the bookstore in Winesburg. Like all old-fashioned country practitioners, Doctor Reefy pulled teeth, and the woman who waited held a handkerchief to her teeth and groaned. Her husband was with her and when the tooth was taken out they both screamed and blood ran down on the woman's white dress. The tall dark girl did not pay any attention. When the woman and the man had gone the doctor smiled. "I will take you driving into the country with me," he said.

For several weeks the tall dark girl and the doctor were together almost every day. The condition that had brought her to him passed in an illness, but she was like one who has discovered the sweetness of the twisted apples, she could not get her mind fixed again upon the round perfect fruit that is eaten in the city apartments. In the fall after the beginning of her acquaintanceship with him she married Doctor Reefy and in the following spring she died. During the winter he read to her all of the odds and ends of thoughts he had scribbled on the bits of paper. After he had read them he laughed and stuffed them away in his pockets to become round hard balls.

Mother

ELIZABETH WILLARD, the mother of George Willard, was tall and gaunt and her face was marked with smallpox scars. Although she was but forty-five, some obscure disease had taken the fire out of her figure. Listlessly she went about the disorderly old hotel looking at the faded wall-paper and the ragged carpets and, when she was able to be about, doing the work of a chambermaid among beds soiled by the slumbers of fat traveling men. Her husband, Tom Willard, a slender, graceful man with square shoulders, a quick military step, and a black mustache, trained to turn sharply up at the ends, tried to put the wife out of his mind. The presence of the tall ghostly figure, moving slowly through the halls, he took as a reproach to himself. When he thought of her he grew angry and swore. The hotel was unprofitable and forever on the edge of failure and he wished himself out of it. He thought of the old house and the woman who lived there with him as things defeated and done for. The hotel in which he had begun life so hopefully was now a mere ghost of what a hotel should be. As he went spruce and businesslike through the streets of Winesburg, he sometimes stopped and turned quickly about as though fearing that the spirit of the hotel and of the woman would follow him even into the streets. "Damn such a life, damn it!" he sputtered aimlessly.

Tom Willard had a passion for village politics and for years had been the leading Democrat in a strongly Republican community. Some day, he told himself, the tide of things political will turn in my favor and the years of ineffectual service count big in the bestowal of rewards. He dreamed of going to Congress and even of becoming governor. Once when a younger member of the party arose at a political conference and began to boast of his faithful service, Tom Willard grew white with fury. "Shut up, you," he roared, glaring about. "What do you know of service? What are you but a boy? Look at what I've done here! I was a Democrat here in Winesburg when it was a crime to be a Democrat. In the old days they fairly hunted us with guns."

Between Elizabeth and her one son George there was a deep unexpressed bond of sympathy, based on a girlhood dream that had long ago died. In the son's presence she was timid and reserved, but sometimes while he hurried about town intent upon his duties as a reporter, she went into his room and closing the door knelt by a little desk, made of a kitchen table, that sat near a window. In the room by the desk she went through a ceremony that was half a prayer, half a demand, addressed to the skies. In the boyish figure she yearned to see something half forgotten that had once been a part of herself recreated. The prayer concerned that. "Even though I die, I will in some way keep defeat from you," she cried, and so deep was her determination that her whole body shook. Her eyes glowed and she clenched her fists. "If I am dead and see him becoming a meaningless drab figure like myself, I will come back," she declared. "I ask God now to give me that privilege. I demand it. I will pay for it. God may beat me with his fists. I will take any blow that may befall if but this my boy be allowed to express something for us both." Pausing uncertainly, the woman stared about the boy's room. "And do not let him become smart and successful either," she added vaguely.

The communion between George Willard and his mother was outwardly a formal thing without meaning. When she was ill and sat by the window in her room he sometimes went in the evening to make her a visit. They sat by a window that looked over the roof of a small frame building into Main Street. By turning their heads they could see, through another window, along an alleyway that ran behind the Main Street stores and into the back door of Abner Groff's bakery. Sometimes as they sat thus a picture of village life presented itself to them. At the back door of his shop appeared Abner Groff with a stick or an empty milk bottle in his hand. For a long time there was a feud between the baker and a grey cat that belonged to Sylvester West, the druggist. The boy and his mother saw the cat creep into the door of the bakery and presently emerge followed by the baker who swore and waved his arms about. The baker's eyes were small and red and his black hair and beard were filled with flour dust. Sometimes he was so angry that, although the cat had disappeared, he hurled sticks, bits of broken glass, and even some of the tools of his trade about. Once he broke a window at the back of Sinnings' Hardware Store. In the alley the grey cat crouched behind barrels filled with torn paper and broken bottles above which flew a black swarm of flies. Once when she was alone, and after watching a prolonged and ineffectual outburst on the part of the baker, Elizabeth Willard put her head down on her long white hands and wept. After that she did not look along the alleyway any more, but tried to forget the contest between the bearded man and the cat. It seemed like a rehearsal of her own life, terrible in its vividness.

In the evening when the son sat in the room with his mother, the silence made them both feel awkward. Darkness came on and the evening train came in at the station. In the street below feet tramped up and down upon a board sidewalk. In the station yard, after the evening train had gone, there was a heavy silence. Perhaps Skinner Leason, the express agent, moved a truck the length of the station platform. Over on Main Street sounded a man's voice, laughing. The door of the express office banged. George Willard arose and crossing the room fumbled for the doorknob. Sometimes he knocked against a chair, making it scrape along the floor. By the window sat the sick woman, perfectly still, listless. Her long hands, white and bloodless, could be seen drooping over the ends of the arms of the chair. "I think you had better be out among the boys. You are too much indoors," she said, striving to relieve the embarrassment of the departure. "I thought I would take a walk," replied George Willard, who felt awkward and confused.

One evening in July, when the transient guests who made the New Willard House their temporary homes had become scarce, and the hallways, lighted only by kerosene lamps turned low, were plunged in gloom, Elizabeth Willard had an adventure. She had been ill in bed for several days and her son had not come to visit her. She was alarmed. The feeble blaze of life that remained in her body was blown into a flame by her anxiety and she crept out of bed, dressed and hurried along the hallway toward her son's room, shaking with exaggerated fears. As she went along she steadied herself with her hand, slipped along the papered walls of the hall and breathed with difficulty. The air whistled through her teeth. As she hurried forward she thought how foolish she was. "He is concerned with boyish affairs," she told herself. "Perhaps he has now begun to walk about in the evening with girls."

Elizabeth Willard had a dread of being seen by guests in the hotel that had once belonged to her father and the ownership of which still stood recorded in her name in the county courthouse. The hotel was continually losing patronage because of its shabbiness and she thought of herself as also shabby. Her own room was in an obscure corner and when she felt able to work she voluntarily worked among the beds, preferring the labor that could be done when the guests were abroad seeking trade among the merchants of Winesburg.

By the door of her son's room the mother knelt upon the floor and listened for some sound from within. When she heard the boy moving about and talking in low tones a smile came to her lips. George Willard had a habit of talking aloud to himself and to hear him doing so had always given his mother a peculiar pleasure. The habit in him, she felt, strengthened the secret bond that existed between them. A thousand times she had whispered to herself of the matter. "He is groping about, trying to find himself," she thought. "He is not a dull clod, all words and smartness. Within him there is a secret something that is striving to grow. It is the thing I let be killed in myself."

In the darkness in the hallway by the door the sick woman arose and started again toward her own room. She was afraid that the door would open and the boy come upon her. When she had reached a safe distance and was about to turn a corner into a second hallway she stopped and bracing herself with her hands waited, thinking to shake off a trembling fit of weakness that had come upon her. The presence of the boy in the room had made her happy. In her bed, during the long hours alone, the little fears that had visited her had become giants. Now they were all gone. "When I get back to my room I shall sleep," she murmured gratefully.

But Elizabeth Willard was not to return to her bed and to sleep. As she stood trembling in the darkness the door of her son's room opened and the boy's father, Tom Willard, stepped out. In the light that streamed out at the door he stood with the knob in his hand and talked. What he said infuriated the woman.

Tom Willard was ambitious for his son. He had always

thought of himself as a successful man, although nothing he had ever done had turned out successfully. However, when he was out of sight of the New Willard House and had no fear of coming upon his wife, he swaggered and began to dramatize himself as one of the chief men of the town. He wanted his son to succeed. He it was who had secured for the boy the position on the *Winesburg Eagle*. Now, with a ring of earnestness in his voice, he was advising concerning some course of conduct. "I tell you what, George, you've got to wake up," he said sharply. "Will Henderson has spoken to me three times concerning the matter. He says you go along for hours not hearing when you are spoken to and acting like a gawky girl. What ails you?" Tom Willard laughed good-naturedly. "Well, I guess you'll get over it," he said. "I told Will that. You're not a fool and you're not a woman. You're Tom Willard's son and you'll wake up. I'm not afraid. What you say clears things up. If being a newspaper man had put the notion of becoming a writer into your mind that's all right. Only I guess you'll have to wake up to do that too, eh?"

Tom Willard went briskly along the hallway and down a flight of stairs to the office. The woman in the darkness could hear him laughing and talking with a guest who was striving to wear away a dull evening by dozing in a chair by the office door. She returned to the door of her son's room. The weakness had passed from her body as by a miracle and she stepped boldly along. A thousand ideas raced through her head. When she heard the scraping of a chair and the sound of a pen scratching upon paper, she again turned and went back along the hallway to her own room.

A definite determination had come into the mind of the defeated wife of the Winesburg Hotel keeper. The determination was the result of long years of quiet and rather ineffectual thinking. "Now," she told herself, "I will act. There is something threatening my boy and I will ward it off." The fact that the conversation between Tom Willard and his son had been rather quiet and natural, as though an understanding existed between them, maddened her. Although for years she had hated her husband, her hatred had always before been a quite impersonal thing. He had been merely a part of something else that she hated. Now, and by the few words at the door, he had become the thing personified. In the darkness of her own room she clenched her fists and glared about. Going to a cloth bag that hung on a nail by the wall she took out a long pair of sewing scissors and held them in her hand like a dagger. "I will stab him," she said aloud. "He has chosen to be the voice of evil and I will kill him. When I have killed him something will snap within myself and I will die also. It will be a release for all of us."

In her girlhood and before her marriage with Tom Willard, Elizabeth had borne a somewhat shaky reputation in Winesburg. For years she had been what is called "stage-struck" and had paraded through the streets with traveling men guests at her father's hotel, wearing loud clothes and urging them to tell her of life in the cities out of which they had come. Once she startled the town by putting on men's clothes and riding a bicycle down Main Street.

In her own mind the tall dark girl had been in those days much confused. A great restlessness was in her and it expressed itself in two ways. First there was an uneasy desire for change, for some big definite movement to her life. It was this feeling that had turned her mind to the stage. She dreamed of joining some company and wandering over the world, seeing always new faces and giving something out of herself to all people. Sometimes at night she was quite beside herself with the thought, but when she tried to talk of the matter to the members of the theatrical companies that came to Winesburg and stopped at her father's hotel, she got nowhere. They did not seem to know what she meant, or if she did get something of her passion expressed, they only laughed. "It's not like that," they said. "It's as dull and uninteresting as this here. Nothing comes of it."

With the traveling men when she walked about with them, and later with Tom Willard, it was quite different. Always they seemed to understand and sympathize with her. On the side streets of the village, in the darkness under the trees, they took hold of her hand and she thought that something unexpressed in herself came forth and became a part of an unexpressed something in them.

And then there was the second expression of her restlessness. When that came she felt for a time released and happy.

She did not blame the men who walked with her and later she did not blame Tom Willard. It was always the same, beginning with kisses and ending, after strange wild emotions, with peace and then sobbing repentance. When she sobbed she put her hand upon the face of the man and had always the same thought. Even though he were large and bearded she thought he had become suddenly a little boy. She wondered why he did not sob also.

In her room, tucked away in a corner of the old Willard House, Elizabeth Willard lighted a lamp and put it on a dressing table that stood by the door. A thought had come into her mind and she went to a closet and brought out a small square box and set it on the table. The box contained material for make-up and had been left with other things by a theatrical company that had once been stranded in Winesburg. Elizabeth Willard had decided that she would be beautiful. Her hair was still black and there was a great mass of it braided and coiled about her head. The scene that was to take place in the office below began to grow in her mind. No ghostly worn-out figure should confront Tom Willard, but something quite unexpected and startling. Tall and with dusky cheeks and hair that fell in a mass from her shoulders, a figure should come striding down the stairway before the startled loungers in the hotel office. The figure would be silent—it would be swift and terrible. As a tigress whose cub had been threatened would she appear, coming out of the shadows, stealing noiselessly along and holding the long wicked scissors in her hand.

With a little broken sob in her throat, Elizabeth Willard blew out the light that stood upon the table and stood weak and trembling in the darkness. The strength that had been as a miracle in her body left and she half reeled across the floor, clutching at the back of the chair in which she had spent so many long days staring out over the tin roofs into the main street of Winesburg. In the hallway there was the sound of footsteps and George Willard came in at the door. Sitting in a chair beside his mother he began to talk. "I'm going to get out of here," he said. "I don't know where I shall go or what I shall do but I am going away."

The woman in the chair waited and trembled. An impulse came to her. "I suppose you had better wake up," she said.

"You think that? You will go to the city and make money, eh? It will be better for you, you think, to be a business man, to be brisk and smart and alive?" She waited and trembled.

The son shook his head. "I suppose I can't make you understand, but oh, I wish I could," he said earnestly. "I can't even talk to father about it. I don't try. There isn't any use. I don't know what I shall do. I just want to go away and look at people and think."

Silence fell upon the room where the boy and woman sat together. Again, as on the other evenings, they were embarrassed. After a time the boy tried again to talk. "I suppose it won't be for a year or two but I've been thinking about it," he said, rising and going toward the door. "Something father said makes it sure that I shall have to go away." He fumbled with the door knob. In the room the silence became unbearable to the woman. She wanted to cry out with joy because of the words that had come from the lips of her son, but the expression of joy had become impossible to her. "I think you had better go out among the boys. You are too much indoors," she said. "I thought I would go for a little walk," replied the son stepping awkwardly out of the room and closing the door.

The Philosopher

DOCTOR PARCIVAL was a large man with a drooping mouth covered by a yellow mustache. He always wore a dirty white waistcoat out of the pockets of which protruded a number of the kind of black cigars known as stogies. His teeth were black and irregular and there was something strange about his eyes. The lid of the left eye twitched; it fell down and snapped up; it was exactly as though the lid of the eye were a window shade and someone stood inside the doctor's head playing with the cord.

Doctor Parcival had a liking for the boy, George Willard. It began when George had been working for a year on the *Winesburg Eagle* and the acquaintanceship was entirely a matter of the doctor's own making.

In the late afternoon Will Henderson, owner and editor of the *Eagle*, went over to Tom Willy's saloon. Along an alleyway he went and slipping in at the back door of the saloon began drinking a drink made of a combination of sloe gin and soda water. Will Henderson was a sensualist and had reached the age of forty-five. He imagined the gin renewed the youth in him. Like most sensualists he enjoyed talking of women, and for an hour he lingered about gossiping with Tom Willy. The saloon keeper was a short, broad-shouldered man with peculiarly marked hands. That flaming kind of birthmark that sometimes paints with red the faces of men and women had touched with red Tom Willy's fingers and the backs of his hands. As he stood by the bar talking to Will Henderson he rubbed the hands together. As he grew more and more excited the red of his fingers deepened. It was as though the hands had been dipped in blood that had dried and faded.

As Will Henderson stood at the bar looking at the red hands and talking of women, his assistant, George Willard, sat in the office of the *Winesburg Eagle* and listened to the talk of Doctor Parcival.

Doctor Parcival appeared immediately after Will Henderson had disappeared. One might have supposed that the doctor had been watching from his office window and had seen the editor going along the alleyway. Coming in at the front door and finding himself a chair, he lighted one of the stogies and crossing his legs began to talk. He seemed intent upon convincing the boy of the advisability of adopting a line of conduct that he was himself unable to define.

"If you have your eyes open you will see that although I call myself a doctor I have mighty few patients," he began. "There is a reason for that. It is not an accident and it is not because I do not know as much of medicine as anyone here. I do not want patients. The reason, you see, does not appear on the surface. It lies in fact in my character, which has, if you think about it, many strange turns. Why I want to talk to you of the matter I don't know. I might keep still and get more credit in your eyes. I have a desire to make you admire me, that's a fact. I don't know why. That's why I talk. It's very amusing, eh?"

Sometimes the doctor launched into long tales concerning himself. To the boy the tales were very real and full of meaning. He began to admire the fat unclean-looking man and, in the afternoon when Will Henderson had gone, looked forward with keen interest to the doctor's coming.

Doctor Parcival had been in Winesburg about five years. He came from Chicago and when he arrived was drunk and got into a fight with Albert Longworth, the baggageman. The fight concerned a trunk and ended by the doctor's being escorted to the village lockup. When he was released he rented a room above a shoe-repairing shop at the lower end of Main Street and put out the sign that announced himself as a doctor. Although he had but few patients and these of the poorer sort who were unable to pay, he seemed to have plenty of money for his needs. He slept in the office that was unspeakably dirty and dined at Biff Carter's lunch room in a small frame building opposite the railroad station. In the summer the lunch room was filled with flies and Biff Carter's white apron was more dirty than his floor. Doctor Parcival did not mind. Into the lunch room he stalked and deposited twenty cents upon the counter. "Feed me what you wish for that," he said laughing. "Use up food that you wouldn't otherwise sell. It makes no difference to me. I am a man of distinction, you see. Why should I concern myself with what I eat."

The tales that Doctor Parcival told George Willard began

nowhere and ended nowhere. Sometimes the boy thought they must all be inventions, a pack of lies. And then again he was convinced that they contained the very essence of truth.

"I was a reporter like you here," Doctor Parcival began. "It was in a town in Iowa—or was it in Illinois? I don't remember and anyway it makes no difference. Perhaps I am trying to conceal my identity and don't want to be very definite. Have you ever thought it strange that I have money for my needs although I do nothing? I may have stolen a great sum of money or been involved in a murder before I came here. There is food for thought in that, eh? If you were a really smart newspaper reporter you would look me up. In Chicago there was a Doctor Cronin who was murdered. Have you heard of that? Some men murdered him and put him in a trunk. In the early morning they hauled the trunk across the city. It sat on the back of an express wagon and they were on the seat as unconcerned as anything. Along they went through quiet streets where everyone was asleep. The sun was just coming up over the lake. Funny, eh—just to think of them smoking pipes and chattering as they drove along as unconcerned as I am now. Perhaps I was one of those men. That would be a strange turn of things, now wouldn't it, eh?" Again Doctor Parcival began his tale: "Well, anyway there I was, a reporter on a paper just as you are here, running about and getting little items to print. My mother was poor. She took in washing. Her dream was to make me a Presbyterian minister and I was studying with that end in view.

"My father had been insane for a number of years. He was in an asylum over at Dayton, Ohio. There you see I have let it slip out! All of this took place in Ohio, right here in Ohio. There is a clew if you ever get the notion of looking me up.

"I was going to tell you of my brother. That's the object of all this. That's what I'm getting at. My brother was a railroad painter and had a job on the Big Four. You know that road runs through Ohio here. With other men he lived in a box car and away they went from town to town painting the railroad property—switches, crossing gates, bridges, and stations.

"The Big Four paints its stations a nasty orange color. How I hated that color! My brother was always covered with it. On pay days he used to get drunk and come home wearing his paint-covered clothes and bringing his money with him. He did not give it to mother but laid it in a pile on our kitchen table.

"About the house he went in the clothes covered with the nasty orange colored paint. I can see the picture. My mother, who was small and had red, sad-looking eyes, would come into the house from a little shed at the back. That's where she spent her time over the washtub scrubbing people's dirty clothes. In she would come and stand by the table, rubbing her eyes with her apron that was covered with soap-suds.

"'Don't touch it! Don't you dare touch that money,' my brother roared, and then he himself took five or ten dollars and went tramping off to the saloons. When he had spent what he had taken he came back for more. He never gave my mother any money at all but stayed about until he had spent it all, a little at a time. Then he went back to his job with the painting crew on the railroad. After he had gone things began to arrive at our house, groceries and such things. Sometimes there would be a dress for mother or a pair of shoes for me.

"Strange, eh? My mother loved my brother much more than she did me, although he never said a kind word to either of us and always raved up and down threatening us if we dared so much as touch the money that sometimes lay on the table three days.

"We got along pretty well. I studied to be a minister and prayed. I was a regular ass about saying prayers. You should have heard me. When my father died I prayed all night, just as I did sometimes when my brother was in town drinking and going about buying the things for us. In the evening after supper I knelt by the table where the money lay and prayed for hours. When no one was looking I stole a dollar or two and put it in my pocket. That makes me laugh now but then it was terrible. It was on my mind all the time. I got six dollars a week from my job on the paper and always took it straight home to mother. The few dollars I stole from my brother's pile I spent on myself, you know, for trifles, candy and cigarettes and such things.

"When my father died at the asylum over at Dayton, I went over there. I borrowed some money from the man for whom I worked and went on the train at night. It was raining. In the asylum they treated me as though I were a king.

"The men who had jobs in the asylum had found out I was a newspaper reporter. That made them afraid. There had been some negligence, some carelessness, you see, when father was ill. They thought perhaps I would write it up in the paper and make a fuss. I never intended to do anything of the kind.

"Anyway, in I went to the room where my father lay dead and blessed the dead body. I wonder what put that notion into my head. Wouldn't my brother, the painter, have laughed, though. There I stood over the dead body and spread out my hands. The superintendent of the asylum and some of his helpers came in and stood about looking sheepish. It was very amusing. I spread out my hands and said, 'Let peace brood over this carcass.' That's what I said."

Jumping to his feet and breaking off the tale, Doctor Parcival began to walk up and down in the office of the *Winesburg Eagle* where George Willard sat listening. He was awkward and, as the office was small, continually knocked against things. "What a fool I am to be talking," he said. "That is not my object in coming here and forcing my acquaintanceship upon you. I have something else in mind. You are a reporter just as I was once and you have attracted my attention. You may end by becoming just such another fool. I want to warn you and keep on warning you. That's why I seek you out."

Doctor Parcival began talking of George Willard's attitude toward men. It seemed to the boy that the man had but one object in view, to make everyone seem despicable. "I want to fill you with hatred and contempt so that you will be a superior being," he declared. "Look at my brother. There was a fellow, eh? He despised everyone, you see. You have no idea with what contempt he looked upon mother and me. And was he not our superior? You know he was. You have not seen him and yet I have made you feel that. I have given you a sense of it. He is dead. Once when he was drunk he lay down on the tracks and the car in which he lived with the other painters ran over him."

One day in August Doctor Parcival had an adventure in Winesburg. For a month George Willard had been going each morning to spend an hour in the doctor's office. The visits came about through a desire on the part of the doctor to read to the boy from the pages of a book he was in the process of writing. To write the book Doctor Parcival declared was the object of his coming to Winesburg to live.

On the morning in August before the coming of the boy, an incident had happened in the doctor's office. There had been an accident on Main Street. A team of horses had been frightened by a train and had run away. A little girl, the daughter of a farmer, had been thrown from a buggy and killed.

On Main Street everyone had become excited and a cry for doctors had gone up. All three of the active practitioners of the town had come quickly but had found the child dead. From the crowd someone had run to the office of Doctor Parcival who had bluntly refused to go down out of his office to the dead child. The useless cruelty of his refusal had passed unnoticed. Indeed, the man who had come up the stairway to summon him had hurried away without hearing the refusal.

All of this, Doctor Parcival did not know and when George Willard came to his office he found the man shaking with terror. "What I have done will arouse the people of this town," he declared excitedly. "Do I not know human nature? Do I not know what will happen? Word of my refusal will be whispered about. Presently men will get together in groups and talk of it. They will come here. We will quarrel and there will be talk of hanging. Then they will come again bearing a rope in their hands."

Doctor Parcival shook with fright. "I have a presentiment," he declared emphatically. "It may be that what I am talking about will not occur this morning. It may be put off until tonight but I will be hanged. Everyone will get excited. I will be hanged to a lamp-post on Main Street."

Going to the door of his dirty little office, Doctor Parcival looked timidly down the stairway leading to the street. When he returned the fright that had been in his eyes was beginning to be replaced by doubt. Coming on tip-toe across the room he tapped George Willard on the shoulder. "If not now, sometime," he whispered, shaking his head. "In the end I will be crucified, uselessly crucified."

Doctor Parcival began to plead with George Willard. "You must pay attention to me," he urged. "If something happens perhaps you will be able to write the book that I may never get written. The idea is very simple, so simple that if you are not careful you will forget it. It is this—that everyone in the world is Christ and they are all crucified. That's what I want to say. Don't you forget that. Whatever happens, don't you dare let yourself forget."

Nobody Knows

LOOKING cautiously about, George Willard arose from his desk in the office of the *Winesburg Eagle* and went hurriedly out at the back door. The night was warm and cloudy and although it was not yet eight o'clock, the alleyway back of the *Eagle* office was pitch dark. A team of horses tied to a post somewhere in the darkness stamped on the hard-baked ground. A cat sprang from under George Willard's feet and ran away into the night. The young man was nervous. All day he had gone about his work like one dazed by a blow. In the alleyway he trembled as though with fright.

In the darkness George Willard walked along the alleyway, going carefully and cautiously. The back doors of the Winesburg stores were open and he could see men sitting about under the store lamps. In Myerbaum's Notion Store Mrs. Willy the saloon keeper's wife stood by the counter with a basket on her arm. Sid Green the clerk was waiting on her. He leaned over the counter and talked earnestly.

George Willard crouched and then jumped through the path of light that came out at the door. He began to run forward in the darkness. Behind Ed Griffith's saloon old Jerry Bird the town drunkard lay asleep on the ground. The runner stumbled over the sprawling legs. He laughed brokenly.

George Willard had set forth upon an adventure. All day he had been trying to make up his mind to go through with the adventure and now he was acting. In the office of the *Winesburg Eagle* he had been sitting since six o'clock trying to think.

There had been no decision. He had just jumped to his feet, hurried past Will Henderson who was reading proof in the print shop and started to run along the alleyway.

Through street after street went George Willard, avoiding the people who passed. He crossed and recrossed the road. When he passed a street lamp he pulled his hat down over his face. He did not dare think. In his mind there was a fear but it was a new kind of fear. He was afraid the adventure on which he had set out would be spoiled, that he would lose courage and turn back.

George Willard found Louise Trunnion in the kitchen of
her father's house. She was washing dishes by the light of a
kerosene lamp. There she stood behind the screen door in the
little shed-like kitchen at the back of the house. George Willard stopped by a picket fence and tried to control the shaking
of his body. Only a narrow potato patch separated him from
the adventure. Five minutes passed before he felt sure enough
of himself to call to her. "Louise! Oh Louise!" he called. The
cry stuck in his throat. His voice became a hoarse whisper.

Louise Trunnion came out across the potato patch holding
the dish cloth in her hand. "How do you know I want to go
out with you," she said sulkily. "What makes you so sure?"

George Willard did not answer. In silence the two stood in the
darkness with the fence between them. "You go on along," she
said. "Pa's in there. I'll come along. You wait by William's barn."

The young newspaper reporter had received a letter from
Louise Trunnion. It had come that morning to the office of
the *Winesburg Eagle*. The letter was brief. "I'm yours if you
want me," it said. He thought it annoying that in the darkness
by the fence she had pretended there was nothing between
them. "She has a nerve! Well, gracious sakes, she has a nerve,"
he muttered as he went along the street and passed a row of
vacant lots where corn grew. The corn was shoulder high and
had been planted right down to the sidewalk.

When Louise Trunnion came out of the front door of her
house she still wore the gingham dress in which she had been
washing dishes. There was no hat on her head. The boy could
see her standing with the doorknob in her hand talking to
someone within, no doubt to old Jake Trunnion, her father.
Old Jake was half deaf and she shouted. The door closed and
everything was dark and silent in the little side street. George
Willard trembled more violently than ever.

In the shadows by William's barn George and Louise stood,
not daring to talk. She was not particularly comely and there
was a black smudge on the side of her nose. George thought
she must have rubbed her nose with her finger after she had
been handling some of the kitchen pots.

The young man began to laugh nervously. "It's warm," he
said. He wanted to touch her with his hand. "I'm not very
bold," he thought. Just to touch the folds of the soiled ging-

ham dress would, he decided, be an exquisite pleasure. She began to quibble. "You think you're better than I am. Don't tell me, I guess I know," she said drawing closer to him.

A flood of words burst from George Willard. He remembered the look that had lurked in the girl's eyes when they had met on the streets and thought of the note she had written. Doubt left him. The whispered tales concerning her that had gone about town gave him confidence. He became wholly the male, bold and aggressive. In his heart there was no sympathy for her. "Ah, come on, it'll be all right. There won't be anyone know anything. How can they know?" he urged.

They began to walk along a narrow brick sidewalk between the cracks of which tall weeds grew. Some of the bricks were missing and the sidewalk was rough and irregular. He took hold of her hand that was also rough and thought it delightfully small. "I can't go far," she said and her voice was quiet, unperturbed.

They crossed a bridge that ran over a tiny stream and passed another vacant lot in which corn grew. The street ended. In the path at the side of the road they were compelled to walk one behind the other. Will Overton's berry field lay beside the road and there was a pile of boards. "Will is going to build a shed to store berry crates here," said George and they sat down upon the boards.

When George Willard got back into Main Street it was past ten o'clock and had begun to rain. Three times he walked up and down the length of Main Street. Sylvester West's Drug Store was still open and he went in and bought a cigar. When Shorty Crandall the clerk came out at the door with him he was pleased. For five minutes the two stood in the shelter of the store awning and talked. George Willard felt satisfied. He had wanted more than anything else to talk to some man. Around a corner toward the New Willard House he went whistling softly.

On the sidewalk at the side of Winney's Dry Goods Store where there was a high board fence covered with circus pictures, he stopped whistling and stood perfectly still in the darkness, attentive, listening as though for a voice calling his name. Then again he laughed nervously. "She hasn't got anything on me. Nobody knows," he muttered doggedly and went on his way.

Godliness

THERE were always three or four old people sitting on the front porch of the house or puttering about the garden of the Bentley farm. Three of the old people were women and sisters to Jesse. They were a colorless, soft-voiced lot. Then there was a silent old man with thin white hair who was Jesse's uncle.

The farmhouse was built of wood, a board outer-covering over a framework of logs. It was in reality not one house but a cluster of houses joined together in a rather haphazard manner. Inside, the place was full of surprises. One went up steps from the living room into the dining room and there were always steps to be ascended or descended in passing from one room to another. At meal times the place was like a beehive. At one moment all was quiet, then doors began to open, feet clattered on stairs, a murmur of soft voices arose and people appeared from a dozen obscure corners.

Beside the old people, already mentioned, many others lived in the Bentley house. There were four hired men, a woman named Aunt Callie Beebe, who was in charge of the housekeeping, a dull-witted girl named Eliza Stoughton, who made beds and helped with the milking, a boy who worked in the stables, and Jesse Bentley himself, the owner and overlord of it all.

By the time the American Civil War had been over for twenty years, that part of Northern Ohio where the Bentley farms lay had begun to emerge from pioneer life. Jesse then owned machinery for harvesting grain. He had built modern barns and most of his land was drained with carefully laid tile drain, but in order to understand the man we will have to go back to an earlier day.

The Bentley family had been in Northern Ohio for several generations before Jesse's time. They came from New York State and took up land when the country was new and land could be had at a low price. For a long time they, in common

36

with all the other Middle Western people, were very poor. The land they had settled upon was heavily wooded and covered with fallen logs and underbrush. After the long hard labor of clearing these away and cutting the timber, there were still the stumps to be reckoned with. Plows run through the fields caught on hidden roots, stones lay all about, on the low places water gathered, and the young corn turned yellow, sickened and died.

When Jesse Bentley's father and brothers had come into their ownership of the place, much of the harder part of the work of clearing had been done, but they clung to old traditions and worked like driven animals. They lived as practically all of the farming people of the time lived. In the spring and through most of the winter the highways leading into the town of Winesburg were a sea of mud. The four young men of the family worked hard all day in the fields, they ate heavily of coarse, greasy food, and at night slept like tired beasts on beds of straw. Into their lives came little that was not coarse and brutal and outwardly they were themselves coarse and brutal. On Saturday afternoons they hitched a team of horses to a three-seated wagon and went off to town. In town they stood about the stoves in the stores talking to other farmers or to the store keepers. They were dressed in overalls and in the winter wore heavy coats that were flecked with mud. Their hands as they stretched them out to the heat of the stoves were cracked and red. It was difficult for them to talk and so they for the most part kept silent. When they had bought meat, flour, sugar, and salt, they went into one of the Winesburg saloons and drank beer. Under the influence of drink the naturally strung lusts of their natures, kept suppressed by the heroic labor of breaking up new ground, were released. A kind of crude and animal-like poetic fervor took possession of them. On the road home they stood up on the wagon seats and shouted at the stars. Sometimes they fought long and bitterly and at other times they broke forth into songs. Once Enoch Bentley, the older one of the boys, struck his father, old Tom Bentley, with the butt of a teamster's whip, and the old man seemed likely to die. For days Enoch lay hid in the straw in the loft of the stable ready to flee if the result of his momentary passion turned out to be murder. He was kept alive with food brought by his mother who also kept him informed of the injured man's condition. When all turned out well he emerged from his hiding place and went back to the work of clearing land as though nothing had happened.

The Civil War brought a sharp turn to the fortunes of the Bentleys and was responsible for the rise of the youngest son, Jesse. Enoch, Edward, Harry, and Will Bentley all enlisted and before the long war ended they were all killed. For a time after they went away to the South, old Tom tried to run the place, but he was not successful. When the last of the four had been killed he sent word to Jesse that he would have to come home.

Then the mother, who had not been well for a year, died suddenly, and the father became altogether discouraged. He talked of selling the farm and moving into town. All day he went about shaking his head and muttering. The work in the fields was neglected and weeds grew high in the corn. Old Tom hired men but he did not use them intelligently. When they had gone away to the fields in the morning he wandered into the woods and sat down on a log. Sometimes he forgot to come home at night and one of the daughters had to go in search of him.

When Jesse Bentley came home to the farm and began to take charge of things he was a slight, sensitive-looking man of twenty-two. At eighteen he had left home to go to school to become a scholar and eventually to become a minister of the Presbyterian Church. All through his boyhood he had been what in our country was called an "odd sheep" and had not got on with his brothers. Of all the family only his mother had understood him and she was now dead. When he came home to take charge of the farm, that had at that time grown to more than six hundred acres, everyone on the farms about and in the nearby town of Winesburg smiled at the idea of his trying to handle the work that had been done by his four strong brothers.

There was indeed good cause to smile. By the standards of his day Jesse did not look like a man at all. He was small and very slender and womanish of body and, true to the traditions of young ministers, wore a long black coat and a narrow black string tie. The neighbors were amused when they saw him, after the years away, and they were even more amused when they saw the woman he had married in the city.

As a matter of fact, Jesse's wife did soon go under. That was perhaps Jesse's fault. A farm in Northern Ohio in the hard years after the Civil War was no place for a delicate woman, and Katherine Bentley was delicate. Jesse was hard with her as he was with everybody about him in those days. She tried to do such work as all the neighbor women about her did and he let her go on without interference. She helped to do the milking and did part of the housework; she made the beds for the men and prepared their food. For a year she worked every day from sunrise until late at night and then after giving birth to a child she died.

As for Jesse Bentley—although he was a delicately built man there was something within him that could not easily be killed. He had brown curly hair and grey eyes that were at times hard and direct, at times wavering and uncertain. Not only was he slender but he was also short of stature. His mouth was like the mouth of a sensitive and very determined child. Jesse Bentley was a fanatic. He was a man born out of his time and place and for this he suffered and made others suffer. Never did he succeed in getting what he wanted out of life and he did not know what he wanted. Within a very short time after he came home to the Bentley farm he made everyone there a little afraid of him, and his wife, who should have been close to him as his mother had been, was afraid also. At the end of two weeks after his coming, old Tom Bentley made over to him the entire ownership of the place and retired into the background. Everyone retired into the background. In spite of his youth and inexperience, Jesse had the trick of mastering the souls of his people. He was so in earnest in everything he did and said that no one understood him. He made everyone on the farm work as they had never worked before and yet there was no joy in the work. If things went well they went well for Jesse and never for the people who were his dependents. Like a thousand other strong men who have come into the world here in America in these later times, Jesse was but half strong. He could master others but he could not master himself. The running of the farm as it had never been run before was easy for him. When he came home from Cleveland where he had been in school, he shut himself off from all of his people and began to make plans. He thought about the farm night and day and that made him successful. Other men on the farms about him worked too hard and were too tired to think, but to think of the farm and to be everlastingly making plans for its success was a relief to Jesse. It partially satisfied something in his passionate nature. Immediately after he came home he had a wing built on to the old house and in a large room facing the west he had windows that looked into the barnyard and other windows that looked off across the fields. By the window he sat down to think. Hour after hour and day after day he sat and looked over the land and thought out his new place in life. The passionate burning thing in his nature flamed up and his eyes became hard. He wanted to make the farm produce as no farm in his state had ever produced before and then he wanted something else. It was the indefinable hunger within that made his eyes waver and that kept him always more and more silent before people. He would have given much to achieve peace and in him was a fear that peace was the thing he could not achieve.

All over his body Jesse Bentley was alive. In his small frame was gathered the force of a long line of strong men. He had always been extraordinarily alive when he was a small boy on the farm and later when he was a young man in school. In the school he had studied and thought of God and the Bible with his whole mind and heart. As time passed and he grew to know people better, he began to think of himself as an extraordinary man, one set apart from his fellows. He wanted terribly to make his life a thing of great importance, and as he looked about at his fellow men and saw how like clods they lived it seemed to him that he could not bear to become also such a clod. Although in his absorption in himself and in his own destiny he was blind to the fact that his young wife was doing a strong woman's work even after she had become large with child and that she was killing herself in his service, he did not intend to be unkind to her. When his father, who was old and twisted with toil, made over to him the ownership of the farm and seemed content to creep away to a corner and wait for death, he shrugged his shoulders and dismissed the old man from his mind.

In the room by the window overlooking the land that had

come down to him sat Jesse thinking of his own affairs. In the stables he could hear the tramping of his horses and the restless movement of his cattle. Away in the fields he could see other cattle wandering over green hills. The voices of men, his men who worked for him, came in to him through the window. From the milkhouse there was the steady thump, thump of a churn being manipulated by the half-witted girl, Eliza Stoughton. Jesse's mind went back to the men of Old Testament days who had also owned lands and herds. He remembered how God had come down out of the skies and talked to these men and he wanted God to notice and to talk to him also. A kind of feverish boyish eagerness to in some way achieve in his own life the flavor of significance that had hung over these men took possession of him. Being a prayerful man he spoke of the matter aloud to God and the sound of his own words strengthened and fed his eagerness.

"I am a new kind of man come into possession of these fields," he declared. "Look upon me, O God, and look Thou also upon my neighbors and all the men who have gone before me here! O God, create in me another Jesse, like that one of old, to rule over men and to be the father of sons who shall be rulers!" Jesse grew excited as he talked aloud and jumping to his feet walked up and down in the room. In fancy he saw himself living in old times and among old peoples. The land that lay stretched out before him became of vast significance, a place peopled by his fancy with a new race of men sprung from himself. It seemed to him that in his day as in those other and older days, kingdoms might be created and new impulses given to the lives of men by the power of God speaking through a chosen servant. He longed to be such a servant. "It is God's work I have come to the land to do," he declared in a loud voice and his short figure straightened and he thought that something like a halo of Godly approval hung over him.

It will perhaps be somewhat difficult for the men and women of a later day to understand Jesse Bentley. In the last fifty years a vast change has taken place in the lives of our people. A revolution has in fact taken place. The coming of industrialism, attended by all the roar and rattle of affairs, the shrill cries of millions of new voices that have come among us from over seas, the going and coming of trains, the growth of cities, the building of the interurban car lines that weave in and out of towns and past farmhouses, and now in these later days the coming of the automobiles has worked a tremendous change in the lives and in the habits of thought of our people of Mid-America. Books, badly imagined and written though they may be in the hurry of our times, are in every household, magazines circulate by the millions of copies, newspapers are everywhere. In our day a farmer standing by the stove in the store in his village has his mind filled to overflowing with the words of other men. The newspapers and the magazines have pumped him full. Much of the old brutal ignorance that had in it also a kind of beautiful childlike innocence is gone forever. The farmer by the stove is brother to the men of the cities, and if you listen you will find him talking as glibly and as senselessly as the best city man of us all.

In Jesse Bentley's time and in the country districts of the whole Middle West in the years after the Civil War it was not so. Men labored too hard and were too tired to read. In them was no desire for words printed upon paper. As they worked in the fields, vague, half-formed thoughts took possession of them. They believed in God and in God's power to control their lives. In the little Protestant churches they gathered on Sunday to hear of God and his works. The churches were the center of the social and intellectual life of the times. The figure of God was big in the hearts of men.

And so, having been born an imaginative child and having within him a great intellectual eagerness, Jesse Bentley had turned wholeheartedly toward God. When the war took his brothers away, he saw the hand of God in that. When his father became ill and could no longer attend to the running of the farm, he took that also as a sign from God. In the city, when the word came to him, he walked about at night through the streets thinking of the matter and when he had come home and had got the work on the farm well under way, he went again at night to walk through the forests and over the low hills and to think of God.

As he walked the importance of his own figure in some divine plan grew in his mind. He grew avaricious and was impatient that the farm contained only six hundred acres. Kneeling in a fence corner at the edge of some meadow, he sent his voice abroad into the silence and looking up he saw the stars shining down at him.

One evening, some months after his father's death, and when his wife Katherine was expecting at any moment to be laid abed of childbirth, Jesse left his house and went for a long walk. The Bentley farm was situated in a tiny valley watered by Wine Creek, and Jesse walked along the banks of the stream to the end of his own land and on through the fields of his neighbors. As he walked the valley broadened and then narrowed again. Great open stretches of field and wood lay before him. The moon came out from behind clouds, and, climbing a low hill, he sat down to think.

Jesse thought that as the true servant of God the entire stretch of country through which he had walked should have come into his possession. He thought of his dead brothers and blamed them that they had not worked harder and achieved more. Before him in the moonlight the tiny stream ran down over stones, and he began to think of the men of old times who like himself had owned flocks and lands.

A fantastic impulse, half fear, half greediness took possession of Jesse Bentley. He remembered how in the old Bible story the Lord had appeared to that other Jesse and told him to send his son David to where Saul and the men of Israel were fighting the Philistines in the Valley of Elah. Into Jesse's mind came the conviction that all of the Ohio farmers who owned land in the valley of Wine Creek were Philistines and enemies of God. "Suppose," he whispered to himself, "there should come from among them one who, like Goliath the Philistine of Gath, could defeat me and take from me my possessions." In fancy he felt the sickening dread that he thought must have lain heavy on the heart of Saul before the coming of David. Jumping to his feet, he began to run through the night. As he ran he called to God. His voice carried far over the low hills. "Jehovah of Hosts," he cried, "send to me this night out of the womb of Katherine, a son. Let thy grace alight upon me. Send me a son to be called David who shall help me to pluck at last all of these lands out of the hands of the Philistines and turn them to Thy service and to the building of Thy kingdom on earth."

Godliness

PART TWO

D AVID HARDY of Winesburg, Ohio was the grandson of
Jesse Bentley, the owner of Bentley farms. When he was
twelve years old he went to the old Bentley place to live. His
mother, Louise Bentley, the girl who came into the world on
that night when Jesse ran through the fields crying to God
that he be given a son, had grown to womanhood on the farm
and had married young John Hardy of Winesburg who became a banker. Louise and her husband did not live happily
together and everyone agreed that she was to blame. She was a
small woman with sharp grey eyes and black hair. From childhood she had been inclined to fits of temper and when not
angry she was often morose and silent. In Winesburg it was
said that she drank. Her husband, the banker, who was a careful, shrewd man, tried hard to make her happy. When he began
to make money he bought for her a large brick house on Elm
Street in Winesburg and he was the first man in that town to
keep a manservant to drive his wife's carriage.

But Louise could not be made happy. She flew into half insane fits of temper during which she was sometimes silent,
sometimes noisy and quarrelsome. She swore and cried out in
her anger. She got a knife from the kitchen and threatened her
husband's life. Once she deliberately set fire to the house, and
often she hid herself away for days in her own room and would
see no one. Her life, lived as a half recluse, gave rise to all sorts
of stories concerning her. It was said that she took drugs and
that she hid herself away from people because she was often so
under the influence of drink that her condition could not be
concealed. Sometimes on summer afternoons she came out of
the house and got into her carriage. Dismissing the driver she
took the reins in her own hands and drove off at top speed
through the streets. If a pedestrian got in her way she drove
straight ahead and the frightened citizen had to escape as best
he could. To the people of the town it seemed as though she
wanted to run them down. When she had driven through

several streets, tearing around corners and beating the horses with the whip, she drove off into the country. On the country roads after she had gotten out of sight of the houses she let the horses slow down to a walk and her wild, reckless mood passed. She became thoughtful and muttered words. Sometimes tears came into her eyes. And then when she came back into town she again drove furiously through the quiet streets. But for the influence of her husband and the respect he inspired in people's minds she would have been arrested more than once by the town marshal.

Young David Hardy grew up in the house with this woman and as can well be imagined there was not much joy in his childhood. He was too young then to have opinions of his own about people, but at times it was difficult for him not to have very definite opinions about the woman who was his mother. David was always a quiet orderly boy and for a long time was thought by the people of Winesburg to be something of a dullard. His eyes were brown and as a child he had a habit of looking at things and people a long time without appearing to see what he was looking at. When he heard his mother spoken of harshly or when he overheard her berating his father, he was frightened and ran away to hide. Sometimes he could not find a hiding place and that confused him. Turning his face toward a tree or if he were indoors toward the wall, he closed his eyes and tried not to think of anything. He had a habit of talking aloud to himself, and early in life a spirit of quiet sadness often took possession of him.

On the occasions when David went to visit his grandfather on the Bentley farm, he was altogether contented and happy. Often he wished that he would never have to go back to town and once when he had come home from the farm after a long visit, something happened that had a lasting effect on his mind.

David had come back into town with one of the hired men. The man was in a hurry to go about his own affairs and left the boy at the head of the street in which the Hardy house stood. It was early dusk of a fall evening and the sky was overcast with clouds. Something happened to David. He could not bear to go into the house where his mother and father lived, and on an impulse he decided to run away from home. He intended to go back to the farm and to his grandfather, but lost his way and for hours he wandered weeping and frightened on country roads. It started to rain and lightning flashed in the sky. The boy's imagination was excited and he fancied that he could see and hear strange things in the darkness. Into his mind came the conviction that he was walking and running in some terrible void where no one had ever been before. The darkness about him seemed limitless. The sound of the wind blowing in trees was terrifying. When a team of horses approached along the road in which he walked he was frightened and climbed a fence. Through a field he ran until he came into another road and getting upon his knees felt of the soft ground with his fingers. But for the figure of his grandfather, whom he was afraid he would never find in the darkness, he thought the world must be altogether empty. When his cries were heard by a farmer who was walking home from town and he was brought back to his father's house, he was so tired and excited that he did not know what was happening to him.

By chance David's father knew that he had disappeared. On the street he had met the farm hand from the Bentley place and knew of his son's return to town. When the boy did not come home an alarm was set up and John Hardy with several men of the town went to search the country. The report that David had been kidnapped ran about through the streets of Winesburg. When he came home there were no lights in the house, but his mother appeared and clutched him eagerly in her arms. David thought she had suddenly become another woman. He could not believe that so delightful a thing had happened. With her own hands Louise Hardy bathed his tired young body and cooked him food. She would not let him go to bed but, when he had put on his nightgown, blew out the lights and sat down in a chair to hold him in her arms. For an hour the woman sat in the darkness and held her boy. All the time she kept talking in a low voice. David could not understand what had so changed her. Her habitually dissatisfied face had become, he thought, the most peaceful and lovely thing he had ever seen. When he began to weep she held him more and more tightly. On and on went her voice. It was not harsh or shrill as when she talked to her husband, but was like rain falling on trees. Presently men began coming to the door to report that he had not been found, but she made him hide and be silent until she had sent them away. He thought it must be a game his mother and the men of the town were playing with him and laughed joyously. Into his mind came the thought that his having been lost and frightened in the darkness was an altogether unimportant matter. He thought that he would have been willing to go through the frightful experience a thousand times to be sure of finding at the end of the long black road a thing so lovely as his mother had suddenly become.

During the last years of young David's boyhood he saw his mother but seldom and she became for him just a woman with whom he had once lived. Still he could not get her figure out of his mind and as he grew older it became more definite. When he was twelve years old he went to the Bentley farm to live. Old Jesse came into town and fairly demanded that he be given charge of the boy. The old man was excited and determined on having his own way. He talked to John Hardy in the office of the Winesburg Savings Bank and then the two men went to the house on Elm Street to talk with Louise. They both expected her to make trouble but were mistaken. She was very quiet and when Jesse had explained his mission and had gone on at some length about the advantages to come through having the boy out of doors and in the quiet atmosphere of the old farmhouse, she nodded her head in approval. "It is an atmosphere not corrupted by my presence," she said sharply. Her shoulders shook and she seemed about to fly into a fit of temper. "It is a place for a man child, although it was never a place for me," she went on. "You never wanted me there and of course the air of your house did me no good. It was like poison in my blood but it will be different with him."

Louise turned and went out of the room, leaving the two men to sit in embarrassed silence. As very often happened she later stayed in her room for days. Even when the boy's clothes were packed and he was taken away she did not appear. The loss of her son made a sharp break in her life and she seemed less inclined to quarrel with her husband. John Hardy thought it had all turned out very well indeed.

And so young David went to live in the Bentley farmhouse with Jesse. Two of the old farmer's sisters were alive and still lived in the house. They were afraid of Jesse and rarely spoke when he was about. One of the women who had been noted for her flaming red hair when she was younger was a born mother and became the boy's caretaker. Every night when he had gone to bed she went into his room and sat on the floor until he fell asleep. When he became drowsy she became bold and whispered things that he later thought he must have dreamed.

Her soft low voice called him endearing names and he dreamed that his mother had come to him and that she had changed so that she was always as she had been that time after he ran away. He also grew bold and reaching out his hand stroked the face of the woman on the floor so that she was ecstatically happy. Everyone in the old house became happy after the boy went there. The hard insistent thing in Jesse Bentley that had kept the people in the house silent and timid and that had never been dispelled by the presence of the girl Louise was apparently swept away by the coming of the boy. It was as though God had relented and sent a son to the man.

The man who had proclaimed himself the only true servant of God in all the valley of Wine Creek, and who had wanted God to send him a sign of approval by way of a son out of the womb of Katherine, began to think that at last his prayers had been answered. Although he was at that time only fifty-five years old he looked seventy and was worn out with much thinking and scheming. The effort he had made to extend his land holdings had been successful and there were few farms in the valley that did not belong to him, but until David came he was a bitterly disappointed man.

There were two influences at work in Jesse Bentley and all his life his mind had been a battleground for these influences. First there was the old thing in him. He wanted to be a man of God and a leader among men of God. His walking in the fields and through the forests at night had brought him close to nature and there were forces in the passionately religious man that ran out to the forces in nature. The disappointment that had come to him when a daughter and not a son had been born to Katherine had fallen upon him like a blow struck by some unseen hand and the blow had somewhat softened his egotism. He still believed that God might at any moment make himself manifest out of the winds or the clouds, but he no longer demanded such recognition. Instead he prayed for it. Sometimes he was altogether doubtful and thought God had deserted the world. He regretted the fate that had not let him live in a simpler and sweeter time when at the beckoning of some strange cloud in the sky men left their lands and houses and went forth into the wilderness to create new races. While he worked night and day to make his farms more productive and to extend his holdings of land, he regretted that he could not use his own restless energy in the building of temples, the slaying of unbelievers and in general in the work of glorifying God's name on earth.

That is what Jesse hungered for and then also he hungered for something else. He had grown into maturity in America in the years after the Civil War and he, like all men of his time, had been touched by the deep influences that were at work in the country during those years when modern industrialism was being born. He began to buy machines that would permit him to do the work of the farms while employing fewer men and he sometimes thought that if he were a younger man he would give up farming altogether and start a factory in Winesburg for the making of machinery. Jesse formed the habit of reading newspapers and magazines. He invented a machine for the making of fence out of wire. Faintly he realized that the atmosphere of old times and places that he had always cultivated in his own mind was strange and foreign to the thing that was growing up in the minds of others. The beginning of the most materialistic age in the history of the world, when wars would be fought without patriotism, when men would forget God and only pay attention to moral standards, when the will to power would replace the will to serve and beauty would be well-nigh forgotten in the terrible headlong rush of mankind toward the acquiring of possessions, was telling its story to Jesse the man of God as it was to the men about him. The greedy thing in him wanted to make money faster than it could be made by tilling the land. More than once he went into Winesburg to talk with his son-in-law John Hardy about it. "You are a banker and you will have chances I never had," he said and his eyes shone. "I am thinking about it all the time. Big things are going to be done in the country and there will be more money to be made than I ever dreamed of. You get into it. I wish I were younger and had your chance." Jesse Bentley walked up and down in the bank office and grew more and more excited as he talked. At one time in his life he had been threatened with paralysis and his left side remained somewhat weakened. As he talked his left eyelid twitched. Later when he drove back home and when night came on and the stars came out it was harder to get back the old feeling of a close and personal God who lived in the sky overhead and who might at any moment reach out his hand, touch him on the shoulder, and appoint for him some heroic task to be done. Jesse's mind was fixed upon the things read in newspapers and magazines, on fortunes to be made almost without effort by shrewd men who bought and sold. For him the coming of the boy David did much to bring back with renewed force the old faith and it seemed to him that God had at last looked with favor upon him.

As for the boy on the farm, life began to reveal itself to him in a thousand new and delightful ways. The kindly attitude of all about him expanded his quiet nature and he lost the half timid, hesitating manner he had always had with his people. At night when he went to bed after a long day of adventures in the stables, in the fields, or driving about from farm to farm with his grandfather he wanted to embrace everyone in the house. If Sherley Bentley, the woman who came each night to sit on the floor by his bedside, did not appear at once, he went to the head of the stairs and shouted, his young voice ringing through the narrow halls where for so long there had been a tradition of silence. In the morning when he awoke and lay still in bed, the sounds that came in to him through the windows filled him with delight. He thought with a shudder of the life in the house in Winesburg and of his mother's angry voice that had always made him tremble. There in the country all sounds were pleasant sounds. When he awoke at dawn the barnyard back of the house also awoke. In the house people stirred about. Eliza Stoughton the half-witted girl was poked in the ribs by a farm hand and giggled noisily, in some distant field a cow bawled and was answered by the cattle in the stables, and one of the farm hands spoke sharply to the horse he was grooming by the stable door. David leaped out of bed and ran to a window. All of the people stirring about excited his mind, and he wondered what his mother was doing in the house in town.

From the windows of his own room he could not see directly into the barnyard where the farm hands had now all assembled to do the morning chores, but he could hear the voices of the men and the neighing of the horses. When one of the men laughed, he laughed also. Leaning out at the open window, he looked into an orchard where a fat sow wandered about with a litter of tiny pigs at her heels. Every morning he counted the pigs. "Four, five, six, seven," he said slowly, wetting his finger and making straight up and down marks on the window ledge. David ran to put on his trousers and shirt. A feverish desire to get out of doors took possession of him. Every morning he made such a noise coming down stairs that Aunt Callie, the housekeeper, declared he was trying to tear the house down. When he had run through the long old house, shutting doors behind him with a bang, he came into the barnyard and looked about with an amazed air of expectancy. It seemed to him that in such a place tremendous things might have happened during the night. The farm hands looked at him and laughed. Henry Strader, an old man who had been on the farm since Jesse came into possession and who before David's time had never been known to make a joke, made the same joke every morning. It amused David so that he laughed and clapped his hands. "See, come here and look," cried the old man, "Grandfather Jesse's white mare has torn the black stocking she wears on her foot."

Day after day through the long summer, Jesse Bentley drove from farm to farm up and down the valley of Wine Creek, and his grandson went with him. They rode in a comfortable old phaeton drawn by the white horse. The old man scratched his thin white beard and talked to himself of his plans for increasing the productiveness of the fields they visited and of God's part in the plans all men made. Sometimes he looked at David and smiled happily and then for a long time he appeared to forget the boy's existence. More and more every day now his mind turned back again to the dreams that had filled his mind when he had first come out of the city to live on the land. One afternoon he startled David by letting his dreams take entire possession of him. With the boy as a witness, he went through a ceremony and brought about an accident that nearly destroyed the companionship that was growing up between them.

Jesse and his grandson were driving in a distant part of the valley some miles from home. A forest came down to the road and through the forest Wine Creek wriggled its way over stones toward a distant river. All the afternoon Jesse had been in a meditative mood and now he began to talk. His mind went back to the night when he had been frightened by thoughts of a giant that might come to rob and plunder him of his possessions, and again as on that night when he had run through the fields crying for a son, he became excited to the edge of insanity. Stopping the horse he got out of the buggy and asked David to get out also. The two climbed over a fence and walked along the bank of the stream. The boy paid no attention to the muttering of his grandfather, but ran along beside him and wondered what was going to happen. When a rabbit jumped up and ran away through the woods, he clapped his hands and danced with delight. He looked at the tall trees and was sorry that he was not a little animal to climb high in the air without being frightened. Stooping, he picked up a small stone and threw it over the head of his grandfather into a clump of bushes. "Wake up, little animal. Go and climb to the top of the trees," he shouted in a shrill voice.

Jesse Bentley went along under the trees with his head bowed and with his mind in a ferment. His earnestness affected the boy who presently became silent and a little alarmed. Into the old man's mind had come the notion that now he could bring from God a word or a sign out of the sky, that the presence of the boy and man on their knees in some lonely spot in the forest would make the miracle he had been waiting for almost inevitable. "It was in just such a place as this that other David tended the sheep when his father came and told him to go down unto Saul," he muttered.

Taking the boy rather roughly by the shoulder, he climbed over a fallen log and when he had come to an open place among the trees, he dropped upon his knees and began to pray in a loud voice.

A kind of terror he had never known before took possession of David. Crouching beneath a tree he watched the man on the ground before him and his own knees began to tremble. It seemed to him that he was in the presence, not only of his grandfather but of someone else, someone who might hurt him, someone who was not kindly but dangerous and brutal. He began to cry and reaching down picked up a small stick which he held tightly gripped in his fingers. When Jesse Bentley, absorbed in his own idea, suddenly arose and advanced toward him, his terror grew until his whole body shook. In the woods an intense silence seemed to lie over everything and suddenly out of the silence came the old man's harsh and insistent voice. Gripping the boy's shoulders, Jesse turned his face to the sky and shouted. The whole left side of his face twitched and his hand on the boy's shoulder twitched also. "Make a sign to me, God," he cried, "here I stand with the boy David. Come down to me out of the sky and make Thy presence known to me."

With a cry of fear, David turned and shaking himself loose from the hands that held him, ran away through the forest. He did not believe that the man who turned up his face and in a harsh voice shouted at the sky, was his grandfather at all. The man did not look like his grandfather. The conviction that something strange and terrible had happened, that by some miracle a new and dangerous person had come into the body of the kindly old man took possession of him. On and on he ran down the hillside sobbing as he ran. When he fell over the roots of a tree and in falling struck his head, he arose and tried to run on again. His head hurt so that presently he fell down and lay still, but it was only after Jesse had carried him to the buggy and he awoke to find the old man's hand stroking his head tenderly, that the terror left him. "Take me away. There is a terrible man back there in the woods," he declared firmly, while Jesse looked away over the tops of the trees and again his lips cried out to God. "What have I done that Thou doest not approve of me," he whispered softly, saying the words over and over as he drove rapidly along the road with the boy's cut and bleeding head held tenderly against his shoulder.

Surrender

PART THREE

THE story of Louise Bentley, who became Mrs. John Hardy and lived with her husband in a brick house on Elm Street in Winesburg, is a story of misunderstanding.

Before such women as Louise can be understood and their lives made livable, much will have to be done. Thoughtful books will have to be written and thoughtful lives lived by people about them.

Born of a delicate and overworked mother, and an impulsive, hard, imaginative father, who did not look with favor upon her coming into the world, Louise was from childhood a neurotic, one of the race of over-sensitive women that in later days industrialism was to bring in such great numbers into the world.

During her early years she lived on the Bentley farm, a silent, moody child, wanting love more than anything else in the world and not getting it. When she was fifteen she went to live in Winesburg with the family of Albert Hardy who had a store for the sale of buggies and wagons, and who was a member of the town board of education.

Louise went into town to be a student in the Winesburg High School and she went to live at the Hardys' because Albert Hardy and her father were friends.

Hardy, the vehicle merchant of Winesburg, like thousands of other men of his times, was an enthusiast on the subject of education. He had made his own way in the world without learning got from books, but he was convinced that had he but known books things would have gone better with him. To everyone who came into his shop he talked of the matter, and in his own household he drove his family distracted by his constant harping on the subject.

He had two daughters and one son, John Hardy, and more than once the daughters threatened to leave school altogether. As a matter of principle they did just enough work in their classes to avoid punishment. "I hate books and I hate anyone

54

who likes books," Harriet, the younger of the two girls, declared passionately.

In Winesburg as on the farm Louise was not happy. For years she had dreamed of the time when she could go forth into the world, and she looked upon the move into the Hardy household as a great step in the direction of freedom. Always when she had thought of the matter, it had seemed to her that in town all must be gaiety and life, that there men and women must live happily and freely, giving and taking friendship and affection as one takes the feel of a wind on the cheek. After the silence and the cheerlessness of life in the Bentley house, she dreamed of stepping forth into an atmosphere that was warm and pulsating with life and reality. And in the Hardy household Louise might have got something of the thing for which she so hungered but for a mistake she made when she had just come to town.

Louise won the disfavor of the two Hardy girls, Mary and Harriet, by her application to her studies in school. She did not come to the house until the day when school was to begin and knew nothing of the feeling they had in the matter. She was timid and during the first month made no acquaintances. Every Friday afternoon one of the hired men from the farm drove into Winesburg and took her home for the week-end, so that she did not spend the Saturday holiday with the town people. Because she was embarrassed and lonely she worked constantly at her studies. To Mary and Harriet, it seemed as though she tried to make trouble for them by her proficiency. In her eagerness to appear well Louise wanted to answer every question put to the class by the teacher. She jumped up and down and her eyes flashed. Then when she had answered some question the others in the class had been unable to answer, she smiled happily. "See, I have done it for you," her eyes seemed to say. "You need not bother about the matter. I will answer all questions. For the whole class it will be easy while I am here."

In the evening after supper in the Hardy house, Albert Hardy began to praise Louise. One of the teachers had spoken highly of her and he was delighted. "Well, again I have heard of it," he began, looking hard at his daughters and then turning to smile at Louise. "Another of the teachers has told me of the good work Louise is doing. Everyone in Winesburg is telling me how smart she is. I am ashamed that they do not speak so of my own girls." Arising, the merchant marched about the room and lighted his evening cigar.

The two girls looked at each other and shook their heads wearily. Seeing their indifference the father became angry. "I tell you it is something for you two to be thinking about," he cried, glaring at them. "There is a big change coming here in America and in learning is the only hope of the coming generations. Louise is the daughter of a rich man but she is not ashamed to study. It should make you ashamed to see what she does."

The merchant took his hat from a rack by the door and prepared to depart for the evening. At the door he stopped and glared back. So fierce was his manner that Louise was frightened and ran upstairs to her own room. The daughters began to speak of their own affairs. "Pay attention to me," roared the merchant. "Your minds are lazy. Your indifference to education is affecting your characters. You will amount to nothing. Now mark what I say—Louise will be so far ahead of you that you will never catch up."

The distracted man went out of the house and into the street shaking with wrath. He went along muttering words and swearing, but when he got into Main Street his anger passed. He stopped to talk of the weather or the crops with some other merchant or with a farmer who had come into town and forgot his daughters altogether or, if he thought of them, only shrugged his shoulders. "Oh, well, girls will be girls," he muttered philosophically.

In the house when Louise came down into the room where the two girls sat, they would have nothing to do with her. One evening after she had been there for more than six weeks and was heartbroken because of the continued air of coldness with which she was always greeted, she burst into tears. "Shut up your crying and go back to your own room and to your books," Mary Hardy said sharply.

The room occupied by Louise was on the second floor of the Hardy house, and her window looked out upon an orchard. There was a stove in the room and every evening young John Hardy carried up an armful of wood and put it in a box that stood by the wall. During the second month after she came to the house, Louise gave up all hope of getting on a friendly footing with the Hardy girls and went to her own room as soon as the evening meal was at an end.

Her mind began to play with thoughts of making friends with John Hardy. When he came into the room with the wood in his arms, she pretended to be busy with her studies but watched him eagerly. When he had put the wood in the box and turned to go out, she put down her head and blushed. She tried to make talk but could say nothing, and after he had gone she was angry at herself for her stupidity.

The mind of the country girl became filled with the idea of drawing close to the young man. She thought that in him might be found the quality she had all her life been seeking in people. It seemed to her that between herself and all the other people in the world, a wall had been built up and that she was living just on the edge of some warm inner circle of life that must be quite open and understandable to others. She became obsessed with the thought that it wanted but a courageous act on her part to make all of her association with people something quite different, and that it was possible by such an act to pass into a new life as one opens a door and goes into a room. Day and night she thought of the matter, but although the thing she wanted so earnestly was something very warm and close it had as yet no conscious connection with sex. It had not become that definite, and her mind had only alighted upon the person of John Hardy because he was at hand and unlike his sisters had not been unfriendly to her.

The Hardy sisters, Mary and Harriet, were both older than Louise. In a certain kind of knowledge of the world they were years older. They lived as all of the young women of Middle Western towns lived. In those days young women did not go out of our towns to eastern colleges and ideas in regard to social classes had hardly begun to exist. A daughter of a laborer was in much the same social position as a daughter of a farmer or a merchant, and there were no leisure classes. A girl was "nice" or she was "not nice." If a nice girl, she had a young man who came to her house to see her on Sunday and on Wednesday evenings. Sometimes she went with her young man to a dance or a church social. At other times she received him at the house and was given the use of the parlor for that purpose. No one intruded upon her. For hours the two sat behind closed doors. Sometimes the lights were turned low and the young man and woman embraced. Cheeks became hot and hair disarranged. After a year or two, if the impulse within them became strong and insistent enough, they married.

One evening during her first winter in Winesburg, Louise had an adventure that gave a new impulse to her desire to break down the wall that she thought stood between her and John Hardy. It was Wednesday and immediately after the evening meal Albert Hardy put on his hat and went away. Young John brought the wood and put it in the box in Louise's room. "You do work hard, don't you?" he said awkwardly, and then before she could answer he also went away.

Louise heard him go out of the house and had a mad desire to run after him. Opening her window she leaned out and called softly. "John, dear John, come back, don't go away." The night was cloudy and she could not see far into the darkness, but as she waited she fancied she could hear a soft little noise as of someone going on tiptoes through the trees in the orchard. She was frightened and closed the window quickly. For an hour she moved about the room trembling with excitement and when she could not longer bear the waiting, she crept into the hall and down the stairs into a closet-like room that opened off the parlor.

Louise had decided that she would perform the courageous act that had for weeks been in her mind. She was convinced that John Hardy had concealed himself in the orchard beneath her window and she was determined to find him and tell him that she wanted him to come close to her, to hold her in his arms, to tell her of his thoughts and dreams and to listen while she told him her thoughts and dreams. "In the darkness it will be easier to say things," she whispered to herself, as she stood in the little room groping for the door.

And then suddenly Louise realized that she was not alone in the house. In the parlor on the other side of the door a man's voice spoke softly and the door opened. Louise just had time to conceal herself in a little opening beneath the stairway when Mary Hardy, accompanied by her young man, came into the little dark room.

For an hour Louise sat on the floor in the darkness and listened. Without words Mary Hardy, with the aid of the man who had come to spend the evening with her, brought to the country girl a knowledge of men and women. Putting her head down until she was curled into a little ball she lay perfectly still. It seemed to her that by some strange impulse of the gods, a great gift had been brought to Mary Hardy and she could not understand the older woman's determined protest.

The young man took Mary Hardy into his arms and kissed her. When she struggled and laughed, he but held her the more tightly. For an hour the contest between them went on and then they went back into the parlor and Louise escaped up the stairs. "I hope you were quiet out there. You must not disturb the little mouse at her studies," she heard Harriet saying to her sister as she stood by her own door in the hallway above.

Louise wrote a note to John Hardy and late that night when all in the house were asleep, she crept downstairs and slipped it under his door. She was afraid that if she did not do the thing at once her courage would fail. In the note she tried to be quite definite about what she wanted. "I want someone to love me and I want to love someone," she wrote. "If you are the one for me I want you to come into the orchard at night and make a noise under my window. It will be easy for me to crawl down over the shed and come to you. I am thinking about it all the time, so if you are to come at all you must come soon."

For a long time Louise did not know what would be the outcome of her bold attempt to secure for herself a lover. In a way she still did not know whether or not she wanted him to come. Sometimes it seemed to her that to be held tightly and kissed was the whole secret of life, and then a new impulse came and she was terribly afraid. The age-old woman's desire to be possessed had taken possession of her, but so vague was her notion of life that it seemed to her just the touch of John Hardy's hand upon her own hand would satisfy. She wondered if he would understand that. At the table next day while Albert Hardy talked and the two girls whispered and laughed, she did not look at John but at the table and as soon as possible escaped. In the evening she went out of the house until she was sure he had taken the wood to her room and gone away. When after several evenings of intense listening she heard no call from the darkness in the orchard, she was half beside herself with grief and decided that for her there was no way to break through the wall that had shut her off from the joy of life.

And then on a Monday evening two or three weeks after the writing of the note, John Hardy came for her. Louise had so entirely given up the thought of his coming that for a long time she did not hear the call that came up from the orchard. On the Friday evening before, as she was being driven back to the farm for the week-end by one of the hired men, she had on an impulse done a thing that had startled her, and as John Hardy stood in the darkness below and called her name softly and insistently, she walked about in her room and wondered what new impulse had led her to commit so ridiculous an act.

The farm hand, a young fellow with black curly hair, had come for her somewhat late on that Friday evening and they drove home in the darkness. Louise, whose mind was filled with thoughts of John Hardy, tried to make talk but the country boy was embarrassed and would say nothing. Her mind began to review the loneliness of her childhood and she remembered with a pang the sharp new loneliness that had just come to her. "I hate everyone," she cried suddenly, and then broke forth into a tirade that frightened her escort. "I hate father and old man Hardy, too," she declared vehemently. "I get my lessons there in the school in town but I hate that also."

Louise frightened the farm hand still more by turning and putting her cheek down upon his shoulder. Vaguely she hoped that he like that young man who had stood in the darkness with Mary would put his arms about her and kiss her, but the country boy was only alarmed. He struck the horse with the whip and began to whistle. "The road is rough, eh?" he said loudly. Louise was so angry that reaching up she snatched his hat from his head and threw it into the road. When he jumped out of the buggy and went to get it, she drove off and left him to walk the rest of the way back to the farm.

Louise Bentley took John Hardy to be her lover. That was not what she wanted but it was so the young man had interpreted her approach to him, and so anxious was she to achieve something else that she made no resistance. When after a few months they were both afraid that she was about to become a mother, they went one evening to the county seat and were married. For a few months they lived in the Hardy house and then took a house of their own. All during the first year Louise tried to make her husband understand the vague and intangible hunger that had led to the writing of the note and that was still unsatisfied. Again and again she crept into his arms and tried to talk of it, but always without success. Filled with his own notions of love between men and women, he did not listen but began to kiss her upon the lips. That confused her so that in the end she did not want to be kissed. She did not know what she wanted.

When the alarm that had tricked them into marriage proved to be groundless, she was angry and said bitter, hurtful things. Later when her son David was born, she could not nurse him and did not know whether she wanted him or not. Sometimes she stayed in the room with him all day, walking about and occasionally creeping close to touch him tenderly with her hands, and then other days came when she did not want to see or be near the tiny bit of humanity that had come into the house. When John Hardy reproached her for her cruelty, she laughed. "It is a man child and will get what it wants anyway," she said sharply. "Had it been a woman child there is nothing in the world I would not have done for it."

Terror

PART FOUR

WHEN David Hardy was a tall boy of fifteen, he, like his mother, had an adventure that changed the whole current of his life and sent him out of his quiet corner into the world. The shell of the circumstances of his life was broken and he was compelled to start forth. He left Winesburg and no one there ever saw him again. After his disappearance, his mother and grandfather both died and his father became very rich. He spent much money in trying to locate his son, but that is no part of this story.

It was in the late fall of an unusual year on the Bentley farms. Everywhere the crops had been heavy. That spring, Jesse had bought part of a long strip of black swamp land that lay in the valley of Wine Creek. He got the land at a low price but had spent a large sum of money to improve it. Great ditches had to be dug and thousands of tile laid. Neighboring farmers shook their heads over the expense. Some of them laughed and hoped that Jesse would lose heavily by the venture, but the old man went silently on with the work and said nothing.

When the land was drained he planted it to cabbages and onions, and again the neighbors laughed. The crop was, however, enormous and brought high prices. In the one year Jesse made enough money to pay for all the cost of preparing the land and had a surplus that enabled him to buy two more farms. He was exultant and could not conceal his delight. For the first time in all the history of his ownership of the farms, he went among his men with a smiling face.

Jesse bought a great many new machines for cutting down the cost of labor and all of the remaining acres in the strip of black fertile swamp land. One day he went into Winesburg and bought a bicycle and a new suit of clothes for David and he gave his two sisters money with which to go to a religious convention at Cleveland, Ohio.

In the fall of that year when the frost came and the trees in the forests along Wine Creek were golden brown, David spent every moment when he did not have to attend school, out in the open. Alone or with other boys he went every afternoon into the woods to gather nuts. The other boys of the country-side, most of them sons of laborers on the Bentley farms, had guns with which they went hunting rabbits and squirrels, but David did not go with them. He made himself a sling with rubber bands and a forked stick and went off by himself to gather nuts. As he went about thoughts came to him. He real-ized that he was almost a man and wondered what he would do in life, but before they came to anything, the thoughts passed and he was a boy again. One day he killed a squirrel that sat on one of the lower branches of a tree and chattered at him. Home he ran with the squirrel in his hand. One of the Bentley sisters cooked the little animal and he ate it with great gusto. The skin he tacked on a board and suspended the board by a string from his bedroom window.

That gave his mind a new turn. After that he never went into the woods without carrying the sling in his pocket and he spent hours shooting at imaginary animals concealed among the brown leaves in the trees. Thoughts of his coming man-hood passed and he was content to be a boy with a boy's impulses.

One Saturday morning when he was about to set off for the woods with the sling in his pocket and a bag for nuts on his shoulder, his grandfather stopped him. In the eyes of the old man was the strained serious look that always a little frightened David. At such times Jesse Bentley's eyes did not look straight ahead but wavered and seemed to be looking at nothing. Something like an invisible curtain appeared to have come be-tween the man and all the rest of the world. "I want you to come with me," he said briefly, and his eyes looked over the boy's head into the sky. "We have something important to do to-day. You may bring the bag for nuts if you wish. It does not matter and anyway we will be going into the woods."

Jesse and David set out from the Bentley farmhouse in the old phaeton that was drawn by the white horse. When they had gone along in silence for a long way they stopped at the edge of a field where a flock of sheep were grazing. Among the sheep was a lamb that had been born out of season, and this David and his grandfather caught and tied so tightly that it looked like a little white ball. When they drove on again Jesse let David hold the lamb in his arms. "I saw it yesterday and it put me in mind of what I have long wanted to do," he said, and again he looked away over the head of the boy with the wavering, uncertain stare in his eyes.

After the feeling of exaltation that had come to the farmer as a result of his successful year, another mood had taken possession of him. For a long time he had been going about feeling very humble and prayerful. Again he walked alone at night thinking of God and as he walked he again connected his own figure with the figures of old days. Under the stars he knelt on the wet grass and raised up his voice in prayer. Now he had decided that like the men whose stories filled the pages of the Bible, he would make a sacrifice to God. "I have been given these abundant crops and God has also sent me a boy who is called David," he whispered to himself. "Perhaps I should have done this thing long ago." He was sorry the idea had not come into his mind in the days before his daughter Louise had been born and thought that surely now when he had erected a pile of burning sticks in some lonely place in the woods and had offered the body of a lamb as a burnt offering, God would appear to him and give him a message.

More and more as he thought of the matter, he thought also of David and his passionate self love was partially forgotten. "It is time for the boy to begin thinking of going out into the world and the message will be one concerning him," he decided. "God will make a pathway for him. He will tell me what place David is to take in life and when he shall set out on his journey. It is right that the boy should be there. If I am fortunate and an angel of God should appear, David will see the beauty and glory of God made manifest to man. It will make a true man of God of him also."

In silence Jesse and David drove along the road until they came to that place where Jesse had once before appealed to God and had frightened his grandson. The morning had been bright and cheerful, but a cold wind now began to blow and clouds hid the sun. When David saw the place to which they had come he began to tremble with fright, and when they stopped by the bridge where the creek came down from among the trees, he wanted to spring out of the phaeton and run away.

A dozen plans for escape ran through David's head, but when Jesse stopped the horse and climbed over the fence into the wood, he followed. "It is foolish to be afraid. Nothing will happen," he told himself as he went along with the lamb in his arms. There was something in the helplessness of the little animal, held so tightly in his arms that gave him courage. He could feel the rapid beating of the beast's heart and that made his own heart beat less rapidly. As he walked swiftly along behind his grandfather, he untied the string with which the four legs of the lamb were fastened together. "If anything happens we will run away together," he thought.

In the woods, after they had gone a long way from the road, Jesse stopped in an opening among the trees where a clearing, overgrown with small bushes, ran up from the creek. He was still silent but began at once to erect a heap of dry sticks which he presently set afire. The boy sat on the ground with the lamb in his arms. His imagination began to invest every movement of the old man with significance and he became every moment more afraid. "I must put the blood of the lamb on the head of the boy," Jesse muttered when the sticks had begun to blaze greedily, and taking a long knife from his pocket he turned and walked rapidly across the clearing toward David.

Terror seized upon the soul of the boy. He was sick with it. For a moment he sat perfectly still and then his body stiffened and he sprang to his feet. His face became as white as the fleece of the lamb, that now finding itself suddenly released, ran down the hill. David ran also. Fear made his feet fly. Over the low bushes and logs he leaped frantically. As he ran he put his hand into his pocket and took out the branched stick from which the sling for shooting squirrels was suspended. When he came to the creek that was shallow and splashed down over the stones, he dashed into the water and turned to look back, and when he saw his grandfather still running toward him with the long knife held tightly in his hand he did not hesitate but reaching down, selected a stone and put it in the sling. With all his strength he drew back the heavy rubber bands and the stone whistled through the air. It hit Jesse, who had entirely forgotten the boy and was pursuing the lamb, squarely in the head. With a groan he pitched forward and fell almost at the boy's feet. When David saw that he lay still and that he was apparently dead, his fright increased immeasurably. It became an insane panic.

With a cry he turned and ran off through the woods weeping convulsively. "I don't care—I killed him, but I don't care," he sobbed. As he ran on and on he decided suddenly that he would never go back again to the Bentley farms or to the town of Winesburg. "I have killed the man of God and now I will myself be a man and go into the world," he said stoutly as he stopped running and walked rapidly down a road that followed the windings of Wine Creek as it ran through fields and forests into the west.

On the ground by the creek Jesse Bentley moved uneasily about. He groaned and opened his eyes. For a long time he lay perfectly still and looked at the sky. When at last he got to his feet, his mind was confused and he was not surprised by the boy's disappearance. By the roadside he sat down on a log and began to talk about God. That is all they ever got out of him. Whenever David's name was mentioned he looked vaguely at the sky and said that a messenger from God had taken the boy. "It happened because I was too greedy for glory," he declared, and would have no more to say in the matter.

A Man of Ideas

HE lived with his mother, a grey, silent woman with a peculiar ashy complexion.

The house in which they lived stood in a little grove of trees beyond where the main street of Winesburg crossed Wine Creek. His name was Joe Welling, and his father had been a man of some dignity in the community, a lawyer and a member of the state legislature at Columbus. Joe himself was small of body and in his character unlike anyone else in town. He was like a tiny little volcano that lies silent for days and then suddenly spouts fire. No, he wasn't like that—he was like a man who is subject to fits, one who walks among his fellow men inspiring fear because a fit may come upon him suddenly and blow him away into a strange uncanny physical state in which his eyes roll and his legs and arms jerk. He was like that, only that the visitation that descended upon Joe Welling was a mental and not a physical thing. He was beset by ideas and in the throes of one of his ideas was uncontrollable. Words rolled and tumbled from his mouth. A peculiar smile came upon his lips. The edges of his teeth that were tipped with gold glistened in the light. Pouncing upon a bystander he began to talk. For the bystander there was no escape. The excited man breathed into his face, peered into his eyes, pounded upon his chest with a shaking forefinger, demanded, compelled attention.

In those days the Standard Oil Company did not deliver oil to the consumer in big wagons and motor trucks as it does now, but delivered instead to retail grocers, hardware stores and the like. Joe was the Standard Oil agent in Winesburg and in several towns up and down the railroad that went through Winesburg. He collected bills, booked orders, and did other things. His father, the legislator, had secured the job for him.

In and out of the stores of Winesburg went Joe Welling—silent, excessively polite, intent upon his business. Men watched him with eyes in which lurked amusement tempered by alarm. They were waiting for him to break forth, preparing to flee. Although the seizures that came upon him were harmless enough, they could not be laughed away. They were over-whelming. Astride an idea, Joe was overmastering. His personality became gigantic. It overrode the man to whom he talked, swept him away, swept all away, all who stood within sound of his voice.

In Sylvester West's Drug Store stood four men who were talking of horse racing. Wesley Moyer's stallion, Tony Tip, was to race at the June meeting at Tiffin, Ohio, and there was a rumor that he would meet the stiffest competition of his career. It was said that Pop Geers, the great racing driver, would himself be there. A doubt of the success of Tony Tip hung heavy in the air of Winesburg.

Into the drug store came Joe Welling, brushing the screen door violently aside. With a strange absorbed light in his eyes he pounced upon Ed Thomas, he who knew Pop Geers and whose opinion of Tony Tip's chances was worth considering.

"The water is up in Wine Creek," cried Joe Welling with the air of Pheidippides bringing news of the victory of the Greeks in the struggle at Marathon. His finger beat a tattoo upon Ed Thomas' broad chest. "By Trunion bridge it is within eleven and a half inches of the flooring," he went on, the words coming quickly and with a little whistling noise from between his teeth. An expression of helpless annoyance crept over the faces of the four.

"I have my facts correct. Depend upon that. I went to Sinnings' Hardware Store and got a rule. Then I went back and measured. I could hardly believe my own eyes. It hasn't rained you see for ten days. At first I didn't know what to think. Thoughts rushed through my head. I thought of subterranean passages and springs. Down under the ground went my mind, delving about. I sat on the floor of the bridge and rubbed my head. There wasn't a cloud in the sky, not one. Come out into the street and you'll see. There wasn't a cloud. There isn't a cloud now. Yes, there was a cloud. I don't want to keep back any facts. There was a cloud in the west down near the horizon, a cloud no bigger than a man's hand.

"Not that I think that has anything to do with it. There it is you see. You understand how puzzled I was.

"Then an idea came to me. I laughed. You'll laugh, too. Of course it rained over in Medina County. That's interesting, eh?

If we had no trains, no mails, no telegraph, we would know that it rained over in Medina County. That's where Wine Creek comes from. Everyone knows that. Little old Wine Creek brought us the news. That's interesting. I laughed. I thought I'd tell you—it's interesting, eh?"

Joe Welling turned and went out at the door. Taking a book from his pocket, he stopped and ran a finger down one of the pages. Again he was absorbed in his duties as agent of the Standard Oil Company. "Hern's Grocery will be getting low on coal oil. I'll see them," he muttered, hurrying along the street, and bowing politely to the right and left at the people walking past.

When George Willard went to work for the *Winesburg Eagle* he was besieged by Joe Welling. Joe envied the boy. It seemed to him that he was meant by Nature to be a reporter on a newspaper. "It is what I should be doing, there is no doubt of that," he declared, stopping George Willard on the sidewalk before Daugherty's Feed Store. His eyes began to glisten and his forefinger to tremble. "Of course I make more money with the Standard Oil Company and I'm only telling you," he added. "I've got nothing against you, but I should have your place. I could do the work at odd moments. Here and there I would run finding out things you'll never see."

Becoming more excited Joe Welling crowded the young reporter against the front of the feed store. He appeared to be lost in thought, rolling his eyes about and running a thin nervous hand through his hair. A smile spread over his face and his gold teeth glittered. "You get out your note book," he commanded. "You carry a little pad of paper in your pocket, don't you? I knew you did. Well, you set this down. I thought of it the other day. Let's take decay. Now what is decay? It's fire. It burns up wood and other things. You never thought of that? Of course not. This sidewalk here and this feed store, the trees down the street there—they're all on fire. They're burning up. Decay you see is always going on. It don't stop. Water and paint can't stop it. If a thing is iron, then what? It rusts, you see. That's fire, too. The world is on fire. Start your pieces in the paper that way. Just say in big letters *'The World Is On Fire.'* That will make 'em look up. They'll say you're a smart one. I don't care. I don't envy you. I just snatched that idea out of the air. I would make a newspaper hum. You got to admit that."

Turning quickly, Joe Welling walked rapidly away. When he had taken several steps he stopped and looked back. "I'm going to stick to you," he said. "I'm going to make you a regular hummer. I should start a newspaper myself, that's what I should do. I'd be a marvel. Everybody knows that."

When George Willard had been for a year on the *Winesburg Eagle*, four things happened to Joe Welling. His mother died, he came to live at the New Willard House, he became involved in a love affair, and he organized the Winesburg Baseball Club.

Joe organized the baseball club because he wanted to be a coach and in that position he began to win the respect of his townsmen. "He is a wonder," they declared after Joe's team had whipped the team from Medina County. "He gets everybody working together. You just watch him."

Upon the baseball field Joe Welling stood by first base, his whole body quivering with excitement. In spite of themselves all of the players watched him closely. The opposing pitcher became confused.

"Now! Now! Now! Now!" shouted the excited man. "Watch me! Watch me! Watch my fingers! Watch my hands! Watch my feet! Watch my eyes! Let's work together here! Watch me! In me you see all the movements of the game! Work with me! Work with me! Watch me! Watch me! Watch me!"

With runners of the Winesburg team on bases, Joe Welling became as one inspired. Before they knew what had come over them, the base runners were watching the man, edging off the bases, advancing, retreating, held as by an invisible cord. The players of the opposing team also watched Joe. They were fascinated. For a moment they watched and then as though to break a spell that hung over them, they began hurling the ball wildly about, and amid a series of fierce animal-like cries from the coach, the runners of the Winesburg team scampered home.

Joe Welling's love affair set the town of Winesburg on edge. When it began everyone whispered and shook his head. When people tried to laugh, the laughter was forced and unnatural. Joe fell in love with Sarah King, a lean, sad-looking woman who lived with her father and brother in a brick house that stood opposite the gate leading to the Winesburg Cemetery.

The two Kings, Edward the father, and Tom the son, were not popular in Winesburg. They were called proud and dangerous. They had come to Winesburg from some place in the South and ran a cider mill on the Trunion Pike. Tom King was reported to have killed a man before he came to Winesburg. He was twenty-seven years old and rode about town on a grey pony. Also he had a long yellow mustache that dropped down over his teeth, and always carried a heavy, wicked-looking walking stick in his hand. Once he killed a dog with the stick. The dog belonged to Win Pawsey, the shoe merchant, and stood on the sidewalk wagging its tail. Tom King killed it with one blow. He was arrested and paid a fine of ten dollars.

Old Edward King was small of stature and when he passed people in the street laughed a queer unmirthful laugh. When he laughed he scratched his left elbow with his right hand. The sleeve of his coat was almost worn through from the habit. As he walked along the street, looking nervously about and laughing, he seemed more dangerous than his silent, fierce looking son.

When Sarah King began walking out in the evening with Joe Welling, people shook their heads in alarm. She was tall and pale and had dark rings under her eyes. The couple looked ridiculous together. Under the trees they walked and Joe talked. His passionate eager protestations of love, heard coming out of the darkness by the cemetery wall, or from the deep shadows of the trees on the hill that ran up to the Fair Grounds from Waterworks Pond, were repeated in the stores. Men stood by the bar in the New Willard House laughing and talking of Joe's courtship. After the laughter came silence. The Winesburg baseball team, under his management, was winning game after game, and the town had begun to respect him. Sensing a tragedy, they waited, laughing nervously.

Late on a Saturday afternoon the meeting between Joe Welling and the two Kings, the anticipation of which had set the town on edge, took place in Joe Welling's room in the New Willard House. George Willard was a witness to the meeting. It came about in this way:

When the young reporter went to his room after the evening meal he saw Tom King and his father sitting in the half darkness in Joe's room. The son had the heavy walking stick in his hand and sat near the door. Old Edward King walked nervously about, scratching his left elbow with his right hand. The hallways were empty and silent.

George Willard went to his own room and sat down at his desk. He tried to write but his hand trembled so that he could not hold the pen. He also walked nervously up and down. Like the rest of the town of Winesburg he was perplexed and knew not what to do.

It was seven-thirty and fast growing dark when Joe Welling came along the station platform toward the New Willard House. In his arms he held a bundle of weeds and grasses. In spite of the terror that made his body shake, George Willard was amused at the sight of the small spry figure holding the grasses and half running along the platform.

Shaking with fright and anxiety, the young reporter lurked in the hallway outside the door of the room in which Joe Welling talked to the two Kings. There had been an oath, the nervous giggle of old Edward King, and then silence. Now the voice of Joe Welling, sharp and clear, broke forth. George Willard began to laugh. He understood. As he had swept all men before him, so now Joe Welling was carrying the two men in the room off their feet with a tidal wave of words. The listener in the hall walked up and down, lost in amazement.

Inside the room Joe Welling had paid no attention to the grumbled threat of Tom King. Absorbed in an idea he closed the door and lighting a lamp, spread the handful of weeds and grasses upon the floor. "I've got something here," he announced solemnly. "I was going to tell George Willard about it, let him make a piece out of it for the paper. I'm glad you're here. I wish Sarah were here also. I've been going to come to your house and tell you of some of my ideas. They're interesting. Sarah wouldn't let me. She said we'd quarrel. That's foolish."

Running up and down before the two perplexed men, Joe Welling began to explain. "Don't you make a mistake now," he cried. "This is something big." His voice was shrill with excitement. "You just follow me, you'll be interested. I know you will. Suppose this—suppose all of the wheat, the corn, the oats, the peas, the potatoes, were all by some miracle swept away. Now here we are, you see, in this county. There is a high fence built all around us. We'll suppose that. No one can get over the fence and all the fruits of the earth are destroyed, nothing left but these wild things, these grasses. Would we be done for? I ask you that. Would we be done for?" Again Tom King growled and for a moment there was silence in the room. Then again Joe plunged into the exposition of his idea. "Things would go hard for a time. I admit that. I've got to admit that. No getting around it. We'd be hard put to it. More than one fat stomach would cave in. But they couldn't down us. I should say not."

Tom King laughed good naturedly and the shivery, nervous laugh of Edward King rang through the house. Joe Welling hurried on. "We'd begin, you see, to breed up new vegetables and fruits. Soon we'd regain all we had lost. Mind, I don't say the new things would be the same as the old. They wouldn't. Maybe they'd be better, maybe not so good. That's interesting, eh? You can think about that. It starts your mind working, now don't it?"

In the room there was silence and then again old Edward King laughed nervously. "Say, I wish Sarah was here," cried Joe Welling. "Let's go up to your house. I want to tell her of this."

There was a scraping of chairs in the room. It was then that George Willard retreated to his own room. Leaning out at the window he saw Joe Welling going along the street with the two Kings. Tom King was forced to take extraordinary long strides to keep pace with the little man. As he strode along, he leaned over, listening—absorbed, fascinated. Joe Welling again talked excitedly. "Take milkweed now," he cried. "A lot might be done with milkweed, eh? It's almost unbelievable. I want you to think about it. I want you two to think about it. There would be a new vegetable kingdom you see. It's interesting, eh? It's an idea. Wait till you see Sarah, she'll get the idea. She'll be interested. Sarah is always interested in ideas. You can't be too smart for Sarah, now can you? Of course you can't. You know that."

Adventure

ALICE HINDMAN, a woman of twenty-seven when George Willard was a mere boy, had lived in Winesburg all her life. She clerked in Winney's Dry Goods Store and lived with her mother who had married a second husband.

Alice's step-father was a carriage painter, and given to drink. His story is an odd one. It will be worth telling some day.

At twenty-seven Alice was tall and somewhat slight. Her head was large and overshadowed her body. Her shoulders were a little stooped and her hair and eyes brown. She was very quiet but beneath a placid exterior a continual ferment went on.

When she was a girl of sixteen and before she began to work in the store, Alice had an affair with a young man. The young man, named Ned Currie, was older than Alice. He, like George Willard, was employed on the *Winesburg Eagle* and for a long time he went to see Alice almost every evening. Together the two walked under the trees through the streets of the town and talked of what they would do with their lives. Alice was then a very pretty girl and Ned Currie took her into his arms and kissed her. He became excited and said things he did not intend to say and Alice, betrayed by her desire to have something beautiful come into her rather narrow life, also grew excited. She also talked. The outer crust of her life, all of her natural diffidence and reserve, was torn away and she gave herself over to the emotions of love. When, late in the fall of her sixteenth year, Ned Currie went away to Cleveland where he hoped to get a place on a city newspaper and rise in the world, she wanted to go with him. With a trembling voice she told him what was in her mind. "I will work and you can work," she said. "I do not want to harness you to a needless expense that will prevent your making progress. Don't marry me now. We will get along without that and we can be together. Even though we live in the same house no one will say anything. In the city we will be unknown and people will pay no attention to us."

Ned Currie was puzzled by the determination and abandon of his sweetheart and was also deeply touched. He had wanted the girl to become his mistress but changed his mind. He wanted to protect and care for her. "You don't know what you're talking about," he said sharply; "you may be sure I'll let you do no such thing. As soon as I get a good job I'll come back. For the present you'll have to stay here. It's the only thing we can do."

On the evening before he left Winesburg to take up his new life in the city, Ned Currie went to call on Alice. They walked about through the streets for an hour and then got a rig from Wesley Moyer's livery and went for a drive in the country. The moon came up and they found themselves unable to talk. In his sadness the young man forgot the resolutions he had made regarding his conduct with the girl.

They got out of the buggy at a place where a long meadow ran down to the bank of Wine Creek and there in the dim light became lovers. When at midnight they returned to town they were both glad. It did not seem to them that anything that could happen in the future could blot out the wonder and beauty of the thing that had happened. "Now we will have to stick to each other, whatever happens we will have to do that," Ned Currie said as he left the girl at her father's door.

The young newspaper man did not succeed in getting a place on a Cleveland paper and went west to Chicago. For a time he was lonely and wrote to Alice almost every day. Then he was caught up by the life of the city; he began to make friends and found new interests in life. In Chicago he boarded at a house where there were several women. One of them attracted his attention and he forgot Alice in Winesburg. At the end of a year he had stopped writing letters, and only once in a long time, when he was lonely or when he went into one of the city parks and saw the moon shining on the grass as it had shone that night on the meadow by Wine Creek, did he think of her at all.

In Winesburg the girl who had been loved grew to be a woman. When she was twenty-two years old her father, who owned a harness repair shop, died suddenly. The harness maker was an old soldier, and after a few months his wife received a widow's pension. She used the first money she got to buy a loom and became a weaver of carpets, and Alice got a place in Winney's store. For a number of years nothing could have induced her to believe that Ned Currie would not in the end return to her.

She was glad to be employed because the daily round of toil in the store made the time of waiting seem less long and uninteresting. She began to save money, thinking that when she had saved two or three hundred dollars she would follow her lover to the city and try if her presence would not win back his affections.

Alice did not blame Ned Currie for what had happened in the moonlight in the field, but felt that she could never marry another man. To her the thought of giving to another what she still felt could belong only to Ned seemed monstrous. When other young men tried to attract her attention she would have nothing to do with them. "I am his wife and shall remain his wife whether he comes back or not," she whispered to herself, and for all of her willingness to support herself could not have understood the growing modern idea of a woman's owning herself and giving and taking for her own ends in life.

Alice worked in the dry goods store from eight in the morning until six at night and on three evenings a week went back to the store to stay from seven until nine. As time passed and she became more and more lonely she began to practice the devices common to lonely people. When at night she went upstairs into her own room she knelt on the floor to pray and in her prayers whispered things she wanted to say to her lover. She became attached to inanimate objects, and because it was her own, could not bear to have anyone touch the furniture of her room. The trick of saving money, begun for a purpose, was carried on after the scheme of going to the city to find Ned Currie had been given up. It became a fixed habit, and when she needed new clothes she did not get them. Sometimes on rainy afternoons in the store she got out her bank book and, letting it lie open before her, spent hours dreaming impossible dreams of saving money enough so that the interest would support both herself and her future husband.

"Ned always liked to travel about," she thought. "I'll give him the chance. Some day when we are married and I can save both his money and my own, we will be rich. Then we can travel together all over the world."

In the dry goods store weeks ran into months and months

into years as Alice waited and dreamed of her lover's return. Her employer, a grey old man with false teeth and a thin grey mustache that drooped down over his mouth, was not given to conversation, and sometimes, on rainy days and in the winter when a storm raged in Main Street, long hours passed when no customers came in. Alice arranged and rearranged the stock. She stood near the front window where she could look down the deserted street and thought of the evenings when she had walked with Ned Currie and of what he had said. "We will have to stick to each other now." The words echoed and re-echoed through the mind of the maturing woman. Tears came into her eyes. Sometimes when her employer had gone out and she was alone in the store she put her head on the counter and wept. "Oh, Ned, I am waiting," she whispered over and over, and all the time the creeping fear that he would never come back grew stronger within her.

In the spring when the rains have passed and before the long hot days of summer have come, the country about Winesburg is delightful. The town lies in the midst of open fields, but beyond the fields are pleasant patches of woodlands. In the wooded places are many little cloistered nooks, quiet places where lovers go to sit on Sunday afternoons. Through the trees they look out across the fields and see farmers at work about the barns or people driving up and down on the roads. In the town bells ring and occasionally a train passes, looking like a toy thing in the distance.

For several years after Ned Currie went away Alice did not go into the wood with other young people on Sunday, but one day after he had been gone for two or three years and when her loneliness seemed unbearable, she put on her best dress and set out. Finding a little sheltered place from which she could see the town and a long stretch of the fields, she sat down. Fear of age and ineffectuality took possession of her. She could not sit still, and arose. As she stood looking out over the land something, perhaps the thought of never ceasing life as it expresses itself in the flow of the seasons, fixed her mind on the passing years. With a shiver of dread, she realized that for her the beauty and freshness of youth had passed. For the first time she felt that she had been cheated. She did not blame Ned Currie and did not know what to blame. Sadness swept over her. Dropping to her knees, she tried to pray, but instead of prayers words of protest came to her lips. "It is not going to come to me. I will never find happiness. Why do I tell myself lies?" she cried, and an odd sense of relief came with this, her first bold attempt to face the fear that had become a part of her everyday life.

In the year when Alice Hindman became twenty-five two things happened to disturb the dull uneventfulness of her days. Her mother married Bush Milton, the carriage painter of Winesburg, and she herself became a member of the Winesburg Methodist Church. Alice joined the church because she had become frightened by the loneliness of her position in life. Her mother's second marriage had emphasized her isolation. "I am becoming old and queer. If Ned comes he will not want me. In the city where he is living men are perpetually young. There is so much going on that they do not have time to grow old," she told herself with a grim little smile, and went resolutely about the business of becoming acquainted with people. Every Thursday evening when the store had closed she went to a prayer meeting in the basement of the church and on Sunday evening attended a meeting of an organization called The Epworth League.

When Will Hurley, a middle-aged man who clerked in a drug store and who also belonged to the church, offered to walk home with her she did not protest. "Of course I will not let him make a practice of being with me, but if he comes to see me once in a long time there can be no harm in that," she told herself, still determined in her loyalty to Ned Currie.

Without realizing what was happening, Alice was trying feebly at first, but with growing determination, to get a new hold upon life. Beside the drug clerk she walked in silence, but sometimes in the darkness as they went stolidly along she put out her hand and touched softly the folds of his coat. When he left her at the gate before her mother's house she did not go indoors, but stood for a moment by the door. She wanted to call to the drug clerk, to ask him to sit with her in the darkness on the porch before the house, but was afraid he would not understand. "It is not him that I want," she told herself; "I want to avoid being so much alone. If I am not careful I will grow unaccustomed to being with people."

During the early fall of her twenty-seventh year a passionate restlessness took possession of Alice. She could not bear to be in the company of the drug clerk, and when, in the evening, he came to walk with her she sent him away. Her mind became intensely active and when, weary from the long hours of standing behind the counter in the store, she went home and crawled into bed, she could not sleep. With staring eyes she looked into the darkness. Her imagination, like a child awakened from long sleep, played about the room. Deep within her there was something that would not be cheated by phantasies and that demanded some definite answer from life.

Alice took a pillow into her arms and held it tightly against her breasts. Getting out of bed, she arranged a blanket so that in the darkness it looked like a form lying between the sheets and, kneeling beside the bed, she caressed it, whispering words over and over, like a refrain. "Why doesn't something happen? Why am I left here alone?" she muttered. Although she sometimes thought of Ned Currie, she no longer depended on him. Her desire had grown vague. She did not want Ned Currie or any other man. She wanted to be loved, to have something answer the call that was growing louder and louder within her.

And then one night when it rained Alice had an adventure. It frightened and confused her. She had come home from the store at nine and found the house empty. Bush Milton had gone off to town and her mother to the house of a neighbor. Alice went upstairs to her room and undressed in the darkness. For a moment she stood by the window hearing the rain beat against the glass and then a strange desire took possession of her. Without stopping to think of what she intended to do, she ran downstairs through the dark house and out into the rain. As she stood on the little grass plot before the house and felt the cold rain on her body a mad desire to run naked through the streets took possession of her.

She thought that the rain would have some creative and wonderful effect on her body. Not for years had she felt so full of youth and courage. She wanted to leap and run, to cry out, to find some other lonely human and embrace him. On the brick sidewalk before the house a man stumbled homeward. Alice started to run. A wild, desperate mood took possession of her. "What do I care who it is. He is alone, and I will go to him," she thought; and then without stopping to consider the possible result of her madness, called softly. "Wait!" she cried. "Don't go away. Whoever you are, you must wait."

The man on the sidewalk stopped and stood listening. He was an old man and somewhat deaf. Putting his hand to his mouth, he shouted: "What? What say?" he called.

Alice dropped to the ground and lay trembling. She was so frightened at the thought of what she had done that when the man had gone on his way she did not dare get to her feet, but crawled on hands and knees through the grass to the house. When she got to her own room she bolted the door and drew her dressing table across the doorway. Her body shook as with a chill and her hands trembled so that she had difficulty getting into her nightdress. When she got into bed she buried her face in the pillow and wept brokenheartedly. "What is the matter with me? I will do something dreadful if I am not careful," she thought, and turning her face to the wall, began trying to force herself to face bravely the fact that many people must live and die alone, even in Winesburg.

Respectability

IF you have lived in cities and have walked in the park on a summer afternoon, you have perhaps seen, blinking in a corner of his iron cage, a huge, grotesque kind of monkey, a creature with ugly, sagging, hairless skin below his eyes and a bright purple underbody. This monkey is a true monster. In the completeness of his ugliness he achieved a kind of perverted beauty. Children stopping before the cage are fascinated, men turn away with an air of disgust, and women linger for a moment, trying perhaps to remember which one of their male acquaintances the thing in some faint way resembles.

Had you been in the earlier years of your life a citizen of the village of Winesburg, Ohio, there would have been for you no mystery in regard to the beast in his cage. "It is like Wash Williams," you would have said. "As he sits in the corner there, the beast is exactly like old Wash sitting on the grass in the station yard on a summer evening after he has closed his office for the night."

Wash Williams, the telegraph operator of Winesburg, was the ugliest thing in town. His girth was immense, his neck thin, his legs feeble. He was dirty. Everything about him was unclean. Even the whites of his eyes looked soiled.

I go too fast. Not everything about Wash was unclean. He took care of his hands. His fingers were fat, but there was something sensitive and shapely in the hand that lay on the table by the instrument in the telegraph office. In his youth Wash Williams had been called the best telegraph operator in the state, and in spite of his degradement to the obscure office at Winesburg, he was still proud of his ability.

Wash Williams did not associate with the men of the town in which he lived. "I'll have nothing to do with them," he said, looking with bleary eyes at the men who walked along the station platform past the telegraph office. Up along Main Street he went in the evening to Ed Griffith's saloon, and after drinking unbelievable quantities of beer staggered off to his room in the New Willard House and to his bed for the night.

Wash Williams was a man of courage. A thing had happened

to him that made him hate life, and he hated it whole-heartedly, with the abandon of a poet. First of all, he hated women. "Bitches," he called them. His feeling toward men was somewhat different. He pitied them. "Does not every man let his life be managed for him by some bitch or another?" he asked.

In Winesburg no attention was paid to Wash Williams and his hatred of his fellows. Once Mrs. White, the banker's wife, complained to the telegraph company, saying that the office in Winesburg was dirty and smelled abominably, but nothing came of her complaint. Here and there a man respected the operator. Instinctively the man felt in him a glowing resentment of something he had not the courage to resent. When Wash walked through the streets such a one had an instinct to pay him homage, to raise his hat or to bow before him. The superintendent who had supervision over the telegraph operators on the railroad that went through Winesburg felt that way. He had put Wash into the obscure office at Winesburg to avoid discharging him, and he meant to keep him there. When he received the letter of complaint from the banker's wife, he tore it up and laughed unpleasantly. For some reason he thought of his own wife as he tore up the letter.

Wash Williams once had a wife. When he was still a young man he married a woman at Dayton, Ohio. The woman was tall and slender and had blue eyes and yellow hair. Wash was himself a comely youth. He loved the woman with a love as absorbing as the hatred he later felt for all women.

In all of Winesburg there was but one person who knew the story of the thing that had made ugly the person and the character of Wash Williams. He once told the story to George Willard and the telling of the tale came about in this way:

George Willard went one evening to walk with Belle Carpenter, a trimmer of women's hats who worked in a millinery shop kept by Mrs. Kate McHugh. The young man was not in love with the woman, who, in fact, had a suitor who worked as bartender in Ed Griffith's saloon, but as they walked about under the trees they occasionally embraced. The night and their own thoughts had aroused something in them. As they were returning to Main Street they passed the little lawn beside the railroad station and saw Wash Williams apparently asleep on the grass beneath a tree. On the next evening the operator and

George Willard walked out together. Down the railroad they went and sat on a pile of decaying railroad ties beside the tracks. It was then that the operator told the young reporter his story of hate.

Perhaps a dozen times George Willard and the strange, shapeless man who lived at his father's hotel had been on the point of talking. The young man looked at the hideous, leering face staring about the hotel dining room and was consumed with curiosity. Something he saw lurking in the staring eyes told him that the man who had nothing to say to others had nevertheless something to say to him. On the pile of railroad ties on the summer evening, he waited expectantly. When the operator remained silent and seemed to have changed his mind about talking, he tried to make conversation. "Were you ever married, Mr. Williams?" he began. "I suppose you were and your wife is dead, is that it?"

Wash Williams spat forth a succession of vile oaths. "Yes, she is dead," he agreed. "She is dead as all women are dead. She is a living-dead thing, walking in the sight of men and making the earth foul by her presence." Staring into the boy's eyes, the man became purple with rage. "Don't have fool notions in your head," he commanded. "My wife, she is dead; yes, surely. I tell you, all women are dead, my mother, your mother, that tall dark woman who works in the millinery store and with whom I saw you walking about yesterday,—all of them, they are all dead. I tell you there is something rotten about them. I was married, sure. My wife was dead before she married me, she was a foul thing come out of a woman more foul. She was a thing sent to make life unbearable to me. I was a fool, do you see, as you are now, and so I married this woman. I would like to see men a little begin to understand women. They are sent to prevent men making the world worth while. It is a trick in Nature. Ugh! They are creeping, crawling, squirming things, they with their soft hands and their blue eyes. The sight of a woman sickens me. Why I don't kill every woman I see I don't know."

Half frightened and yet fascinated by the light burning in the eyes of the hideous old man, George Willard listened, afire with curiosity. Darkness came on and he leaned forward trying to see the face of the man who talked. When, in the gathering darkness, he could no longer see the purple, bloated face and the burning eyes, a curious fancy came to him. Wash Williams talked in low even tones that made his words seem the more terrible. In the darkness the young reporter found himself imagining that he sat on the railroad ties beside a comely young man with black hair and black shining eyes. There was something almost beautiful in the voice of Wash Williams, the hideous, telling his story of hate.

The telegraph operator of Winesburg, sitting in the darkness on the railroad ties, had become a poet. Hatred had raised him to that elevation. "It is because I saw you kissing the lips of that Belle Carpenter that I tell you my story," he said. "What happened to me may next happen to you. I want to put you on your guard. Already you may be having dreams in your head. I want to destroy them."

Wash Williams began telling the story of his married life with the tall blonde girl with blue eyes whom he had met when he was a young operator at Dayton, Ohio. Here and there his story was touched with moments of beauty intermingled with strings of vile curses. The operator had married the daughter of a dentist who was the youngest of three sisters. On his marriage day, because of his ability, he was promoted to a position as dispatcher at an increased salary and sent to an office at Columbus, Ohio. There he settled down with his young wife and began buying a house on the installment plan.

The young telegraph operator was madly in love. With a kind of religious fervor he had managed to go through the pitfalls of his youth and to remain virginal until after his marriage. He made for George Willard a picture of his life in the house at Columbus, Ohio, with the young wife. "In the garden back of our house we planted vegetables," he said, "you know, peas and corn and such things. We went to Columbus in early March and as soon as the days became warm I went to work in the garden. With a spade I turned up the black ground while she ran about laughing and pretending to be afraid of the worms I uncovered. Late in April came the planting. In the little paths among the seed beds she stood holding a paper bag in her hand. The bag was filled with seeds. A few at a time she handed me the seeds that I might thrust them into the warm, soft ground."

For a moment there was a catch in the voice of the man talking in the darkness. "I loved her," he said. "I don't claim not to be a fool. I love her yet. There in the dusk in the spring evening I crawled along the black ground to her feet and groveled before her. I kissed her shoes and the ankles above her shoes. When the hem of her garment touched my face I trembled. When after two years of that life I found she had managed to acquire three other lovers who came regularly to our house when I was away at work, I didn't want to touch them or her. I just sent her home to her mother and said nothing. There was nothing to say. I had four hundred dollars in the bank and I gave her that. I didn't ask her reasons. I didn't say anything. When she had gone I cried like a silly boy. Pretty soon I had a chance to sell the house and I sent that money to her."

Wash Williams and George Willard arose from the pile of railroad ties and walked along the tracks toward town. The operator finished his tale quickly, breathlessly.

"Her mother sent for me," he said. "She wrote me a letter and asked me to come to their house at Dayton. When I got there it was evening about this time."

Wash Williams' voice rose to a half scream. "I sat in the parlor of that house two hours. Her mother took me in there and left me. Their house was stylish. They were what is called respectable people. There were plush chairs and a couch in the room. I was trembling all over. I hated the men I thought had wronged her. I was sick of living alone and wanted her back. The longer I waited the more raw and tender I became. I thought that if she came in and just touched me with her hand I would perhaps faint away. I ached to forgive and forget."

Wash Williams stopped and stood staring at George Willard. The boy's body shook as from a chill. Again the man's voice became soft and low. "She came into the room naked," he went on. "Her mother did that. While I sat there she was taking the girl's clothes off, perhaps coaxing her to do it. First I heard voices at the door that led into a little hallway and then it opened softly. The girl was ashamed and stood perfectly still staring at the floor. The mother didn't come into the room. When she had pushed the girl in through the door she stood in the hallway waiting, hoping we would—well, you see—waiting."

George Willard and the telegraph operator came into the main street of Winesburg. The lights from the store windows lay bright and shining on the sidewalks. People moved about laughing and talking. The young reporter felt ill and weak. In imagination, he also became old and shapeless. "I didn't get the mother killed," said Wash Williams, staring up and down the street. "I struck her once with a chair and then the neighbors came in and took it away. She screamed so loud you see. I won't ever have a chance to kill her now. She died of a fever a month after that happened."

The Thinker

THE house in which Seth Richmond of Winesburg lived with his mother had been at one time the show place of the town, but when young Seth lived there its glory had become somewhat dimmed. The huge brick house which Banker White had built on Buckeye Street had overshadowed it. The Richmond place was in a little valley far out at the end of Main Street. Farmers coming into town by a dusty road from the south passed by a grove of walnut trees, skirted the Fair Ground with its high board fence covered with advertisements, and trotted their horses down through the valley past the Richmond place into town. As much of the country north and south of Winesburg was devoted to fruit and berry raising, Seth saw wagon-loads of berry pickers—boys, girls, and women —going to the fields in the morning and returning covered with dust in the evening. The chattering crowd, with their rude jokes cried out from wagon to wagon, sometimes irritated him sharply. He regretted that he also could not laugh boisterously, shout meaningless jokes and make of himself a figure in the endless stream of moving, giggling activity that went up and down the road.

The Richmond house was built of limestone, and although it was said in the village to have become run down, had in reality grown more beautiful with every passing year. Already time had begun a little to color the stone, lending a golden richness to its surface and in the evening or on dark days touching the shaded places beneath the eaves with wavering patches of browns and blacks.

The house had been built by Seth's grandfather, a stone quarryman, and it, together with the stone quarries on Lake Erie eighteen miles to the north, had been left to his son, Clarence Richmond, Seth's father. Clarence Richmond, a quiet passionate man extraordinarily admired by his neighbors, had been killed in a street fight with the editor of a newspaper in Toledo, Ohio. The fight concerned the publication of Clarence Richmond's name coupled with that of a woman school teacher, and as the dead man had begun the row by firing upon the editor, the effort to punish the slayer was unsuccessful. After the quarryman's death it was found that much of the money left to him had been squandered in speculation and in insecure investments made through the influence of friends.

Left with but a small income, Virginia Richmond had settled down to a retired life in the village and to the raising of her son. Although she had been deeply moved by the death of the husband and father, she did not at all believe the stories concerning him that ran about after his death. To her mind, the sensitive, boyish man whom all had instinctively loved, was but an unfortunate, a being too fine for everyday life. "You'll be hearing all sorts of stories, but you are not to believe what you hear," she said to her son. "He was a good man, full of tenderness for everyone, and should not have tried to be a man of affairs. No matter how much I were to plan and dream of your future, I could not imagine anything better for you than that you turn out as good a man as your father."

Several years after the death of her husband, Virginia Richmond had become alarmed at the growing demands upon her income and had set herself to the task of increasing it. She had learned stenography and through the influence of her husband's friends got the position of court stenographer at the county seat. There she went by train each morning during the sessions of the court and when no court sat, spent her days working among the rosebushes in her garden. She was a tall, straight figure of a woman with a plain face and a great mass of brown hair.

In the relationship between Seth Richmond and his mother, there was a quality that even at eighteen had begun to color all of his traffic with men. An almost unhealthy respect for the youth kept the mother for the most part silent in his presence. When she did speak sharply to him he had only to look steadily into her eyes to see dawning there the puzzled look he had already noticed in the eyes of others when he looked at them.

The truth was that the son thought with remarkable clearness and the mother did not. She expected from all people certain conventional reactions to life. A boy was your son, you scolded him and he trembled and looked at the floor. When you had scolded enough he wept and all was forgiven. After the weeping and when he had gone to bed, you crept into his room and kissed him.

Virginia Richmond could not understand why her son did not do these things. After the severest reprimand, he did not tremble and look at the floor but instead looked steadily at her, causing uneasy doubts to invade her mind. As for creeping into his room—after Seth had passed his fifteenth year, she would have been half afraid to do anything of the kind.

Once when he was a boy of sixteen, Seth in company with two other boys, ran away from home. The three boys climbed into the open door of an empty freight car and rode some forty miles to a town where a fair was being held. One of the boys had a bottle filled with a combination of whiskey and blackberry wine, and the three sat with legs dangling out of the car door drinking from the bottle. Seth's two companions sang and waved their hands to idlers about the stations of the towns through which the train passed. They planned raids upon the baskets of farmers who had come with their families to the fair. "We will live like kings and won't have to spend a penny to see the fair and horse races," they declared boastfully.

After the disappearance of Seth, Virginia Richmond walked up and down the floor of her home filled with vague alarms. Although on the next day she discovered, through an inquiry made by the town marshal, on what adventure the boys had gone, she could not quiet herself. All through the night she lay awake hearing the clock tick and telling herself that Seth, like his father, would come to a sudden and violent end. So determined was she that the boy should this time feel the weight of her wrath that, although she would not allow the marshal to interfere with his adventure, she got out pencil and paper and wrote down a series of sharp, stinging reproofs she intended to pour out upon him. The reproofs she committed to memory, going about the garden and saying them aloud like an actor memorizing his part.

And when, at the end of the week, Seth returned, a little weary and with coal soot in his ears and about his eyes, she again found herself unable to reprove him. Walking into the house he hung his cap on a nail by the kitchen door and stood looking steadily at her. "I wanted to turn back within an hour after we had started," he explained. "I didn't know what to do. I knew you would be bothered, but I knew also that if I didn't go on I would be ashamed of myself. I went through with the thing for my own good. It was uncomfortable, sleeping on wet straw, and two drunken negroes came and slept with us. When I stole a lunch basket out of a farmer's wagon I couldn't help thinking of his children going all day without food. I was sick of the whole affair, but I was determined to stick it out until the other boys were ready to come back."

"I'm glad you did stick it out," replied the mother, half resentfully, and kissing him upon the forehead pretended to busy herself with the work about the house.

On a summer evening Seth Richmond went to the New Willard House to visit his friend, George Willard. It had rained during the afternoon, but as he walked through Main Street, the sky had partially cleared and a golden glow lit up the west. Going around a corner, he turned in at the door of the hotel and began to climb the stairway leading up to his friend's room. In the hotel office the proprietor and two traveling men were engaged in a discussion of politics.

On the stairway Seth stopped and listened to the voices of the men below. They were excited and talked rapidly. Tom Willard was berating the traveling men. "I am a Democrat but your talk makes me sick," he said. "You don't understand McKinley. McKinley and Mark Hanna are friends. It is impossible perhaps for your mind to grasp that. If anyone tells you that a friendship can be deeper and bigger and more worth while than dollars and cents, or even more worth while than state politics, you snicker and laugh."

The landlord was interrupted by one of the guests, a tall grey-mustached man who worked for a wholesale grocery house. "Do you think that I've lived in Cleveland all these years without knowing Mark Hanna?" he demanded. "Your talk is piffle. Hanna is after money and nothing else. This McKinley is his tool. He has McKinley bluffed and don't you forget it."

The young man on the stairs did not linger to hear the rest of the discussion, but went on up the stairway and into a little dark hall. Something in the voices of the men talking in the hotel office started a chain of thoughts in his mind. He was lonely and had begun to think that loneliness was a part of his character, something that would always stay with him. Stepping into a side hall he stood by a window that looked into an alleyway. At the back of his shop stood Abner Groff, the town baker. His tiny bloodshot eyes looked up and down the alleyway. In his shop someone called the baker who pretended not to hear. The baker had an empty milk bottle in his hand and an angry sullen look in his eyes.

In Winesburg, Seth Richmond was called the "deep one." "He's like his father," men said as he went through the streets. "He'll break out some of these days. You wait and see."

The talk of the town and the respect with which men and boys instinctively greeted him, as all men greet silent people, had affected Seth Richmond's outlook on life and on himself. He, like most boys, was deeper than boys are given credit for being, but he was not what the men of the town, and even his mother, thought him to be. No great underlying purpose lay back of his habitual silence, and he had no definite plan for his life. When the boys with whom he associated were noisy and quarrelsome, he stood quietly at one side. With calm eyes he watched the gesticulating lively figures of his companions. He wasn't particularly interested in what was going on, and sometimes wondered if he would ever be particularly interested in anything. Now, as he stood in the half-darkness by the window watching the baker, he wished that he himself might become thoroughly stirred by something, even by the fits of sullen anger for which Baker Groff was noted. "It would be better for me if I could become excited and wrangle about politics like windy old Tom Willard," he thought, as he left the window and went again along the hallway to the room occupied by his friend, George Willard.

George Willard was older than Seth Richmond, but in the rather odd friendship between the two, it was he who was forever courting and the younger boy who was being courted. The paper on which George worked had one policy. It strove to mention by name in each issue, as many as possible of the inhabitants of the village. Like an excited dog, George Willard ran here and there, noting on his pad of paper who had gone on business to the county seat or had returned from a visit to a neighboring village. All day he wrote little facts upon the pad.

"A. P. Wringlet has received a shipment of straw hats. Ed Byer-baum and Tom Marshall were in Cleveland Friday. Uncle Tom Sinnings is building a new barn on his place on the Valley Road."

The idea that George Willard would some day become a writer had given him a place of distinction in Winesburg, and to Seth Richmond he talked continually of the matter. "It's the easiest of all lives to live," he declared, becoming excited and boastful. "Here and there you go and there is no one to boss you. Though you are in India or in the South Seas in a boat, you have but to write and there you are. Wait till I get my name up and then see what fun I shall have."

In George Willard's room, which had a window looking down into an alleyway and one that looked across railroad tracks to Biff Carter's Lunch Room facing the railroad station, Seth Richmond sat in a chair and looked at the floor. George Willard who had been sitting for an hour idly playing with a lead pencil, greeted him effusively. "I've been trying to write a love story," he explained, laughing nervously. Lighting a pipe he began walking up and down the room. "I know what I'm going to do. I'm going to fall in love. I've been sitting here and thinking it over and I'm going to do it."

As though embarrassed by his declaration, George went to a window and turning his back to his friend leaned out. "I know who I'm going to fall in love with," he said sharply. "It's Helen White. She is the only girl in town with any 'get-up' to her."

Struck with a new idea, young Willard turned and walked towards his visitor. "Look here," he said. "You know Helen White better than I do. I want you to tell her what I said. You just get to talking to her and say that I'm in love with her. See what she says to that. See how she takes it, and then you come and tell me."

Seth Richmond arose and went towards the door. The words of his comrade irritated him unbearably. "Well, good-bye," he said briefly.

George was amazed. Running forward he stood in the dark-ness trying to look into Seth's face. "What's the matter? What are you going to do? You stay here and let's talk," he urged.

A wave of resentment directed against his friend, the men of the town who were, he thought, perpetually talking of nothing, and most of all, against his own habit of silence, made Seth half desperate. "Aw, speak to her yourself," he burst forth and then going quickly through the door, slammed it sharply in his friend's face. "I'm going to find Helen White and talk to her, but not about him," he muttered.

Seth went down the stairway and out at the front door of the hotel muttering with wrath. Crossing a little dusty street and climbing a low iron railing, he went to sit upon the grass in the station yard. George Willard he thought a profound fool, and he wished that he had said so more vigorously. Although his acquaintanceship with Helen White, the banker's daughter, was outwardly but casual, she was often the subject of his thoughts and he felt that she was something private and personal to himself. "The busy fool with his love stories," he muttered, staring back over his shoulder at George Willard's room, "why does he never tire of his eternal talking."

It was berry harvest time in Winesburg and upon the station platform men and boys loaded the boxes of red, fragrant berries into two express cars that stood upon the siding. A June moon was in the sky, although in the west a storm threatened, and no street lamps were lighted. In the dim light the figures of the men standing upon the express truck and pitching the boxes in at the doors of the cars were but dimly discernible. Upon the iron railing that protected the station lawn sat other men. Pipes were lighted. Village jokes went back and forth. Away in the distance a train whistled and the men loading the boxes into the cars worked with renewed activity.

Seth arose from his place on the grass and went silently past the men perched upon the railing and into Main Street. He had come to a resolution. "I'll get out of here," he told himself. "What good am I here? I'm going to some city and go to work. I'll tell mother about it to-morrow."

Seth Richmond went slowly along Main Street, past Wacker's Cigar Store and the Town Hall, and into Buckeye Street. He was depressed by the thought that he was not a part of the life in his own town, but the depression did not cut deeply as he did not think of himself as at fault. In the heavy shadows of a big tree before Dr. Welling's house, he stopped and stood watching half-witted Turk Smollet, who was pushing a wheelbarrow in the road. The old man with his absurdly boyish mind had a dozen long boards on the wheelbarrow, and as he hurried along the road, balanced the load with extreme nicety. "Easy there, Turk! Steady now, old boy!" the old man shouted to himself, and laughed so that the load of boards rocked dangerously.

Seth knew Turk Smollet, the half dangerous old wood chopper whose peculiarities added so much of color to the life of the village. He knew that when Turk got into Main Street he would become the center of a whirlwind of cries and comments, that in truth the old man was going far out of his way in order to pass through Main Street and exhibit his skill in wheeling the boards. "If George Willard were here, he'd have something to say," thought Seth. "George belongs to this town. He'd shout at Turk and Turk would shout at him. They'd both be secretly pleased by what they had said. It's different with me. I don't belong. I'll not make a fuss about it, but I'm going to get out of here."

Seth stumbled forward through the half darkness, feeling himself an outcast in his own town. He began to pity himself, but a sense of the absurdity of his thoughts made him smile. In the end he decided that he was simply old beyond his years and not at all a subject for self-pity. "I'm made to go to work. I may be able to make a place for myself by steady working, and I might as well be at it," he decided.

Seth went to the house of Banker White and stood in the darkness by the front door. On the door hung a heavy brass knocker, an innovation introduced into the village by Helen White's mother, who had also organized a woman's club for the study of poetry. Seth raised the knocker and let it fall. Its heavy clatter sounded like a report from distant guns. "How awkward and foolish I am," he thought. "If Mrs. White comes to the door, I don't know what to say."

It was Helen White who came to the door and found Seth standing at the edge of the porch. Blushing with pleasure, she stepped forward, closing the door softly. "I'm going to get out of town. I don't know what I'll do, but I'm going to get out of here and go to work. I think I'll go to Columbus," he said. "Perhaps I'll get into the State University down there. Anyway, I'm going. I'll tell mother to-night." He hesitated and looked doubtfully about. "Perhaps you wouldn't mind coming to walk with me?"

Seth and Helen walked through the streets beneath the trees. Heavy clouds had drifted across the face of the moon, and before them in the deep twilight went a man with a short ladder upon his shoulder. Hurrying forward, the man stopped at the street crossing and, putting the ladder against the wooden lamp post, lighted the village lights so that their way was half lighted, half darkened, by the lamps and by the deepening shadows cast by the low-branched trees. In the tops of the trees the wind began to play, disturbing the sleeping birds so that they flew about calling plaintively. In the lighted space before one of the lamps, two bats wheeled and circled, pursuing the gathering swarm of night flies.

Since Seth had been a boy in knee trousers there had been a half expressed intimacy between him and the maiden who now for the first time walked beside him. For a time she had been beset with a madness for writing notes which she addressed to Seth. He had found them concealed in his books at school and one had been given him by a child met in the street, while several had been delivered through the village post office.

The notes had been written in a round, boyish hand and had reflected a mind inflamed by novel reading. Seth had not answered them, although he had been moved and flattered by some of the sentences scrawled in pencil upon the stationery of the banker's wife. Putting them into the pocket of his coat, he went through the street or stood by the fence in the school yard with something burning at his side. He thought it fine that he should be thus selected as the favorite of the richest and most attractive girl in town.

Helen and Seth stopped by a fence near where a low dark building faced the street. The building had once been a factory for the making of barrel staves but was now vacant. Across the street upon the porch of a house a man and woman talked of their childhood, their voices coming clearly across to the half-embarrassed youth and maiden. There was the sound of scraping chairs and the man and woman came down the gravel path to a wooden gate. Standing outside the gate, the man leaned over and kissed the woman. "For old times' sake," he said and, turning, walked rapidly away along the sidewalk.

"That's Belle Turner," whispered Helen, and put her hand boldly into Seth's hand. "I didn't know she had a fellow. I

thought she was too old for that." Seth laughed uneasily. The
hand of the girl was warm and a strange, dizzy feeling crept
over him. Into his mind came a desire to tell her something he
had been determined not to tell. "George Willard's in love
with you," he said, and in spite of his agitation his voice was
low and quiet. "He's writing a story, and he wants to be in
love. He wants to know how it feels. He wanted me to tell you
and see what you said."

Again Helen and Seth walked in silence. They came to the
garden surrounding the old Richmond place and going
through a gap in the hedge sat on a wooden bench beneath a
bush.

On the street as he walked beside the girl new and daring
thoughts had come into Seth Richmond's mind. He began to
regret his decision to get out of town. "It would be something
new and altogether delightful to remain and walk often
through the streets with Helen White," he thought. In imagination he saw himself putting his arm about her waist and
feeling her arms clasped tightly about his neck. One of those
odd combinations of events and places made him connect the
idea of love-making with this girl and a spot he had visited
some days before. He had gone on an errand to the house of a
farmer who lived on a hillside beyond the Fair Ground and
had returned by a path through a field. At the foot of the hill
below the farmer's house Seth had stopped beneath a sycamore
tree and looked about him. A soft humming noise had greeted
his ears. For a moment he had thought the tree must be the
home of a swarm of bees.

And then, looking down, Seth had seen the bees everywhere
all about him in the long grass. He stood in a mass of weeds
that grew waist-high in the field that ran away from the hillside.
The weeds were abloom with tiny purple blossoms and gave
forth an overpowering fragrance. Upon the weeds the bees
were gathered in armies, singing as they worked.

Seth imagined himself lying on a summer evening, buried
deep among the weeds beneath the tree. Beside him, in the
scene built in his fancy, lay Helen White, her hand lying in his
hand. A peculiar reluctance kept him from kissing her lips, but
he felt he might have done that if he wished. Instead, he lay

perfectly still, looking at her and listening to the army of bees that sang the sustained masterful song of labor above his head.

On the bench in the garden Seth stirred uneasily. Releasing the hand of the girl, he thrust his hands into his trouser pockets. A desire to impress the mind of his companion with the importance of the resolution he had made came over him and he nodded his head toward the house. "Mother'll make a fuss, I suppose," he whispered. "She hasn't thought at all about what I'm going to do in life. She thinks I'm going to stay on here forever just being a boy."

Seth's voice became charged with boyish earnestness. "You see, I've got to strike out. I've got to get to work. It's what I'm good for."

Helen White was impressed. She nodded her head and a feeling of admiration swept over her. "This is as it should be," she thought. "This boy is not a boy at all, but a strong, purposeful man." Certain vague desires that had been invading her body were swept away and she sat up very straight on the bench. The thunder continued to rumble and flashes of heat lightning lit up the eastern sky. The garden that had been so mysterious and vast, a place that with Seth beside her might have become the background for strange and wonderful adventures, now seemed no more than an ordinary Winesburg back yard, quite definite and limited in its outlines.

"What will you do up there?" she whispered.

Seth turned half around on the bench, striving to see her face in the darkness. He thought her infinitely more sensible and straightforward than George Willard, and was glad he had come away from his friend. A feeling of impatience with the town that had been in his mind returned, and he tried to tell her of it. "Everyone talks and talks," he began. "I'm sick of it. I'll do something, get into some kind of work where talk don't count. Maybe I'll just be a mechanic in a shop. I don't know. I guess I don't care much. I just want to work and keep quiet. That's all I've got in my mind."

Seth arose from the bench and put out his hand. He did not want to bring the meeting to an end but could not think of anything more to say. "It's the last time we'll see each other," he whispered.

A wave of sentiment swept over Helen. Putting her hand upon Seth's shoulder, she started to draw his face down towards her own upturned face. The act was one of pure affection and cutting regret that some vague adventure that had been present in the spirit of the night would now never be realized. "I think I'd better be going along," she said, letting her hand fall heavily to her side. A thought came to her. "Don't you go with me; I want to be alone," she said. "You go and talk with your mother. You'd better do that now."

Seth hesitated and, as he stood waiting, the girl turned and ran away through the hedge. A desire to run after her came to him, but he only stood staring, perplexed and puzzled by her action as he had been perplexed and puzzled by all of the life of the town out of which she had come. Walking slowly toward the house, he stopped in the shadow of a large tree and looked at his mother sitting by a lighted window busily sewing. The feeling of loneliness that had visited him earlier in the evening returned and colored his thoughts of the adventure through which he had just passed. "Huh!" he exclaimed, turning and staring in the direction taken by Helen White. "That's how things'll turn out. She'll be like the rest. I suppose she'll begin now to look at me in a funny way." He looked at the ground and pondered this thought. "She'll be embarrassed and feel strange when I'm around," he whispered to himself. "That's how it'll be. That's how everything'll turn out. When it comes to loving some one, it won't never be me. It'll be some one else—some fool—some one who talks a lot—some one like that George Willard."

Tandy

UNTIL she was seven years old she lived in an old unpainted house on an unused road that led off Trunion Pike. Her father gave her but little attention and her mother was dead. The father spent his time talking and thinking of religion. He proclaimed himself an agnostic and was so absorbed in destroying the ideas of God that had crept into the minds of his neighbors that he never saw God manifesting himself in the little child that, half forgotten, lived here and there on the bounty of her dead mother's relatives.

A stranger came to Winesburg and saw in the child what the father did not see. He was a tall, red-haired young man who was almost always drunk. Sometimes he sat in a chair before the New Willard House with Tom Hard, the father. As Tom talked, declaring there could be no God, the stranger smiled and winked at the bystanders. He and Tom became friends and were much together.

The stranger was the son of a rich merchant of Cleveland and had come to Winesburg on a mission. He wanted to cure himself of the habit of drink, and thought that by escaping from his city associates and living in a rural community he would have a better chance in the struggle with the appetite that was destroying him.

His sojourn in Winesburg was not a success. The dullness of the passing hours led to his drinking harder than ever. But he did succeed in doing something. He gave a name rich with meaning to Tom Hard's daughter.

One evening when he was recovering from a long debauch the stranger came reeling along the main street of the town. Tom Hard sat in a chair before the New Willard House with his daughter, then a child of five, on his knees. Beside him on the board sidewalk sat young George Willard. The stranger dropped into a chair beside them. His body shook and when he tried to talk his voice trembled.

It was late evening and darkness lay over the town and over the railroad that ran along the foot of a little incline before the hotel. Somewhere in the distance, off to the west, there was a prolonged blast from the whistle of a passenger engine. A dog that had been sleeping in the roadway arose and barked. The stranger began to babble and made a prophecy concerning the child that lay in the arms of the agnostic.

"I came here to quit drinking," he said, and tears began to run down his cheeks. He did not look at Tom Hard, but leaned forward and stared into the darkness as though seeing a vision. "I ran away to the country to be cured, but I am not cured. There is a reason." He turned to look at the child who sat up very straight on her father's knee and returned the look.

The stranger touched Tom Hard on the arm. "Drink is not the only thing to which I am addicted," he said. "There is something else. I am a lover and have not found my thing to love. That is a big point if you know enough to realize what I mean. It makes my destruction inevitable, you see. There are few who understand that."

The stranger became silent and seemed overcome with sadness, but another blast from the whistle of the passenger engine aroused him. "I have not lost faith. I proclaim that. I have only been brought to the place where I know my faith will not be realized," he declared hoarsely. He looked hard at the child and began to address her, paying no more attention to the father. "There is a woman coming," he said, and his voice was now sharp and earnest. "I have missed her, you see. She did not come in my time. You may be the woman. It would be like fate to let me stand in her presence once, on such an evening as this, when I have destroyed myself with drink and she is as yet only a child."

The shoulders of the stranger shook violently, and when he tried to roll a cigarette the paper fell from his trembling fingers. He grew angry and scolded. "They think it's easy to be a woman, to be loved, but I know better," he declared. Again he turned to the child. "I understand," he cried. "Perhaps of all men I alone understand."

His glance again wandered away to the darkened street. "I know about her, although she has never crossed my path," he said softly. "I know about her struggles and her defeats. It is because of her defeats that she is to me the lovely one. Out of her defeats has been born a new quality in woman. I have a name for it. I call it Tandy. I made up the name when I was a true dreamer and before my body became vile. It is the quality of being strong to be loved. It is something men need from women and that they do not get."

The stranger arose and stood before Tom Hard. His body rocked back and forth and he seemed about to fall, but instead he dropped to his knees on the sidewalk and raised the hands of the little girl to his drunken lips. He kissed them ecstatically. "Be Tandy, little one," he plead. "Dare to be strong and courageous. That is the road. Venture anything. Be brave enough to dare to be loved. Be something more than man or woman. Be Tandy."

The stranger arose and staggered off down the street. A day or two later he got aboard a train and returned to his home in Cleveland. On the summer evening, after the talk before the hotel, Tom Hard took the girl child to the house of a relative where she had been invited to spend the night. As he went along in the darkness under the trees he forgot the babbling voice of the stranger and his mind returned to the making of arguments by which he might destroy men's faith in God. He spoke his daughter's name and she began to weep.

"I don't want to be called that," she declared. "I want to be called Tandy—Tandy Hard." The child wept so bitterly that Tom Hard was touched and tried to comfort her. He stopped beneath a tree and, taking her into his arms, began to caress her. "Be good, now," he said sharply; but she would not be quieted. With childish abandon she gave herself over to grief, her voice breaking the evening stillness of the street. "I want to be Tandy. I want to be Tandy. I want to be Tandy Hard," she cried, shaking her head and sobbing as though her young strength were not enough to bear the vision the words of the drunkard had brought to her.

The Strength of God

THE Reverend Curtis Hartman was pastor of the Presbyterian Church of Winesburg, and had been in that position ten years. He was forty years old, and by his nature very silent and reticent. To preach, standing in the pulpit before the people, was always a hardship for him and from Wednesday morning until Saturday evening he thought of nothing but the two sermons that must be preached on Sunday. Early on Sunday morning he went into a little room called a study in the bell tower of the church and prayed. In his prayers there was one note that always predominated. "Give me strength and courage for Thy work, O Lord!" he plead, kneeling on the bare floor and bowing his head in the presence of the task that lay before him.

The Reverend Hartman was a tall man with a brown beard. His wife, a stout, nervous woman, was the daughter of a manufacturer of underwear at Cleveland, Ohio. The minister himself was rather a favorite in the town. The elders of the church liked him because he was quiet and unpretentious and Mrs. White, the banker's wife, thought him scholarly and refined.

The Presbyterian Church held itself somewhat aloof from the other churches of Winesburg. It was larger and more imposing and its minister was better paid. He even had a carriage of his own and on summer evenings sometimes drove about town with his wife. Through Main Street and up and down Buckeye Street he went, bowing gravely to the people, while his wife, afire with secret pride, looked at him out of the corners of her eyes and worried lest the horse become frightened and run away.

For a good many years after he came to Winesburg things went well with Curtis Hartman. He was not one to arouse keen enthusiasm among the worshippers in his church but on the other hand he made no enemies. In reality he was much in earnest and sometimes suffered prolonged periods of remorse because he could not go crying the word of God in the highways and byways of the town. He wondered if the flame of the spirit really burned in him and dreamed of a day when a strong sweet new current of power would come like a great wind into his voice and his soul and the people would tremble before the spirit of God made manifest in him. "I am a poor stick and that will never really happen to me," he mused dejectedly and then a patient smile lit up his features. "Oh well, I suppose I'm doing well enough," he added philosophically.

The room in the bell tower of the church, where on Sunday mornings the minister prayed for an increase in him of the power of God, had but one window. It was long and narrow and swung outward on a hinge like a door. On the window, made of little leaded panes, was a design showing the Christ laying his hand upon the head of a child. One Sunday morning in the summer as he sat by his desk in the room with a large Bible opened before him, and the sheets of his sermon scattered about, the minister was shocked to see, in the upper room of the house next door, a woman lying in her bed and smoking a cigarette while she read a book. Curtis Hartman went on tiptoe to the window and closed it softly. He was horror stricken at the thought of a woman smoking and trembled also to think that his eyes, just raised from the pages of the book of God, had looked upon the bare shoulders and white throat of a woman. With his brain in a whirl he went down into the pulpit and preached a long sermon without once thinking of his gestures or his voice. The sermon attracted unusual attention because of its power and clearness. "I wonder if she is listening, if my voice is carrying a message into her soul," he thought and began to hope that on future Sunday mornings he might be able to say words that would touch and awaken the woman apparently far gone in secret sin.

The house next door to the Presbyterian Church, through the windows of which the minister had seen the sight that had so upset him, was occupied by two women. Aunt Elizabeth Swift, a grey competent-looking widow with money in the Winesburg National Bank, lived there with her daughter Kate Swift, a school teacher. The school teacher was thirty years old and had a neat trim-looking figure. She had few friends and bore a reputation of having a sharp tongue. When he began to think about her, Curtis Hartman remembered that she had been to Europe and had lived for two years in New York City. "Perhaps after all her smoking means nothing," he thought.

He began to remember that when he was a student in college and occasionally read novels, good, although somewhat worldly women, had smoked through the pages of a book that had once fallen into his hands. With a rush of new determination he worked on his sermons all through the week and forgot, in his zeal to reach the ears and the soul of this new listener, both his embarrassment in the pulpit and the necessity of prayer in the study on Sunday mornings.

Reverend Hartman's experience with women had been somewhat limited. He was the son of a wagon maker from Muncie, Indiana, and had worked his way through college. The daughter of the underwear manufacturer had boarded in a house where he lived during his school days and he had married her after a formal and prolonged courtship, carried on for the most part by the girl herself. On his marriage day the underwear manufacturer had given his daughter five thousand dollars and he promised to leave her at least twice that amount in his will. The minister had thought himself fortunate in marriage and had never permitted himself to think of other women. He did not want to think of other women. What he wanted was to do the work of God quietly and earnestly.

In the soul of the minister a struggle awoke. From wanting to reach the ears of Kate Swift, and through his sermons to delve into her soul, he began to want also to look again at the figure lying white and quiet in the bed. On a Sunday morning when he could not sleep because of his thoughts he arose and went to walk in the streets. When he had gone along Main Street almost to the old Richmond place he stopped and picking up a stone rushed off to the room in the bell tower. With the stone he broke out a corner of the window and then locked the door and sat down at the desk before the open Bible to wait. When the shade of the window to Kate Swift's room was raised he could see, through the hole, directly into her bed, but she was not there. She also had arisen and had gone for a walk and the hand that raised the shade was the hand of Aunt Elizabeth Swift.

The minister almost wept with joy at this deliverence from the carnal desire to "peep" and went back to his own house praising God. In an ill moment he forgot, however, to stop the hole in the window. The piece of glass broken out at the corner of the window just nipped off the bare heel of the boy standing motionless and looking with rapt eyes into the face of the Christ.

Curtis Hartman forgot his sermon on that Sunday morning. He talked to his congregation and in his talk said that it was a mistake for people to think of their minister as a man set aside and intended by nature to lead a blameless life. "Out of my own experience I know that we, who are the ministers of God's word, are beset by the same temptations that assail you," he declared. "I have been tempted and have surrendered to temptation. It is only the hand of God, placed beneath my head, that has raised me up. As he has raised me so also will he raise you. Do not despair. In your hour of sin raise your eyes to the skies and you will be again and again saved."

Resolutely the minister put the thoughts of the woman in the bed out of his mind and began to be something like a lover in the presence of his wife. One evening when they drove out together he turned the horse out of Buckeye Street and in the darkness on Gospel Hill, above Waterworks Pond, put his arm about Sarah Hartman's waist. When he had eaten breakfast in the morning and was ready to retire to his study at the back of his house he went around the table and kissed his wife on the cheek. When thoughts of Kate Swift came into his head, he smiled and raised his eyes to the skies. "Intercede for me, Master," he muttered, "keep me in the narrow path intent on Thy work."

And now began the real struggle in the soul of the brown-bearded minister. By chance he discovered that Kate Swift was in the habit of lying in her bed in the evenings and reading a book. A lamp stood on a table by the side of the bed and the light streamed down upon her white shoulders and bare throat. On the evening when he made the discovery the minister sat at the desk in the study from nine until after eleven and when her light was put out stumbled out of the church to spend two more hours walking and praying in the streets. He did not want to kiss the shoulders and the throat of Kate Swift and had not allowed his mind to dwell on such thoughts. He did not know what he wanted. "I am God's child and he must save me from myself," he cried, in the darkness under the trees as he wandered in the streets. By a tree he stood and looked at the sky that was covered with hurrying clouds. He began to talk to God intimately and closely. "Please, Father, do not forget me. Give me power to go to-morrow and repair the hole in the window. Lift my eyes again to the skies. Stay with me, Thy servant, in his hour of need."

Up and down through the silent streets walked the minister and for days and weeks his soul was troubled. He could not understand the temptation that had come to him nor could he fathom the reason for its coming. In a way he began to blame God, saying to himself that he had tried to keep his feet in the true path and had not run about seeking sin. "Through my days as a young man and all through my life here I have gone quietly about my work," he declared. "Why now should I be tempted? What have I done that this burden should be laid on me?"

Three times during the early fall and winter of that year Curtis Hartman crept out of his house to the room in the bell tower to sit in the darkness looking at the figure of Kate Swift lying in her bed and later went to walk and pray in the streets. He could not understand himself. For weeks he would go along scarcely thinking of the school teacher and telling himself that he had conquered the carnal desire to look at her body. And then something would happen. As he sat in the study of his own house, hard at work on a sermon, he would become nervous and begin to walk up and down the room. "I will go out into the streets," he told himself and even as he let himself in at the church door he persistently denied to himself the cause of his being there. "I will not repair the hole in the window and I will train myself to come here at night and sit in the presence of this woman without raising my eyes. I will not be defeated in this thing. The Lord has devised this temptation as a test of my soul and I will grope my way out of darkness into the light of righteousness."

One night in January when it was bitter cold and snow lay deep on the streets of Winesburg Curtis Hartman paid his last visit to the room in the bell tower of the church. It was past nine o'clock when he left his own house and he set out so hurriedly that he forgot to put on his overshoes. In Main Street no one was abroad but Hop Higgins the night watchman and in the whole town no one was awake but the watchman and young George Willard, who sat in the office of the *Winesburg Eagle* trying to write a story. Along the street to the church went the minister, plowing through the drifts and thinking that this time he would utterly give way to sin. "I want to look at the woman and to think of kissing her shoulders and I am going to let myself think what I choose," he declared bitterly and tears came into his eyes. He began to think that he would get out of the ministry and try some other way of life. "I shall go to some city and get into business," he declared. "If my nature is such that I cannot resist sin, I shall give myself over to sin. At least I shall not be a hypocrite, preaching the word of God with my mind thinking of the shoulders and neck of a woman who does not belong to me."

It was cold in the room of the bell tower of the church on that January night and almost as soon as he came into the room Curtis Hartman knew that if he stayed he would be ill. His feet were wet from tramping in the snow and there was no fire. In the room in the house next door Kate Swift had not yet appeared. With grim determination the man sat down to wait. Sitting in the chair and gripping the edge of the desk on which lay the Bible he stared into the darkness thinking the blackest thoughts of his life. He thought of his wife and for the moment almost hated her. "She has always been ashamed of passion and has cheated me," he thought. "Man has a right to expect living passion and beauty in a woman. He has no right to forget that he is an animal and in me there is something that is Greek. I will throw off the woman of my bosom and seek other women. I will besiege this school teacher. I will fly in the face of all men and if I am a creature of carnal lusts I will live then for my lusts."

The distracted man trembled from head to foot, partly from cold, partly from the struggle in which he was engaged. Hours passed and a fever assailed his body. His throat began to hurt and his teeth chattered. His feet on the study floor felt like two cakes of ice. Still he would not give up. "I will see this woman and will think the thoughts I have never dared to think," he told himself, gripping the edge of the desk and waiting.

Curtis Hartman came near dying from the effects of that night of waiting in the church, and also he found in the thing that happened what he took to be the way of life for him. On other evenings when he had waited he had not been able to see, through the little hole in the glass, any part of the school teacher's room except that occupied by her bed. In the darkness he had waited until the woman suddenly appeared sitting in the bed in her white night-robe. When the light was turned up she propped herself up among the pillows and read a book. Sometimes she smoked one of the cigarettes. Only her bare shoulders and throat were visible.

On the January night, after he had come near dying with cold and after his mind had two or three times actually slipped away into an odd land of fantasy so that he had by an exercise of will power to force himself back into consciousness, Kate Swift appeared. In the room next door a lamp was lighted and the waiting man stared into an empty bed. Then upon the bed before his eyes a naked woman threw herself. Lying face downward she wept and beat with her fists upon the pillow. With a final outburst of weeping she half arose, and in the presence of the man who had waited to look and to think thoughts the woman of sin began to pray. In the lamplight her figure, slim and strong, looked like the figure of the boy in the presence of the Christ on the leaded window.

Curtis Hartman never remembered how he got out of the church. With a cry he arose, dragging the heavy desk along the floor. The Bible fell, making a great clatter in the silence. When the light in the house next door went out he stumbled down the stairway and into the street. Along the street he went and ran in at the door of the *Winesburg Eagle*. To George Willard, who was tramping up and down in the office undergoing a struggle of his own, he began to talk half incoherently. "The ways of God are beyond human understanding," he cried, running in quickly and closing the door. He began to advance upon the young man, his eyes glowing and his voice ringing with fervor. "I have found the light," he cried. "After ten years in this town, God has manifested himself to me in the body of a woman." His voice dropped and he began to whisper. "I did not understand," he said. "What I took to be a trial of my soul was only a preparation for a new and more beautiful fervor of the spirit. God has appeared to me in the person of Kate Swift, the school teacher, kneeling naked on a bed. Do you know

Kate Swift? Although she may not be aware of it, she is an instrument of God, bearing the message of truth."

Reverend Curtis Hartman turned and ran out of the office. At the door he stopped, and after looking up and down the deserted street, turned again to George Willard. "I am delivered. Have no fear." He held up a bleeding fist for the young man to see. "I smashed the glass of the window," he cried. "Now it will have to be wholly replaced. The strength of God was in me and I broke it with my fist."

The Teacher

S NOW lay deep in the streets of Winesburg. It had begun to snow about ten o'clock in the morning and a wind sprang up and blew the snow in clouds along Main Street. The frozen mud roads that led into town were fairly smooth and in places ice covered the mud. "There will be good sleighing," said Will Henderson, standing by the bar in Ed Griffith's saloon. Out of the saloon he went and met Sylvester West the druggist stumbling along in the kind of heavy overshoes called arctics. "Snow will bring the people into town on Saturday," said the druggist. The two men stopped and discussed their affairs. Will Henderson, who had on a light overcoat and no overshoes, kicked the heel of his left foot with the toe of the right. "Snow will be good for the wheat," observed the druggist sagely.

Young George Willard, who had nothing to do, was glad because he did not feel like working that day. The weekly paper had been printed and taken to the post office on Wednesday evening and the snow began to fall on Thursday. At eight o'clock, after the morning train had passed, he put a pair of skates in his pocket and went up to Waterworks Pond but did not go skating. Past the pond and along a path that followed Wine Creek he went until he came to a grove of beech trees. There he built a fire against the side of a log and sat down at the end of the log to think. When the snow began to fall and the wind to blow he hurried about getting fuel for the fire.

The young reporter was thinking of Kate Swift who had once been his school teacher. On the evening before he had gone to her house to get a book she wanted him to read and had been alone with her for an hour. For the fourth or fifth time the woman had talked to him with great earnestness and he could not make out what she meant by her talk. He began to believe she might be in love with him and the thought was both pleasing and annoying.

Up from the log he sprang and began to pile sticks on the fire. Looking about to be sure he was alone he talked aloud pretending he was in the presence of the woman. "Oh, you're just letting on, you know you are," he declared. "I am going to find out about you. You wait and see."

The young man got up and went back along the path toward town leaving the fire blazing in the wood. As he went through the streets the skates clanked in his pocket. In his own room in the New Willard House he built a fire in the stove and lay down on top of the bed. He began to have lustful thoughts and pulling down the shade of the window closed his eyes and turned his face to the wall. He took a pillow into his arms and embraced it thinking first of the school teacher, who by her words had stirred something within him and later of Helen White, the slim daughter of the town banker, with whom he had been for a long time half in love.

By nine o'clock of that evening snow lay deep in the streets and the weather had become bitter cold. It was difficult to walk about. The stores were dark and the people had crawled away to their houses. The evening train from Cleveland was very late but nobody was interested in its arrival. By ten o'clock all but four of the eighteen hundred citizens of the town were in bed.

Hop Higgins, the night watchman, was partially awake. He was lame and carried a heavy stick. On dark nights he carried a lantern. Between nine and ten o'clock he went his rounds. Up and down Main Street he stumbled through the drifts trying the doors of the stores. Then he went into alleyways and tried the back doors. Finding all tight he hurried around the corner to the New Willard House and beat on the door. Through the rest of the night he intended to stay by the stove. "You go to bed. I'll keep the stove going," he said to the boy who slept on a cot in the hotel office.

Hop Higgins sat down by the stove and took off his shoes. When the boy had gone to sleep he began to think of his own affairs. He intended to paint his house in the spring and sat by the stove calculating the cost of paint and labor. That led him into other calculations. The night watchman was sixty years old and wanted to retire. He had been a soldier in the Civil War and drew a small pension. He hoped to find some new method of making a living and aspired to become a professional breeder of ferrets. Already he had four of the strangely shaped savage little creatures, that are used by sportsmen in the pursuit of rabbits, in the cellar of his house. "Now I have one male and three females," he mused. "If I am lucky by spring I shall have twelve or fifteen. In another year I shall be able to begin advertising ferrets for sale in the sporting papers."

The night watchman settled into his chair and his mind became a blank. He did not sleep. By years of practice he had trained himself to sit for hours through the long nights neither asleep nor awake. In the morning he was almost as refreshed as though he had slept.

With Hop Higgins safely stowed away in the chair behind the stove only three people were awake in Winesburg. George Willard was in the office of the *Eagle* pretending to be at work on the writing of a story but in reality continuing the mood of the morning by the fire in the wood. In the bell tower of the Presbyterian Church the Reverend Curtis Hartman was sitting in the darkness preparing himself for a revelation from God, and Kate Swift, the school teacher, was leaving her house for a walk in the storm.

It was past ten o'clock when Kate Swift set out and the walk was unpremeditated. It was as though the man and the boy, by thinking of her, had driven her forth into the wintry streets. Aunt Elizabeth Swift had gone to the county seat concerning some business in connection with mortgages in which she had money invested and would not be back until the next day. By a huge stove, called a base burner, in the living room of the house sat the daughter reading a book. Suddenly she sprang to her feet and, snatching a cloak from a rack by the front door, ran out of the house.

At the age of thirty Kate Swift was not known in Winesburg as a pretty woman. Her complexion was not good and her face was covered with blotches that indicated ill health. Alone in the night in the winter streets she was lovely. Her back was straight, her shoulders square and her features were as the features of a tiny goddess on a pedestal in a garden in the dim light of a summer evening.

During the afternoon the school teacher had been to see Dr. Welling concerning her health. The doctor had scolded her and had declared she was in danger of losing her hearing. It was foolish for Kate Swift to be abroad in the storm, foolish and perhaps dangerous.

The woman in the streets did not remember the words of the doctor and would not have turned back had she remembered. She was very cold but after walking for five minutes no longer minded the cold. First she went to the end of her own street and then across a pair of hay scales set in the ground before a feed barn and into Trunion Pike. Along Trunion Pike she went to Ned Winters' barn and turning east followed a street of low frame houses that led over Gospel Hill and into Sucker Road that ran down a shallow valley past Ike Smead's chicken farm to Waterworks Pond. As she went along, the bold, excited mood that had driven her out of doors passed and then returned again.

There was something biting and forbidding in the character of Kate Swift. Everyone felt it. In the schoolroom she was silent, cold, and stern, and yet in an odd way very close to her pupils. Once in a long while something seemed to have come over her and she was happy. All of the children in the schoolroom felt the effect of her happiness. For a time they did not work but sat back in their chairs and looked at her.

With hands clasped behind her back the school teacher walked up and down in the schoolroom and talked very rapidly. It did not seem to matter what subject came into her mind. Once she talked to the children of Charles Lamb and made up strange intimate little stories concerning the life of the dead writer. The stories were told with the air of one who had lived in a house with Charles Lamb and knew all the secrets of his private life. The children were somewhat confused, thinking Charles Lamb must be someone who had once lived in Winesburg.

On another occasion the teacher talked to the children of Benvenuto Cellini. That time they laughed. What a bragging, blustering, brave, lovable fellow she made of the old artist! Concerning him also she invented anecdotes. There was one of a German music teacher who had a room above Cellini's lodgings in the city of Milan that made the boys guffaw. Sugars McNutts, a fat boy with red cheeks, laughed so hard that he became dizzy and fell off his seat and Kate Swift laughed with him. Then suddenly she became again cold and stern.

On the winter night when she walked through the deserted snow-covered streets, a crisis had come into the life of the school teacher. Although no one in Winesburg would have suspected it, her life had been very adventurous. It was still adventurous. Day by day as she worked in the schoolroom or walked in the streets, grief, hope, and desire fought within her. Behind a cold exterior the most extraordinary events transpired in her mind. The people of the town thought of her as a confirmed old maid and because she spoke sharply and went her own way thought her lacking in all the human feeling that did so much to make and mar their own lives. In reality she was the most eagerly passionate soul among them, and more than once, in the five years since she had come back from her travels to settle in Winesburg and become a school teacher, had been compelled to go out of the house and walk half through the night fighting out some battle raging within. Once on a night when it rained she had stayed out six hours and when she came home had a quarrel with Aunt Elizabeth Swift. "I am glad you're not a man," said the mother sharply. "More than once I've waited for your father to come home, not knowing what new mess he had got into. I've had my share of uncertainty and you cannot blame me if I do not want to see the worst side of him reproduced in you."

Kate Swift's mind was ablaze with thoughts of George Willard. In something he had written as a school boy she thought she had recognized the spark of genius and wanted to blow on the spark. One day in the summer she had gone to the *Eagle* office and finding the boy unoccupied had taken him out Main Street to the fair ground, where the two sat on a grassy bank and talked. The school teacher tried to bring home to the mind of the boy some conception of the difficulties he would have to face as a writer. "You will have to know life," she declared, and her voice trembled with earnestness. She took hold of George Willard's shoulders and turned him about so that she could look into his eyes. A passer-by might have thought them about to embrace. "If you are to become a writer you'll have to stop fooling with words," she explained. "It would be better to give up the notion of writing until you are better prepared. Now it's time to be living. I don't want to frighten you, but I would like to make you understand the import of what you think of attempting. You must not become a mere peddler of words. The thing to learn is to know what people are thinking about, not what they say."

On the evening before that stormy Thursday night, when the Reverend Curtis Hartman sat in the bell tower of the church waiting to look at her body, young Willard had gone to visit the teacher and to borrow a book. It was then the thing happened that confused and puzzled the boy. He had the book under his arm and was preparing to depart. Again Kate Swift talked with great earnestness. Night was coming on and the light in the room grew dim. As he turned to go she spoke his name softly and with an impulsive movement took hold of his hand. Because the reporter was rapidly becoming a man something of his man's appeal, combined with the winsomeness of the boy, stirred the heart of the lonely woman. A passionate desire to have him understand the import of life, to learn to interpret it truly and honestly, swept over her. Leaning forward, her lips brushed his cheek. At the same moment he for the first time became aware of the marked beauty of her features. They were both embarrassed, and to relieve her feeling she became harsh and domineering. "What's the use? It will be ten years before you begin to understand what I mean when I talk to you," she cried passionately.

On the night of the storm and while the minister sat in the church waiting for her, Kate Swift went to the office of the *Winesburg Eagle*, intending to have another talk with the boy. After the long walk in the snow she was cold, lonely, and tired. As she came through Main Street she saw the light from the print shop window shining on the snow and on an impulse opened the door and went in. For an hour she sat by the stove in the office talking of life. She talked with passionate earnestness. The impulse that had driven her out into the snow poured itself out into talk. She became inspired as she sometimes did in the presence of the children in school. A great eagerness to open the door of life to the boy, who had been her pupil and whom she thought might possess a talent for the understanding of life, had possession of her. So strong was her passion that it became something physical. Again her hands took hold

of his shoulders and she turned him about. In the dim light
her eyes blazed. She arose and laughed, not sharply as was
customary with her, but in a queer, hesitating way. "I must be
going," she said. "In a moment, if I stay, I'll be wanting to kiss
you."

In the newspaper office a confusion arose. Kate Swift turned
and walked to the door. She was a teacher but she was also
a woman. As she looked at George Willard, the passionate desire to be loved by a man, that had a thousand times before
swept like a storm over her body, took possession of her. In the
lamplight George Willard looked no longer a boy, but a man
ready to play the part of a man.

The school teacher let George Willard take her into his
arms. In the warm little office the air became suddenly heavy
and the strength went out of her body. Leaning against a low
counter by the door she waited. When he came and put a hand
on her shoulder she turned and let her body fall heavily against
him. For George Willard the confusion was immediately increased. For a moment he held the body of the woman tightly
against his body and then it stiffened. Two sharp little fists
began to beat on his face. When the school teacher had run
away and left him alone, he walked up and down in the office
swearing furiously.

It was into this confusion that the Reverend Curtis Hartman protruded himself. When he came in George Willard
thought the town had gone mad. Shaking a bleeding fist in the
air, the minister proclaimed the woman George had only a
moment before held in his arms an instrument of God bearing
a message of truth.

George blew out the lamp by the window and locking the
door of the print shop went home. Through the hotel office,
past Hop Higgins lost in his dream of the raising of ferrets, he
went and up into his own room. The fire in the stove had gone
out and he undressed in the cold. When he got into bed the
sheets were like blankets of dry snow.

George Willard rolled about in the bed on which he had lain
in the afternoon hugging the pillow and thinking thoughts of
Kate Swift. The words of the minister, who he thought had
gone suddenly insane, rang in his ears. His eyes stared about

the room. The resentment, natural to the baffled male, passed and he tried to understand what had happened. He could not make it out. Over and over he turned the matter in his mind. Hours passed and he began to think it must be time for another day to come. At four o'clock he pulled the covers up about his neck and tried to sleep. When he became drowsy and closed his eyes, he raised a hand and with it groped about in the darkness. "I have missed something. I have missed something Kate Swift was trying to tell me," he muttered sleepily. Then he slept and in all Winesburg he was the last soul on that winter night to go to sleep.

Loneliness

HE was the son of Mrs. Al Robinson who once owned a farm on a side road leading off Trunion Pike, east of Winesburg and two miles beyond the town limits. The farmhouse was painted brown and the blinds to all of the windows facing the road were kept closed. In the road before the house a flock of chickens, accompanied by two guinea hens, lay in the deep dust. Enoch lived in the house with his mother in those days and when he was a young boy went to school at the Winesburg High School. Old citizens remembered him as a quiet, smiling youth inclined to silence. He walked in the middle of the road when he came into town and sometimes read a book. Drivers of teams had to shout and swear to make him realize where he was so that he would turn out of the beaten track and let them pass.

When he was twenty-one years old Enoch went to New York City and was a city man for fifteen years. He studied French and went to an art school, hoping to develop a faculty he had for drawing. In his own mind he planned to go to Paris and to finish his art education among the masters there, but that never turned out.

Nothing ever turned out for Enoch Robinson. He could draw well enough and he had many odd delicate thoughts hidden away in his brain that might have expressed themselves through the brush of a painter, but he was always a child and that was a handicap to his worldly development. He never grew up and of course he couldn't understand people and he couldn't make people understand him. The child in him kept bumping against things, against actualities like money and sex and opinions. Once he was hit by a street car and thrown against an iron post. That made him lame. It was one of the many things that kept things from turning out for Enoch Robinson.

In New York City, when he first went there to live and before he became confused and disconcerted by the facts of life, Enoch went about a good deal with young men. He got into a group of other young artists, both men and women, and in the evenings they sometimes came to visit him in his room. Once

118

he got drunk and was taken to a police station where a police magistrate frightened him horribly, and once he tried to have an affair with a woman of the town met on the sidewalk before his lodging house. The woman and Enoch walked together three blocks and then the young man grew afraid and ran away. The woman had been drinking and the incident amused her. She leaned against the wall of a building and laughed so heartily that another man stopped and laughed with her. The two went away together, still laughing, and Enoch crept off to his room trembling and vexed.

The room in which young Robinson lived in New York faced Washington Square and was long and narrow like a hallway. It is important to get that fixed in your mind. The story of Enoch is in fact the story of a room almost more than it is the story of a man.

And so into the room in the evening came young Enoch's friends. There was nothing particularly striking about them except that they were artists of the kind that talk. Everyone knows of the talking artists. Throughout all of the known history of the world they have gathered in rooms and talked. They talk of art and are passionately, almost feverishly, in earnest about it. They think that it matters much more than it does.

And so these people gathered and smoked cigarettes and talked and Enoch Robinson, the boy from the farm near Winesburg, was there. He stayed in a corner and for the most part said nothing. How his big blue childlike eyes stared about! On the walls were pictures he had made, crude things, half finished. His friends talked of these. Leaning back in their chairs, they talked and talked with their heads rocking from side to side. Words were said about line and values and composition, lots of words, such as are always being said.

Enoch wanted to talk too but he didn't know how. He was too excited to talk coherently. When he tried he sputtered and stammered and his voice sounded strange and squeaky to him. That made him stop talking. He knew what he wanted to say, but he knew also that he could never by any possibility say it. When a picture he had painted was under discussion, he wanted to burst out with something like this: "You don't get the point," he wanted to explain: "the picture you see doesn't consist of the things you see and say words about. There is something else, something you don't see at all, something you aren't intended to see. Look at this one over here, by the door here, where the light from the window falls on it. The dark spot by the road that you might not notice at all is, you see, the beginning of everything. There is a clump of elders there such as used to grow beside the road before our house back in Winesburg, Ohio, and in among the elders there is something hidden. It is a woman, that's what it is. She has been thrown from a horse and the horse has run away out of sight. Do you not see how the old man who drives a cart looks anxiously about? That is Thad Grayback who has a farm up the road. He is taking corn to Winesburg to be ground into meal at Comstock's mill. He knows there is something in the elders, something hidden away, and yet he doesn't quite know.

"It's a woman you see, that's what it is! It's a woman and, oh, she is lovely! She is hurt and is suffering but she makes no sound. Don't you see how it is? She lies quite still, white and still, and the beauty comes out from her and spreads over everything. It is in the sky back there and all around everywhere. I didn't try to paint the woman, of course. She is too beautiful to be painted. How dull to talk of composition and such things! Why do you not look at the sky and then run away as I used to do when I was boy back there in Winesburg, Ohio?"

That is the kind of thing young Enoch Robinson trembled to say to the guests who came into his room when he was a young fellow in New York City, but he always ended by saying nothing. Then he began to doubt his own mind. He was afraid the things he felt were not getting expressed in the pictures he painted. In a half indignant mood he stopped inviting people into his room and presently got into the habit of locking the door. He began to think that enough people had visited him, that he did not need people any more. With quick imagination he began to invent his own people to whom he could really talk and to whom he explained the things he had been unable to explain to living people. His room began to be inhabited by the spirits of men and women among whom he went, in his turn saying words. It was as though every one Enoch Robinson had ever seen had left with him some essence of himself, something he could mould and change to suit his own fancy, something that understood all about such things as the wounded woman behind the elders in the pictures.

The mild, blue-eyed young Ohio boy was a complete egotist, as all children are egotists. He did not want friends for the quite simple reason that no child wants friends. He wanted most of all the people of his own mind, people with whom he could really talk, people he could harangue and scold by the hour, servants, you see, to his fancy. Among these people he was always self-confident and bold. They might talk, to be sure, and even have opinions of their own, but always he talked last and best. He was like a writer busy among the figures of his brain, a kind of tiny blue-eyed king he was, in a six-dollar room facing Washington Square in the city of New York.

Then Enoch Robinson got married. He began to get lonely and to want to touch actual flesh and bone people with his hands. Days passed when his room seemed empty. Lust visited his body and desire grew in his mind. At night strange fevers, burning within, kept him awake. He married a girl who sat in a chair next to his own in the art school and went to live in an apartment house in Brooklyn. Two children were born to the woman he married, and Enoch got a job in a place where illustrations are made for advertisements.

That began another phase of Enoch's life. He began to play at a new game. For a while he was very proud of himself in the rôle of producing citizen of the world. He dismissed the essence of things and played with realities. In the fall he voted at an election and he had a newspaper thrown on his porch each morning. When in the evening he came home from work he got off a street car and walked sedately along behind some business man, striving to look very substantial and important. As a payer of taxes he thought he should post himself on how things are run. "I'm getting to be of some moment, a real part of things, of the state and the city and all that," he told himself with an amusing miniature air of dignity. Once coming home from Philadelphia, he had a discussion with a man met on a train. Enoch talked about the advisability of the government's owning and operating the railroads and the man gave him a cigar. It was Enoch's notion that such a move on the part of the government would be a good thing, and he grew quite excited as he talked. Later he remembered his own words with pleasure. "I gave him something to think about, that fellow," he muttered to himself as he climbed the stairs to his Brooklyn apartment.

To be sure, Enoch's marriage did not turn out. He himself brought it to an end. He began to feel choked and walled in by the life in the apartment, and to feel toward his wife and even toward his children as he had felt concerning the friends who once came to visit him. He began to tell little lies about business engagements that would give him freedom to walk alone in the street at night and, the chance offering, he secretly re-rented the room facing Washington Square. Then Mrs. Al Robinson died on the farm near Winesburg, and he got eight thousand dollars from the bank that acted as trustee of her estate. That took Enoch out of the world of men altogether. He gave the money to his wife and told her he could not live in the apartment any more. She cried and was angry and threatened, but he only stared at her and went his own way. In reality the wife did not care much. She thought Enoch slightly insane and was a little afraid of him. When it was quite sure that he would never come back, she took the two children and went to a village in Connecticut where she had lived as a girl. In the end she married a man who bought and sold real estate and was contented enough.

And so Enoch Robinson stayed in the New York room among the people of his fancy, playing with them, talking to them, happy as a child is happy. They were an odd lot, Enoch's people. They were made, I suppose, out of real people he had seen and who had for some obscure reason made an appeal to him. There was a woman with a sword in her hand, an old man with a long white beard who went about followed by a dog, a young girl whose stockings were always coming down and hanging over her shoe tops. There must have been two dozen of the shadow people, invented by the child-mind of Enoch Robinson, who lived in the room with him.

And Enoch was happy. Into the room he went and locked the door. With an absurd air of importance he talked aloud, giving instructions, making comments on life. He was happy and satisfied to go on making his living in the advertising place until something happened. Of course something did happen. That is why he went back to live in Winesburg and why we know about him. The thing that happened was a woman. It would be that way. He was too happy. Something had to come into his world. Something had to drive him out of the New York room to live out his life, an obscure, jerky little figure, bobbing up and down on the streets of an Ohio town at evening when the sun was going down behind the roof of Wesley Moyer's livery barn.

About the thing that happened. Enoch told George Willard about it one night. He wanted to talk to someone, and he chose the young newspaper reporter because the two happened to be thrown together at a time when the younger man was in a mood to understand.

Youthful sadness, young man's sadness, the sadness of a growing boy in a village at the year's end opened the lips of the old man. The sadness was in the heart of George Willard and was without meaning, but it appealed to Enoch Robinson.

It rained on the evening when the two met and talked, a drizzly wet October rain. The fruition of the year had come and the night should have been fine with a moon in the sky and the crisp sharp promise of frost in the air, but it wasn't that way. It rained and little puddles of water shone under the street lamps on Main Street. In the woods in the darkness beyond the Fair Ground water dripped from the black trees. Beneath the trees wet leaves were pasted against tree roots that protruded from the ground. In gardens back of houses in Winesburg dry shriveled potato vines lay sprawling on the ground. Men who had finished the evening meal and who had planned to go uptown to talk the evening away with other men at the back of some store changed their minds. George Willard tramped about in the rain and was glad that it rained. He felt that way. He was like Enoch Robinson on the evenings when the old man came down out of his room and wandered alone in the streets. He was like that only that George Willard had become a tall young man and did not think it manly to weep and carry on. For a month his mother had been very ill and that had something to do with his sadness, but not much. He thought about himself and to the young that always brings sadness.

Enoch Robinson and George Willard met beneath a wooden awning that extended out over the sidewalk before Voight's wagon shop on Maumee Street just off the main street of

Winesburg. They went together from there through the rain-washed streets to the older man's room on the third floor of the Heffner Block. The young reporter went willingly enough. Enoch Robinson asked him to go after the two had talked for ten minutes. The boy was a little afraid but had never been more curious in his life. A hundred times he had heard the old man spoken of as a little off his head and he thought himself rather brave and manly to go at all. From the very beginning, in the street in the rain, the old man talked in a queer way, trying to tell the story of the room in Washington Square and of his life in the room. "You'll understand if you try hard enough," he said conclusively. "I have looked at you when you went past me on the street and I think you can understand. It isn't hard. All you have to do is to believe what I say, just listen and believe, that's all there is to it."

It was past eleven o'clock that evening when Old Enoch, talking to George Willard in the room in the Heffner Block, came to the vital thing, the story of the woman and of what drove him out of the city to live out his life alone and defeated in Winesburg. He sat on a cot by the window with his head in his hand and George Willard was in a chair by a table. A kerosene lamp sat on the table and the room, although almost bare of furniture, was scrupulously clean. As the man talked George Willard began to feel that he would like to get out of the chair and sit on the cot also. He wanted to put his arms about the little old man. In the half darkness the man talked and the boy listened, filled with sadness.

"She got to coming in there after there hadn't been anyone in the room for years," said Enoch Robinson. "She saw me in the hallway of the house and we got acquainted. I don't know just what she did in her own room. I never went there. I think she was a musician and played a violin. Every now and then she came and knocked at the door and I opened it. In she came and sat down beside me, just sat and looked about and said nothing. Anyway, she said nothing that mattered."

The old man arose from the cot and moved about the room. The overcoat he wore was wet from the rain and drops of water kept falling with a soft little thump on the floor. When he again sat upon the cot George Willard got out of the chair and sat beside him.

"I had a feeling about her. She sat there in the room with me and she was too big for the room. I felt that she was driving everything else away. We just talked of little things, but I couldn't sit still. I wanted to touch her with my fingers and to kiss her. Her hands were so strong and her face was so good and she looked at me all the time."

The trembling voice of the old man became silent and his body shook as from a chill. "I was afraid," he whispered. "I was terribly afraid. I didn't want to let her come in when she knocked at the door but I couldn't sit still. 'No, no,' I said to myself, but I got up and opened the door just the same. She was so grown up, you see. She was a woman. I thought she would be bigger than I was there in that room."

Enoch Robinson stared at George Willard, his childlike blue eyes shining in the lamplight. Again he shivered. "I wanted her and all the time I didn't want her," he explained. "Then I began to tell her about my people, about everything that meant anything to me. I tried to keep quiet, to keep myself to myself, but I couldn't. I felt just as I did about opening the door. Sometimes I ached to have her go away and never come back any more."

The old man sprang to his feet and his voice shook with excitement. "One night something happened. I became mad to make her understand me and to know what a big thing I was in that room. I wanted her to see how important I was. I told her over and over. When she tried to go away, I ran and locked the door. I followed her about. I talked and talked and then all of a sudden things went to smash. A look came into her eyes and I knew she did understand. Maybe she had understood all the time. I was furious. I couldn't stand it. I wanted her to understand but, don't you see, I couldn't let her understand. I felt that then she would know everything, that I would be submerged, drowned out, you see. That's how it is. I don't know why."

The old man dropped into a chair by the lamp and the boy listened, filled with awe. "Go away, boy," said the man. "Don't stay here with me any more. I thought it might be a good thing to tell you but it isn't. I don't want to talk any more. Go away."

George Willard shook his head and a note of command

came into his voice. "Don't stop now. Tell me the rest of it," he commanded sharply. "What happened? Tell me the rest of the story."

Enoch Robinson sprang to his feet and ran to the window that looked down into the deserted main street of Winesburg. George Willard followed. By the window the two stood, the tall awkward boy-man and the little wrinkled man-boy. The childish, eager voice carried forward the tale. "I swore at her," he explained. "I said vile words. I ordered her to go away and not to come back. Oh, I said terrible things. At first she pretended not to understand but I kept at it. I screamed and stamped on the floor. I made the house ring with my curses. I didn't want ever to see her again and I knew, after some of the things I said, that I never would see her again."

The old man's voice broke and he shook his head. "Things went to smash," he said quietly and sadly. "Out she went through the door and all the life there had been in the room followed her out. She took all of my people away. They all went out through the door after her. That's the way it was."

George Willard turned and went out of Enoch Robinson's room. In the darkness by the window, as he went through the door, he could hear the thin old voice whimpering and complaining. "I'm alone, all alone here," said the voice. "It was warm and friendly in my room but now I'm all alone."

An Awakening

BELLE CARPENTER had a dark skin, grey eyes and thick lips. She was tall and strong. When black thoughts visited her she grew angry and wished she were a man and could fight someone with her fists. She worked in the millinery shop kept by Mrs. Kate McHugh and during the day sat trimming hats by a window at the rear of the store. She was the daughter of Henry Carpenter, bookkeeper in the First National Bank of Winesburg, and lived with him in a gloomy old house far out at the end of Buckeye Street. The house was surrounded by pine trees and there was no grass beneath the trees. A rusty tin eaves-trough had slipped from its fastenings at the back of the house and when the wind blew it beat against the roof of a small shed, making a dismal drumming noise that sometimes persisted all through the night.

When she was a young girl Henry Carpenter made life almost unbearable for Belle, but as she emerged from girlhood into womanhood he lost his power over her. The bookkeeper's life was made up of innumerable little pettinesses. When he went to the bank in the morning he stepped into a closet and put on a black alpaca coat that had become shabby with age. At night when he returned to his home he donned another black alpaca coat. Every evening he pressed the clothes worn in the streets. He had invented an arrangement of boards for the purpose. The trousers to his street suit were placed between the boards and the boards were clamped together with heavy screws. In the morning he wiped the boards with a damp cloth and stood them upright behind the dining room door. If they were moved during the day he was speechless with anger and did not recover his equilibrium for a week.

The bank cashier was a little bully and was afraid of his daughter. She, he realized, knew the story of his brutal treatment of her mother and hated him for it. One day she went home at noon and carried a handful of soft mud, taken from the road, into the house. With the mud she smeared the face of the boards used for the pressing of trousers and then went back to her work feeling relieved and happy.

Belle Carpenter occasionally walked out in the evening with George Willard. Secretly she loved another man, but her love affair, about which no one knew, caused her much anxiety. She was in love with Ed Handby, bartender in Ed Griffith's Saloon, and went about with the young reporter as a kind of relief to her feelings. She did not think that her station in life would permit her to be seen in the company of the bartender and walked about under the trees with George Willard and let him kiss her to relieve a longing that was very insistent in her nature. She felt that she could keep the younger man within bounds. About Ed Handby she was somewhat uncertain.

Handby, the bartender, was a tall, broad-shouldered man of thirty who lived in a room upstairs above Griffith's saloon. His fists were large and his eyes unusually small, but his voice, as though striving to conceal the power back of his fists, was soft and quiet.

At twenty-five the bartender had inherited a large farm from an uncle in Indiana. When sold, the farm brought in eight thousand dollars which Ed spent in six months. Going to Sandusky, on Lake Erie, he began an orgy of dissipation, the story of which afterward filled his home town with awe. Here and there he went throwing the money about, driving carriages through the streets, giving wine parties to crowds of men and women, playing cards for high stakes and keeping mistresses whose wardrobes cost him hundreds of dollars. One night at a resort called Cedar Point, he got into a fight and ran amuck like a wild thing. With his fist he broke a large mirror in the wash room of a hotel and later went about smashing windows and breaking chairs in dance halls for the joy of hearing the glass rattle on the floor and seeing the terror in the eyes of clerks who had come from Sandusky to spend the evening at the resort with their sweethearts.

The affair between Ed Handby and Belle Carpenter on the surface amounted to nothing. He had succeeded in spending but one evening in her company. On that evening he hired a horse and buggy at Wesley Moyer's livery barn and took her for a drive. The conviction that she was the woman his nature demanded and that he must get her settled upon him and he told her of his desires. The bartender was ready to marry and to begin trying to earn money for the support of his wife, but so simple was his nature that he found it difficult to explain his intentions. His body ached with physical longing and with his body he expressed himself. Taking the milliner into his arms and holding her tightly in spite of her struggles, he kissed her until she became helpless. Then he brought her back to town and let her out of the buggy. "When I get hold of you again I'll not let you go. You can't play with me," he declared as he turned to drive away. Then, jumping out of the buggy, he gripped her shoulders with his strong hands. "I'll keep you for good the next time," he said. "You might as well make up your mind to that. It's you and me for it and I'm going to have you before I get through."

One night in January when there was a new moon George Willard, who was in Ed Handby's mind the only obstacle to his getting Belle Carpenter, went for a walk. Early that evening George went into Ransom Surbeck's pool room with Seth Richmond and Art Wilson, son of the town butcher. Seth Richmond stood with his back against the wall and remained silent, but George Willard talked. The pool room was filled with Winesburg boys and they talked of women. The young reporter got into that vein. He said that women should look out for themselves, that the fellow who went out with a girl was not responsible for what happened. As he talked he looked about, eager for attention. He held the floor for five minutes and then Art Wilson began to talk. Art was learning the barber's trade in Cal Prouse's shop and already began to consider himself an authority in such matters as baseball, horse racing, drinking, and going about with women. He began to tell of a night when he with two men from Winesburg went into a house of prostitution at the county seat. The butcher's son held a cigar in the side of his mouth and as he talked spat on the floor. "The women in the place couldn't embarrass me although they tried hard enough," he boasted. "One of the girls in the house tried to get fresh, but I fooled her. As soon as she began to talk I went and sat in her lap. Everyone in the room laughed when I kissed her. I taught her to let me alone."

George Willard went out of the pool room and into Main Street. For days the weather had been bitter cold with a high wind blowing down on the town from Lake Erie, eighteen miles to the north, but on that night the wind had died away and a new moon made the night unusually lovely. Without thinking where he was going or what he wanted to do, George went out of Main Street and began walking in dimly lighted streets filled with frame houses.

Out of doors under the black sky filled with stars he forgot his companions of the pool room. Because it was dark and he was alone he began to talk aloud. In a spirit of play he reeled along the street imitating a drunken man and then imagined himself a soldier clad in shining boots that reached to the knees and wearing a sword that jingled as he walked. As a soldier he pictured himself as an inspector, passing before a long line of men who stood at attention. He began to examine the accoutrements of the men. Before a tree he stopped and began to scold. "Your pack is not in order," he said sharply. "How many times will I have to speak of this matter? Everything must be in order here. We have a difficult task before us and no difficult task can be done without order."

Hypnotized by his own words, the young man stumbled along the board sidewalk saying more words. "There is a law for armies and for men too," he muttered, lost in reflection. "The law begins with little things and spreads out until it covers everything. In every little thing there must be order, in the place where men work, in their clothes, in their thoughts. I myself must be orderly. I must learn that law. I must get myself into touch with something orderly and big that swings through the night like a star. In my little way I must begin to learn something, to give and swing and work with life, with the law."

George Willard stopped by a picket fence near a street lamp and his body began to tremble. He had never before thought such thoughts as had just come into his head and he wondered where they had come from. For the moment it seemed to him that some voice outside of himself had been talking as he walked. He was amazed and delighted with his own mind and when he walked on again spoke of the matter with fervor. "To come out of Ransom Surbeck's pool room and think things like that," he whispered. "It is better to be alone. If I talked like Art Wilson the boys would understand me but they wouldn't understand what I've been thinking down here."

In Winesburg, as in all Ohio towns of twenty years ago, there was a section in which lived day laborers. As the time of factories had not yet come, the laborers worked in the fields or were section hands on the railroads. They worked twelve hours a day and received one dollar for the long day of toil. The houses in which they lived were small cheaply constructed wooden affairs with a garden at the back. The more comfortable among them kept cows and perhaps a pig, housed in a little shed at the rear of the garden.

With his head filled with resounding thoughts, George Willard walked into such a street on the clear January night. The street was dimly lighted and in places there was no sidewalk. In the scene that lay about him there was something that excited his already aroused fancy. For a year he had been devoting all of his odd moments to the reading of books and now some tale he had read concerning life in old world towns of the middle ages came sharply back to his mind so that he stumbled forward with the curious feeling of one revisiting a place that had been a part of some former existence. On an impulse he turned out of the street and went into a little dark alleyway behind the sheds in which lived the cows and pigs.

For a half hour he stayed in the alleyway, smelling the strong smell of animals too closely housed and letting his mind play with the strange new thoughts that came to him. The very rankness of the smell of manure in the clear sweet air awoke something heady in his brain. The poor little houses lighted by kerosene lamps, the smoke from the chimneys mounting straight up into the clear air, the grunting of pigs, the women clad in cheap calico dresses and washing dishes in the kitchens, the footsteps of men coming out of the houses and going off to the stores and saloons of Main Street, the dogs barking and the children crying—all of these things made him seem, as he lurked in the darkness, oddly detached and apart from all life.

The excited young man, unable to bear the weight of his own thoughts, began to move cautiously along the alleyway. A dog attacked him and had to be driven away with stones, and a man appeared at the door of one of the houses and swore at the dog. George went into a vacant lot and throwing back his head looked up at the sky. He felt unutterably big and remade by the simple experience through which he had been passing and in a kind of fervor of emotion put up his hands, thrusting them into the darkness above his head and muttering words.

The desire to say words overcame him and he said words without meaning, rolling them over on his tongue and saying them because they were brave words, full of meaning. "Death," he muttered, "night, the sea, fear, loveliness."

George Willard came out of the vacant lot and stood again on the sidewalk facing the houses. He felt that all of the people in the little street must be brothers and sisters to him and he wished he had the courage to call them out of their houses and to shake their hands. "If there were only a woman here I would take hold of her hand and we would run until we were both tired out," he thought. "That would make me feel better." With the thought of a woman in his mind he walked out of the street and went toward the house where Belle Carpenter lived. He thought she would understand his mood and that he could achieve in her presence a position he had long been wanting to achieve. In the past when he had been with her and had kissed her lips he had come away filled with anger at himself. He had felt like one being used for some obscure purpose and had not enjoyed the feeling. Now he thought he had suddenly become too big to be used.

When George got to Belle Carpenter's house there had already been a visitor there before him. Ed Handby had come to the door and calling Belle out of the house had tried to talk to her. He had wanted to ask the woman to come away with him and to be his wife, but when she came and stood by the door he lost his self-assurance and became sullen. "You stay away from that kid," he growled, thinking of George Willard, and then, not knowing what else to say, turned to go away. "If I catch you together I will break your bones and his too," he added. The bartender had come to woo, not to threaten, and was angry with himself because of his failure.

When her lover had departed Belle went indoors and ran hurriedly upstairs. From a window at the upper part of the house she saw Ed Handby cross the street and sit down on a horse block before the house of a neighbor. In the dim light the man sat motionless holding his head in his hands. She was made happy by the sight, and when George Willard came to the door she greeted him effusively and hurriedly put on her hat. She thought that, as she walked through the streets with young Willard, Ed Handby would follow and she wanted to make him suffer.

For an hour Belle Carpenter and the young reporter walked about under the trees in the sweet night air. George Willard was full of big words. The sense of power that had come to him during the hour in the darkness in the alleyway remained with him and he talked boldly, swaggering along and swinging his arms about. He wanted to make Belle Carpenter realize that he was aware of his former weakness and that he had changed. "You'll find me different," he declared, thrusting his hands into his pockets and looking boldly into her eyes. "I don't know why but it is so. You've got to take me for a man or let me alone. That's how it is."

Up and down the quiet streets under the new moon went the woman and the boy. When George had finished talking they turned down a side street and went across a bridge into a path that ran up the side of a hill. The hill began at Waterworks Pond and climbed upwards to the Winesburg Fair Grounds. On the hillside grew dense bushes and small trees and among the bushes were little open spaces carpeted with long grass, now stiff and frozen.

As he walked behind the woman up the hill George Willard's heart began to beat rapidly and his shoulders straightened. Suddenly he decided that Belle Carpenter was about to surrender herself to him. The new force that had manifested itself in him had, he felt, been at work upon her and had led to her conquest. The thought made him half drunk with the sense of masculine power. Although he had been annoyed that as they walked about she had not seemed to be listening to his words, the fact that she had accompanied him to this place took all his doubts away. "It is different. Everything has become different," he thought and taking hold of her shoulder turned her about and stood looking at her, his eyes shining with pride.

Belle Carpenter did not resist. When he kissed her upon the lips she leaned heavily against him and looked over his shoulder into the darkness. In her whole attitude there was a suggestion of waiting. Again, as in the alleyway, George Willard's mind ran off into words and, holding the woman tightly he whispered the words into the still night. "Lust," he whispered, "lust and night and women."

George Willard did not understand what happened to him that night on the hillside. Later, when he got to his own room, he wanted to weep and then grew half insane with anger and hate. He hated Belle Carpenter and was sure that all his life he would continue to hate her. On the hillside he had led the woman to one of the little open spaces among the bushes and had dropped to his knees beside her. As in the vacant lot, by the laborers' houses, he had put up his hands in gratitude for the new power in himself and was waiting for the woman to speak when Ed Handby appeared.

The bartender did not want to beat the boy, who he thought had tried to take his woman away. He knew that beating was unnecessary, that he had power within himself to accomplish his purpose without using his fists. Gripping George by the shoulder and pulling him to his feet, he held him with one hand while he looked at Belle Carpenter seated on the grass. Then with a quick wide movement of his arm he sent the younger man sprawling away into the bushes and began to bully the woman, who had risen to her feet. "You're no good," he said roughly. "I've half a mind not to bother with you. I'd let you alone if I didn't want you so much."

On his hands and knees in the bushes George Willard stared at the scene before him and tried hard to think. He prepared to spring at the man who had humiliated him. To be beaten seemed to be infinitely better than to be thus hurled ignominiously aside.

Three times the young reporter sprang at Ed Handby and each time the bartender, catching him by the shoulder, hurled him back into the bushes. The older man seemed prepared to keep the exercise going indefinitely but George Willard's head struck the root of a tree and he lay still. Then Ed Handby took Belle Carpenter by the arm and marched her away.

George heard the man and woman making their way through the bushes. As he crept down the hillside his heart was sick within him. He hated himself and he hated the fate that had brought about his humiliation. When his mind went back to the hour alone in the alleyway he was puzzled and stopping in the darkness listened, hoping to hear again the voice outside himself that had so short a time before put new courage into his heart. When his way homeward led him again into the street of frame houses he could not bear the sight and began to run, wanting to get quickly out of the neighborhood that now seemed to him utterly squalid and commonplace.

"Queer"

FROM his seat on a box in the rough board shed that stuck like a burr on the rear of Cowley & Son's store in Winesburg, Elmer Cowley, the junior member of the firm, could see through a dirty window into the printshop of the *Winesburg Eagle*. Elmer was putting new shoelaces in his shoes. They did not go in readily and he had to take the shoes off. With the shoes in his hand he sat looking at a large hole in the heel of one of his stockings. Then looking quickly up he saw George Willard, the only newspaper reporter in Winesburg, standing at the back door of the *Eagle* printshop and staring absent-mindedly about. "Well, well, what next!" exclaimed the young man with the shoes in his hand, jumping to his feet and creeping away from the window.

A flush crept into Elmer Cowley's face and his hands began to tremble. In Cowley & Son's store a Jewish traveling salesman stood by the counter talking to his father. He imagined the reporter could hear what was being said and the thought made him furious. With one of the shoes still held in his hand he stood in a corner of the shed and stamped with a stockinged foot upon the board floor.

Cowley & Son's store did not face the main street of Winesburg. The front was on Maumee Street and beyond it was Voight's wagon shop and a shed for the sheltering of farmers' horses. Beside the store an alleyway ran behind the main street stores and all day drays and delivery wagons, intent on bringing in and taking out goods, passed up and down. The store itself was indescribable. Will Henderson once said of it that it sold everything and nothing. In the window facing Maumee Street stood a chunk of coal as large as an apple barrel, to indicate that orders for coal were taken, and beside the black mass of the coal stood three combs of honey grown brown and dirty in their wooden frames.

The honey had stood in the store window for six months. It was for sale as were also the coat hangers, patent suspender buttons, cans of roof paint, bottles of rheumatism cure and a substitute for coffee that companioned the honey in its patient willingness to serve the public.

Ebenezer Cowley, the man who stood in the store listening to the eager patter of words that fell from the lips of the traveling man, was tall and lean and looked unwashed. On his scrawny neck was a large wen partially covered by a grey beard. He wore a long Prince Albert coat. The coat had been purchased to serve as a wedding garment. Before he became a merchant Ebenezer was a farmer and after his marriage he wore the Prince Albert coat to church on Sundays and on Saturday afternoons when he came into town to trade. When he sold the farm to become a merchant he wore the coat constantly. It had become brown with age and was covered with grease spots, but in it Ebenezer always felt dressed up and ready for the day in town.

As a merchant Ebenezer was not happily placed in life and he had not been happily placed as a farmer. Still he existed. His family, consisting of a daughter named Mabel and the son, lived with him in rooms above the store and it did not cost them much to live. His troubles were not financial. His unhappiness as a merchant lay in the fact that when a traveling man with wares to be sold came in at the front door he was afraid. Behind the counter he stood shaking his head. He was afraid, first that he would stubbornly refuse to buy and thus lose the opportunity to sell again; second that he would not be stubborn enough and would in a moment of weakness buy what could not be sold.

In the store on the morning when Elmer Cowley saw George Willard standing and apparently listening at the back door of the *Eagle* printshop, a situation had arisen that always stirred the son's wrath. The traveling man talked and Ebenezer listened, his whole figure expressing uncertainty. "You see how quickly it is done," said the traveling man who had for sale a small flat metal substitute for collar buttons. With one hand he quickly unfastened a collar from his shirt and then fastened it on again. He assumed a flattering wheedling tone. "I tell you what, men have come to the end of all this fooling with collar buttons and you are the man to make money out of the change that is coming. I am offering you the exclusive agency for this town. Take twenty dozen of these fasteners and I'll not visit any other store. I'll leave the field to you."

The traveling man leaned over the counter and tapped with his finger on Ebenezer's breast. "It's an opportunity and I want you to take it," he urged. "A friend of mine told me about you. 'See that man Cowley,' he said. 'He's a live one.'"

The traveling man paused and waited. Taking a book from his pocket he began writing out the order. Still holding the shoe in his hand Elmer Cowley went through the store, past the two absorbed men, to a glass show case near the front door. He took a cheap revolver from the case and began to wave it about. "You get out of here!" he shrieked. "We don't want any collar fasteners here." An idea came to him. "Mind, I'm not making any threat," he added. "I don't say I'll shoot. Maybe I just took this gun out of the case to look at it. But you better get out. Yes sir, I'll say that. You better grab up your things and get out."

The young storekeeper's voice rose to a scream and going behind the counter he began to advance upon the two men. "We're through being fools here!" he cried. "We ain't going to buy any more stuff until we begin to sell. We ain't going to keep on being queer and have folks staring and listening. You get out of here!"

The traveling man left. Raking the samples of collar fasteners off the counter into a black leather bag, he ran. He was a small man and very bow-legged and he ran awkwardly. The black bag caught against the door and he stumbled and fell. "Crazy, that's what he is—crazy!" he sputtered as he arose from the sidewalk and hurried away.

In the store Elmer Cowley and his father stared at each other. Now that the immediate object of his wrath had fled, the younger man was embarrassed. "Well, I meant it. I think we've been queer long enough," he declared, going to the showcase and replacing the revolver. Sitting on a barrel he pulled on and fastened the shoe he had been holding in his hand. He was waiting for some word of understanding from his father but when Ebenezer spoke his words only served to reawaken the wrath in the son and the young man ran out of the store without replying. Scratching his grey beard with his long dirty fingers, the merchant looked at his son with the same wavering uncertain stare with which he had confronted the traveling man. "I'll be starched," he said softly. "Well, well, I'll be washed and ironed and starched!"

Elmer Cowley went out of Winesburg and along a country road that paralleled the railroad track. He did not know where he was going or what he was going to do. In the shelter of a deep cut where the road, after turning sharply to the right, dipped under the tracks he stopped and the passion that had been the cause of his outburst in the store began to again find expression. "I will not be queer—one to be looked at and listened to," he declared aloud. "I'll be like other people. I'll show that George Willard. He'll find out. I'll show him!"

The distraught young man stood in the middle of the road and glared back at the town. He did not know the reporter George Willard and had no special feeling concerning the tall boy who ran about town gathering the town news. The reporter had merely come, by his presence in the office and in the printshop of the *Winesburg Eagle*, to stand for something in the young merchant's mind. He thought the boy who passed and repassed Cowley & Son's store and who stopped to talk to people in the street must be thinking of him and perhaps laughing at him. George Willard, he felt, belonged to the town, typified the town, represented in his person the spirit of the town. Elmer Cowley could not have believed that George Willard had also his days of unhappiness, that vague hungers and secret unnamable desires visited also his mind. Did he not represent public opinion and had not the public opinion of Winesburg condemned the Cowleys to queerness? Did he not walk whistling and laughing through Main Street? Might not one by striking his person strike also the greater enemy—the thing that smiled and went its own way—the judgment of Winesburg?

Elmer Cowley was extraordinarily tall and his arms were long and powerful. His hair, his eyebrows, and the downy beard that had begun to grow upon his chin, were pale almost to whiteness. His teeth protruded from between his lips and his eyes were blue with the colorless blueness of the marbles called "aggies" that the boys of Winesburg carried in their pockets. Elmer had lived in Winesburg for a year and had made no friends. He was, he felt, one condemned to go through life without friends and he hated the thought.

Sullenly the tall young man tramped along the road with his hands stuffed into his trouser pockets. The day was cold with a raw wind, but presently the sun began to shine and the road became soft and muddy. The tops of the ridges of frozen mud that formed the road began to melt and the mud clung to Elmer's shoes. His feet became cold. When he had gone several miles he turned off the road, crossed a field and entered a wood. In the wood he gathered sticks to build a fire by which he sat trying to warm himself, miserable in body and in mind.

For two hours he sat on the log by the fire and then, arising and creeping cautiously through a mass of underbrush, he went to a fence and looked across fields to a small farmhouse surrounded by low sheds. A smile came to his lips and he began making motions with his long arms to a man who was husking corn in one of the fields.

In his hour of misery the young merchant had returned to the farm where he had lived through boyhood and where there was another human being to whom he felt he could explain himself. The man on the farm was a half-witted old fellow named Mook. He had once been employed by Ebenezer Cowley and had stayed on the farm when it was sold. The old man lived in one of the unpainted sheds back of the farmhouse and puttered about all day in the fields.

Mook the half-wit lived happily. With childlike faith he believed in the intelligence of the animals that lived in the sheds with him, and when he was lonely held long conversations with the cows, the pigs, and even with the chickens that ran about the barnyard. He it was who had put the expression regarding being "laundered" into the mouth of his former employer. When excited or surprised by anything he smiled vaguely and muttered: "I'll be washed and ironed. Well, well, I'll be washed and ironed and starched."

When the half-witted old man left his husking of corn and came into the wood to meet Elmer Cowley, he was neither surprised nor especially interested in the sudden appearance of the young man. His feet also were cold and he sat on the log by the fire, grateful for the warmth and apparently indifferent to what Elmer had to say.

Elmer talked earnestly and with great freedom, walking up and down and waving his arms about. "You don't understand what's the matter with me so of course you don't care," he declared. "With me it's different. Look how it has always been with me. Father is queer and mother was queer, too. Even the clothes mother used to wear were not like other people's clothes, and look at that coat in which father goes about there in town, thinking he's dressed up, too. Why don't he get a new one? It wouldn't cost much. I'll tell you why. Father doesn't know and when mother was alive she didn't know either. Mabel is different. She knows but she won't say anything. I will, though. I'm not going to be stared at any longer. Why look here, Mook, father doesn't know that his store there in town is just a queer jumble, that he'll never sell the stuff he buys. He knows nothing about it. Sometimes he's a little worried that trade doesn't come and then he goes and buys something else. In the evenings he sits by the fire upstairs and says trade will come after a while. He isn't worried. He's queer. He doesn't know enough to be worried."

The excited young man became more excited. "He don't know but I know," he shouted, stopping to gaze down into the dumb, unresponsive face of the half-wit. "I know too well. I can't stand it. When we lived out here it was different. I worked and at night I went to bed and slept. I wasn't always seeing people and thinking as I am now. In the evening, there in town, I go to the post office or to the depot to see the train come in, and no one says anything to me. Everyone stands around and laughs and they talk but they say nothing to me. Then I feel so queer that I can't talk either. I go away. I don't say anything. I can't."

The fury of the young man became uncontrollable. "I won't stand it," he yelled, looking up at the bare branches of the trees. "I'm not made to stand it."

Maddened by the dull face of the man on the log by the fire, Elmer turned and glared at him as he had glared back along the road at the town of Winesburg. "Go on back to work," he screamed. "What good does it do me to talk to you?" A thought came to him and his voice dropped. "I'm a coward too, eh?" he muttered. "Do you know why I came clear out here afoot? I had to tell some one and you were the only one I could tell. I hunted out another queer one, you see. I ran away, that's what I did. I couldn't stand up to some one like that George Willard. I had to come to you. I ought to tell him and I will."

Again his voice arose to a shout and his arms flew about. "I will tell him. I won't be queer. I don't care what they think. I won't stand it."

Elmer Cowley ran out of the woods leaving the half-wit sitting on the log before the fire. Presently the old man arose and climbing over the fence went back to his work in the corn. "I'll be washed and ironed and starched," he declared. "Well, well, I'll be washed and ironed." Mook was interested. He went along a lane to a field where two cows stood nibbling at a straw stack. "Elmer was here," he said to the cows. "Elmer is crazy. You better get behind the stack where he don't see you. He'll hurt someone yet, Elmer will."

At eight o'clock that evening Elmer Cowley put his head in at the front door of the office of the *Winesburg Eagle* where George Willard sat writing. His cap was pulled down over his eyes and a sullen determined look was on his face. "You come on outside with me," he said, stepping in and closing the door. He kept his hand on the knob as though prepared to resist anyone else coming in. "You just come along outside. I want to see you."

George Willard and Elmer Cowley walked through the main street of Winesburg. The night was cold and George Willard had on a new overcoat and looked very spruce and dressed up. He thrust his hands into the overcoat pockets and looked inquiringly at his companion. He had long been wanting to make friends with the young merchant and find out what was in his mind. Now he thought he saw a chance and was delighted. "I wonder what he's up to? Perhaps he thinks he has a piece of news for the paper. It can't be a fire because I haven't heard the fire bell and there isn't anyone running," he thought.

In the main street of Winesburg, on the cold November evening, but few citizens appeared and these hurried along bent on getting to the stove at the back of some store. The windows of the stores were frosted and the wind rattled the tin sign that hung over the entrance to the stairway leading to Doctor Welling's office. Before Hern's Grocery a basket of apples and a rack filled with new brooms stood on the sidewalk. Elmer Cowley stopped and stood facing George Willard. He tried to talk and his arms began to pump up and down. His face worked spasmodically. He seemed about to shout. "Oh, you go on back," he cried. "Don't stay out here with me. I ain't got anything to tell you. I don't want to see you at all."

For three hours the distracted young merchant wandered through the resident streets of Winesburg blind with anger, brought on by his failure to declare his determination not to be queer. Bitterly the sense of defeat settled upon him and he wanted to weep. After the hours of futile sputtering at nothingness that had coupled the afternoon and his failure in the presence of the young reporter, he thought he could see no hope of a future for himself.

And then a new idea dawned for him. In the darkness that surrounded him he began to see a light. Going to the now darkened store, where Cowley & Son had for over a year waited vainly for trade to come, he crept stealthily in and felt about in a barrel that stood by the stove at the rear. In the barrel beneath shavings lay a tin box, containing Cowley & Son's cash. Every evening Ebenezer Cowley put the box in the barrel when he closed the store and went upstairs to bed. "They wouldn't never think of a careless place like that," he told himself, thinking of robbers.

Elmer took twenty dollars, two ten dollar bills, from the little roll containing perhaps four hundred dollars, the cash left from the sale of the farm. Then replacing the box beneath the shavings he went quietly out at the front door and walked again in the streets.

The idea that he thought might put an end to all of his unhappiness was very simple. "I will get out of here, run away from home," he told himself. He knew that a local freight train passed through Winesburg at midnight and went on to Cleveland where it arrived at dawn. He would steal a ride on the local and when he got to Cleveland would lose himself in the crowds there. He would get work in some shop and become friends with the other workmen. Gradually he would become like other men and would be indistinguishable. Then he could talk and laugh. He would no longer be queer and would make friends. Life would begin to have warmth and meaning for him as it had for others.

The tall awkward young man, striding through the streets, laughed at himself because he had been angry and had been half afraid of George Willard. He decided he would have his talk with the young reporter before he left town, that he would tell him about things, perhaps challenge him, challenge all of Winesburg through him.

Aglow with new confidence Elmer went to the office of the New Willard House and pounded on the door. A sleep-eyed boy slept on a cot in the office. He received no salary but was fed at the hotel table and bore with pride the title of "night clerk." Before the boy Elmer was bold, insistent. "You wake him up," he commanded. "You tell him to come down by the depot. I got to see him and I'm going away on the local. Tell him to dress and come on down. I ain't got much time."

The midnight local had finished its work in Winesburg and the trainsmen were coupling cars, swinging lanterns and preparing to resume their flight east. George Willard, rubbing his eyes and again wearing the new overcoat, ran down to the station platform afire with curiosity. "Well, here I am. What do you want? You've got something to tell me, eh?" he said.

Elmer tried to explain. He wet his lips with his tongue and looked at the train that had begun to groan and get under way. "Well, you see," he began, and then lost control of his tongue. "I'll be washed and ironed. I'll be washed and ironed and starched," he muttered half incoherently.

Elmer Cowley danced with fury beside the groaning train in the darkness on the station platform. Lights leaped into the air and bobbed up and down before his eyes. Taking the two ten dollar bills from his pocket he thrust them into George Willard's hand. "Take them," he cried. "I don't want them. Give them to father. I stole them." With a snarl of rage he turned and his long arms began to flay the air. Like one struggling for release from hands that held him he struck out, hitting George Willard blow after blow on the breast, the neck, the mouth. The young reporter rolled over on the platform half unconscious, stunned by the terrific force of the blows. Springing aboard the passing train and running over the tops of cars, Elmer sprang down to a flat car and lying on his face looked back, trying to see the fallen man in the darkness. Pride surged up in him. "I showed him," he cried. "I guess I showed him. I ain't so queer. I guess I showed him I ain't so queer."

The Untold Lie

R AY PEARSON and Hal Winters were farm hands employed on a farm three miles north of Winesburg. On Saturday afternoons they came into town and wandered about through the streets with other fellows from the country.

Ray was a quiet, rather nervous man of perhaps fifty with a brown beard and shoulders rounded by too much and too hard labor. In his nature he was as unlike Hal Winters as two men can be unlike.

Ray was an altogether serious man and had a little sharp featured wife who had also a sharp voice. The two, with half a dozen thin legged children, lived in a tumble-down frame house beside a creek at the back end of the Wills farm where Ray was employed.

Hal Winters, his fellow employee, was a young fellow. He was not of the Ned Winters family, who were very respectable people in Winesburg, but was one of the three sons of the old man called Windpeter Winters who had a sawmill near Unionville, six miles away, and who was looked upon by everyone in Winesburg as a confirmed old reprobate.

People from the part of Northern Ohio in which Winesburg lies will remember old Windpeter by his unusual and tragic death. He got drunk one evening in town and started to drive home to Unionville along the railroad tracks. Henry Brattenburg, the butcher, who lived out that way, stopped him at the edge of the town and told him he was sure to meet the down train but Windpeter slashed at him with his whip and drove on. When the train struck and killed him and his two horses a farmer and his wife who were driving home along a nearby road saw the accident. They said that old Windpeter stood up on the seat of his wagon, raving and swearing at the onrushing locomotive, and that he fairly screamed with delight when the team, maddened by his incessant slashing at them, rushed straight ahead to certain death. Boys like young George Willard and Seth Richmond will remember the incident quite vividly because, although everyone in our town said that the old man would go straight to hell and that the community was better off without him, they had a secret conviction that he knew what he was doing and admired his foolish courage. Most boys have seasons of wishing they could die gloriously instead of just being grocery clerks and going on with their humdrum lives.

But this is not the story of Windpeter Winters nor yet of his son Hal who worked on the Wills farm with Ray Pearson. It is Ray's story. It will, however, be necessary to talk a little of young Hal so that you will get into the spirit of it.

Hal was a bad one. Everyone said that. There were three of the Winters boys in that family, John, Hal, and Edward, all broad shouldered big fellows like old Windpeter himself and all fighters and woman-chasers and generally all-around bad ones.

Hal was the worst of the lot and always up to some devilment. He once stole a load of boards from his father's mill and sold them in Winesburg. With the money he bought himself a suit of cheap, flashy clothes. Then he got drunk and when his father came raving into town to find him, they met and fought with their fists on Main Street and were arrested and put into jail together.

Hal went to work on the Wills farm because there was a country school teacher out that way who had taken his fancy. He was only twenty-two then but had already been in two or three of what were spoken of in Winesburg as "women scrapes." Everyone who heard of his infatuation for the school teacher was sure it would turn out badly. "He'll only get her into trouble, you'll see," was the word that went around.

And so these two men, Ray and Hal, were at work in a field on a day in the late October. They were husking corn and occasionally something was said and they laughed. Then came silence. Ray, who was the more sensitive and always minded things more, had chapped hands and they hurt. He put them into his coat pockets and looked away across the fields. He was in a sad distracted mood and was affected by the beauty of the country. If you knew the Winesburg country in the fall and how the low hills are all splashed with yellows and reds you would understand his feeling. He began to think of the time, long ago when he was a young fellow living with his father, then a baker in Winesburg, and how on such days he had wandered away to the woods to gather nuts, hunt rabbits, or just to loaf about and smoke his pipe. His marriage had come about through one of his days of wandering. He had induced a girl who waited on trade in his father's shop to go with him and something had happened. He was thinking of that afternoon and how it had affected his whole life when a spirit of protest awoke in him. He had forgotten about Hal and muttered words. "Tricked by Gad, that's what I was, tricked by life and made a fool of," he said in a low voice.

As though understanding his thoughts, Hal Winters spoke up. "Well, has it been worth while? What about it, eh? What about marriage and all that?" he asked and then laughed. Hal tried to keep on laughing but he too was in an earnest mood. He began to talk earnestly. "Has a fellow got to do it?" he asked. "Has he got to be harnessed up and driven through life like a horse?"

Hal didn't wait for an answer but sprang to his feet and began to walk back and forth between the corn shocks. He was getting more and more excited. Bending down suddenly he picked up an ear of the yellow corn and threw it at the fence. "I've got Nell Gunther in trouble," he said. "I'm telling you, but you keep your mouth shut."

Ray Pearson arose and stood staring. He was almost a foot shorter than Hal, and when the younger man came and put his two hands on the older man's shoulders they made a picture. There they stood in the big empty field with the quiet corn shocks standing in rows behind them and the red and yellow hills in the distance, and from being just two indifferent workmen they had become all alive to each other. Hal sensed it and because that was his way he laughed. "Well, old daddy," he said awkwardly, "come on, advise me. I've got Nell in trouble. Perhaps you've been in the same fix yourself. I know what every one would say is the right thing to do, but what do you say? Shall I marry and settle down? Shall I put myself into the harness to be worn out like an old horse? You know me, Ray. There can't any one break me but I can break myself. Shall I do it or shall I tell Nell to go to the devil? Come on, you tell me. Whatever you say, Ray, I'll do."

Ray couldn't answer. He shook Hal's hands loose and turning walked straight away toward the barn. He was a sensitive man and there were tears in his eyes. He knew there was only one thing to say to Hal Winters, son of old Windpeter Winters, only one thing that all his own training and all the beliefs of the people he knew would approve, but for his life he couldn't say what he knew he should say.

At half-past four that afternoon Ray was puttering about the barnyard when his wife came up the lane along the creek and called him. After the talk with Hal he hadn't returned to the corn field but worked about the barn. He had already done the evening chores and had seen Hal, dressed and ready for a roistering night in town, come out of the farmhouse and go into the road. Along the path to his own house he trudged behind his wife, looking at the ground and thinking. He couldn't make out what was wrong. Every time he raised his eyes and saw the beauty of the country in the failing light he wanted to do something he had never done before, shout or scream or hit his wife with his fists or something equally unexpected and terrifying. Along the path he went scratching his head and trying to make it out. He looked hard at his wife's back but she seemed all right.

She only wanted him to go into town for groceries and as soon as she had told him what she wanted began to scold. "You're always puttering," she said. "Now I want you to hustle. There isn't anything in the house for supper and you've got to get to town and back in a hurry."

Ray went into his own house and took an overcoat from a hook back of the door. It was torn about the pockets and the collar was shiny. His wife went into the bedroom and presently came out with a soiled cloth in one hand and three silver dollars in the other. Somewhere in the house a child wept bitterly and a dog that had been sleeping by the stove arose and yawned. Again the wife scolded. "The children will cry and cry. Why are you always puttering?" she asked.

Ray went out of the house and climbed the fence into a field. It was just growing dark and the scene that lay before him was lovely. All the low hills were washed with color and even the little clusters of bushes in the corners by the fences were alive with beauty. The whole world seemed to Ray Pearson to have become alive with something just as he and Hal had suddenly become alive when they stood in the corn field staring into each other's eyes.

The beauty of the country about Winesburg was too much for Ray on that fall evening. That is all there was to it. He could not stand it. Of a sudden he forgot all about being a quiet old farm hand and throwing off the torn overcoat began to run across the field. As he ran he shouted a protest against his life, against all life, against everything that makes life ugly. "There was no promise made," he cried into the empty spaces that lay about him. "I didn't promise my Minnie anything and Hal hasn't made any promise to Nell. I know he hasn't. She went into the woods with him because she wanted to go. What he wanted she wanted. Why should I pay? Why should Hal pay? Why should any one pay? I don't want Hal to become old and worn out. I'll tell him. I won't let it go on. I'll catch Hal before he gets to town and I'll tell him."

Ray ran clumsily and once he stumbled and fell down. "I must catch Hal and tell him," he kept thinking and although his breath came in gasps he kept running harder and harder. As he ran he thought of things that hadn't come into his mind for years—how at the time he married he had planned to go west to his uncle in Portland, Oregon—how he hadn't wanted to be a farm hand, but had thought when he got out west he would go to sea and be a sailor or get a job on a ranch and ride a horse into western towns, shouting and laughing and waking the people in the houses with his wild cries. Then as he ran he remembered his children and in fancy felt their hands clutching at him. All of his thoughts of himself were involved with the thoughts of Hal and he thought the children were clutching at the younger man also. "They are the accidents of life, Hal," he cried. "They are not mine or yours. I had nothing to do with them."

Darkness began to spread over the fields as Ray Pearson ran on and on. His breath came in little sobs. When he came to the fence at the edge of the road and confronted Hal Winters, all dressed up and smoking a pipe as he walked jauntily along, he could not have told what he thought or what he wanted.

Ray Pearson lost his nerve and this is really the end of the story of what happened to him. It was almost dark when he got to the fence and he put his hands on the top bar and stood staring. Hal Winters jumped a ditch and coming up close to Ray put his hands into his pockets and laughed. He seemed to have lost his own sense of what had happened in the corn field and when he put up a strong hand and took hold of the lapel of Ray's coat he shook the old man as he might have shaken a dog that had misbehaved.

"You came to tell me, eh?" he said. "Well, never mind telling me anything. I'm not a coward and I've already made up my mind." He laughed again and jumped back across the ditch. "Nell ain't no fool," he said. "She didn't ask me to marry her. I want to marry her. I want to settle down and have kids."

Ray Pearson also laughed. He felt like laughing at himself and all the world.

As the form of Hal Winters disappeared in the dusk that lay over the road that led to Winesburg, he turned and walked slowly back across the fields to where he had left his torn overcoat. As he went some memory of pleasant evenings spent with the thin-legged children in the tumble-down house by the creek must have come into his mind, for he muttered words. "It's just as well. Whatever I told him would have been a lie," he said softly, and then his form also disappeared into the darkness of the fields.

Drink

Tom Foster came to Winesburg from Cincinnati when he was still young and could get many new impressions. His grandmother had been raised on a farm near the town and as a young girl had gone to school there when Winesburg was a village of twelve or fifteen houses clustered about a general store on the Trunion Pike.

What a life the old woman had led since she went away from the frontier settlement and what a strong, capable little old thing she was! She had been in Kansas, in Canada, and in New York City, traveling about with her husband, a mechanic, before he died. Later she went to stay with her daughter who had also married a mechanic and lived in Covington, Kentucky, across the river from Cincinnati.

Then began the hard years for Tom Foster's grandmother. First her son-in-law was killed by a policeman during a strike and then Tom's mother became an invalid and died also. The grandmother had saved a little money, but it was swept away by the illness of the daughter and by the cost of the two funerals. She became a half worn-out old woman worker and lived with the grandson above a junk shop on a side street in Cincinnati. For five years she scrubbed the floors in an office building and then got a place as dish washer in a restaurant. Her hands were all twisted out of shape. When she took hold of a mop or a broom handle the hands looked like the dried stems of an old creeping vine clinging to a tree.

The old woman came back to Winesburg as soon as she got the chance. One evening as she was coming home from work she found a pocket-book containing thirty-seven dollars, and that opened the way. The trip was a great adventure for the boy. It was past seven o'clock at night when the grandmother came home with the pocket-book held tightly in her old hands and she was so excited she could scarcely speak. She insisted on leaving Cincinnati that night, saying that if they stayed until morning the owner of the money would be sure to find them out and make trouble. Tom, who was then sixteen years old, had to go trudging off to the station with the old woman bearing all of their earthly belongings done up in a worn-out blanket and slung across his back. By his side walked the grandmother urging him forward. Her toothless old mouth twitched nervously, and when Tom grew weary and wanted to put the pack down at a street crossing she snatched it up and if he had not prevented would have slung it across her own back. When they got into the train and it had run out of the city she was as delighted as a girl and talked as the boy had never heard her talk before.

All through the night as the train rattled along, the grand-mother told Tom tales of Winesburg and of how he would enjoy his life working in the fields and shooting wild things in the wood there. She could not believe that the tiny village of fifty years before had grown into a thriving town in her absence, and in the morning when the train came to Winesburg did not want to get off. "It isn't what I thought. It may be hard for you here," she said, and then the train went on its way and the two stood confused, not knowing where to turn, in the presence of Albert Longworth, the Winesburg baggage master.

But Tom Foster did get along all right. He was one to get along anywhere. Mrs. White, the banker's wife, employed his grandmother to work in the kitchen and he got a place as stable boy in the banker's new brick barn.

In Winesburg servants were hard to get. The woman who wanted help in her housework employed a "hired girl" who insisted on sitting at the table with the family. Mrs. White was sick of hired girls and snatched at the chance to get hold of the old city woman. She furnished a room for the boy Tom up-stairs in the barn. "He can mow the lawn and run errands when the horses do not need attention," she explained to her husband.

Tom Foster was rather small for his age and had a large head covered with stiff black hair that stood straight up. The hair emphasized the bigness of his head. His voice was the softest thing imaginable, and he was himself so gentle and quiet that he slipped into the life of the town without attracting the least bit of attention.

One could not help wondering where Tom Foster got his gentleness. In Cincinnati he had lived in a neighborhood where gangs of tough boys prowled through the streets, and all through his early formative years he ran about with tough boys. For a while he was messenger for a telegraph company and delivered messages in a neighborhood sprinkled with houses of prostitution. The women in the houses knew and loved Tom Foster and the tough boys in the gangs loved him also.

He never asserted himself. That was one thing that helped him escape. In an odd way he stood in the shadow of the wall of life, was meant to stand in the shadow. He saw the men and women in the houses of lust, sensed their casual and horrible love affairs, saw boys fighting and listened to their tales of thieving and drunkenness unmoved and strangely unaffected.

Once Tom did steal. That was while he still lived in the city. The grandmother was ill at the time and he himself was out of work. There was nothing to eat in the house, and so he went into a harness shop on a side street and stole a dollar and seventy-five cents out of the cash drawer.

The harness shop was run by an old man with a long mustache. He saw the boy lurking about and thought nothing of it. When he went out into the street to talk to a teamster Tom opened the cash drawer and taking the money walked away. Later he was caught and his grandmother settled the matter by offering to come twice a week for a month and scrub the shop. The boy was ashamed, but he was rather glad, too. "It is all right to be ashamed and makes me understand new things," he said to the grandmother, who didn't know what the boy was talking about but loved him so much that it didn't matter whether she understood or not.

For a year Tom Foster lived in the banker's stable and then lost his place there. He didn't take very good care of the horses and he was a constant source of irritation to the banker's wife. She told him to mow the lawn and he forgot. Then she sent him to the store or to the post office and he did not come back but joined a group of men and boys and spent the whole afternoon with them, standing about, listening and occasionally, when addressed, saying a few words. As in the city in the houses of prostitution and with the rowdy boys running through the streets at night, so in Winesburg among its citizens he had always the power to be a part of and yet distinctly apart from the life about him.

After Tom lost his place at Banker White's he did not live with his grandmother, although often in the evening she came to visit him. He rented a room at the rear of a little frame building belonging to old Rufus Whiting. The building was on Duane Street, just off Main Street, and had been used for years as a law office by the old man who had become too feeble and forgetful for the practice of his profession but did not realize his inefficiency. He liked Tom and let him have the room for a dollar a month. In the late afternoon when the lawyer had gone home the boy had the place to himself and spent hours lying on the floor by the stove and thinking of things. In the evening the grandmother came and sat in the lawyer's chair to smoke a pipe while Tom remained silent, as he always did in the presence of every one.

Often the old woman talked with great vigor. Sometimes she was angry about some happening at the banker's house and scolded away for hours. Out of her own earnings she bought a mop and regularly scrubbed the lawyer's office. Then when the place was spotlessly clean and smelled clean she lighted her clay pipe and she and Tom had a smoke together. "When you get ready to die then I will die also," she said to the boy lying on the floor beside her chair.

Tom Foster enjoyed life in Winesburg. He did odd jobs, such as cutting wood for kitchen stoves and mowing the grass before houses. In late May and early June he picked strawberries in the fields. He had time to loaf and he enjoyed loafing. Banker White had given him a cast-off coat which was too large for him, but his grandmother cut it down, and he had also an overcoat, got at the same place, that was lined with fur. The fur was worn away in spots, but the coat was warm and in the winter Tom slept in it. He thought his method of getting along good enough and was happy and satisfied with the way life in Winesburg had turned out for him.

The most absurd little things made Tom Foster happy. That, I suppose, was why people loved him. In Hern's grocery they would be roasting coffee on Friday afternoon, preparatory to the Saturday rush of trade, and the rich odor invaded lower Main Street. Tom Foster appeared and sat on a box at the rear of the store. For an hour he did not move but sat perfectly still, filling his being with the spicy odor that made him half drunk with happiness. "I like it," he said gently. "It makes me think of things far away, places and things like that."

One night Tom Foster got drunk. That came about in a curious way. He never had been drunk before, and indeed in all his life had never taken a drink of anything intoxicating, but he felt he needed to be drunk that one time and so went and did it.

In Cincinnati, when he lived there, Tom had found out many things, things about ugliness and crime and lust. Indeed, he knew more of these things than any one else in Winesburg. The matter of sex in particular had presented itself to him in a quite horrible way and had made a deep impression on his mind. He thought, after what he had seen of the women standing before the squalid houses on cold nights and the look he had seen in the eyes of the men who stopped to talk to them, that he would put sex altogether out of his own life. One of the women of the neighborhood tempted him once and he went into a room with her. He never forgot the smell of the room nor the greedy look that came into the eyes of the woman. It sickened him and in a very terrible way left a scar on his soul. He had always before thought of women as quite innocent things, much like his grandmother, but after that one experience in the room he dismissed women from his mind. So gentle was his nature that he could not hate anything and not being able to understand he decided to forget.

And Tom did forget until he came to Winesburg. After he had lived there for two years something began to stir in him. On all sides he saw youth making love and he was himself a youth. Before he knew what had happened he was in love also. He fell in love with Helen White, daughter of the man for whom he had worked, and found himself thinking of her at night.

That was a problem for Tom and he settled it in his own way. He let himself think of Helen White whenever her figure came into his mind and only concerned himself with the manner of his thoughts. He had a fight, a quiet determined little fight of his own, to keep his desires in the channel where he thought they belonged, but on the whole he was victorious.

And then came the spring night when he got drunk. Tom was wild on that night. He was like an innocent young buck of the forest that has eaten of some maddening weed. The thing began, ran its course, and was ended in one night, and you may be sure that no one in Winesburg was any the worse for Tom's outbreak.

In the first place, the night was one to make a sensitive nature drunk. The trees along the residence streets of the town were all newly clothed in soft green leaves, in the gardens behind the houses men were puttering about in vegetable gardens, and in the air there was a hush, a waiting kind of silence very stirring to the blood.

Tom left his room on Duane Street just as the young night began to make itself felt. First he walked through the streets, going softly and quietly along, thinking thoughts that he tried to put into words. He said that Helen White was a flame dancing in the air and that he was a little tree without leaves standing out sharply against the sky. Then he said that she was a wind, a strong terrible wind, coming out of the darkness of a stormy sea and that he was a boat left on the shore of the sea by a fisherman.

That idea pleased the boy and he sauntered along playing with it. He went into Main Street and sat on the curbing before Wacker's tobacco store. For an hour he lingered about listening to the talk of men, but it did not interest him much and he slipped away. Then he decided to get drunk and went into Willy's saloon and bought a bottle of whiskey. Putting the bottle into his pocket, he walked out of town, wanting to be alone to think more thoughts and to drink the whiskey.

Tom got drunk sitting on a bank of new grass beside the road about a mile north of town. Before him was a white road and at his back an apple orchard in full bloom. He took a drink out of the bottle and then lay down on the grass. He thought of mornings in Winesburg and of how the stones in the graveled driveway by Banker White's house were wet with dew and glistened in the morning light. He thought of the nights in the barn when it rained and he lay awake hearing the drumming of the rain drops and smelling the warm smell of horses and of hay. Then he thought of a storm that had gone roaring through Winesburg several days before and, his mind going back, he relived the night he had spent on the train with his grandmother when the two were coming from Cincinnati.

Sharply he remembered how strange it had seemed to sit quietly in the coach and to feel the power of the engine hurling
the train along through the night.

Tom got drunk in a very short time. He kept taking drinks
from the bottle as the thoughts visited him and when his head
began to reel got up and walked along the road going away
from Winesburg. There was a bridge on the road that ran out
of Winesburg north to Lake Erie and the drunken boy made
his way along the road to the bridge. There he sat down. He
tried to drink again, but when he had taken the cork out of the
bottle he became ill and put it quickly back. His head was
rocking back and forth and so he sat on the stone approach to
the bridge and sighed. His head seemed to be flying about like
a pin wheel and then projecting itself off into space and his
arms and legs flopped helplessly about.

At eleven o'clock Tom got back into town. George Willard
found him wandering about and took him into the *Eagle*
printshop. Then he became afraid that the drunken boy would
make a mess on the floor and helped him into the alleyway.

The reporter was confused by Tom Foster. The drunken
boy talked of Helen White and said he had been with her on
the shore of a sea and had made love to her. George had seen
Helen White walking in the street with her father during the
evening and decided that Tom was out of his head. A sentiment concerning Helen White that lurked in his own heart
flamed up and he became angry. "Now you quit that," he said.
"I won't let Helen White's name be dragged into this. I won't
let that happen." He began shaking Tom's shoulder, trying to
make him understand. "You quit it," he said again.

For three hours the two young men, thus strangely thrown
together, stayed in the printshop. When he had a little recovered George took Tom for a walk. They went into the country
and sat on a log near the edge of wood. Something in the still
night drew them together and when the drunken boy's head
began to clear they talked.

"It was good to be drunk," Tom Foster said. "It taught me
something. I won't have to do it again. I will think more clearly
after this. You see how it is."

George Willard did not see, but his anger concerning Helen
White passed and he felt drawn towards the pale, shaken boy

as he had never before been drawn towards any one. With motherly solicitude, he insisted that Tom get to his feet and walk about. Again they went back to the printshop and sat in silence in the darkness.

The reporter could not get the purpose of Tom Foster's action straightened out in his mind. When Tom spoke again of Helen White he again grew angry and began to scold. "You quit that," he said sharply. "You haven't been with her. What makes you say you have? What makes you keep saying such things? Now you quit it, do you hear?"

Tom was hurt. He couldn't quarrel with George Willard because he was incapable of quarreling, so he got up to go away. When George Willard was insistent he put out his hand, laying it on the older boy's arm, and tried to explain.

"Well," he said softly, "I don't know how it was. I was happy. You see how that was. Helen White made me happy and the night did too. I wanted to suffer, to be hurt somehow. I thought that was what I should do. I wanted to suffer, you see, because every one suffers and does wrong. I thought of a lot of things to do, but they wouldn't work. They all hurt some one else."

Tom Foster's voice arose, and for once in his life he became almost excited. "It was like making love, that's what I mean," he explained. "Don't you see how it is? It hurt me to do what I did and made everything strange. That's why I did it. I'm glad, too. It taught me something, that's it, that's what I wanted. Don't you understand? I wanted to learn things, you see. That's why I did it."

Death

THE stairway leading up to Dr. Reefy's office, in the Heffner Block above the Paris Dry Goods Store, was but dimly lighted. At the head of the stairway hung a lamp with a dirty chimney that was fastened by a bracket to the wall. The lamp had a tin reflector, brown with rust and covered with dust. The people who went up the stairway followed with their feet the feet of many who had gone before. The soft boards of the stairs had yielded under the pressure of feet and deep hollows marked the way.

At the top of the stairway a turn to the right brought you to the doctor's door. To the left was a dark hallway filled with rubbish. Old chairs, carpenter's horses, step ladders and empty boxes lay in the darkness waiting for shins to be barked. The pile of rubbish belonged to the Paris Dry Goods Co. When a counter or a row of shelves in the store became useless, clerks carried it up the stairway and threw it on the pile.

Doctor Reefy's office was as large as a barn. A stove with a round paunch sat in the middle of the room. Around its base was piled sawdust, held in place by heavy planks nailed to the floor. By the door stood a huge table that had once been a part of the furniture of Herrick's Clothing Store and that had been used for displaying custom-made clothes. It was covered with books, bottles and surgical instruments. Near the edge of the table lay three or four apples left by John Spaniard, a tree nurseryman who was Doctor Reefy's friend, and who had slipped the apples out of his pocket as he came in at the door.

At middle age Doctor Reefy was tall and awkward. The grey beard he later wore had not yet appeared, but on the upper lip grew a brown mustache. He was not a graceful man, as when he grew older, and was much occupied with the problem of disposing of his hands and feet.

On summer afternoons, when she had been married many years and when her son George was a boy of twelve or fourteen, Elizabeth Willard sometimes went up the worn steps to Doctor Reefy's office. Already the woman's naturally tall figure had begun to droop and to drag itself listlessly about. Ostensibly she went to see the doctor because of her health, but on the half dozen occasions when she had been to see him the outcome of the visits did not primarily concern her health. She and the doctor talked of that but they talked most of her life, of their two lives and of the ideas that had come to them as they lived their lives in Winesburg.

In the big empty office the man and the woman sat looking at each other and they were a good deal alike. Their bodies were different as were also the color of their eyes, the length of their noses and the circumstances of their existence, but something inside them meant the same thing, wanted the same release, would have left the same impression on the memory of an onlooker. Later, and when he grew older and married a young wife, the doctor often talked to her of the hours spent with the sick woman and expressed a good many things he had been unable to express to Elizabeth. He was almost a poet in his old age and his notion of what happened took a poetic turn. "I had come to the time in my life when prayer became necessary and so I invented gods and prayed to them," he said. "I did not say my prayers in words nor did I kneel down but sat perfectly still in my chair. In the late afternoon when it was hot and quiet on Main Street or in the winter when the days were gloomy, the gods came into the office and I thought no one knew about them. Then I found that this woman Elizabeth knew, that she worshipped also the same gods. I have a notion that she came to the office because she thought the gods would be there but she was happy to find herself not alone just the same. It was an experience that cannot be explained, although I suppose it is always happening to men and women in all sorts of places."

On the summer afternoons when Elizabeth and the doctor sat in the office and talked of their two lives they talked of other lives also. Sometimes the doctor made philosophic epigrams. Then he chuckled with amusement. Now and then after a period of silence, a word was said or a hint given that strangely illuminated the life of the speaker, a wish became a desire, or a dream, half dead, flared suddenly into life. For the most part the words came from the woman and she said them without looking at the man.

Each time she came to see the doctor the hotel keeper's wife talked a little more freely and after an hour or two in his presence went down the stairway into Main Street feeling renewed and strengthened against the dullness of her days. With something approaching a girlhood swing to her body she walked along, but when she had got back to her chair by the window of her room and when darkness had come on and a girl from the hotel dining room brought her dinner on a tray, she let it grow cold. Her thoughts ran away to her girlhood with its passionate longing for adventure and she remembered the arms of men that had held her when adventure was a possible thing for her. Particularly she remembered one who had for a time been her lover and who in the moment of his passion had cried out to her more than a hundred times, saying the same words madly over and over: "You dear! You dear! You lovely dear!" The words she thought expressed something she would have liked to have achieved in life.

In her room in the shabby old hotel the sick wife of the hotel keeper began to weep and putting her hands to her face rocked back and forth. The words of her one friend, Doctor Reefy, rang in her ears. "Love is like a wind stirring the grass beneath trees on a black night," he had said. "You must not try to make love definite. It is the divine accident of life. If you try to be definite and sure about it and to live beneath the trees, where soft night winds blow, the long hot day of disappointment comes swiftly and the gritty dust from passing wagons gathers upon lips inflamed and made tender by kisses."

Elizabeth Willard could not remember her mother who had died when she was but five years old. Her girlhood had been lived in the most haphazard manner imaginable. Her father was a man who had wanted to be let alone and the affairs of the hotel would not let him alone. He also had lived and died a sick man. Every day he arose with a cheerful face, but by ten o'clock in the morning all the joy had gone out of his heart. When a guest complained of the fare in the hotel dining room or one of the girls who made up the beds got married and went away, he stamped on the floor and swore. At night when he went to bed he thought of his daughter growing up among the stream of people that drifted in and out of the hotel and was overcome with sadness. As the girl grew older and began to walk out in the evening with men he wanted to talk to her, but when he tried was not successful. He always forgot what he wanted to say and spent the time complaining of his own affairs.

In her girlhood and young womanhood Elizabeth had tried to be a real adventurer in life. At eighteen life had so gripped her that she was no longer a virgin but, although she had a half dozen lovers before she married Tom Willard, she had never entered upon an adventure prompted by desire alone. Like all the women in the world, she wanted a real lover. Always there was something she sought blindly, passionately, some hidden wonder in life. The tall beautiful girl with the swinging stride who had walked under the trees with men was forever putting out her hand into the darkness and trying to get hold of some other hand. In all the babble of words that fell from the lips of the men with whom she adventured she was trying to find what would be for her the true word.

Elizabeth had married Tom Willard, a clerk in her father's hotel, because he was at hand and wanted to marry at the time when the determination to marry came to her. For a while, like most young girls, she thought marriage would change the face of life. If there was in her mind a doubt of the outcome of the marriage with Tom she brushed it aside. Her father was ill and near death at the time and she was perplexed because of the meaningless outcome of an affair in which she had just been involved. Other girls of her age in Winesburg were marrying men she had always known, grocery clerks or young farmers. In the evening they walked in Main Street with their husbands and when she passed they smiled happily. She began to think that the fact of marriage might be full of some hidden significance. Young wives with whom she talked spoke softly and shyly. "It changes things to have a man of your own," they said.

On the evening before her marriage the perplexed girl had a talk with her father. Later she wondered if the hours alone with the sick man had not led to her decision to marry. The father talked of his life and advised the daughter to avoid being led into another such muddle. He abused Tom Willard, and that led Elizabeth to come to the clerk's defense. The sick man became excited and tried to get out of bed. When she would not let him walk about he began to complain. "I've never been let alone," he said. "Although I've worked hard I've not made the hotel pay. Even now I owe money at the bank. You'll find that out when I'm gone."

The voice of the sick man became tense with earnestness. Being unable to arise, he put out his hand and pulled the girl's head down beside his own. "There's a way out," he whispered. "Don't marry Tom Willard or any one else here in Winesburg. There is eight hundred dollars in a tin box in my trunk. Take it and go away."

Again the sick man's voice became querulous. "You've got to promise," he declared. "If you won't promise not to marry, give me your word that you'll never tell Tom about the money. It is mine and if I give it to you I've the right to make that demand. Hide it away. It is to make up to you for my failure as a father. Some time it may prove to be a door, a great open door to you. Come now, I tell you I'm about to die, give me your promise."

In Doctor Reefy's office, Elizabeth, a tired gaunt old woman at forty-one, sat in a chair near the stove and looked at the floor. By a small desk near the window sat the doctor. His hands played with a lead pencil that lay on the desk. Elizabeth talked of her life as a married woman. She became impersonal and forgot her husband, only using him as a lay figure to give point to her tale. "And then I was married and it did not turn out at all," she said bitterly. "As soon as I had gone into it I began to be afraid. Perhaps I knew too much before and then perhaps I found out too much during my first night with him. I don't remember.

"What a fool I was. When father gave me the money and tried to talk me out of the thought of marriage, I would not listen. I thought of what the girls who were married had said of it and I wanted marriage also. It wasn't Tom I wanted, it was marriage. When father went to sleep I leaned out of the window and thought of the life I had led. I didn't want to be a bad woman. The town was full of stories about me. I even began to be afraid Tom would change his mind."

The woman's voice began to quiver with excitement. To Doctor Reefy, who without realizing what was happening had begun to love her, there came an odd illusion. He thought that as she talked the woman's body was changing, that she was becoming younger, straighter, stronger. When he could not shake off the illusion his mind gave it a professional twist. "It is good for both her body and her mind, this talking," he muttered.

The woman began telling of an incident that had happened one afternoon a few months after her marriage. Her voice became steadier. "In the late afternoon I went for a drive alone," she said. "I had a buggy and a little grey pony I kept in Moyer's Livery. Tom was painting and repapering rooms in the hotel. He wanted money and I was trying to make up my mind to tell him about the eight hundred dollars father had given to me. I couldn't decide to do it. I didn't like him well enough. There was always paint on his hands and face during those days and he smelled of paint. He was trying to fix up the old hotel, make it new and smart."

The excited woman sat up very straight in her chair and made a quick girlish movement with her hand as she told of the drive alone on the spring afternoon. "It was cloudy and a storm threatened," she said. "Black clouds made the green of the trees and the grass stand out so that the colors hurt my eyes. I went out Trunion Pike a mile or more and then turned into a side road. The little horse went quickly along up hill and down. I was impatient. Thoughts came and I wanted to get away from my thoughts. I began to beat the horse. The black clouds settled down and it began to rain. I wanted to go at a terrible speed, to drive on and on forever. I wanted to get out of town, out of my clothes, out of my marriage, out of my body, out of everything. I almost killed the horse, making him run, and when he could not run any more I got out of the buggy and ran afoot into the darkness until I fell and hurt my side. I wanted to run away from everything but I wanted to run towards something too. Don't you see, dear, how it was?"

Elizabeth sprang out of the chair and began to walk about in the office. She walked as Doctor Reefy thought he had never seen any one walk before. To her whole body there was a swing, a rhythm that intoxicated him. When she came and knelt on the floor beside his chair he took her into his arms and began to kiss her passionately. "I cried all the way home," she said, as she tried to continue the story of her wild ride, but he did not listen. "You dear! You lovely dear! Oh you lovely dear!" he muttered and thought he held in his arms, not the tired out woman of forty-one but a lovely and innocent girl who had been able by some miracle to project herself out of the husk of the body of the tired-out woman.

Doctor Reefy did not see the woman he had held in his arms again until after her death. On the summer afternoon in the office when he was on the point of becoming her lover a half grotesque little incident brought his love-making quickly to an end. As the man and woman held each other tightly heavy feet came tramping up the office stairs. The two sprang to their feet and stood listening and trembling. The noise on the stairs was made by a clerk from the Paris Dry Goods Store Co. With a loud bang he threw an empty box on the pile of rubbish in the hallway and then went heavily down the stairs. Elizabeth followed him almost immediately. The thing that had come to life in her as she talked to her one friend died suddenly. She was hysterical, as was also Doctor Reefy, and did not want to continue the talk. Along the street she went with the blood still singing in her body, but when she turned out of Main Street and saw ahead the lights of the New Willard House, she began to tremble and her knees shook so that for a moment she thought she would fall in the street.

The sick woman spent the last few months of her life hungering for death. Along the road of death she went, seeking, hungering. She personified the figure of death and made him, now a strong black-haired youth running over hills, now a stern quiet man marked and scarred by the business of living. In the darkness of her room she put out her hand, thrusting it from under the covers of her bed, and she thought that death like a living thing put out his hand to her. "Be patient, lover," she whispered. "Keep yourself young and beautiful and be patient."

On the evening when disease laid its heavy hand upon her and defeated her plans for telling her son George of the eight hundred dollars hidden away, she got out of bed and crept half across the room pleading with death for another hour of life. "Wait, dear! The boy! The boy! The boy!" she pleaded as she tried with all of her strength to fight off the arms of the lover she had wanted so earnestly.

Elizabeth died one day in March in the year when her son George became eighteen, and the young man had but little sense of the meaning of her death. Only time could give him that. For a month he had seen her lying white and still and speechless in her bed, and then one afternoon the doctor stopped him in the hallway and said a few words.

The young man went into his room and closed the door. He had a queer empty feeling in the region of his stomach. For a moment he sat staring at the floor and then jumping up went for a walk. Along the station platform he went, and around through residence streets past the high school building, thinking almost entirely of his own affairs. The notion of death could not get hold of him and he was in fact a little annoyed that his mother had died on that day. He had just received a note from Helen White, the daughter of the town banker, in answer to one from him. "Tonight I could have gone to see her and now it will have to be put off," he thought half angrily.

Elizabeth died on a Friday afternoon at three o'clock. It had been cold and rainy in the morning but in the afternoon the sun came out. Before she died she lay paralyzed for six days unable to speak or move and with only her mind and her eyes alive. For three of the six days she struggled, thinking of her boy, trying to say some few words in regard to his future, and in her eyes there was an appeal so touching that all who saw it kept the memory of the dying woman in their minds for years. Even Tom Willard who had always half resented his wife forgot his resentment and the tears ran out of his eyes and lodged in his mustache. The mustache had begun to turn grey and Tom colored it with dye. There was oil in the preparation he used for the purpose and the tears, catching in the mustache and being brushed away by his hand, formed a fine mist-like vapor. In his grief Tom Willard's face looked like the face of a little dog that has been out a long time in bitter weather.

George came home along Main Street at dark on the day of his mother's death and, after going to his own room to brush his hair and clothes, went along the hallway and into the room where the body lay. There was a candle on the dressing table by the door and Doctor Reefy sat in a chair by the bed. The doctor arose and started to go out. He put out his hand as though to greet the younger man and then awkwardly drew it back again. The air of the room was heavy with the presence of the two self-conscious human beings, and the man hurried away.

The dead woman's son sat down in a chair and looked at the floor. He again thought of his own affairs and definitely decided he would make a change in his life, that he would leave Winesburg. "I will go to some city. Perhaps I can get a job on some newspaper," he thought and then his mind turned to the girl with whom he was to have spent this evening and again he was half angry at the turn of events that had prevented his going to her.

In the dimly lighted room with the dead woman the young man began to have thoughts. His mind played with thoughts of life as his mother's mind had played with the thought of death. He closed his eyes and imagined that the red young lips of Helen White touched his own lips. His body trembled and his hands shook. And then something happened. The boy sprang to his feet and stood stiffly. He looked at the figure of the dead woman under the sheets and shame for his thoughts swept over him so that he began to weep. A new notion came into his mind and he turned and looked guiltily about as though afraid he would be observed.

George Willard became possessed of a madness to lift the sheet from the body of his mother and look at her face. The thought that had come into his mind gripped him terribly. He became convinced that not his mother but some one else lay in the bed before him. The conviction was so real that it was almost unbearable. The body under the sheets was long and in death looked young and graceful. To the boy, held by some strange fancy, it was unspeakably lovely. The feeling that the body before him was alive, that in another moment a lovely woman would spring out of the bed and confront him became so overpowering that he could not bear the suspense. Again and again he put out his hand. Once he touched and half lifted the white sheet that covered her, but his courage failed and he, like Doctor Reefy, turned and went out of the room. In the hallway outside the door he stopped and trembled so that he had to put a hand against the wall to support himself. "That's not my mother. That's not my mother in there," he whispered to himself and again his body shook with fright and uncertainty. When Aunt Elizabeth Swift, who had come to watch over the body, came out of an adjoining room he put his hand into hers and began to sob, shaking his head from side to side, half blind with grief. "My mother is dead," he said, and then forgetting the woman he turned and stared at the door through which he had just come. "The dear, the dear, oh the lovely dear," the boy, urged by some impulse outside himself, muttered aloud.

As for the eight hundred dollars, the dead woman had kept hidden so long and that was to give George Willard his start in the city, it lay in the tin box behind the plaster by the foot of his mother's bed. Elizabeth had put it there a week after her marriage, breaking the plaster away with a stick. Then she got one of the workmen her husband was at that time employing about the hotel to mend the wall. "I jammed the corner of the bed against it," she had explained to her husband, unable at the moment to give up her dream of release, the release that after all came to her but twice in her life, in the moments when her lovers Death and Doctor Reefy held her in their arms.

Sophistication

I T was early evening of a day in the late fall and the Wines-burg County Fair had brought crowds of country people into town. The day had been clear and the night came on warm and pleasant. On the Trunion Pike, where the road after it left town stretched away between berry fields now covered with dry brown leaves, the dust from passing wagons arose in clouds. Children, curled into little balls, slept on the straw scattered on wagon beds. Their hair was full of dust and their fingers black and sticky. The dust rolled away over the fields and the departing sun set it ablaze with colors.

In the main street of Winesburg crowds filled the stores and the sidewalks. Night came on, horses whinnied, the clerks in the stores ran madly about, children became lost and cried lustily, an American town worked terribly at the task of amus-ing itself.

Pushing his way through the crowds in Main Street, young George Willard concealed himself in the stairway leading to Doctor Reefy's office and looked at the people. With feverish eyes he watched the faces drifting past under the store lights. Thoughts kept coming into his head and he did not want to think. He stamped impatiently on the wooden steps and looked sharply about. "Well, is she going to stay with him all day? Have I done all this waiting for nothing?" he muttered.

George Willard, the Ohio village boy, was fast growing into manhood and new thoughts had been coming into his mind. All that day, amid the jam of people at the Fair, he had gone about feeling lonely. He was about to leave Winesburg to go away to some city where he hoped to get work on a city news-paper and he felt grown up. The mood that had taken posses-sion of him was a thing known to men and unknown to boys. He felt old and a little tired. Memories awoke in him. To his mind his new sense of maturity set him apart, made of him a half-tragic figure. He wanted someone to understand the feel-ing that had taken possession of him after his mother's death.

There is a time in the life of every boy when he for the first time takes the backward view of life. Perhaps that is the moment when he crosses the line into manhood. The boy is walking through the street of his town. He is thinking of the future and of the figure he will cut in the world. Ambitions and regrets awake within him. Suddenly something happens; he stops under a tree and waits as for a voice calling his name. Ghosts of old things creep into his consciousness; the voices outside of himself whisper a message concerning the limitations of life. From being quite sure of himself and his future he becomes not at all sure. If he be an imaginative boy a door is torn open and for the first time he looks out upon the world, seeing, as though they marched in procession before him, the countless figures of men who before his time have come out of nothingness into the world, lived their lives and again disappeared into nothingness. The sadness of sophistication has come to the boy. With a little gasp he sees himself as merely a leaf blown by the wind through the streets of his village. He knows that in spite of all the stout talk of his fellows he must live and die in uncertainty, a thing blown by the winds, a thing destined like corn to wilt in the sun. He shivers and looks eagerly about. The eighteen years he has lived seem but a moment, a breathing space in the long march of humanity. Already he hears death calling. With all his heart he wants to come close to some other human, touch someone with his hands, be touched by the hand of another. If he prefers that the other be a woman, that is because he believes that a woman will be gentle, that she will understand. He wants, most of all, understanding.

When the moment of sophistication came to George Willard his mind turned to Helen White, the Winesburg banker's daughter. Always he had been conscious of the girl growing into womanhood as he grew into manhood. Once on a summer night when he was eighteen, he had walked with her on a country road and in her presence had given way to an impulse to boast, to make himself appear big and significant in her eyes. Now he wanted to see her for another purpose. He wanted to tell her of the new impulses that had come to him. He had tried to make her think of him as a man when he knew nothing of manhood and now he wanted to be with her and to try to make her feel the change he believed had taken place in his nature.

As for Helen White, she also had come to a period of change. What George felt, she in her young woman's way felt also. She was no longer a girl and hungered to reach into the grace and beauty of womanhood. She had come home from Cleveland, where she was attending college, to spend a day at the Fair. She also had begun to have memories. During the day she sat in the grandstand with a young man, one of the instructors from the college, who was a guest of her mother's. The young man was of a pedantic turn of mind and she felt at once he would not do for her purpose. At the Fair she was glad to be seen in his company as he was well dressed and a stranger. She knew that the fact of his presence would create an impression. During the day she was happy, but when night came on she began to grow restless. She wanted to drive the instructor away, to get out of his presence. While they sat together in the grand-stand and while the eyes of former schoolmates were upon them, she paid so much attention to her escort that he grew interested. "A scholar needs money. I should marry a woman with money," he mused.

Helen White was thinking of George Willard even as he wandered gloomily through the crowds thinking of her. She remembered the summer evening when they had walked together and wanted to walk with him again. She thought that the months she had spent in the city, the going to theatres and the seeing of great crowds wandering in lighted thoroughfares, had changed her profoundly. She wanted him to feel and be conscious of the change in her nature.

The summer evening together that had left its mark on the memory of both the young man and woman had, when looked at quite sensibly, been rather stupidly spent. They had walked out of town along a country road. Then they had stopped by a fence near a field of young corn and George had taken off his coat and let it hang on his arm. "Well, I've stayed here in Winesburg—yes—I've not yet gone away but I'm growing up," he had said. "I've been reading books and I've been thinking. I'm going to try to amount to something in life.

"Well," he explained, "that isn't the point. Perhaps I'd better quit talking."

The confused boy put his hand on the girl's arm. His voice trembled. The two started to walk back along the road toward town. In his desperation George boasted, "I'm going to be a big man, the biggest that ever lived here in Winesburg," he declared. "I want you to do something, I don't know what. Perhaps it is none of my business. I want you to try to be different from other women. You see the point. It's none of my business I tell you. I want you be a beautiful woman. You see what I want."

The boy's voice failed and in silence the two came back into town and went along the street to Helen White's house. At the gate he tried to say something impressive. Speeches he had thought out came into his head, but they seemed utterly pointless. "I thought—I used to think—I had it in my mind you would marry Seth Richmond. Now I know you won't," was all he could find to say as she went through the gate and toward the door of her house.

On the warm fall evening as he stood in the stairway and looked at the crowd drifting through Main Street, George thought of the talk beside the field of young corn and was ashamed of the figure he had made of himself. In the street the people surged up and down like cattle confined in a pen. Buggies and wagons almost filled the narrow thoroughfare. A band played and small boys raced along the sidewalk, diving between the legs of men. Young men with shining red faces walked awkwardly about with girls on their arms. In a room above one of the stores, where a dance was to be held, the fiddlers tuned their instruments. The broken sounds floated down through an open window and out across the murmer of voices and the loud blare of the horns of the band. The medley of sounds got on young Willard's nerves. Everywhere, on all sides, the sense of crowding, moving life closed in about him. He wanted to run away by himself and think. "If she wants to stay with that fellow she may. Why should I care? What difference does it make to me?" he growled and went along Main Street and through Hern's grocery into a side street.

George felt so utterly lonely and dejected that he wanted to weep but pride made him walk rapidly along, swinging his arms. He came to Wesley Moyer's livery barn and stopped in the shadows to listen to a group of men who talked of a race Wesley's stallion, Tony Tip, had won at the Fair during the afternoon. A crowd had gathered in front of the barn and before the crowd walked Wesley, prancing up and down and boasting. He held a whip in his hand and kept tapping the ground. Little puffs of dust arose in the lamplight. "Hell, quit your talking," Wesley exclaimed. "I wasn't afraid, I knew I had 'em beat all the time. I wasn't afraid."

Ordinarily George Willard would have been intensely interested in the boasting of Moyer, the horseman. Now it made him angry. He turned and hurried away along the street. "Old windbag," he sputtered. "Why does he want to be bragging? Why don't he shut up?"

George went into a vacant lot and as he hurried along, fell over a pile of rubbish. A nail protruding from an empty barrel tore his trousers. He sat down on the ground and swore. With a pin he mended the torn place and then arose and went on. "I'll go to Helen White's house, that's what I'll do. I'll walk right in. I'll say that I want to see her. I'll walk right in and sit down, that's what I'll do," he declared, climbing over a fence and beginning to run.

On the veranda of Banker White's house Helen was restless and distraught. The instructor sat between the mother and daughter. His talk wearied the girl. Although he had also been raised in an Ohio town, the instructor began to put on the airs of the city. He wanted to appear cosmopolitan. "I like the chance you have given me to study the background out of which most of our girls come," he declared. "It was good of you, Mrs. White, to have me down for the day." He turned to Helen and laughed. "Your life is still bound up with the life of this town?" he asked. "There are people here in whom you are interested?" To the girl his voice sounded pompous and heavy.

Helen arose and went into the house. At the door leading to a garden at the back she stopped and stood listening. Her mother began to talk. "There is no one here fit to associate with a girl of Helen's breeding," she said.

Helen ran down a flight of stairs at the back of the house and into the garden. In the darkness she stopped and stood trembling. It seemed to her that the world was full of meaningless people saying words. Afire with eagerness she ran through a garden gate and turning a corner by the banker's barn, went into a little side street. "George! Where are you,

George?" she cried, filled with nervous excitement. She stopped running, and leaned against a tree to laugh hysterically. Along the dark little street came George Willard, still saying words. "I'm going to walk right into her house. I'll go right in and sit down," he declared as he came up to her. He stopped and stared stupidly. "Come on," he said and took hold of her hand. With hanging heads they walked away along the street under the trees. Dry leaves rustled under foot. Now that he had found her George wondered what he had better do and say.

At the upper end of the fair ground, in Winesburg, there is a half decayed old grand-stand. It has never been painted and the boards are all warped out of shape. The fair ground stands on top of a low hill rising out of the valley of Wine Creek and from the grand-stand one can see at night, over a cornfield, the lights of the town reflected against the sky.

George and Helen climbed the hill to the fair ground, coming by the path past Waterworks Pond. The feeling of loneliness and isolation that had come to the young man in the crowded streets of his town was both broken and intensified by the presence of Helen. What he felt was reflected in her.

In youth there are always two forces fighting in people. The warm unthinking little animal struggles against the thing that reflects and remembers, and the older, the more sophisticated thing had possession of George Willard. Sensing his mood, Helen walked beside him filled with respect. When they got to the grand-stand they climbed up under the roof and sat down on one of the long bench-like seats.

There is something memorable in the experience to be had by going into a fair ground that stands at the edge of a Middle Western town on a night after the annual fair has been held. The sensation is one never to be forgotten. On all sides are ghosts, not of the dead, but of living people. Here, during the day just passed, have come the people pouring in from the town and the country around. Farmers with their wives and children and all the people from the hundreds of little frame houses have gathered within these board walls. Young girls have laughed and men with beards have talked of the affairs of their lives. The place has been filled to overflowing with life. It has itched and squirmed with life and now it is night and the life has all gone away. The silence is almost terrifying. One conceals oneself standing silently beside the trunk of a tree and what there is of a reflective tendency in his nature is intensified. One shudders at the thought of the meaninglessness of life while at the same instant, and if the people of the town are his people, one loves life so intensely that tears come into the eyes.

In the darkness under the roof of the grand-stand, George Willard sat beside Helen White and felt very keenly his own insignificance in the scheme of existence. Now that he had come out of town where the presence of the people stirring about, busy with a multitude of affairs, had been so irritating the irritation was all gone. The presence of Helen renewed and refreshed him. It was as though her woman's hand was assisting him to make some minute readjustment of the machinery of his life. He began to think of the people in the town where he had always lived with something like reverence. He had reverence for Helen. He wanted to love and to be loved by her, but he did not want at the moment to be confused by her womanhood. In the darkness he took hold of her hand and when she crept close put a hand on her shoulder. A wind began to blow and he shivered. With all his strength he tried to hold and to understand the mood that had come upon him. In that high place in the darkness the two oddly sensitive human atoms held each other tightly and waited. In the mind of each was the same thought. "I have come to this lonely place and here is this other," was the substance of the thing felt.

In Winesburg the crowded day had run itself out into the long night of the late fall. Farm horses jogged away along lonely country roads pulling their portion of weary people. Clerks began to bring samples of goods in off the sidewalks and lock the doors of stores. In the Opera House a crowd had gathered to see a show and further down Main Street the fiddlers, their instruments tuned, sweated and worked to keep the feet of youth flying over a dance floor.

In the darkness in the grand-stand Helen White and George Willard remained silent. Now and then the spell that held them was broken and they turned and tried in the dim light to see into each others eyes. They kissed but that impulse did not last. At the upper end of the fair ground a half dozen men worked over horses that had raced during the afternoon. The men had built a fire and were heating kettles of water. Only their legs could be seen as they passed back and forth in the light. When the wind blew the little flames of the fire danced crazily about.

George and Helen arose and walked away into the darkness. They went along a path past a field of corn that had not yet been cut. The wind whispered among the dry corn blades. For a moment during the walk back into town the spell that held them was broken. When they had come to the crest of Waterworks Hill they stopped by a tree and George again put his hands on the girl's shoulders. She embraced him eagerly and then again they drew quickly back from that impulse. They stopped kissing and stood a little apart. Mutual respect grew big in them. They were both embarrassed and to relieve their embarrassment dropped into the animalism of youth. They laughed and began to pull and haul at each other. In some way chastened and purified by the mood they had been in they became, not man and woman, not boy and girl, but excited little animals.

It was so they went down the hill. In the darkness they played like two splendid young things in a young world. Once, running swiftly forward, Helen tripped George and he fell. He squirmed and shouted. Shaking with laughter, he rolled down the hill. Helen ran after him. For just a moment she stopped in the darkness. There is no way of knowing what woman's thoughts went through her mind but, when the bottom of the hill was reached and she came up to the boy, she took his arm and walked beside him in dignified silence. For some reason they could not have explained they had both got from their silent evening together the thing needed. Man or boy, woman or girl, they had for a moment taken hold of the thing that makes the mature life of men and women in the modern world possible.

Departure

YOUNG George Willard got out of bed at four in the morning. It was April and the young tree leaves were just coming out of their buds. The trees along the residence streets in Winesburg are maple and the seeds are winged. When the wind blows they whirl crazily about, filling the air and making a carpet underfoot.

George came down stairs into the hotel office carrying a brown leather bag. His trunk was packed for departure. Since two o'clock he had been awake thinking of the journey he was about to take and wondering what he would find at the end of his journey. The boy who slept in the hotel office lay on a cot by the door. His mouth was open and he snored lustily. George crept past the cot and went out into the silent deserted main street. The east was pink with the dawn and long streaks of light climbed into the sky where a few stars still shone.

Beyond the last house on Trunion Pike in Winesburg there is a great stretch of open fields. The fields are owned by farmers who live in town and drive homeward at evening along Trunion Pike in light creaking wagons. In the fields are planted berries and small fruits. In the late afternoon in the hot summers when the road and the fields are covered with dust, a smoky haze lies over the great flat basin of land. To look across it is like looking out across the sea. In the spring when the land is green the effect is somewhat different. The land becomes a wide green billiard table on which tiny human insects toil up and down.

All through his boyhood and young manhood George Willard had been in the habit of walking on Trunion Pike. He had been in the midst of the great open place on winter nights when it was covered with snow and only the moon looked down at him; he had been there in the fall when bleak winds blew and on summer evenings when the air vibrated with the song of insects. On the April morning he wanted to go there again, to walk again in the silence. He did walk to where the road dipped down by a little stream two miles from town and then turned and walked silently back again. When he got to

Main Street clerks were sweeping the sidewalks before the stores. "Hey, you George. How does it feel to be going away?" they asked.

The west bound train leaves Winesburg at seven forty-five in the morning. Tom Little is conductor. His train runs from Cleveland to where it connects with a great trunk line railroad with terminals in Chicago and New York. Tom has what in railroad circles is called an "easy run." Every evening he returned to his family. In the fall and spring he spends his Sundays fishing in Lake Erie. He has a round red face and small blue eyes. He knows the people in the towns along his railroad better than a city man knows the people who live in his apartment building.

George came down the little incline from the New Willard House at seven o'clock. Tom Willard carried his bag. The son had become taller than the father.

On the station platform everyone shook the young man's hand. More than a dozen people waited about. Then they talked of their own affairs. Even Will Henderson, who was lazy and often slept until nine, had got out of bed. George was embarrassed. Gertrude Wilmot, a tall thin woman of fifty who worked in the Winesburg post office, came along the station platform. She had never before paid any attention to George. Now she stopped and put out her hand. In two words she voiced what everyone felt. "Good luck," she said sharply and then turning went on her way.

When the train came into the station George felt relieved. He scampered hurriedly aboard. Helen White came running along Main Street hoping to have a parting word with him, but he had found a seat and did not see her. When the train started Tom Little punched his ticket, grinned and, although he knew George well and knew on what adventure he was just setting out, made no comment. Tom had seen a thousand George Willards go out of their towns to the city. It was a commonplace enough incident with him. In the smoking car there was a man who had just invited Tom to go on a fishing trip to Sandusky Bay. He wanted to accept the invitation and talk over details.

George glanced up and down the car to be sure no one was looking then took out his pocketbook and counted his money.

His mind was occupied with a desire not to appear green. Almost the last words his father had said to him concerned the matter of his behavior when he got to the city. "Be a sharp one," Tom Willard had said. "Keep your eyes on your money. Be awake. That's the ticket. Don't let any one think you're a greenhorn."

After George counted his money he looked out of the window and was surprised to see that the train was still in Winesburg.

The young man, going out of his town to meet the adventure of life, began to think but he did not think of anything very big or dramatic. Things like his mother's death, his departure from Winesburg, the uncertainty of his future life in the city, the serious and larger aspects of his life did not come into his mind.

He thought of little things—Turk Smollet wheeling boards through the main street of his town in the morning, a tall woman, beautifully gowned, who had once stayed overnight at his father's hotel, Butch Wheeler the lamp lighter of Winesburg hurrying through the streets on a summer evening and holding a torch in his hand, Helen White standing by a window in the Winesburg post office and putting a stamp on an envelope.

The young man's mind was carried away by his growing passion for dreams. One looking at him would not have thought him particularly sharp. With the recollection of little things occupying his mind he closed his eyes and leaned back in the car seat. He stayed that way for a long time and when he aroused himself and again looked out of the car window the town of Winesburg had disappeared and his life there had become but a background on which to paint the dreams of his manhood.

THE TRIUMPH OF THE EGG

A BOOK OF IMPRESSIONS
FROM AMERICAN LIFE
IN TALES AND POEMS

> In the fields
> Seeds on the air floating.
> In the towns
> Black smoke for a shroud.
> In my breast
> Understanding awake.
> —*Mid-American Chants*

TO
ROBERT AND JOHN
ANDERSON

Tales are people who sit on the doorstep of the house of my mind.
It is cold outside and they sit waiting.
I look out at a window.

> *The tales have cold hands,*
> *Their hands are freezing.*

A short thickly-built tale arises and threshes his arms about.
His nose is red and he has two gold teeth.

There is an old female tale sitting hunched up in a cloak.

Many tales come to sit for a few moments on the doorstep and
*   then go away.*
It is too cold for them outside.
The street before the door of the house of my mind is filled with
*   tales.*
They murmur and cry out, they are dying of cold and hunger.

I am a helpless man—my hands tremble.
I should be sitting on a bench like a tailor.
I should be weaving warm cloth out of the threads of thought.
The tales should be clothed.
They are freezing on the doorstep of the house of my mind.

I am a helpless man—my hands tremble.
I feel in the darkness but cannot find the doorknob.
I look out at a window.
Many tales are dying in the street before the house of my mind.

Impressions in Clay
by
Tennessee Mitchell

PHOTOGRAPHS BY EUGENE HUTCHINSON

Labor

"They are squarer with kids,
I don't know why."

For I WANT TO KNOW WHY

She worked her way through college

Well-to-do

The Old Scholar

For THE EGG

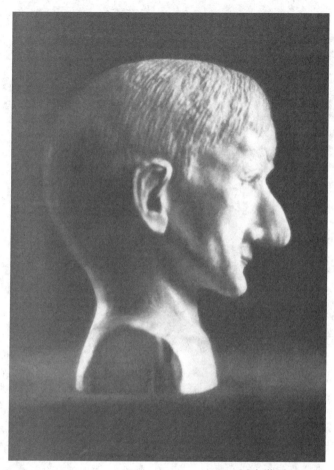

Melville Stoner

For OUT OF NOWHERE INTO NOTHING

CONTENTS

The Dumb Man

THERE is a story.—I cannot tell it.—I have no words.
The story is almost forgotten but sometimes I remember.

The story concerns three men in a house in a street.
If I could say the words I would sing the story.
I would whisper it into the ears of women, of mothers.
I would run through the streets saying it over and over.
My tongue would be torn loose—it would rattle against my
    teeth.

The three men are in a room in the house.
One is young and dandified.
He continually laughs.

There is a second man who has a long white beard.
He is consumed with doubt but occasionally his doubt leaves
    him and he sleeps.

A third man there is who has wicked eyes and who moves
    nervously about the room rubbing his hands together.
The three men are waiting—waiting.

Upstairs in the house there is a woman standing with her back
    to a wall, in half darkness by a window.

That is the foundation of my story and everything I will ever
    know is distilled in it.

I remember that a fourth man came to the house, a white silent
    man.
Everything was as silent as the sea at night.
His feet on the stone floor of the room where the three men
    were made no sound.

The man with the wicked eyes became like a boiling liquid—he
    ran back and forth like a caged animal.

203

The old grey man was infected by his nervousness—he kept
  pulling at his beard.

The fourth man, the white one, went upstairs to the woman.

There she was—waiting.

How silent the house was—how loudly all the clocks in the
  neighborhood ticked.
The woman upstairs craved love. That must have been the
  story. She hungered for love with her whole being. She
  wanted to create in love.
When the white silent man came into her presence she sprang
  forward.

Her lips were parted.
There was a smile on her lips.

The white one said nothing.
In his eyes there was no rebuke, no question.
His eyes were as impersonal as stars.

Down stairs the wicked one whined and ran back and forth
  like a little lost hungry dog.
The grey one tried to follow him about but presently grew
  tired and lay down on the floor to sleep.
He never awoke again.

The dandified fellow lay on the floor too.
He laughed and played with his tiny black mustache.

I have no words to tell what happened in my story.
I cannot tell the story.

The white silent one may have been Death.

The waiting eager woman may have been Life.

Both the old grey bearded man and the wicked one puzzle me.
I think and think but cannot understand them.

Most of the time however I do not think of them at all.
I keep thinking about the dandified man who laughed all
    through my story.

If I could understand him I could understand everything.
I could run through the world telling a wonderful story.
I would no longer be dumb.

Why was I not given words?
Why am I dumb?

I have a wonderful story to tell but know no way to tell it.

I Want to Know Why

WE got up at four in the morning, that first day in the east. On the evening before we had climbed off a freight train at the edge of town, and with the true instinct of Kentucky boys had found our way across town and to the race track and the stables at once. Then we knew we were all right. Hanley Turner right away found a nigger we knew. It was Bildad Johnson who in the winter works at Ed Becker's livery barn in our home town, Beckersville. Bildad is a good cook as almost all our niggers are and of course he, like everyone in our part of Kentucky who is anyone at all, likes the horses. In the spring Bildad begins to scratch around. A nigger from our country can flatter and wheedle anyone into letting him do most anything he wants. Bildad wheedles the stable men and the trainers from the horse farms in our country around Lexington. The trainers come into town in the evening to stand around and talk and maybe get into a poker game. Bildad gets in with them. He is always doing little favors and telling about things to eat, chicken browned in a pan, and how is the best way to cook sweet potatoes and corn bread. It makes your mouth water to hear him.

When the racing season comes on and the horses go to the races and there is all the talk on the streets in the evenings about the new colts, and everyone says when they are going over to Lexington or to the spring meeting at Churchill Downs or to Latonia, and the horsemen that have been down to New Orleans or maybe at the winter meeting at Havana in Cuba come home to spend a week before they start out again, at such a time when everything talked about in Beckersville is just horses and nothing else and the outfits start out and horse racing is in every breath of air you breathe, Bildad shows up with a job as cook for some outfit. Often when I think about it, his always going all season to the races and working in the livery barn in the winter where horses are and where men like to come and talk about horses, I wish I was a nigger. It's a foolish thing to say, but that's the way I am about being around horses, just crazy. I can't help it.

Well, I must tell you about what we did and let you in on what I'm talking about. Four of us boys from Beckersville, all whites and sons of men who live in Beckersville regular, made up our minds we were going to the races, not just to Lexington or Louisville, I don't mean, but to the big eastern track we were always hearing our Beckersville men talk about, to Saratoga. We were all pretty young then. I was just turned fifteen and I was the oldest of the four. It was my scheme. I admit that and I talked the others into trying it. There was Hanley Turner and Henry Rieback and Tom Tumberton and myself. I had thirty-seven dollars I had earned during the winter working nights and Saturdays in Enoch Myer's grocery. Henry Rieback had eleven dollars and the others, Hanley and Tom had only a dollar or two each. We fixed it all up and laid low until the Kentucky spring meetings were over and some of our men, the sportiest ones, the ones we envied the most, had cut out—then we cut out too.

I won't tell you the trouble we had beating our way on freights and all. We went through Cleveland and Buffalo and other cities and saw Niagara Falls. We bought things there, souvenirs and spoons and cards and shells with pictures of the falls on them for our sisters and mothers, but thought we had better not send any of the things home. We didn't want to put the folks on our trail and maybe be nabbed.

We got into Saratoga as I said at night and went to the track. Bildad fed us up. He showed us a place to sleep in hay over a shed and promised to keep still. Niggers are all right about things like that. They won't squeal on you. Often a white man you might meet, when you had run away from home like that, might appear to be all right and give you a quarter or a half dollar or something, and then go right and give you away. White men will do that, but not a nigger. You can trust them. They are squarer with kids. I don't know why.

At the Saratoga meeting that year there were a lot of men from home. Dave Williams and Arthur Mulford and Jerry Myers and others. Then there was a lot from Louisville and Lexington Henry Rieback knew but I didn't. They were professional gamblers and Henry Rieback's father is one too. He is what is called a sheet writer and goes away most of the year to tracks. In the winter when he is home in Beckersville he don't stay there much but goes away to cities and deals faro. He is a nice man and generous, is always sending Henry presents, a bicycle and a gold watch and a boy scout suit of clothes and things like that.

My own father is a lawyer. He's all right, but don't make much money and can't buy me things and anyway I'm getting so old now I don't expect it. He never said nothing to me against Henry, but Hanley Turner and Tom Tumberton's fathers did. They said to their boys that money so come by is no good and they didn't want their boys brought up to hear gamblers' talk and be thinking about such things and maybe embrace them.

That's all right and I guess the men know what they are talking about, but I don't see what it's got to do with Henry or with horses either. That's what I'm writing this story about. I'm puzzled. I'm getting to be a man and want to think straight and be O. K., and there's something I saw at the race meeting at the eastern track I can't figure out.

I can't help it, I'm crazy about thoroughbred horses. I've always been that way. When I was ten years old and saw I was growing to be big and couldn't be a rider I was so sorry I nearly died. Harry Hellinfinger in Beckersville, whose father is Postmaster, is grown up and too lazy to work, but likes to stand around in the street and get up jokes on boys like sending them to a hardware store for a gimlet to bore square holes and other jokes like that. He played one on me. He told me that if I would eat a half a cigar I would be stunted and not grow any more and maybe could be a rider. I did it. When father wasn't looking I took a cigar out of his pocket and gagged it down some way. It made me awful sick and the doctor had to be sent for, and then it did no good. I kept right on growing. It was a joke. When I told what I had done and why most fathers would have whipped me but mine didn't.

Well, I didn't get stunted and didn't die. It serves Harry Hellinfinger right. Then I made up my mind I would like to be a stable boy, but had to give that up too. Mostly niggers do that work and I knew father wouldn't let me go into it. No use to ask him.

If you've never been crazy about thoroughbreds it's because you've never been around where they are much and don't know

any better. They're beautiful. There isn't anything so lovely
and clean and full of spunk and honest and everything as some
race horses. On the big horse farms that are all around our
town Beckersville there are tracks and the horses run in the
early morning. More than a thousand times I've got out of bed
before daylight and walked two or three miles to the tracks.
Mother wouldn't of let me go but father always says, "Let him
alone," so I got some bread out of the bread box and some
butter and jam, gobbled it and lit out.

At the tracks you sit on the fence with men, whites and niggers, and they chew tobacco and talk, and then the colts are
brought out. It's early and the grass is covered with shiny dew
and in another field a man is plowing and they are frying things
in a shed where the track niggers sleep, and you know how a
nigger can giggle and laugh and say things that make you laugh.
A white man can't do it and some niggers can't but a track
nigger can every time.

And so the colts are brought out and some are just galloped
by stable boys, but almost every morning on a big track owned
by a rich man who lives maybe in New York, there are always,
nearly every morning, a few colts and some of the old race
horses and geldings and mares that are cut loose.

It brings a lump up into my throat when a horse runs. I
don't mean all horses but some. I can pick them nearly every
time. It's in my blood like in the blood of race track niggers
and trainers. Even when they just go slop-jogging along with a
little nigger on their backs I can tell a winner. If my throat
hurts and it's hard for me to swallow, that's him. He'll run like
Sam Hill when you let him out. If he don't win every time
it'll be a wonder and because they've got him in a pocket behind another or he was pulled or got off bad at the post or
something. If I wanted to be a gambler like Henry Rieback's
father I could get rich. I know I could and Henry says so too.
All I would have to do is to wait 'til that hurt comes when I
see a horse and then bet every cent. That's what I would do if
I wanted to be a gambler, but I don't.

When you're at the tracks in the morning—not the race tracks
but the training tracks around Beckersville—you don't see a
horse, the kind I've been talking about, very often, but it's nice

anyway. Any thoroughbred, that is sired right and out of a good mare and trained by a man that knows how, can run. If he couldn't what would he be there for and not pulling a plow?

Well, out of the stables they come and the boys are on their backs and it's lovely to be there. You hunch down on top of the fence and itch inside you. Over in the sheds the niggers giggle and sing. Bacon is being fried and coffee made. Everything smells lovely. Nothing smells better than coffee and manure and horses and niggers and bacon frying and pipes being smoked out of doors on a morning like that. It just gets you, that's what it does.

But about Saratoga. We was there six days and not a soul from home seen us and everything came off just as we wanted it to, fine weather and horses and races and all. We beat our way home and Bildad gave us a basket with fried chicken and bread and other eatables in, and I had eighteen dollars when we got back to Beckersville. Mother jawed and cried but Pop didn't say much. I told everything we done except one thing. I did and saw that alone. That's what I'm writing about. It got me upset. I think about it at night. Here it is.

At Saratoga we laid up nights in the hay in the shed Bildad had showed us and ate with the niggers early and at night when the race people had all gone away. The men from home stayed mostly in the grandstand and betting field, and didn't come out around the places where the horses are kept except to the paddocks just before a race when the horses are saddled. At Saratoga they don't have paddocks under an open shed as at Lexington and Churchill Downs and other tracks down in our country, but saddle the horses right out in an open place under trees on a lawn as smooth and nice as Banker Bohon's front yard here in Beckersville. It's lovely. The horses are sweaty and nervous and shine and the men come out and smoke cigars and look at them and the trainers are there and the owners, and your heart thumps so you can hardly breathe.

Then the bugle blows for post and the boys that ride come running out with their silk clothes on and you run to get a place by the fence with the niggers.

I always am wanting to be a trainer or owner, and at the risk of being seen and caught and sent home I went to the paddocks before every race. The other boys didn't but I did.

We got to Saratoga on a Friday and on Wednesday the next week the big Mullford Handicap was to be run. Middlestride was in it and Sunstreak. The weather was fine and the track fast. I couldn't sleep the night before.

What had happened was that both these horses are the kind it makes my throat hurt to see. Middlestride is long and looks awkward and is a gelding. He belongs to Joe Thompson, a little owner from home who only has a half dozen horses. The Mullford Handicap is for a mile and Middlestride can't untrack fast. He goes away slow and is always way back at the half, then he begins to run and if the race is a mile and a quarter he'll just eat up everything and get there.

Sunstreak is different. He is a stallion and nervous and belongs on the biggest farm we've got in our country, the Van Riddle place that belongs to Mr. Van Riddle of New York. Sunstreak is like a girl you think about sometimes but never see. He is hard all over and lovely too. When you look at his head you want to kiss him. He is trained by Jerry Tillford who knows me and has been good to me lots of times, lets me walk into a horse's stall to look at him close and other things. There isn't anything as sweet as that horse. He stands at the post quiet and not letting on, but he is just burning up inside. Then when the barrier goes up he is off like his name, Sunstreak. It makes you ache to see him. It hurts you. He just lays down and runs like a bird dog. There can't anything I ever see run like him except Middlestride when he gets untracked and stretches himself.

Gee! I ached to see that race and those two horses run, ached and dreaded it too. I didn't want to see either of our horses beaten. We had never sent a pair like that to the races before. Old men in Beckersville said so and the niggers said so. It was a fact.

Before the race I went over to the paddocks to see. I looked a last look at Middlestride, who isn't such a much standing in a paddock that way, then I went to see Sunstreak.

It was his day. I knew when I see him. I forgot all about being seen myself and walked right up. All the men from Beckersville were there and no one noticed me except Jerry Tillford. He saw me and something happened. I'll tell you about that.

I was standing looking at that horse and aching. In some way,

I can't tell how, I knew just how Sunstreak felt inside. He was quiet and letting the niggers rub his legs and Mr. Van Riddle himself put the saddle on, but he was just a raging torrent inside. He was like the water in the river at Niagara Falls just before it goes plunk down. That horse wasn't thinking about running. He don't have to think about that. He was just thinking about holding himself back 'til the time for the running came. I knew that. I could just in a way see right inside him. He was going to do some awful running and I knew it. He wasn't bragging or letting on much or prancing or making a fuss, but just waiting. I knew it and Jerry Tillford his trainer knew. I looked up and then that man and I looked into each other's eyes. Something happened to me. I guess I loved the man as much as I did the horse because he knew what I knew. Seemed to me there wasn't anything in the world but that man and the horse and me. I cried and Jerry Tillford had a shine in his eyes. Then I came away to the fence to wait for the race. The horse was better than me, more steadier, and now I know better than Jerry. He was the quietest and he had to do the running.

Sunstreak ran first of course and he busted the world's record for a mile. I've seen that if I never see anything more. Everything came out just as I expected. Middlestride got left at the post and was way back and closed up to be second, just as I knew he would. He'll get a world's record too some day. They can't skin the Beckersville country on horses.

I watched the race calm because I knew what would happen. I was sure. Hanley Turner and Henry Rieback and Tom Tumberton were all more excited than me.

A funny thing had happened to me. I was thinking about Jerry Tillford the trainer and how happy he was all through the race. I liked him that afternoon even more than I ever liked my own father. I almost forgot the horses thinking that way about him. It was because of what I had seen in his eyes as he stood in the paddocks beside Sunstreak before the race started. I knew he had been watching and working with Sunstreak since the horse was a baby colt, had taught him to run and be patient and when to let himself out and not to quit, never. I knew that for him it was like a mother seeing her child do something brave or wonderful. It was the first time I ever felt for a man like that.

After the race that night I cut out from Tom and Hanley and Henry. I wanted to be by myself and I wanted to be near Jerry Tillford if I could work it. Here is what happened.

The track in Saratoga is near the edge of town. It is all polished up and trees around, the evergreen kind, and grass and everything painted and nice. If you go past the track you get to a hard road made of asphalt for automobiles, and if you go along this for a few miles there is a road turns off to a little rummy-looking farm house set in a yard.

That night after the race I went along that road because I had seen Jerry and some other men go that way in an automobile. I didn't expect to find them. I walked for a ways and then sat down by a fence to think. It was the direction they went in. I wanted to be as near Jerry as I could. I felt close to him. Pretty soon I went up the side road—I don't know why—and came to the rummy farm house. I was just lonesome to see Jerry, like wanting to see your father at night when you are a young kid. Just then an automobile came along and turned in. Jerry was in it and Henry Rieback's father, and Arthur Bedford from home, and Dave Williams and two other men I didn't know. They got out of the car and went into the house, all but Henry Rieback's father who quarreled with them and said he wouldn't go. It was only about nine o'clock, but they were all drunk and the rummy looking farm house was a place for bad women to stay in. That's what it was. I crept up along a fence and looked through a window and saw.

It's what give me the fantods. I can't make it out. The women in the house were all ugly mean-looking women, not nice to look at or be near. They were homely too, except one who was tall and looked a little like the gelding Middlestride, but not clean like him, but with a hard ugly mouth. She had red hair. I saw everything plain. I got up by an old rose bush by an open window and looked. The women had on loose dresses and sat around in chairs. The men came in and some sat on the women's laps. The place smelled rotten and there was rotten talk, the kind a kid hears around a livery stable in a town like Beckersville in the winter but don't ever expect to hear talked when there are women around. It was rotten. A nigger wouldn't go into such a place.

I looked at Jerry Tillford. I've told you how I had been feeling about him on account of his knowing what was going on in-side of Sunstreak in the minute before he went to the post for the race in which he made a world's record.

Jerry bragged in that bad woman house as I know Sunstreak wouldn't never have bragged. He said that he made that horse, that it was him that won the race and made the record. He lied and bragged like a fool. I never heard such silly talk.

And then, what do you suppose he did! He looked at the woman in there, the one that was lean and hard-mouthed and looked a little like the gelding Middlestride, but not clean like him, and his eyes began to shine just as they did when he looked at me and at Sunstreak in the paddocks at the track in the afternoon. I stood there by the window—gee!—but I wished I hadn't gone away from the tracks, but had stayed with the boys and the niggers and the horses. The tall rotten looking woman was between us just as Sunstreak was in the paddocks in the afternoon.

Then, all of a sudden, I began to hate that man. I wanted to scream and rush in the room and kill him. I never had such a feeling before. I was so mad clean through that I cried and my fists were doubled up so my finger nails cut my hands.

And Jerry's eyes kept shining and he waved back and forth, and then he went and kissed that woman and I crept away and went back to the tracks and to bed and didn't sleep hardly any, and then next day I got the other kids to start home with me and never told them anything I seen.

I been thinking about it ever since. I can't make it out. Spring has come again and I'm nearly sixteen and go to the tracks mornings same as always, and I see Sunstreak and Middlestride and a new colt named Strident I'll bet will lay them all out, but no one thinks so but me and two or three niggers.

But things are different. At the tracks the air don't taste as good or smell as good. It's because a man like Jerry Tillford, who knows what he does, could see a horse like Sunstreak run, and kiss a woman like that the same day. I can't make it out. Darn him, what did he want to do like that for? I keep thinking about it and it spoils looking at horses and smelling things and hearing niggers laugh and everything. Sometimes I'm so mad about it I want to fight someone. It gives me the fantods. What did he do it for? I want to know why.

Seeds

H E was a small man with a beard and was very nervous. I remember how the cords of his neck were drawn taut.

For years he had been trying to cure people of illness by the method called psychoanalysis. The idea was the passion of his life. "I came here because I am tired," he said dejectedly. "My body is not tired but something inside me is old and worn-out. I want joy. For a few days or weeks I would like to forget men and women and the influences that make them the sick things they are."

There is a note that comes into the human voice by which you may know real weariness. It comes when one has been trying with all his heart and soul to think his way along some difficult road of thought. Of a sudden he finds himself unable to go on. Something within him stops. A tiny explosion takes place. He bursts into words and talks, perhaps foolishly. Little side currents of his nature he didn't know were there run out and get themselves expressed. It is at such times that a man boasts, uses big words, makes a fool of himself in general.

And so it was the doctor became shrill. He jumped up from the steps where we had been sitting, talking and walked about. "You come from the West. You have kept away from people. You have preserved yourself—damn you! I haven't—" His voice had indeed become shrill. "I have entered into lives. I have gone beneath the surface of the lives of men and women. Women especially I have studied—our own women, here in America."

"You have loved them?" I suggested.

"Yes," he said. "Yes—you are right there. I have done that. It is the only way I can get at things. I have to try to love. You see how that is? It's the only way. Love must be the beginning of things with me."

I began to sense the depths of his weariness. "We will go swim in the lake," I urged.

"I don't want to swim or do any damn plodding thing. I want to run and shout," he declared. "For awhile, for a few hours, I want to be like a dead leaf blown by the winds over these hills. I have one desire and one only—to free myself."

We walked in a dusty country road. I wanted him to know that I thought I understood, so I put the case in my own way.

When he stopped and stared at me I talked. "You are no more and no better than myself," I declared. "You are a dog that has rolled in offal, and because you are not quite a dog you do not like the smell of your own hide."

In turn my voice became shrill. "You blind fool," I cried impatiently. "Men like you are fools. You cannot go along that road. It is given to no man to venture far along the road of lives."

I became passionately in earnest. "The illness you pretend to cure is the universal illness," I said. "The thing you want to do cannot be done. Fool—do you expect love to be understood?"

We stood in the road and looked at each other. The suggestion of a sneer played about the corners of his mouth. He put a hand on my shoulder and shook me. "How smart we are— how aptly we put things!"

He spat the words out and then turned and walked a little away. "You think you understand, but you don't understand," he cried. "What you say can't be done can be done. You're a liar. You cannot be so definite without missing something vague and fine. You miss the whole point. The lives of people are like young trees in a forest. They are being choked by climbing vines. The vines are old thoughts and beliefs planted by dead men. I am myself covered by crawling creeping vines that choke me."

He laughed bitterly. "And that's why I want to run and play," he said. "I want to be a leaf blown by the wind over hills. I want to die and be born again and I am only a tree covered with vines and slowly dying. I am, you see, weary and want to be made clean. I am an amateur venturing timidly into lives," he concluded. "I am weary and want to be made clean. I am covered by creeping crawling things."

A woman from Iowa came here to Chicago and took a room in a house on the west-side. She was about twenty-seven years old and ostensibly she came to the city to study advanced methods for teaching music.

A certain young man also lived in the west-side house. His room faced a long hall on the second floor of the house and the one taken by the woman was across the hall facing his room.

In regard to the young man—there is something very sweet in his nature. He is a painter but I have often wished he would decide to become a writer. He tells things with understanding and he does not paint brilliantly.

And so the woman from Iowa lived in the west-side house and came home from the city in the evening. She looked like a thousand other women one sees in the streets every day. The only thing that at all made her stand out among the women in the crowds was that she was a little lame. Her right foot was slightly deformed and she walked with a limp. For three months she lived in the house—where she was the only woman except the landlady—and then a feeling in regard to her began to grow up among the men of the house.

The men all said the same thing concerning her. When they met in the hall way at the front of the house they stopped, laughed and whispered. "She wants a lover," they said and winked. "She may not know it but a lover is what she needs."

One knowing Chicago and Chicago men would think that an easy want to be satisfied. I laughed when my friend—whose name is LeRoy—told me the story, but he did not laugh. He shook his head. "It wasn't so easy," he said. "There would be no story were the matter that simple."

LeRoy tried to explain. "Whenever a man approached her she became alarmed," he said. Men kept smiling and speaking to her. They invited her to dinner and to the theatre, but nothing would induce her to walk in the streets with a man. She never went into the streets at night. When a man stopped and tried to talk with her in the hallway she turned her eyes to the floor and then ran into her room. Once a young drygoods clerk who lived there induced her to sit with him on the steps before the house.

He was a sentimental fellow and took hold of her hand. When she began to cry he was alarmed and arose. He put a hand on her shoulder and tried to explain, but under the touch of his fingers her whole body shook with terror. "Don't touch me," she cried, "don't let your hands touch me!" She began to scream and people passing in the street stopped to listen. The drygoods clerk was alarmed and ran upstairs to his own room.

He bolted the door and stood listening. "It is a trick," he declared in a trembling voice. "She is trying to make trouble. I did nothing to her. It was an accident and anyway what's the matter? I only touched her arm with my fingers."

Perhaps a dozen times LeRoy has spoken to me of the experience of the Iowa woman in the west-side house. The men there began to hate her. Although she would have nothing to do with them she would not let them alone. In a hundred ways she continually invited approaches that when made she repelled. When she stood naked in the bathroom facing the hallway where the men passed up and down she left the door slightly ajar. There was a couch in the living room down stairs, and when men were present she would sometimes enter and without saying a word throw herself down before them. On the couch she lay with lips drawn slightly apart. Her eyes stared at the ceiling. Her whole physical being seemed to be waiting for something. The sense of her filled the room. The men standing about pretended not to see. They talked loudly. Embarrassment took possession of them and one by one they crept quietly away.

One evening the woman was ordered to leave the house. Someone, perhaps the drygoods clerk, had talked to the landlady and she acted at once. "If you leave tonight I shall like it that much better," LeRoy heard the elder woman's voice saying. She stood in the hallway before the Iowa woman's room. The landlady's voice rang through the house.

LeRoy the painter is tall and lean and his life has been spent in devotion to ideas. The passions of his brain have consumed the passions of his body. His income is small and he has not married. Perhaps he has never had a sweetheart. He is not without physical desire but he is not primarily concerned with desire.

On the evening when the Iowa woman was ordered to leave the west-side house, she waited until she thought the landlady had gone down stairs, and then went into LeRoy's room. It was about eight o'clock and he sat by a window reading a book. The woman did not knock but opened the door. She said nothing but ran across the floor and knelt at his feet. LeRoy said that her twisted foot made her run like a wounded bird, that her eyes were burning and that her breath came in little gasps. "Take me," she said, putting her face down upon his knees and trembling violently. "Take me quickly. There must be a beginning to things. I can't stand the waiting. You must take me at once."

You may be quite sure LeRoy was perplexed by all this. From what he has said I gathered that until that evening he had hardly noticed the woman. I suppose that of all the men in the house he had been the most indifferent to her. In the room something happened. The landlady followed the woman when she ran to LeRoy, and the two women confronted him. The woman from Iowa knelt trembling and frightened at his feet. The landlady was indignant. LeRoy acted on impulse. An inspiration came to him. Putting his hand on the kneeling woman's shoulder he shook her violently. "Now behave yourself," he said quickly. "I will keep my promise." He turned to the landlady and smiled. "We have been engaged to be married," he said. "We have quarreled. She came here to be near me. She has been unwell and excited. I will take her away. Please don't let yourself be annoyed. I will take her away."

When the woman and LeRoy got out of the house she stopped weeping and put her hand into his. Her fears had all gone away. He found a room for her in another house and then went with her into a park and sat on a bench.

Everything LeRoy has told me concerning this woman strengthens my belief in what I said to the man that day in the mountains. You cannot venture along the road of lives. On the bench he and the woman talked until midnight and he saw and talked with her many times later. Nothing came of it. She went back, I suppose, to her place in the West.

In the place from which she had come the woman had been a teacher of music. She was one of four sisters, all engaged in the same sort of work and, LeRoy says, all quiet capable women. Their father had died when the eldest girl was not yet ten, and five years later the mother died also. The girls had a house and a garden.

In the nature of things I cannot know what the lives of the women were like but of this, one may be quite certain—they talked only of women's affairs, thought only of women's affairs. No one of them ever had a lover. For years no man came near the house.

Of them all only the youngest, the one who came to Chicago, was visibly affected by the utterly feminine quality of their lives. It did something to her. All day and every day she taught music to young girls and then went home to the women. When she was twenty-five she began to think and to dream of men. During the day and through the evening she talked with women of women's affairs, and all the time she wanted desperately to be loved by a man. She went to Chicago with that hope in mind. LeRoy explained her attitude in the matter and her strange behavior in the west-side house by saying she had thought too much and acted too little. "The life force within her became decentralized," he declared. "What she wanted she could not achieve. The living force within could not find expression. When it could not get expressed in one way it took another. Sex spread itself out over her body. It permeated the very fibre of her being. At the last she was sex personified, sex become condensed and impersonal. Certain words, the touch of a man's hand, sometimes even the sight of a man passing in the street did something to her."

Yesterday I saw LeRoy and he talked to me again of the woman and her strange and terrible fate.

We walked in the park by the lake. As we went along the figure of the woman kept coming into my mind. An idea came to me.

"You might have been her lover," I said. "That was possible. She was not afraid of you."

LeRoy stopped. Like the doctor who was so sure of his ability to walk into lives he grew angry and scolded. For a moment he stared at me and then a rather odd thing happened. Words said by the other man in the dusty road in the hills came to LeRoy's lips and were said over again. The suggestion of a sneer played about the corners of his mouth. "How smart we are. How aptly we put things," he said.

The voice of the young man who walked with me in the park by the lake in the city became shrill. I sensed the weariness in him. Then he laughed and said quietly and softly, "It isn't so simple. By being sure of yourself you are in danger of losing all of the romance of life. You miss the whole point. Nothing in life can be settled so definitely. The woman—you see—was like a young tree choked by a climbing vine. The thing that wrapped her about had shut out the light. She was a grotesque as many trees in the forest are grotesques. Her problem was such a difficult one that thinking of it has changed the whole current of my life. At first I was like you. I was quite sure. I thought I would be her lover and settle the matter."

LeRoy turned and walked a little away. Then he came back and took hold of my arm. A passionate earnestness took possession of him. His voice trembled. "She needed a lover, yes, the men in the house were quite right about that," he said. "She needed a lover and at the same time a lover was not what she needed. The need of a lover was, after all, a quite secondary thing. She needed to be loved, to be long and quietly and patiently loved. To be sure she is a grotesque, but then all the people in the world are grotesques. We all need to be loved. What would cure her would cure the rest of us also. The disease she had is, you see, universal. We all want to be loved and the world has no plan for creating our lovers."

LeRoy's voice dropped and he walked beside me in silence. We turned away from the lake and walked under trees. I looked closely at him. The cords of his neck were drawn taut. "I have seen under the shell of life and I am afraid," he mused. "I am myself like the woman. I am covered with creeping crawling vine-like things. I cannot be a lover. I am not subtle or patient enough. I am paying old debts. Old thoughts and beliefs—seeds planted by dead men—spring up in my soul and choke me."

For a long time we walked and LeRoy talked, voicing the thoughts that came into his mind. I listened in silence. His mind struck upon the refrain voiced by the man in the mountains. "I would like to be a dead dry thing," he muttered looking at the leaves scattered over the grass. "I would like to be a leaf blown away by the wind." He looked up and his eyes turned to where among the trees we could see the lake in the distance. "I am weary and want to be made clean. I am a man covered by creeping crawling things. I would like to be dead and blown by the wind over limitless waters," he said. "I want more than anything else in the world to be clean."

The Other Woman

"I AM in love with my wife," he said—a superfluous remark, as I had not questioned his attachment to the woman he had married. We walked for ten minutes and then he said it again. I turned to look at him. He began to talk and told me the tale I am now about to set down.

The thing he had on his mind happened during what must have been the most eventful week of his life. He was to be married on Friday afternoon. On Friday of the week before he got a telegram announcing his appointment to a government position. Something else happened that made him very proud and glad. In secret he was in the habit of writing verses and during the year before several of them had been printed in poetry magazines. One of the societies that give prizes for what they think the best poems published during the year put his name at the head of its list. The story of his triumph was printed in the newspapers of his home city and one of them also printed his picture.

As might have been expected he was excited and in a rather highly strung nervous state all during that week. Almost every evening he went to call on his fiancée, the daughter of a judge. When he got there the house was filled with people and many letters, telegrams and packages were being received. He stood a little to one side and men and women kept coming up to speak to him. They congratulated him upon his success in getting the government position and on his achievement as a poet. Everyone seemed to be praising him and when he went home and to bed he could not sleep. On Wednesday evening he went to the theatre and it seemed to him that people all over the house recognized him. Everyone nodded and smiled. After the first act five or six men and two women left their seats to gather about him. A little group was formed. Strangers sitting along the same row of seats stretched their necks and looked. He had never received so much attention before, and now a fever of expectancy took possession of him.

As he explained when he told me of his experience, it was for him an altogether abnormal time. He felt like one floating in air. When he got into bed after seeing so many people and hearing so many words of praise his head whirled round and round. When he closed his eyes a crowd of people invaded his room. It seemed as though the minds of all the people of his city were centred on himself. The most absurd fancies took possession of him. He imagined himself riding in a carriage through the streets of a city. Windows were thrown open and people ran out at the doors of houses. "There he is. That's him," they shouted, and at the words a glad cry arose. The carriage drove into a street blocked with people. A hundred thousand pairs of eyes looked up at him. "There you are! What a fellow you have managed to make of yourself!" the eyes seemed to be saying.

My friend could not explain whether the excitement of the people was due to the fact that he had written a new poem or whether, in his new government position, he had performed some notable act. The apartment where he lived at that time was on a street perched along the top of a cliff far out at the edge of his city, and from his bedroom window he could look down over trees and factory roofs to a river. As he could not sleep and as the fancies that kept crowding in upon him only made him more excited, he got out of bed and tried to think.

As would be natural under such circumstances, he tried to control his thoughts, but when he sat by the window and was wide awake a most unexpected and humiliating thing happened. The night was clear and fine. There was a moon. He wanted to dream of the woman who was to be his wife, to think out lines for noble poems or make plans that would affect his career. Much to his surprise his mind refused to do anything of the sort.

At a corner of the street where he lived there was a small cigar store and newspaper stand run by a fat man of forty and his wife, a small active woman with bright grey eyes. In the morning he stopped there to buy a paper before going down to the city. Sometimes he saw only the fat man, but often the man had disappeared and the woman waited on him. She was, as he assured me at least twenty times in telling me his tale, a very ordinary person with nothing special or notable about her, but for some reason he could not explain, being in her presence stirred him profoundly. During that week in the midst of his distraction she was the only person he knew who stood out clear and distinct in his mind. When he wanted so much to think noble thoughts he could think only of her. Before he knew what was happening his imagination had taken hold of the notion of having a love affair with the woman.

"I could not understand myself," he declared, in telling me the story. "At night, when the city was quiet and when I should have been asleep, I thought about her all the time. After two or three days of that sort of thing the consciousness of her got into my daytime thoughts. I was terribly muddled. When I went to see the woman who is now my wife I found that my love for her was in no way affected by my vagrant thoughts. There was but one woman in the world I wanted to live with and to be my comrade in undertaking to improve my own character and my position in the world, but for the moment, you see, I wanted this other woman to be in my arms. She had worked her way into my being. On all sides people were saying I was a big man who would do big things, and there I was. That evening when I went to the theatre I walked home because I knew I would be unable to sleep, and to satisfy the annoying impulse in myself I went and stood on the sidewalk before the tobacco shop. It was a two story building, and I knew the woman lived upstairs with her husband. For a long time I stood in the darkness with my body pressed against the wall of the building, and then I thought of the two of them up there and no doubt in bed together. That made me furious.

"Then I grew more furious with myself. I went home and got into bed, shaken with anger. There are certain books of verse and some prose writings that have always moved me deeply, and so I put several books on a table by my bed.

"The voices in the books were like the voices of the dead. I did not hear them. The printed words would not penetrate into my consciousness. I tried to think of the woman I loved, but her figure had also become something far away, something with which I for the moment seemed to have nothing to do. I rolled and tumbled about in the bed. It was a miserable experience.

"On Thursday morning I went into the store. There stood the woman alone. I think she knew how I felt. Perhaps she had been thinking of me as I had been thinking of her. A doubtful hesitating smile played about the corners of her mouth. She had on a dress made of cheap cloth and there was a tear on the shoulder. She must have been ten years older than myself. When I tried to put my pennies on the glass counter, behind which she stood, my hand trembled so that the pennies made a sharp rattling noise. When I spoke the voice that came out of my throat did not sound like anything that had ever belonged to me. It barely arose above a thick whisper. 'I want you,' I said. 'I want you very much. Can't you run away from your husband? Come to me at my apartment at seven tonight.'

"The woman did come to my apartment at seven. That morning she didn't say anything at all. For a minute perhaps we stood looking at each other. I had forgotten everything in the world but just her. Then she nodded her head and I went away. Now that I think of it I cannot remember a word I ever heard her say. She came to my apartment at seven and it was dark. You must understand this was in the month of October. I had not lighted a light and I had sent my servant away.

"During that day I was no good at all. Several men came to see me at my office, but I got all muddled up in trying to talk with them. They attributed my rattle-headedness to my approaching marriage and went away laughing.

"It was on that morning, just the day before my marriage, that I got a long and very beautiful letter from my fiancée. During the night before she also had been unable to sleep and had got out of bed to write the letter. Everything she said in it was very sharp and real, but she herself, as a living thing, seemed to have receded into the distance. It seemed to me that she was like a bird, flying far away in distant skies, and that I was like a perplexed bare-footed boy standing in the dusty road before a farm house and looking at her receding figure. I wonder if you will understand what I mean?

"In regard to the letter. In it she, the awakening woman, poured out her heart. She of course knew nothing of life, but she was a woman. She lay, I suppose, in her bed feeling nervous and wrought up as I had been doing. She realized that a great change was about to take place in her life and was glad and afraid too. There she lay thinking of it all. Then she got out of bed and began talking to me on the bit of paper. She told me how afraid she was and how glad too. Like most young women she had heard things whispered. In the letter she was very sweet and fine. 'For a long time, after we are married, we will forget we are a man and woman,' she wrote. 'We will be human beings. You must remember that I am ignorant and often I will be very stupid. You must love me and be very patient and kind. When I know more, when after a long time you have taught me the way of life, I will try to repay you. I will love you tenderly and passionately. The possibility of that is in me or I would not want to marry at all. I am afraid but I am also happy. O, I am so glad our marriage time is near at hand!'

"Now you see clearly enough what a mess I was in. In my office, after I had read my fiancée's letter, I became at once very resolute and strong. I remember that I got out of my chair and walked about, proud of the fact that I was to be the husband of so noble a woman. Right away I felt concerning her as I had been feeling about myself before I found out what a weak thing I was. To be sure I took a strong resolution that I would not be weak. At nine that evening I had planned to run in to see my fiancée. 'I'm all right now', I said to myself. 'The beauty of her character has saved me from myself. I will go home now and send the other woman away.' In the morning I had telephoned to my servant and told him that I did not want him to be at the apartment that evening and I now picked up the telephone to tell him to stay at home.

"Then a thought came to me. 'I will not want him there in any event,' I told myself. 'What will he think when he sees a woman coming in my place on the evening before the day I am to be married?' I put the telephone down and prepared to go home. 'If I want my servant out of the apartment it is because I do not want him to hear me talk with the woman. I cannot be rude to her. I will have to make some kind of an explanation,' I said to myself.

"The woman came at seven o'clock, and, as you may have guessed, I let her in and forgot the resolution I had made. It is likely I never had any intention of doing anything else. There was a bell on my door, but she did not ring, but knocked very softly. It seems to me that everything she did that evening was soft and quiet, but very determined and quick. Do I make myself clear? When she came I was standing just within the door where I had been standing and waiting for a half hour.

My hands were trembling as they had trembled in the morning when her eyes looked at me and when I tried to put the pennies on the counter in the store. When I opened the door she stepped quickly in and I took her into my arms. We stood together in the darkness. My hands no longer trembled. I felt very happy and strong.

"Although I have tried to make everything clear I have not told you what the woman I married is like. I have emphasized, you see, the other woman. I make the blind statement that I love my wife, and to a man of your shrewdness that means nothing at all. To tell the truth, had I not started to speak of this matter I would feel more comfortable. It is inevitable that I give you the impression that I am in love with the tobacconist's wife. That's not true. To be sure I was very conscious of her all during the week before my marriage, but after she had come to me at my apartment she went entirely out of my mind.

"Am I telling the truth? I am trying very hard to tell what happened to me. I am saying that I have not since that evening thought of the woman who came to my apartment. Now, to tell the facts of the case, that is not true. On that evening I went to my fiancée at nine, as she had asked me to do in her letter. In a kind of way I cannot explain the other woman went with me. This is what I mean—you see I had been thinking that if anything happened between me and the tobacconist's wife I would not be able to go through with my marriage. 'It is one thing or the other with me,' I had said to myself.

"As a matter of fact I went to see my beloved on that evening filled with a new faith in the outcome of our life together. I am afraid I muddle this matter in trying to tell it. A moment ago I said the other woman, the tobacconist's wife, went with me. I do not mean she went in fact. What I am trying to say is that something of her faith in her own desires and her courage in seeing things through went with me. Is that clear to you? When I got to my fiancée's house there was a crowd of people standing about. Some were relatives from distant places I had not seen before. She looked up quickly when I came into the room. My face must have been radiant. I never saw her so moved. She thought her letter had affected me deeply, and of course it had. Up she jumped and ran to meet me. She was like a glad child. Right before the people who turned and looked inquiringly at us, she said the thing that was in her mind. 'O, I am so happy,' she cried. 'You have understood. We will be two human beings. We will not have to be husband and wife.'

"As you may suppose everyone laughed, but I did not laugh. The tears came into my eyes. I was so happy I wanted to shout. Perhaps you understand what I mean. In the office that day when I read the letter my fiancée had written I had said to myself, 'I will take care of the dear little woman.' There was something smug, you see, about that. In her house when she cried out in that way, and when everyone laughed, what I said to myself was something like this: 'We will take care of ourselves.' I whispered something of the sort into her ears. To tell you the truth I had come down off my perch. The spirit of the other woman did that to me. Before all the people gathered about I held my fiancée close and we kissed. They thought it very sweet of us to be so affected at the sight of each other. What they would have thought had they known the truth about me God only knows!

"Twice now I have said that after that evening I never thought of the other woman at all. That is partially true but, sometimes in the evening when I am walking alone in the street or in the park as we are walking now, and when evening comes softly and quickly as it has come to-night, the feeling of her comes sharply into my body and mind. After that one meeting I never saw her again. On the next day I was married and I have never gone back into her street. Often however as I am walking along as I am doing now, a quick sharp earthy feeling takes possession of me. It is as though I were a seed in the ground and the warm rains of the spring had come. It is as though I were not a man but a tree.

"And now you see I am married and everything is all right. My marriage is to me a very beautiful fact. If you were to say that my marriage is not a happy one I could call you a liar and be speaking the absolute truth. I have tried to tell you about this other woman. There is a kind of relief in speaking of her. I have never done it before. I wonder why I was so silly as to be afraid that I would give you the impression I am not in love with my wife. If I did not instinctively trust your understanding I would not have spoken. As the matter stands I have a little stirred myself up. To-night I shall think of the other woman. That sometimes occurs. It will happen after I have gone to bed. My wife sleeps in the next room to mine and the door is always left open. There will be a moon to-night, and when there is a moon long streaks of light fall on her bed. I shall awake at midnight to-night. She will be lying asleep with one arm thrown over her head.

"What is it that I am now talking about? A man does not speak of his wife lying in bed. What I am trying to say is that, because of this talk, I shall think of the other woman to-night. My thoughts will not take the form they did during the week before I was married. I will wonder what has become of the woman. For a moment I will again feel myself holding her close. I will think that for an hour I was closer to her than I have ever been to anyone else. Then I will think of the time when I will be as close as that to my wife. She is still, you see, an awakening woman. For a moment I will close my eyes and the quick, shrewd, determined eyes of that other woman will look into mine. My head will swim and then I will quickly open my eyes and see again the dear woman with whom I have undertaken to live out my life. Then I will sleep and when I awake in the morning it will be as it was that evening when I walked out of my dark apartment after having had the most notable experience of my life. What I mean to say, you understand is that, for me, when I awake, the other woman will be utterly gone."

The Egg

M Y father was, I am sure, intended by nature to be a cheerful, kindly man. Until he was thirty-four years old he
worked as a farm-hand for a man named Thomas Butterworth
whose place lay near the town of Bidwell, Ohio. He had then a
horse of his own and on Saturday evenings drove into town to
spend a few hours in social intercourse with other farm-hands.
In town he drank several glasses of beer and stood about in Ben
Head's saloon—crowded on Saturday evenings with visiting
farm-hands. Songs were sung and glasses thumped on the bar.
At ten o'clock father drove home along a lonely country road,
made his horse comfortable for the night and himself went to
bed, quite happy in his position in life. He had at that time no
notion of trying to rise in the world.

It was in the spring of his thirty-fifth year that father married
my mother, then a country school-teacher, and in the following spring I came wriggling and crying into the world. Something happened to the two people. They became ambitious. The
American passion for getting up in the world took possession
of them.

It may have been that mother was responsible. Being a
school-teacher she had no doubt read books and magazines.
She had, I presume, read of how Garfield, Lincoln, and other
Americans rose from poverty to fame and greatness and as I lay
beside her—in the days of her lying-in—she may have dreamed
that I would some day rule men and cities. At any rate she induced father to give up his place as a farm-hand, sell his horse
and embark on an independent enterprise of his own. She was
a tall silent woman with a long nose and troubled grey eyes.
For herself she wanted nothing. For father and myself she was
incurably ambitious.

The first venture into which the two people went turned out
badly. They rented ten acres of poor stony land on Griggs's
Road, eight miles from Bidwell, and launched into chicken
raising. I grew into boyhood on the place and got my first
impressions of life there. From the beginning they were impressions of disaster and if, in my turn, I am a gloomy man

inclined to see the darker side of life, I attribute it to the fact that what should have been for me the happy joyous days of childhood were spent on a chicken farm.

One unversed in such matters can have no notion of the many and tragic things that can happen to a chicken. It is born out of an egg, lives for a few weeks as a tiny fluffy thing such as you will see pictured on Easter cards, then becomes hideously naked, eats quantities of corn and meal bought by the sweat of your father's brow, gets diseases called pip, cholera, and other names, stands looking with stupid eyes at the sun, becomes sick and dies. A few hens and now and then a rooster, intended to serve God's mysterious ends, struggle through to maturity. The hens lay eggs out of which come other chickens and the dreadful cycle is thus made complete. It is all unbelievably complex. Most philosophers must have been raised on chicken farms. One hopes for so much from a chicken and is so dreadfully disillusioned. Small chickens, just setting out on the journey of life, look so bright and alert and they are in fact so dreadfully stupid. They are so much like people they mix one up in one's judgments of life. If disease does not kill them they wait until your expectations are thoroughly aroused and then walk under the wheels of a wagon—to go squashed and dead back to their maker. Vermin infest their youth, and fortunes must be spent for curative powders. In later life I have seen how a literature has been built up on the subject of fortunes to be made out of the raising of chickens. It is intended to be read by the gods who have just eaten of the tree of the knowledge of good and evil. It is a hopeful literature and declares that much may be done by simple ambitious people who own a few hens. Do not be led astray by it. It was not written for you. Go hunt for gold on the frozen hills of Alaska, put your faith in the honesty of a politician, believe if you will that the world is daily growing better and that good will triumph over evil, but do not read and believe the literature that is written concerning the hen. It was not written for you.

I, however, digress. My tale does not primarily concern itself with the hen. If correctly told it will centre on the egg. For ten years my father and mother struggled to make our chicken farm pay and then they gave up that struggle and began another. They moved into the town of Bidwell, Ohio and embarked in

the restaurant business. After ten years of worry with incuba-
tors that did not hatch, and with tiny—and in their own way
lovely—balls of fluff that passed on into semi-naked pullethood
and from that into dead henhood, we threw all aside and packing our belongings on a wagon drove down Griggs's Road
toward Bidwell, a tiny caravan of hope looking for a new place
from which to start on our upward journey through life.

We must have been a sad looking lot, not, I fancy, unlike
refugees fleeing from a battlefield. Mother and I walked in the
road. The wagon that contained our goods had been borrowed
for the day from Mr. Albert Griggs, a neighbor. Out of its sides
stuck the legs of cheap chairs and at the back of the pile of
beds, tables, and boxes filled with kitchen utensils was a crate
of live chickens, and on top of that the baby carriage in which
I had been wheeled about in my infancy. Why we stuck to the
baby carriage I don't know. It was unlikely other children
would be born and the wheels were broken. People who have
few possessions cling tightly to those they have. That is one of
the facts that make life so discouraging.

Father rode on top of the wagon. He was then a bald-headed
man of forty-five, a little fat and from long association with
mother and the chickens he had become habitually silent and
discouraged. All during our ten years on the chicken farm he
had worked as a laborer on neighboring farms and most of the
money he had earned had been spent for remedies to cure
chicken diseases, on Wilmer's White Wonder Cholera Cure or
Professor Bidlow's Egg Producer or some other preparations
that mother found advertised in the poultry papers. There
were two little patches of hair on father's head just above his
ears. I remember that as a child I used to sit looking at him
when he had gone to sleep in a chair before the stove on Sunday afternoons in the winter. I had at that time already begun
to read books and have notions of my own and the bald path
that led over the top of his head was, I fancied, something
like a broad road, such a road as Caesar might have made on
which to lead his legions out of Rome and into the wonders of
an unknown world. The tufts of hair that grew above father's
ears were, I thought, like forests. I fell into a half-sleeping,
half-waking state and dreamed I was a tiny thing going along

the road into a far beautiful place where there were no chicken farms and where life was a happy eggless affair.

One might write a book concerning our flight from the chicken farm into town. Mother and I walked the entire eight miles—she to be sure that nothing fell from the wagon and I to see the wonders of the world. On the seat of the wagon beside father was his greatest treasure. I will tell you of that.

On a chicken farm where hundreds and even thousands of chickens come out of eggs surprising things sometimes happen. Grotesques are born out of eggs as out of people. The accident does not often occur—perhaps once in a thousand births. A chicken is, you see, born that has four legs, two pairs of wings, two heads or what not. The things do not live. They go quickly back to the hand of their maker that has for a moment trembled. The fact that the poor little things could not live was one of the tragedies of life to father. He had some sort of notion that if he could but bring into henhood or rooster-hood a five-legged hen or a two-headed rooster his fortune would be made. He dreamed of taking the wonder about to county fairs and of growing rich by exhibiting it to other farm-hands.

At any rate he saved all the little monstrous things that had been born on our chicken farm. They were preserved in alcohol and put each in its own glass bottle. These he had carefully put into a box and on our journey into town it was carried on the wagon seat beside him. He drove the horses with one hand and with the other clung to the box. When we got to our destination the box was taken down at once and the bottles removed. All during our days as keepers of a restaurant in the town of Bidwell, Ohio, the grotesques in their little glass bottles sat on a shelf back of the counter. Mother sometimes protested but father was a rock on the subject of his treasure. The grotesques were, he declared, valuable. People, he said, liked to look at strange and wonderful things.

Did I say that we embarked in the restaurant business in the town of Bidwell, Ohio? I exaggerated a little. The town itself lay at the foot of a low hill and on the shore of a small river. The railroad did not run through the town and the station was a mile away to the north at a place called Pickleville. There had been a cider mill and pickle factory at the station, but before the time of our coming they had both gone out of business. In the morning and in the evening busses came down to the station along a road called Turner's Pike from the hotel on the main street of Bidwell. Our going to the out of the way place to embark in the restaurant business was mother's idea. She talked of it for a year and then one day went off and rented an empty store building opposite the railroad station. It was her idea that the restaurant would be profitable. Travelling men, she said, would be always waiting around to take trains out of town and town people would come to the station to await incoming trains. They would come to the restaurant to buy pieces of pie and drink coffee. Now that I am older I know that she had another motive in going. She was ambitious for me. She wanted me to rise in the world, to get into a town school and become a man of the towns.

At Pickleville father and mother worked hard as they always had done. At first there was the necessity of putting our place into shape to be a restaurant. That took a month. Father built a shelf on which he put tins of vegetables. He painted a sign on which he put his name in large red letters. Below his name was the sharp command—"EAT HERE"—that was so seldom obeyed. A show case was bought and filled with cigars and tobacco. Mother scrubbed the floor and the walls of the room. I went to school in the town and was glad to be away from the farm and from the presence of the discouraged, sad-looking chickens. Still I was not very joyous. In the evening I walked home from school along Turner's Pike and remembered the children I had seen playing in the town school yard. A troop of little girls had gone hopping about and singing. I tried that. Down along the frozen road I went hopping solemnly on one leg. "Hippity Hop To The Barber Shop," I sang shrilly. Then I stopped and looked doubtfully about. I was afraid of being seen in my gay mood. It must have seemed to me that I was doing a thing that should not be done by one who, like myself, had been raised on a chicken farm where death was a daily visitor.

Mother decided that our restaurant should remain open at night. At ten in the evening a passenger train went north past our door followed by a local freight. The freight crew had switching to do in Pickleville and when the work was done they came to our restaurant for hot coffee and food. Sometimes one of them ordered a fried egg. In the morning at four they returned north-bound and again visited us. A little trade began to grow up. Mother slept at night and during the day tended the restaurant and fed our boarders while father slept. He slept in the same bed mother had occupied during the night and I went off to the town of Bidwell and to school. During the long nights, while mother and I slept, father cooked meats that were to go into sandwiches for the lunch baskets of our boarders. Then an idea in regard to getting up in the world came into his head. The American spirit took hold of him. He also became ambitious.

In the long nights when there was little to do father had time to think. That was his undoing. He decided that he had in the past been an unsuccessful man because he had not been cheerful enough and that in the future he would adopt a cheerful outlook on life. In the early morning he came upstairs and got into bed with mother. She woke and the two talked. From my bed in the corner I listened.

It was father's idea that both he and mother should try to entertain the people who came to eat at our restaurant. I cannot now remember his words, but he gave the impression of one about to become in some obscure way a kind of public entertainer. When people, particularly young people from the town of Bidwell, came into our place, as on very rare occasions they did, bright entertaining conversation was to be made. From father's words I gathered that something of the jolly inn-keeper effect was to be sought. Mother must have been doubtful from the first, but she said nothing discouraging. It was father's notion that a passion for the company of himself and mother would spring up in the breasts of the younger people of the town of Bidwell. In the evening bright happy groups would come singing down Turner's Pike. They would troop shouting with joy and laughter into our place. There would be song and festivity. I do not mean to give the impression that father spoke so elaborately of the matter. He was as I have said an uncommunicative man. "They want some place to go. I tell you they want some place to go," he said over and over. That was as far as he got. My own imagination has filled in the blanks.

For two or three weeks this notion of father's invaded our house. We did not talk much, but in our daily lives tried earnestly to make smiles take the place of glum looks. Mother smiled at the boarders and I, catching the infection, smiled at our cat. Father became a little feverish in his anxiety to please. There was no doubt, lurking somewhere in him, a touch of the spirit of the showman. He did not waste much of his ammunition on the railroad men he served at night but seemed to be waiting for a young man or woman from Bidwell to come in to show what he could do. On the counter in the restaurant there was a wire basket kept always filled with eggs, and it must have been before his eyes when the idea of being entertaining was born in his brain. There was something pre-natal about the way eggs kept themselves connected with the development of his idea. At any rate an egg ruined his new impulse in life. Late one night I was awakened by a roar of anger coming from father's throat. Both mother and I sat upright in our beds. With trembling hands she lighted a lamp that stood on a table by her head. Downstairs the front door of our restaurant went shut with a bang and in a few minutes father tramped up the stairs. He held an egg in his hand and his hand trembled as though he were having a chill. There was a half insane light in his eyes. As he stood glaring at us I was sure he intended throwing the egg at either mother or me. Then he laid it gently on the table beside the lamp and dropped on his knees beside mother's bed. He began to cry like a boy and I, carried away by his grief, cried with him. The two of us filled the little upstairs room with our wailing voices. It is ridiculous, but of the picture we made I can remember only the fact that mother's hand continually stroked the bald path that ran across the top of his head. I have forgotten what mother said to him and how she induced him to tell her of what had happened downstairs. His explanation also has gone out of my mind. I remember only my own grief and fright and the shiny path over father's head glowing in the lamp light as he knelt by the bed.

As to what happened downstairs. For some unexplainable reason I know the story as well as though I had been a witness to my father's discomfiture. One in time gets to know many unexplainable things. On that evening young Joe Kane, son of a merchant of Bidwell, came to Pickleville to meet his father, who was expected on the ten o'clock evening train from the South. The train was three hours late and Joe came into our place to loaf about and to wait for its arrival. The local freight train came in and the freight crew were fed. Joe was left alone in the restaurant with father.

From the moment he came into our place the Bidwell young man must have been puzzled by my father's actions. It was his notion that father was angry at him for hanging around. He noticed that the restaurant keeper was apparently disturbed by his presence and he thought of going out. However, it began to rain and he did not fancy the long walk to town and back. He bought a five-cent cigar and ordered a cup of coffee. He had a newspaper in his pocket and took it out and began to read. "I'm waiting for the evening train. It's late," he said apologetically.

For a long time father, whom Joe Kane had never seen before, remained silently gazing at his visitor. He was no doubt suffering from an attack of stage fright. As so often happens in life he had thought so much and so often of the situation that now confronted him that he was somewhat nervous in its presence.

For one thing, he did not know what to do with his hands. He thrust one of them nervously over the counter and shook hands with Joe Kane. "How-de-do," he said. Joe Kane put his newspaper down and stared at him. Father's eye lighted on the basket of eggs that sat on the counter and he began to talk. "Well," he began hesitatingly, "well, you have heard of Christopher Columbus, eh?" He seemed to be angry. "That Christopher Columbus was a cheat," he declared emphatically. "He talked of making an egg stand on its end. He talked, he did, and then he went and broke the end of the egg."

My father seemed to his visitor to be beside himself at the duplicity of Christopher Columbus. He muttered and swore. He declared it was wrong to teach children that Christopher Columbus was a great man when, after all, he cheated at the critical moment. He had declared he would make an egg stand on end and then when his bluff had been called he had done a trick. Still grumbling at Columbus, father took an egg from the basket on the counter and began to walk up and down. He rolled the egg between the palms of his hands. He smiled genially. He began to mumble words regarding the effect to be produced on an egg by the electricity that comes out of the human body. He declared that without breaking its shell and by virtue of rolling it back and forth in his hands he could stand the egg on its end. He explained that the warmth of his hands and the gentle rolling movement he gave the egg created a new centre of gravity, and Joe Kane was mildly interested. "I have handled thousands of eggs," father said. "No one knows more about eggs than I do."

He stood the egg on the counter and it fell on its side. He tried the trick again and again, each time rolling the egg between the palms of his hands and saying the words regarding the wonders of electricity and the laws of gravity. When after a half hour's effort he did succeed in making the egg stand for a moment he looked up to find that his visitor was no longer watching. By the time he had succeeded in calling Joe Kane's attention to the success of his effort the egg had again rolled over and lay on its side.

Afire with the showman's passion and at the same time a good deal disconcerted by the failure of his first effort, father now took the bottles containing the poultry monstrosities down from their place on the shelf and began to show them to his visitor. "How would you like to have seven legs and two heads like this fellow?" he asked, exhibiting the most remarkable of his treasures. A cheerful smile played over his face. He reached over the counter and tried to slap Joe Kane on the shoulder as he had seen men do in Ben Head's saloon when he was a young farm-hand and drove to town on Saturday evenings. His visitor was made a little ill by the sight of the body of the terribly deformed bird floating in the alcohol in the bottle and got up to go. Coming from behind the counter father took hold of the young man's arm and led him back to his seat. He grew a little angry and for a moment had to turn his face away and force himself to smile. Then he put the bottles back on the shelf. In a outburst of generosity he fairly compelled Joe Kane to have a fresh cup of coffee and another cigar at his expense. Then he took a pan and filling it with vinegar, taken from a jug that sat beneath the counter, he declared himself about to do a new trick. "I will heat this egg in this pan of vinegar," he said. "Then I will put it through the neck of a bottle without breaking the shell. When the egg is inside the bottle it will resume its normal shape and the shell will become hard again. Then I will give the bottle with the egg in it to you. You can take it about with you wherever you go. People will want to know how you got the egg in the bottle. Don't tell them. Keep them guessing. That is the way to have fun with this trick."

Father grinned and winked at his visitor. Joe Kane decided that the man who confronted him was mildly insane but harmless. He drank the cup of coffee that had been given him and began to read his paper again. When the egg had been heated in vinegar father carried it on a spoon to the counter and going into a back room got an empty bottle. He was angry because his visitor did not watch him as he began to do his trick, but nevertheless went cheerfully to work. For a long time he struggled, trying to get the egg to go through the neck of the bottle. He put the pan of vinegar back on the stove, intending to reheat the egg, then picked it up and burned his fingers. After a second bath in the hot vinegar the shell of the egg had been softened a little but not enough for his purpose. He worked and worked and a spirit of desperate determination took possession of him. When he thought that at last the trick was about to be consummated the delayed train came in at the station and Joe Kane started to go nonchalantly out at the door. Father made a last desperate effort to conquer the egg and make it do the thing that would establish his reputation as one who knew how to entertain guests who came into his restaurant. He worried the egg. He attempted to be somewhat rough with it. He swore and the sweat stood out on his forehead. The egg broke under his hand. When the contents spurted over his clothes, Joe Kane, who had stopped at the door, turned and laughed.

A roar of anger rose from my father's throat. He danced and shouted a string of inarticulate words. Grabbing another egg from the basket on the counter, he threw it, just missing the head of the young man as he dodged through the door and escaped.

Father came upstairs to mother and me with an egg in his hand. I do not know what he intended to do. I imagine he had some idea of destroying it, of destroying all eggs, and that he intended to let mother and me see him begin. When, however, he got into the presence of mother something happened to him. He laid the egg gently on the table and dropped on his knees by the bed as I have already explained. He later decided to close the restaurant for the night and to come upstairs and get into bed. When he did so he blew out the light and after much muttered conversation both he and mother went to sleep. I suppose I went to sleep also, but my sleep was troubled. I awoke at dawn and for a long time looked at the egg that lay on the table. I wondered why eggs had to be and why from the egg came the hen who again laid the egg. The question got into my blood. It has stayed there, I imagine, because I am the son of my father. At any rate, the problem remains unsolved in my mind. And that, I conclude, is but another evidence of the complete and final triumph of the egg—at least as far as my family is concerned.

Unlighted Lamps

MARY COCHRAN went out of the rooms where she lived with her father, Doctor Lester Cochran, at seven o'clock on a Sunday evening. It was June of the year nineteen hundred and eight and Mary was eighteen years old. She walked along Tremont to Main Street and across the railroad tracks to Upper Main, lined with small shops and shoddy houses, a rather quiet cheerless place on Sundays when there were few people about. She had told her father she was going to church but did not intend doing anything of the kind. She did not know what she wanted to do. "I'll get off by myself and think," she told herself as she walked slowly along. The night she thought promised to be too fine to be spent sitting in a stuffy church and hearing a man talk of things that had apparently nothing to do with her own problem. Her own affairs were approaching a crisis and it was time for her to begin thinking seriously of her future.

The thoughtful serious state of mind in which Mary found herself had been induced in her by a conversation had with her father on the evening before. Without any preliminary talk and quite suddenly and abruptly he had told her that he was a victim of heart disease and might die at any moment. He had made the announcement as they stood together in the Doctor's office, back of which were the rooms in which the father and daughter lived.

It was growing dark outside when she came into the office and found him sitting alone. The office and living rooms were on the second floor of an old frame building in the town of Huntersburg, Illinois, and as the Doctor talked he stood beside his daughter near one of the windows that looked down into Tremont Street. The hushed murmur of the town's Saturday night life went on in Main Street just around a corner, and the evening train, bound to Chicago fifty miles to the east, had just passed. The hotel bus came rattling out of Lincoln Street and went through Tremont toward the hotel on Lower Main. A cloud of dust kicked up by the horses' hoofs floated on the quiet air. A straggling group of people followed the bus and the row of hitching posts on Tremont Street was already lined with buggies in which farmers and their wives had driven into town for the evening of shopping and gossip.

After the station bus had passed three or four more buggies were driven into the street. From one of them a young man helped his sweetheart to alight. He took hold of her arm with a certain air of tenderness, and a hunger to be touched thus tenderly by a man's hand, that had come to Mary many times before, returned at almost the same moment her father made the announcement of his approaching death.

As the Doctor began to speak Barney Smithfield, who owned a livery barn that opened into Tremont Street directly opposite the building in which the Cochrans lived, came back to his place of business from his evening meal. He stopped to tell a story to a group of men gathered before the barn door and a shout of laughter arose. One of the loungers in the street, a strongly built young man in a checkered suit, stepped away from the others and stood before the liveryman. Having seen Mary he was trying to attract her attention. He also began to tell a story and as he talked he gesticulated, waved his arms and from time to time looked over his shoulder to see if the girl still stood by the window and if she were watching.

Doctor Cochran had told his daughter of his approaching death in a cold quiet voice. To the girl it had seemed that everything concerning her father must be cold and quiet. "I have a disease of the heart," he said flatly, "have long suspected there was something of the sort the matter with me and on Thursday when I went into Chicago I had myself examined. The truth is I may die at any moment. I would not tell you but for one reason—I will leave little money and you must be making plans for the future."

The Doctor stepped nearer the window where his daughter stood with her hand on the frame. The announcement had made her a little pale and her hand trembled. In spite of his apparent coldness he was touched and wanted to reassure her. "There now," he said hesitatingly, "it'll likely be all right after all. Don't worry. I haven't been a doctor for thirty years without knowing there's a great deal of nonsense about these pronouncements on the part of experts. In a matter like this, that is to say when a man has a disease of the heart, he may putter about for years." He laughed uncomfortably. "I've even heard it said that the best way to insure a long life is to contract a disease of the heart."

With these words the Doctor had turned and walked out of his office, going down a wooden stairway to the street. He had wanted to put his arm about his daughter's shoulder as he talked to her, but never having shown any feeling in his relations with her could not sufficiently release some tight thing in himself.

Mary had stood for a long time looking down into the street. The young man in the checkered suit, whose name was Duke Yetter, had finished telling his tale and a shout of laughter arose. She turned to look toward the door through which her father had passed and dread took possession of her. In all her life there had never been anything warm and close. She shivered although the night was warm and with a quick girlish gesture passed her hand over her eyes.

The gesture was but an expression of a desire to brush away the cloud of fear that had settled down upon her but it was misinterpreted by Duke Yetter who now stood a little apart from the other men before the livery barn. When he saw Mary's hand go up he smiled and turning quickly to be sure he was unobserved began jerking his head and making motions with his hand as a sign that he wished her to come down into the street where he would have an opportunity to join her.

On the Sunday evening Mary, having walked through Upper Main, turned into Wilmott, a street of workmen's houses. During that year the first sign of the march of factories westward from Chicago into the prairie towns had come to Huntersburg. A Chicago manufacturer of furniture had built a plant in the sleepy little farming town, hoping thus to escape the labor organizations that had begun to give him trouble in the city. At the upper end of town, in Wilmott, Swift, Harrison and Chestnut Streets and in cheap, badly-constructed frame houses, most of the factory workers lived. On the warm summer evening they were gathered on the porches at the front of the houses and a mob of children played in the dusty streets. Red-faced men in white shirts and without collars and coats slept in chairs or lay sprawled on strips of grass or on the hard earth before the doors of the houses.

The laborers' wives had gathered in groups and stood gossiping by the fences that separated the yards. Occasionally the voice of one of the women arose sharp and distinct above the steady flow of voices that ran like a murmuring river through the hot little streets.

In the roadway two children had got into a fight. A thick-shouldered red-haired boy struck another boy who had a pale sharp-featured face, a blow on the shoulder. Other children came running. The mother of the red-haired boy brought the promised fight to an end. "Stop it Johnny, I tell you to stop it. I'll break your neck if you don't," the woman screamed.

The pale boy turned and walked away from his antagonist. As he went slinking along the sidewalk past Mary Cochran his sharp little eyes, burning with hatred, looked up at her.

Mary went quickly along. The strange new part of her native town with the hubbub of life always stirring and asserting itself had a strong fascination for her. There was something dark and resentful in her own nature that made her feel at home in the crowded place where life carried itself off darkly, with a blow and an oath. The habitual silence of her father and the mystery concerning the unhappy married life of her father and mother, that had affected the attitude toward her of the people of the town, had made her own life a lonely one and had encouraged in her a rather dogged determination to in some way think her own way through the things of life she could not understand.

And back of Mary's thinking there was an intense curiosity and a courageous determination toward adventure. She was like a little animal of the forest that has been robbed of its mother by the gun of a sportsman and has been driven by hunger to go forth and seek food. Twenty times during the year she had walked alone at evening in the new and fast growing factory district of her town. She was eighteen and had begun to look like a woman, and she felt that other girls of the town of her own age would not have dared to walk in such a place alone. The feeling made her somewhat proud and as she went along she looked boldly about.

Among the workers in Wilmott Street, men and women who had been brought to town by the furniture manufacturer, were many who spoke in foreign tongues. Mary walked among them and liked the sound of the strange voices. To be in the street made her feel that she had gone out of her town and on a voyage into a strange land. In Lower Main Street or in the residence streets in the eastern part of town where lived the young men and women she had always known and where lived also the merchants, the clerks, the lawyers and the more well-to-do American workmen of Huntersburg, she felt always a secret antagonism to herself. The antagonism was not due to anything in her own character. She was sure of that. She had kept so much to herself that she was in fact but little known. "It is because I am the daughter of my mother," she told herself and did not walk often in the part of town where other girls of her class lived.

Mary had been so often in Wilmott Street that many of the people had begun to feel acquainted with her. "She is the daughter of some farmer and has got into the habit of walking into town," they said. A red-haired, broad-hipped woman who came out at the front door of one of the houses nodded to her. On a narrow strip of grass beside another house sat a young man with his back against a tree. He was smoking a pipe, but when he looked up and saw her he took the pipe from his mouth. She decided he must be an Italian, his hair and eyes were so black. "Ne bella! si fai un onore a passare di qua," he called waving his hand and smiling.

Mary went to the end of Wilmott Street and came out upon a country road. It seemed to her that a long time must have passed since she left her father's presence although the walk had in fact occupied but a few minutes. By the side of the road and on top of a small hill there was a ruined barn, and before the barn a great hole filled with the charred timbers of what had once been a farmhouse. A pile of stones lay beside the hole and these were covered with creeping vines. Between the site of the house and the barn there was an old orchard in which grew a mass of tangled weeds.

Pushing her way in among the weeds, many of which were covered with blossoms, Mary found herself a seat on a rock that had been rolled against the trunk of an old apple tree. The weeds half concealed her and from the road only her head was visible. Buried away thus in the weeds she looked like a quail that runs in the tall grass and that on hearing some unusual sound, stops, throws up its head and looks sharply about.

The doctor's daughter had been to the decayed old orchard many times before. At the foot of the hill on which it stood the streets of the town began, and as she sat on the rock she could hear faint shouts and cries coming out of Wilmott Street. A hedge separated the orchard from the fields on the hillside. Mary intended to sit by the tree until darkness came creeping over the land and to try to think out some plan regarding her future. The notion that her father was soon to die seemed both true and untrue, but her mind was unable to take hold of the thought of him as physically dead. For the moment death in relation to her father did not take the form of a cold inanimate body that was to be buried in the ground, instead it seemed to her that her father was not to die but to go away somewhere on a journey. Long ago her mother had done that. There was a strange hesitating sense of relief in the thought. "Well," she told herself, "when the time comes I also shall be setting out, I shall get out of here and into the world." On several occasions Mary had gone to spend a day with her father in Chicago and she was fascinated by the thought that soon she might be going there to live. Before her mind's eye floated a vision of long streets filled with thousands of people all strangers to herself. To go into such streets and to live her life among strangers would be like coming out of a waterless desert and into a cool forest carpeted with tender young grass.

In Huntersburg she had always lived under a cloud and now she was becoming a woman and the close stuffy atmosphere she had always breathed was becoming constantly more and more oppressive. It was true no direct question had ever been raised touching her own standing in the community life, but she felt that a kind of prejudice against her existed. While she was still a baby there had been a scandal involving her father and mother. The town of Huntersburg had rocked with it and when she was a child people had sometimes looked at her with mocking sympathetic eyes. "Poor child! It's too bad," they said. Once, on a cloudy summer evening when her father had driven off to the country and she sat alone in the darkness by his office window, she heard a man and woman in the street mention her name. The couple stumbled along in the darkness on the sidewalk below the office window. "That daughter of Doc Cochran's is a nice girl," said the man. The woman laughed. "She's growing up and attracting men's attention now. Better keep your eyes in your head. She'll turn out bad. Like mother, like daughter," the woman replied.

For ten or fifteen minutes Mary sat on the stone beneath the tree in the orchard and thought of the attitude of the town toward herself and her father. "It should have drawn us together," she told herself, and wondered if the approach of death would do what the cloud that had for years hung over them had not done. It did not at the moment seem to her cruel that the figure of death was soon to visit her father. In a way Death had become for her and for the time a lovely and gracious figure intent upon good. The hand of death was to open the door out of her father's house and into life. With the cruelty of youth she thought first of the adventurous possibilities of the new life.

Mary sat very still. In the long weeds the insects that had been disturbed in their evening song began to sing again. A robin flew into the tree beneath which she sat and struck a clear sharp note of alarm. The voices of people in the town's new factory district came softly up the hillside. They were like bells of distant cathedrals calling people to worship. Something within the girl's breast seemed to break and putting her head into her hands she rocked slowly back and forth. Tears came accompanied by a warm tender impulse toward the living men and women of Huntersburg.

And then from the road came a call. "Hello there kid," shouted a voice, and Mary sprang quickly to her feet. Her mellow mood passed like a puff of wind and in its place hot anger came.

In the road stood Duke Yetter who from his loafing place before the livery barn had seen her set out for the Sunday evening walk and had followed. When she went through Upper Main Street and into the new factory district he was sure of his conquest. "She doesn't want to be seen walking with me," he had told himself, "that's all right. She knows well enough I'll follow but doesn't want me to put in an appearance until she is well out of sight of her friends. She's a little stuck up and needs to be brought down a peg, but what do I care? She's gone out of her way to give me this chance and maybe she's only afraid of her dad."

Duke climbed the little incline out of the road and came into the orchard, but when he reached the pile of stones covered by vines he stumbled and fell. He arose and laughed. Mary had not waited for him to reach her but had started toward him, and when his laugh broke the silence that lay over the orchard she sprang forward and with her open hand struck him a sharp blow on the cheek. Then she turned and as he stood with his feet tangled in the vines ran out to the road. "If you follow or speak to me I'll get someone to kill you," she shouted.

Mary walked along the road and down the hill toward Wilmott Street. Broken bits of the story concerning her mother that had for years circulated in town had reached her ears. Her mother, it was said, had disappeared on a summer night long ago and a young town rough, who had been in the habit of loitering before Barney Smithfield's Livery Barn, had gone away with her. Now another young rough was trying to make up to her. The thought made her furious.

Her mind groped about striving to lay hold of some weapon with which she could strike a more telling blow at Duke Yetter. In desperation it lit upon the figure of her father already broken in health and now about to die. "My father just wants the chance to kill some such fellow as you," she shouted, turning to face the young man, who having got clear of the mass of vines in the orchard, had followed her into the road. "My father just wants to kill someone because of the lies that have been told in this town about mother."

Having given way to the impulse to threaten Duke Yetter Mary was instantly ashamed of her outburst and walked rapidly along, the tears running from her eyes. With hanging head Duke walked at her heels. "I didn't mean no harm, Miss Cochran," he pleaded. "I didn't mean no harm. Don't tell your father. I was only funning with you. I tell you I didn't mean no harm."

The light of the summer evening had begun to fall and the faces of the people made soft little ovals of light as they stood grouped under the dark porches or by the fences in Wilmott

Street. The voices of the children had become subdued and they also stood in groups. They became silent as Mary passed and stood with upturned faces and staring eyes. "The lady doesn't live very far. She must be almost a neighbor," she heard a woman's voice saying in English. When she turned her head she saw only a crowd of dark-skinned men standing before a house. From within the house came the sound of a woman's voice singing a child to sleep.

The young Italian, who had called to her earlier in the evening and who was now apparently setting out of his own Sunday evening's adventures, came along the sidewalk and walked quickly away into the darkness. He had dressed himself in his Sunday clothes and had put on a black derby hat and a stiff white collar, set off by a red necktie. The shining whiteness of the collar made his brown skin look almost black. He smiled boyishly and raised his hat awkwardly but did not speak.

Mary kept looking back along the street to be sure Duke Yetter had not followed but in the dim light could see nothing of him. Her angry excited mood went away.

She did not want to go home and decided it was too late to go to church. From Upper Main Street there was a short street that ran eastward and fell rather sharply down a hillside to a creek and a bridge that marked the end of the town's growth in that direction. She went down along the street to the bridge and stood in the failing light watching two boys who were fishing in the creek.

A broad-shouldered man dressed in rough clothes came down along the street and stopping on the bridge spoke to her. It was the first time she had ever heard a citizen of her home town speak with feeling of her father. "You are Doctor Cochran's daughter?" he asked hesitatingly. "I guess you don't know who I am but your father does." He pointed toward the two boys who sat with fishpoles in their hands on the weed-grown bank of the creek. "Those are my boys and I have four other children," he explained. "There is another boy and I have three girls. One of my daughters has a job in a store. She is as old as yourself." The man explained his relations with Doctor Cochran. He had been a farm laborer, he said, and had but recently moved to town to work in the furniture factory. During the previous winter he had been ill for a long time and had no money. While he lay in bed one of his boys fell out of a barn loft and there was a terrible cut in his head.

"Your father came every day to see us and he sewed up my Tom's head." The laborer turned away from Mary and stood with his cap in his hand looking toward the boys. "I was down and out and your father not only took care of me and the boys but he gave my old woman money to buy the things we had to have from the stores in town here, groceries and medicines." The man spoke in such low tones that Mary had to lean forward to hear his words. Her face almost touched the laborer's shoulder. "Your father is a good man and I don't think he is very happy," he went on. "The boy and I got well and I got work here in town but he wouldn't take any money from me. 'You know how to live with your children and with your wife. You know how to make them happy. Keep your money and spend it on them,' that's what he said to me."

The laborer went on across the bridge and along the creek bank toward the spot where his two sons sat fishing and Mary leaned on the railing of the bridge and looked at the slow moving water. It was almost black in the shadows under the bridge and she thought that it was thus her father's life had been lived. "It has been like a stream running always in shadows and never coming out into the sunlight," she thought, and fear that her own life would run on in darkness gripped her. A great new love for her father swept over her and in fancy she felt his arms about her. As a child she had continually dreamed of caresses received at her father's hands and now the dream came back. For a long time she stood looking at the stream and she resolved that the night should not pass without an effort on her part to make the old dream come true. When she again looked up the laborer had built a little fire of sticks at the edge of the stream. "We catch bullheads here," he called. "The light of the fire draws them close to the shore. If you want to come and try your hand at fishing the boys will lend you one of the poles."

"O, I thank you, I won't do it tonight," Mary said, and then fearing she might suddenly begin weeping and that if the man spoke to her again she would find herself unable to answer, she hurried away. "Good bye!" shouted the man and the two boys. The words came quite spontaneously out of the three throats and created a sharp trumpet-like effect that rang like a glad cry across the heaviness of her mood.

When his daughter Mary went out for her evening walk Doctor Cochran sat for an hour alone in his office. It began to grow dark and the men who all afternoon had been sitting on chairs and boxes before the livery barn across the street went home for the evening meal. The noise of voices grew faint and sometimes for five or ten minutes there was silence. Then from some distant street came a child's cry. Presently church bells began to ring.

The Doctor was not a very neat man and sometimes for several days he forgot to shave. With a long lean hand he stroked his half grown beard. His illness had struck deeper than he had admitted even to himself and his mind had an inclination to float out of his body. Often when he sat thus his hands lay in his lap and he looked at them with a child's absorption. It seemed to him they must belong to someone else. He grew philosophic. "It's an odd thing about my body. Here I've lived in it all these years and how little use I have had of it. Now it's going to die and decay never having been used. I wonder why it did not get another tenant." He smiled sadly over this fancy but went on with it. "Well I've had thoughts enough concerning people and I've had the use of these lips and a tongue but I've let them lie idle. When my Ellen was here living with me I let her think me cold and unfeeling while something within me was straining and straining trying to tear itself loose."

He remembered how often, as a young man, he had sat in the evening in silence beside his wife in this same office and how his hands had ached to reach across the narrow space that separated them and touch her hands, her face, her hair.

Well, everyone in town had predicted his marriage would turn out badly! His wife had been an actress with a company that came to Huntersburg and got stranded there. At the same time the girl became ill and had no money to pay for her room at the hotel. The young doctor had attended to that and when the girl was convalescent took her to ride about the country in his buggy. Her life had been a hard one and the notion of leading a quiet existence in the little town appealed to her.

And then after the marriage and after the child was born she had suddenly found herself unable to go on living with the silent cold man. There had been a story of her having run away with a young sport, the son of a saloon keeper who had disappeared from town at the same time, but the story was untrue. Lester Cochran had himself taken her to Chicago where she got work with a company going into the far western states. Then he had taken her to the door of her hotel, had put money into her hands and in silence and without even a farewell kiss had turned and walked away.

The Doctor sat in his office living over that moment and other intense moments when he had been deeply stirred and had been on the surface so cool and quiet. He wondered if the woman had known. How many times he had asked himself that question. After he left her that night at the hotel door she never wrote. "Perhaps she is dead," he thought for the thousandth time.

A thing happened that had been happening at odd moments for more than a year. In Doctor Cochran's mind the remembered figure of his wife became confused with the figure of his daughter. When at such moments he tried to separate the two figures, to make them stand out distinct from each other, he was unsuccessful. Turning his head slightly he imagined he saw a white girlish figure coming through a door out of the rooms in which he and his daughter lived. The door was painted white and swung slowly in a light breeze that came in at an open window. The wind ran softly and quietly through the room and played over some papers lying on a desk in a corner. There was a soft swishing sound as of a woman's skirts. The doctor arose and stood trembling. "Which is it? Is it you Mary or is it Ellen?" he asked huskily.

On the stairway leading up from the street there was the sound of heavy feet and the outer door opened. The doctor's weak heart fluttered and he dropped heavily back into his chair.

A man came into the room. He was a farmer, one of the doctor's patients, and coming to the centre of the room he struck a match, held it above his head and shouted. "Hello!" he called. When the doctor arose from his chair and answered he was so startled that the match fell from his hand and lay burning faintly at his feet.

The young farmer had sturdy legs that were like two pillars

of stone supporting a heavy building, and the little flame of the match that burned and fluttered in the light breeze on the floor between his feet threw dancing shadows along the walls of the room. The doctor's confused mind refused to clear itself of his fancies that now began to feed upon this new situation.

He forgot the presence of the farmer and his mind raced back over his life as a married man. The flickering light on the wall recalled another dancing light. One afternoon in the summer during the first year after his marriage his wife Ellen had driven with him into the country. They were then furnishing their rooms and at a farmer's house Ellen had seen an old mirror, no longer in use, standing against a wall in a shed. Because of something quaint in the design the mirror had taken her fancy and the farmer's wife had given it to her. On the drive home the young wife had told her husband of her pregnancy and the doctor had been stirred as never before. He sat holding the mirror on his knees while his wife drove and when she announced the coming of the child she looked away across the fields.

How deeply etched, that scene in the sick man's mind! The sun was going down over young corn and oat fields beside the road. The prairie land was black and occasionally the road ran through short lanes of trees that also looked black in the waning light.

The mirror on his knees caught the rays of the departing sun and sent a great ball of golden light dancing across the fields and among the branches of trees. Now as he stood in the presence of the farmer and as the little light from the burning match on the floor recalled that other evening of dancing lights, he thought he understood the failure of his marriage and of his life. On that evening long ago when Ellen had told him of the coming of the great adventure of their marriage he had remained silent because he had thought no words he could utter would express what he felt. There had been a defense for himself built up. "I told myself she should have understood without words and I've all my life been telling myself the same thing about Mary. I've been a fool and a coward. I've always been silent because I've been afraid of expressing myself—like a blundering fool. I've been a proud man and a coward.

"Tonight I'll do it. If it kills me I'll make myself talk to the girl," he said aloud, his mind coming back to the figure of his daughter.

"Hey! What's that?" asked the farmer who stood with his hat in his hand waiting to tell of his mission.

The doctor got his horse from Barney Smithfield's livery and drove off to the country to attend the farmer's wife who was about to give birth to her first child. She was a slender narrow-hipped woman and the child was large, but the doctor was feverishly strong. He worked desperately and the woman, who was frightened, groaned and struggled. Her husband kept coming in and going out of the room and two neighbor women appeared and stood silently about waiting to be of service. It was past ten o'clock when everything was done and the doctor was ready to depart for town.

The farmer hitched his horse and brought it to the door and the doctor drove off feeling strangely weak and at the same time strong. How simple now seemed the thing he had yet to do. Perhaps when he got home his daughter would have gone to bed but he would ask her to get up and come into the office. Then he would tell the whole story of his marriage and its failure sparing himself no humiliation. "There was something very dear and beautiful in my Ellen and I must make Mary understand that. It will help her to be a beautiful woman," he thought, full of confidence in the strength of his resolution.

He got to the door of the livery barn at eleven o'clock and Barney Smithfield with young Duke Yetter and two other men sat talking there. The liveryman took his horse away into the darkness of the barn and the doctor stood for a moment leaning against the wall of the building. The town's night watchman stood with the group by the barn door and a quarrel broke out between him and Duke Yetter, but the doctor did not hear the hot words that flew back and forth or Duke's loud laughter at the night watchman's anger. A queer hesitating mood had taken possession of him. There was something he passionately desired to do but could not remember. Did it have to do with his wife Ellen or Mary his daughter? The figures of the two women were again confused in his mind and to add to the confusion there was a third figure, that of the woman he had just assisted through child birth. Everything was confusion.

He started across the street toward the entrance of the stairway leading to his office and then stopped in the road and stared about. Barney Smithfield having returned from putting his horse in the stall shut the door of the barn and a hanging lantern over the door swung back and forth. It threw grotesque dancing shadows down over the faces and forms of the men standing and quarreling beside the wall of the barn.

Mary sat by a window in the doctor's office awaiting his return. So absorbed was she in her own thoughts that she was unconscious of the voice of Duke Yetter talking with the men in the street.

When Duke had come into the street the hot anger of the early part of the evening had returned and she again saw him advancing toward her in the orchard with the look of arrogant male confidence in his eyes but presently she forgot him and thought only of her father. An incident of her childhood returned to haunt her. One afternoon in the month of May when she was fifteen her father had asked her to accompany him on an evening drive into the country. The doctor went to visit a sick woman at a farmhouse five miles from town and as there had been a great deal of rain the roads were heavy. It was dark when they reached the farmer's house and they went into the kitchen and ate cold food off a kitchen table. For some reason her father had, on that evening, appeared boyish and almost gay. On the road he had talked a little. Even at that early age Mary had grown tall and her figure was becoming womanly. After the cold supper in the farm kitchen he walked with her around the house and she sat on a narrow porch. For a moment her father stood before her. He put his hands into his trouser pockets and throwing back his head laughed almost heartily. "It seems strange to think you will soon be a woman," he said. "When you do become a woman what do you suppose is going to happen, eh? What kind of a life will you lead? What will happen to you?"

The doctor sat on the porch beside the child and for a moment she had thought he was about to put his arm around her. Then he jumped up and went into the house leaving her to sit alone in the darkness.

As she remembered the incident Mary remembered also

that on that evening of her childhood she had met her father's advances in silence. It seemed to her that she, not her father, was to blame for the life they had led together. The farm laborer she had met on the bridge had not felt her father's coldness. That was because he had himself been warm and generous in his attitude toward the man who had cared for him in his hour of sickness and misfortune. Her father had said that the laborer knew how to be a father and Mary remembered with what warmth the two boys fishing by the creek had called to her as she went away into the darkness. "Their father has known how to be a father because his children have known how to give themselves," she thought guiltily. She also would give herself. Before the night had passed she would do that. On that evening long ago and as she rode home beside her father he had made another unsuccessful effort to break through the wall that separated them. The heavy rains had swollen the streams they had to cross and when they had almost reached town he had stopped the horse on a wooden bridge. The horse danced nervously about and her father held the reins firmly and occasionally spoke to him. Beneath the bridge the swollen stream made a great roaring sound and beside the road in a long flat field there was a lake of flood water. At that moment the moon had come out from behind clouds and the wind that blew across the water made little waves. The lake of flood water was covered with dancing lights. "I'm going to tell you about your mother and myself," her father said huskily, but at that moment the timbers of the bridge began to crack dangerously and the horse plunged forward. When her father had regained control of the frightened beast they were in the streets of the town and his diffident silent nature had reasserted itself.

Mary sat in the darkness by the office window and saw her father drive into the street. When his horse had been put away he did not, as was his custom, come at once up the stairway to the office but lingered in the darkness before the barn door. Once he started to cross the street and then returned into the darkness.

Among the men who for two hours had been sitting and talking quietly a quarrel broke out. Jack Fisher the town nightwatchman had been telling the others the story of a battle in which he had fought during the Civil War and Duke Yetter had begun bantering him. The nightwatchman grew angry. Grasping his nightstick he limped up and down. The loud voice of Duke Yetter cut across the shrill angry voice of the victim of his wit. "You ought to a flanked the fellow, I tell you Jack. Yes sir 'ee, you ought to a flanked that reb and then when you got him flanked you ought to a knocked the stuffings out of the cuss. That's what I would a done," Duke shouted, laughing boisterously. "You would a raised hell, you would," the night watchman answered, filled with ineffectual wrath.

The old soldier went off along the street followed by the laughter of Duke and his companions and Barney Smithfield, having put the doctor's horse away, came out and closed the barn door. A lantern hanging above the door swung back and forth. Doctor Cochran again started across the street and when he had reached the foot of the stairway turned and shouted to the men. "Good night," he called cheerfully. A strand of hair was blown by the light summer breeze across Mary's cheek and she jumped to her feet as though she had been touched by a hand reached out to her from the darkness. A hundred times she had seen her father return from drives in the evening but never before had he said anything at all to the loiterers by the barn door. She became half convinced that not her father but some other man was now coming up the stairway.

The heavy dragging footsteps rang loudly on the wooden stairs and Mary heard her father set down the little square medicine case he always carried. The strange cheerful hearty mood of the man continued but his mind was in a confused riot. Mary imagined she could see his dark form in the doorway. "The woman has had a baby," said the hearty voice from the landing outside the door. "Who did that happen to? Was it Ellen or that other woman or my little Mary?"

A stream of words, a protest came from the man's lips. "Who's been having a baby? I want to know. Who's been having a baby? Life doesn't work out. Why are babies always being born?" he asked.

A laugh broke from the doctor's lips and his daughter leaned forward and gripped the arms of her chair. "A babe has been born," he said again. "It's strange eh, that my hands should have helped a baby be born while all the time death stood at my elbow?"

Doctor Cochran stamped upon the floor of the landing. "My feet are cold and numb from waiting for life to come out of life," he said heavily. "The woman struggled and now I must struggle."

Silence followed the stamping of feet and the tired heavy declaration from the sick man's lips. From the street below came another loud shout of laughter from Duke Yetter.

And then Doctor Cochran fell backward down the narrow stairs to the street. There was no cry from him, just the clatter of his shoes upon the stairs and the terrible subdued sound of the body falling.

Mary did not move from her chair. With closed eyes she waited. Her heart pounded. A weakness complete and overmastering had possession of her and from feet to head ran little waves of feeling as though tiny creatures with soft hair-like feet were playing upon her body.

It was Duke Yetter who carried the dead man up the stairs and laid him on a bed in one of the rooms back of the office. One of the men who had been sitting with him before the door of the barn followed lifting his hands and dropping them nervously. Between his fingers he held a forgotten cigarette the light from which danced up and down in the darkness.

Senility

He was an old man and he sat on the steps of the railroad station in a small Kentucky town.

A well dressed man, some traveler from the city, approached and stood before him.

The old man became self-conscious.

His smile was like the smile of a very young child. His face was all sunken and wrinkled and he had a huge nose.

"Have you any coughs, colds, consumption or bleeding sickness?" he asked. In his voice there was a pleading quality.

The stranger shook his head. The old man arose.

"The sickness that bleeds is a terrible nuisance," he said. His tongue protruded from between his teeth and he rattled it about. He put his hand on the stranger's arm and laughed.

"Bully, pretty," he exclaimed. "I cure them all—coughs, colds, consumption and the sickness that bleeds. I take warts from the hand—I cannot explain how I do it—it is a mystery—I charge nothing—my name is Tom—do you like me?"

The stranger was cordial. He nodded his head. The old man became reminiscent.

"My father was a hard man," he declared. "He was like me, a blacksmith by trade, but he wore a plug hat. When the corn was high he said to the poor, 'go into the fields and pick' but when the war came he made a rich man pay five dollars for a bushel of corn."

"I married against his will. He came to me and he said, 'Tom I do not like that girl.'"

"'But I love her,' I said.

"'I don't,' he said.

"My father and I sat on a log. He was a pretty man and wore a plug hat. 'I will get the license,' I said.

"'I will give you no money,' he said.

"My marriage cost me twenty-one dollars—I worked in the corn—it rained and the horses were blind—the clerk said, 'Are you over twenty-one?' I said 'yes' and she said 'yes.' We had chalked it on our shoes. My father said, 'I give you your freedom.'

We had no money. My marriage cost twenty-one dollars. She is dead."

The old man looked at the sky. It was evening and the sun had set. The sky was all mottled with grey clouds. "I paint beautiful pictures and give them away," he declared. "My brother is in the penitentiary. He killed a man who called him an ugly name."

The decrepit old man held his hands before the face of the stranger. He opened and shut them. They were black with grime. "I pick out warts," he explained plaintively. "They are as soft as your hands."

"I play on an accordion. You are thirty-seven years old. I sat beside my brother in the penitentiary. He is a pretty man with pompadour hair. 'Albert,' I said, 'are you sorry you killed a man?' 'No,' he said, 'I am not sorry. I would kill ten, a hundred, a thousand!'"

The old man began to weep and to wipe his hands with a soiled handkerchief. He attempted to take a chew of tobacco and his false teeth became displaced. He covered his mouth with his hands and was ashamed.

"I am old. You are thirty-seven years old but I am older than that," he whispered.

"My brother is a bad man—he is full of hate—he is pretty and has pompadour hair, but he would kill and kill. I hate old age—I am ashamed that I am old.

"I have a pretty new wife. I wrote her four letters and she replied. She came here and we married—I love to see her walk —O, I buy her pretty clothes.

"Her foot is not straight—it is twisted—my first wife is dead —I pick warts off the hand with my fingers and no blood comes—I cure coughs, colds, consumption and the sickness that bleeds—people can write to me and I answer the letters— if they send me no money it is no matter—all is free."

Again the old man wept and the stranger tried to comfort him. "You are a happy man?" the stranger asked.

"Yes," said the old man, "and a good man too. Ask everywhere about me—my name is Tom, a blacksmith—my wife walks prettily although she has a twisted foot—I have bought her a long dress—she is thirty and I am seventy-five—she has many pairs of shoes—I have bought them for her, but her foot is twisted—I buy straight shoes—

"She thinks I do not know—everybody thinks Tom does not know—I have bought her a long dress that comes down to the ground—my name is Tom, a blacksmith—I am seventy-five and I hate old age—I take warts off the hands and no blood comes—people may write to me and I answer the letters —all is free."

The Man in the Brown Coat

> Napoleon went down into a battle riding on a horse.
> Alexander went down into a battle riding on a horse.
> General Grant got off a horse and walked in a wood.
> General Hindenburg stood on a hill.
> The moon came up out of a clump of bushes.

I AM writing a history of the things men do. I have written three such histories and I am but a young man. Already I have written three hundred, four hundred thousand words.

My wife is somewhere in this house where for hours now I have been sitting and writing. She is a tall woman with black hair, turning a little grey. Listen, she is going softly up a flight of stairs. All day she goes softly about, doing the housework in our house.

I came here to this town from another town in the state of Iowa. My father was a workman, a house painter. He did not rise in the world as I have done. I worked my way through college and became an historian. We own this house in which I sit. This is my room in which I work. Already I have written three histories of peoples. I have told how states were formed and battles fought. You may see my books standing straight up on the shelves of libraries. They stand up like sentries.

I am tall like my wife and my shoulders are a little stooped. Although I write boldly I am a shy man. I like being at work alone in this room with the door closed. There are many books here. Nations march back and forth in the books. It is quiet here but in the books a great thundering goes on.

> Napoleon rides down a hill and into a battle.
> General Grant walks in a wood.
> Alexander rides down a hill and into a battle.

My wife has a serious, almost stern look. Sometimes the thoughts I have concerning her frighten me. In the afternoon she leaves our house and goes for a walk. Sometimes she goes to stores, sometimes to visit a neighbor. There is a yellow house opposite our house. My wife goes out at a side door and passes along the street between our house and the yellow house.

The side door of our house bangs. There is a moment of waiting. My wife's face floats across the yellow background of a picture.

> General Pershing rode down a hill and into a battle.
> Alexander rode down a hill and into a battle.

Little things are growing big in my mind. The window before my desk makes a little framed place like a picture. Every day I sit staring. I wait with an odd sensation of something impending. My hand trembles. The face that floats through the picture does something I don't understand. The face floats, then it stops. It goes from the right hand side to the left hand side, then it stops.

The face comes into my mind and goes out—the face floats in my mind. The pen has fallen from my fingers. The house is silent. The eyes of the floating face are turned away from me.

My wife is a girl who came here to this town from another town in the state of Ohio. We keep a servant but my wife often sweeps the floors and she sometimes makes the bed in which we sleep together. We sit together in the evening but I do not know her. I cannot shake myself out of myself. I wear a brown coat and I cannot come out of my coat. I cannot come out of myself. My wife is very gentle and she speaks softly but she cannot come out of herself.

My wife has gone out of the house. She does not know that I know every little thought of her life. I know what she thought when she was a child and walked in the streets of an Ohio town. I have heard the voices of her mind. I have heard the little voices. I heard the voice of fear crying when she was first overtaken with passion and crawled into my arms. Again I heard the voices of fear when her lips said words of courage to me as we sat together on the first evening after we were married and moved into this house.

It would be strange if I could sit here, as I am doing now, while my own face floated across the picture made by the yellow house and the window. It would be strange and beautiful if I could meet my wife, come into her presence.

The woman whose face floated across my picture just now knows nothing of me. I know nothing of her. She has gone off, along a street. The voices of her mind are talking. I am here in this room, as alone as ever any man God made.

It would be strange and beautiful if I could float my face across my picture. If my floating face could come into her presence, if it could come into the presence of any man or any woman—that would be a strange and beautiful thing to have happen.

> Napoleon went down into a battle riding on a horse.
> General Grant went into a wood.
> Alexander went down into a battle riding on a horse.

I'll tell you what—sometimes the whole life of this world floats in a human face in my mind. The unconscious face of the world stops and stands still before me.

Why do I not say a word out of myself to the others? Why, in all our life together, have I never been able to break through the wall to my wife? Already I have written three hundred, four hundred thousand words. Are there no words that lead into life? Some day I shall speak to myself. Some day I shall make a testament unto myself.

Brothers

I AM at my house in the country and it is late October. It rains. Back of my house is a forest and in front there is a road and beyond that open fields. The country is one of low hills, flattening suddenly into plains. Some twenty miles away, across the flat country, lies the huge city Chicago.

On this rainy day the leaves of the trees that line the road before my window are falling like rain, the yellow, red and golden leaves fall straight down heavily. The rain beats them brutally down. They are denied a last golden flash across the sky. In October leaves should be carried away, out over the plains, in a wind. They should go dancing away.

Yesterday morning I arose at daybreak and went for a walk. There was a heavy fog and I lost myself in it. I went down into the plains and returned to the hills, and everywhere the fog was as a wall before me. Out of it trees sprang suddenly, grotesquely, as in a city street late at night people come suddenly out of the darkness into the circle of light under a street lamp. Above there was the light of day forcing itself slowly into the fog. The fog moved slowly. The tops of trees moved slowly. Under the trees the fog was dense, purple. It was like smoke lying in the streets of a factory town.

An old man came up to me in the fog. I know him well. The people here call him insane. "He is a little cracked," they say. He lives alone in a little house buried deep in the forest and has a small dog he carries always in his arms. On many mornings I have met him walking on the road and he has told me of men and women who are his brothers and sisters, his cousins, aunts, uncles, brothers-in-law. It is confusing. He cannot draw close to people near at hand so he gets hold of a name out of a newspaper and his mind plays with it. On one morning he told me he was a cousin to the man named Cox who at the time when I write is a candidate for the presidency. On another morning he told me that Caruso the singer had married a woman who was his sister-in-law. "She is my wife's sister," he said, holding the little dog close. His grey watery eyes looked appealing up to me. He wanted me to believe. "My wife was a sweet slim girl," he declared. "We lived together in a big house and in the morning walked about arm in arm. Now her sister has married Caruso the singer. He is of my family now."

As someone had told me the old man had never married, I went away wondering. One morning in early September I came upon him sitting under a tree beside a path near his house. The dog barked at me and then ran and crept into his arms. At that time the Chicago newspapers were filled with the story of a millionaire who had got into trouble with his wife because of an intimacy with an actress. The old man told me that the actress was his sister. He is sixty years old and the actress whose story appeared in the newspapers is twenty but he spoke of their childhood together. "You would not realize it to see us now but we were poor then," he said. "It's true. We lived in a little house on the side of a hill. Once when there was a storm, the wind nearly swept our house away. How the wind blew! Our father was a carpenter and he built strong houses for other people but our own house he did not build very strong!" He shook his head sorrowfully. "My sister the actress has got into trouble. Our house is not built very strongly," he said as I went away along the path.

For a month, two months, the Chicago newspapers, that are delivered every morning in our village, have been filled with the story of a murder. A man there has murdered his wife and there seems no reason for the deed. The tale runs something like this—

The man, who is now on trial in the courts and will no doubt be hanged, worked in a bicycle factory where he was a foreman and lived with his wife and his wife's mother in an apartment in Thirty-second Street. He loved a girl who worked in the office of the factory where he was employed. She came from a town in Iowa and when she first came to the city lived with her aunt who has since died. To the foreman, a heavy stolid looking man with grey eyes, she seemed the most beautiful woman in the world. Her desk was by a window at an angle of the factory, a sort of wing of the building, and the foreman, down in the shop had a desk by another window. He sat at his desk making out sheets containing the record of the work done by each man in his department. When he looked up he could see the girl sitting at work at her desk. The notion got into his head that she was peculiarly lovely. He did not think of trying to draw close to her or of winning her love. He looked at her as one might look at a star or across a country of low hills in October when the leaves of the trees are all red and yellow gold. "She is a pure, virginal thing," he thought vaguely. "What can she be thinking about as she sits there by the window at work."

In fancy the foreman took the girl from Iowa home with him to his apartment in Thirty-second Street and into the presence of his wife and his mother-in-law. All day in the shop and during the evening at home he carried her figure about with him in his mind. As he stood by a window in his apartment and looked out toward the Illinois Central railroad tracks and beyond the tracks to the lake, the girl was there beside him. Down below women walked in the street and in every woman he saw there was something of the Iowa girl. One woman walked as she did, another made a gesture with her hand that reminded of her. All the women he saw except his wife and his mother-in-law were like the girl he had taken inside himself.

The two women in his own house puzzled and confused him. They became suddenly unlovely and commonplace. His wife in particular was like some strange unlovely growth that had attached itself to his body.

In the evening after the day at the factory he went home to his own place and had dinner. He had always been a silent man and when he did not talk no one minded. After dinner he with his wife went to a picture show. There were two children and his wife expected another. They came into the apartment and sat down. The climb up two flights of stairs had wearied his wife. She sat in a chair beside her mother groaning with weariness.

The mother-in-law was the soul of goodness. She took the place of a servant in the home and got no pay. When her daughter wanted to go to a picture show she waved her hand and smiled. "Go on," she said. "I don't want to go. I'd rather sit here." She got a book and sat reading. The little boy of nine awoke and cried. He wanted to sit on the po-po. The mother-in-law attended to that.

After the man and his wife came home the three people sat in silence for an hour or two before bed time. The man pretended to read a newspaper. He looked at his hands. Although he had washed them carefully grease from the bicycle frames left dark stains under the nails. He thought of the Iowa girl and of her white quick hands playing over the keys of a typewriter. He felt dirty and uncomfortable.

The girl at the factory knew the foreman had fallen in love with her and the thought excited her a little. Since her aunt's death she had gone to live in a rooming house and had nothing to do in the evening. Although the foreman meant nothing to her she could in a way use him. To her he became a symbol. Sometimes he came into the office and stood for a moment by the door. His large hands were covered with black grease. She looked at him without seeing. In his place in her imagination stood a tall slender young man. Of the foreman she saw only the grey eyes that began to burn with a strange fire. The eyes expressed eagerness, a humble and devout eagerness. In the presence of a man with such eyes she felt she need not be afraid.

She wanted a lover who would come to her with such a look in his eyes. Occasionally, perhaps once in two weeks, she stayed a little late at the office, pretending to have work that must be finished. Through the window she could see the foreman waiting. When everyone had gone she closed her desk and went into the street. At the same moment the foreman came out at the factory door.

They walked together along the street a half dozen blocks to where she got aboard her car. The factory was in a place called South Chicago and as they went along evening was coming on. The streets were lined with small unpainted frame houses and dirty faced children ran screaming in the dusty roadway. They crossed over a bridge. Two abandoned coal barges lay rotting in the stream.

He went by her side walking heavily and striving to conceal his hands. He had scrubbed them carefully before leaving the factory but they seemed to him like heavy dirty pieces of waste matter hanging at his side. Their walking together happened but a few times and during one summer. "It's hot," he said. He never spoke to her of anything but the weather. "It's hot," he said. "I think it may rain."

She dreamed of the lover who would some time come, a tall fair young man, a rich man owning houses and lands. The workingman who walked beside her had nothing to do with her conception of love. She walked with him, stayed at the office until the others had gone to walk unobserved with him because of his eyes, because of the eager thing in his eyes that was at the same time humble, that bowed down to her. In his presence there was no danger, could be no danger. He would never attempt to approach too closely, to touch her with his hands. She was safe with him.

In his apartment in the evening the man sat under the electric light with his wife and his mother-in-law. In the next room his two children were asleep. In a short time his wife would have another child. He had been with her to a picture show and in a short time they would get into bed together.

He would lie awake thinking, would hear the creaking of the springs of a bed where, in another room, his mother-in-law was crawling between the sheets. Life was too intimate. He would lie awake eager, expectant—expecting, what?

Nothing. Presently one of the children would cry. It wanted to get out of bed and sit on the po-po. Nothing strange or unusual or lovely would or could happen. Life was too close, intimate. Nothing that could happen in the apartment could in any way stir him; the things his wife might say, her occasional half-hearted outbursts of passion, the goodness of his mother-in-law who did the work of a servant without pay—

He sat in the apartment under the electric light pretending to read a newspaper—thinking. He looked at his hands. They were large, shapeless, a workingman's hands.

The figure of the girl from Iowa walked about the room. With her he went out of the apartment and walked in silence through miles of streets. It was not necessary to say words. He walked with her by a sea, along the crest of a mountain. The night was clear and silent and the stars shone. She also was a star. It was not necessary to say words.

Her eyes were like stars and her lips were like soft hills rising out of dim, star lit plains. "She is unattainable, she is far off like the stars," he thought. "She is unattainable like the stars but unlike the stars she breathes, she lives, like myself she has being."

One evening, some six weeks ago, the man who worked as foreman in the bicycle factory killed his wife and he is now in the courts being tried for murder. Every day the newspapers are filled with the story. On the evening of the murder he had taken his wife as usual to a picture show and they started home at nine. In Thirty-second Street, at a corner near their apartment building, the figure of a man darted suddenly out of an alleyway and then darted back again. The incident may have put the idea of killing his wife into the man's head.

They got to the entrance to the apartment building and stepped into a dark hallway. Then quite suddenly and apparently without thought the man took a knife out of his pocket. "Suppose that man who darted into the alleyway had intended to kill us," he thought. Opening the knife he whirled about and struck at his wife. He struck twice, a dozen times—madly. There was a scream and his wife's body fell.

The janitor had neglected to light the gas in the lower hallway. Afterwards, the foreman decided, that was the reason he did it, that and the fact that the dark slinking figure of a man darted out of an alleyway and then darted back again. "Surely," he told himself, "I could never have done it had the gas been lighted."

He stood in the hallway thinking. His wife was dead and with her had died her unborn child. There was a sound of doors opening in the apartments above. For several minutes nothing happened. His wife and her unborn child were dead— that was all.

He ran upstairs thinking quickly. In the darkness on the lower stairway he had put the knife back into his pocket and, as it turned out later, there was no blood on his hands or on his clothes. The knife he later washed carefully in the bathroom, when the excitement had died down a little. He told everyone the same story. "There has been a holdup," he explained. "A man came slinking out of an alleyway and followed me and my wife home. He followed us into the hallway of the building and there was no light. The janitor has neglected to light the gas." Well—there had been a struggle and in the darkness his wife had been killed. He could not tell how it had happened. "There was no light. The janitor has neglected to light the gas," he kept saying.

For a day or two they did not question him specially and he had time to get rid of the knife. He took a long walk and threw it away into the river in South Chicago where the two abandoned coal barges lay rotting under the bridge, the bridge he had crossed when on the summer evenings he walked to the street car with the girl who was virginal and pure, who was far off and unattainable, like a star and yet not like a star.

And then he was arrested and right away he confessed—told everything. He said he did not know why he killed his wife and was careful to say nothing of the girl at the office. The newspapers tried to discover the motive for the crime. They are still trying. Someone had seen him on the few evenings when he walked with the girl and she was dragged into the affair and had her picture printed in the papers. That has been annoying for her as of course she has been able to prove she had nothing to do with the man.

Yesterday morning a heavy fog lay over our village here at the edge of the city and I went for a long walk in the early morning. As I returned out of the lowlands into our hill country I met the old man whose family has so many and such strange ramifications. For a time he walked beside me holding the little dog in his arms. It was cold and the dog whined and shivered. In the fog the old man's face was indistinct. It moved slowly back and forth with the fog banks of the upper air and with the tops of trees. He spoke of the man who has killed his wife and whose name is being shouted in the pages of the city newspapers that come to our village each morning. As he walked beside me he launched into a long tale concerning a life he and his brother, who has now become a murderer, once lived together. "He is my brother," he said over and over, shaking his head. He seemed afraid I would not believe. There was a fact that must be established. "We were boys together that man and I," he began again. "You see we played together in a barn back of our father's house. Our father went away to sea in a ship. That is the way our names became confused. You understand that. We have different names, but we are brothers. We had the same father. We played together in a barn back of our father's house. For hours we lay together in the hay in the barn and it was warm there."

In the fog the slender body of the old man became like a little gnarled tree. Then it became a thing suspended in air. It swung back and forth like a body hanging on the gallows. The face beseeched me to believe the story the lips were trying to tell. In my mind everything concerning the relationship of men and women became confused, a muddle. The spirit of the man who had killed his wife came into the body of the little old man there by the roadside. It was striving to tell me the story it would never be able to tell in the court room in the city, in the presence of the judge. The whole story of mankind's loneliness, of the effort to reach out to unattainable beauty tried to get itself expressed from the lips of a mumbling old man, crazed with loneliness, who stood by the side of a country road on a foggy morning holding a little dog in his arms.

The arms of the old man held the dog so closely that it began to whine with pain. A sort of convulsion shook his body. The soul seemed striving to wrench itself out of the body, to fly away through the fog, down across the plain to the city, to the singer, the politician, the millionaire, the murderer, to its brothers, cousins, sisters, down in the city. The intensity of the old man's desire was terrible and in sympathy my body began to tremble. His arms tightened about the body of the little dog so that it cried with pain. I stepped forward and tore the arms away and the dog fell to the ground and lay whining. No doubt it had been injured. Perhaps ribs had been crushed. The old man stared at the dog lying at his feet as in the hallway of the apartment building the worker from the bicycle factory had stared at his dead wife. "We are brothers," he said again. "We have different names but we are brothers. Our father you understand went off to sea."

I am sitting in my house in the country and it rains. Before my eyes the hills fall suddenly away and there are the flat plains and beyond the plains the city. An hour ago the old man of the house in the forest went past my door and the little dog was not with him. It may be that as we talked in the fog he crushed the life out of his companion. It may be that the dog like the workman's wife and her unborn child is now dead. The leaves of the trees that line the road before my window are falling like rain—the yellow, red and golden leaves fall straight down, heavily. The rain beat them brutally down. They are denied a last golden flash across the sky. In October leaves should be carried away, out over the plains, in a wind. They should be dancing away.

The Door of the Trap

WINIFRED WALKER understood some things clearly enough. She understood that when a man is put behind iron bars he is in prison. Marriage was marriage to her.

It was that to her husband Hugh Walker, too, as he found out. Still he didn't understand. It might have been better had he understood, then he might at least have found himself. He didn't. After his marriage five or six years passed like shadows of wind blown trees playing on a wall. He was in a drugged, silent state. In the morning and evening every day he saw his wife. Occasionally something happened within him and he kissed her. Three children were born. He taught mathematics in the little college at Union Valley, Illinois, and waited.

For what? He began to ask himself that question. It came to him at first faintly like an echo. Then it became an insistent question. "I want answering," the question seemed to say. "Stop fooling along. Give your attention to me."

Hugh walked through the streets of the Illinois town. "Well, I'm married. I have children," he muttered.

He went home to his own house. He did not have to live within his income from the little college, and so the house was rather large and comfortably furnished. There was a negro woman who took care of the children and another who cooked and did the housework. One of the women was in the habit of crooning low soft negro songs. Sometimes Hugh stopped at the house door and listened. He could see through the glass in the door into the room where his family was gathered. Two children played with blocks on the floor. His wife sat sewing. The old negress sat in a rocking chair with his youngest child, a baby, in her arms. The whole room seemed under the spell of the crooning voice. Hugh fell under the spell. He waited in silence. The voice carried him far away somewhere, into forests, along the edges of swamps. There was nothing very definite about his thinking. He would have given a good deal to be able to be definite.

He went inside the house. "Well, here I am," his mind

seemed to say, "here I am. This is my house, these are my children."

He looked at his wife Winifred. She had grown a little plump since their marriage. "Perhaps it is the mother in her coming out, she has had three children," he thought.

The crooning old negro woman went away, taking the youngest child with her. He and Winifred held a fragmentary conversation. "Have you been well to-day, dear?" she asked. "Yes," he answered.

If the two older children were intent on their play his chain of thought was not broken. His wife never broke it as the children did when they came running to pull and tear at him. Throughout the early evening, after the children went to bed, the surface of the shell of him was not broken at all. A brother college professor and his wife came in or he and Winifred went to a neighbor's house. There was talk. Even when he and Winifred were alone together in the house there was talk. "The shutters are becoming loose," she said. The house was an old one and had green shutters. They were continually coming loose and at night blew back and forth on their hinges making a loud banging noise.

Hugh made some remark. He said he would see a carpenter about the shutters. Then his mind began playing away, out of his wife's presence, out of the house, in another sphere. "I am a house and my shutters are loose," his mind said. He thought of himself as a living thing inside a shell, trying to break out. To avoid distracting conversation he got a book and pretended to read. When his wife had also begun to read he watched her closely, intently. Her nose was so and so and her eyes so and so. She had a little habit with her hands. When she became lost in the pages of a book the hand crept up to her cheek, touched it and then was put down again. Her hair was not in very good order. Since her marriage and the coming of the children she had not taken good care of her body. When she read her body slumped down in the chair. It became bag-like. She was one whose race had been run.

Hugh's mind played all about the figure of his wife but did not really approach the woman who sat before him. It was so with his children. Sometimes, just for a moment, they were living things to him, things as alive as his own body. Then for long periods they seemed to go far away like the crooning voice of the negress.

It was odd that the negress was always real enough. He felt an understanding existed between himself and the negress. She was outside his life. He could look at her as at a tree. Sometimes in the evening when she had been putting the children to bed in the upper part of the house and when he sat with a book in his hand pretending to read, the old black woman came softly through the room, going toward the kitchen. She did not look at Winifred, but at Hugh. He thought there was a strange, soft light in her old eyes. "I understand you, my son," her eyes seemed to say.

Hugh was determined to get his life cleaned up if he could manage it. "All right, then," he said, as though speaking to a third person in the room. He was quite sure there was a third person there and that the third person was within himself, inside his body. He addressed the third person.

"Well, there is this woman, this person I married, she has the air of something accomplished," he said, as though speaking aloud. Sometimes it almost seemed to him he had spoken aloud and he looked quickly and sharply at his wife. She continued reading, lost in her book. "That may be it," he went on. "She has had these children. They are accomplished facts to her. They came out of her body, not out of mine. Her body has done something. Now it rests. If she is becoming a little bag-like, that's all right."

He got up and making some trivial excuse got out of the room and out of the house. In his youth and young manhood the long periods of walking straight ahead through the country, that had come upon him like visitations of some recurring disease, had helped. Walking solved nothing. It only tired his body, but when his body was tired he could sleep. After many days of walking and sleeping something occurred. The reality of life was in some queer way re-established in his mind. Some little thing happened. A man walking in the road before him threw a stone at a dog that ran barking out of a farm-house. It was evening perhaps, and he walked in a country of low hills. Suddenly he came out upon the top of one of the hills. Before him the road dipped down into darkness but to the west, across fields, there was a farm-house. The sun had gone down, but a faint glow lit the western horizon. A woman came out of the farmhouse and went toward a barn. He could not see her figure distinctly. She seemed to be carrying something, no doubt a milk pail; she was going to a barn to milk a cow.

The man in the road who had thrown the stone at the farm dog had turned and seen Hugh in the road behind him. He was a little ashamed of having been afraid of the dog. For a moment he seemed about to wait and speak to Hugh, and then was overcome with confusion and hurried away. He was a middle-aged man, but quite suddenly and unexpectedly he looked like a boy.

As for the farm woman, dimly seen going toward a distant barn, she also stopped and looked toward him. It was impossible she should have seen him. She was dressed in white and he could see her but dimly against the blackish green of the trees of an orchard behind her. Still she stood looking and seemed to look directly into his eyes. He had a queer sensation of her having been lifted by an unseen hand and brought to him. It seemed to him he knew all about her life, all about the life of the man who had thrown the stone at the dog.

In his youth, when life had stepped out of his grasp, Hugh had walked and walked until several such things had occurred and then suddenly he was all right again and could again work and live among men.

After his marriage and after such an evening at home he started walking rapidly as soon as he left the house. As quickly as possible he got out of town and struck out along a road that led over the rolling prairie. "Well, I can't walk for days and days as I did once," he thought. "There are certain facts in life and I must face facts. Winifred, my wife, is a fact, and my children are facts. I must get my fingers on facts. I must live by them and with them. It's the way lives are lived."

Hugh got out of town and on to a road that ran between cornfields. He was an athletic looking man and wore loose fitting clothes. He went along distraught and puzzled. In a way he felt like a man capable of taking a man's place in life and in another way he didn't at all.

The country spread out, wide, in all directions. It was always night when he walked thus and he could not see, but the realization of distances was always with him. "Everything goes on and on but I stand still," he thought. He had been a professor in the little college for six years. Young men and women had come into a room and he had taught them. It was nothing. Words and figures had been played with. An effort had been made to arouse minds.

For what?

There was the old question, always coming back, always wanting answering as a little animal wants food. Hugh gave up trying to answer. He walked rapidly, trying to grow physically tired. He made his mind attend to little things in the effort to forget distances. One night he got out of the road and walked completely around a cornfield. He counted the stalks in each hill of corn and computed the number of stalks in a whole field. "It should yield twelve hundred bushels of corn, that field," he said to himself dumbly, as though it mattered to him. He pulled a little handful of cornsilk out of the top of an ear of corn and played with it. He tried to fashion himself a yellow moustache. "I'd be quite a fellow with a trim yellow moustache," he thought.

One day in his class-room Hugh suddenly began to look with new interest at his pupils. A young girl attracted his attention. She sat beside the son of a Union Valley merchant and the young man was writing something on the back of a book. She looked at it and then turned her head away. The young man waited.

It was winter and the merchant's son had asked the girl to go with him to a skating party. Hugh, however, did not know that. He felt suddenly old. When he asked the girl a question she was confused. Her voice trembled.

When the class was dismissed an amazing thing happened. He asked the merchant's son to stay for a moment and, when the two were alone together in the room, he grew suddenly and furiously angry. His voice was, however, cold and steady. "Young man," he said, "you do not come into this room to write on the back of a book and waste your time. If I see anything of the kind again I'll do something you don't expect. I'll throw you out through a window, that's what I'll do."

Hugh made a gesture and the young man went away, white and silent. Hugh felt miserable. For several days he thought

about the girl who had quite accidentally attracted his attention. "I'll get acquainted with her. I'll find out about her," he
thought.

It was not an unusual thing for professors in the college at
Union Valley to take students home to their houses. Hugh
decided he would take the girl to his home. He thought about
it several days and late one afternoon saw her going down the
college hill ahead of him.

The girl's name was Mary Cochran and she had come to the
school but a few months before from a place called Huntersburg, Illinois, no doubt just such another place as Union Valley. He knew nothing of her except that her father was dead,
her mother too, perhaps. He walked rapidly down the hill to
overtake her. "Miss Cochran," he called, and was surprised to
find that his voice trembled a little. "What am I so eager
about?" he asked himself.

A new life began in Hugh Walker's house. It was good for
the man to have some one there who did not belong to him,
and Winifred Walker and the children accepted the presence of
the girl. Winifred urged her to come again. She did come several times a week.

To Mary Cochran it was comforting to be in the presence of
a family of children. On winter afternoons she took Hugh's
two sons and a sled and went to a small hill near the house.
Shouts arose. Mary Cochran pulled the sled up the hill and the
children followed. Then they all came tearing down together.

The girl, developing rapidly into womanhood, looked upon
Hugh Walker as something that stood completely outside her
own life. She and the man who had become suddenly and intensely interested in her had little to say to each other and
Winifred seemed to have accepted her without question as an
addition to the household. Often in the afternoon when the
two negro women were busy she went away leaving the two
older children in Mary's charge.

It was late afternoon and perhaps Hugh had walked home
with Mary from the college. In the spring he worked in the
neglected garden. It had been plowed and planted, but he
took a hoe and rake and puttered about. The children played
about the house with the college girl. Hugh did not look at
them but at her. "She is one of the world of people with whom

I live and with whom I am supposed to work here," he thought. "Unlike Winifred and these children she does not belong to me. I could go to her now, touch her fingers, look at her and then go away and never see her again."

That thought was a comfort to the distraught man. In the evening when he went out to walk the sense of distance that lay all about him did not tempt him to walk and walk, going half insanely forward for hours, trying to break through an intangible wall

He thought about Mary Cochran. She was a girl from a country town. She must be like millions of American girls. He wondered what went on in her mind as she sat in his classroom, as she walked beside him along the streets of Union Valley, as she played with the children in the yard beside his house.

In the winter, when in the growing darkness of a late afternoon Mary and the children built a snow man in the yard, he went upstairs and stood in the darkness to look out a window. The tall straight figure of the girl, dimly seen, moved quickly about. "Well, nothing has happened to her. She may be anything or nothing. Her figure is like a young tree that has not borne fruit," he thought. He went away to his own room and sat for a long time in the darkness. That night when he left the house for his evening's walk he did not stay long but hurried home and went to his own room. He locked the door. Unconsciously he did not want Winifred to come to the door and disturb his thoughts. Sometimes she did that.

All the time she read novels. She read the novels of Robert Louis Stevenson. When she had read them all she began again.

Sometimes she came upstairs and stood talking by his door. She told some tale, repeated some wise saying that had fallen unexpectedly from the lips of the children. Occasionally she came into the room and turned out the light. There was a couch by a window. She went to sit on the edge of the couch. Something happened. It was as it had been before their marriage. New life came into her figure. He also went to sit on the couch and she put up her hand and touched his face.

Hugh did not want that to happen now. He stood within the room for a moment and then unlocked the door and went to the head of the stairs. "Be quiet when you come up, Winifred. I have a headache and am going to try to sleep," he lied.

When he had gone back to his own room and locked the door again he felt safe. He did not undress but threw himself on the couch and turned out the light.

He thought about Mary Cochran, the school girl, but was sure he thought about her in a quite impersonal way. She was like the woman going to milk cows he had seen across hills when he was a young fellow and walked far and wide over the country to cure the restlessness in himself. In his life she was like the man who threw the stone at the dog.

"Well, she is unformed; she is like a young tree," he told himself again. "People are like that. They just grow up suddenly out of childhood. It will happen to my own children. My little Winifred that cannot yet say words will suddenly be like this girl. I have not selected her to think about for any particular reason. For some reason I have drawn away from life and she has brought me back. It might have happened when I saw a child playing in the street or an old man going up a stairway into a house. She does not belong to me. She will go away out of my sight. Winifred and the children will stay on and on here and I will stay on and on. We are imprisoned by the fact that we belong to each other. This Mary Cochran is free, or at least she is free as far as this prison is concerned. No doubt she will, after a while, make a prison of her own and live in it, but I will have nothing to do with the matter."

By the time Mary Cochran was in her third year in the college at Union Valley she had become almost a fixture in the Walker household. Still she did not know Hugh. She knew the children better than he did, perhaps better than their mother. In the fall she and the two boys went to the woods to gather nuts. In the winter they went skating on a little pond near the house.

Winifred accepted her as she accepted everything, the service of the two negroes, the coming of the children, the habitual silence of her husband.

And then quite suddenly and unexpectedly Hugh's silence, that had lasted all through his married life, was broken up. He walked homeward with a German who had the chair of modern languages in the school and got into a violent quarrel. He stopped to speak to men on the street. When he went to putter about in the garden he whistled and sang.

One afternoon in the fall he came home and found the whole family assembled in the living room of the house. The children were playing on the floor and the negress sat in the chair by the window with his youngest child in her arms, crooning one of the negro songs. Mary Cochran was there. She sat reading a book.

Hugh walked directly toward her and looked over her shoulder. At that moment Winifred came into the room. He reached forward and snatched the book out of the girl's hands. She looked up startled. With an oath he threw it into the fire that burned in an open grate at the side of the room. A flood of words ran from him. He cursed books and people and schools. "Damn it all," he said. "What makes you want to read about life? What makes people want to think about life? Why don't they live? Why don't they leave books and thoughts and schools alone?"

He turned to look at his wife who had grown pale and stared at him with a queer fixed uncertain stare. The old negro woman got up and went quickly away. The two older children began to cry. Hugh was miserable. He looked at the startled girl in the chair who also had tears in her eyes, and at his wife. His fingers pulled nervously at his coat. To the two women he looked like a boy who had been caught stealing food in a pantry. "I am having one of my silly irritable spells," he said, looking at his wife but in reality addressing the girl. "You see I am more serious than I pretend to be. I was not irritated by your book but by something else. I see so much that can be done in life and I do so little."

He went upstairs to his own room wondering why he had lied to the two women, why he continually lied to himself.

Did he lie to himself? He tried to answer the question but couldn't. He was like one who walks in the darkness of the hallway of a house and comes to a blank wall. The old desire to run away from life, to wear himself out physically, came back upon him like a madness.

For a long time he stood in the darkness inside his own room. The children stopped crying and the house became quiet again. He could hear his wife's voice speaking softly and presently the back door of the house banged and he knew the schoolgirl had gone away.

Life in the house began again. Nothing happened. Hugh ate his dinner in silence and went for a long walk. For two weeks Mary Cochran did not come to his house and then one day he saw her on the college grounds. She was no longer one of his pupils. "Please do not desert us because of my rudeness," he said. The girl blushed and said nothing. When he got home that evening she was in the yard beside the house playing with the children. He went at once to his own room. A hard smile came and went on his face. "She isn't like a young tree any more. She is almost like Winifred. She is almost like a person who belongs here, who belongs to me and my life," he thought.

Mary Cochran's visits to the Walker household came to an end very abruptly. One evening when Hugh was in his room she came up the stairway with the two boys. She had dined with the family and was putting the two boys into their beds. It was a privilege she claimed when she dined with the Walkers.

Hugh had hurried upstairs immediately after dining. He knew where his wife was. She was downstairs, sitting under a lamp, reading one of the books of Robert Louis Stevenson.

For a long time Hugh could hear the voices of his children on the floor above. Then the thing happened.

Mary Cochran came down the stairway that led past the door of his room. She stopped, turned back and climbed the stairs again to the room above. Hugh arose and stepped into the hallway. The schoolgirl had returned to the children's room because she had been suddenly overtaken with a hunger to kiss Hugh's oldest boy, now a lad of nine. She crept into the room and stood for a long time looking at the two boys, who unaware of her presence had gone to sleep. Then she stole forward and kissed the boy lightly. When she went out of the room Hugh stood in the darkness waiting for her. He took hold of her hand and led her down the stairs to his own room.

She was terribly afraid and her fright in an odd way pleased him. "Well," he whispered, "you can't understand now what's going to happen here but some day you will. I'm going to kiss you and then I'm going to ask you to go out of this house and never come back."

He held the girl against his body and kissed her upon the cheeks and lips. When he led her to the door she was so weak with fright and with new, strange, trembling desires that she could with difficulty make her way down the stair and into his wife's presence. "She will lie now," he thought, and heard her voice coming up the stairs like an echo to his thoughts. "I have a terrible headache. I must hurry home," he heard her voice saying. The voice was dull and heavy. It was not the voice of a young girl.

"She is no longer like a young tree," he thought. He was glad and proud of what he had done. When he heard the door at the back of the house close softly his heart jumped. A strange quivering light came into his eyes. "She will be imprisoned but I will have nothing to do with it. She will never belong to me. My hands will never build a prison for her," he thought with grim pleasure.

The New Englander

Her name was Elsie Leander and her girlhood was spent on her father's farm in Vermont. For several generations the Leanders had all lived on the same farm and had all married thin women, and so she was thin. The farm lay in the shadow of a mountain and the soil was not very rich. From the beginning and for several generations there had been a great many sons and few daughters in the family. The sons had gone west or to New York City and the daughters had stayed at home and thought such thoughts as come to New England women who see the sons of their fathers' neighbors slipping away, one by one, into the West.

Her father's house was a small white frame affair and when you went out at the back door, past a small barn and chicken house, you got into a path that ran up the side of a hill and into an orchard. The trees were all old and gnarled. At the back of the orchard the hill dropped away and bare rocks showed.

Inside the fence a large grey rock stuck high up out of the ground. As Elsie sat with her back to the rock, with a mangled hillside at her feet, she could see several large mountains, apparently but a short distance away, and between herself and the mountains lay many tiny fields surrounded by neatly built stone walls. Everywhere rocks appeared. Large ones, too heavy to be moved, stuck out of the ground in the centre of the fields. The fields were like cups filled with a green liquid that turned grey in the fall and white in the winter. The mountains, far off but apparently near at hand, were like giants ready at any moment to reach out their hands and take the cups one by one and drink off the green liquid. The large rocks in the fields were like the thumbs of the giants.

Elsie had three brothers, born before her, but they had all gone away. Two of them had gone to live with her uncle in the West and her oldest brother had gone to New York City where he had married and prospered. All through his youth and manhood her father had worked hard and had lived a hard life, but his son in New York City had begun to send money home,

285

and after that things went better. He still worked every day about the barn or in the fields but he did not worry about the future. Elsie's mother did house work in the mornings and in the afternoons sat in a rocking chair in her tiny living room and thought of her sons while she crocheted table covers and tidies for the backs of chairs. She was a silent woman, very thin and with very thin bony hands. She did not ease herself into a rocking chair but sat down and got up suddenly, and when she crocheted her back was as straight as the back of a drill sergeant.

The mother rarely spoke to the daughter. Sometimes in the afternoons as the younger woman went up the hillside to her place by the rock at the back of the orchard, her father came out of the barn and stopped her. He put a hand on her shoulder and asked her where she was going. "To the rock," she said and her father laughed. His laughter was like the creaking of a rusty barn door hinge and the hand he had laid on her shoulders was thin like her own hands and like her mother's hands. The father went into the barn shaking his head. "She's like her mother. She is herself like a rock," he thought. At the head of the path that led from the house to the orchard there was a great cluster of bayberry bushes. The New England farmer came out of his barn to watch his daughter go along the path, but she had disappeared behind the bushes. He looked away past his house to the fields and to the mountains in the distance. He also saw the green cup-like fields and the grim mountains. There was an almost imperceptible tightening of the muscles of his half worn-out old body. For a long time he stood in silence and then, knowing from long experience the danger of having thoughts, he went back into the barn and busied himself with the mending of an agricultural tool that had been mended many times before.

The son of the Leanders who went to live in New York City was the father of one son, a thin sensitive boy who looked like Elsie. The son died when he was twenty-three years old and some years later the father died and left his money to the old people on the New England farm. The two Leanders who had gone west had lived there with their father's brother, a farmer, until they grew into manhood. Then Will, the younger, got a job on a railroad. He was killed one winter morning. It was a cold snowy day and when the freight train he was in charge of as conductor left the city of Des Moines, he started to run over the tops of the cars. His feet slipped and he shot down into space. That was the end of him.

Of the new generation there was only Elsie and her brother Tom, whom she had never seen, left alive. Her father and mother talked of going west to Tom for two years before they came to a decision. Then it took another year to dispose of the farm and make preparations. During the whole time Elsie did not think much about the change about to take place in her life.

The trip west on the railroad train jolted Elsie out of herself. In spite of her detached attitude toward life she became excited. Her mother sat up very straight and stiff in the seat in the sleeping car and her father walked up and down in the aisle. After a night when the younger of the two women did not sleep but lay awake with red burning cheeks and with her thin fingers incessantly picking at the bed clothes in her berth while the train went through towns and cities, crawled up the sides of hills and fell down into forest-clad valleys, she got up and dressed to sit all day looking at a new kind of land. The train ran for a day and through another sleepless night in a flat land where every field was as large as a farm in her own country. Towns appeared and disappeared in a continual procession. The whole land was so unlike anything she had ever known that she began to feel unlike herself. In the valley where she had been born and where she had lived all her days everything had an air of finality. Nothing could be changed. The tiny fields were chained to the earth. They were fixed in their places and surrounded by aged stone walls. The fields like the mountains that looked down at them were as unchangeable as the passing days. She had a feeling they had always been so, would always be so.

Elsie sat like her mother, upright in the car seat and with a back like the back of a drill sergeant. The train ran swiftly along through Ohio and Indiana. Her thin hands like her mother's hands were crossed and locked. One passing casually through the car might have thought both women prisoners handcuffed and bound to their seats. Night came on and she again got into her berth. Again she lay awake and her thin cheeks became flushed, but she thought new thoughts. Her hands were no longer gripped together and she did not pick at the bed clothes. Twice during the night she stretched herself and yawned, a thing she had never in her life done before. The train stopped at a town on the prairies, and as there was something the matter with one of the wheels of the car in which she lay the trainsmen came with flaming torches to tinker with it. There was a great pounding and shouting. When the train went on its way she wanted to get out of her berth and run up and down in the aisle of the car. The fancy had come to her that the men tinkering with the car wheel were new men out of the new land who with strong hammers had broken away the doors of her prison. They had destroyed forever the programme she had made for her life.

Elsie was filled with joy at the thought that the train was still going on into the West. She wanted to go on forever in a straight line into the unknown. She fancied herself no longer on a train and imagined she had become a winged thing flying through space. Her long years of sitting alone by the rock on the New England farm had got her into the habit of expressing her thoughts aloud. Her thin voice broke the silence that lay over the sleeping car and her father and mother, both also lying awake, sat up in their berth to listen.

Tom Leander, the only living male representative of the new generation of Leanders, was a loosely built man of forty inclined to corpulency. At twenty he had married the daughter of a neighboring farmer, and when his wife inherited some money she and Tom moved into the town of Apple Junction in Iowa where Tom opened a grocery. The venture prospered as did Tom's matrimonial venture. When his brother died in New York City and his father, mother, and sister decided to come west Tom was already the father of a daughter and four sons.

On the prairies north of town and in the midst of a vast level stretch of cornfields, there was a partly completed brick house that had belonged to a rich farmer named Russell who had begun to build the house intending to make it the most magnificent place in the county, but when it was almost completed he had found himself without money and heavily in debt. The farm, consisting of several hundred acres of corn land, had been split into three farms and sold. No one had wanted the huge unfinished brick house. For years it had stood vacant, its windows staring out over the fields that had been planted almost up to the door.

In buying the Russell house Tom was moved by two motives. He had a notion that in New England the Leanders had been rather magnificent people. His memory of his father's place in the Vermont valley was shadowy, but in speaking of it to his wife he became very definite. "We had good blood in us, we Leanders," he said, straightening his shoulders. "We lived in a big house. We were important people."

Wanting his father and mother to feel at home in the new place, Tom had also another motive. He was not a very energetic man and, although he had done well enough as keeper of a grocery, his success was largely due to the boundless energy of his wife. She did not pay much attention to her household and her children, like little animals, had to take care of themselves, but in any matter concerning the store her word was law.

To have his father the owner of the Russell place Tom felt would establish him as a man of consequence in the eyes of his neighbors. "I can tell you what, they're used to a big house," he said to his wife. "I tell you what, my people are used to living in style."

The exaltation that had come over Elsie on the train wore away in the presence of the grey empty Iowa fields, but something of the effect of it remained with her for months. In the big brick house life went on much as it had in the tiny New England house where she had always lived. The Leanders installed themselves in three or four rooms on the ground floor. After a few weeks the furniture that had been shipped by freight arrived and was hauled out from town in one of Tom's grocery wagons. There were three or four acres of ground covered with great piles of boards the unsuccessful farmer had intended to use in the building of stables. Tom sent men to haul the boards away and Elsie's father prepared to plant a garden. They had come west in April and as soon as they were installed in the house ploughing and planting began in the fields nearby. The habit of a lifetime returned to the daughter of the house. In the new place there was no gnarled orchard surrounded by a half-ruined stone fence. All of the fences in all of the fields that stretched away out of sight to the north, south, east, and west were made of wire and looked like spider webs against the blackness of the ground when it had been freshly ploughed.

There was however the house itself. It was like an island rising out of the sea. In an odd way the house, although it was less than ten years old, was very old. Its unnecessary bigness represented an old impulse in men. Elsie felt that. At the east side there was a door leading to a stairway that ran into the upper part of the house that was kept locked. Two or three stone steps led up to it. Elsie could sit on the top step with her back against the door and gaze into the distance without being disturbed. Almost at her feet began the fields that seemed to go on and on forever. The fields were like the waters of a sea. Men came to plough and plant. Giant horses moved in a procession across the prairies. A young man who drove six horses came directly toward her. She was fascinated. The breasts of the horses as they came forward with bowed heads seemed like the breasts of giants. The soft spring air that lay over the fields was also like a sea. The horses were giants walking on the floor of a sea. With their breasts they pushed the waters of the sea before them. They were pushing the waters out of the basin of the sea. The young man who drove them also was a giant.

Elsie pressed her body against the closed door at the top of the steps. In the garden back of the house she could hear her father at work. He was raking dry masses of weeds off the ground preparatory to spading it for a family garden. He had always worked in a tiny confined place and would do the same thing here. In this vast open place he would work with small tools, doing little things with infinite care, raising little vegetables. In the house her mother would crochet little tidies. She herself would be small. She would press her body against the door of the house, try to get herself out of sight. Only the feeling that sometimes took possession of her, and that did not form itself into a thought would be large.

The six horses turned at the fence and the outside horse got entangled in the traces. The driver swore vigorously. Then he turned and started at the pale New Englander and with another oath pulled the heads of the horses about and drove away into the distance. The field in which he was ploughing contained two hundred acres. Elsie did not wait for him to return but went into the house and sat with folded arms in a room. The house she thought was a ship floating in a sea on the floor of which giants went up and down.

May came and then June. In the great fields work was always going on and Elsie became somewhat used to the sight of the young man in the field that came down to the steps. Sometimes when he drove his horses down to the wire fence he smiled and nodded.

In the month of August, when it is very hot, the corn in Iowa fields grows until the corn stalks resemble young trees. The corn fields become forests. The time for the cultivating of the corn has passed and weeds grow thick between the corn rows. The men with their giant horses have gone away. Over the immense fields silence broods.

When the time of the laying-by of the crop came that first summer after Elsie's arrival in the West her mind, partially awakened by the strangeness of the railroad trip, awakened again. She did not feel like a staid thin woman with a back like the back of a drill sergeant, but like something new and as strange as the new land into which she had come to live. For a time she did not know what was the matter. In the field the corn had grown so high that she could not see into the distance. The corn was like a wall and the little bare spot of land on which her father's house stood was like a house built behind the walls of a prison. For a time she was depressed, thinking that she had come west into a wide open country, only to find herself locked up more closely than ever.

An impulse came to her. She arose and going down three or four steps seated herself almost on a level with the ground.

Immediately she got a sense of release. She could not see over the corn but she could see under it. The corn had long wide leaves that met over the rows. The rows became long tunnels running away into infinity. Out of the black ground grew weeds that made a soft carpet of green. From above light sifted down. The corn rows were mysteriously beautiful. They were

warm passageways running out into life. She got up from the
steps and, walking timidly to the wire fence that separated her
from the field, put her hand between the wires and took hold
of one of the corn stalks. For some reason after she had
touched the strong young stalk and had held it for a moment
firmly in her hand she grew afraid. Running quickly back to
the step she sat down and covered her face with her hands.
Her body trembled. She tried to imagine herself crawling
through the fence and wandering along one of the passageways. The thought of trying the experiment fascinated but at
the same time terrified. She got quickly up and went into the
house.

One Saturday night in August Elsie found herself unable to
sleep. Thoughts, more definite than any she had ever known
before, came into her mind. It was a quiet hot night and her
bed stood near a window. Her room was the only one the Leanders occupied on the second floor of the house. At midnight
a little breeze came up from the south and when she sat up in
bed the floor of corn tassels lying below her line of sight looked
in the moonlight like the face of a sea just stirred by a gentle
breeze.

   A murmuring began in the corn and murmuring thoughts
and memories awoke in her mind. The long wide succulent
leaves had begun to dry in the intense heat of the August days
and as the wind stirred the corn they rubbed against each
other. A call, far away, as of a thousand voices arose. She imagined the voices were like the voices of children. They were not
like her brother Tom's children, noisy boisterous little animals,
but something quite different, tiny little things with large eyes
and thin sensitive hands. One after another they crept into her
arms. She became so excited over the fancy that she sat up in
bed and taking a pillow into her arms held it against her breast.
The figure of her cousin, the pale sensitive young Leander who
had lived with his father in New York City and who had died
at the age of twenty-three, came into her mind. It was as
though the young man had come suddenly into the room. She
dropped the pillow and sat waiting, intense, expectant.

   Young Harry Leander had come to visit his cousin on the
New England farm during the late summer of the year before

he died. He had stayed there for a month and almost every afternoon had gone with Elsie to sit by the rock at the back of the orchard. One afternoon when they had both been for a long time silent he began to talk. "I want to go live in the West," he said. "I want to go live in the West. I want to grow strong and be a man," he repeated. Tears came into his eyes.

They got up to return to the house, Elsie walking in silence beside the young man. The moment marked a high spot in her life. A strange trembling eagerness for something she had not realized in her experience of life had taken possession of her. They went in silence through the orchard but when they came to the bayberry bush her cousin stopped in the path and turned to face her. "I want you to kiss me," he said eagerly, stepping toward her.

A fluttering uncertainty had taken possession of Elsie and had been transmitted to her cousin. After he had made the sudden and unexpected demand and had stepped so close to her that his breath could be felt on her cheek, his own cheeks became scarlet and his hand that had taken her hand trembled. "Well, I wish I were strong. I only wish I were strong," he said hesitatingly and turning walked away along the path toward the house.

And in the strange new house, set like an island in its sea of corn, Harry Leander's voice seemed to arise again above the fancied voices of the children that had been coming out of the fields. Elsie got out of bed and walked up and down in the dim light coming through the window. Her body trembled violently. "I want you to kiss me," the voice said again and to quiet it and to quiet also the answering voice in herself she went to kneel by the bed and taking the pillow again into her arms pressed it against her face.

Tom Leander came with his wife and family to visit his father and mother on Sundays. The family appeared at about ten o'clock in the morning. When the wagon turned out of the road that ran past the Russell place Tom shouted. There was a field between the house and the road and the wagon could not be seen as it came along the narrow way through the corn. After Tom had shouted, his daughter Elizabeth, a tall girl of sixteen, jumped out of the wagon. All five children came tearing toward the house through the corn. A series of wild shouts arose on the still morning air.

The groceryman had brought food from the store. When the horse had been unhitched and put into a shed he and his wife began to carry packages into the house. The four Leander boys, accompanied by their sister, disappeared into the near-by fields. Three dogs that had trotted out from town under the wagon accompanied the children. Two or three children and occasionally a young man from a neighboring farm had come to join in the fun. Elsie's sister-in-law dismissed them all with a wave of her hand. With a wave of her hand she also brushed Elsie aside. Fires were lighted and the house reeked with the smell of cooking. Elsie went to sit on the step at the side of the house. The corn fields that had been so quiet rang with shouts and with the barking of dogs.

Tom Leander's oldest child, Elizabeth, was like her mother, full of energy. She was thin and tall like the women of her father's house but very strong and alive. In secret she wanted to be a lady but when she tried her brothers, led by her father and mother, made fun of her. "Don't put on airs," they said. When she got into the country with no one but her brothers and two or three neighboring farm boys she herself became a boy. With the boys she went tearing through the fields, following the dogs in pursuit of rabbits. Sometimes a young man came with the children from a near-by farm. Then she did not know what to do with herself. She wanted to walk demurely along the rows through the corn but was afraid her brothers would laugh and in desperation outdid the boys in roughness and noisiness. She screamed and shouted and running wildly tore her dress on the wire fences as she scrambled over in pursuit of the dogs. When a rabbit was caught and killed she rushed in and tore it out of the grasp of the dogs. The blood of the little dying animal dripped on her clothes. She swung it over her head and shouted.

The farm hand who had worked all summer in the field within sight of Elsie became enamoured of the young woman from town. When the groceryman's family appeared on Sunday mornings he also appeared but did not come to the house. When the boys and dogs came tearing through the fields he joined them. He also was self-conscious and did not want the boys to know the purpose of his coming and when he and Elizabeth found themselves alone together he became embarrassed. For a moment they walked together in silence. In a wide circle about them, in the forest of the corn, ran the boys and dogs. The young man had something he wanted to say, but when he tried to find words his tongue became thick and his lips felt hot and dry. "Well," he began, "let's you and me—"

Words failed him and Elizabeth turned and ran after her brothers and for the rest of the day he could not manage to get her out of their sight. When he went to join them she became the noisiest member of the party. A frenzy of activity took possession of her. With hair hanging down her back, with clothes torn and with cheeks and hands scratched and bleeding she led her brothers in the endless wild pursuit of the rabbits.

The Sunday in August that followed Elsie Leander's sleepless night was hot and cloudy. In the morning she was half ill and as soon as the visitors from town arrived she crept away to sit on the step at the side of the house. The children ran away into the fields. An almost overpowering desire to run with them, shouting and playing along the corn rows took possession of her. She arose and went to the back of the house. Her father was at work in the garden, pulling weeds from between rows of vegetables. Inside the house she could hear her sister-in-law moving about. On the front porch her brother Tom was asleep with his mother beside him. Elsie went back to the step and then arose and went to where the corn came down to the fence. She climbed awkwardly over and went a little way along one of the rows. Putting out her hand she touched the firm stalks and then, becoming afraid, dropped to her knees on the carpet of weeds that covered the ground. For a long time she stayed thus listening to the voices of the children in the distance.

An hour slipped away. Presently it was time for dinner and her sister-in-law came to the back door and shouted. There was an answering whoop from the distance and the children came running through the fields. They climbed over the fence and ran shouting across her father's garden. Elsie also arose. She was about to attempt to climb back over the fence unobserved when she heard a rustling in the corn. Young Elizabeth

Leander appeared. Beside her walked the ploughman who but a few months earlier had planted the corn in the field where Elsie now stood. She could see the two people coming slowly along the rows. An understanding had been established between them. The man reached through between the corn stalks and touched the hand of the girl who laughed awkwardly and running to the fence climbed quickly over. In her hand she held the limp body of a rabbit the dogs had killed.

The farm hand went away and when Elizabeth had gone into the house Elsie climbed over the fence. Her niece stood just within the kitchen door holding the dead rabbit by one leg. The other leg had been torn away by the dogs. At sight of the New England woman, who seemed to look at her with hard unsympathetic eyes, she was ashamed and went quickly into the house. She threw the rabbit upon a table in the parlor and then ran out of the room. Its blood ran out on the delicate flowers of a white crocheted table cover that had been made by Elsie's mother.

The Sunday dinner with all the living Leanders gathered about the table was gone through in a heavy lumbering silence. When the dinner was over and Tom and his wife had washed the dishes they went to sit with the older people on the front porch. Presently they were both asleep. Elsie returned to the step at the side of the house but when the desire to go again into the cornfields came sweeping over her she got up and went indoors.

The woman of thirty-five tip-toed about the big house like a frightened child. The dead rabbit that lay on the table in the parlour had become cold and stiff. Its blood had dried on the white table cover. She went upstairs but did not go to her own room. A spirit of adventure had hold of her. In the upper part of the house there were many rooms and in some of them no glass had been put into the windows. The windows had been boarded up and narrow streaks of light crept in through the cracks between the boards.

Elsie tip-toed up the flight of stairs past the room in which she slept and opening doors went into other rooms. Dust lay thick on the floors. In the silence she could hear her brother snoring as he slept in the chair on the front porch. From what seemed a far away place there came the shrill cries of the children. The cries became soft. They were like the cries of unborn children that had called to her out of the fields on the night before.

Into her mind came the intense silent figure of her mother sitting on the porch beside her son and waiting for the day to wear itself out into night. The thought brought a lump into her throat. She wanted something and did not know what it was. Her own mood frightened her. In a windowless room at the back of the house one of the boards over a window had been broken and a bird had flown in and become imprisoned.

The presence of the woman frightened the bird. It flew wildly about. Its beating wings stirred up dust that danced in the air. Elsie stood perfectly still, also frightened, not by the presence of the bird but by the presence of life. Like the bird she was a prisoner. The thought gripped her. She wanted to go outdoors where her niece Elizabeth walked with the young ploughman through the corn, but was like the bird in the room —a prisoner. She moved restlessly about. The bird flew back and forth across the room. It alighted on the window sill near the place where the board was broken away. She stared into the frightened eyes of the bird that in turn stared into her eyes. Then the bird flew away, out through the window, and Elsie turned and ran nervously downstairs and out into the yard. She climbed over the wire fence and ran with stooped shoulders along one of the tunnels.

Elsie ran into the vastness of the cornfields filled with but one desire. She wanted to get out of her life and into some new and sweeter life she felt must be hidden away somewhere in the fields. After she had run a long way she came to a wire fence and crawled over. Her hair became unloosed and fell down over her shoulders. Her cheeks became flushed and for the moment she looked like a young girl. When she climbed over the fence she tore a great hole in the front of her dress. For a moment her tiny breasts were exposed and then her hand clutched and held nervously the sides of the tear. In the distance she could hear the voices of the boys and the barking of the dogs. A summer storm had been threatening for days and now black clouds had begun to spread themselves over the sky. As she ran nervously forward, stopping to listen and then running on again, the dry corn blades brushed against her shoulders and a fine shower of yellow dust from the corn tassels fell on her hair. A continued crackling noise accompanied her progress. The dust made a golden crown about her head. From the sky overhead a low rumbling sound, like the growling of giant dogs, came to her ears.

The thought that having at last ventured into the corn she would never escape became fixed in the mind of the running woman. Sharp pains shot through her body. Presently she was compelled to stop and sit on the ground. For a long time she sat with closed eyes. Her dress became soiled. Little insects that live in the ground under the corn came out of their holes and crawled over her legs.

Following some obscure impulse the tired woman threw herself on her back and lay still with closed eyes. Her fright passed. It was warm and close in the room-like tunnels. The pain in her side went away. She opened her eyes and between the wide green corn blades could see patches of a black threatening sky. She did not want to be alarmed and so closed her eyes again. Her thin hand no longer gripped the tear in her dress and her little breasts were exposed. They expanded and contracted in spasmodic jerks. She threw her hands back over her head and lay still.

It seemed to Elsie that hours passed as she lay thus, quiet and passive under the corn. Deep within her there was a feeling that something was about to happen, something that would lift her out of herself, that would tear her away from her past and the past of her people. Her thoughts were not definite. She lay still and waited as she had waited for days and months by the rock at the back of the orchard on the Vermont farm when she was a girl. A deep grumbling noise went on in the sky overhead but the sky and everything she had ever known seemed very far away, no part of herself.

After a long silence, when it seemed to her that she had gone out of herself as in a dream, Elsie heard a man's voice calling. "Aho, aho, aho," shouted the voice and after another period of silence there arose answering voices and then the sound of bodies crashing through the corn and the excited chatter of children. A dog came running along the row where she lay and stood beside her. His cold nose touched her face and she sat up. The dog ran away. The Leander boys passed. She could see their bare legs flashing in and out across one of the tunnels. Her brother had become alarmed by the rapid approach of the thunder storm and wanted to get his family to town. His voice kept calling from the house and the voices of the children answered from the fields.

Elsie sat on the ground with her hands pressed together. An odd feeling of disappointment had possession of her. She arose and walked slowly along in the general direction taken by the children. She came to a fence and crawled over, tearing her dress in a new place. One of her stockings had become un-loosed and had slipped down over her shoe top. The long sharp weeds had scratched her leg so that it was criss-crossed with red lines, but she was not conscious of any pain.

The distraught woman followed the children until she came within sight of her father's house and then stopped and again sat on the ground. There was another loud crash of thunder and Tom Leander's voice called again, this time half angrily. The name of the girl Elizabeth was shouted in loud masculine tones that rolled and echoed like the thunder along the aisles under the corn.

And then Elizabeth came into sight accompanied by the young ploughman. They stopped near Elsie and the man took the girl into his arms. At the sound of their approach Elsie had thrown herself face downward on the ground and had twisted herself into a position where she could see without being seen. When their lips met her tense hands grasped one of the corn stalks. Her lips pressed themselves into the dust. When they had gone on their way she raised her head. A dusty powder covered her lips.

What seemed another long period of silence fell over the fields. The murmuring voices of unborn children, her imagina-tion had created in the whispering fields, became a vast shout. The wind blew harder and harder. The corn stalks were twisted and bent. Elizabeth went thoughtfully out of the field and climbing the fence confronted her father. "Where you been? What you been a doing?" he asked. "Don't you think we got to get out of here?"

When Elizabeth went toward the house Elsie followed, creeping on her hands and knees like a little animal, and when she had come within sight of the fence surrounding the house she sat on the ground and put her hands over her face. Something within herself was being twisted and whirled about as the tops of the corn stalks were now being twisted and whirled by the wind. She sat so that she did not look toward the house and when she opened her eyes she could again see along the long mysterious aisles.

Her brother with his wife and children went away. By turning her head Elsie could see them driving at a trot out of the yard back of her father's house. With the going of the younger woman the farm house in the midst of the cornfield rocked by the winds seemed the most desolate place in the world.

Her mother came out at the back door of the house. She ran to the steps where she knew her daughter was in the habit of sitting and then in alarm began to call. It did not occur to Elsie to answer. The voice of the older woman did not seem to have anything to do with herself. It was a thin voice and was quickly lost in the wind and in the crashing sound that arose out of the fields. With her head turned toward the house Elsie stared at her mother who ran wildly around the house and then went indoors. The back door of the house went shut with a bang.

The storm that had been threatening broke with a roar. Broad sheets of water swept over the cornfields. Sheets of water swept over the woman's body. The storm that had for years been gathering in her also broke. Sobs arose out of her throat. She abandoned herself to a storm of grief that was only partially grief. Tears ran out of her eyes and made little furrows through the dust on her face. In the lulls that occasionally came in the storm she raised her head and heard, through the tangled mass of wet hair that covered her ears and above the sound of millions of rain-drops that alighted on the earthen floor inside the house of the corn, the thin voices of her mother and father calling to her out of the Leander house.

War

THE story came to me from a woman met on a train. The car was crowded and I took the seat beside her. There was a man in the offing who belonged with her—a slender girlish figure of a man in a heavy brown canvas coat such as teamsters wear in the winter. He moved up and down in the aisle of the car, wanting my place by the woman's side, but I did not know that at the time.

The woman had a heavy face and a thick nose. Something had happened to her. She had been struck a blow or had a fall. Nature could never have made a nose so broad and thick and ugly. She had talked to me in very good English. I suspect now that she was temporarily weary of the man in the brown canvas coat, that she had travelled with him for days, perhaps weeks, and was glad of the chance to spend a few hours in the company of some one else.

Everyone knows the feeling of a crowded train in the middle of the night. We ran along through western Iowa and eastern Nebraska. It had rained for days and the fields were flooded. In the clear night the moon came out and the scene outside the car-window was strange and in an odd way very beautiful. You get the feeling: the black bare trees standing up in clusters as they do out in that country, the pools of water with the moon reflected and running quickly as it does when the train hurries along, the rattle of the car-trucks, the lights in isolated farmhouses, and occasionally the clustered lights of a town as the train rushed through it into the west.

The woman had just come out of war-ridden Poland, had got out of that stricken land with her lover by God knows what miracles of effort. She made me feel the war, that woman did, and she told me the tale that I want to tell you.

I do not remember the beginning of our talk, nor can I tell you of how the strangeness of my mood grew to match her mood until the story she told became a part of the mystery of the still night outside the car-window and very pregnant with meaning to me.

There was a company of Polish refugees moving along a

road in Poland in charge of a German. The German was a man of perhaps fifty, with a beard. As I got him, he was much such a man as might be professor of foreign languages in a college in our country, say at Des Moines, Iowa, or Springfield, Ohio. He would be sturdy and strong of body and given to the eating of rather rank foods, as such men are. Also he would be a fellow of books and in his thinking inclined toward the ranker philosophies. He was dragged into the war because he was a German, and he had steeped his soul in the German philosophy of might. Faintly, I fancy, there was another notion in his head that kept bothering him, and so to serve his government with a whole heart he read books that would re-establish his feeling for the strong, terrible thing for which he fought. Because he was past fifty he was not on the battle line, but was in charge of the refugees, taking them out of their destroyed village to a camp near a railroad where they could be fed.

The refugees were peasants, all except the woman in the American train with me, her lover and her mother, an old woman of sixty-five. They had been small landowners and the others in their party had worked on their estate.

Along a country road in Poland went this party in charge of the German who tramped heavily along, urging them forward. He was brutal in his insistence, and the old woman of sixty-five, who was a kind of leader of the refugees, was almost equally brutal in her constant refusal to go forward. In the rainy night she stopped in the muddy road and her party gathered about her. Like a stubborn horse she shook her head and muttered Polish words. "I want to be let alone, that's what I want. All I want in the world is to be let alone," she said, over and over; and then the German came up and putting his hand on her back pushed her along, so that their progress through the dismal night was a constant repetition of the stopping, her muttered words, and his pushing. They hated each other with whole-hearted hatred, that old Polish woman and the German.

The party came to a clump of trees on the bank of a shallow stream and the German took hold of the old woman's arm and dragged her through the stream while the others followed. Over and over she said the words: "I want to be let alone. All I want in the world is to be let alone."

In the clump of trees the German started a fire. With

incredible efficiency he had it blazing high in a few minutes, taking the matches and even some bits of dry wood from a little rubber-lined pouch carried in his inside coat pocket. Then he got out tobacco and, sitting down on the protruding root of a tree, smoked and stared at the refugees, clustered about the old woman on the opposite side of the fire.

The German went to sleep. That was what started his trouble. He slept for an hour and when he awoke the refugees were gone. You can imagine him jumping up and tramping heavily back through the shallow stream and along the muddy road to gather his party together again. He would be angry through and through, but he would not be alarmed. It was only a matter, he knew, of going far enough back along the road as one goes back along a road for strayed cattle.

And then, when the German came up to the party, he and the old woman began to fight. She stopped muttering the words about being let alone and sprang at him. One of her old hands gripped his beard and the other buried itself in the thick skin of his neck.

The struggle in the road lasted a long time. The German was tired and not as strong as he looked, and there was that faint thing in him that kept him from hitting the old woman with his fist. He took hold of her thin shoulders and pushed, and she pulled. The struggle was like a man trying to lift himself by his boot straps. The two fought and were full of the determination that will not stop fighting, but they were not very strong physically.

And so their two souls began to struggle. The woman in the train made me understand that quite clearly, although it may be difficult to get the sense of it over to you. I had the night and the mystery of the moving train to help me. It was a physical thing, the fight of the two souls in the dim light of the rainy night on that deserted muddy road. The air was full of the struggle and the refugees gathered about and stood shivering. They shivered with cold and weariness, of course, but also with something else. In the air everywhere about them they could feel the vague something going on. The woman said that she would gladly have given her life to have it stopped, or to have someone strike a light, and that her man felt the same way. It was like two winds struggling, she said, like a soft yielding cloud become hard and trying vainly to push another cloud out of the sky.

Then the struggle ended and the old woman and the German fell down exhausted in the road. The refugees gathered about and waited. They thought something more was going to happen, knew in fact something more would happen. The feeling they had persisted, you see, and they huddled together and perhaps whimpered a little.

What happened is the whole point of the story. The woman in the train explained it very clearly. She said that the two souls, after struggling, went back into the two bodies, but that the soul of the old woman went into the body of the German and the soul of the German into the body of the old woman.

After that, of course, everything was quite simple. The German sat down by the road and began shaking his head and saying he wanted to be let alone, declared that all he wanted in the world was to be let alone, and the Polish woman took papers out of his pocket and began driving her companions back along the road, driving them harshly and brutally along, and when they grew weary pushing them with her hands.

There was more of the story after that. The woman's lover, who had been a school-teacher, took the papers and got out of the country, taking his sweetheart with him. But my mind has forgotten the details. I only remember the German sitting by the road and muttering that he wanted to be let alone, and the old tired mother-in-Poland saying the harsh words and forcing her weary companions to march through the night back into their own country.

Motherhood

BELOW the hill there was a swamp in which cattails grew. The wind rustled the dry leaves of a walnut tree that grew on top of the hill.

She went beyond the tree to where the grass was long and matted. In the farmhouse a door banged and in the road before the house a dog barked.

For a long time there was no sound. Then a wagon came jolting and bumping over the frozen road. The little noises ran along the ground to where she was lying on the grass and seemed like fingers playing over her body. A fragrance arose from her. It took a long time for the wagon to pass.

Then another sound broke the stillness. A young man from a neighboring farm came stealthily across a field and climbed a fence. He also came to the hill but for a time did not see her lying almost at his feet. He looked toward the house and stood with hands in pockets, stamping on the frozen ground like a horse.

Then he knew she was there. The aroma of her crept into his consciousness.

He ran to kneel beside her silent figure. Everything was different than it had been when they crept to the hill on the other evenings. The time of talking and waiting was over. She was different. He grew bold and put his hands on her face, her neck, her breasts, her hips. There was a strange new firmness and hardness in her body. When he kissed her lips she did not move and for a moment he was afraid. Then courage came and he went down to lie with her.

He had been a farm boy all his life and had plowed many acres of rich black land.

He became sure of himself.

He plowed her deeply.

He planted the seeds of a son in the warm rich quivering soil.

She carried the seeds of a son within herself. On winter evenings she went along a path at the foot of a small hill and turned up the hill to a barn where she milked cows. She was large and strong. Her legs went swinging along. The son within her went swinging along.

He learned the rhythm of little hills.

He learned the rhythm of flat places.

He learned the rhythm of legs walking.

He learned the rhythm of firm strong hands pulling at the teats of cows.

There was a field that was barren and filled with stones. In the spring when the warm nights came and when she was big with him she went to the fields. The heads of little stones stuck out of the ground like the heads of buried children. The field, washed with moonlight, sloped gradually downward to a murmuring brook. A few sheep went among the stones nibbling the sparse grass.

A thousand children were buried in the barren field. They struggled to come out of the ground. They struggled to come to her. The brook ran over stones and its voice cried out. For a long time she stayed in the field, shaken with sorrow.

She arose from her seat on a large stone and went to the farmhouse. The voices of the darkness cried to her as she went along a lane and past a silent barn.

Within herself only the one child struggled. When she got into bed his heels beat upon the walls of his prison. She lay still and listened. Only one small voice seemed coming to her out of the silence of the night.

Out of Nowhere into Nothing

I

ROSALIND WESCOTT, a tall strong looking woman of twenty-seven, was walking on the railroad track near the town of Willow Springs, Iowa. It was about four in the afternoon of a day in August, and the third day since she had come home to her native town from Chicago, where she was employed.

At that time Willow Springs was a town of about three thousand people. It has grown since. There was a public square with the town hall in the centre and about the four sides of the square and facing it were the merchandising establishments. The public square was bare and grassless, and out of it ran streets of frame houses, long straight streets that finally became country roads running away into the flat prairie country.

Although she had told everyone that she had merely come home for a short visit because she was a little homesick, and although she wanted in particular to have a talk with her mother in regard to a certain matter, Rosalind had been unable to talk with anyone. Indeed she had found it difficult to stay in the house with her mother and father and all the time, day and night, she was haunted by a desire to get out of town. As she went along the railroad tracks in the hot afternoon sunshine she kept scolding herself. "I've grown moody and no good. If I want to do it why don't I just go ahead and not make a fuss," she thought.

For two miles the railroad tracks, eastward out of Willow Springs, went through corn fields on a flat plain. Then there was a little dip in the land and a bridge over Willow Creek. The Creek was altogether dry now but trees grew along the edge of the grey streak of cracked mud that in the fall, winter and spring would be the bed of the stream. Rosalind left the tracks and went to sit under one of the trees. Her cheeks were flushed and her forehead wet. When she took off her hat her hair fell down in disorder and strands of it clung to her hot wet face. She sat in what seemed a kind of great bowl on the sides of which the corn grew rank. Before her and following the bed of the stream there was a dusty path along which cows came at evening from distant pastures. A great pancake formed of cow dung lay nearby. It was covered with grey dust and over it crawled shiny black beetles. They were rolling the dung into balls in preparation for the germination of a new generation of beetles.

Rosalind had come on the visit to her home town at a time of the year when everyone wished to escape from the hot dusty place. No one had expected her and she had not written to announce her coming. One hot morning in Chicago she had got out of bed and had suddenly begun packing her bag, and on that same evening there she was in Willow Springs, in the house where she had lived until her twenty-first year, among her own people. She had come up from the station in the hotel bus and had walked into the Wescott house unannounced. Her father was at the pump by the kitchen door and her mother came into the living room to greet her wearing a soiled kitchen apron. Everything in the house was just as it always had been. "I just thought I would come home for a few days," she said, putting down her bag and kissing her mother.

Ma and Pa Wescott had been glad to see their daughter. On the evening of her arrival they were excited and a special supper was prepared. After supper Pa Wescott went up town as usual, but he stayed only a few minutes. "I just want to run to the postoffice and get the evening paper," he said apologetically. Rosalind's mother put on a clean dress and they all sat in the darkness on the front porch. There was talk, of a kind. "Is it hot in Chicago now? I'm going to do a good deal of canning this fall. I thought later I would send you a box of canned fruit. Do you live in the same place on the North Side? It must be nice in the evening to be able to walk down to the park by the lake."

Rosalind sat under the tree near the railroad bridge two miles from Willow Springs and watched the tumble bugs at work. Her whole body was hot from the walk in the sun and the thin dress she wore clung to her legs. It was being soiled by the dust on the grass under the tree.

She had run away from town and from her mother's house.

All during the three days of her visit she had been doing that. She did not go from house to house to visit her old schoolgirl friends, the girls who unlike herself had stayed in Willow Springs, had got married and settled down there. When she saw one of these women on the street in the morning, pushing a baby carriage and perhaps followed by a small child, she stopped. There was a few minutes of talk. "It's hot. Do you live in the same place in Chicago? My husband and I hope to take the children and go away for a week or two. It must be nice in Chicago where you are so near the lake." Rosalind hurried away.

All the hours of her visit to her mother and to her home town had been spent in an effort to hurry away.

From what? Rosalind defended herself. There was something she had come from Chicago hoping to be able to say to her mother. Did she really want to talk with her about things? Had she thought, by again breathing the air of her home town, to get strength to face life and its difficulties?

There was no point in her taking the hot uncomfortable trip from Chicago only to spend her days walking in dusty country roads or between rows of cornfields in the stifling heat along the railroad tracks.

"I must have hoped. There is a hope that cannot be fulfilled," she thought vaguely.

Willow Springs was a rather meaningless, dreary town, one of thousands of such towns in Indiana, Illinois, Wisconsin, Kansas, Iowa, but her mind made it more dreary.

She sat under the tree by the dry bed of Willow Creek thinking of the street in town where her mother and father lived, where she had lived until she had become a woman. It was only because of a series of circumstances she did not live there now. Her one brother, ten years older than herself, had married and moved to Chicago. He had asked her to come for a visit and after she got to the city she stayed. Her brother was a traveling salesman and spent a good deal of time away from home. "Why don't you stay here with Bess and learn stenography," he asked. "If you don't want to use it you don't have to. Dad can look out for you all right. I just thought you might like to learn."

"That was six years ago," Rosalind thought wearily. "I've been a city woman for six years." Her mind hopped about. Thoughts came and went. In the city, after she became a stenographer, something for a time awakened her. She wanted to be an actress and went in the evening to a dramatic school. In an office where she worked there was a young man, a clerk. They went out together, to the theatre or to walk in the park in the evening. They kissed.

Her thoughts came sharply back to her mother and father, to her home in Willow Springs, to the street in which she had lived until her twenty-first year.

It was but an end of a street. From the windows at the front of her mother's house six other houses could be seen. How well she knew the street and the people in the houses! Did she know them? From her eighteenth and until her twenty-first year she had stayed at home, helping her mother with the housework, waiting for something. Other young women in town waited just as she did. They like herself had graduated from the town highschool and their parents had no intention of sending them away to college. There was nothing to do but wait. Some of the young women—their mothers and their mothers' friends still spoke of them as girls—had young men friends who came to see them on Sunday and perhaps also on Wednesday or Thursday evenings. Others joined the church, went to prayer meetings, became active members of some church organization. They fussed about.

Rosalind had done none of these things. All through those three trying years in Willow Springs she had just waited. In the morning there was the work to do in the house and then, in some way, the day wore itself away. In the evening her father went up town and she sat with her mother. Nothing much was said. After she had gone to bed she lay awake, strangely nervous, eager for something to happen that never would happen. The noises of the Wescott house cut across her thoughts. What things went through her mind!

There was a procession of people always going away from her. Sometimes she lay on her belly at the edge of a ravine. Well it was not a ravine. It had two walls of marble and on the marble face of the walls strange figures were carved. Broad steps led down—always down and away. People walked along the steps, between the marble walls, going down and away from her.

What people! Who were they? Where did they come from? Where were they going? She was not asleep but wide awake. Her bedroom was dark. The walls and ceiling of the room receded. She seemed to hang suspended in space, above the ravine —the ravine with walls of white marble over which strange beautiful lights played.

The people who went down the broad steps and away into infinite distance—they were men and women. Sometime a young girl like herself but in some way sweeter and purer than herself, passed alone. The young girl walked with a swinging stride, going swiftly and freely like a beautiful young animal. Her legs and arms were like the slender top branches of trees swaying in a gentle wind. She also went down and away.

Others followed along the marble steps. Young boys walked alone. A dignified old man followed by a sweet faced woman passed. What a remarkable man! One felt infinite power in his old frame. There were deep wrinkles in his face and his eyes were sad. One felt he knew everything about life but had kept something very precious alive in himself. It was that precious thing that made the eyes of the woman who followed him burn with a strange fire. They also went down along the steps and away.

Down and away along the steps went others—how many others, men and women, boys and girls, single old men, old women who leaned on sticks and hobbled along.

In the bed in her father's house as she lay awake Rosalind's head grew light. She tried to clutch at something, understand something.

She couldn't. The noises of the house cut across her waking dream. Her father was at the pump by the kitchen door. He was pumping a pail of water. In a moment he would bring it into the house and put it on a box by the kitchen sink. A little of the water would slop over on the floor. There would be a sound like a child's bare foot striking the floor. Then her father would go to wind the clock. The day was done. Presently there would be the sound of his heavy feet on the floor of the bedroom above and he would get into bed to lie beside Rosalind's mother.

The night noises of her father's house had been in some way terrible to the girl in the years when she was becoming a woman. After chance had taken her to the city she never wanted to think of them again. Even in Chicago where the silence of nights was cut and slashed by a thousand noises, by automobiles whirling through the streets, by the belated footsteps of men homeward bound along the cement sidewalks after midnight, by the shouts of quarreling men drunk on summer nights, even in the great hubbub of noises there was comparative quiet. The insistent clanging noises of the city nights were not like the homely insistent noises of her father's house. Certain terrible truths about life did not abide in them, they did not cling so closely to life and did not frighten as did the noises in the one house on the quiet street in the town of Willow Springs. How often, there in the city, in the midst of the great noises she had fought to escape the little noises! Her father's feet were on the steps leading into the kitchen. Now he was putting the pail of water on the box by the kitchen sink. Upstairs her mother's body fell heavily into bed. The visions of the great marble-lined ravine down along which went the beautiful people flew away. There was the little slap of water on the kitchen floor. It was like a child's bare foot striking the floor. Rosalind wanted to cry out. Her father closed the kitchen door. Now he was winding the clock. In a moment his feet would be on the stairs—

There were six houses to be seen from the windows of the Wescott house. In the winter smoke from six brick chimneys went up into the sky. There was one house, the next one to the Wescott's place, a small frame affair, in which lived a man who was thirty-five years old when Rosalind became a woman of twenty-one and went away to the city. The man was unmarried and his mother, who had been his housekeeper, had died during the year in which Rosalind graduated from the high school. After that the man lived alone. He took his dinner and supper at the hotel, down town on the square, but he got his own breakfast, made his own bed and swept out his own house. Sometimes he walked slowly along the street past the Wescott house when Rosalind sat alone on the front porch. He raised his hat and spoke to her. Their eyes met. He had a long, hawk-like nose and his hair was long and uncombed.

Rosalind thought about him sometimes. It bothered her a little that he sometimes went stealing softly, as though not to disturb her, across her daytime fancies.

As she sat that day by the dry creek bed Rosalind thought about the bachelor, who had now passed the age of forty and who lived on the street where she had lived during her girlhood. His house was separated from the Wescott house by a picket fence. Sometimes in the morning he forgot to pull his blinds and Rosalind, busy with the housework in her father's house, had seen him walking about in his underwear. It was—uh, one could not think of it.

The man's name was Melville Stoner. He had a small income and did not have to work. On some days he did not leave his house and go to the hotel for his meals but sat all day in a chair with his nose buried in a book.

There was a house on the street occupied by a widow who raised chickens. Two or three of her hens were what the people who lived on the street called 'high flyers.' They flew over the fence of the chicken yard and escaped and almost always they came at once into the yard of the bachelor. The neighbors laughed about it. It was significant, they felt. When the hens had come into the yard of the bachelor, Stoner, the widow with a stick in her hand ran after them. Melville Stoner came out of his house and stood on a little porch in front. The widow ran through the front gate waving her arms wildly and the hens made a great racket and flew over the fence. They ran down the street toward the widow's house. For a moment she stood by the Stoner gate. In the summer time when the windows of the Wescott house were open Rosalind could hear what the man and woman said to each other. In Willow Springs it was not thought proper for an unmarried woman to stand talking to an unmarried man near the door of his bachelor establishment. The widow wanted to observe the conventions. Still she did linger a moment, her bare arm resting on the gate post. What bright eager little eyes she had! "If those hens of mine bother you I wish you would catch them and kill them," she said fiercely. "I am always glad to see them coming along the road," Melville Stoner replied, bowing. Rosalind thought he was making fun of the widow. She liked him for that. "I'd never see you if you did not have to come here after your hens. Don't let anything happen to them," he said, bowing again.

For a moment the man and woman lingered looking into each other's eyes. From one of the windows of the Wescott house Rosalind watched the woman. Nothing more was said. There was something about the woman she had not understood —well the widow's senses were being fed. The developing woman in the house next door had hated her.

Rosalind jumped up from under the tree and climbed up the railroad embankment. She thanked the gods she had been lifted out of the life of the town of Willow Springs and that chance had set her down to live in a city. "Chicago is far from beautiful. People say it is just a big noisy dirty village and per-haps that's what it is, but there is something alive there," she thought. In Chicago, or at least during the last two or three years of her life there, Rosalind felt she had learned a little something of life. She had read books for one thing, such books as did not come to Willow Springs, books that Willow Springs knew nothing about, she had gone to hear the Sym-phony Orchestra, she had begun to understand something of the possibility of line and color, had heard intelligent, under-standing men speak of these things. In Chicago, in the midst of the twisting squirming millions of men and women there were voices. One occasionally saw men or at least heard of the existence of men who, like the beautiful old man who had walked away down the marble stairs in the vision of her girl-hood nights, had kept some precious thing alive in themselves.

And there was something else—it was the most important thing of all. For the last two years of her life in Chicago she had spent hours, days in the presence of a man to whom she could talk. The talks had awakened her. She felt they had made her a woman, had matured her.

"I know what these people here in Willow Springs are like and what I would have been like had I stayed here," she thought. She felt relieved and almost happy. She had come home at a crisis of her own life hoping to be able to talk a little with her mother, or if talk proved impossible hoping to get some sense of sisterhood by being in her presence. She had thought there was something buried away, deep within every woman, that at a certain call would run out to other women. Now she felt that the hope, the dream, the desire she had cherished was altogether futile. Sitting in the great flat bowl in the midst of the corn lands two miles from her home town where no breath of air stirred and seeing the beetles at their work of preparing to propagate a new generation of beetles, while she thought of the town and its people, had settled something for her. Her visit to Willow Springs had come to something after all.

Rosalind's figure had still much of the spring and swing of youth in it. Her legs were strong and her shoulders broad. She went swinging along the railroad track toward town, going westward. The sun had begun to fall rapidly down the sky. Away over the tops of the corn in one of the great fields she could see in the distance to where a man was driving a motor along a dusty road. The wheels of the car kicked up dust through which the sunlight played. The floating cloud of dust became a shower of gold that settled down over the fields. "When a woman most wants what is best and truest in another woman, even in her own mother, she isn't likely to find it," she thought grimly. "There are certain things every woman has to find out for herself, there is a road she must travel alone. It may only lead to some more ugly and terrible place, but if she doesn't want death to overtake her and live within her while her body is still alive she must set out on that road."

Rosalind walked for a mile along the railroad track and then stopped. A freight train had gone eastward as she sat under the tree by the creek bed and now, there beside the tracks, in the grass was the body of a man. It lay still, the face buried in the deep burned grass. At once she concluded the man had been struck and killed by the train. The body had been thrown thus aside. All her thoughts went away and she turned and started to tiptoe away, stepping carefully along the railroad ties, making no noise. Then she stopped again. The man in the grass might not be dead, only hurt, terribly hurt. It would not do to leave him there. She imagined him mutilated but still struggling for life and herself trying to help him. She crept back along the ties. The man's legs were not twisted and beside him lay his hat. It was as though he had put it there before lying down to sleep, but a man did not sleep with his face buried in the grass in such a hot uncomfortable place. She drew nearer. "O, you Mister," she called, "O, you—are you hurt?"

The man in the grass sat up and looked at her. He laughed.

It was Melville Stoner, the man of whom she had just been thinking and in thinking of whom she had come to certain settled conclusions regarding the futility of her visit to Willow Springs. He got to his feet and picked up his hat. "Well, hello, Miss Rosalind Wescott," he said heartily. He climbed a small embankment and stood beside her. "I knew you were at home on a visit but what are you doing out here?" he asked and then added, "What luck this is! Now I shall have the privilege of walking home with you. You can hardly refuse to let me walk with you after shouting at me like that."

They walked together along the tracks he with his hat in his hand. Rosalind thought he looked like a gigantic bird, an aged wise old bird, "perhaps a vulture" she thought. For a time he was silent and then he began to talk, explaining his lying with his face buried in the grass. There was a twinkle in his eyes and Rosalind wondered if he was laughing at her as she had seen him laugh at the widow who owned the hens.

He did not come directly to the point and Rosalind thought it strange that they should walk and talk together. At once his words interested her. He was so much older than herself and no doubt wiser. How vain she had been to think herself so much more knowing than all the people of Willow Springs. Here was this man and he was talking and his talk did not sound like anything she had ever expected to hear from the lips of a native of her home town. "I want to explain myself but we'll wait a little. For years I've been wanting to get at you, to talk with you, and this is my chance. You've been away now five or six years and have grown into womanhood.

"You understand it's nothing specially personal, my wanting to get at you and understand you a little," he added quickly. "I'm that way about everyone. Perhaps that's the reason I live alone, why I've never married or had personal friends. I'm too eager. It isn't comfortable to others to have me about."

Rosalind was caught up by this new view point of the man. She wondered. In the distance along the tracks the houses of the town came into sight. Melville Stoner tried to walk on one of the iron rails but after a few steps lost his balance and fell off. His long arms whirled about. A strange intensity of mood and feeling had come over Rosalind. In one moment Melville Stoner was like an old man and then he was like a boy. Being with him made her mind, that had been racing all afternoon, race faster than ever.

When he began to talk again he seemed to have forgotten the explanation he had intended making. "We've lived side by side but we've hardly spoken to each other," he said. "When I was a young man and you were a girl I used to sit in the house thinking of you. We've really been friends. What I mean is we've had the same thoughts."

He began to speak of life in the city where she had been living, condemning it. "It's dull and stupid here but in the city you have your own kind of stupidity too," he declared. "I'm glad I do not live there."

In Chicago when she had first gone there to live a thing had sometimes happened that had startled Rosalind. She knew no one but her brother and his wife and was sometimes very lonely. When she could no longer bear the eternal sameness of the talk in her brother's house she went out to a concert or to the theatre. Once or twice when she had no money to buy a theatre ticket she grew bold and walked alone in the streets, going rapidly along without looking to the right or left. As she sat in the theatre or walked in the street an odd thing sometimes happened. Someone spoke her name, a call came to her. The thing happened at a concert and she looked quickly about. All the faces in sight had that peculiar, half bored, half expectant expression one grows accustomed to seeing on the faces of people listening to music. In the entire theatre no one seemed aware of her. On the street or in the park the call had come when she was utterly alone. It seemed to come out of the air, from behind a tree in the park.

And now as she walked on the railroad tracks with Melville Stoner the call seemed to come from him. He walked along apparently absorbed with his own thoughts, the thoughts he was trying to find words to express. His legs were long and he walked with a queer loping gait. The idea of some great bird, perhaps a sea-bird stranded far inland, stayed in Rosalind's mind but the call did not come from the bird part of him. There was something else, another personality hidden away. Rosalind fancied the call came this time from a young boy, from such another clear-eyed boy as she had once seen in her waking dreams at night in her father's house, from one of the boys who walked on the marble stairway, walked down and away. A thought came that startled her. "The boy is hidden away in the body of this strange bird-like man," she told herself. The thought awoke fancies within her. It explained much in the lives of men and women. An expression, a phrase, remembered from her childhood when she had gone to Sunday School in Willow Springs, came back to her mind. "And God spoke to me out of a burning bush." She almost said the words aloud.

Melville Stoner loped along, walking on the railroad ties and talking. He seemed to have forgotten the incident of his lying with his nose buried in the grass and was explaining his life lived alone in the house in town. Rosalind tried to put her own thoughts aside and to listen to his words but did not succeed very well. "I came home here hoping to get a little closer to life, to get, for a few days, out of the company of a man so I could think about him. I fancied I could get what I wanted by being near mother, but that hasn't worked. It would be strange if I got what I am looking for by this chance meeting with another man," she thought. Her mind went on recording thoughts. She heard the spoken words of the man beside her but her own mind went on, also making words. Something within herself felt suddenly relaxed and free. Ever since she had got off the train at Willow Springs three days before there had been a great tenseness. Now it was all gone. She looked at Melville Stoner who occasionally looked at her. There was something in his eyes, a kind of laughter—a mocking kind of laughter. His eyes were grey, of a cold greyness, like the eyes of a bird.

"It has come into my mind—I have been thinking—well you see you have not married in the six years since you went to live in the city. It would be strange and a little amusing if you are like myself, if you cannot marry or come close to any other person," he was saying.

Again he spoke of the life he led in his house. "I sometimes sit in my house all day, even when the weather is fine outside," he said. "You have no doubt seen me sitting there. Sometimes I forget to eat. I read books all day, striving to forget myself and then night comes and I cannot sleep.

"If I could write or paint or make music, if I cared at all

about expressing what goes on in my mind it would be different. However, I would not write as others do. I would have
but little to say about what people do. What do they do? In
what way does it matter? Well you see they build cities such as
you live in and towns like Willow Springs, they have built this
railroad track on which we are walking, they marry and raise
children, commit murders, steal, do kindly acts. What does it
matter? You see we are walking here in the hot sun. In five
minutes more we will be in town and you will go to your house
and I to mine. You will eat supper with your father and mother.
Then your father will go up town and you and your mother
will sit together on the front porch. There will be little said.
Your mother will speak of her intention to can fruit. Then your
father will come home and you will all go to bed. Your father
will pump a pail of water at the pump by the kitchen door. He
will carry it indoors and put it on a box by the kitchen sink. A
little of the water will be spilled. It will make a soft little slap on
the kitchen floor—"

"Ha!"

Melville Stoner turned and looked sharply at Rosalind who
had grown a little pale. Her mind raced madly, like an engine
out of control. There was a kind of power in Melville Stoner
that frightened her. By the recital of a few commonplace facts
he had suddenly invaded her secret places. It was almost as
though he had come into the bedroom in her father's house
where she lay thinking. He had in fact got into her bed. He
laughed again, an unmirthful laugh. "I'll tell you what, we
know little enough here in America, either in the towns or in
the cities," he said rapidly. "We are all on the rush. We are all
for action. I sit still and think. If I wanted to write I'd do
something. I'd tell what everyone thought. It would startle
people, frighten them a little, eh? I would tell you what you
have been thinking this afternoon while you walked here on
this railroad track with me. I would tell you what your mother
has been thinking at the same time and what she would like to
say to you."

Rosalind's face had grown chalky white and her hands
trembled. They got off the railroad tracks and into the streets
of Willow Springs. A change came over Melville Stoner. Of a
sudden he seemed just a man of forty, a little embarrassed by

the presence of the younger woman, a little hesitant. "I'm going to the hotel now and I must leave you here," he said. His feet made a shuffling sound on the sidewalk. "I intended to tell you why you found me lying out there with my face buried in the grass," he said. A new quality had come into his voice. It was the voice of the boy who had called to Rosalind out of the body of the man as they walked and talked on the tracks. "Sometimes I can't stand my life here," he said almost fiercely and waved his long arms about. "I'm alone too much. I grow to hate myself. I have to run out of town."

The man did not look at Rosalind but at the ground. His big feet continued shuffling nervously about. "Once in the winter time I thought I was going insane," he said. "I happened to remember an orchard, five miles from town where I had walked one day in the late fall when the pears were ripe. A notion came into my head. It was bitter cold but I walked the five miles and went into the orchard. The ground was frozen and covered with snow but I brushed the snow aside. I pushed my face into the grass. In the fall when I had walked there the ground was covered with ripe pears. A fragrance arose from them. They were covered with bees that crawled over them, drunk, filled with a kind of ecstacy. I had remembered the fragrance. That's why I went there and put my face into the frozen grass. The bees were in an ecstasy of life and I had missed life. I have always missed life. It always goes away from me. I always imagined people walking away. In the spring this year I walked on the railroad track out to the bridge over Willow Creek. Violets grew in the grass. At that time I hardly noticed them but today I remembered. The violets were like the people who walk away from me. A mad desire to run after them had take possession of me. I felt like a bird flying through space. A conviction that something had escaped me and that I must pursue it had taken possession of me."

Melville Stoner stopped talking. His face also had grown white and his hands also trembled. Rosalind had an almost irresistible desire to put out her hand and touch his hand. She wanted to shout, crying—"I am here. I am not dead. I am alive." Instead she stood in silence, staring at him, as the widow who owned the high flying hens had stared. Melville Stoner struggled to recover from the ecstasy into which he had been thrown by his own words. He bowed and smiled. "I hope you are in the habit of walking on railroad tracks," he said. "I shall in the future know what to do with my time. When you come to town I shall camp on the railroad tracks. No doubt, like the violets, you have left your fragrance out there." Rosalind looked at him. He was laughing at her as he had laughed when he talked to the widow standing at his gate. She did not mind. When he had left her she went slowly through the streets. The phrase that had come into her mind as they walked on the tracks came back and she said it over and over. "And God spoke to me out of a burning bush." She kept repeating the phrase until she got back into the Wescott house.

Rosalind sat on the front porch of the house where her girlhood had been spent. Her father had not come home for the evening meal. He was a dealer in coal and lumber and owned a number of unpainted sheds facing a railroad siding west of town. There was a tiny office with a stove and a desk in a corner by a window. The desk was piled high with unanswered letters and with circulars from mining and lumber companies. Over them had settled a thick layer of coal dust. All day he sat in his office looking like an animal in a cage, but unlike a caged animal he was apparently not discontented and did not grow restless. He was the one coal and lumber dealer in Willow Springs. When people wanted one of these commodities they had to come to him. There was no other place to go. He was content. In the morning as soon as he got to his office he read the Des Moines paper and then if no one came to disturb him he sat all day, by the stove in winter and by an open window through the long hot summer days, apparently unaffected by the marching change of seasons pictured in the fields, without thought, without hope, without regret that life was becoming an old worn out thing for him.

In the Wescott house Rosalind's mother had already begun the canning of which she had several times spoken. She was making gooseberry jam. Rosalind could hear the pots boiling in the kitchen. Her mother walked heavily. With the coming of age she was beginning to grow fat.

The daughter was weary from much thinking. It had been a day of many emotions. She took off her hat and laid it on the porch beside her. Melville Stoner's house next door had windows that were like eyes staring at her, accusing her. "Well now, you see, you have gone too fast," the house declared. It sneered at her. "You thought you knew about people. After all you knew nothing." Rosalind held her head in her hands. It was true she had misunderstood. The man who lived in the house was no doubt like other people in Willow Springs. He was not, as she had smartly supposed, a dull citizen of a dreary town, one who knew nothing of life. Had he not said words that had startled her, torn her out of herself?

Rosalind had an experience not uncommon to tired nervous people. Her mind, weary of thinking, did not stop thinking but went on faster than ever. A new plane of thought was reached. Her mind was like a flying machine that leaves the ground and leaps into the air.

It took hold upon an idea expressed or implied in something Melville Stoner had said. "In every human being there are two voices, each striving to make itself heard."

A new world of thought had opened itself before her. After all human beings might be understood. It might be possible to understand her mother and her mother's life, her father, the man she loved, herself. There was the voice that said words. Words came forth from lips. They conformed, fell into a certain mold. For the most part the words had no life of their own. They had come down out of old times and many of them were no doubt once strong living words, coming out of the depth of people, out of the bellies of people. The words had escaped out of a shut-in place. They had once expressed living truth. Then they had gone on being said, over and over, by the lips of many people, endlessly, wearily.

She thought of men and women she had seen together, that she had heard talking together as they sat in the street cars or in apartments or walked in a Chicago park. Her brother, the traveling salesman, and his wife had talked half wearily through the long evenings she had spent with them in their apartment. It was with them as with the other people. A thing happened. The lips said certain words but the eyes of the people said other words. Sometimes the lips expressed affection while hatred shone out of the eyes. Sometimes it was the other way about. What a confusion!

It was clear there was something hidden away within people that could not get itself expressed except accidentally. One was startled or alarmed and then the words that fell from the lips became pregnant words, words that lived.

The vision that had sometimes visited her in her girlhood as she lay in bed at night came back. Again she saw the people on the marble stairway, going down and away, into infinity. Her own mind began to make words that struggled to get themselves expressed through her lips. She hungered for someone to whom to say the words and half arose to go to her mother, to where her mother was making gooseberry jam in the kitchen, and then sat down again. "They were going down into the hall of the hidden voices," she whispered to herself. The words excited and intoxicated her as had the words from the lips of Melville Stoner. She thought of herself as having quite suddenly grown amazingly, spiritually, even physically. She felt relaxed, young, wonderfully strong. She imagined herself as walking, as had the young girl she had seen in the vision, with swinging arms and shoulders, going down a marble stairway—down into the hidden places in people, into the hall of the little voices. "I shall understand after this, what shall I not understand?" she asked herself.

Doubt came and she trembled a little. As she walked with him on the railroad track Melville Stoner had gone down within herself. Her body was a house, through the door of which he had walked. He had known about the night noises in her father's house—her father at the well by the kitchen door, the slap of the spilled water on the floor. Even when she was a young girl and had thought herself alone in the bed in the darkness in the room upstairs in the house before which she now sat, she had not been alone. The strange bird-like man who lived in the house next door had been with her, in her room, in her bed. Years later he had remembered the terrible little noises of the house and had known how they had terrified her. There was something terrible in his knowledge too. He had spoken, given forth his knowledge, but as he did so there was laughter in his eyes, perhaps a sneer.

In the Wescott house the sounds of housekeeping went on. A man who had been at work in a distant field, who had already begun his fall plowing, was unhitching his horses from the plow. He was far away, beyond the street's end, in a field that swelled a little out of the plain. Rosalind stared. The man was hitching the horses to a wagon. She saw him as through the large end of a telescope. He would drive the horses away to a distant farmhouse and put them into a barn. Then he would go into a house where there was a woman at work. Perhaps the woman like her mother would be making gooseberry jam. He would grunt as her father did when at evening he came home from the little hot office by the railroad siding. "Hello," he would say, flatly, indifferently, stupidly. Life was like that.

Rosalind became weary of thinking. The man in the distant field had got into his wagon and was driving away. In a moment there would be nothing left of him but a thin cloud of dust that floated in the air. In the house the gooseberry jam had boiled long enough. Her mother was preparing to put it into glass jars. The operation produced a new little side current of sounds. She thought again of Melville Stoner. For years he had been sitting, listening to sounds. There was a kind of madness in it.

She had got herself into a half frenzied condition. "I must stop it," she told herself. "I am like a stringed instrument on which the strings have been tightened too much." She put her face into her hands, wearily.

And then a thrill ran through her body. There was a reason for Melville Stoner's being what he had become. There was a locked gateway leading to the marble stairway that led down and away, into infinity, into the hall of the little voices and the key to the gateway was love. Warmth came back into Rosalind's body. "Understanding need not lead to weariness," she thought. Life might after all be a rich, a triumphant thing. She would make her visit to Willow Springs count for something significant in her life. For one thing she would really approach her mother, she would walk into her mother's life. "It will be my first trip down the marble stairway," she thought and tears came to her eyes. In a moment her father would be coming home for the evening meal but after supper he would go away. The two women would be alone together. Together they would explore a little into the mystery of life, they would find sisterhood. The thing she had wanted to talk about with another understanding woman could be talked about then.

There might yet be a beautiful outcome to her visit to Willow Springs and to her mother.

II

The story of Rosalind's six years in Chicago is the story of thousands of unmarried women who work in offices in the city. Necessity had not driven her to work nor kept her at her task and she did not think of herself as a worker, one who would always be a worker. For a time after she came out of the stenographic school she drifted from office to office, acquiring always more skill, but with no particular interest in what she was doing. It was a way to put in the long days. Her father, who in addition to the coal and lumber yards owned three farms, sent her a hundred dollars a month. The money her work brought was spent for clothes so that she dressed better than the women she worked with.

Of one thing she was quite sure. She did not want to return to Willow Springs to live with her father and mother, and after a time she knew she could not continue living with her brother and his wife. For the first time she began seeing the city that spread itself out before her eyes. When she walked at the noon hour along Michigan Boulevard or went into a restaurant or in the evening went home in the street car she saw men and women together. It was the same when on Sunday afternoons in the summer she walked in the park or by the lake. On a street car she saw a small round-faced woman put her hand into the hand of her male companion. Before she did it she looked cautiously about. She wanted to assure herself of something. To the other women in the car, to Rosalind and the others the act said something. It was as though the woman's voice had said aloud, "He is mine. Do not draw too close to him."

There was no doubt that Rosalind was awakening out of the Willow Springs torpor in which she had lived out her young womanhood. The city had at least done that for her. The city was wide. It flung itself out. One had but to let his feet go thump, thump upon the pavements to get into strange streets, see always new faces.

On Saturday afternoon and all day Sunday one did not work.

In the summer it was a time to go to places—to the park, to walk among the strange colorful crowds in Halsted Street, with a half dozen young people from the office, to spend a day on the sand dunes at the foot of Lake Michigan. One got excited and was hungry, hungry, always hungry—for companionship. That was it. One wanted to possess something—a man—to take him along on jaunts, be sure of him, yes—own him.

She read books—always written by men or by manlike women. There was an essential mistake in the viewpoint of life set forth in the books. The mistake was always being made. In Rosalind's time it grew more pronounced. Someone had got hold of a key with which the door to the secret chamber of life could be unlocked. Others took the key and rushed in. The secret chamber of life was filled with a noisy vulgar crowd. All the books that dealt with life at all dealt with it through the lips of the crowd that had newly come into the sacred place. The writer had hold of the key. It was his time to be heard. "Sex," he cried. "It is by understanding sex I will untangle the mystery."

It was all very well and sometimes interesting but one grew tired of the subject.

She lay abed in her room at her brother's house on a Sunday night in the summer. During the afternoon she had gone for a walk and on a street on the Northwest Side had come upon a religious procession. The Virgin was being carried through the streets. The houses were decorated and women leaned out at the windows of houses. Old priests dressed in white gowns waddled along. Strong young men carried the platform on which the Virgin rested. The procession stopped. Someone started a chant in a loud clear voice. Other voices took it up. Children ran about gathering in money. All the time there was a loud hum of ordinary conversation going on. Women shouted across the street to other women. Young girls walked on the sidewalks and laughed softly as the young men in white, clustered about the Virgin, turned to stare at them. On every street corner merchants sold candies, nuts, cool drinks—

In her bed at night Rosalind put down the book she had been reading. "The worship of the Virgin is a form of sex expression," she read.

"Well what of it? If it be true what does it matter?"

She got out of bed and took off her nightgown. She was herself a virgin. What did that matter? She turned herself slowly about, looking at her strong young woman's body. It was a thing in which sex lived. It was a thing upon which sex in others might express itself. What did it matter?

There was her brother sleeping with his wife in another room near at hand. In Willow Springs, Iowa, her father was at just this moment pumping a pail of water at the well by the kitchen door. In a moment he would carry it into the kitchen to set it on the box by the kitchen sink.

Rosalind's cheeks were flushed. She made an odd and lovely figure standing nude before the glass in her room there in Chicago. She was so much alive and yet not alive. Her eyes shone with excitement. She continued to turn slowly round and round twisting her head to look at her naked back. "Perhaps I am learning to think," she decided. There was some sort of essential mistake in people's conception of life. There was something she knew and it was of as much importance as the things the wise men knew and put into books. She also had found out something about life. Her body was still the body of what was called a virgin. What of it? "If the sex impulse within it had been gratified in what way would my problem be solved? I am lonely now. It is evident that after that had happened I would still be lonely."

III

Rosalind's life in Chicago had been like a stream that apparently turns back toward its source. It ran forward, then stopped, turned, twisted. At just the time when her awakening became a half realized thing she went to work at a new place, a piano factory on the Northwest Side facing a branch of the Chicago River. She became secretary to a man who was treasurer of the company. He was a slender, rather small man of thirty-eight with thin white restless hands and with gray eyes that were clouded and troubled. For the first time she became really interested in the work that ate up her days. Her employer was charged with the responsibility of passing upon the credit of the firm's customers and was unfitted for the task. He was not shrewd and within a short time had made two costly mistakes by which the company had lost money. "I have too much to do. My time is too much taken up with details. I need help here," he had explained, evidently irritated, and Rosalind had been engaged to relieve him of details.

Her new employer, named Walter Sayers, was the only son of a man who in his time had been well known in Chicago's social and club life. Everyone had thought him wealthy and he had tried to live up to people's estimate of his fortune. His son Walter had wanted to be a singer and had expected to inherit a comfortable fortune. At thirty he had married and three years later when his father died he was already the father of two children.

And then suddenly he had found himself quite penniless. He could sing but his voice was not large. It wasn't an instrument with which one could make money in any dignified way. Fortunately his wife had some money of her own. It was her money, invested in the piano manufacturing business, that had secured him the position as treasurer of the company. With his wife he withdrew from social life and they went to live in a comfortable house in a suburb.

Walter Sayers gave up music, apparently surrendered even his interest in it. Many men and women from his suburb went to hear the orchestra on Friday afternoons but he did not go. "What's the use of torturing myself and thinking of a life I cannot lead?" he said to himself. To his wife he pretended a growing interest in his work at the factory. "It's really fascinating. It's a game, like moving men back and forth on a chess board. I shall grow to love it," he said.

He had tried to build up interest in his work but had not been successful. Certain things would not get into his consciousness. Although he tried hard he could not make the fact that profit or loss to the company depended upon his judgment seem important to himself. It was a matter of money lost or gained and money meant nothing to him. "It's father's fault," he thought. "While he lived money never meant anything to me. I was brought up wrong. I am ill prepared for the battle of life." He became too timid and lost business that should have come to the company quite naturally. Then he became too bold in the extension of credit and other losses followed.

His wife was quite happy and satisfied with her life. There were four or five acres of land about the suburban house and she became absorbed in the work of raising flowers and vegetables. For the sake of the children she kept a cow. With a young negro gardener she puttered about all day, digging in the earth, spreading manure about the roots of bushes and shrubs, planting and transplanting. In the evening when he had come home from his office in his car she took him by the arm and led him eagerly about. The two children trotted at their heels. She talked glowingly. They stood at a low spot at the foot of the garden and she spoke of the necessity of putting in tile. The prospect seemed to excite her. "It will be the best land on the place when it's drained," she said. She stooped and with a trowel turned over the soft black soil. An odor arose. "See! Just see how rich and black it is!" she exclaimed eagerly. "It's a little sour now because water has stood on it." She seemed to be apologizing as for a wayward child. "When it's drained I shall use lime to sweeten it," she added. She was like a mother leaning over the cradle of a sleeping babe. Her enthusiasm irritated him.

When Rosalind came to take the position in his office the slow fires of hatred that had been burning beneath the surface of Walter Sayers' life had already eaten away much of his vigor and energy. His body sagged in the office chair and there were heavy sagging lines at the corners of his mouth. Outwardly he remained always kindly and cheerful but back of the clouded, troubled eyes the fires of hatred burned slowly, persistently. It was as though he was trying to awaken from a troubled dream that gripped him, a dream that frightened a little, that was unending. He had contracted little physical habits. A sharp paper cutter lay on his desk. As he read a letter from one of the firm's customers he took it up and jabbed little holes in the leather cover of his desk. When he had several letters to sign he took up his pen and jabbed it almost viciously into the inkwell. Then before signing he jabbed it in again. Sometimes he did the thing a dozen times in succession.

Sometimes the things that went on beneath the surface of

Walter Sayers frightened him. In order to do what he called "putting in his Saturday afternoons and Sundays" he had taken up photography. The camera took him away from his own house and the sight of the garden where his wife and the negro were busy digging, and into the fields and into stretches of woodland at the edge of the suburban village. Also it took him away from his wife's talk, from her eternal planning for the garden's future. Here by the house tulip bulbs were to be put in in the fall. Later there would be a hedge of lilac bushes shutting off the house from the road. The men who lived in the other houses along the suburban street spent their Saturday afternoons and Sunday mornings tinkering with motor cars. On Sunday afternoons they took their families driving, sitting up very straight and silent at the driving wheel. They consumed the afternoon in a swift dash over country roads. The car ate up the hours. Monday morning and the work in the city was there, at the end of the road. They ran madly toward it.

For a time the use of the camera made Walter Sayers almost happy. The study of light, playing on the trunk of a tree or over the grass in a field appealed to some instinct within. It was an uncertain delicate business. He fixed himself a dark room upstairs in the house and spent his evenings there. One dipped the films into the developing liquid, held them to the light and then dipped them again. The little nerves that controlled the eyes were aroused. One felt oneself being enriched, a little—

One Sunday afternoon he went to walk in a strip of woodland and came out upon the slope of a low hill. He had read somewhere that the low hill country southwest of Chicago, in which his suburb lay, had once been the shore of Lake Michigan. The low hills sprang out of the flat land and were covered with forests. Beyond them the flat lands began again. The prairies went on indefinitely, into infinity. People's lives went on so. Life was too long. It was to be spent in the endless doing over and over of an unsatisfactory task. He sat on the slope and looked out across the land.

He thought of his wife. She was back there, in the suburb in the hills, in her garden making things grow. It was a noble sort of thing to be doing. One shouldn't be irritated.

Well he had married her expecting to have money of his own. Then he would have worked at something else. Money would not have been involved in the matter and success would not have been a thing one must seek. He had expected his own life would be motivated. No matter how much or how hard he worked he would not have been a great singer. What did that matter? There was a way to live—a way of life in which such things did not matter. The delicate shades of things might be sought after. Before his eyes, there on the grass covered flat lands, the afternoon light was playing. It was like a breath, a vapor of color blown suddenly from between red lips out over the grey dead burned grass. Song might be like that. The beauty might come out of himself, out of his own body.

Again he thought of his wife and the sleeping light in his eyes flared up, it became a flame. He felt himself being mean, unfair. It didn't matter. Where did the truth lie? Was his wife, digging in her garden, having always a succession of small triumphs, marching forward with the seasons—well, was she becoming a little old, lean and sharp, a little vulgarized?

It seemed so to him. There was something smug in the way in which she managed to fling green growing flowering things over the black land. It was obvious the thing could be done and that there was satisfaction in doing it. It was a little like running a business and making money by it. There was a deep seated vulgarity involved in the whole matter. His wife put her hands into the black ground. They felt about, caressed the roots of the growing things. She laid hold of the slender trunk of a young tree in a certain way—as though she possessed it.

One could not deny that the destruction of beautiful things was involved. Weeds grew in the garden, delicate shapely things. She plucked them out without thought. He had seen her do it.

As for himself, he also had been pulled out of something. Had he not surrendered to the fact of a wife and growing children? Did he not spend his days doing work he detested? The anger within him burned bright. The fire came into his conscious self. Why should a weed that is to be destroyed pretend to a vegetable existence? As for puttering about with a camera—was it not a form of cheating? He did not want to be a photographer. He had once wanted to be a singer.

He arose and walked along the hillside, still watching the shadows play over the plains below. At night—in bed with his wife—well, was she not sometimes with him as she was in the garden? Something was plucked out of him and another thing grew in its place—something she wanted to have grow. Their love making was like his puttering with a camera—to make the weekends pass. She came at him a little too determinedly—sure. She was plucking delicate weeds in order that things she had determined upon—"vegetables," he exclaimed in disgust —in order that vegetables might grow. Love was a fragrance, the shading of a tone over the lips, out of the throat. It was like the afternoon light on the burned grass. Keeping a garden and making flowers grow had nothing to do with it.

Walter Sayers' fingers twitched. The camera hung by a strap over his shoulder. He took hold of the strap and walked to a tree. He swung the box above his head and brought it down with a thump against the tree trunk. The sharp breaking sound —the delicate parts of the machine being broken—was sweet to his ears. It was as though a song had come suddenly from between his lips. Again he swung the box and again brought it down against the tree trunk.

IV

Rosalind at work in Walter Sayers' office was from the beginning something different, apart from the young woman from Iowa who had been drifting from office to office, moving from rooming house to rooming house on Chicago's North Side, striving feebly to find out something about life by reading books, going to the theatre and walking alone in the streets. In the new place her life at once began to have point and purpose, but at the same time the perplexity that was later to send her running to Willow Springs and to the presence of her mother began to grow in her.

Walter Sayers' office was a rather large room on the third floor of the factory whose walls went straight up from the river's edge. In the morning Rosalind arrived at eight and went into the office and closed the door. In a large room across a narrow hallway and shut off from her retreat by two thick, clouded-glass partitions was the company's general office. It contained the desks of salesmen, several clerks, a bookkeeper and two stenographers. Rosalind avoided becoming acquainted with these people. She was in a mood to be alone, to spend as many hours as possible alone with her own thoughts.

She got to the office at eight and her employer did not arrive until nine-thirty or ten. For an hour or two in the morning and in the late afternoon she had the place to herself. Immediately she shut the door into the hallway and was alone she felt at home. Even in her father's house it had never been so. She took off her wraps and walked about the room touching things, putting things to rights. During the night a negro woman had scrubbed the floor and wiped the dust off her employer's desk but she got a cloth and wiped the desk again. Then she opened the letters that had come in and after reading arranged them in little piles. She wanted to spend a part of her wages for flowers and imagined clusters of flowers arranged in small hanging baskets along the grey walls. "I'll do that later, perhaps," she thought.

The walls of the room enclosed her. "What makes me so happy here?" she asked herself. As for her employer—she felt she scarcely knew him. He was a shy man, rather small—

She went to a window and stood looking out. Near the factory a bridge crossed the river and over it went a stream of heavily loaded wagons and motor trucks. The sky was grey with smoke. In the afternoon, after her employer had gone for the day, she would stand again by the window. As she stood thus she faced westward and in the afternoon saw the sun fall down the sky. It was glorious to be there alone during the late hours of the afternoon. What a tremendous thing this city in which she had come to live! For some reason after she went to work for Walter Sayers the city seemed, like the room in which she worked, to have accepted her, taken her into itself. In the late afternoon the rays of the departing sun fell across great banks of clouds. The whole city seemed to reach upwards. It left the ground and ascended into the air. There was an illusion produced. Stark grim factory chimneys, that all day were stiff cold formal things sticking up into the air and belching forth black smoke, were now slender upreaching pencils of light and wavering color. The tall chimneys detached themselves from the buildings and sprang into the air. The factory in which Rosalind stood had such a chimney. It also was leaping upward. She felt herself being lifted, an odd floating sensation was achieved. With what a stately tread the day went away, over the city! The city, like the factory chimneys yearned after it, hungered for it.

In the morning gulls came in from Lake Michigan to feed on the sewage floating in the river below. The river was the color of chrysoprase. The gulls floated above it as sometimes in the evening the whole city seemed to float before her eyes. They were graceful, living, free things. They were triumphant. The getting of food, even the eating of sewage was done thus gracefully, beautifully. The gulls turned and twisted in the air. They wheeled and floated and then fell downward to the river in a long curve, just touching, caressing the surface of the water and then rising again.

Rosalind raised herself on her toes. At her back beyond the two glass partitions were other men and women, but there, in that room, she was alone. She belonged there. What an odd feeling she had. She also belonged to her employer, Walter Sayers. She scarcely knew the man and yet she belonged to him. She threw her arms above her head, trying awkwardly to imitate some movement of the birds.

Her awkwardness shamed her a little and she turned and walked about the room. "I'm twenty-five years old and it's a little late to begin trying to be a bird, to be graceful," she thought. She resented the slow stupid heavy movements of her father and mother, the movements she had imitated as a child. "Why was I not taught to be graceful and beautiful in mind and body, why in the place I came from did no one think it worth while to try to be graceful and beautiful?" she whispered to herself.

How conscious of her own body Rosalind was becoming! She walked across the room, trying to go lightly and gracefully. In the office beyond the glass partitions someone spoke suddenly and she was startled. She laughed foolishly. For a long time after she went to work in the office of Walter Sayers she thought the desire in herself to be physically more graceful and beautiful and to rise also out of the mental stupidity and sloth of her young womanhood was due to the fact that the factory windows faced the river and the western sky, and that in the morning she saw the gulls feeding and in the afternoon the sun going down through the smoke clouds in a riot of colors.

V

On the August evening as Rosalind sat on the porch before her father's house in Willow Springs, Walter Sayers came home from the factory by the river and to his wife's suburban garden. When the family had dined he came out to walk in the paths with the two children, boys, but they soon tired of his silence and went to join their mother. The young negro came along a path by the kitchen door and joined the party. Walter went to sit on a garden seat that was concealed behind bushes. He lighted a cigarette but did not smoke. The smoke curled quietly up through his fingers as it burned itself out.

Closing his eyes Walter sat perfectly still and tried not to think. The soft evening shadows began presently to close down and around him. For a long time he sat thus motionless, like a carved figure placed on the garden bench. He rested. He lived and did not live. The intense body, usually so active and alert, had become a passive thing. It was thrown aside, on to the bench, under the bush, to sit there, waiting to be reinhabited.

This hanging suspended between consciousness and unconsciousness was a thing that did not happen often. There was something to be settled between himself and a woman and the woman had gone away. His whole plan of life had been disturbed. Now he wanted to rest. The details of his life were forgotten. As for the woman he did not think of her, did not want to think of her. It was ridiculous that he needed her so much. He wondered if he had ever felt that way about Cora, his wife. Perhaps he had. Now she was near him, but a few yards away. It was almost dark but she with the negro remained at work, digging in the ground—somewhere near—caressing the soil, making things grow.

When his mind was undisturbed by thoughts and lay like a lake in the hills on a quiet summer evening little thoughts did come. "I want you as a lover—far away. Keep yourself far away." The words trailed through his mind as the smoke from the cigarette trailed slowly upwards through his fingers. Did the words refer to Rosalind Wescott? She had been gone from him three days. Did he hope she would never come back or did the words refer to his wife?

His wife's voice spoke sharply. One of the children in playing about, had stepped on a plant. "If you are not careful I shall have to make you stay out of the garden altogether." She raised her voice and called, "Marian!" A maid came from the house and took the children away. They went along the path toward the house protesting. Then they ran back to kiss their mother. There was a struggle and then acceptance. The kiss was acceptance of their fate—to obey. "O, Walter," the mother's voice called, but the man on the bench did not answer. Tree toads began to cry. "The kiss is acceptance. Any physical contact with another is acceptance," he reflected.

The little voices within Walter Sayers were talking away at a great rate. Suddenly he wanted to sing. He had been told that his voice was small, not of much account, that he would never be a singer. It was quite true no doubt but here, in the garden on the quiet summer night, was a place and a time for a small voice. It would be like the voice within himself that whispered sometimes when he was quiet, relaxed. One evening when he had been with the woman, Rosalind, when he had taken her into the country in his car, he had suddenly felt as he did now. They sat together in the car that he had run into a field. For a long time they had remained silent. Some cattle came and stood nearby, their figures soft in the night. Suddenly he had felt like a new man in a new world and had begun to sing. He sang one song over and over, then sat in silence for a time and after that drove out of the field and through a gate into the road. He took the woman back to her place in the city.

In the quiet of the garden on the summer evening he opened his lips to sing the same song. He would sing with the tree toad hidden away in the fork of a tree somewhere. He would lift his voice up from the earth, up into the branches, of trees, away from the ground in which people were digging, his wife and the young negro.

The song did not come. His wife began speaking and the sound of her voice took away the desire to sing. Why had she not, like the other woman, remained silent?

He began playing a game. Sometimes, when he was alone the thing happened to him that had now happened. His body became like a tree or a plant. Life ran through it unobstructed. He had dreamed of being a singer but at such a moment he wanted also to be a dancer. That would have been sweetest of all things—to sway like the tops of young trees when a wind blew, to give himself as grey weeds in a sunburned field gave themself to the influence of passing shadows, changing color constantly, becoming every moment something new, to live in life and in death too, always to live, to be unafraid of life, to let it flow through his body, to let the blood flow through his body, not to struggle, to offer no resistance, to dance.

Walter Sayers' children had gone into the house with the nurse girl Marian. It had become too dark for his wife to dig in the garden. It was August and the fruitful time of the year for farms and gardens had come, but his wife had forgotten fruitfulness. She was making plans for another year. She came along the garden path followed by the negro. "We will set out strawberry plants there," she was saying. The soft voice of the young negro murmured his assent. It was evident the young man lived in her conception of the garden. His mind sought out her desire and gave itself.

The children Walter Sayers had brought into life through the body of his wife Cora had gone into the house and to bed. They bound him to life, to his wife, to the garden where he sat, to the office by the riverside in the city.

They were not his children. Suddenly he knew that quite clearly. His own children were quite different things. "Men have children just as women do. The children come out of their bodies. They play about," he thought. It seemed to him that children, born of his fancy, were at that very moment playing about the bench where he sat. Living things that dwelt within him and that had at the same time the power to depart out of him were now running along paths, swinging from the branches of trees, dancing in the soft light.

His mind sought out the figure of Rosalind Wescott. She had gone away, to her own people in Iowa. There had been a note at the office saying she might be gone for several days. Between himself and Rosalind the conventional relationship of employer and employee had long since been swept quite away.

It needed something in a man he did not possess to maintain that relationship with either men or women.

At the moment he wanted to forget Rosalind. In her there was a struggle going on. The two people had wanted to be lovers and he had fought against that. They had talked about it. "Well," he said, "it will not work out. We will bring unnecessary unhappiness upon ourselves."

He had been honest enough in fighting off the intensification of their relationship. "If she were here now, in this garden with me, it wouldn't matter. We could be lovers and then forget about being lovers," he told himself.

His wife came along the path and stopped nearby. She continued talking in a low voice, making plans for another year of gardening. The negro stood near her, his figure making a dark wavering mass against the foliage of a low growing bush. His wife wore a white dress. He could see her figure quite plainly. In the uncertain light it looked girlish and young. She put her hand up and took hold of the body of a young tree. The hand became detached from her body. The pressure of her leaning body made the young tree sway a little. The white hand moved slowly back and forth in space.

Rosalind Wescott had gone home to tell her mother of her love. In her note she had said nothing of that but Walter Sayers knew that was the object of her visit to the Iowa town. It was an odd sort of thing to try to do—to tell people of love, to try to explain it to others.

The night was a thing apart from Walter Sayers, the male being sitting in silence in the garden. Only the children of his fancy understood it. The night was a living thing. It advanced upon him, enfolded him. "Night is the sweet little brother of Death," he thought.

His wife stood very near. Her voice was soft and low and the voice of the negro when he answered her comments on the future of the garden was soft and low. There was music in the negro's voice, perhaps a dance in it. Walter remembered about him.

The young negro had been in trouble before he came to the Sayers. He had been an ambitious young black and had listened to the voices of people, to the voices that filled the air of

America, rang through the houses of America. He had wanted to get on in life and had tried to educate himself. The black had wanted to be a lawyer.

How far away he had got from his own people, from the blacks of the African forests! He had wanted to be a lawyer in a city in America. What a notion!

Well he had got into trouble. He had managed to get through college and had opened a law office. Then one evening he went out to walk and chance led him into a street where a woman, a white woman, had been murdered an hour before. The body of the woman was found and then he was found walking in the street. Mrs. Sayers' brother, a lawyer, had saved him from being punished as a murderer and after the trial, and the young negro's acquittal, had induced his sister to take him as gardener. His chances as a professional man in the city were no good. "He has had a terrible experience and has just escaped by a fluke" the brother had said. Cora Sayers had taken the young man. She had bound him to herself, to her garden.

It was evident the two people were bound together. One cannot bind another without being bound. His wife had no more to say to the negro who went away along the path that led to the kitchen door. He had a room in a little house at the foot of the garden. In the room he had books and a piano. Sometimes in the evening he sang. He was going now to his place. By educating himself he had cut himself off from his own people.

Cora Sayers went into the house and Walter sat alone. After a time the young negro came silently down the path. He stopped by the tree where a moment before the white woman had stood talking to him. He put his hand on the trunk of the young tree where her hand had been and then went softly away. His feet made no sound on the garden path.

An hour passed. In his little house at the foot of the garden the negro began to sing softly. He did that sometimes in the middle of the night. What a life he had led too! He had come away from his black people, from the warm brown girls with the golden colors playing through the blue black of their skins and had worked his way through a Northern college, had accepted the patronage of impertinent people who wanted to uplift the black race, had listened to them, had bound himself to them, had tried to follow the way of life they had suggested.

Now he was in the little house at the foot of the Sayers' garden. Walter remembered little things his wife had told him about the man. The experience in the court room had frightened him horribly and he did not want to go off the Sayers' place. Education, books had done something to him. He could not go back to his own people. In Chicago, for the most part, the blacks lived crowded into a few streets on the South Side. "I want to be a slave," he had said to Cora Sayers. "You may pay me money if it makes you feel better but I shall have no use for it. I want to be your slave. I would be happy if I knew I would never have to go off your place."

The black sang a low voiced song. It ran like a little wind on the surface of a pond. It had no words. He had remembered the song from his father who had got it from his father. In the South, in Alabama and Mississippi the blacks sang it when they rolled cotton bales onto the steamers in the rivers. They had got it from other rollers of cotton bales long since dead. Long before there were any cotton bales to roll black men in boats on rivers in Africa had sung it. Young blacks in boats floated down rivers and came to a town they intended to attack at dawn. There was bravado in singing the song then. It was addressed to the women in the town to be attacked and contained both a caress and a threat. "In the morning your husbands and brothers and sweethearts we shall kill. Then we shall come into your town to you. We shall hold you close. We shall make you forget. With our hot love and our strength we shall make you forget." That was the old significance of the song.

Walter Sayers remembered many things. On other nights when the negro sang and when he lay in his room upstairs in the house, his wife came to him. There were two beds in their room. She sat upright in her bed. "Do you hear, Walter?" she asked. She came to sit on his bed, sometimes she crept into his arms. In the African villages long ago when the song floated up from the river men arose and prepared for battle. The song was a defiance, a taunt. That was all gone now. The young negro's house was at the foot of the garden and Walter with his wife lay upstairs in the larger house situated on high ground. It was a sad song, filled with race sadness. There was something in the ground that wanted to grow, buried deep in the ground. Cora Sayers understood that. It touched something instinctive in her. Her hand went out and touched, caressed her husband's face, his body. The song made her want to hold him tight, possess him.

The night was advancing and it grew a little cold in the garden. The negro stopped singing. Walter Sayers arose and went along the path toward the house but did not enter. Instead he went through a gate into the road and along the suburban streets until he got into the open country. There was no moon but the stars shone brightly. For a time he hurried along looking back as though afraid of being followed, but when he got out into a broad flat meadow he went more slowly. For an hour he walked and then stopped and sat on a tuft of dry grass. For some reason he knew he could not return to his house in the suburb that night. In the morning he would go to the office and wait there until Rosalind came. Then? He did not know what he would do then. "I shall have to make up some story. In the morning I shall have to telephone Cora and make up some silly story," he thought. It was an absurd thing that he, a grown man, could not spend a night abroad, in the fields without the necessity of explanations. The thought irritated him and he arose and walked again. Under the stars in the soft night and on the wide flat plains the irritation soon went away and he began to sing softly, but the song he sang was not the one he had repeated over and over on that other night when he sat with Rosalind in the car and the cattle came. It was the song the negro sang, the river song of the young black warriors that slavery had softened and colored with sadness. On the lips of Walter Sayers the song had lost much of its sadness. He walked almost gaily along and in the song that flowed from his lips there was a taunt, a kind of challenge.

VI

At the end of the short street on which the Wescotts lived in Willow Springs there was a cornfield. When Rosalind was a child it was a meadow and beyond was an orchard.

On summer afternoons the child often went there to sit alone on the banks of a tiny stream that wandered away eastward toward Willow Creek, draining the farmer's fields on the way. The creek had made a slight depression in the level contour of the land and she sat with her back against an old apple tree and with her bare feet almost touching the water. Her mother did not permit her to run bare footed through the streets but when she got into the orchard she took her shoes off. It gave her a delightful naked feeling.

Overhead and through the branches the child could see the great sky. Masses of white clouds broke into fragments and then the fragments came together again. The sun ran in behind one of the cloud masses and grey shadows slid silently over the face of distant fields. The world of her child life, the Wescott household, Melville Stoner sitting in his house, the cries of other children who lived in her street, all the life she knew went far away. To be there in that silent place was like lying awake in bed at night only in some way sweeter and better. There were no dull household sounds and the air she breathed was sweeter, cleaner. The child played a little game. All the apple trees in the orchard were old and gnarled and she had given all the trees names. There was one fancy that frightened her a little but was delicious too. She fancied that at night when she had gone to bed and was asleep and when all the town of Willow Springs had gone to sleep the trees came out of the ground and walked about. The grasses beneath the trees, the bushes that grew beside the fence—all came out of the ground and ran madly here and there. They danced wildly. The old trees, like stately old men, put their heads together and talked. As they talked their bodies swayed slightly—back and forth, back and forth. The bushes and flowering weeds ran in great circles among the little grasses. The grasses hopped straight up and down.

Sometimes when she sat with her back against the tree on warm bright afternoons the child Rosalind had played the game of dancing-life until she grew afraid and had to give it up. Nearby in the fields men were cultivating corn. The breasts of the horses and their wide strong shoulders pushed the young corn aside and made a low rustling sound. Now and then a man's voice was raised in a shout. "Hi, there you Joe!

Get in there Frank!" The widow of the hens owned a little woolly dog that occasionally broke into a spasm of barking, apparently without cause, senseless, eager, barking. Rosalind shut all the sounds out. She closed her eyes and struggled, trying to get into the place beyond human sounds. After a time her desire was accomplished. There was a low sweet sound like the murmuring of voices far away. Now the thing was happening. With a kind of tearing sound the trees came up to stand on top of the ground. They moved with stately tread toward each other. Now the mad bushes and the flowering weeds came running, dancing madly, now the joyful grasses hopped. Rosalind could not stay long in her world of fancy. It was too mad, too joyful. She opened her eyes and jumped to her feet. Everything was all right. The trees stood solidly rooted in the ground, the weeds and bushes had gone back to their places by the fence, the grasses lay asleep on the ground. She felt that her father and mother, her brother, everyone she knew would not approve of her being there among them. The world of dancing life was a lovely but a wicked world. She knew. Sometimes she was a little mad herself and then she was whipped or scolded. The mad world of her fancy had to be put away. It frightened her a little. Once after the thing appeared she cried, went down to the fence crying. A man who was cultivating corn came along and stopped his horses. "What's the matter?" he asked sharply. She couldn't tell him so she told a lie. "A bee stung me," she said. The man laughed. "It'll get well. Better put on your shoes," he advised.

The time of the marching trees and the dancing grasses was in Rosalind's childhood. Later when she had graduated from the Willow Springs High School and had the three years of waiting about the Wescott house before she went to the city she had other experiences in the orchard. Then she had been reading novels and had talked with other young women. She knew many things that after all she did not know. In the attic of her mother's house there was a cradle in which she and her brother had slept when they were babies. One day she went up there and found it. Bedding for the cradle was packed away in a trunk and she took it out. She arranged the cradle for the reception of a child. Then after she did it she was ashamed. Her mother might come up the attic stairs and see it. She put the bedding quickly back into the trunk and went down stairs, her cheeks burning with shame.

What a confusion! One day she went to the house of a schoolgirl friend who was about to be married. Several other girls came and they were all taken into a bedroom where the bride's trousseau was laid out on a bed. What soft lovely things! All the girls went forward and stood over them, Rosalind among them. Some of the girls were shy, others bold. There was one, a thin girl who had no breasts. Her body was flat like a door and she had a thin sharp voice and a thin sharp face. She began to cry out strangely. "How sweet, how sweet, how sweet," she cried over and over. The voice was not like a human voice. It was like something being hurt, an animal in the forest, far away somewhere by itself, being hurt. Then the girl dropped to her knees beside the bed and began to weep bitterly. She declared she could not bear the thought of her schoolgirl friend being married. "Don't do it! O, Mary don't do it!" she pleaded. The other girls laughed but Rosalind couldn't stand it. She hurried out of the house.

That was one thing that had happened to Rosalind and there were other things. Once she saw a young man on the street. He clerked in a store and Rosalind did not know him. However her fancy played with the thought that she had married him. Her own thoughts made her ashamed.

Everything shamed her. When she went into the orchard on summer afternoons she sat with her back against the apple tree and took off her shoes and stockings just as she had when she was a child, but the world of her childhood fancy was gone, nothing could bring it back.

Rosalind's body was soft but all her flesh was firm and strong. She moved away from the tree and lay on the ground. She pressed her body down into the grass, into the firm hard ground. It seemed to her that her mind, her fancy, all the life within her, except just her physical life, went away. The earth pressed upwards against her body. Her body was pressed against the earth. There was darkness. She was imprisoned. She pressed against the walls of her prison. Everything was dark and there was in all the earth silence. Her fingers clutched a handful of the grasses, played in the grasses.

Then she grew very still but did not sleep. There was something that had nothing to do with the ground beneath her or the trees or the clouds in the sky, that seemed to want to come to her, come into her, a kind of white wonder of life.

The thing couldn't happen. She opened her eyes and there was the sky overhead and the trees standing silently about. She went again to sit with her back against one of the trees. She thought with dread of the evening coming on and the necessity of going out of the orchard and to the Wescott house. She was weary. It was the weariness that made her appear to others a rather dull stupid young woman. Where was the wonder of life? It was not within herself, not in the ground. It must be in the sky overhead. Presently it would be night and the stars would come out. Perhaps the wonder did not really exist in life. It had something to do with God. She wanted to ascend upwards, to go at once up into God's house, to be there among the light strong men and women who had died and left dullness and heaviness behind them on the earth. Thinking of them took some of her weariness away and sometimes she went out of the orchard in the late afternoon walking almost lightly. Something like grace seemed to have come into her tall strong body.

Rosalind had gone away from the Wescott house and from Willow Springs, Iowa, feeling that life was essentially ugly. In a way she hated life and people. In Chicago sometimes it was unbelievable how ugly the world had become. She tried to shake off the feeling but it clung to her. She walked through the crowded streets and the buildings were ugly. A sea of faces floated up to her. They were the faces of dead people. The dull death that was in them was in her also. They too could not break through the walls of themselves to the white wonder of life. After all perhaps there was no such thing as the white wonder of life. It might be just a thing of the mind. There was something essentially dirty about life. The dirt was on her and in her. Once as she walked at evening over the Rush Street bridge to her room on the North Side she looked up suddenly and saw the chrysoprase river running inland from the lake. Near at hand stood a soap factory. The men of the city had turned the river about, made it flow inland from the lake. Someone had erected a great soap factory there near the river's

entrance to the city, to the land of men. Rosalind stopped and
stood looking along the river toward the lake. Men and women,
wagons, automobiles rushed past her. They were dirty. She was
dirty. "The water of an entire sea and millions of cakes of soap
will not wash me clean," she thought. The dirtiness of life
seemed a part of her very being and an almost overwhelming
desire to climb upon the railing of the bridge and leap down
into the chrysoprase river swept over her. Her body trembled
violently and putting down her head and staring at the flooring of the bridge she hurried away.

And now Rosalind, a grown woman, was in the Wescott house
at the supper table with her father and mother. None of the
three people ate. They fussed about with the food Ma Wescott
had prepared. Rosalind looked at her mother and thought of
what Melville Stoner had said.

"If I wanted to write I'd do something. I'd tell what everyone thought. It would startle people, frighten them a little, eh?
I would tell what you have been thinking this afternoon while
you walked here on this railroad track with me. I would tell
what your mother has been thinking at the same time and
what she would like to say to you."

What had Rosalind's mother been thinking all through the
three days since her daughter had so unexpectedly come home
from Chicago? What did mothers think in regard to the lives
led by their daughters? Had mothers something of importance
to say to daughters and if they did when did the time come
when they were ready to say it?

She looked at her mother sharply. The older woman's face
was heavy and sagging. She had grey eyes like Rosalind's but
they were dull like the eyes of a fish lying on a slab of ice in the
window of a city meat market. The daughter was a little frightened by what she saw in her mother's face and something
caught in her throat. There was an embarrassing moment. A
strange sort of tenseness came into the air of the room and all
three people suddenly got up from the table.

Rosalind went to help her mother with the dishes and her
father sat in a chair by a window and read a paper. The daughter avoided looking again into her mother's face. "I must
gather myself together if I am to do what I want to do," she

thought. It was strange—in fancy she saw the lean bird-like face of Melville Stoner and the eager tired face of Walter Sayers floating above the head of her mother who leaned over the kitchen sink, washing the dishes. Both of the men's faces sneered at her. "You think you can but you can't. You are a young fool," the men's lips seemed to be saying.

Rosalind's father wondered how long his daughter's visit was to last. After the evening meal he wanted to clear out of the house, go up town, and he had a guilty feeling that in doing so he was being discourteous to his daughter. While the two women washed the dishes he put on his hat and going into the back yard began chopping wood. Rosalind went to sit on the front porch. The dishes were all washed and dried but for a half hour her mother would putter about in the kitchen. She always did that. She would arrange and rearrange. Pick up dishes and put them down again. She clung to the kitchen. It was as though she dreaded the hours that must pass before she could go upstairs and to bed and asleep, to fall into the oblivion of sleep.

When Henry Wescott came around the corner of the house and confronted his daughter he was a little startled. He did not know what was the matter but he felt uncomfortable. For a moment he stopped and looked at her. Life radiated from her figure. A fire burned in her eyes, in her grey intense eyes. Her hair was yellow like cornsilk. She was, at the moment, a complete, a lovely daughter of the cornlands, a being to be loved passionately, completely by some son of the cornlands—had there been in the land a son as alive as this daughter it had thrown aside. The father had hoped to escape from the house unnoticed. "I'm going up town a little while," he said hesitatingly. Still he lingered a moment. Some old sleeping thing awoke in him, was awakened in him by the startling beauty of his daughter. A little fire flared up among the charred rafters of the old house that was his body. "You look pretty, girly," he said sheepishly and then turned his back to her and went along the path to the gate and the street.

Rosalind followed her father to the gate and stood looking as he went slowly along the short street and around a corner. The mood induced in her by her talk with Melville Stoner had returned. Was it possible that her father also felt as Melville

Stoner sometimes did? Did loneliness drive him to the door of insanity and did he also run through the night seeking some lost, some hidden and half forgotten loveliness?

When her father had disappeared around the corner she went through the gate and into the street. "I'll go sit by the tree in the orchard until mother has finished puttering about the kitchen," she thought.

Henry Wescott went along the streets until he came to the square about the court house and then went into Emanuel Wilson's Hardware Store. Two or three other men presently joined him there. Every evening he sat among these men of his town saying nothing. It was an escape from his own house and his wife. The other men came for the same reason. A faint perverted kind of male fellowship was achieved. One of the men of the party, a little old man who followed the house-painters trade, was unmarried and lived with his mother. He was himself nearing the age of sixty but his mother was still alive. It was a thing to be wondered about. When in the evening the house painter was a trifle late at the rendezvous a mild flurry of speculation arose, floated in the air for a moment and then settled like dust in an empty house. Did the old house painter do the housework in his own house, did he wash the dishes, cook the food, sweep and make the beds or did his feeble old mother do these things? Emanuel Wilson told a story he had often told before. In a town in Ohio where he had lived as a young man he had once heard a tale. There was an old man like the house painter whose mother was also still alive and lived with him. They were very poor and in the winter had not enough bedclothes to keep them both warm. They crawled into a bed together. It was an innocent enough matter, just like a mother taking her child into her bed.

Henry Wescott sat in the store listening to the tale Emanuel Wilson told for the twentieth time and thought about his daughter. Her beauty made him feel a little proud, a little above the men who were his companions. He had never before thought of his daughter as a beautiful woman. Why had he never before noticed her beauty? Why had she come from Chicago, there by the lake, to Willow Springs, in the hot month of August? Had she come home from Chicago because she really wanted to see her father and mother? For a moment he was ashamed of his own heavy body, of his shabby clothes and his unshaven face and then the tiny flame that had flared up within him burned itself out. The house painter came in and the faint flavor of male companionship to which he clung so tenaciously was reestablished.

In the orchard Rosalind sat with her back against the tree in the same spot where her fancy had created the dancing life of her childhood and where as a young woman graduate of the Willow Springs High School she had come to try to break through the wall that separated her from life. The sun had disappeared and the grey shadows of night were creeping over the grass, lengthening the shadows cast by the trees. The orchard had long been neglected and many of the trees were dead and without foliage. The shadows of the dead branches were like long lean arms that reached out, felt their way forward over the grey grass. Long lean fingers reached and clutched. There was no wind and the night would be dark and without a moon, a hot dark starlit night of the plains.

In a moment more it would be black night. Already the creeping shadows on the grass were barely discernible. Rosalind felt death all about her, in the orchard, in the town. Something Walter Sayers had once said to her came sharply back into her mind. "When you are in the country alone at night sometime try giving yourself to the night, to the darkness, to the shadows cast by trees. The experience, if you really give yourself to it, will tell you a startling story. You will find that, although the white men have owned the land for several generations now and although they have built towns everywhere, dug coal out of the ground, covered the land with railroads, towns and cities, they do not own an inch of the land in the whole continent. It still belongs to a race who in their physical life are now dead. The red men, although they are practically all gone still own the American continent. Their fancy has peopled it with ghosts, with gods and devils. It is because in their time they loved the land. The proof of what I say is to be seen everywhere. We have given our towns no beautiful names of our own because we have not built the towns beautifully. When an American town has a beautiful name it was stolen from another race, from a race that still owns the land in which we live. We are all strangers here. When you are alone at night in the country, anywhere in America, try giving yourself to the night. You will find that death only resides in the conquering whites and that life remains in the red men who are gone."

The spirits of the two men, Walter Sayers and Melville Stoner, dominated the mind of Rosalind. She felt that. It was as though they were beside her, sitting beside her on the grass in the orchard. She was quite certain that Melville Stoner had come back to his house and was now sitting within sound of her voice, did she raise her voice to call. What did they want of her? Had she suddenly begun to love two men, both older than herself? The shadows of the branches of trees made a carpet on the floor of the orchard, a soft carpet spun of some delicate material on which the footsteps of men could make no sound. The two men were coming toward her, advancing over the carpet. Melville Stoner was near at hand and Walter Sayers was coming from far away, out of the distance. The spirit of him was creeping toward her. The two men were in accord. They came bearing some male knowledge of life, something they wanted to give her.

She arose and stood by the tree, trembling. Into what a state she had got herself! How long would it endure? Into what knowledge of life and death was she being led? She had come home on a simple mission. She loved Walter Sayers, wanted to offer herself to him but before doing so had felt the call to come home to her mother. She had thought she would be bold and would tell her mother the story of her love. She would tell her and then take what the older woman offered. If her mother understood and sympathized, well that would be a beautiful thing to have happen. If her mother did not understand—at any rate she would have paid some old debt, would have been true to some old, unexpressed obligation.

The two men—what did they want of her? What had Melville Stoner to do with the matter? She put the figure of him out of her mind. In the figure of the other man, Walter Sayers, there was something less aggressive, less assertive. She clung to that.

She put her arm about the trunk of the old apple tree and

laid her cheek against its rough bark. Within herself she was so intense, so excited that she wanted to rub her cheeks against the bark of the tree until the blood came, until physical pain came to counteract the tenseness within that had become pain.

Since the meadow between the orchard and the street end had been planted to corn she would have to reach the street by going along a lane, crawling under a wire fence and crossing the yard of the widowed chicken raiser. A profound silence reigned over the orchard and when she had crawled under the fence and reached the widow's back yard she had to feel her way through a narrow opening between a chicken house and a barn by running her fingers forward over the rough boards.

Her mother sat on the porch waiting and on the narrow porch before his house next door sat Melville Stoner. She saw him as she hurried past and shivered slightly. "What a dark vulture-like thing he is! He lives off the dead, off dead glimpses of beauty, off dead old sounds heard at night," she thought. When she got to the Wescott house she threw herself down on the porch and lay on her back with her arms stretched above her head. Her mother sat on a rocking chair beside her. There was a street lamp at the corner at the end of the street and a little light came through the branches of trees and lighted her mother's face. How white and still and death-like it was. When she had looked Rosalind closed her eyes. "I mustn't. I shall lose courage," she thought.

There was no hurry about delivering the message she had come to deliver. It would be two hours before her father came home. The silence of the village street was broken by a hubbub that arose in the house across the street. Two boys playing some game ran from room to room through the house, slamming doors, shouting. A baby began to cry and then a woman's voice protested. "Quit it! Quit it!" the voice called. "Don't you see you have wakened the baby? Now I shall have a time getting him to sleep again."

Rosalind's fingers closed and her hands remained clenched. "I came home to tell you something. I have fallen in love with a man and can't marry him. He is a good many years older than myself and is already married. He has two children. I love him and I think he loves me—I know he does. I want him to have me too. I wanted to come home and tell you before it happened," she said speaking in a low clear voice. She wondered if Melville Stoner could hear her declaration.

Nothing happened. The chair in which Rosalind's mother sat had been rocking slowly back and forth and making a slight creaking sound. The sound continued. In the house across the street the baby stopped crying. The words Rosalind had come from Chicago to say to her mother were said and she felt relieved and almost happy. The silence between the two women went on and on. Rosalind's mind wandered away. Presently there would be some sort of reaction from her mother. She would be condemned. Perhaps her mother would say nothing until her father came home and would then tell him. She would be condemned as a wicked woman, ordered to leave the house. It did not matter.

Rosalind waited. Like Walter Sayers, sitting in his garden, her mind seemed to float away, out of her body. It ran away from her mother to the man she loved.

One evening, on just such another quiet summer evening as this one, she had gone into the country with Walter Sayers. Before that he had talked to her, at her, on many other evenings and during long hours in the office. He had found in her someone to whom he could talk, to whom he wanted to talk. What doors of life he had opened for her! The talk had gone on and on. In her presence the man was relieved, he relaxed out of the tenseness that had become the habit of his body. He had told her of how he had wanted to be a singer and had given up the notion. "It isn't my wife's fault nor the children's fault," he had said. "They could have lived without me. The trouble is I could not have lived without them. I am a defeated man, was intended from the first to be a defeated man and I needed something to cling to, something with which to justify my defeat. I realize that now. I am a dependent. I shall never try to sing now because I am one who has at least one merit. I know defeat. I can accept defeat."

That is what Walter Sayers had said and then on the summer evening in the country as she sat beside him in his car he had suddenly begun to sing. He had opened a farm gate and had driven the car silently along a grass covered lane and into a meadow. The lights had been put out and the car crept along. When it stopped some cattle came and stood nearby.

Then he began to sing, softly at first and with increasing boldness as he repeated the song over and over. Rosalind was so happy she had wanted to cry out. "It is because of myself he can sing now," she had thought proudly. How intensely, at the moment she loved the man, and yet perhaps the thing she felt was not love after all. There was pride in it. It was for her a moment of triumph. He had crept up to her out of a dark place, out of the dark cave of defeat. It had been her hand reached down that had given him courage.

She lay on her back, at her mother's feet, on the porch of the Wescott house trying to think, striving to get her own impulses clear in her mind. She had just told her mother that she wanted to give herself to the man, Walter Sayers. Having made the statement she already wondered if it could be quite true. She was a woman and her mother was a woman. What would her mother have to say to her? What did mothers say to daughters? The male element in life—what did it want? Her own desires and impulses were not clearly realized within herself. Perhaps what she wanted in life could be got in some sort of communion with another woman, with her mother. What a strange and beautiful thing it would be if mothers could suddenly begin to sing to their daughters, if out of the darkness and silence of old women song could come.

Men confused Rosalind, they had always confused her. On that very evening her father for the first time in years had really looked at her. He had stopped before her as she sat on the porch and there had been something in his eyes. A fire had burned in his old eyes as it had sometimes burned in the eyes of Walter. Was the fire intended to consume her quite? Was it the fate of women to be consumed by men and of men to be consumed by women?

In the orchard, an hour before she had distinctly felt the two men, Melville Stoner and Walter Sayers coming toward her, walking silently on the soft carpet made of the dark shadows of trees.

They were again coming toward her. In their thoughts they

approached nearer and nearer to her, to the inner truth of her. The street and the town of Willow Springs were covered with a mantle of silence. Was it the silence of death? Had her mother died? Did her mother sit there now a dead thing in the chair beside her?

The soft creaking of the rocking chair went on and on. Of the two men whose spirits seemed hovering about one, Melville Stoner, was bold and cunning. He was too close to her, knew too much of her. He was unafraid. The spirit of Walter Sayers was merciful. He was gentle, a man of understanding. She grew afraid of Melville Stoner. He was too close to her, knew too much of the dark, stupid side of her life. She turned on her side and stared into the darkness toward the Stoner house remembering her girlhood. The man was too physically close. The faint light from the distant street lamp that had lighted her mother's face crept between branches of trees and over the tops of bushes and she could see dimly the figure of Melville Stoner sitting before his house. She wished it were possible with a thought to destroy him, wipe him out, cause him to cease to exist. He was waiting. When her mother had gone to bed and when she had gone upstairs to her own room to lie awake he would invade her privacy. Her father would come home, walking with dragging footsteps along the sidewalk. He would come into the Wescott house and through to the back door. He would pump the pail of water at the pump and bring it into the house to put it on the box by the kitchen sink. Then he would wind the clock. He would—

Rosalind stirred uneasily. Life in the figure of Melville Stoner had her, it gripped her tightly. She could not escape. He would come into her bedroom and invade her secret thoughts. There was no escape for her. She imagined his mocking laughter ringing through the silent house, the sound rising above the dreadful commonplace sounds of everyday life there. She did not want that to happen. The sudden death of Melville Stoner would bring sweet silence. She wished it possible with a thought to destroy him, to destroy all men. She wanted her mother to draw close to her. That would save her from the men. Surely, before the evening had passed her mother would have something to say, somthing living and true.

Rosalind forced the figure of Melville Stoner out of her

mind. It was as though she had got out of her bed in the room upstairs and had taken the man by the arm to lead him to the door. She had put him out of the room and had closed the door.

Her mind played her a trick. Melville Stoner had no sooner gone out of her mind than Walter Sayers came in. In imagination she was with Walter in the car on the summer evening in the pasture and he was singing. The cattle with their soft broad noses and the sweet grass-flavored breaths were crowding in close.

There was sweetness in Rosalind's thoughts now. She rested and waited, waited for her mother to speak. In her presence Walter Sayers had broken his long silence and soon the old silence between mother and daughter would also be broken.

The singer who would not sing had begun to sing because of her presence. Song was the true note of life, it was the triumph of life over death.

What sweet solace had come to her that time when Walter Sayers sang! How life had coursed through her body! How alive she had suddenly become! It was at that moment she had decided definitely, finally, that she wanted to come closer to the man, that she wanted with him the ultimate physical closeness—to find in physical expression through him what in his song he was finding through her.

It was in expressing physically her love of the man she would find the white wonder of life, the wonder of which, as a clumsy and crude girl, she had dreamed as she lay on the grass in the orchard. Through the body of the singer she would approach, touch the white wonder of life. "I shall willingly sacrifice everything else on the chance that may happen," she thought.

How peaceful and quiet the summer night had become! How clearly now she understood life! The song Walter Sayers had sung in the field, in the presence of the cattle was in a tongue she had not understood, but now she understood everything, even the meaning of the strange foreign words.

The song was about life and death. What else was there to sing about? The sudden knowledge of the content of the song had not come out of her own mind. The spirit of Walter was coming toward her. It had pushed the mocking spirit of Melville Stoner aside. What things had not the mind of Walter

Sayers already done to her mind, to the awakening woman within her. Now it was telling her the story of the song. The words of the song itself seemed to float down the silent street of the Iowa town. They described the sun going down in the smoke clouds of a city and the gulls coming from a lake to float over the city.

Now the gulls floated over a river. The river was the color of chrysoprase. She, Rosalind Wescott, stood on a bridge in the heart of the city and she had become entirely convinced of the filth and ugliness of life. She was about to throw herself into the river, to destroy herself in an effort to make herself clean.

It did not matter. Strange sharp cries came from the birds. The cries of the birds were like the voice of Melville Stoner. They whirled and turned in the air overhead. In a moment more she would throw herself into the river and then the birds would fall straight down in a long graceful line. The body of her would be gone, swept away by the stream, carried away to decay but what was really alive in herself would arise with the birds, in the long graceful upward line of the flight of the birds.

Rosalind lay tense and still on the porch at her mother's feet. In the air above the hot sleeping town, buried deep in the ground beneath all towns and cities, life went on singing, it persistently sang. The song of life was in the humming of bees, in the calling of tree toads, in the throats of negroes rolling cotton bales on a boat in a river.

The song was a command. It told over and over the story of life and of death, life forever defeated by death, death forever defeated by life.

The long silence of Rosalind's mother was broken and Rosalind tried to tear herself away from the spirit of the song that had begun to sing itself within her—

> The sun sank down into the western sky over a city—
> > Life defeated by death,
> > Death defeated by life.
> The factory chimneys had become pencils of light—
> > Life defeated by death,
> > Death defeated by life.

The rocking chair in which Rosalind's mother sat kept creaking. Words came haltingly from between her white lips. The test of Ma Wescott's life had come. Always she had been defeated. Now she must triumph in the person of Rosalind, the daughter who had come out of her body. To her she must make clear the fate of all women. Young girls grew up dreaming, hoping, believing. There was a conspiracy. Men made words, they wrote books and sang songs about a thing called love. Young girls believed. They married or entered into close relationships with men without marriage. On the marriage night there was a brutal assault and after that the woman had to try to save herself as best as she could. She withdrew within herself, further and further within herself. Ma Wescott had stayed all her life hidden away within her own house, in the kitchen of her house. As the years passed and after the children came her man had demanded less and less of her. Now this new trouble had come. Her daughter was to have the same experience, to go through the experience that had spoiled life for her.

How proud she had been of Rosalind, going out into the world, making her own way. Her daughter dressed with a certain air, walked with a certain air. She was a proud, upstanding, triumphant thing. She did not need a man.

"God, Rosalind, don't do it, don't do it," she muttered over and over.

How much she had wanted Rosalind to keep clear and clean! Once she also had been a young woman, proud, upstanding. Could anyone think she had ever wanted to become Ma Wescott, fat, heavy and old? All through her married life she had stayed in her own house, in the kitchen of her own house, but in her own way she had watched, she had seen how things went with women. Her man had known how to make money, he had always housed her comfortably. He was a slow, silent man but in his own way he was as good as any of the men of Willow Springs. Men worked for money, they ate heavily and then at night they came home to the woman they had married.

Before she married, Ma Wescott had been a farmer's daughter. She had seen things among the beasts, how the male pursued the female. There was a certain hard insistence, cruelty. Life perpetuated itself that way. The time of her own marriage was a dim, terrible time. Why had she wanted to marry? She tried to tell Rosalind about it. "I saw him on the Main Street of town here, one Saturday evening when I had come to town with father, and two weeks after that I met him again at a dance out in the country," she said. She spoke like one who has been running a long distance and who has some important, some immediate message to deliver. "He wanted me to marry him and I did it. He wanted me to marry him and I did it."

She could not get beyond the fact of her marriage. Did her daughter think she had no vital thing to say concerning the relationship of men and women? All through her married life she had stayed in her husband's house, working as a beast might work, washing dirty clothes, dirty dishes, cooking food.

She had been thinking, all through the years she had been thinking. There was a dreadful lie in life, the whole fact of life was a lie.

She had thought it all out. There was a world somewhere unlike the world in which she lived. It was a heavenly place in which there was no marrying or giving in marriage, a sexless quiet windless place where mankind lived in a state of bliss. For some unknown reason mankind had been thrown out of that place, had been thrown down upon the earth. It was a punishment for an unforgivable sin, the sin of sex.

The sin had been in her as well as in the man she had married. She had wanted to marry. Why else did she do it? Men and women were condemned to commit the sin that destroyed them. Except for a few rare sacred beings no man or woman escaped.

What thinking she had done! When she had just married and after her man had taken what he wanted of her he slept heavily but she did not sleep. She crept out of bed and going to a window looked at the stars. The stars were quiet. With what a slow stately tread the moon moved across the sky. The stars did not sin. They did not touch one another. Each star was a thing apart from all other stars, a sacred inviolate thing. On the earth, under the stars everything was corrupt, the trees, flowers, grasses, the beasts of the field, men and women. They were all corrupt. They lived for a moment and then fell into decay. She herself was falling into decay. Life was a lie. Life perpetuated itself by the lie called love. The truth was that life itself came out of sin, perpetuated itself only by sin.

"There is no such thing as love. The word is a lie. The man you are telling me about wants you for the purpose of sin," she said and getting heavily up went into the house.

Rosalind heard her moving about in the darkness. She came to the screen door and stood looking at her daughter lying tense and waiting on the porch. The passion of denial was so strong in her that she felt choked. To the daughter it seemed that her mother standing in the darkness behind her had become a great spider, striving to lead her down into some web of darkness. "Men only hurt women," she said, "they can't help wanting to hurt women. They are made that way. The thing they call love doesn't exist. It's a lie."

"Life is dirty. Letting a man touch her dirties a woman." Ma Wescott fairly screamed forth the words. They seemed torn from her, from some deep inner part of her being. Having said them she moved off into the darkness and Rosalind heard her going slowly toward the stairway that led to the bedroom above. She was weeping in the peculiar half choked way in which old fat women weep. The heavy feet that had begun to mount the stair stopped and there was silence. Ma Wescott had said nothing of what was in her mind. She had thought it all out, what she wanted to say to her daughter. Why would the words not come? The passion for denial within her was not satisfied. "There is no love. Life is a lie. It leads to sin, to death and decay," she called into the darkness.

A strange, almost uncanny thing happened to Rosalind. The figure of her mother went out of her mind and she was in fancy again a young girl and had gone with other young girls to visit a friend about to be married. With the others she stood in a room where white dresses lay on a bed. One of her companions, a thin, flat breasted girl fell on her knees beside the bed. A cry arose. Did it come from the girl or from the old tired defeated woman within the Wescott house? "Don't do it. O, Rosalind don't do it," pleaded a voice broken with sobs.

The Wescott house had become silent like the street outside and like the sky sprinkled with stars into which Rosalind gazed. The tenseness within her relaxed and she tried again to think.

There was a thing that balanced, that swung backward and forward. Was it merely her heart beating? Her mind cleared.

The song that had come from the lips of Walter Sayers was still singing within her—

> Life the conqueror over death,
> Death the conqueror over life.

She sat up and put her head into her hands. "I came here to Willow Springs to put myself to a test. Is it the test of life and death?" she asked herself. Her mother had gone up the stairway, into the darkness of the bedroom above.

The song singing within Rosalind went on—

> Life the conquerer over death,
> Death the conquerer over life.

Was the song a male thing, the call of the male to the female, a lie, as her mother had said? It did not sound like a lie. The song had come from the lips of the man Walter and she had left him and had come to her mother. Then Melville Stoner, another male, had come to her. In him also was singing the song of life and death. When the song stopped singing within one did death come? Was death but denial? The song was singing within herself. What a confusion!

After her last outcry Ma Wescott had gone weeping up the stairs and to her own room and to bed. After a time Rosalind followed. She threw herself onto her own bed without undressing. Both women lay waiting. Outside in the darkness before his house sat Melville Stoner, the male, the man who knew of all that had passed between mother and daughter. Rosalind thought of the bridge over the river near the factory in the city and of the gulls floating in the air high above the river. She wished herself there, standing on the bridge. "It would be sweet now to throw my body down into the river," she thought. She imagined herself falling swiftly and the swifter fall of the birds down out of the sky. They were swooping down to pick up the life she was ready to drop, sweeping swiftly and beautifully down. That was what the song Walter had sung was about.

Henry Wescott came home from his evening at Emanuel Wilson's store. He went heavily through the house to the back door and the pump. There was the slow creaking sound of the pump working and then he came into the house and put the pail of water on the box by the kitchen sink. A little of the water spilled. There was a soft little slap—like a child's bare feet striking the floor—

Rosalind arose. The dead cold weariness that had settled down upon her went away. Cold dead hands had been gripping her. Now they were swept aside. Her bag was in a closet but she had forgotten it. Quickly she took off her shoes and holding them in her hands went out into the hall in her stockinged feet. Her father came heavily up the stairs past her as she stood breathless with her body pressed against the wall in the hallway.

How quick and alert her mind had become! There was a train Eastward bound toward Chicago that passed through Willow Springs at two in the morning. She would not wait for it. She would walk the eight miles to the next town to the east. That would get her out of town. It would give her something to do. "I need to be moving now," she thought as she ran down the stairs and went silently out of the house.

She walked on the grass beside the sidewalk to the gate before Melville Stoner's house and he came down to the gate to meet her. He laughed mockingly. "I fancied I might have another chance to walk with you before the night was gone," he said bowing. Rosalind did not know how much of the conversation between herself and her mother he had heard. It did not matter. He knew all Ma Wescott had said, all she could say and all Rosalind could say or understand. The thought was infinitely sweet to Rosalind. It was Melville Stoner who lifted the town of Willow Springs up out of the shadow of death. Words were unnecessary. With him she had established the thing beyond words, beyond passion—the fellowship in living, the fellowship in life.

They walked in silence to the town's edge and then Melville Stoner put out his hand. "You'll come with me?" she asked, but he shook his head and laughed. "No," he said, "I'll stay here. My time for going passed long ago. I'll stay here until I die. I'll stay here with my thoughts."

He turned and walked away into the darkness beyond the round circle of light cast by the last street lamp on the street that now became a country road leading to the next town to the east. Rosalind stood to watch him go and something in his long loping gait again suggested to her mind the figure of a gigantic bird. "He is like the gulls that float above the river in Chicago," she thought. "His spirit floats above the town of Willow Springs. When the death in life comes to the people here he swoops down, with his mind, plucking out the beauty of them."

She walked at first slowly along the road between corn fields. The night was a vast quiet place into which she could walk in peace. A little breeze rustled the corn blades but there were no dreadful significant human sounds, the sounds made by those who lived physically but who in spirit were dead, had accepted death, believed only in death. The corn blades rubbed against each other and there was a low sweet sound as though something was being born, old dead physical life was being torn away, cast aside. Perhaps new life was coming into the land.

Rosalind began to run. She had thrown off the town and her father and mother as a runner might throw off a heavy and unnecessary garment. She wished also to throw off the garments that stood between her body and nudity. She wanted to be naked, new born. Two miles out of town a bridge crossed Willow Creek. It was now empty and dry but in the darkness she imagined it filled with water, swift running water, water the color of chrysoprase. She had been running swiftly and now she stopped and stood on the bridge her breath coming in quick little gasps.

After a time she went on again, walking until she had regained her breath and then running again. Her body tingled with life. She did not ask herself what she was going to do, how she was to meet the problem she had come to Willow Springs half hoping to have solved by a word from her mother. She ran. Before her eyes the dusty road kept coming up to her out of darkness. She ran forward, always forward into a faint streak of light. The darkness unfolded before her. There was joy in the running and with every step she took she achieved a new sense of escape. A delicious notion came into her mind. As she ran she thought the light under her feet became more distinct. It was, she thought, as though the darkness had grown afraid in her presence and sprang aside, out of her path.

There was a sensation of boldness. She had herself become something that within itself contained light. She was a creator of light. At her approach darkness grew afraid and fled away into the distance. When that thought came she found herself able to run without stopping to rest and half wished she might run on forever, through the land, through towns and cities, driving darkness away with her presence.

The Man with the Trumpet

I STATED it as definitely as I could.
   I was in a room with them.
   They had tongues like me, and hair and eyes.
   I got up out of my chair and said it as definitely as I could.
   Their eyes wavered. Something slipped out of their grasp. Had I been white and strong and young enough I might have plunged through walls, gone outward into nights and days, gone into prairies, into distances—gone outward to the doorstep of the house of God, gone to God's throne room with their hands in mine.
   What I am trying to say is this—
   By God I made their minds flee out of them.
   Their minds came out of them as clear and straight as anything could be.
   I said they might build temples to their lives.
   I threw my words at faces floating in a street.
   I threw my words like stones, like building stones.
   I scattered words in alleyways like seeds.
   I crept at night and threw my words in empty rooms of houses in a street.
   I said that life was life, that men in streets and cities might build temples to their souls.
   I whispered words at night into a telephone.
   I told my people life was sweet, that men might live.
   I said a million temples might be built, that doorsteps might be cleaned.
   At their fleeing harried minds I hurled a stone.
   I said they might build temples to themselves.

HORSES AND MEN

Tales, long and short, from
our American life

TO THEODORE DREISER

In whose presence I have sometimes had
the same refreshed feeling as when in
the presence of a thoroughbred horse.

FOREWORD

Did you ever have a notion of this kind—there is an orange, or say an apple, lying on a table before you. You put out your hand to take it. Perhaps you eat it, make it a part of your physical life. Have you touched? Have you eaten? That's what I wonder about.

The whole subject is only important to me because I want the apple. What subtle flavors are concealed in it—how does it taste, smell, feel? Heavens, man, the way the apple feels in the hand is something—isn't it?

For a long time I thought only of eating the apple. Then later its fragrance became something of importance too. The fragrance stole out through my room, through a window and into the streets. It made itself a part of all the smells of the streets. The devil!—in Chicago or Pittsburgh, Youngstown or Cleveland it would have had a rough time.

That doesn't matter.

The point is that after the form of the apple began to take my eye I often found myself unable to touch at all. My hands went toward the object of my desire and then came back.

There I sat, in the room with the apple before me, and hours passed. I had pushed myself off into a world where nothing has any existence. Had I done that, or had I merely stepped, for the moment, out of the world of darkness into the light?

It may be that my eyes are blind and that I cannot see.

It may be I am deaf.

My hands are nervous and tremble. How much do they tremble? Now, alas, I am absorbed in looking at my own hands.

With these nervous and uncertain hands may I really feel for the form of things concealed in the darkness?

DREISER

Heavy, heavy, hangs over thy head,
Fine, or superfine?

Theodore Dreiser is old—he is very, very old. I do not know how many years he has lived, perhaps forty, perhaps fifty, but he is very old. Something grey and bleak and hurtful, that has been in the world perhaps forever, is personified in him.

When Dreiser is gone men shall write books, many of them, and in the books they shall write there will be so many of the qualities Dreiser lacks. The new, the younger men shall have a sense of humor, and everyone knows Dreiser has no sense of humor. More than that, American prose writers shall have grace, lightness of touch, a dream of beauty breaking through the husks of life.

O, those who follow him shall have many things that Dreiser does not have. That is a part of the wonder and beauty of Theodore Dreiser, the things that others shall have, because of him.

Long ago, when he was editor of the *Delineator*, Dreiser went one day, with a woman friend, to visit an orphan asylum. The woman once told me the story of that afternoon in the big, ugly grey building, with Dreiser, looking heavy and lumpy and old, sitting on a platform, folding and refolding his pocket-handkerchief and watching the children—all in their little uniforms, trooping in.

"The tears ran down his cheeks and he shook his head," the woman said, and that is a real picture of Theodore Dreiser. He is old in spirit and he does not know what to do with life, so he tells about it as he sees it, simply and honestly. The tears run down his cheeks and he folds and refolds the pocket-handkerchief and shakes his head.

Heavy, heavy, the feet of Theodore. How easy to pick some of his books to pieces, to laugh at him for so much of his heavy prose.

The feet of Theodore are making a path, the heavy brutal feet. They are tramping through the wilderness of lies, making a path. Presently the path will be a street, with great arches overhead and delicately carved spires piercing the sky. Along

368

the street will run children, shouting, "Look at me. See what I and my fellows of the new day have done"—forgetting the heavy feet of Dreiser.

The fellows of the ink-pots, the prose writers in America who follow Dreiser, will have much to do that he has never done. Their road is long but, because of him, those who follow will never have to face the road through the wilderness of Puritan denial, the road that Dreiser faced alone.

> *Heavy, heavy, hangs over thy head,*
> *Fine, or superfine?*

TALES OF THE BOOK

I'm a Fool

IT was a hard jolt for me, one of the most bitterest I ever had to face. And it all came about through my own foolishness, too. Even yet sometimes, when I think of it, I want to cry or swear or kick myself. Perhaps, even now, after all this time, there will be a kind of satisfaction in making myself look cheap by telling of it.

It began at three o'clock one October afternoon as I sat in the grand stand at the fall trotting and pacing meet at Sandusky, Ohio.

To tell the truth, I felt a little foolish that I should be sitting in the grand stand at all. During the summer before I had left my home town with Harry Whitehead and, with a nigger named Burt, had taken a job as swipe with one of the two horses Harry was campaigning through the fall race meets that year. Mother cried and my sister Mildred, who wanted to get a job as a school teacher in our town that fall, stormed and scolded about the house all during the week before I left. They both thought it something disgraceful that one of our family should take a place as a swipe with race horses. I've an idea Mildred thought my taking the place would stand in the way of her getting the job she'd been working so long for.

But after all I had to work, and there was no other work to be got. A big lumbering fellow of nineteen couldn't just hang around the house and I had got too big to mow people's lawns and sell newspapers. Little chaps who could get next to people's sympathies by their sizes were always getting jobs away from me. There was one fellow who kept saying to everyone who wanted a lawn mowed or a cistern cleaned, that he was saving money to work his way through college, and I used to lay awake nights thinking up ways to injure him without being found out. I kept thinking of wagons running over him and bricks falling on his head as he walked along the street. But never mind him.

I got the place with Harry and I liked Burt fine. We got along splendid together. He was a big nigger with a lazy sprawling body and soft, kind eyes, and when it came to a fight he could

373

hit like Jack Johnson. He had Bucephalus, a big black pacing stallion that could do 2.09 or 2.10, if he had to, and I had a little gelding named Doctor Fritz that never lost a race all fall when Harry wanted him to win.

We set out from home late in July in a box car with the two horses and after that, until late November, we kept moving along to the race meets and the fairs. It was a peachy time for me, I'll say that. Sometimes now I think that boys who are raised regular in houses, and never have a fine nigger like Burt for best friend, and go to high schools and college, and never steal anything, or get drunk a little, or learn to swear from fellows who know how, or come walking up in front of a grand stand in their shirt sleeves and with dirty horsey pants on when the races are going on and the grand stand is full of people all dressed up—What's the use of talking about it? Such fellows don't know nothing at all. They've never had no opportunity.

But I did. Burt taught me how to rub down a horse and put the bandages on after a race and steam a horse out and a lot of valuable things for any man to know. He could wrap a bandage on a horse's leg so smooth that if it had been the same color you would think it was his skin, and I guess he'd have been a big driver, too, and got to the top like Murphy and Walter Cox and the others if he hadn't been black.

Gee whizz, it was fun. You got to a county seat town, maybe say on a Saturday or Sunday, and the fair began the next Tuesday and lasted until Friday afternoon. Doctor Fritz would be, say in the 2.25 trot on Tuesday afternoon and on Thursday afternoon Bucephalus would knock 'em cold in the "free-for-all" pace. It left you a lot of time to hang around and listen to horse talk, and see Burt knock some yap cold that got too gay, and you'd find out about horses and men and pick up a lot of stuff you could use all the rest of your life, if you had some sense and salted down what you heard and felt and saw.

And then at the end of the week when the race meet was over, and Harry had run home to tend up to his livery stable business, you and Burt hitched the two horses to carts and drove slow and steady across country, to the place for the next meeting, so as to not over-heat the horses, etc., etc., you know.

Gee whizz, Gosh amighty, the nice hickorynut and beech-nut and oaks and other kinds of trees along the roads, all brown and red, and the good smells, and Burt singing a song that was called Deep River, and the country girls at the windows of houses and everything. You can stick your colleges up your nose for all me. I guess I know where I got my education.

Why, one of those little burgs of towns you come to on the way, say now on a Saturday afternoon, and Burt says, "let's lay up here." And you did.

And you took the horses to a livery stable and fed them, and you got your good clothes out of a box and put them on.

And the town was full of farmers gaping, because they could see you were race horse people, and the kids maybe never see a nigger before and was afraid and run away when the two of us walked down their main street.

And that was before prohibition and all that foolishness, and so you went into a saloon, the two of you, and all the yaps come and stood around, and there was always someone pretended he was horsey and knew things and spoke up and began asking questions, and all you did was to lie and lie all you could about what horses you had, and I said I owned them, and then some fellow said "will you have a drink of whiskey" and Burt knocked his eye out the way he could say, off-hand like, "Oh well, all right, I'm agreeable to a little nip. I'll split a quart with you." Gee whizz.

But that isn't what I want to tell my story about. We got home late in November and I promised mother I'd quit the race horses for good. There's a lot of things you've got to promise a mother because she don't know any better.

And so, there not being any work in our town any more than when I left there to go to the races, I went off to Sandusky and got a pretty good place taking care of horses for a man who owned a teaming and delivery and storage and coal and real estate business there. It was a pretty good place with good eats, and a day off each week, and sleeping on a cot in a big barn, and mostly just shovelling in hay and oats to a lot of big good-enough skates of horses, that couldn't have trotted a race with a toad. I wasn't dissatisfied and I could send money home.

And then, as I started to tell you, the fall races come to

Sandusky and I got the day off and I went. I left the job at noon and had on my good clothes and my new brown derby hat, I'd just bought the Saturday before, and a stand-up collar.

First of all I went down-town and walked about with the dudes. I've always thought to myself, "put up a good front" and so I did it. I had forty dollars in my pocket and so I went into the West House, a big hotel, and walked up to the cigar stand. "Give me three twenty-five cent cigars," I said. There was a lot of horsemen and strangers and dressed-up people from other towns standing around in the lobby and in the bar, and I mingled amongst them. In the bar there was a fellow with a cane and a Windsor tie on, that it made me sick to look at him. I like a man to be a man and dress up, but not to go put on that kind of airs. So I pushed him aside, kind of rough, and had me a drink of whiskey. And then he looked at me, as though he thought maybe he'd get gay, but he changed his mind and didn't say anything. And then I had another drink of whiskey, just to show him something, and went out and had a hack out to the races, all to myself, and when I got there I bought myself the best seat I could get up in the grand stand, but didn't go in for any of these boxes. That's putting on too many airs.

And so there I was, sitting up in the grand stand as gay as you please and looking down on the swipes coming out with their horses, and with their dirty horsey pants on and the horse blankets swung over their shoulders, same as I had been doing all the year before. I liked one thing about the same as the other, sitting up there and feeling grand and being down there and looking up at the yaps and feeling grander and more important, too. One thing's about as good as another, if you take it just right. I've often said that.

Well, right in front of me, in the grand stand that day, there was a fellow with a couple of girls and they was about my age. The young fellow was a nice guy all right. He was the kind maybe that goes to college and then comes to be a lawyer or maybe a newspaper editor or something like that, but he wasn't stuck on himself. There are some of that kind are all right and he was one of the ones.

He had his sister with him and another girl and the sister looked around over his shoulder, accidental at first, not intending to start anything—she wasn't that kind—and her eyes and mine happened to meet.

You know how it is. Gee, she was a peach! She had on a soft dress, kind of a blue stuff and it looked carelessly made, but was well sewed and made and everything. I knew that much. I blushed when she looked right at me and so did she. She was the nicest girl I've ever seen in my life. She wasn't stuck on herself and she could talk proper grammar without being like a school teacher or something like that. What I mean is, she was O. K. I think maybe her father was well-to-do, but not rich to make her chesty because she was his daughter, as some are. Maybe he owned a drug store or a drygoods store in their home town, or something like that. She never told me and I never asked.

My own people are all O. K. too, when you come to that. My grandfather was Welsh and over in the old country, in Wales he was— But never mind that.

The first heat of the first race come off and the young fellow setting there with the two girls left them and went down to make a bet. I knew what he was up to, but he didn't talk big and noisy and let everyone around know he was a sport, as some do. He wasn't that kind. Well, he come back and I heard him tell the two girls what horse he'd bet on, and when the heat was trotted they all half got to their feet and acted in the excited, sweaty way people do when they've got money down on a race, and the horse they bet on is up there pretty close at the end, and they think maybe he'll come on with a rush, but he never does because he hasn't got the old juice in him, come right down to it.

And then, pretty soon, the horses came out for the 2.18 pace and there was a horse in it I knew. He was a horse Bob French had in his string but Bob didn't own him. He was a horse owned by a Mr. Mathers down at Marietta, Ohio.

This Mr. Mathers had a lot of money and owned some coal mines or something, and he had a swell place out in the country, and he was stuck on race horses, but was a Presbyterian or something, and I think more than likely his wife was one, too, maybe a stiffer one than himself. So he never raced his horses hisself, and the story round the Ohio race tracks was that when one of his horses got ready to go to the races he turned him over to Bob French and pretended to his wife he was sold.

So Bob had the horses and he did pretty much as he pleased and you can't blame Bob, at least, I never did. Sometimes he was out to win and sometimes he wasn't. I never cared much about that when I was swiping a horse. What I did want to know was that my horse had the speed and could go out in front, if you wanted him to.

And, as I'm telling you, there was Bob in this race with one of Mr. Mathers' horses, was named "About Ben Ahem" or something like that, and was fast as a streak. He was a gelding and had a mark of 2.21, but could step in .08 or .09.

Because when Burt and I were out, as I've told you, the year before, there was a nigger, Burt knew, worked for Mr. Mathers and we went out there one day when we didn't have no race on at the Marietta Fair and our boss Harry was gone home.

And so everyone was gone to the fair but just this one nigger and he took us all through Mr. Mathers' swell house and he and Burt tapped a bottle of wine Mr. Mathers had hid in his bedroom, back in a closet, without his wife knowing, and he showed us this Ahem horse. Burt was always stuck on being a driver but didn't have much chance to get to the top, being a nigger, and he and the other nigger gulped that whole bottle of wine and Burt got a little lit up.

So the nigger let Burt take this About Ben Ahem and step him a mile in a track Mr. Mathers had all to himself, right there on the farm. And Mr. Mathers had one child, a daughter, kinda sick and not very good looking, and she came home and we had to hustle and get About Ben Ahem stuck back in the barn.

I'm only telling you to get everything straight. At Sandusky, that afternoon I was at the fair, this young fellow with the two girls was fussed, being with the girls and losing his bet. You know how a fellow is that way. One of them was his girl and the other his sister. I had figured that out.

"Gee whizz," I says to myself, "I'm going to give him the dope."

He was mighty nice when I touched him on the shoulder. He and the girls were nice to me right from the start and clear to the end. I'm not blaming them.

And so he leaned back and I give him the dope on About Ben Ahem. "Don't bet a cent on this first heat because he'll go like an oxen hitched to a plow, but when the first heat is over go right down and lay on your pile." That's what I told him.

Well, I never saw a fellow treat any one sweller. There was a fat man sitting beside the little girl, that had looked at me twice by this time, and I at her, and both blushing, and what did he do but have the nerve to turn and ask the fat man to get up and change places with me so I could set with his crowd.

Gee whizz, craps amighty. There I was. What a chump I was to go and get gay up there in the West House bar, and just because that dude was standing there with a cane and that kind of a necktie on, to go and get all balled up and drink that whiskey, just to show off.

Of course she would know, me setting right beside her and letting her smell of my breath. I could have kicked myself right down out of that grand stand and all around that race track and made a faster record than most of the skates of horses they had there that year.

Because that girl wasn't any mutt of a girl. What wouldn't I have give right then for a stick of chewing gum to chew, or a lozenger, or some liquorice, or most anything. I was glad I had those twenty-five cent cigars in my pocket and right away I give that fellow one and lit one myself. Then that fat man got up and we changed places and there I was, plunked right down beside her.

They introduced themselves and the fellow's best girl, he had with him, was named Miss Elinor Woodbury, and her father was a manufacturer of barrels from a place called Tiffin, Ohio. And the fellow himself was named Wilbur Wessen and his sister was Miss Lucy Wessen.

I suppose it was their having such swell names got me off my trolley. A fellow, just because he has been a swipe with a race horse, and works taking care of horses for a man in the teaming, delivery, and storage business, isn't any better or worse than any one else. I've often thought that, and said it too.

But you know how a fellow is. There's something in that kind of nice clothes, and the kind of nice eyes she had, and the way she had looked at me, awhile before, over her brother's shoulder, and me looking back at her, and both of us blushing.

I couldn't show her up for a boob, could I?

I made a fool of myself, that's what I did. I said my name was Walter Mathers from Marietta, Ohio, and then I told all three of them the smashingest lie you ever heard. What I said was that my father owned the horse About Ben Ahem and that he had let him out to this Bob French for racing purposes, because our family was proud and had never gone into racing that way, in our own name, I mean. Then I had got started and they were all leaning over and listening, and Miss Lucy Wessen's eyes were shining, and I went the whole hog.

I told about our place down at Marietta, and about the big stables and the grand brick house we had on a hill, up above the Ohio River, but I knew enough not to do it in no bragging way. What I did was to start things and then let them drag the rest out of me. I acted just as reluctant to tell as I could. Our family hasn't got any barrel factory, and, since I've known us, we've always been pretty poor, but not asking anything of any one at that, and my grandfather, over in Wales—but never mind that.

We set there talking like we had known each other for years and years, and I went and told them that my father had been expecting maybe this Bob French wasn't on the square, and had sent me up to Sandusky on the sly to find out what I could.

And I bluffed it through I had found out all about the 2.18 pace, in which About Ben Ahem was to start.

I said he would lose the first heat by pacing like a lame cow and then he would come back and skin 'em alive after that. And to back up what I said I took thirty dollars out of my pocket and handed it to Mr. Wilbur Wessen and asked him, would he mind, after the first heat, to go down and place it on About Ben Ahem for whatever odds he could get. What I said was that I didn't want Bob French to see me and none of the swipes.

Sure enough the first heat come off and About Ben Ahem went off his stride, up the back stretch, and looked like a wooden horse or a sick one, and come in to be last. Then this Wilbur Wessen went down to the betting place under the grand stand and there I was with the two girls, and when that Miss Woodbury was looking the other way once, Lucy Wessen kinda, with her shoulder you know, kinda touched me. Not just tucking down, I don't mean. You know how a woman can do. They get close, but not getting gay either. You know what they do. Gee whizz.

And then they give me a jolt. What they had done, when I didn't know, was to get together, and they had decided Wilbur Wessen would bet fifty dollars, and the two girls had gone and put in ten dollars each, of their own money, too. I was sick then, but I was sicker later.

About the gelding, About Ben Ahem, and their winning their money, I wasn't worried a lot about that. It come out O.K. Ahem stepped the next three heats like a bushel of spoiled eggs going to market before they could be found out, and Wilbur Wessen had got nine to two for the money. There was something else eating at me.

Because Wilbur come back, after he had bet the money, and after that he spent most of his time talking to that Miss Woodbury, and Lucy Wessen and I was left alone together like on a desert island. Gee, if I'd only been on the square or if there had been any way of getting myself on the square. There ain't any Walter Mathers, like I said to her and them, and there hasn't ever been one, but if there was, I bet I'd go to Marietta, Ohio, and shoot him to-morrow.

There I was, big boob that I am. Pretty soon the race was over, and Wilbur had gone down and collected our money, and we had a hack down-town, and he stood us a swell supper at the West House, and a bottle of champagne beside.

And I was with that girl and she wasn't saying much, and I wasn't saying much either. One thing I know. She wasn't stuck on me because of the lie about my father being rich and all that. There's a way you know. . . . Craps amighty. There's a kind of girl, you see just once in your life, and if you don't get busy and make hay, then you're gone for good and all, and might as well go jump off a bridge. They give you a look from inside of them somewhere, and it ain't no vamping, and what it means is—you want that girl to be your wife, and you want nice things around her like flowers and swell clothes, and you want her to have the kids you're going to have, and you want good music played and no rag time. Gee whizz.

There's a place over near Sandusky, across a kind of bay, and

it's called Cedar Point. And after we had supper we went over
to it in a launch, all by ourselves. Wilbur and Miss Lucy and
that Miss Woodbury had to catch a ten o'clock train back to
Tiffin, Ohio, because, when you're out with girls like that you
can't get careless and miss any trains and stay out all night, like
you can with some kinds of Janes.

And Wilbur blowed himself to the launch and it cost him
fifteen cold plunks, but I wouldn't never have knew if I hadn't
listened. He wasn't no tin horn kind of a sport.

Over at the Cedar Point place, we didn't stay around where
there was a gang of common kind of cattle at all.

There was big dance halls and dining places for yaps, and
there was a beach you could walk along and get where it was
dark, and we went there.

She didn't talk hardly at all and neither did I, and I was thinking how glad I was my mother was all right, and always made
us kids learn to eat with a fork at table, and not swill soup, and
not be noisy and rough like a gang you see around a race track
that way.

Then Wilbur and his girl went away up the beach and Lucy
and I sat down in a dark place, where there was some roots of
old trees the water had washed up, and after that the time, till
we had to go back in the launch and they had to catch their
trains, wasn't nothing at all. It went like winking your eye.

Here's how it was. The place we were setting in was dark,
like I said, and there was the roots from that old stump sticking up like arms, and there was a watery smell, and the night
was like—as if you could put your hand out and feel it—so
warm and soft and dark and sweet like an orange.

I most cried and I most swore and I most jumped up and
danced, I was so mad and happy and sad.

When Wilbur come back from being alone with his girl, and
she saw him coming, Lucy she says, "we got to go to the train
now," and she was most crying too, but she never knew nothing I knew, and she couldn't be so all busted up. And then,
before Wilbur and Miss Woodbury got up to where we was,
she put her face up and kissed me quick and put her head up
against me and she was all quivering and—Gee whizz.

Sometimes I hope I have cancer and die. I guess you know what I mean. We went in the launch across the bay to the train like that, and it was dark, too. She whispered and said it was like she and I could get out of the boat and walk on the water, and it sounded foolish, but I knew what she meant.

And then quick we were right at the depot, and there was a big gang of yaps, the kind that goes to the fairs, and crowded and milling around like cattle, and how could I tell her? "It won't be long because you'll write and I'll write to you." That's all she said.

I got a chance like a hay barn afire. A swell chance I got.

And maybe she would write me, down at Marietta that way, and the letter would come back, and stamped on the front of it by the U.S.A. "there ain't any such guy," or something like that, whatever they stamp on a letter that way.

And me trying to pass myself off for a bigbug and a swell— to her, as decent a little body as God ever made. Craps amighty —a swell chance I got!

And then the train come in, and she got on it, and Wilbur Wessen he come and shook hands with me, and that Miss Woodbury was nice too and bowed to me, and I at her, and the train went and I busted out and cried like a kid.

Gee, I could have run after that train and made Dan Patch look like a freight train after a wreck but, socks amighty, what was the use? Did you ever see such a fool?

I'll bet you what—if I had an arm broke right now or a train had run over my foot—I wouldn't go to no doctor at all. I'd go set down and let her hurt and hurt—that's what I'd do.

I'll bet you what—if I hadn't a drunk that booze I'd a never been such a boob as to go tell such a lie—that couldn't never be made straight to a lady like her.

I wish I had that fellow right here that had on a Windsor tie and carried a cane. I'd smash him for fair. Gosh darn his eyes. He's a big fool—that's what he is.

And if I'm not another you just go find me one and I'll quit working and be a bum and give him my job. I don't care nothing for working, and earning money, and saving it for no such boob as myself.

The Triumph of a Modern
Or, Send for the Lawyer

INASMUCH as I have put to myself the task of trying to tell you a curious story in which I am myself concerned—in a strictly secondary way you must of course understand—I will begin by giving you some notion of myself.

Very well then, I am a man of thirty-two, rather small in size, with sandy hair. I wear glasses. Until two years ago I lived in Chicago, where I had a position as clerk in an office that afforded me a good enough living. I have never married, being somewhat afraid of women—in the flesh, in a way of speaking. In fancy and in my imagination I have always been very bold but in the flesh women have always frightened me horribly. They have a way of smiling quietly as though to say——. But we will not go into that now.

Since boyhood I have had an ambition to be a painter, not, I will confess, because of a desire to produce some great masterpiece of the arts, but simply and solely because I have always thought the life painters lead would appeal to me.

I have always liked the notion (let's be honest if we can) of going about, wearing a hat, tipped a little to the side of my head, sporting a moustache, carrying a cane and speaking in an off-hand way of such things as form, rhythm, the effects of light and masses, surfaces, etc., etc. During my life I have read a good many books concerning painters and their work, their friendships and their loves and when I was in Chicago and poor and was compelled to live in a small room alone, I assure you I carried off many a dull weary evening by imagining myself a painter of wide renown in the world.

It was afternoon and having finished my day's work I went strolling off to the studio of another painter. He was still at work and there were two models in the room, women in the nude sitting about. One of them smiled at me, I thought a little wistfully, but pshaw, I am too blasé for anything of that sort.

I go across the room to my friend's canvas and stand looking at it.

Now he is looking at me, a little anxiously. I am the greater

384

man, you understand. That is frankly and freely acknowledged. Whatever else may be said against my friend he never claimed to be my equal. In fact it is generally understood, wherever I go, that I am the greater man.

"Well?" says my friend. You see he is fairly hanging on my words, as the saying goes; in short, he is waiting for me to speak with the air of one about to be hanged.

Why? The devil! Why does he put everything up to me? One gets tired carrying such responsibility upon one's shoulders. A painter should be the judge of his own work and not embarrass his fellow painters by asking questions. That is my method.

Very well then. If I speak sharply you have only yourself to blame. "The yellow you have been using is a little muddy. The arm of this woman is not felt. In painting one should feel the arm of a woman. What I advise is that you change your palette. You have scattered too much. Pull it together. A painting should stick together as a wet snow ball thrown by a boy clings to a wall."

When I had reached the age of thirty, that is to say two years ago, I received from my aunt, the sister of my father to be exact, a small fortune I had long been dreaming I might possibly inherit.

My aunt I had never seen, but I had always been saying to myself, "I must go see my aunt. The old lady will be sore at me and when she dies will not leave me a cent."

And then, lucky fellow that I am, I did go to see her just before she died.

Filled with determination to put the thing through I set out from Chicago, and it is not my fault that I did not spend the day with her. Even although my aunt is (as I am not fool enough not to know that you know) a woman I would have spent the day with her but that it was impossible.

She lived at Madison, Wisconsin, and I went there on Saturday morning. The house was locked and the windows boarded up. Fortunately, at just that moment, a mail carrier came along and, upon my telling him that I was my aunt's nephew, gave me her address. He also gave me some news concerning her.

For years she had been a sufferer from hay-fever and every summer had to have a change of climate.

That was an opportunity for me. I went at once to a hotel

and wrote her a letter telling of my visit and expressing, to the utmost of my ability, my sorrow in not having found her at home. "I have been a long time doing this job but now that I am at it I fancy I shall do it rather well," I said to myself.

A sort of feeling came into my hand, as it were. I can't just say what it was but as soon as I sat down I knew very well I should be eloquent. For the moment I was positively a poet.

In the first place, and as one should in writing a letter to a lady, I spoke of the sky. "The sky is full of mottled clouds," I said. Then, and I frankly admit in a brutally casual way, I spoke of myself as one practically prostrated with grief. To tell the truth I did not just know what I was doing. I had got the fever for writing words, you see. They fairly flowed out of my pen.

I had come, I said, on a long and weary journey to the home of my only female relative, and here I threw into the letter some reference to the fact that I was an orphan. "Imagine," I wrote, "the sorrow and desolation in my heart at finding the house unoccupied and the windows boarded up."

It was there, sitting in the hotel at Madison, Wisconsin, with the pen in my hand, that I made my fortune. Something bold and heroic came into my mood and, without a moment's hesitation, I mentioned in my letter what should never be mentioned to a woman, unless she be an elderly woman of one's own family, and then only by a physician perhaps—I spoke of my aunt's breasts, using the plural.

I had hoped, I said, to lay my tired head on her breasts. To tell the truth I had become drunken with words and now, how glad I am that I did. Mr. George Moore, Clive Bell, Paul Rosenfeld, and others of the most skillful writers of our English speech, have written a great deal about painters and, as I have already explained, there was not a book or magazine article in English and concerning painters, their lives and works, procurable in Chicago, I had not read.

What I am now striving to convey to you is something of my own pride in my literary effort in the hotel at Madison, Wisconsin, and surely, if I was, at that moment an artist, no other artist has ever had such quick and wholehearted recognition.

Having spoken of putting my tired head on my aunt's breasts (poor woman, she died, never having seen me) I went on to give the general impression—which by the way was quite

honest and correct—of a somewhat boyish figure, rather puzzled, wandering in a confused way through life. The imaginary
but correct enough figure of myself, born at the moment in
my imagination, had made its way through dismal swamps of
gloom, over the rough hills of adversity and through the dry
deserts of loneliness, toward the one spot in all this world
where it had hoped to find rest and peace—that is to say upon
the bosom of its aunt. However, as I have already explained,
being a thorough modern and full of the modern boldness, I
did not use the word bosom, as an old-fashioned writer might
have done. I used the word breasts. When I had finished writing tears were in my eyes.

The letter I wrote on that day covered some seven sheets of
hotel paper—finely written to the margins—and cost four
cents to mail.

"Shall I mail it or shall I not?" I said to myself as I came out
of the hotel office and stood before a mail box. The letter was
balanced between my finger and thumb.

> "Eeny, meeny, miny, mo,
> Catch a nigger by the toe."

The forefinger of my left hand—I was holding the letter in
my right hand—touched my nose, mouth, forehead, eyes, chin,
neck, shoulder, arm, hand and then tapped the letter itself. No
doubt I fully intended, from the first, to drop it. I had been
doing the work of an artist. Well, artists are always talking of
destroying their own work but few do it, and those who do are
perhaps the real heroes of life.

And so down into the mail box it went with a thud and my
fortune was made. The letter was received by my aunt, who
was lying abed of an illness that was to destroy her—she had, it
seems, other things beside hay-fever the matter with her—and
she altered her will in my favor. She had intended leaving her
money, a tidy sum yielding an income of five thousand a year,
to a fund to be established for the study of methods for the
cure of hay-fever—that is to say, really you see, to her fellow
sufferers—but instead left it to me. My aunt could not find her
spectacles and a nurse—may the gods bring her bright days
and a good husband—read the letter aloud. Both women were
deeply touched and my aunt wept. I am only telling you the

facts, you understand, but I would like to suggest that this whole incident might well be taken as proof of the power of modern art. From the first I have been a firm believer in the moderns. I am one who, as an art critic might word it, has been right down through the moments. At first I was an impressionist and later a cubist, a post-impressionist, and even a vorticist. Time after time, in my imaginary life, as a painter, I have been quite swept off my feet. For example I remember Picasso's blue period . . . but we'll not go into that.

What I am trying to say is that, having this faith in modernity, if one may use the word thus, I did find within myself a peculiar boldness as I sat in the hotel writing room at Madison, Wisconsin. I used the word breasts (in the plural, you understand) and everyone will admit that it is a bold and modern word to use in a letter to an aunt one has never seen. It brought my aunt and me into one family. Her modesty never could have admitted anything else.

And then, my aunt was really touched. Afterward I talked to the nurse and made her a rather handsome present for her part in the affair. When the letter had been read my aunt felt overwhelmingly drawn to me. She turned her face to the wall and her shoulders shook. Do not think that I am not also touched as I write this. "Poor lad," my aunt said to the nurse, "I will make things easier for him. Send for the lawyer."

"Unused"

A TALE OF LIFE IN OHIO

"UNUSED," that was one of the words the Doctor used that day in speaking of her. He, the doctor, was an extraordinarily large and immaculately clean man, by whom I was at that time employed. I swept out his office, mowed the lawn before his residence, took care of the two horses in his stable and did odd jobs about the yard and kitchen—such as bringing in firewood, putting water in a tub in the sun behind a grape arbor for the doctor's bath and even sometimes, during his bath, scrubbing for him those parts of his broad back he himself could not reach.

The doctor had a passion in life with which he early infected me. He loved fishing and as he knew all of the good places in the river, several miles west of town, and in Sandusky Bay, some nineteen or twenty miles to the north, we often went off for long delightful days together.

It was late in the afternoon of such a fishing day in the late June, when the doctor and I were together in a boat on the bay, that a farmer came running to the shore, waving his arms and calling to the doctor. Little May Edgley's body had been found floating near a river's mouth half a mile away, and, as she had been dead for several days, as the doctor had just had a good bite, and as there was nothing he could do anyway, it was all nonsense, his being called. I remembered how he growled and grumbled. He did not then know what had happened but the fish were just beginning to bite splendidly, I had just landed a fine bass and the good evening's fishing was all ahead of us. Well, you know how it is—a doctor is always at everyone's beck and call.

"Dang it all! That's the way it always goes! Here we are—as good a fishing evening as we'll find this summer—wind just right and the sky clouding over—and will you look at my dang luck? A doctor in the neighborhood and that farmer knows it and so, just to accommodate me, he goes and stubs his toe, like as not, or his boy falls out of a barn loft, or his old woman gets the toothache. Like as not it's one of his women folks. I

389

know 'em! His wife's got an unmarried sister living with her. Dang sentimental old maid! She's got a nervous complaint— gets all worked up and thinks she's going to die. Die nothing! I know that kind. Lots of 'em like to have a doctor fooling around. Let a doctor come near, so they can get him alone in a room, and they'll spend hours talking about themselves—if he'll let 'em."

The doctor was reeling in his line, grumbling and complaining as he did so and then, suddenly, with the characteristic cheerfulness that I had seen carry him with a smile on his lips through whole days and nights of work and night driving over rough frozen earth roads in the winter, he picked up the oars and rowed vigorously ashore. When I offered to take the oars he shook his head. "No kid, it's good for the figure," he said, looking down at his huge paunch. He smiled. "I got to keep my figure. If I don't I'll be losing some of my practice among the unmarried women."

As for the business ashore—there was May Edgley, of our town, drowned in that out of the way place, and her body had been in the water several days. It had been found among some willows that grew near the mouth of a deep creek that emptied into the bay, had lodged in among the roots of the willows, and when we got ashore the farmer, his son and the hired man, had got it out and had laid it on some boards near a barn that faced the bay.

That was my own first sight of death and I shall not forget the moment when I followed the doctor in among the little group of silent people standing about and saw the dead, discolored and bloated body of the woman lying there.

The doctor was used to that sort of thing, but to me it was all new and terrifying. I remember that I looked once and then ran away. Dashing into the barn I went to lean against the feedbox of a stall, where an old farm-horse was eating hay. The warm day outside had suddenly seemed cold and chill but in the barn it was warm again. Oh, what a lovely thing to a boy is a barn, with the rich warm comforting smell of the cured hay and the animal life, lying like a soft bed over it all. At the doctor's house, while I lived and worked there, the doctor's wife used to put on my bed, on winter nights, a kind of soft warm bed cover called a "comfortable." That's what it was like to me that day in the barn when we had just found May Edgley's body.

As for the body—well, May Edgley had been a small woman with small firm hands and in one of her hands, tightly gripped, when they had found her, was a woman's hat—a great broad-brimmed gaudy thing it must have been, and there had been a huge ostrich feather sticking out of the top, such an ostrich feather as you see sometimes sticking out of the hat of a kind of big flashy woman at the horse races or at second-rate summer resorts near cities.

It stayed in my mind, that bedraggled ostrich feather, little May Edgley's hand had gripped so determinedly when death came, and as I stood shivering in the barn I could see it again, as I had so often seen it perched on the head of big bold Lil Edgley, May Edgley's sister, as she went, half-defiantly always, through the streets of our town, Bidwell, Ohio.

And then as I stood shivering with boyish dread of death in that old barn, the farm-horse put his head through an opening at the front of the stall and rubbed his soft warm nose against my cheek. The farmer, on whose place we were, must have been one who was kind to his animals. The old horse rubbed his nose up and down my cheek. "You are a long ways from death, my lad, and when the time comes for you you won't shiver so much. I am old and I know. Death is a kind comforting thing to those who are through with their lives."

Something of that sort the old farmhorse seemed to be saying and at any rate he quieted me, took the fear and the chill all out of me.

It was when the doctor and I were driving home together that evening in the dusk, and after all arrangements for sending May Edgley's body back to town and to her people had been made, that he spoke of her and used the word I am now using as the title for her story. The doctor said a great many things that evening that I cannot now remember and I only remember how the night came softly on and how the grey road faded out of sight, and then how the moon came out and the road that had been grey became silvery white, with patches of inky blackness where the shadows of trees fell across it. The doctor was one sane enough not to talk down to a boy. How often he spoke intimately to me of his impressions of men and events! There were many things in the fat old doctor's mind of which his patients knew nothing, but of which his stable boy knew.

The doctor's old bay horse went steadily along, doing his work as cheerfully as the doctor did his and the doctor smoked a cigar. He spoke of the dead woman, May Edgley, and of what a bright girl she had been.

As for her story—he did not tell it completely. I was myself much alive that evening—that is to say the imaginative side of myself was much alive—and the doctor was as a sower, sowing seed in a fertile soil. He was as one who goes through a wide long field, newly plowed by the hand of Death, the plowman, and as he went along he flung wide the seeds of May Edgley's story, wide, far over the land, over the rich fertile land of a boy's awakening imagination.

CHAPTER I

There were three boys and as many girls in the Edgley family of Bidwell, Ohio, and of the girls Lillian and Kate were known in a dozen towns along the railroad that ran between Cleveland and Toledo. The fame of Lillian, the eldest, went far. On the streets of the neighboring towns of Clyde, Norwalk, Fremont, Tiffin, and even in Toledo and Cleveland, she was well known. On summer evenings she went up and down our main street wearing a huge hat with a white ostrich feather that fell down almost to her shoulder. She, like her sister Kate, who never succeeded in attaining to a position of prominence in the town's life, was a blonde with cold staring blue eyes. On almost any Friday evening she might have been seen setting forth on some adventure, from which she did not return until the following Monday or Tuesday. It was evident the adventures were profitable, as the Edgley family were working folk and it is certain her brothers did not purchase for her the endless number of new dresses in which she arrayed herself.

It was a Friday evening in the summer and Lillian appeared on the upper main street of Bidwell. Two dozen men and boys loafed by the station platform, awaiting the arrival of the New York Central train, eastward bound. They stared at Lillian who stared back at them. In the west, from which direction the train was presently to come, the sun went down over young corn fields. A dusky golden splendor lit the skies and the loafers were awed into silence, hushed, both by the beauty of the evening and by the challenge in Lillian's eyes.

Then the train arrived and the spell of silence was broken. The conductor and brakeman jumped to the station platform and waved their hands at Lillian and the engineer put his head out of the cab.

Aboard the train Lillian found a seat by herself and as soon as the train had started and the fares were collected the conductor came to sit with her. When the train arrived at the next town and the conductor was compelled to attend to his affairs, the brakeman came to lean over her seat. The men talked in undertones and occasionally the silence in the car was broken by outbursts of laughter. Other women from Bidwell, going to visit relatives in distant towns, were embarrassed. They turned their heads to look out at car windows and their cheeks grew red.

On the station platform at Bidwell, where darkness was settling down over the scene, the men and boys still lingered about speaking of Lillian and her adventures. "She can ride anywhere she pleases and never has to pay a cent of fare," declared a tall bearded man who leaned against the station door. He was a buyer of pigs and cattle and was compelled to go to the Cleveland market once every week. The thought of Lillian, the light o' love traveling free over the railroads filled his heart with envy and anger.

The entire Edgley family bore a shaky reputation in Bidwell but with the exception of May, the youngest of the girls, they were people who knew how to take care of themselves. For years Jake, the eldest of the boys, tended bar for Charley Shuter in a saloon in lower Main Street and then, to everyone's surprise, he bought out the place. "Either Lillian gave him the money or he stole it from Charley," the men said, but nevertheless, and throwing moral standards aside, they went into the bar to buy drinks. In Bidwell vice, while openly condemned, was in secret looked upon as a mark of virility in young manhood.

Frank and Will Edgley were teamsters and draymen like their

father John and were hard working men. They owned their own teams and asked favors of no man and when they were not at work did not seek the society of others. Late on Saturday afternoons, when the week's work was done and the horses cleaned, fed and bedded down for the night they dressed themselves in black suits, put on white collars and black derby hats and went into our main street to drink themselves drunk. By ten o'clock they had succeeded and went reeling homeward. When in the darkness under the maple trees on Vine or Walnut Streets they met a Bidwell citizen, also homeward bound, a row started. "Damn you, get out of our way. Get off the sidewalk," Frank Edgley shouted and the two men rushed forward intent on a fight.

One evening in the month of June, when there was a moon and when insects sang loudly in the long grass between the sidewalks and the road, the Edgley brothers met Ed Pesch, a young German farmer, out for an evening's walk with Caroline Dupee, daughter of a Bidwell drygoods merchant, and the fight the Edgley boys had long been looking for took place. Frank Edgley shouted and he and his brother plunged forward but Ed Pesch did not run into the road and leave them to go triumphantly homeward. He fought and the brothers were badly beaten, and on Monday morning appeared driving their team and with faces disfigured and eyes blackened. For a week they went up and down alleyways and along residence streets, delivering ice and coal to houses and merchandise to the stores without lifting their eyes or speaking. The town was delighted and clerks ran from store to store making comments, they longed to repeat within hearing of one of the brothers. "Have you seen the Edgley boys?" they asked one another. "They got what was coming to them. Ed Pesch gave them what for." The more excitable and imaginative of the clerks spoke of the fight in the darkness as though they had been on hand and had seen every blow struck. "They are bullies and can be beaten by any man who stands up for his rights," declared Walter Wills, a slender, nervous young man who worked for Albert Twist, the grocer. The clerk hungered to be such another fighter as Ed Pesch had proven himself. At night he went home from the store in the soft darkness and imagined himself as meeting the Edgleys. "I'll show you—you big bullies," he muttered and his fists shot out, striking at nothingness. An eager strained feeling ran along the muscles of his back and arms but his night time courage did not abide with him through the day. On Wednesday when Will Edgley came to the back door of the store, his wagon loaded with salt in barrels, Walter went into the alleyway to enjoy the sight of the cut lips and blackened eyes. Will stood with hands in pockets looking at the ground. An uncomfortable silence ensued and in the end it was broken by the voice of the clerk. "There's no one here and those barrels are heavy," he said heartily. "I might as well make myself useful and help you unload." Taking off his coat Walter Wills voluntarily helped at the task that belonged to Will Edgley, the drayman.

If May Edgley, during her girlhood, rose higher than any of the others of the Edgley family she also fell lower. "She had her chance and threw it away," was the word that went round and surely no one else in that family ever had so completely the town's sympathy. Lillian Edgley was outside the pale of the town's life, and Kate was but a lesser edition of her sister. She waited on table at the Fownsby House, and on almost any evening might have been seen walking out with some traveling man. She also took the evening train to neighboring towns but returned to Bidwell later on the same night or at daylight the next morning. She did not prosper as Lillian did and grew tired of the dullness of small town life. At twenty-two she went to live in Cleveland where she got a job as cloak model in a large store. Later she went on the road as an actress, in a burlesque show, and Bidwell heard no more of her.

As for May Edgley, all through her childhood and until her seventeenth year she was a model of good behavior. Everyone spoke of it. She was, unlike the other Edgleys, small and dark, and unlike her sisters dressed herself in plain neat-fitting clothes. As a young girl in the public school she began to attract attention because of her proficiency in the classes. Both Lillian and Kate Edgley had been slovenly students, who spent their time ogling boys and the men teachers but May looked at no one and as soon as school was dismissed in the afternoon went home to her mother, a tall tired-looking woman who seldom went out of her own house.

In Bidwell, Tom Means, who later became a soldier and

who has recently won high rank in the army because of his proficiency in training recruits for the World War, was the prize pupil in the schools. Tom was working for his appointment to West Point, and did not spend his evenings loafing on the streets, as did other young men. He stayed in his own house, intent on his studies. Tom's father was a lawyer and his mother was third cousin to a Kentucky woman who had married an English baronet. The son aspired to be a soldier and a gentleman and to live on the intellectual plane, and had a good deal of contempt for the mental capacities of his fellow students, and when one of the Edgley family set up as his rival he was angry and embarrassed and the schoolroom was delighted. Day after day and year after year the contest between him and May Edgley went on and in a sense the whole town of Bidwell got back of the girl. In all such things as history and English literature Tom swept all before him but in spelling, arithmetic, and geography May defeated him without effort. At her desk she sat like a little terrier in the presence of a trap filled with rats. A question was asked or a problem in arithmetic put on the blackboard and like a terrier she jumped. Her hand went up and her sensitive mouth quivered. Fingers were snapped vigorously. "I know," she said, and the entire class knew she did. When she had answered the question or had gone to the blackboard to solve the problem the half-grown children along the rows of benches laughed and Tom Means stared out through a window. May returned to her seat, half triumphant, half ashamed of her victory.

The country lying west of Bidwell, like all the Ohio country down that way, is given to small fruit and berry raising, and in June and after school has been dismissed for the year all the younger men, boys, and girls, with most of the women of the town go to work in the fruit harvest. To the fields immediately after breakfast the citizens go trooping away. Lunches are carried in baskets and until the sun goes down everyone stays in the fields.

And in the berry fields as in the schoolroom May was a notable figure. She did not walk or ride to the work with the other young girls, or join the parties at lunch at the noon hour, but everyone understood that that was because of her family. "I know how she feels, if I came from a family like that I wouldn't ask or want other people's attention," said one of the women, the wife of a carpenter, who trudged along with the others in the dust of the road.

In a berry field, belonging to a farmer named Peter Short, some thirty women, young men and tall awkward boys crawled over the ground, picking the red fragrant berries. Ahead of them, in a row by herself, went May, the exclusive, the woman who walked by herself. Her hands flitted in and out of the berry vines as the tail of a squirrel disappears among the leaves of a tree when one walks in a wood. The other pickers went slowly, stopping occasionally to eat berries and talk and when one had crawled a little ahead of the others he stopped and waited, sitting on his haunches. The pickers were paid in proportion to the number of quarts picked during the day but, as they often said, "pay was not everything." The berry picking was in a way a social function, and who were the pickers, wives, sons and daughters of prosperous artisans, to kill themselves for a few paltry dollars?

With May Edgley they understood it was different. Everyone knew that she and her mother got practically no money from John Edgley, the father—from the boys, Jake, Frank and Will—or from the girls, Lilian and Kate, who spent their takings on clothes for themselves. If she were to be decently dressed, she had to earn the money for the purpose during the vacation time when she could stay out of school. Later it was understood she planned to be a school teacher herself, and to attain to that position it was necessary that she keep herself well dressed and show herself industrious and alert in affairs.

Tirelessly, therefore, May worked and the boxes of berries, filled by her ever alert fingers, grew into mountains. Peter Short with his son came walking down the rows to gather the filled crates and put them aboard a wagon to be hauled to town. He looked at May with pride in his eyes and the other pickers lumbering slowly along became the target for his scorn. "Ah, you talking women and you big lazy boys, you're not much good," he cried. "Ain't you ashamed of yourselves? Look at you there, Sylvester and Al—letting yourself be beat, twice over, by a girl so little you could almost carry her home in your pocket."

It was in the summer of her seventeenth year that May fell

down from her high place in the life of the town of Bidwell.
Two vital and dramatic events had happened to her that year.
Her mother died in April and she graduated from the high
school in June, second only in honors to Tom Means. As
Tom's father had been on the school board for years the town
shook its head over the decision that placed him ahead of May
and in everyone's eyes May had really walked off with the
prize. When she went into the fields, and when they remembered the fact of her mother's recent death, even the women
were ready to forget and forgive the fact of her being a member
of the Edgley family. As for May, it seemed to her at that moment that nothing that could happen to her could very much
matter.

And then the unexpected. As more than one Bidwell wife
said afterwards to her husband. "It was then that blood showed
itself."

A man named Jerome Hadley first found out about May. He
went that year to Peter Short's field, as he himself said, "just
for fun," and he found it. Jerome was pitcher for the Bidwell
baseball nine and worked as mail clerk on the railroad. After he
had returned from a run he had several days' rest and went to
the berry field because the town was deserted. When he saw
May working off by herself he winked at the other young men
and going to her got down on his knees and began picking at
a speed almost as great as her own. "Come on here, little
woman," he said, "I'm a mail clerk and have got my hand in,
sorting letters. My fingers can go pretty fast. Come on now,
let's see if you can keep up with me."

For an hour Jerome and May went up and down in the rows
and then the thing happened that set the town by the ears.
The girl, who had never talked to others, began talking to Jerome and the other pickers turned to look and wonder. She no
longer picked at lightning speed but loitered along, stopping
to rest and put choice berries into her mouth. "Eat that," she
said boldly passing a great red berry across the row to the man.
She put a handful of berries into his box. "You won't make as
much as seventy-five cents all day if you don't get a move on
you," she said, smiling shyly.

At the noon hour the other pickers found out the truth. The
tired workers had gone to the pump by Peter Short's house

and then to a near-by orchard to sit under the trees and rest after the eating of lunches.

There was no doubt something had happened to May. Everyone felt it. It was later understood that she had, during that noon hour in June and quite calmly and deliberately, decided to become like her two sisters and go on the town.

The berry pickers as usual ate their lunches in groups, the women and girls sitting under one tree and the young men and boys under another. Peter Short's wife brought hot coffee and tin cups were filled. Jokes went back and forth and the girls giggled.

In spite of the unexpectedness of May's attitude toward Jerome, a bachelor and quite legitimate game for the unmarried women, no one suspected anything serious would happen. Flirtations were always going on in the berry fields. They came, played themselves out, and passed like the clouds in the June sky. In the evening, when the young men had washed the dirt of the fields away and had put on their Sunday clothes, things were different. Then a girl must look out for herself. When she went to walk in the evening with a young man under the trees or out into country lanes—then anything might happen.

But in the fields, with all the older women about—to have thought anything at all of a young man and a girl working together and blushing and laughing, would have been to misunderstand the whole spirit of the berry picking season.

And it was evident May had misunderstood. Later no one blamed Jerome, at least none of the young fellows did. As the pickers ate lunch May sat a little apart from the others. That was her custom and Jerry lay in the long grass at the edge of the orchard also a little apart. A sudden tenseness crept into the groups under the trees. May had not gone to the pump with the others when she came in from the field but sat with her back braced against a tree and the hand that held the sandwich was black with the soil of her morning labors. It trembled and once the sandwich fell out of her hand.

Suddenly she got to her feet and put her lunch basket into the fork of a tree, and then, with a look of defiance in her eyes, she climbed over a fence and started along a lane past Peter Short's barn. The lane ran down to a meadow, crossed a bridge and went on beside a waving wheatfield to a wood.

May went a little way along the lane and then stopped to look back and the other pickers stared at her, wondering what was the matter. Then Jerome Hadley got to his feet. He was ashamed and climbed awkwardly over the fence and walked away without looking back.

Everyone was quite sure it had all been arranged. As the girls and women got to their feet and stood watching, May and Jerome went out of the lane and into the wood. The older women shook their heads. "Well, well," they exclaimed while the boys and young men began slapping each other on the back and prancing grotesquely about.

It was unbelievable. Before they had got out of sight of the others under the tree Jerome had put his arm about May's waist and she had put her head down on his shoulder. It was as though May Edgley who, as all the older women agreed, had been treated almost as an equal by all of the others had wanted to throw something ugly right in their faces.

Jerome and May stayed for two hours in the wood and then came back together to the field where the others were at work. May's cheeks were pale and she looked as though she had been crying. She picked alone as before and after a few moments of awkward silence Jerome put on his coat and went off along a road toward town. May made a little mountain of filled berry boxes during that afternoon but two or three times filled boxes dropped out of her hands. The spilled fruit lay red and shining against the brown and black of the soil.

No one saw May in the berry fields after that, and Jerome Hadley had something of which to boast. In the evening when he came among the young fellows he spoke of his adventure at length.

"You couldn't blame me for taking the chance when I had it," he said laughing. He explained in detail what had occurred in the wood, while other young men stood about filled with envy. As he talked he grew both proud and a little ashamed of the public attention his adventure was attaining. "It was easy," he said. "That May Edgley's the easiest thing that ever lived in this town. A fellow don't have to ask to get what he wants. That's how easy it is."

CHAPTER II

In Bidwell, and after she had fairly flung herself against the wall of village convention by going into the wood with Jerome, May lived at home, doing the work her mother had formerly done in the Edgley household. She washed the clothes, cooked the food and made the beds. There was, for the time, something sweet to her in the thoughts of doing lowly tasks and she washed and ironed the dresses in which Lillian and Kate were to array themselves and the heavy overalls worn by her father and brothers with a kind of satisfaction in the task. "It makes me tired and I can sleep and won't be thinking," she told herself. As she worked over the washtubs, among the beds soiled by the heavy slumbers of her brothers who on the evening before had perhaps come home drunk, or stood over the hot stove in the kitchen, she kept thinking of her dead mother. "I wonder what she would think," she asked herself and then added, "If she hadn't died it wouldn't have happened. If I had someone, I could go to and talk with, things would be different."

During the day when the men of the household were gone with their teams and when Lillian was away from town May had the house to herself. It was a two-storied frame building, standing at the edge of a field near the town's edge, and had once been painted yellow. Now, water washing from the roofs had discolored the paint, and the side walls of the old building were all mottled and streaked. The house stood on a little hill and the land fell sharply away from the kitchen door. There was a creek under the hill and beyond the creek a field that at certain times during the year became a swamp. At the creek's edge willows and elders grew and often in the afternoon, when there was no one about, May went softly out at the kitchen door, looking to be sure there was no one in the road that ran past the front of the house, and if the coast was clear went down the hill and crept in among the fragrant elders and willows. "I am lost here and no one can see me or find me," she thought, and the thought gave her intense satisfaction. Her cheeks grew flushed and hot and she pressed the cool green leaves of the willows against them. When a wagon passed in the road or someone walked along the board sidewalk at the roadside she drew herself into a little lump and closed her eyes. The passing sounds seemed far away and to herself it seemed that she had in some way escaped from life. How warm and close it was there, buried amid the dark green shadows of the willows. The gnarled twisted limbs of the trees were like arms but unlike the arms of the man with whom she had lain in the wood they did not grasp her with terrifying convulsive strength. For hours she lay still in the shadows and nothing came to frighten her and her lacerated spirit began to heal a little. "I have made myself an outlaw among people but I am not an outlaw here," she told herself.

Having heard of the incident with Jerome Hadley, in the berry field, Lillian and Kate Edgley were irritated and angry and one evening when they were both at the house and May was at work in the kitchen they spoke about it. Lillian was very angry and had decided to give May what she spoke of as "a piece of her mind." "What'd she want to go in the cheap for?" she asked. "It makes me sick when I think of it—a fellow like that Jerome Hadley! If she was going to cut loose what made her want to go on the cheap?"

In the Edgley family it had always been understood that May was of a different clay and old John Edgley and the boys had always paid her a kind of crude respect. They did not swear at her as they sometimes did at Lillian and Kate, and in secret they thought of her as a link between themselves and the more respectable life of the town. Ma Edgley was respectable enough but she was old and tired and never went out of the house and it was in May the family held up its head. The two brothers were proud of their sister because of her record in the town school. They themselves were working men and never expected to be anything else but, they thought, "that sister of ours has shown the town that an Edgley can beat them at their own game. She is smarter than any of them. See how she has forced the town to pay attention to her."

As for Lillian—before the incident with Jerome Hadley, she continually talked of her sister. In Norwalk, Fremont, Clyde and the other towns she visited she had many friends. Men liked her because, as they often said, she was a woman to be trusted. One could talk to her, say anything, and she would keep her mouth shut and in her presence one felt comfortably free and easy. Among her secret associates were members of churches, lawyers, owners of prosperous businesses, heads of respectable families. To be sure they saw Lillian in secret but she seemed to understand and respect their desire for secrecy. "You don't need to make no bones about it with me. I know you got to be careful," she said.

On a summer evening, in one of the towns she was in the habit of visiting, an arrangement was made. The man with whom she was to spend the evening waited until darkness had come and then, hiring a horse at a livery stable, drove to an appointed place. Side curtains were put on the buggy and the pair set forth into the darkness and loneliness of country roads. As the evening advanced and the more ardent mood of the occasion passed, a sudden sense of freedom swept over the man. "It is better not to fool around with a young girl or with some other man's wife. With Lillian one does not get found out and get into trouble," he thought.

The horse went slowly, along out of the way roads—bars were let down and the couple drove into a field. For hours they sat in the buggy and talked. The men talked to Lillian as they could talk to no other woman they had ever known. She was shrewd and in her own way capable and often the men spoke of their affairs, asking her advice. "Now what do you think, Lil'—if you were me would you buy or sell?" one of them asked.

Other and more intimate things crept into the conversations. "Well, Lil', my wife and I are all right. We get along well enough, but we ain't what you might speak of as lovers," Lillian's temporary intimate said. "She jaws me a lot when I smoke too much or when I don't want to go to church. And then, you see, we're worried about the kids. My oldest girl is running around a lot with young Harry Garvner and I keep asking myself, 'Is he any good?' I can't make up my mind. You've seen him around, Lil', what do you think?"

Having taken part in many such conversations Lillian had come to depend on her sister May to furnish her with a topic of conversation. "I know how you feel. I feel that way about May," she said. More than a hundred times she had explained that May was different from the rest of the Edgleys. "She's smart," she explained. "I tell you what, she's the smartest girl that ever went to the high school in Bidwell."

Having so often used May as an example of what an Edgley could be Lillian was shocked when she heard of the affair in the berry field. For several weeks she said nothing and then one evening in July when the two were alone in the house together she spoke. She had intended to be motherly, direct and kind—if firm, but when the words came her voice trembled and she grew angry. "I hear, May, you been fooling with a man," she began as they sat together on the front porch of the house. It was a hot evening and dark and a thunder storm threatened and for a long time after Lillian had spoken there was silence and then May put her head into her hands and leaning forward began to cry softly. Her body rocked back and forth and occasionally a dry broken sob broke the silence. "Well," Lillian added sharply, being determined to terminate her remarks before she also broke into tears, "well, May, you've made a darn fool of yourself. I didn't think it of you. I didn't think you'd turn out a fool."

In the attempt to control her own unhappiness and to conceal it, Lillian became more and more angry. Her voice continued to tremble and to regain control of it she got up and went inside the house. When she came out again May still sat in the chair at the edge of the porch with her head held in her hands. Lillian was moved to pity. "Well, don't break your heart about it, kid. I'm only an old fool after all. Don't pay too much attention to me. I guess Kate and I haven't set you such a good example," she said softly.

Lillian sat on the edge of the porch and put her hand on May's knee and when she felt the trembling of the younger woman's body a sharp mother feeling awakened within her. "I say, kid," she began again, "a girl gets notions into her head. I've had them myself. A girl thinks she'll find a man that's all right. She kinda dreams of a man that doesn't exist. She wants to be good and at the same time she wants to be something else. I guess I know how you felt but, believe me, kid, it's bunk. Take it from me, kid, I know what I'm talking about. I been with men enough. I ought to know something."

Intent now on giving advice and having for the first time definitely accepted her sister as a comrade Lillian did not realize that what she now had to say would hurt May more than her anger. "I've often wondered about mother," she said reminiscently. "She was always so glum and silent. When Kate and I went on the turf she never had nothing to say and even when I was a kid and began running around with men evenings, she kept still. I remember the first time I went over to Fremont with a man and stayed out all night. I was ashamed to come home. 'I'll catch hell,' I thought but she never said nothing at all and it was the same way with Kate. She never said nothing to her. I guess Kate and I thought she was like the rest of the family—she was banking on you."

"To Ballyhack with Dad and the boys," Lillian added sharply. "They're men and don't care about anything but getting filled up with booze and when they're tired sleeping like dogs. They're like all the other men only not so much stuck on themselves."

Lillian became angry again. "I was pretty proud of you, May, and now I don't know what to think," she said. "I've bragged about you a thousand times and I suppose Kate has. It makes me sore to think of it, you an Edgley and being as smart as you are, to fall for a cheap one like that Jerome Hadley. I bet he didn't even give you any money or promise to marry you either."

May arose from her chair, her whole body trembling as with a chill, and Lillian arose and stood beside her. The older woman got down to the kernel of what she wanted to say. "You ain't that way are you, sis—you ain't going to have a kid?" she asked. May stood by the door, leaning against the door jamb and the rain that had been threatening began to fall. "No, Lillian," she said. Like a child begging for mercy she held out her hand. Her face was white and in a flash of lightning Lillian could see it plainly. It seemed to leap out of the darkness toward her. "Don't talk about it any more, Lillian, please don't. I won't ever do it again," she pleaded.

Lillian was determined. When May went indoors and up the stairway to her room above she followed to the foot of the stairs and finished what she felt she had to say. "I don't want you to do it, May," she said, "I don't want you to do it. I want to see there be one Edgley that goes straight but if you intend to go crooked don't be a fool. Don't take up with a cheap one, like Jerome Hadley, who just give you soft talk. If you are

going to do it anyway you just come to me. I'll get you in with
men who have money and I'll fix it so you don't have no
trouble. If you're going to go on the turf, like Kate and I did,
don't be a fool. You just come to me."

In all her life May had never achieved a friendship with another
woman, although often she had dreamed of such a possibility.
When she was still a school girl she saw other girls going
homeward in the evening. They loitered along, their arms
linked, and how much they had to say to each other. When
they came to a corner, where their ways parted, they could not
bear to leave each other. "You go a piece with me to-night and
to-morrow night I'll go a piece with you," one of them said.

May hurried homeward alone, her heart filled with envy,
and after she had finished her time in the school and, more
than ever after the incident in the berry field—always spoken
of by Lillian as the time of her troubles—the dream of a possible friendship with some other woman grew more intense.

During the summer of that last year of her life in Bidwell a
young woman from another town moved into a house on her
street. Her father had a job on the Nickel Plate Railroad and
Bidwell was at the end of a section of that road. The railroad
man was seldom at home, his wife had died a few months before and his daughter, whose name was Maud, was not well
and did not go about town with the other young women.
Every afternoon and evening she sat on the front porch of her
father's house, and May, who was sometimes compelled to go
to one of the stores, often saw her sitting there. The newcomer
in Bidwell was tall and slender and looked like an invalid. Her
cheeks were pale and she looked tired. During the year before
she had been operated upon and some part of her internal
machinery had been taken away and her paleness and the look
of weariness on her face, touched May's heart. "She looks as
though she might be wanting company," she thought hopefully.

After his wife's death an unmarried sister had become the
railroad man's housekeeper. She was a short strongly built
woman with hard grey eyes and a determined jaw and sometimes she sat with the new girl. Then May hurried past without
looking, but, when Maud sat alone, she went slowly, looking

slyly at the pale face and drooped figure in the rocking chair. One day she smiled and the smile was returned. May lingered a moment. "It's hot," she said leaning over the fence, but before a conversation could be started she grew alarmed and hurried away.

When the evening's work was done on that evening and when the Edgley men had gone up town, May went into the street. Lillian was away from home and the sidewalk further up the street was deserted. The Edgley house was the last one on the street, and in the direction of town and on the same side of the street, there was—first a vacant lot, then a shed that had once been used as a blacksmith shop but that was now deserted, and after that the house where the new girl had come to live.

When the soft darkness of the summer evening came May went a little way along the street and stopped by the deserted shed. The girl in the rocking chair on the porch saw her there, and seemed to understand May's fear of her aunt. Arising she opened the door and peered into the house to be sure she was unobserved and then came down a brick walk to the gate and along the street to May, occasionally looking back to be sure she had escaped unnoticed. A large stone lay at the edge of the sidewalk before the shed and May urged the new girl to sit down beside her and rest herself.

May was flushed with excitement. "I wonder if she knows? I wonder if she knows about me?" she thought.

"I saw you wanted to be friendly and I thought I'd come and talk," the new girl said. She was filled with a vague curiosity. "I heard something about you but I know it ain't true," she said.

May's heart jumped and her hands trembled. "I've let myself in for something," she thought. The impulse to jump to her feet and run away along the sidewalk, to escape at once from the situation her hunger for companionship had created, almost overcame her and she half arose from the stone and then sat down again. She became suddenly angry and when she spoke her voice was firm, filled with indignation. "I know what you mean," she said sharply, "you mean the fool story about me and Jerome Hadley in the woods?" The new girl nodded. "I don't believe it," she said. "My aunt heard it from a woman."

Now that Maud had boldly mentioned the affair, that had, May knew, made her an outlaw in the town's life May felt suddenly free, bold, capable of meeting any situation that might arise and was lost in wonder at her own display of courage. Well, she had wanted to love the new girl, take her as a friend, but now that impulse was lost in another passion that swept through her. She wanted to conquer, to come out of a bad situation with flying colors. With the boldness of another Lillian she began to speak, to tell lies. "It just shows what happens," she said quickly. A re-creation of the incident in the wood with Jerome had come to her swiftly, like a flash of sunlight on a dark day. "I went into the woods with Jerome Hadley —why? You won't believe it when I tell you, maybe," she added.

May began laying the foundation of her lie. "He said he was in trouble and wanted to speak with me, off somewhere where no one could hear, in some secret place," she explained. "I said, 'If you're in trouble let's go over into the woods at noon.' It was my idea, our going off together that way. When he told me he was in trouble his eyes looked so hurt I never thought of reputation or nothing. I just said I'd go and I been paid for it. A girl always has to pay if she's good to a man I suppose."

May tried to look and talk like a wise woman, as she imagined Lillian would have talked under the circumstances. "I've got a notion to tell what that Jerome Hadley talked to me about all the time when we were in there—in the woods—but I won't," she declared. "He lied about me afterwards because I wouldn't do what he wanted me to, but I'll keep my word. I won't tell you any names but I'll tell you this much—I know enough to have Jerome Hadley sent to jail if I wanted to do it."

May watched her companion. To Maud, whose life had always been a dull affair, the evening was like going to a theatre. It was better than that. It was like going to the theatre where the star is your friend, where you sit among strangers and have the sense of superiority that comes with knowing, as a person much like yourself, the hero in the velvet gown with the sword clanking at his side. "Oh, do tell me all you dare. I want to know," she said.

"It was about a woman he was in trouble," May answered. "One of these days maybe the whole town will find out what I alone know." She leaned forward and touched Maud's arm. The lie she was telling made her feel glad and free. As on a dark day, when the sun suddenly breaks through clouds, everything in life now seemed bright and glowing and her imagination took a great leap forward. She had been inventing a tale to save herself but went on for the joy of seeing what she could do with the story that had come suddenly, unexpectedly, to her lips. As when she was a girl in school her mind worked swiftly, eagerly. "Listen," she said impressively, "and don't you never tell no one. Jerome Hadley wanted to kill a man here in this town, because he was in love with the man's woman. He had got poison and intended to give it to the woman. She is married and rich too. Her husband is a big man here in Bidwell. Jerome was to give the poison to the woman and she was to put it in her husband's coffee and, when the man died, the woman was to marry Jerome. I put a stop to it. I prevented the murder. Now do you understand why I went into the woods with that man?"

The fever of excitement that had taken possession of May was transmitted to her companion. It drew them closer together and now Maud put her arm about May's waist. "The nerve of him," May said boldly, "he wanted me to take the stuff to the woman's house and he offered me money too. He said the rich woman would give me a thousand dollars, but I laughed at him. 'If anything happens to that man I'll tell and you'll get hung for murder,' that's what I said to him."

May described the scene that had taken place there in the deep dark forest with the man, intent upon murder. They fought, she said, for more than two hours and the man tried to kill her. She would have had him arrested at once, she explained, but to do so involved telling the story of the poison plot and she had given her word to save him, and if he reformed, she would not tell. After a long time, when the man saw she was not to be moved and would neither take part in the plot or allow it to be carried out, he grew quieter. Then, as they were coming out of the woods, he sprang upon her again and tried to choke her. Some berry pickers in a field, among whom she had been working during the morning, saw the struggle.

"They went and told lies about me," May said emphatically.

"They saw us struggling and they went and said he was making love to me. A girl there, who was in love with Jerome herself and was jealous when she saw us together, started the story. It spread all over town and now I'm so ashamed I hardly dare to show my face."

With an air of helpless annoyance May arose. "Well," she said, "I promised him I wouldn't tell the name of the man he was going to murder or nothing about it and I won't. I've told you too much as it is but you gave me your word you wouldn't tell. It's got to be a secret between us." She started off along the sidewalk toward the Edgley house and then turned and ran back to the new girl, who had got almost to her own gate. "You keep still," May whispered dramatically. "If you go talking now remember you may get a man hung."

CHAPTER III

A new life began to unfold itself to May Edgley. After the affair in the berry field, and until the time of the conversation with Maud Welliver, she had felt as one dead. As she went about in the Edgley household, doing the daily work, she sometimes stopped and stood still, on the stairs or in the kitchen by the stove. A whirlwind seemed to be going on around her while she stood thus, becalmed—fear made her body tremble. It had happened even in the moments when she was hidden under the elders by the creek. At such times the trunks of the willow trees and the fragrance of the elders comforted but did not comfort enough. There was something wanting. They were too impersonal, too sure of themselves.

To herself, at such moments, May was like one sealed up in a vessel of glass. The light of days came to her and from all sides came the sound of life going on but she herself did not live. She but breathed, ate food, slept and awakened but what she wanted out of life seemed far away, lost to her. In a way, and ever since she had been conscious of herself, it had been so.

She remembered faces she had seen, expressions that had come suddenly to peoples' faces as she passed them on the streets. In particular old men had always been kind to her. They stopped to speak to her. "Hello, little girl," they said. For her benefit eyes had been lifted, lips had smiled, kindly words had been spoken, and at such moments it had seemed to her that some tiny sluiceway out of the great stream of human life had been opened to her. The stream flowed on somewhere, in the distance, on the further side of a wall, behind a mountain of iron—just out of sight, out of hearing—but a few drops of the living waters of life had reached her, had bathed her. Understanding of the secret thing that went on within herself was not impossible. It could exist.

In the days after the talk with Lillian the puzzled woman in the yellow house thought much about life. Her mind, naturally a busy active one, could not remain passive and for the time she dared not think much of herself and of her own future. She thought abstractly.

She had done a thing and how natural and yet how strange the doing of it had been. There she was at work in a berry field —it was morning, the sun shone, boys, young girls, and mature women laughed and talked in the rows behind her. Her fingers were very busy but she listened while a woman's voice talked of canning fruit. "Cherries take so much sugar," the voice said. A young girl's voice talked endlessly of some boy and girl affair. There was a tale of a ride into the country on a hay wagon, and an involved recital of "he saids" and "I saids."

And then the man had come along the rows and had got down on his knees to work beside herself—May Edgley. He was a man out of the town's life, and had come thus, suddenly, unexpectedly. No one had ever come to her in that way. Oh, people had been kind. They had smiled and nodded, and had gone their own ways.

May had not seen the sly winks Jerome Hadley had bestowed on the other berry pickers and had taken his impulse to come to her as a simple and lovely fact in life. Perhaps he was lonely like herself. For a time the two had worked together in silence and then a bantering conversation began. May had found herself able to carry her end of a conversation, to give and take with the man. She laughed at him because, although his fingers were skilled, he could not fill the berry boxes as fast as herself.

And then, quite suddenly, the tone of the conversation had changed. The man became bold and his boldness had excited May. What words he had said. "I'd like to hold you in my arms. I'd like to have you alone where I could kiss you. I'd like to be alone with you in the woods or somewhere." The others working, now far away along the rows, young girls and women, too, must also have heard just such words from the lips of men. It was the fact that they had heard such words and responded to them in kind that differentiated them from herself. It was by responding to such words that a woman got herself a lover, got married, connected herself with the stream of life. She heard such words and something within herself stirred, as it was stirring now in herself. Like a flower she opened to receive life. Strange beautiful things happened and her experience became the experience of all life, of trees, of flowers, of grasses and most of all of other women. Something arose within her and then broke. The wall of life was broken down. She became a living thing, receiving life, giving it forth, one with all life.

In the berry field that morning May had gone on working after the words were said. Her fingers automatically picked berries and put them in the boxes slowly, hesitatingly. She turned to the man and laughed. How wonderful that she could control herself so.

Her mind had raced. What a thing her mind was. It was always doing that—racing, running madly, a little out of control. Her fingers moved more slowly. She picked berries and put them in the man's box, and now and then gave him large fine round berries to eat and was conscious that the others in the field were looking in her direction. They were listening, wondering, and she grew resentful. "What did they want? What did all this have to do with them?"

Her mind took a new turn. "What would it be like to be held in the arms of a man, to have a man's lips pressed down upon her lips. It was an experience all women, who had lived, had known. It had come to her own mother, to the married women, working with her in the field, to young girls, too, to many much younger than herself." She imagined arms soft and yet firm, strong arms, holding her closely, and sank into a dim, splendid world of emotion. The stream of life in which she had always wanted to float had picked her up—it carried her along. All life became colorful. The red berries in the boxes—how red they were, the green of the vines, what a living green! The colors merged—they ran together, the stream of life was flowing over them, over her.

What a terrible day that had been for May. Later she could not focus her mind upon it, dared not do so. The actual experience with the man in the forest had been quite brutal—an assault had been made upon her. She had consented—yes—but not to what happened. Why had she gone into the woods with him? Well, she had gone, and by her manner she had invited, urged him to follow, but she had not expected anything really to happen.

It had been her own fault, everything had been her own fault. She had got up from among the berry pickers, angry at them—resentful. They knew too much and not enough and she had hated their knowledge, their smartness. She had got up and walked away from them, looking back, expecting him.

What had she expected? What she had expected could not get itself put into words. She knew nothing of poets and their efforts, of the things they live to try to do, of things men try to paint into canvasses, translate into song. She was an Ohio woman, an Edgley, the daughter of a teamster, the sister of Lillian Edgley who had gone on the turf. May expected to walk into a new world, into life—she expected to bathe herself in the living waters of life. There was to be something warm, close, comforting, secure. Hands were to arise out of darkness and grasp her hands, her hands covered with the stain of red berries and the yellow dust of fields. She was to be held closely in the warm place and then like a flower she was to break open, throw herself, her fragrance into the air.

What had been the matter with her, with her notion of life? May had asked herself that question a thousand times, had asked it until she was weary of asking, could not ask any more. She had known her mother—thought she had known her—if she had not, no Edgley had. Had none of the others cared? Her mother had met a man and had been held in his arms, she had become the mother of sons and daughters, and the sons and daughters had gone their own way, lived brutally. They had gone after what they thought they wanted from life, directly, brutally—like animals. And her mother had stood aside. How long ago she must have died, really. It was then only flesh and blood that went on living, working, making beds, cooking, lying with a husband.

It was plain that was true of her mother—it must have been true. If it were not true why had she not spoken, why had no words come to her lips. Day after day May had worked with her mother. Well, then she was a virgin, young, tender and her mother had not kissed her, had not held her closely. No word had been said. It was not true, as Lillian had said, that her mother had counted on her. It was because of death that she was silent, when Lillian and then Kate went on the turf. The dead did not care! The dead are dead!

May wondered if she herself had passed out of life, if she had died. "It may be," she thought, "I may never have lived and my thinking I was alive may only have been a trick of mind."

"I'm smart," May thought. Lillian had said that, her brothers had said it, the whole town had said it. How she hated her own smartness.

The others had been proud of it, glad of it. The whole town had been proud of her, had hailed her. It was because she was smart, because she thought quicker and faster than others, it was because of that the women schoolteachers had smiled at her, because of that old men spoke to her on the streets.

Once an old man had met her on the sidewalk in front of one of the stores and taking her by the hand had led her inside and had bought her a bag of candy. The man was a merchant in Bidwell and had a daughter who was a teacher in the schools, but May had never seen him before, had heard nothing of him, knew nothing about him. He came up to her out of nothingness, out of the stream of life. He had heard about May, of her quick active mind, that always defeated the other children in the school room, that in every test came out ahead. Her imagination played about his figure.

At that time May went every Sunday morning to the Presbyterian Sunday School, as there was a tradition in the Edgley family that Ma Edgley had once been a Presbyterian. None of the other children had ever gone, but for a time she did and they all seemed to want her to go. She remembered the men, the Sunday School teachers were always talking about. There was a gigantic strong old man named Abraham who walked in God's footsteps. He must have been huge, strong, and good, too. His children were like the sands of the seas for numbers, and was that not a sign of strength. How many children! All the children in the world could not be more than that! The man who had taken hold of her hand and had led her into the store to buy the candy for her was, she imagined just such another. He also must own lands and be the father of innumerable children and no doubt he could ride all day on a fast horse and never get off his own possessions. It was possible he thought her one of his innumerable children.

There was no doubt he was a mighty man. He looked like one and he had admired her. "I'm giving you this candy because my daughter says you are the smartest girl in school," he said. She remembered that another man stood in the store and that, as she ran away with the bag of candy gripped in her small fingers, the old man, the mighty one, turned to him. He said something to the man. "They are all cattle except her, just cattle," he had said. Later she had thought out what he meant. He meant her family, the Edgleys.

How many things she had thought out as she went back and forth to school, always alone. There was always plenty of time for thinking things out—in the late afternoons as she helped her mother with the housework and in the long winter evenings when she went to bed early and for a long time did not go to sleep. The old man in the store had admired her quick brain—for that he had forgiven her being an Edgley, one of the cattle. Her thoughts went round and round in circles. Even as a child she had always felt shut in, walled in from life. She struggled to escape out of herself, out into life.

And now she was a woman who had experienced life, tested it, and she stood, silent and attentive on the stairway of the Edgley house or by the stove in the kitchen and with an effort forced herself to quit thinking. On another street, in another house, a door banged. Her sense of hearing was extraordinarily acute, and it seemed to her she could hear every sound made by every man, woman, and child in town. The circle of thoughts began again and again she fought to think, to feel her way out of herself. On another street, in another house a woman was doing housework, just as she had been doing—making beds, washing dishes, cooking food. The woman had just passed from one room of her house to another and a door had shut with a bang. "Well," May thought, "she is a human being, she feels things as I do, she thinks, eats food, sleeps, dreams, walks about her house."

It didn't matter who the woman was. Being or not being an Edgley made no difference. Any woman would do for the purposes of May's thoughts. All people who lived, lived! Men walked about too, and had thoughts, young girls laughed. She had heard a girl in school, when no one was speaking to her— paying any attention to her—burst suddenly into loud laughter. What was she laughing about?

How cruelly the town had patronized May, setting her apart from the others, calling her smart. They had cared about her because of her smartness. She was smart. Her mind was quick, it reached out. And she was one of the Edgleys—"cattle," the bearded man in the store had said.

And what of that—what was an Edgley—why were they cattle? An Edgley also slept, ate food, had dreams, walked about. Lillian had said that an Edgley man was like all other men, only less stuck on himself.

May's mind fought to realize herself in the world of people, she wanted to be a part of all life, to function in life—did not want to be a special thing—smart—patted on the head—smiled at because she was smart.

What was smartness? She could work out problems in school quickly, swiftly, but as each problem was solved she forgot it. It meant nothing to her. A merchant in Egypt wanted to transport goods across the desert and had 370 pounds of tea and such another number of pounds of dried fruits and spices. There was a problem concerning the matter. Camels were to be loaded. How far away? The result of all her quick thinking was some number like twelve or eighteen, arrived at before the others. There was a little trick. It consisted in throwing everything else out of the mind and concentrating on the one thing —and that was smartness.

But what did it matter to her about the loading of camels? It might have meant something could she have seen into the mind, the soul of the man who owned all that merchandise and who was to carry it so far, if she could have understood him, if she could have understood anyone, if anyone could have understood her.

May stood in the kitchen of the Edgley house, quiet, attentive—for ten minutes, a half hour. Once a dish she held in her hand fell to the floor and broke, awakening her suddenly and to awaken was like coming back to the Edgley house after a long journey, during which she had traveled far, over mountains, rivers, seas—it was like coming back to a place she wanted to leave for good.

"And all the time," she told herself, "life swept on, other people lived, laughed, achieved life."

And then, through the lie she had told Maud Welliver, May stepped into a new world, a world of boundless release. Through the lie and the telling of it she found out that, if she could not live in the life about her, she could create a life. If she was walled in, shut off from participation in the life of the Ohio town—hated, feared by the town—she could come out of the town. The people would not really look at her, try to understand her and they would not let her look down into themselves.

The lie she had told was the foundation stone, the first of the foundation stones. A tower was to be built, a tall tower on which she could stand, from the ramparts of which she could look down into a world created by herself, by her own mind. If her mind was really what Lillian, the teachers in the school, all the others, had said, she would use it, it would become the tool which in her hands, would force stone after stone into its place in her tower.

In the Edgley house May had a room of her own, a tiny room at the back of the house and there was one window looking down into the field, that every spring and fall became a swamp. In the winter sometimes it was covered with ice and boys came there to skate. On the evening she had told Maud Welliver the great lie—recreated the incident in the wood with Jerome Hadley—she hurried home and went up to her room and, pulling a chair to the window, sat down. What a thing she had done! The encounter with Jerome Hadley in the wood had been terrible—she had been unable to think about it, did not dare to think about it, and trying not to think had almost upset her reason.

And now it was gone. The whole thing had really never

happened. What had happened was this other thing, or something like that, something no one knew about. There had really been an attempt at murder. May sat by the window and
smiled sadly. "I stretched it a little," she thought. "Of course I
stretched it, but what was the use trying to tell what happened.
I couldn't make it understood. I can't understand it myself."

All through the weeks that had passed since that day in the
wood May had been obsessed by the notion that she was unclean, physically unclean. Doing the housework she wore calico
dresses—she had several of them and two or three times a day
she changed her dress and the soiled dress she could not leave
hanging in a closet until washday but washed the dress at once
and hung it on a line in the back yard. The wind blowing
through it gave her a comforting feeling.

The Edgleys had no bathroom or bathtub. Few people in
towns in her day owned any such luxurious appendages to life.
And a washtub was kept in the woodshed by the kitchen door
and what baths were taken were taken in the tub. It was a ceremony that did not often occur in the family, and when it did
occur the tub was filled from the cistern and set in the sun to
warm. Then it was carried into the shed. The candidate for
cleanliness went into the shed and closed the door. In the
winter the ceremony took place in the kitchen and Ma Edgley
came at the last moment and poured a kettle of boiling water
into the cold water in the tub. In the summer in the shed that
was not necessary. The bather undressed and put his clothes
about, on the piles of wood, and there was a great splashing.

During that summer May took a bath every afternoon, but
did not bother to put the water out in the sun. How good it
felt to have it cold! Often when there was no one about, she
filled the tub and got into it again before going to bed. Her
small body, dark and strong, sank into the cold water and she
took strong soap and scrubbed her legs, her breasts, her neck
where Jerome Hadley's kisses had alighted. Her neck and
breasts she wished she could scrub quite away.

Her body was strong and wiry. All the Edgleys, even Ma
Edgley, had been strong. They were all, except May, large
people and in her the family strength seemed to have concentrated. She was never physically weary and after the time of her
intensive thinking began, and when she often slept little at

night her body seemed to grow constantly stronger. Her breasts grew larger and her figure changed slightly. It grew less boyish. She was becoming a woman.

After the telling of the lie, May's body became for a time no more than a tree growing in a forest through which she walked. It was something through which life made itself manifest; it was a house within which she lived, a house, in which, and in spite of the enmity of the town, life went on. "I'm not dead like those who die while their bodies are still alive," May thought, and there was intense comfort in the thought.

She sat by the window of her room in the darkness thinking. Jerome Hadley had tried to commit a murder and how often such attempts must have been made in the history of other men and women—and how often they must have succeeded. The spirit within was killed. Boys and girls grew up full of notions, brave notions too. In Bidwell, as in other towns, they went to schools and Sunday schools. Words were said—they heard many brave words—but within themselves, within their own tiny houses, all life was uncertain, hesitating. They looked abroad and saw men and women, bearded men, kind strong women. How many were dead! How many of the houses were but empty haunted places! Their town was not the town they had thought it and some day they would have to find that out. It was not a place of warm friendly closeness. Feeling instinctively the uncertainty of life, the difficulty of arriving at truth the people did not draw together. They were not humble in the face of the great mystery. The mystery was to be solved with lies, with truth put away. A great noise must be made. Everything was to be covered up. There must be a great noise and bustle, the firing of cannons, the roll of drums, the shouting of many words. The spirit within must be killed. "What liars people are," May thought breathlessly. It seemed to her that all the people of her town stood before her, were in a way being judged by her, and her own lie, told to defeat a universal lie, now seemed a small, a white innocent thing.

There was a very tender delicate thing within her, many people had wanted to kill—that was certain. To kill the delicate thing within was a passion that obsessed mankind. All men and women tried to do it. First the man or woman killed the thing within himself, and then tried to kill it in others. Men and women were afraid to let the thing live.

May sat in the darkness in her room in the Edgley house having such thoughts as had never come to her before and the night seemed alive as no other night of her life had been. For her gods walked abroad in the land. The Edgley house was but a poor little affair of boards—of thin walls—and she looked out, in the dim wavering light of the night, into a field, that at times during the year became a bog where cattle sank in black mud to their knees. Her town was but a dot on the huge map of her country—she knew that. It was not necessary to travel to find out. Had she not been at the top of her class in geography? In her country alone lived some sixty, eighty, a hundred million people—she could not remember the number—it changed yearly. When the country was new millions of buffalo walked up and down on the plains. She was a she-calf among the buffalo but she had found lodgment in a town, in a house made of boards and painted yellow, but the field below the house was dry now and long grass grew there. However, tiny pools remained and frogs lived in them and croaked loudly while crickets sang in the dry grass. Her life was sacred—the house in which she lived, the room in which she sat, became a church, a temple, a tower. The lie she had told had started a new force within her and the new temple, on which she was to live, was now being built.

Thoughts like giant clouds, seen in a dim night sky, floated through her mind. Tears came to her eyes and her throat seemed to be swelling. She put her head down on the window sill and convulsive sobs shook her.

That was, she knew, because she had been brave enough and quick-witted enough to tell the lie, to reestablish the romance of existence within herself. The foundation stone for the temple had been laid.

May did not think anything out clearly, did not try to do that. She felt—she knew her own truth. Words heard, read in books in school, in other books loaned her by the school-teachers, words said casually, without feeling—by thin-lipped, flat-breasted young women who were teachers at the Sunday school, words that had seemed as nothing to her when said, now made a great sound in her mind. They were repeated to her in stately measure by some force, seemingly outside herself and were like the steady rhythmical tread of an army marching on earth roads. No, they were like rain on the roof over her head, on the roof of the house that was herself. All her life she had lived in a house and the rains had come unheeded—and the words she had heard and now remembered were like rain drops falling on roofs. There was a subtle perfume remaining. "The stone which the builders refused is become the head-stone of the corner."

As the thoughts marched through May's mind her small shoulders shook with sobs, but she was happy—strangely happy and something within herself was singing. The singing was a song that was always alive somewhere in the world, it was the song of life, the song that crickets sang, the song the frogs croaked hoarsely. It ran away out of her room, out of the darkness into the night, into days, into far lands—it was the old song, the sweet song.

May kept thinking about buildings and builders. "The stone which the builders refused is become the headstone of the corner." Someone had said that and others had felt what she now felt—they had had the feeling she could not put into words and they had tried putting it into words. She was not alone in the world. It was not a strange path she walked in life, but many had walked it, many were walking it now. Even as she sat in the window, thinking so strangely, many men and women in many places and many lands sat at other windows having the same thoughts. In a world, where many men and women had killed the thing within themselves, the path of the rejected was the true path and how many had walked the path! The trees along the way were marked. Signs had been hung up by those who wanted to show others the way. "The stone which the builders refused is become the headstone of the corner."

Lillian had said, "men are no good," and it was clear Lillian had also killed the thing within herself, had let it be killed. She had let some Jerome Hadley kill it, and then she had grown slowly and steadily more and more angry at life, had come to hate life, had thrown it away. And the thing had happened to her mother, too. That was the reason for her life of silence—death walking about. "The dead rise up to strike the dead."

The story May had told to Maud Welliver was not a lie—it

was the living truth. He had tried to kill and had come near succeeding. May had walked in the valley of the shadow of death. She knew that now. Her own sister, Lillian, had come to her when she walked with Death and wanted Life. "If you are going to go on the turf I'll get you in with men who have money," Lillian had said. She had got no closer to understanding than that.

May decided that after all she would not try to be Maud Welliver's friend. She would see her and talk to her but, for the present, she would keep herself to herself. The living thing within her had been wounded and needed time to recover. Of all the feelings, the strong emotion, that swept through her on that evening, cleansing her internally, as she had been trying by splashing in the tub in the woodshed to cleanse herself externally, one impulse got itself definitely expressed. "I'll go it alone, that's what I'll do," she murmured between sobs as she sat by the window with her head in her hands, and heard the sweet song of the insects, singing of life in the darkness of the fields.

CHAPTER IV

"There was a man here. For weeks he lay sick to the point of death, in our house, and all the time I did not dare sleep. Night and day I was on the watch. How often at night I have crept down across this very field, in the middle of the night, in the darkness looking for the black, trying to discover if he was still on the trail."

It was early summer and May sat talking with Maud Welliver by a tree in the field back of the Edgley's kitchen door— building steadily her tower of romance. Two or three times each week, since that first talk by the blacksmith shop, Maud had managed to get to the Edgley house unobserved by her aunt. In her passionate devotion to the little dark-skinned woman, who had lived through so many and such romantic adventures in life, she was ready to risk anything, even to the wrath of her father's iron-jawed housekeeper.

To the Edgley house she came always at night, and the necessity of that was understood by May and perhaps better understood by Lillian Edgley. On the next day, after the meeting by the blacksmith shop, Maud's father had spoken his mind concerning the Edgleys. The Welliver family sat at supper in the evening. "Maud," John Welliver began, looking sternly at his daughter, "I don't want you should have anything to do with that Edgley family that lives on this street." The railroad man cursed the ill luck that had led him to take a house on the same street where such cattle lived. One of his brother employees on the road, he said, had told him the story of the Edgleys. "They are such an outfit," he declared wrathfully. "God only knows why they are allowed to stay here. They should be tarred and feathered and run out of town. Why, to live on the same street with them is like living in the midst of cattle."

The railroad man looked hard at his daughter. To him she was a young woman and a virgin, and by these tokens walked a dangerous trail through life. On dark streets, adventurous men lay in wait for all such women and they employed other women, of the Edgley stripe, to decoy innocent virgins into their hands. There was much he would have liked to say to his daughter but not much he could say. Among themselves men could speak openly of such women as the Edgley sisters. They were a thing—well. To tell the truth—during young manhood almost every man went to see such women, went with other men into a house inhabited by such women. To go to such a place one needed to have been drinking a little. It happened. Several young men were together and went from place to place drinking. "Let's go down the line," one of them said. The men went straggling off along a street, two by two. Little was said and they were all a little ashamed of their mission. Then they came to a house, always on a dark foul street, and one of the young men, a bold fellow, knocked at the door. A fat woman, with a hard face, came to let them in and they went into a room and stood about, looking foolish. "O, girls,—company," the fat woman shouted and several women came and stood about. The women looked bored and tired.

John Welliver had himself been to such places. Well, that was when he was a young workman. Later a man met a good woman and married her, tried to forget the other women, did forget them. In spite of all the things said, most men after marriage went straight. They had a living to make and children growing up and there was no time for any such nonsense. Among his fellow workmen, the railroad man often spoke of the kind of women he believed the three Edgley women to be. "It's my notion," he said, "that it's better to have such places in order that good women may be let alone, but they ought to be off by themselves somewhere. A good woman never ought to see or know about such cattle."

In the presence of his daughter and of his sister, the house-keeper, now that the subject of the Edgleys had been broached the railroad man was embarrassed. He kept his eye on the plate before him and stole a shy look at his daughter's face. How white and pure it looked. "I wish I had kept my mouth shut," he thought—but a sense of the necessity of the occasion led him on. "My Maud might be led to take up with the Edgley women, knowing nothing," he thought. "Well," he said, "there are three women in that family and they are all alike. There is one, who works at the hotel—where she meets travel-ing men—and the oldest one doesn't work at all. And there is another, too, the youngest that everyone thought was going to turn out all right because she stood high in school and is said to be smart. Everyone thought she would be different but she isn't, you see. Why, right before everyone, in a berry field, where she was at work, she went into a wood with a man."

"I know about it and I've told Maud," the railroad man's sister said sharply. "We don't need to talk about it no more."

Maud Welliver had listened with flushed cheeks to her father's words, and even as he talked had made up her mind she would see May again and soon. Since coming to Bidwell she had not left the house at night, but now she felt suddenly quite strong and well. When the supper was finished and darkness came on she got up from her chair on the porch and spoke to her aunt, at work inside the house. "I feel better than I have for months, aunty," she said, "and I'm going for a little walk. You know the doctor said I was to walk all I could and I can't walk during the day on account of the heat. I'll just go uptown a little while."

Maud went cautiously along the sidewalk toward the busi-ness section of town and then crossed over and returning on the opposite side, stole along, walking on the grass at the edge of lawns. What an adventure! She felt like one being admitted into some strange world filled with romance. For her May Edgley's tales had become golden apples of existence, to taste which she would risk anything. "What a person!" she thought as she crept forward in the darkness, lifting and putting down her feet on the grass like a kitten compelled to walk in water. She thought of May Edgley's adventure in the wood with Jerome Hadley. How stupid her father had been, how stupid everyone in the town of Bidwell! "It must be so with men and women everywhere," she thought vaguely. "They go on thinking they know what's happening, and they know nothing." She thought of May Edgley, small and a woman, alone in the forest with a man—a dark determined man, intent upon murder. The man held in his hand a little package containing a white powder. A few grains of it in a cup of coffee and a human life would go out. A man who walked and talked and went about the streets of Bidwell with other men would become a white lifeless bit of clay. Maud had been at several times in her life close to the door of death. She imagined a scene. There was a rich man's home with soft carpets, woven of priceless stuffs, brought from the Orient. One walking on the carpets made no sound. The feet sank softly into the velvety stuff and soft-voiced servants moved about. A man entered and sat at breakfast. The movies had not at that time come to Bidwell but Maud had read many popular novels and several times, at Fort Wayne, had been to the theatre.

There was a woman in the rich man's house—his guilty wife. She was slender and willowy. Ah, there was something serpentine about her. In Maud's imagination she lay on a silken couch beside the table, at which the man now sat down to eat his breakfast. A wood fire burned in the fireplace. The woman's hand stole forward and a tiny pinch of the white powder went into the coffee cup; then she raised a white hand and stroked the man's cheek. She closed her eyes and lay back on the silken couch. The dastardly deed was done and the woman did not care. She was not even curious as to how death would come. She yawned and waited.

The man drank his coffee and arising moved about the room and then a sudden pallor came upon his cheeks. It was quite noticeable as he was a ruddy-cheeked man with soft grey hair—a strong commanding figure of a man, a leader among men. Maud pictured him as the president of a great railroad system. She had never seen a railroad president but her father had often spoken of the president of the Nickel Plate and had described him as a big fine looking fellow.

What a thing is passion, so terrible, so strange. It takes such unimaginable turns. The woman on the silken couch, the willowy serpentine woman, had turned from her husband, from the commander of men, from the strong man, the powerful one who swept all before him, and had given her illicit but powerfully fascinating love to a railroad mail clerk.

Maud had seen Jerome Hadley. When the Wellivers had first come to Bidwell she, with her aunt and father, had been driven about town with a real-estate man and his wife. They were looking for a house in which to live and as they drove about the real-estate man's wife, who sat on the back seat of a surrey with Maud and her aunt, had pointed to Jerome Hadley, walking past in the street, and had told in a whisper the story of his going into the wood with May Edgley. Maud was half sick on that day and had not listened. The railroad journey from Fort Wayne to Bidwell had given her a headache.

However, she had looked at Jerome. He had sloping shoulders, pale grey eyes and sandy hair, and when he walked he toed out badly and his trousers were baggy. And for that man the woman on the silken couch, the railroad president's wife, was ready to commit murder. What an unexplainable, what a strange thing is love! The windings and twistings of its pathway through life cannot be followed by the human mind.

The scene being enacted in Maud Welliver's mind played itself out. The strong man in the richly furnished room put his hand to his throat and staggered. He reeled from side to side and clutched at the backs of chairs. The noiseless servants had all gone out of the room. The woman half arose from the couch as the man fell to the floor and in falling struck his head on the corner of a table so that his blood ran out upon the silken carpets. The woman smiled sardonically. It was terrible. She cared not the least in the world and a slow cruel smile came and remained fixed on her face. Then there was the sound of running feet. The servants were coming, they were running, running desperately. The woman lay back on the couch and yawned again. "I had better scream and then faint," she thought and she did the two things, did them with the air of a tired actor rehearsing a well known part for a play. It was all for love, for a strange and mysterious thing called passion. She did it for Jerome Hadley's sake, that she might be free to walk with him the illicit paths of love.

Maud Welliver tiptoed cautiously forward on the lawns on the further side of Duane Street in Bidwell, looking across at the dark house where she had come to live. In Fort Wayne she had known nothing like this. What a terrible thing might have happened in Bidwell but for May Edgley! The scene in the rich man's home faded and was replaced by another. She saw May standing in the forest with Jerome Hadley. How he had changed! He stood alert, intent, determined, holding the poison package in his hand and he was threatening, threatening and pleading. In the other hand he held money, a great package of bills. He thrust the bills forward and pleaded with May Edgley and then grew angry and threatened again.

Before him stood the small, white-faced woman, frightened now, but terribly determined also. The word "never" was upon her lips. And now the man threw the money away into the bushes and sprang forward. His hand was at the woman's throat, the murderous hand of the infuriated mail clerk. It pressed hard. May fell to the ground.

Jerome Hadley did not quite dare let the woman die. Too many people had seen the two go into the wood together. He stood over her until she had a little recovered and then the threatening and pleading began again, but all the time the little woman stood firm, shaking her head and saying the brave word "never." "Kill me if you will," she said, "but I'll take no part in this murder. My reputation is gone and I am an outlaw among men and women but I'll take no part in this murder, and if you go on with it I will betray you."

The September evening when May uttered the startling sentences, regarding a strange man and a mysterious black, set down at the head of this section of the story of her adventures, was warm and clear. Brightly the stars shone in the sky and in the field back of the Edgley's kitchen door all the little ponds had become dry. Since that first evening when she had met

May a great change had taken place in Maud. May had led her up to the ramparts of the tower of romance and as often as possible now the two sat together under a tree in the field or on the floor by the open window in May's room. To the field they went through the kitchen door, along the creek where the elders and willows grew and over stones in the bed of the creek itself, to a wire fence. How alone and how far away from the life of the town they were in the field at night! Buggies and the few automobiles then owned in Bidwell passed on distant roads, and over the town, soft lights played on the sky and soft lights seemed to play over the spirits of the two women. On a distant street, that led down to the town waterworks, a group of young men went tramping along on a board sidewalk. They were singing a song. "Listen, May," Maud said. The voices died away and another sound came. Jerry Haden, a cripple who walked with a crutch and who delivered evening papers, went along quickly, his crutch making a sharp clicking sound on the sidewalks. What a hurry he was in. "Click! click!" went the crutch.

It was a time and place for the growth of romance. A desire to reach out to life, to command life grew within Maud. One evening she, alone and unaided, mounted the tower of romance and told May of how a young man in Fort Wayne had wanted to marry her. "He was the son of the president of a railroad company," she said. The matter was of no importance and she only spoke of it to show what men were like. For a long time he came to the house almost every evening and when he did not come he sent flowers and candy. Maud had cared nothing for him. There was a certain air he had that wearied her. He seemed to think himself in some way of better blood than the Wellivers. The idea was absurd. Maud's father knew his father and knew that he had once been no more than a section hand on the railroad. His pretensions wearied Maud and she finally sent him away.

Maud told May, on several evenings of the imaginary young man whom, because of his pride of blood, she had cast adrift, and on the September evening wanted to speak of something else. For two or three evenings she had been on the point of saying what was in her mind but could not bring the matter to her lips. It trembled within her like a wild bird caught and held in her hand, as, in the dim light, she looked at May. "She won't do it. I'll never get her to do it," she thought.

In Fort Wayne, before she came to Bidwell, and when she had just graduated from the high school Maud had for a time walked upon the border line of love, had stood for a moment in the very pathway of Cupid's darts. Near the house where the Wellivers then lived there was a grocery run by an alert erect little man of forty-five, whose wife had died. Maud often went to the store to buy supplies for the Welliver home and one evening she arrived just as the grocer, a man named Hunt, was locking the store for the night. He unlocked the door and let her in. "You won't mind if I don't light the lights again," he said. He explained that the grocerymen of Fort Wayne had made an agreement among themselves that they would sell no goods after seven in the evening. "If I light the lights and people see us in here they will be coming in and wanting to be waited on," he explained.

Maud stood in the uncertain light by a counter while the grocer wrapped her packages. At the back of the store there was a lamp fastened to a bracket on the wall and burning dimly and the soft yellow light fell on her hair and on her white smiling face as the grocer fumbled in the darkness back of the counter and from time to time looked up at her. How beautiful her long pale face in that light! He was stirred and delayed the matter of getting the packages wrapped. "My wife and I were not very happy together but I was happy when I lived alone with my mother," he thought. He let Maud out at the door, locked it and went along beside her carrying the packages. "I'm going your way," he said vaguely. He began to speak of his boyhood in a town in Ohio and told of how he had married at the age of twenty-three and had come to Fort Wayne where his wife's father owned the store that was now his own. He spoke to Maud as to one who knew most of the details of his life. "Well, my wife and her father are both dead and I own the place—I've come out all right," he said. "I wonder why I left my mother. I thought more of her than anyone else in the world but I got married and went away and left her, went away and left her, to live alone until she died," he said. They came to a corner and he put the packages into Maud's arms. "You got me started thinking of mother. You're like her," he said suddenly and then hurried away.

Maud had got into the habit of going to the store, just at closing time in the evening and when she did not come the grocer was upset. He closed the store and, walking to a nearby corner, stood under an awning before a hardware store, also closed for the night, and looked down along the street where Maud lived. Then he took a heavy silver watch from his pocket and looked at it. "Huh!" he exclaimed and went off along another street to his boarding house, stopping several times in the first block to look back.

It was early June and the Wellivers had lived in Bidwell, for four months and, during the last year of her life at Fort Wayne Maud had been so continually ill that she had seldom seen the grocer, but now a letter had come from him. The letter came from the city of Cleveland. "I am here at a convention of the K of Ps," he wrote, "and I have met a man here who is a widower like myself. We are in the same room at the hotel. I want to stop to see you on the way home and would like to bring my friend along. Can't you get another girl and we'll all spend an evening together. If you can do it, you get a surrey and meet us at the seven-fifty train next Friday evening. I'll pay for the surrey of course and we'll go off somewhere to the country. I've got something very important I want to say to you. You write me here and let me know if it's all right."

Maud sat in the field beside May and thought of the letter. An answer must be sent at once. In fancy she saw the little bright-eyed grocer standing before May, the hero of the passage in the wood with Jerome Hadley, the woman who lived the romance of which she herself dreamed. At the postoffice during the afternoon she had heard two young men talking of a dance to be given at a place called the Dewdrop. It was to be held on Friday evening, and a bold impulse had led her to go to a livery stable and make inquiry about the place. It was twenty miles away and on the shores of Sandusky Bay. "We will go there," she had thought, and had engaged the surrey and horses and now she was face to face with May and the thought of the little grocer and his companion frightened her.

Freeman Hunt the widower had a bald head and a grey mustache. What would his friend be like? Fear made Maud's body tremble and when she tried to speak, to tell May of her plan, the words would not come. "She'll never do it. I'll never get her to do it," she thought again.

"There was a man here. For weeks he lay sick to the point of death in our house and all the time I did not dare sleep."

May Edgley was building high her tower of romance. Having several times listened, as Maud told of the imaginary son of the railroad president who had been determined to marry her, she had set about making a romantic lover of her own. Books she had read, the remembrance of childhood tales of love and romantic adventure poured in upon her mind. "There was a man here. He was just twenty-four but what a life he had led," she said absentmindedly. She appeared to be lost in thought and for a long time was silent. Then she got suddenly to her feet and ran to where two large maple trees stood on a little hill in the midst of the field. Maud also got to her feet and her body shook with a new fear. The grocer was forgotten. May returned and again sat on the grass. "I thought I saw someone snooping there behind that tree," she said. "You see I have to be careful. A man's life depends on my being careful."

Warning Maud that whatever happened she was not to tell the secret, now for the first time to be told to another, May launched into her tale. On a dark night, when it was raining and when the trees shook in the wind, she had got out of bed in the Edgley house and had opened her window to behold the storm. She could not imagine what had led her to do it. It was something she had never done before. To tell the truth a voice outside herself seemed to be calling her, commanding her. Well, she had thrown up the window and had stood looking out. How the wind screamed and shrieked! Furies seemed abroad in the night. The house itself trembled on its foundations and great trees bent almost to the ground. Now and then there was a flash of lightning and she could see the whole outdoors as plain as day—"I could even see the leaves on the tree." May had thought the world must be coming to an end but for some strange reason she was not in the least afraid. It was impossible to explain the feeling she had on that night.

Well, she couldn't sleep. Something, outside there, in the darkness, seemed to be calling, calling to her. "All of this happened more than two years ago, when I was just a young girl in school," she explained.

On that night when the storm raged May had seen, during one of the flashes of lightning, a man running desperately across the very field, where now she and Maud sat so quietly. Even from where she stood by the window in the upstairs room she could see that he was white and that his face was drawn and tired from long running. Behind him, perhaps a dozen strides behind, was another man, a giant black, with a club in his hand. In a moment May knew, she knew everything, knowledge came into her mind and illuminated it as the lightning had illuminated the scene in the field. The giant black with the club was about to kill the other man, the white man in the field. In a moment she knew she would see a murder done. The fleeing man could not escape. At every stride the black gained. There came a second flash of lightning and then the white man stumbled and fell. May threw up her hands and screamed. She had always been ashamed of the fact but why deny it—she fainted.

What a night that had turned out to be! Even to speak of it made May shudder, even yet. Her father had heard her scream and came running to her room. She recovered—she sat up—in a few quick words she told her father what she had seen.

Well, you see, her father and she had got out of the house somehow. They were both in their night dresses and in the woodshed back of the house her father had fumbled about and had got hold of an axe. It was the only weapon of any kind he could lay his hands on about the place.

And there they were, in the darkness. No more flashes of lightning came and it began to rain. It poured. The rain came in torrents and the wind blew so that the trees seemed to be shouting to each other, calling to each other like friends lost in some dark pit.

There was plenty of shouting after that but neither May nor her father was afraid. They were perhaps too excited for fear to take hold of them. May didn't know exactly how she felt. No words could describe how she felt.

Followed by her father she ran, down the little hill back of the kitchen, got across the creek, stumbled and fell several times, picked herself up and ran on again. They came to the fence at the edge of the field. Well, they got over somehow. It was strange how the field, across which they had both walked so many times in the daytime (as a child May had always played there and she thought she knew every blade of grass, every little pond, and hillock)—it was strange how it had changed. It was exactly as though she and her father had run out upon a wide treeless plain. They ran, it seemed for hours and hours, and still they were in the field. Later when May thought of the experiences of that night she understood how men came to write fairy tales. Why, the ground in the field might have been made of rubber that stretched out as they ran.

They could see no trees, no buildings—nothing. For a time she and her father kept close together, running desperately, into nothingness, into a wall of darkness.

Then her father got lost from her, was swallowed up in the darkness.

What a roaring of voices went on. Trees somewhere, away off in the distance, were shouting to each other. The very blades of grass seemed to be talking—in excited whispers, you understand.

It was terrible! Now and then May could hear her father's voice. He just swore. "Gol darn you," he shouted over and over. The words were grunted forth.

Then there was another and terrible voice—it must have been the voice of the black, intent upon murder. May could not understand what he said. He, of course, just shouted words in some strange foreign language—a gibberish of words.

Then May stopped running. She was too exhausted to run any more and sat down on the ground at the edge of one of the little ponds. Her hair had all fallen about her face. Well, she wasn't afraid. The thing that had happened was too big to be afraid of. It was like being in the presence of God and one couldn't be afraid. How could one? A blade of grass isn't afraid in the presence of the sun, coming up. That's the way May felt—little you see—a tiny thing in the vast night—nothing.

How wet she was! Her clothes clung to her. All about the voices went on and on and the storm raged. She sat with her feet in a puddle of water and things seemed to fly past her, dark figures running, screaming, swearing, saying strange words. She herself did not doubt—when she thought of it all after it was over—that the giant black and her father had both run past her a dozen times, had passed so close to her that she might have put out her hand and touched them.

How long did she sit there in the darkness? That was something she never knew and her father was like her about it too. Later he couldn't have said, for the life of him, how long he ran about in the darkness, trying to strike something with the axe. Once he ran against a tree. Well, he drew back and sank the axe into the tree. Sometime—in the daytime—May would show Maud the tree with the great gash in it. Her father sank the axe so deeply into the body of the tree that he had work getting it out again and even in the midst of his excitement he had to laugh to think of what a silly fool he had been.

And there was May sitting with her feet in the puddle, the hair clinging to her bare shoulders, her head in her hands, trying to think, trying perhaps to catch some meaningful word in the strange roar of voices. Well, what was she thinking about? She didn't know.

And then a hand touched her, a white strong firm hand. It just crept up out of the darkness, seemed to come out of the very ground under her. There was one thing sure—although she lived to be a thousand years old, May would never know why she didn't scream, faint away, get up and run madly, butting her head against things.

"Love is a strange thing," she told Maud Welliver, as the two sat in the field that warm clear starlit evening. Her voice trembled. "I knew a man had come to whom I would be faithful unto death," she explained.

That was the beginning of the strangest and most exciting time in May's whole life. Never had she thought she would tell anyone in the world about it, at least not until the time came for her marriage, and when all the dangers that still faced the man she loved had passed like a cloud.

On that terrible night, and while the storm still raged, the hand that had crept so strangely and unexpectedly into hers had at once quieted and reassured her. It was too dark to see the face and the body of the man back of the hand, but for some reason she knew at once that he was beautiful and good.

She loved the man at once and completely, that was the truth. Later he had told her that his own experience was the same. For him also there came a great peace of the spirit, after his hand found hers in the midst of that roaring darkness.

They got out of that field and into the Edgley house somehow, crawled along together and when they got to the house they did not light a lamp or anything but sat on the floor of May's room hand in hand, talking in low quiet tones. After a long time, perhaps an hour, May's father came home. He had got out of the field and had wandered on a country road and as he went along he heard stealthy footsteps behind him. That was the black following the wrong man and it's a wonder he didn't kill John Edgley. What happened was that the drayman began to run and got into a grove of trees and there lost his pursuer. Then he took off his shoes and managed to find his way home barefooted. The black's having followed the wrong man turned out to be a good thing. The man up in May's room was free, for the first time in more than two years, he was free.

It had turned out that the man was quite badly injured, the black having, in his excitement, aimed a blow at his head that would have done for him had it struck fair. However, the blow glanced off and only bruised his head and made it bleed and as he sat in the darkness on the floor in May's room with his hand in hers, telling her his story, the blood kept dropping thump, thump, on the floor. May had thought, at the time, it was water falling from her hair. It just went to show what a man he was, afraid of nothing, enduring everything without a murmur. Later he was sick with a fever for weeks and May never left his room, but gradually nursed him back to health and strength, and no one in Bidwell had ever known of his presence in the house. Later he left town at night, on a dark night when, to save yourself, you couldn't see your hand before your face.

As to the man's story—it had never been told to anyone and if May told it to Maud Welliver it was because she had to have at least one friend who knew all. Even her father, who had risked his life, did not know.

May put her hands over her face and leaned forward and for a long time she was silent. In the grass the insects kept singing and on a distant street Maud could hear the footsteps of people

walking. What a world she had come into when she left Fort
Wayne and came to Bidwell! Indiana was not like Ohio! The
very air was different. She breathed deeply and looked about
into the soft darkness. Had she been alone she could not have
stood being in a place where such wonderful things as had just
been described to her could happen. How quiet it was in the
field now. She put out a hand softly and touched May's dress
and tried to think but her own thoughts were vague, they
swam away into a strange world. To go to a theatre, to read
books, to hear of the commonplace adventures of other people
—how dull and uneventful her life had been before she knew
May. Once her father had been in a wreck on the railroad and
by a miracle had escaped uninjured and, when company came
to the Welliver house, he always told of the wreck, how the
cars were piled up and how he, walking over the tops of cars in
the darkness of a rainy night was pitched off and went flying,
head over heels, only by a pure miracle to land on his feet in
dense bushes, uninjured, only badly shaken up. Maud had
thought the tale exciting, she had been stupid enough to think
it exciting. What contempt she now had for such weak commonplace adventures. What a vast change knowing May Edgley had made in her life!

"You won't tell. You promise on your life you won't tell."
May's hand gripped Maud's and the two women sat in silence,
intent, shaken with some vast emotion that seemed to run
over the dry grass in the field, through the branches of distant
trees, and that seemed to effect even the stars in the sky. To
Maud the stars appeared about to speak. They came down
close out of the sky. "Be cautious," they seemed to be saying.
Had she lived in old times, in Judea, and had she been permitted to go into the room where Jesus sat at the last supper with
his disciples, she could not have felt more completely humble
and thankful that she, of all the people in the world had been
permitted to be where she was at the moment.

"He was a prince in his own country," May said suddenly
breaking the silence that had become so intense that in another
moment Maud thought she would have screamed. "He lived,
Oh, far away. In his own country the father, a king, had decided to marry the prince to the princess of a neighboring
kingdom, and on the same day his sister was to marry the

brother of his betrothed. Neither he nor his sister had ever seen the man and woman they were to marry. Princes and princesses don't, you know. That is the way such things are arranged when princes and princesses are concerned.

"He thought nothing about it, was all ready for the marriage, and then one night something came into his head and he had an almost overpowering desire to see the woman, who was to be his wife, and the man who was to be his sister's husband. Well, he went at night and crept up the side of a great wall to the window of a tower, and through the window saw the man and woman. How ugly they were—horrible! He shuddered. For a time he thought he would let go his hold on the stone face of the wall and be dashed to bits on the rocks beneath. He was ready to die with horror—didn't care much.

"And then he thought of his sister, the beautiful princess. Whatever happened she had to be saved from such a marriage.

"And so home the prince went and confronted his father and there was a terrible scene, the father swearing the marriage would have to be consummated. The neighboring king was powerful and his kingdom was of vast extent and the marriage would make the son, born of the marriage, the most powerful king in the whole world. The prince and the king stood in the castle and looked at each other. Neither of them would give in an inch.

"There was one thing of which the prince was sure—if he did not marry his sister would not have to. If he went away there would be a quarrel between the two old kings. He was sure of that.

"First though he gave the king, his father, his chance. 'I won't do it,' he declared and he stuck to his word. The king was furious. 'I'll disinherit you,' he cried, and then he ordered his son to go out of his presence and not to come back until he had made up his mind to go ahead with the marriage.

"What the king did not expect was that he would be taken at his word. For what the young man, the prince, did, you see, was to just walk out of the castle and right on out into the world.

"Poor man, his hands were then as soft as a woman's," May explained. "You see in all his former life he had never even lifted his hand to do a thing. When he dressed he didn't even button his own clothes. A prince never did.

"And so the prince ran away and managed, after unbelievable hardships, to make his way to a seaport, where he got a place as sailor on a ship just leaving for foreign parts. The captain of the ship did not know, and the other sailors did not know that he was a king's son, nor did they know that a great outcry was going up and horsemen riding madly over the whole country, trying to find the lost prince.

"So he got away and was a sailor and in the castle his father was so furious he would not speak to anyone. He shut himself up in a room of the castle and just swore and swore.

"And then one day he called to him a giant black, one who had been his slave since he was born, and was the strongest, the fleetest of foot and the smartest man too, of all the king's servants. 'Go over land and sea,' shouted the king. 'Go into all strange far away lands and amongst all peoples. Do not let me ever see your face again until you have found my son and have brought him back to marry the woman I have decided shall be his wife. If you find him and he will not come strike him down if you must, but do not kill him. Stun him and bring him to me. Do not let me see your face again until you have done my bidding.' He threw a handful of gold at the black's feet. That was to pay the fares on railroads and buy his meals at hotels," May explained.

"And all the time the king's son was sailing on and on, over unknown seas. He passed icebergs, islands and continents, and saw great whales and at night heard the growling of wild beasts on strange shores.

"He wasn't afraid, not he. And all the time he kept getting stronger and his hands got harder, and he could do more work and do it quicker than almost any man on the ship. Almost every day the captain called him aside. 'Well,' he said, 'you are my bravest and best sailor. How shall I reward you?'

"But the young prince wanted no reward. He was so glad to escape from that horrible king's daughter. How homely she was. Why her teeth stuck out of her mouth like tusks and she was all covered with wrinkles and haggard.

"And the ship sailed and sailed, and it hit a hidden rock, sticking up in the bottom of the ocean, and was split right in two. All but the prince were drowned.

"He swam and swam and came at last to an island that had a

mountain on it, and no one lived there, and the mountain was filled with gold. After a long time a passing ship took him off but he told no one of the golden mountain. He sailed and sailed and came to America, and started out to get money to buy a ship and go get the gold and go back to his own country, rich enough so he could marry almost anyone he chose. He had worked and worked and saved money, and then the giant black got on his trail. He tried to escape, time after time he tried to escape. He had been trying that time May found him half-dead in the field.

"The way that came about was that he was on a train passing through Bidwell at night and it was the nine-fifty, that didn't stop but only threw off a mail sack. He was on that train and the black was on it, too, and, as the train went flying through Bidwell in the terrible storm, the prince opened a door and jumped and the black jumped after him. They ran and ran.

"By a miracle neither of them was hurt by the leap from the train, and then they had got into the field where May had seen them.

"I can't think what kept me awake on that night," May said again. She arose and walked toward the Edgley house. "We are betrothed. He has gone to earn money to buy a ship and get the gold. Then he will come for me," she said in a matter of fact tone.

The two women went to the wire fence, crawled over and got into the Edgley back yard. It was nearly midnight and Maud Welliver had never before been out so late. In the Welliver house her aunt and father sat waiting for her, fright-ened and nervous. "If she doesn't come soon I'll get the police to look for her. I'm afraid something dreadful has happened."

Maud did not, however, think of her father or of the recep-tion that awaited her in the Welliver house. Other and more sombre thoughts occupied her mind. She had come on that evening to the Edgley house, intending to ask May to go with her on the excursion to the Dewdrop with the two grocers, and that was now an impossibility. One who was loved by a prince, who was secretly betrothed to a prince, would never let herself be seen in the company of a grocer, and, beside May, Maud knew no other woman in Bidwell she felt she could ask to go on the trip, on which she did not feel she could go alone.

The whole thing would have to be given up. With a catch in her throat she realized what the trip had meant to her. In Fort Wayne, in the presence of the grocer Hunt, she had felt as she had never felt in the presence of another man. He was old, yes, but there was something in his eyes when he looked at her that made her feel strange inside. He had written that he had something to say to her. Now it could never be said.

In the darkness the two women passed around the Edgley house and came to the front gate, and then Maud gave way to the grief struggling for expression within. May was astonished and tried to comfort her. "What's the matter? What's the matter?" she asked anxiously. Stepping through the gate she put an arm about Maud Welliver's shoulders and for a long time the two figures rocked back and forth in the darkness, and then May managed to get her to come to the Edgley front porch and sit beside her. Maud told the story of the proposed trip and of what it had meant to her—spoke of it as a thing of the past, as a hopeless dream that had faded. "I wouldn't dare ask you to go," she said.

It was ten minutes later when Maud got up to go home and May was silent, absorbed in her own thoughts. The tale of the prince was forgotten and she thought only of the town, of what it had done to her, what it would do again when the chance offered. The two grocers were both, however, from another place and knew nothing of her. She thought of the long ride to the shore of Sandusky Bay. Maud had conveyed to her some notion of what the trip meant to her. May's mind raced. "I could not be alone with a man. I wouldn't dare," she thought. Maud had said they would go in a surrey and there was something, that could be used now, in the story she had told about the prince. She could insist that, because of the prince, Maud was not to leave her alone with another man, with the strange grocer, not for a moment.

May arose and stood irresolutely by the front door of the Edgley house and watched Maud go through the gate. How her shoulders drooped. "Oh, well, I'll go. You fix it up. Don't you tell anyone in the world, but I'll go," she said and then, before Maud Welliver could recover from her surprise, and from the glad thrill that ran through her body, May had opened the door and had disappeared into the Edgley house.

CHAPTER V

The Dewdrop, where the dance Maud and May were to attend was to be held was, in May Edgley's day and no doubt is now, a dreary enough place. An east and west trunk line here came down almost to the water's edge, touching and then swinging off inland again, and on a narrow strip of land between the tracks and the bay several huge ice houses had been built. To the west of the ice houses were four other buildings, buildings less huge but equally stark and unsightly. The shore of the bay, turned beyond the ice houses, leaving the four latter buildings standing at some distance from the railroad, and during ten months of the year they were uninhabited and stared with curtainless windows—that looked like great dead eyes—out over the water.

The buildings had been erected by an ice company, with headquarters at Cleveland, for the housing of its workmen during the ice-cutting season, and the upper floors, reached by outside stairways, had rickety balconies running about the four sides. The balconies served as entry ways to small sleeping rooms each provided with a bunk built against the inner wall and filled with straw.

Still further west was the village of Dewdrop itself, a place of some eight or ten small unpainted frame houses, inhabited by men who combined fishing with small farming, and on the shore before each house a small sailing craft was drawn, during the winter months, far up on the sand out of the reach of storms.

All summer long the Dewdrop remained a quiet sleepy place and, far away, over the water, smoke from factory chimneys in the growing industrial city of Sandusky, at the foot of the bay, could be seen—a cloud of smoke that drifted slowly across the horizon and was torn and tossed by a wind. On summer days, on the long beaches a few fishermen launched their boats and went to visit the nets while their children played in the sand at the water's edge. Inland the farming country—black land, partially covered at certain seasons of the year with stagnant water—was not very prosperous and the road leading down to the Dewdrop from the towns of Fremont, Bellevue, Clyde, Tiffin, and Bidwell was often impassable.

On June days, however, in May Edgley's time, parties came down along the road to the beach and there was the screaming of town children, the laughter of women and the gruff voices of men. They stayed for a day and an evening and went, leaving upon the beach many empty tin cans, rusty cooking utensils and bits of paper that lay rotting at the base of trees and among the bushes back from the shore.

The hot months of July and August came and brought a little life. The summer crew came to take the ice out of the ice houses and load it into cars. They came in the morning and departed in the evening, and, as they were quiet workmen with families of their own, did nothing to disturb the quiet of the place. At the noon hour they sat in the shade of one of the ice houses and ate their luncheons while they discussed such problems as whether it was better for a workman to pay rent or to own his own house, going into debt and paying on the installment plan.

Night came and an adventurous girl, daughter of one of the fishermen, went to walk on the beach. Thanks to wind and rain the beach kept itself always quite clean. Great tree stumps and logs had been carried up on to the sand by winter storms but the wind and water had mellowed these and touched them with delightful color. On moonlight nights the old roots, clinging to the tree trunks, were like gaunt arms reached up to the sky, and on stormy nights these moved back and forth in the wind and sent a thrill of terror through the breast of the girl. She pressed her body against the wall of one of the ice houses and listened. Far away, over the water, were the massed lights of the great town of Sandusky and over her shoulder the few feeble lights of her own fishing town. A group of tramps had dropped off a freight train that afternoon and were making a night of it about the empty workingmen's lodging houses. They had jerked doors off their hinges and were throwing them down from the balconies above and soon a great fire would be lit and all night the fishing families would be disturbed by oaths and shouts. The adventurous girl ran swiftly along the beach but was seen by one of the road adventurers. The fire had been lighted and he took a burning stick in his hand and hurled it over her head. "Run little rabbit," he called as the burning stick, after making a long arch through the air, fell with a hiss into the water.

That was a prelude to the coming of winter and the time of terror. In the hard month of January, when the whole bay was covered with thick ice, a fat man in a heavy fur overcoat, got off a train, that stopped beside the ice houses, and from a car at the front of the train a great multitude of boxes, kegs and crates were pitched into the deep snow at the track side. The world of the cities was coming to break the winter silence of the Dewdrop and the fur coated man and his helpers had come to set the stage for the drama. Hundreds of thousands of tons of ice were to be cut and stored in sawdust in the great ice houses and for weeks, the quiet secluded spot would be astir with life. The silence would be torn by cries, oaths, bits of drunken song—fights would be started and blood would flow.

The fat man waded through the snow to the four empty houses and began to look about. From the little cluster of native houses thin columns of smoke went up into the winter sky. He spoke to one of his helpers. "Who lives in those shacks?" he asked. He himself had much money invested at the Dewdrop but visited the place but once each year and then stayed but a few days. He walked through the big dining room and along the upper galleries where the ice cutters slept, swearing softly. During the year much of his property had been destroyed. Windows had been broken and doors torn from their hinges and he took pencil and paper from his pocket and began to figure. "We'll have to spend all of three hundred dollars this year," he meditated. The thoughts of the money, thus thrown away, brought a flush to his cheeks and he looked again along the shore towards the tiny houses. Almost every year he decided he would go to the houses and do what he called "raising the devil." If doors were torn from hinges and windows smashed these people must have done it. No one else lived at the Dewdrop. "Well I suppose they are a rough gang and I'd better let them alone," he concluded, "I'll send a couple of carpenters down tomorrow and have them do just what has to be done. It's better to keep the ice cutters filled up with beer than to waste money giving them luxurious quarters."

The fat man went away and other men came. Fires were

lighted in the kitchens of the great boarding-houses, carpenters nailed doors back on hinges and replaced broken windows and the Dewdrop was ready again for its season of feverish activity.

The fisher folk hid themselves completely away. On the day when the first of the ice cutters arrived one of them spoke to his assembled family. He looked at his daughter, a somewhat comely girl of fifteen, who could sail a boat through the roughest storm that ever swept down the bay. "I want you to keep out of sight," he said. One winter night a fire had broken out in the dining room of the smallest of the houses where the ice cutters boarded and the fishermen with their wives had gone to help put it out. That was an event they could never forget. As the men worked, carrying buckets of water from a hole cut in the ice of the bay, a group of young roughs, from Cleveland, tried to drag their wives into another of the houses. Screams and cries arose on the winter air and the men ran to the defense of their women. A battle began, some of the ice cutters fighting on the side of the fishermen, some on the side of the young roughs, but the fishermen never knew they had helpers in the struggle. Out of a mass of swearing, laughing men they had managed to drag their women and escape to their own houses and the thoughts of what might have happened, had they been unsuccessful, had brought the fear of man upon them. "I want you to keep out of sight," the fisherman said to his assembled family, but as he said it he looked at his daughter. He imagined her dragged into the upper galleries of the boarding-houses and handed about among the city men —something like that had come near happening to her mother. He stared hard at his daughter and she was frightened by the look in his eyes. "You," he began again, "now you—well you keep yourself out of sight. Those men are looking for just such girls as you." The fisherman went out of the room and his daughter stood by a window. Sometimes, on Sundays, during the ice-cutting time, the men who had not gone to spend the day in the city walked in the afternoon along the beach past the houses of the fishermen and, more than once, she had peeked out at them from behind a curtain. Sometimes they stopped before one of the houses and shouted and a wit among them exercised his powers. "Hey, there house," he shouted, "is there any woman in there wants a louse for a lover." The wit leaped upon the shoulders of one of his companions and with his teeth snatched the cap off his head. Turning towards the house he made an elaborate bow. "I'm only a little louse but I'm cold. Let me crawl into your nest," he shouted.

There were six young men from Bidwell who went to the dance given at the Dewdrop on the June evening when May went there with Maud and the two widowed grocers, homeward bound from the K. of P. convention at Cleveland. The dance was held in one of the large rooms, on the first floor of one of the boarding-houses, one of the rooms used as a dining and drinking place by the ice cutters in the months of January and February. A group of farmers' sons gave the dance and Rat Gould, a one-eyed fiddler from Clyde, came with two other fiddlers, to furnish the music. The dance was open to all who paid fifty cents at the door, and women paid nothing. Rat Gould had announced it at other dances given at Clyde, Bellevue, Castalia and on the floors of newly built barns. There was an idea. At all dances, where Rat had officiated, for several weeks previously, the announcement had been made. "There will be a dance at the Dewdrop two weeks from next Friday night," he had cried out in a shrill voice. "A prize will be given. The best dressed lady gets a new calico dress."

Three of the young men from Bidwell who came to the dance, were railroad employees, brakemen on freight trains. They, like John Welliver, worked for the Nickel Plate and their names were Sid Gould, Herman Sanford and Will Smith. With them, to the dance, went Harry Kingsley, Michael Tompkins and Cal Mosher, all known in Bidwell as young sports. Cal Mosher tended bar at the Crescent Saloon near the Nickel Plate station in Bidwell and Michael Tompkins and Harry Kingsley were house painters.

The going of the six young men to the dance was unpremeditated. They had met at the Crescent Saloon early on that June evening and there was a good deal of drinking. There had been a ball game between the baseball teams of Clyde and Bidwell during the week before, and that was talked over, and, thinking and speaking of the defeat of the Bidwell team, all six of the young men grew angry. "Let's go over to Clyde," Cal

Mosher said. The young men went to a livery stable and hired a team and surrey and set out, taking with them a plentiful supply of whiskey in bottles. It was decided they would make a night of it. As they drove along Turner's Pike, between Bidwell and Clyde they stopped before farmhouses. "Hey, go to bed you rubes. Get the cows milked and go on to bed," they shouted. Michael Tompkins, called Mike, was the wit of the party and he decided upon a stroke to win applause. At one of the farmhouses he went to the door and told the woman who came to answer his knock that a friend of hers wanted to speak to her in the road and the woman, a plump red-cheeked farmer's wife, came boldly out and stood in the road beside the surrey. Mike crept up behind her and throwing his arms about her neck pulled her quickly backward. The woman screamed with fright as Mike kissed her on the cheek and, jumping into the surrey, Mike joined in the laughter of his companions. "Tell your husband your lover has been here," he shouted at the woman, now fleeing toward the house. Cal Mosher slapped him on the back. "You got a nerve, Mike," he said filled with admiration. He slapped his knees with his hands. "She'll have something to talk about for ten years, eh? She won't get over talking about that kiss Mike gave her for ten years."

At Clyde, the Bidwell young men went into Charley Shuter's saloon and there got into trouble. Sid Gould was pitcher for the Bidwell team and during the game at Clyde, during the week before, had been hurt by a swiftly pitched ball that struck him on the side of the head as he stood at bat. He had been unable to continue pitching, and the man who took his place was unskillful and the game was lost, and now, standing at the bar in Charley Shuter's saloon, Sid remembered his injury and began to talk in a loud voice, challenging another group of young men at another end of the bar. Charley Shuter's bartender became alarmed. "Here, now, don't you go starting nothing. Don't you go trying to start nothing in this place," he growled.

Sid turned to his friends. "Well, the cowardly pup, he beaned me," he said. "Well, I had the team, this town thinks so much of, eating out of my hand. For five innings they never got a smell of a hit. Then what did they do, eh? They fixed it up with their cowardly pitcher to bean me—that's what they did."

One of the young men of Clyde, loafing the evening away in the saloon, was an outfielder on the Clyde ball team and as Sid talked he went out at the front door. From store to store and from saloon to saloon he ran hurriedly, whispering, sending messengers out in all directions. He was a tall blue-eyed soft-voiced man but he had now become intensely excited. A dozen other young men gathered about him and the crowd started for Shuter's saloon but when they had got there the young men from Bidwell had come out to the sidewalk, had unhitched their horses from the railing before the saloon door and were preparing to depart. "Yah, you," bawled the blue-eyed out-fielder. "Don't tell lies and then sneak out of town. Stand up and take your medicine."

The fight at Clyde was short and sharp and when it had lasted three minutes, and when Sid Gould had lost two teeth and two of his companions had acquired bleeding heads, they managed to struggle into the surrey and start the horses. The blue-eyed outfielder, white with wrath and disappointment, sprang on the steps. "Come back, you cheap skates," he cried. The surrey rattled off over the cobblestones and several Clyde young men ran in the road behind. Sid Gould drew back his arm and caught the outfielder a swinging blow on the nose and the blow knocked him out of the surrey to the road so that a wheel ran over his legs. Leaning out, and mad now with joy, Sid issued a challenge. "Come over to Bidwell, one at a time, and I'll clean up your whole town alone. All I want is to get at you fellows one or two at a time," he challenged.

In the road north of Clyde, Cal Mosher, who was driving, stopped the horses and there was a discussion as to whether the journey should be continued on to the town of Fremont, in search of new and perhaps more enticing adventures, or whether it would be better to go back to Bidwell and mend broken teeth, cut lips and blackened eyes. Sid Gould, the most badly injured member of the party, settled the matter. "There's a dance down at the Dewdrop tonight. Let's go down there and stir up the farmers. This night is just started for me," he said, and the heads of the horses were turned northward. On the back seat Will Smith and Harry Kingsley fell into a troubled sleep, Herman Sanford and Michael Tompkins attempted a song and Cal Mosher talked to Sid. "We'll get up another game with that bunch from Clyde," he said. "Now you listen and I'll tell you how to work it. You pitch the game, see. Well, you fan every man that faces you for eight innings. That will show them up, show what mutts they are. Then, when it comes to the ninth inning, you start to bean 'em. You can lay out three or four of that gang before the game ends in a scrap, and when that time comes we'll have our own gang on hand."

At the Dewdrop, when the six young men from Bidwell arrived at about eleven o'clock, the dance was in full swing. The doors and windows to the dining room of one of the big frame boarding-houses had been thrown open and the floor carefully swept, and over the windows and doorways green branches of trees had been hung. The night was fine—with a moon—and, on a white beach, twenty feet away, the waters of the bay made a faint murmuring sound. At one end of the dance hall and on a little raised platform sat Rat Gould with his brother Will, a small grey-haired man who played a base viol larger than himself. Two other men, fiddlers like Rat himself filled out the orchestra. Nearly every dance announced was a square dance and Rat did the "calling off," his shrill voice rising above the shuffle of feet and the low continuous hum of conversations. "Swing your pardners round and round. Bow your heads down to the ground. Kick your heels and let her fly. The night is fine and the moon's on high," he sang.

In a corner of the big room with her escort, the grocer, from the town of Muncie in Indiana, sat May Edgley. He was a rather heavy and fleshy man of forty-five, whose wife had died during the year before, and for the first time since that event he was with a woman and the thought had excited him. There was a round bald spot on the top of his head and blushes kept running up his cheeks, into his hair and out upon the bald spot, like waves upon a beach. May had put on a white dress, bought for the ceremony of graduation from the Bidwell high school and, the owner being out of town, had borrowed from Lillian,—unknown to her—a huge white hat, decorated with a long ostrich feather, of the variety known as a willow plume.

She had never before been to a dance and her escort had not danced since boyhood but at Maud Welliver's suggestion they had tried to take part in a square dance. "It's easy," Maud had said. "All you got to do is to watch and do what everyone else is doing."

The attempt turned out a failure, and all the other dancers giggled and laughed at the fat man from Muncie as he rolled and capered about. He ran in the wrong direction, grabbed other men's partners, whirled them about and even got into the wrong set. A madness of embarrassment seized him and he rushed for May, as one hurries into the house at the coming of a sudden storm, and taking her by the arm started to get off the floor, out of sight of the laughing people—but Rat Gould shouted at him. "Come back, fat man," he shrieked and the grocer, not knowing what else to do, started to whirl May about. She also laughed and protested but before she could make him understand that she did not want to dance any more his feet flew out from under him and he sat down, pulling May down to sit upon his round paunch.

For May that evening was terrible and the time spent at the dance hung fire like a long unused and rusty old gun. It seemed to her that every passing minute was heavily freighted with possibilities of evil for herself. In the surrey, coming out from Bidwell, she had remained silent, filled with vague fears and Maud Welliver was also silent. In a way she wished May had not come. Alone with Grover Hunt on such a night, she felt she might have had something to say, but all the time, in her mind floated vague visions of May—alone in the wood with Jerome Hadley, May struggling for life there, in the darkness of the field on that other night—and grasping the hand of a prince. Grover Hunt's hand took hold of hers and he also became silent with embarrassment. When they had got to the Dewdrop, and when they had danced in two square dances, Maud went to May. "Mr. Hunt and I are going to take a little walk together," she said. "We won't be gone long." Through a window May saw the two figures go off along the beach in the moonlight.

The man who had brought May to the dance was named Wilder, and he also wanted May to go walk with him, into the moonlight outside, but could not bring himself to the point of asking so bold a favor. He lit a cigar and held it outside the window, taking occasional puffs and blowing the smoke into the outer air and told May of the K. of P. convention at

Cleveland, of a ride the delegates had taken in automobiles and of a dinner given in their honor by the business men of Cleveland. "It was one of the largest affairs ever held in the city," he said. The Mayor had come and there was present a United States Senator. Well, there was one man there. He was a fat fellow who could say such funny things that everyone in the room rocked with laughter. He was the master of ceremonies and all evening kept telling the funniest stories. As for the Muncie grocer, he had been unable to eat. Well, he laughed until his sides ached. Grocer Wilder tried to reproduce one of the tales told by the Cleveland funny man. "There were two farmers," he began, "they went to the city of Philadelphia, to a church convention, and at the same time and in the same city a convention of brewers was being held. The two farmers got into the wrong place."

May's escort stopped talking and growing suddenly red, leaned out at the window and puffed hard at his cigar. "Well, I can't remember," he declared. It had come into his mind that the story he had started to tell was one a man could not tell to a woman. "Gee, I nearly put me foot into it! I came near making a break," he thought.

May looked from her escort to the men and women dancing on the floor. In her eyes fear lurked. "I wonder if anyone here knows me, I wonder if anyone knows about me and Jerome Hadley," she thought. Fear, like a little hungry mouse, gnawed at May's soul. Two red-cheeked country girls sitting on a near-by bench put their heads together and whispered "Oh, I don't believe it," one of them shouted and they both gave way to a spasm of giggles. May turned to look at them and something gripped at her heart. A young farm hand, with a shiny red face and with a white handkerchief tied about his neck, beckoned to another young man and the two went outside into the moonlight. They also whispered and laughed. One of them turned to look back at May's white face and then they lit cigars and walked away. May could no longer hear the voice of grocer Wilder telling of his adventures at the convention at Cleveland. "They know me, I'm sure they know me. They have heard that story. Something dreadful will happen to me before the night is over," she thought.

May had always wanted to be in some such place as the one

to which she had now come, some place where many strange people had congregated and where she could move freely about among strange people. Before the Jerome Hadley incident, and the giving up of the idea of becoming a schoolteacher she had thought a great deal of what she would do when she became a teacher. Everything had been carefully planned. She would get a place as teacher in some town or in the country, far from Bidwell and from the Edgleys and there she would live her own life and make her own way. There would be no handicap of birth and she could stand upon her own feet. Well, that would be a chance. Her natural smartness would at last count for something real and in the new place she would go about to dances and to other social gatherings. Being the schoolteacher, and in a way responsible for the future of their children, people would be glad to invite her into their houses, and all she wanted was a chance, the opportunity to step unknown into the presence of people who had never been to Bidwell and had never heard of the Edgleys.

Then she would show what she could do! She would go—well, to a dance or to a house where many people had congregated to have a good time. She would move about, saying things, laughing, keeping everyone on tiptoes. What things her quick mind would make up to say! Words would become little sharp swords with which she played. How many pictures her mind had made of herself in the midst of such an assemblage. It was not her fault if she found herself the centre toward which all eyes looked and, in spite of the fact that she was the outstanding figure in any assemblage of people among whom she went, she would always remain modest. After all, she would not say things that would hurt people. Indeed she would not do that! Such a thing would not be necessary. It would all be very lovely. Several people would be talking and up she would come and for a moment she would listen, to catch the drift of what was being said, and then her own word would be said. Well it would startle people. She would have a new, a novel, a startling but attractive point of view on any subject that was brought up. Her mind was extraordinarily quick. It would attend to things.

With her fancy thus filled with the thoughts of the possibilities of herself as a glowing social figure May turned toward her escort who, puzzled by her apparent indifference, was striving manfully to remember the funny things the Cleveland man had said at the dinner given for the K. of Ps. Many of the man's stories could not be repeated to a lady—it had been what is called a stag dinner—but others could be. Of the ones that could be told anywhere—they were called parlor stories—he remembered one and launched into it. May pitied him. He forgot the point, could not remember where the story began and ended. "Well," he began, "there was a man and woman on a train. It was on a train on the B. and O. No, I think the man said it was on the Lake Shore and Michigan Southern. Perhaps they were riding on a train on the Pennsylvania Railroad. I have forgotten what the woman said to the man. It was about a dog another woman was trying to conceal in a basket. They do not allow dogs in passenger cars on railroads, you know. Something very funny happened. I thought I would die laughing when the man told about it."

"If I had that story to tell I could make something out of it," May thought. She imagined herself telling the story of the man and the woman and the dog. How she would decorate it, add little touches. That fat man in Cleveland might have been funny but had she been intrusted with the telling of the story, she was sure he would have been outdone. Her mind began to recast the story and then the fear, that had all evening been lurking within, came back and she forgot the man, the woman and the dog on the train. Again her eyes searched the faces in the room and when a new man or woman came in she trembled. "Suppose Jerome Hadley were to come here tonight," she thought and the thought made her ill. It was a thing that might happen. Jerome was a young man and a bachelor and he no doubt went about to places, to dances and to shows at the Bidwell Opera House, and he might now, at any moment, come into the very room in which she was sitting and walk directly to her. In the berry field he had been bold and had not cared what he said and, if he came to the dance, he would walk directly to her and might even take her by the arm. "I want you," he would say. "Come outside with me."

May tried to think what she would do if such a thing happened. Would she struggle and refuse to go, thus attracting the attention of everyone in the room, or would she go quietly

and make her struggle with the man outside alone in the darkness? Her mind ran into a tangle of thoughts. It was true that
Jerome Hadley had done something quite terrible to her, had
tried to kill something within her, but after all she had surrendered to him. She had lain with the man—filled with fear,
trembling to be sure—but the thing had been done. In a
strange sort of way she belonged to Jerome Hadley and suppose he were to come and demand again that she submit.
Could she refuse? Had she become, and in spite of herself, the
property of the man?

With her head a whirlpool of thought May stared, half
wildly, about. If in her own room in the Edgley house, and
when she had hidden herself away by the willows by the creek,
she had built herself a tower of romance in which she could
live and from the windows of which she could look down upon
life, striving to understand it, to understand people, the tower
was now being destroyed. Hands were tearing at it, strong,
determined hands. She had felt them as she sat in the surrey
with Maud and the two grocers, outbound from Bidwell.
Then as now she wondered why she had consented to come to
the dance. Well, she had come because not to come would
bring a disappointment to Maud Welliver, the only woman
who had come in any way close to herself, and now she was at
the dance and Maud had gone away, outdoors into darkness.
She had gone away with a man and it had been understood that
would not happen. There was the matter of the prince, her
lover. It had been understood that, because of the prince,
Maud would not leave her alone with another man, and she
had left, had gone outdoors with a grocer and had left another
grocer sitting beside May.

Hands were tearing at her tower of romance, the tower she
had built so slowly and painfully, the tower in which she had
found the prince, the tower in which she had found a way to
live and to be happy in spite of the ugliness of actuality. Dust
arose from the walls. An army of men and women, male and
female Jerome Hadleys, were charging down upon it. There
would be rape and murder and how could she, left alone,
withstand them. The prince had gone away. He was now far,
far away, and the invaders would clamor over the walls. They

would throw her down from the walls. The beautiful hangings in the tower, the rich silken gowns, the stones from strange lands, all the treasures of the tower would be destroyed.

May had worked herself into a state of mind that made her want to scream. In the room the dance went on, the shrill voice of Rat Gould called off and the fiddles made dance music to which heavy feet scraped over rough boards. By her side sat Grocer Wilder, still talking of the K. of P. convention at Cleveland and May felt that, in coming to the dance, she had raised a knife that in a moment would be plunged into her own breast. She arose to go out of the room, out into the night, out of the sight of people—but for a moment stood uncertain, looking vaguely about. Then she sat heavily down. Grocer Wilder also arose and his face grew red. "I've made a break," he thought. He wondered what he had said that had offended May. "Maybe she didn't want me to smoke," he told himself and threw the end of his cigar out through a window. The moment reminded him of many moments of his married life. It was like having his wife back, this feeling of having offended a woman, without knowing in just what the offense lay.

And then, through a door at the front, the six Bidwell young men came into the room. They had stopped outside for a final drink out of the bottles carried in their hip pockets and, the appetite for drink being satisfied, another appetite had come into the ascendency. They wanted women.

Sid Gould, accompanied by Cal Mosher, led the way into the dance hall. His face had become badly swollen during the drive north from Clyde and he walked uncertainly.

He walked directly toward May, who turned her face to the wall and tried to hide herself. She looked like a rabbit, cornered by dogs, and when she turned on her seat and half knelt, trying to hide her face, the rim of Lillian Edgley's white dress hat struck against the wall and the hat fell to the floor. Trembling with excitement she turned and picked it up. Her face was chalky white.

Sid Gould was well known in the Edgley household. One summer evening, in the year before May's mother's death, he had got into a row with the Edgleys. Being a little under the

influence of drink and wanting a woman he shouted at Kate
Edgley, walking through the streets of Bidwell with a traveling
man, and a fight had been started in which the traveling man
blackened Sid's eyes. Later he was taken into the mayor's office
and fined and the whole affair had given the Edgley men and
women a good deal of satisfaction and had been discussed
endlessly at the table. Old John Edgley and the sons had sworn
they also would beat the ball player. "Just let me catch him
alone somewhere, so I don't get stuck for no fine, and I'll
pound the head off'n him," they declared.

In the dance hall, and when his eyes alighted upon the figure
of May Edgley, Sid Gould remembered his beating at the
hands of the traveling man and the ten dollar fine he had been
compelled to pay for fighting on the street. "Well, look here,"
he cried turning to his companions, now straggling into the
room, "here's one of the Edgley chickens, a long ways from
the home coop."

"There she is—that little chicken over there by the wall." Sid
laughed and leaning over slapped his knees with his hands.
The twisted swollen face made the laugh a grotesque, something horrible. Sid's companions gathered about him. "There
she is," he said, again pointing a wavering forefinger. "It's the
youngest of that Edgley gang, the one that's just gone on
the turf, the one that was so blamed smart in school. Jerome
Hadley says she's all right, and I say she's mine. I saw her first."

In the hall all became quiet and many eyes were turned toward the laughing man and the shrinking trembling woman by
the wall. May tried to stand erect, to be defiant, but her knees
shook so that she sat quickly down on the bench. Grover
Wilder, now utterly confused, touched her on the arm, intending to ask for an explanation of her strange behavior, but at the
touch of his finger she again sprang to her feet. She was like
some little automatic toy that goes stiffly through certain
movements when you touch some hidden spring. "What's the
matter, what's the matter?" Grocer Wilder asked wildly.

Sid Gould walked to where May stood and took hold of her
arm and she went meekly when he led her toward the door,
walking demurely beside him. He was amazed, having expected a struggle. "Well," he thought, "I got into trouble over
that Kate Edgley but this one is different. She knows how to

behave. I'll have a good time with this kid." He remembered the trial and the ten dollars he had been compelled to pay for his first attempt to get into the good graces of one of the Edgley women. "I'll get the worth of my money now and I won't pay this one a cent," he thought. He turned to his companions still straggling at his heels. "Get out," he cried. "Get your own women. I saw this one first. You go get one of your own."

Sid and May had got outside and nearly to the beach before strength came back into May's body and mind. She walked beside Sid on the white sand and toward the beach. "Don't be afraid little kid. I won't hurt you," he said. May laughed nervously and he loosened the grip of his hand on her arm.

And then, with a cry of joy she sprang away from him and leaning quickly down grasped one of the pieces of driftwood with which the sand was strewn. The stick whistled through the air and descended upon Sid's head, knocking him to his knees. "You, you!" he stuttered and then cried out. "Hey, rubes!" he called and two of his companions, who had been standing at the door of the dance hall, ran toward him. Swinging the stick about her head May ran past them and in her nervous fright struck Sid again. In her mind the thing that was happening was in some odd way connected with the affair in the wood with Jerome. It was the same affair. Sid Gould and Jerome were one man, they stood for the same thing, were the same thing. They were something strange and terrible she had to meet, with which she had to struggle. The thing they represented had defeated her once, had got the best of her. She had surrendered to it, had opened the gates that led into the tower of romance, that was herself, that walled in her own secret and precious life. Something terribly crude, without understanding had happened then—it must not, could not happen again! She had been a child and had understood nothing but now she did understand. There was a thing within herself that must not be touched by unclean hands. A terrible fear of people swept over her. There was Maud Welliver, whom she had tried to take as a friend, and Lillian who had tried to be a sister to her, had wanted to help her achieve life. As for Maud—she knew nothing, she was a child—and Lillian was crude, she understood nothing.

May's mind put all men in a class with Jerome Hadley. There

was something men wanted from women, that Jerome had
wanted and now this other man, Sid Gould. They were all, like
the Edgleys—Lillian and Kate and the two boys—people who
went after the thing they wanted brutally, directly. That was
not May's way and she decided she wanted nothing more to
do with such people. "I'll never go back to Bidwell," she kept
saying over and over as she ran in the uncertain light along the
beach.

Sid Gould's companions, having run out of the dance hall,
could not understand that he had been knocked over by the
slight girl he had led into the darkness, and when they heard his
curses and groans and saw him reeling about, quite overcome
by the second blow May had aimed at his head—combined
with the liquor within—they imagined some man had come to
May's rescue. When they ran forward and saw May with the
stick in her hand and swinging it wildly about they paid little
attention to her but began at once looking for her companion.
Two of them followed May as she ran along the beach and the
others returned to the dance hall. A group of young farmers
came crowding to the door and Cal Mosher hit one of them a
swinging blow with his fist. "Get out of the way," he cried,
"we're going to clean up this place."

May ran like a frightened rabbit along the beach, stopping
occasionally to listen. From the dance hall came an uproar and
oaths and cries broke the silence of the night. At her heels two
men ran, lumbering along slowly. The drink within had taken
effect and one of them fell. As she ran May came presently into
the place of huge stumps and logs, thrown up by the storms of
winter, and saw Maud Welliver standing at the edge of the
water with the grocer Hunt—who had his arm about Maud's
waist. The frightened woman ran so close to them that she
might have touched Maud's dress but they were unconscious
of her presence and, as for May, she was in an odd way afraid of
them also. She was afraid of everything human. "It all comes
to something ugly and terrible," she thought frantically.

May ran for nearly two miles, along the beach, among the
tree stumps, the roots of which stuck up into the air like arms
raised in supplication to the moon. Perhaps the dry withered
old tree arms, sticking up thus, kept her physical fear alive, as it
is not likely Sid Gould's drunken companions followed her far.

She ran clinging to Lillian Edgley's hat—she had borrowed
without permission—and that, I presume, seemed a thing of
beauty to her. Something conscientious and fine in her made
her cling desperately to the hat and she had held it in her left
hand and safely out of harm's way, even in the moment when
she was belaboring Sid Gould with the stick of driftwood.

And now she ran, still clinging to the hat, and was afraid
with a fear that was no longer physical. The new fear that swept
in upon her comprehended something more than the grotesque masses of tree roots, that now appeared to dance madly
in the moonlight, something more than Sid Gould, Cal
Mosher and Jerome Hadley—that had become a fear of life
itself, of all she had ever known of life, all she had ever been
permitted to see of life—that fear was now heavy upon her.

Little May Edgley did not want to live any more. "Death is
a kind and comforting thing to those who are through with
life," an old farm horse had seemed to say to a boy, who, a few
days later, ran in terror from the sight of May Edgley's dead
body to lean trembling on the old horse's manger.

What actually happened on that terrible night when May ran
so madly was that she came in her flight to where a creek runs
down into the bay. There are good fishing places off the mouth
of the creek. At the creek's mouth the water spreads itself out,
so that the small stream looks, from a distance, like a strong
river, but one coming along the beach—running along the
beach, in the moonlight, let us say—from the west would run
almost to the eastern bank in the shallow water, that came only
to the shoe tops.

One would run thus, in the shallow water, and the clear
white beach—east of the creek's mouth—would seem but a
few steps away, and then one would be plunged suddenly
down into the narrow deep current, sweeping under the eastern bank, the current that carried the main body of the water
of the stream.

And May Edgley plunged in there, still clinging to Lillian's
white hat—the white willow plume bobbing up and down in
the swift current—and was swept into the bay. Her body, caught
by an eddy was carried in and lodged among the submerged
tree roots, where it stayed, lodged, until the farmer and his

hired man accidentally found it and laid it tenderly on the boards beside the farmer's barn.

The little hard fist clung to the hat, the white grotesque hat that Lil Edgley was in the habit of putting on when she wanted to look her best—when she wanted, I presume, to be beautiful.

May may have thought the hat was beautiful. She may have thought of it as the most beautiful thing she had ever seen in the actuality of her life.

Of that one cannot speak too definitely, and I only know that, if the hat ever had been beautiful, it had lost its beauty when, a few days later, it fell under the eyes of a boy who saw the bedraggled remains of it, clutched in the drowned woman's hand.

A Chicago Hamlet

THERE was one time in Tom's life when he came near dying, came so close to it that for several days he held his own life in his hand, as a boy would hold a ball. He had only to open his fingers to let it drop.

How vividly I remember the night when he told me the story. We had gone to dine together at a little combined saloon and restaurant in what is now Wells Street in Chicago. It was a wet cold night in early October. In Chicago October and November are usually the most charming months of the year but that year the first weeks of October were cold and rainy. Everyone who lives in our industrial lake cities has a disease of the nasal passages and a week of such weather starts everyone coughing and sneezing. The warm little den into which Tom and I had got seemed cosy and comfortable. We had drinks of whiskey to drive the chill out of our bodies and then, after eating, Tom began to talk.

Something had come into the air of the place where we sat, a kind of weariness. At times all Chicagoans grow weary of the almost universal ugliness of Chicago and everyone sags. One feels it in the streets, in the stores, in the homes. The bodies of the people sag and a cry seems to go up out of a million throats,—"we are set down here in this continual noise, dirt and ugliness. Why did you put us down here? There is no rest. We are always being hurried about from place to place, to no end. Millions of us live on the vast Chicago West Side, where all streets are equally ugly and where the streets go on and on forever, out of nowhere into nothing. We are tired, tired! What is it all about? Why did you put us down here, mother of men?" All the moving bodies of the people in the streets seem to be saying something like the words set down above and some day, perhaps, that Chicago poet, Carl Sandburg, will sing a song about it. Oh, he will make you feel then the tired voices coming out of tired people. Then, it may be, we will all begin singing it and realizing something long forgotten among us.

But I grow too eloquent. I will return to Tom and the restaurant in Wells Street. Carl Sandburg works on a newspaper and sits at a desk writing about the movies in Wells Street, Chicago.

In the restaurant two men stood at the bar talking to the bartender. They were trying to hold a friendly conversation, but there was something in the air that made friendly conversations impossible. The bartender looked like pictures one sees of famous generals—he was the type—a red-faced, well-fed looking man, with a grey moustache.

The two men facing him and with their feet resting on the bar rail had got into a meaningless wrangle concerning the relationship of President McKinley and his friend Mark Hanna. Did Mark Hanna control McKinley or was McKinley only using Mark Hanna to his own ends. The discussion was of no special interest to the men engaged in it—they did not care. At that time the newspapers and political magazines of the country were always wrangling over the same subject. It filled space that had to be filled, I should say.

At any rate the two men had taken it up and were using it as a vehicle for their weariness and disgust with life. They spoke of McKinley and Hanna as Bill and Mark.

"Bill is a smooth one, I tell you what. He has Mark eating out of his hand."

"Eating out of his hand, hell! Mark whistles and Bill comes running, like that, like a little dog."

Meaningless vicious sentences, opinions thrown out by tired brains. One of the men grew sullenly angry. "Don't look at me like that, I tell you. I'll stand a good deal from a friend but not any such looks. I'm a fellow who loses his temper. Sometimes I bust someone on the jaw."

The bartender was taking the situation in hand. He tried to change the subject. "Who's going to lick that Fitzsimmons? How long they going to let that Australian strut around in this country? Ain't they no guy can take him?" he asked, with pumped up enthusiasm.

I sat with my head in my hands. "Men jangling with men! Men and women in houses and apartments jangling! Tired people going home to Chicago's West Side, going home from the factories! Children crying fretfully!"

Tom tapped me on the shoulder, and then tapped with his empty glass on the table. He laughed.

"Ladybug, ladybug, why do you roam?
Ladybug, ladybug, fly away home,"

he recited. When the whiskey had come he leaned forward and made one of the odd and truthful observations on life that were always coming out of him at unexpected moments. "I want you to notice something," he began; "You have seen a lot of bartenders—well, if you'll notice, there is a striking similarity in appearance between bartenders, great generals, diplomats, presidents and all such people. I just happened to think why it is. It's because they are all up to the same game. They have to spend their lives handling weary dissatisfied people and they learn the trick of giving things just a little twist, out of one dull meaningless channel into another. That is their game and practising it makes them all look alike."

I smiled sympathetically. Now that I come to write of my friend I find it somewhat difficult not to misrepresent him on the sentimental side. I forget times when I was with him and he was unspeakably dull, when he also talked often for hours of meaningless things. It was all foolishness, this trying to be anything but a dull business man, he sometimes said, and declared that both he and I were fools. Better for us both that we become more alert, more foxy, as he put it. But for the fact that we were both fools we would both join the Chicago Athletic Club, play golf, ride about in automobiles, pick up flashy young girls and take them out to road-houses to dinner, go home later and make up cock and bull stories to quiet our wives, go to church on Sunday, talk continuously of money making, woman and golf, and in general enjoy our lives. At times he half convinced me he thought the fellows he described led gay and cheerful lives.

And there were times, too, when he, as a physical being, seemed to fairly disintegrate before my eyes. His great bulk grew a little loose and flabby, he talked and talked, saying nothing.

And then, when I had quite made up my mind he had gone the same road I and all the men about me were no doubt going, the road of surrender to ugliness and to dreary meaningless living, something would happen. He would have talked thus, as I have just described, aimlessly, through a long evening, and then, when we parted for the night, he would scribble a few words on a bit of paper and push it awkwardly into my pocket. I watched his lumbering figure go away along a street and going to a street lamp read what he had written.

"I am very weary. I am not the silly ass I seem but I am as tired as a dog, trying to find out what I am," were the words he had scrawled.

But to return to the evening in the place in Wells Street. When the whiskey came we drank it and sat looking at each other. Then he put his hand on the table and closing the fingers, so that they made a little cup, opened the hand slowly and listlessly. "Once I had life, like that, in my hand, my own life. I could have let go of it as easily as that. Just why I didn't I've never quite figured out. I can't think why I kept my fingers cupped, instead of opening my hand and letting go," he said. If, a few minutes before, there had been no integrity in the man there was enough of it now.

He began telling the story of an evening and a night of his youth.

It was when he was still on his father's farm, a little rented farm down in Southeastern Ohio, and when he was but eighteen years old. That would have been in the fall before he left home and started on his adventures in the world. I knew something of his history.

It was late October and he and his father had been digging potatoes in a field. I suppose they both wore torn shoes as, in telling the story, Tom made a point of the fact that their feet were cold, and that the black dirt had worked into their shoes and discolored their feet.

The day was cold and Tom wasn't very well and was in a bitter mood. He and his father worked rather desperately and in silence. The father was tall, had a sallow complexion and wore a beard, and in the mental picture I have of him, he is always stopping—as he walks about the farmyard or works in the fields he stops and runs his fingers nervously through his beard.

As for Tom, one gets the notion of him as having been at that time rather nice, one having an inclination toward the nicer things of life without just knowing he had the feeling, and certainly without an opportunity to gratify it.

Tom had something the matter with him, a cold with a bit of fever perhaps and sometimes as he worked his body shook as with a chill and then, after a few minutes, he felt hot all over. The two men had been digging the potatoes all afternoon and as night began to fall over the field, they started to pick up. One picks up the potatoes in baskets and carries them to the ends of the rows where they are put into two-bushel grain bags.

Tom's step-mother came to the kitchen door and called. "Supper," she cried in her peculiarly colorless voice. Her husband was a little angry and fretful. Perhaps for a long time he had been feeling very deeply the enmity of his son. "All right," he called back, "we'll come pretty soon. We got to get done picking up." There was something very like a whine in his voice. "You can keep the things hot for a time," he shouted.

Tom and his father both worked with feverish haste, as though trying to outdo each other and every time Tom bent over to pick up a handful of the potatoes his head whirled and he thought he might fall. A kind of terrible pride had taken possession of him and with the whole strength of his being he was determined not to let his father—who, if ineffectual, was nevertheless sometimes very quick and accurate at tasks—get the better of him. They were picking up potatoes—that was the task before them at the moment—and the thing was to get all the potatoes picked up and in the bags before darkness came. Tom did not believe in his father and was he to let such an ineffectual man outdo him at any task, no matter how ill he might be?

That was somewhat the nature of Tom's thoughts and feelings at the moment.

And then the darkness had come and the task was done. The filled sacks were set along a fence at the end of the field. It was to be a cold frosty night and now the moon was coming up and the filled sacks looked like grotesque human beings, standing there along the fence—standing with grey sagging bodies, such as Tom's step-mother had—sagged bodies and dull eyes —standing and looking at the two men, so amazingly not in accord with each other.

As the two walked across the field Tom let his father go ahead. He was afraid he might stagger and did not want his father to see there was anything the matter with him. In a way boyish pride was involved too. "He might think he could wear me out working," Tom thought. The moon coming up was a huge yellow ball in the distance. It was larger than the house towards which they were walking and the figure of Tom's father seemed to walk directly across the yellow face of the moon.

When they got to the house the children Tom's father had got—thrown in with the woman, as it were, when he made his second marriage—were standing about. After he left home Tom could never remember anything about the children except that they always had dirty faces and were clad in torn dirty dresses and that the youngest, a baby, wasn't very well and was always crying fretfully.

When the two men came into the house the children, from having been fussing at their mother because the meal was delayed, grew silent. With the quick intuition of children they sensed something wrong between father and son. Tom walked directly across the small dining room and opening a door entered a stairway that led up to his bedroom. "Ain't you going to eat any supper?" his father asked. It was the first word that had passed between father and son for hours.

"No," Tom answered and went up the stairs. At the moment his mind was concentrated on the problem of not letting anyone in the house know he was ill and the father let him go without protest. No doubt the whole family were glad enough to have him out of the way.

He went upstairs and into his own room and got into bed without taking off his clothes, just pulled off the torn shoes and crawling in pulled the covers up over himself. There was an old quilt, not very clean.

His brain cleared a little and as the house was small he could hear everything going on down stairs. Now the family were all seated at the table and his father was doing a thing called "saying grace." He always did that and sometimes, while the others waited, he prayed intermittently.

Tom was thinking, trying to think. What was it all about, his father's praying that way? When he got at it the man seemed to forget everyone else in the world. There he was, alone with God, facing God alone and the people about him seemed to have no existence. He prayed a little about food, and then went on to speak with God, in a strange confidential way, about other things, his own frustrated desires mostly.

All his life he had wanted to be a Methodist minister but could not be ordained because he was uneducated, had never been to the schools or colleges. There was no chance at all for his becoming just the thing he wanted to be and still he went on and on praying about it, and in a way seemed to think there might be a possibility that God, feeling strongly the need of more Methodist ministers, would suddenly come down out of the sky, off the judgment seat as it were, and would go to the administrating board, or whatever one might call it, of the Methodist Church and say, "Here you, what are you up to? Make this man a Methodist minister and be quick about it. I don't want any fooling around."

Tom lay on the bed upstairs listening to his father praying down below. When he was a lad and his own mother was alive he had always been compelled to go with his father to the church on Sundays and to the prayer meetings on Wednesday evenings. His father always prayed, delivered sermons to the other sad-faced men and women sitting about, under the guise of prayers, and the son sat listening and no doubt it was then, in childhood, his hatred of his father was born. The man who was then the minister of the little country church, a tall, raw-boned young man, who was as yet unmarried, sometimes spoke of Tom's father as one powerful in prayer.

And all the time there was something in Tom's mind. Well he had seen a thing. One day when he was walking alone through a strip of wood, coming back barefooted from town to the farm he had seen—he never told anyone what he had seen. The minister was in the wood, sitting alone on a log. There was something. Some rather nice sense of life in Tom was deeply offended. He had crept away unseen.

And now he was lying on the bed in the half darkness up-stairs in his father's house, shaken with a chill, and downstairs his father was praying and there was one sentence always creeping into his prayers. "Give me the gift, O God, give me the great gift." Tom thought he knew what that meant—"the gift of the gab and the opportunity to exercise it, eh?"

There was a door at the foot of Tom's bed and beyond the

door another room, at the front of the house upstairs. His father slept in there with the new woman he had married and
the three children slept in a small room beside it. The baby
slept with the man and woman. It was odd what terrible
thoughts sometimes came into one's head. The baby wasn't
very well and was always whining and crying. Chances were it
would grow up to be a yellow-skinned thing, with dull eyes,
like the mother. Suppose . . . well suppose . . . some night
. . . one did not voluntarily have such thoughts—suppose
either the man or woman might, quite accidentally, roll over
on the baby and crush it, smother it, rather.

Tom's mind slipped a little out of his grasp. He was trying to
hold on to something—what was it? Was it his own life? That
was an odd thought. Now his father had stopped praying and
downstairs the family were eating the evening meal. There was
silence in the house. People, even dirty half-ill children, grew
silent when they ate. That was a good thing. It was good to
be silent sometimes.

And now Tom was in the wood, going barefooted through
the wood and there was that man, the minister, sitting alone
there on the log. Tom's father wanted to be a minister, wanted
God to arbitrarily make him a minister, wanted God to break
the rules, bust up the regular order of things just to make him
a minister. And he a man who could barely make a living on
the farm, who did everything in a half slipshod way, who, when
he felt he had to have a second wife, had gone off and got one
with four sickly kids, one who couldn't cook, who did the
work of his house in a slovenly way.

Tom slipped off into unconsciousness and lay still for a long
time. Perhaps he slept.

When he awoke—or came back into consciousness—there
was his father's voice still praying and Tom had thought the
grace-saying was over. He lay still, listening. The voice was
loud and insistent and now seemed near at hand. All of the rest
of the house was silent. None of the children were crying.

Now there was a sound, the rattling of dishes downstairs in
the kitchen and Tom sat up in bed and leaning far over looked
through the open door into the room occupied by his father
and his father's new wife. His mind cleared.

After all, the evening meal was over and the children had

been put to bed and now the woman downstairs had put the three older children into their bed and was washing the dishes at the kitchen stove. Tom's father had come upstairs and had prepared for bed by taking off his clothes and putting on a long soiled white nightgown. Then he had gone to the open window at the front of the house and kneeling down had begun praying again.

A kind of cold fury took possession of Tom and without a moment's hesitation he got silently out of bed. He did not feel ill now but very strong. At the foot of his bed, leaning against the wall, was a whippletree, a round piece of hard wood, shaped something like a baseball bat, but tapering at both ends. At each end there was an iron ring. The whippletree had been left there by his father who was always leaving things about, in odd unexpected places. He leaned a whippletree against the wall in his son's bedroom and then, on the next day, when he was hitching a horse to a plow and wanted it, he spent hours going nervously about rubbing his fingers through his beard and looking.

Tom took the whippletree in his hand and crept barefooted through the open door into his father's room. "He wants to be like that fellow in the woods—that's what he's always praying about." There was in Tom's mind some notion—from the beginning there must have been a great deal of the autocrat in him—well, you see, he wanted to crush out impotence and sloth.

He had quite made up his mind to kill his father with the whippletree and crept silently across the floor, gripping the hardwood stick firmly in his right hand. The sickly looking baby had already been put into the one bed in the room and was asleep. Its little face looked out from above another dirty quilt and the clear cold moonlight streamed into the room and fell upon the bed and upon the kneeling figure on the floor by the window.

Tom had got almost across the room when he noticed something—his father's bare feet sticking out from beneath the white nightgown. The heels and the little balls of flesh below the toes were black with the dirt of the fields but in the centre of each foot there was a place. It was not black but yellowish white in the moonlight.

Tom crept silently back into his own room and closed softly the door between himself and his father. After all he did not want to kill anyone. His father had not thought it necessary to wash his feet before kneeling to pray to his God, and he had himself come upstairs and had got into bed without washing his own feet.

His hands were trembling now and his body shaking with the chill but he sat on the edge of the bed trying to think. When he was a child and went to church with his father and mother there was a story he had heard told. A man came into a feast, after walking a long time on dusty roads, and sat down at the feast. A woman came and washed his feet. Then she put precious ointments on them and later dried the feet with her hair.

The story had, when he heard it, no special meaning to the boy but now . . . He sat on the bed smiling half foolishly. Could one make of one's own hands a symbol of what the woman's hands must have meant on that occasion, long ago, could not one make one's own hands the humble servants to one's soiled feet, to one's soiled body?

It was a strange notion, this business of making oneself the keeper of the clean integrity of oneself. When one was ill one got things a little distorted. In Tom's room there was a tin wash-basin, and a pail of water, he himself brought each morning from the cistern at the back of the house. He had always been one who fancied waiting on himself and perhaps, at that time, he had in him something he afterward lost, or only got hold of again at long intervals, the sense of the worth of his own young body, the feeling that his own body was a temple, as one might put it.

At any rate he must have had some such feeling on that night of his childhood and I shall never forget a kind of illusion I had concerning him that time in the Wells Street place when he told me the tale. At the moment something seemed to spring out of his great hulking body, something young hard clean and white.

But I must walk carefully. Perhaps I had better stick to my tale, try only to tell it simply, as he did.

Anyway he got off the bed, there in the upper room of that strangely disorganized and impotent household, and standing in the centre of the room took off his clothes. There was a towel hanging on a hook on the wall but it wasn't very clean.

By chance he did have, however, a white nightgown that had not been worn and he now got it out of the drawer of a small rickety dresser that stood by the wall and recklessly tore off a part of it to serve as a washcloth. Then he stood up and with the tin washbasin on the floor at his feet washed himself carefully in the icy cold water.

No matter what illusions I may have had regarding him when he told me the tale, that night in Wells Street, surely on that night of his youth he must have been, as I have already described him, something young hard clean and white. Surely and at that moment his body was a temple.

As for the matter of his holding his own life in his hands—that came later, when he had got back into the bed, and that part of his tale I do not exactly understand. Perhaps he fumbled it in the telling and perhaps my own understanding fumbled.

I remember that he kept his hand lying on the table in the Wells Street place and that he kept opening and closing the fingers as though that would explain everything. It didn't for me, not then at any rate. Perhaps it will for you who read.

"I got back into bed," he said, "and taking my own life into my hand tried to decide whether I wanted to hold on to it or not. All that night I held it like that, my own life I mean," he said.

There was some notion, he was evidently trying to explain, concerning other lives being things outside his own, things not to be touched, not to be fooled with. How much of that could have been in his mind that night of his youth, long ago, and how much came later I do not know and one takes it for granted he did not know either.

He seemed however to have had the notion that for some hours that night, after his father's wife came upstairs and the two elder people got into bed and the house was silent, that there came certain hours when his own life belonged to him to hold or to drop as easily as one spreads out the fingers of a hand lying on a table in a saloon in Wells Street, Chicago.

"I had a fancy not to do it," he said, "not to spread out my fingers, not to open my hand. You see, I couldn't feel any very definite purpose in life, but there was something. There was a feeling I had as I stood naked in the cold washing my body. Perhaps I just wanted to have that feeling of washing myself again sometime. You know what I mean—I was really cleansing myself, there in the moonlight, that night.

"And so I got back into bed and kept my fingers closed, like this, like a cup. I held my own life in my hand and when I felt like opening my fingers and letting my life slip away I remembered myself washing myself in the moonlight.

"And so I didn't open out my fingers. I kept my fingers closed like this, like a cup," he said, again slowly drawing his fingers together.

PART TWO

For a good many years Tom wrote advertisements in an office in Chicago where I was also employed. He had grown middle-aged and was unmarried and in the evenings and on Sundays sat in his apartment reading or playing rather badly on a piano. Outside business hours he had few associates and although his youth and young manhood had been a time of hardship, he continually, in fancy, lived in the past.

He and I had been intimate, in a loose detached sort of way, for a good many years. Although I was a much younger man we often got half-drunk together.

Little fluttering tag-like ends of his personal history were always leaking out of him and, of all the men and women I have known, he gave me the most material for stories. His own talks, things remembered or imagined, were never quite completely told. They were fragments caught up, tossed in the air as by a wind and then abruptly dropped.

All during the late afternoon we had been standing together at a bar and drinking. We had talked of our work and as Tom grew more drunken he played with the notion of the importance of advertising writing. At that time his more mature point of view puzzled me a little. "I'll tell you what, that lot of advertisements on which you are now at work is very important. Do put all your best self into your work. It is very important that the American house-wife buy Star laundry soap, rather than Arrow laundry soap. And there is something else—the daughter of the man who owns the soap factory, that is at present indirectly employing you, is a very pretty girl. I saw her once. She is nineteen now but soon she will be out of college and, if her father makes a great deal of money it will profoundly affect her life. The very man she is to marry may be decided by the success or failure of the advertisements you are now writing. In an obscure way you are fighting her battles. Like a knight of old you have tipped your lance, or shall I say typewriter, in her service. Today as I walked past your desk and saw you sitting there, scratching your head, and trying to think whether to say, "buy Star Laundry Soap—it's best," or whether to be a bit slangy and say, "Buy Star—You win!"—well, I say, my heart went out to you and to this fair young girl you have never seen, may never see. I tell you what, I was touched." He hiccoughed and leaning forward tapped me affectionately on the shoulder. "I tell you what, young fellow," he added smiling, "I thought of the middle ages and of the men, women and children who once set out toward the Holy Land in the service of the Virgin. They didn't get as well paid as you do. I tell you what, we advertising men are too well paid. There would be more dignity in our profession if we went barefooted and walked about dressed in old ragged cloaks and carrying staffs. We might, with a good deal more dignity, carry beggar's bowls, in our hands, eh!"

He was laughing heartily now, but suddenly stopped laughing. There was always an element of sadness in Tom's mirth.

We walked out of the saloon, he going forward a little unsteadily for, even when he was quite sober, he was not too steady on his legs. Life did not express itself very definitely in his body and he rolled awkwardly about, his heavy body at times threatening to knock some passerby off the sidewalk.

For a time we stood at a corner, at La Salle and Lake Streets in Chicago, and about us surged the home-going crowds while over our heads rattled the elevated trains. Bits of newspaper and clouds of dust were picked up by a wind and blown in our faces and the dust got into our eyes. We laughed together, a little nervously.

At any rate for us the evening had just begun. We would walk and later dine together. He plunged again into the saloon out of which we had just come, and in a moment returned with a bottle of whiskey in his pocket.

"It is horrible stuff, this whiskey, eh, but after all this is a horrible town. One couldn't drink wine here. Wine belongs to a sunny, laughing people and clime," he said. He had a notion that drunkenness was necessary to men in such a modern industrial city as the one in which we lived. "You wait," he said, "you'll see what will happen. One of these days the reformers will manage to take whiskey away from us, and what then? We'll sag down, you see. We'll become like old women, who have had too many children. We'll all sag spiritually and then you'll see what'll happen. Without whiskey no people can stand up against all this ugliness. It can't be done, I say. We'll become empty and bag-like—we will—all of us. We'll be like old women who were never loved but who have had too many children."

We had walked through many streets and had come to a bridge over a river. It was growing dark now and we stood for a time in the dusk and in the uncertain light the structures, built to the very edge of the stream, great warehouses and factories, began to take on strange shapes. The river ran through a canyon formed by the buildings, a few boats passed up and down, and over other bridges, in the distance, street cars passed. They were like moving clusters of stars against the dark purple of the sky.

From time to time he sucked at the whiskey bottle and occasionally offered me a drink but often he forgot me and drank alone. When he had taken the bottle from his lips he held it before him and spoke to it softly, "Little mother," he said, "I am always at your breast, eh? You cannot wean me, can you?"

He grew a little angry. "Well, then why did you drop me down here? Mothers should drop their children in places where men have learned a little to live. Here there is only a desert of buildings."

He took another drink from the bottle and then held it for a moment against his cheek before passing it to me. "There is something feminine about a whiskey bottle," he declared. "As long as it contains liquor one hates to part with it and passing it to a friend is a little like inviting a friend to go in to your wife. They do that, I'm told, in some of the Oriental countries—a rather delicate custom. Perhaps they are more civilized than ourselves, and then, you know, perhaps, it's just possible, they have found out that the women sometimes like it too, eh?"

I tried to laugh but did not succeed very well. Now that I am writing of my friend, I find I am not making a very good likeness of him after all. It may be that I overdo the note of sadness I get into my account of him. There was always that element present but it was tempered in him, as I seem to be unable to temper it in my account of him.

For one thing he was not very clever and I seem to be making him out a rather clever fellow. On many evenings I have spent with him he was silent and positively dull and for hours walked awkwardly along, talking of some affair at the office. There was a long rambling story. He had been at Detroit with the president of the company and the two men had visited an advertiser. There was a long dull account of what had been said—of "he saids," and, "I saids."

Or again he told a story of some experience of his own, as a newspaper man, before he got into advertising. He had been on the copy desk in some Chicago newspaper, the *Tribune*, perhaps. One grew accustomed to a little peculiarity of his mind. It traveled sometimes in circles and there were certain oft-told tales always bobbing up. A man had come into the newspaper office, a cub reporter with an important piece of news, a great scoop in fact. No one would believe the reporter's story. He was just a kid. There was a murderer, for whom the whole town was on the watchout, and the cub reporter had picked him up and had brought him into the office.

There he sat, the dangerous murderer. The cub reporter had found him in a saloon and going up to him had said, "You might as well give yourself up. They will get you anyway and it will go better with you if you come in voluntarily."

And so the dangerous murderer had decided to come and the cub reporter had escorted him, not to the police station but to the newspaper office. It was a great scoop. In a moment now the forms would close, the newspaper would go to press. The dead line was growing close and the cub reporter ran about the room from one man to another. He kept pointing at the murderer, a mild-looking little man with blue eyes, sitting on a bench, waiting. The cub reporter was almost insane. He danced up and down and shouting "I tell you that's Murdock, sitting there. Don't be a lot of damn fools. I tell you that's Murdock, sitting there."

Now one of the editors has walked listlessly across the room and is speaking to the little man with blue eyes, and suddenly the whole tone of the newspaper office has changed. "My God! It's the truth! Stop everything! Clear the front page! My God! It is Murdock! What a near thing! We almost let it go! My God! It's Murdock!"

The incident in the newspaper office had stayed in my friend's mind. It swam about in his mind as in a pool. At recurring times, perhaps once every six months, he told the story, using always the same words and the tenseness of that moment in the newspaper office was reproduced in him over and over. He grew excited. Now the men in the office were all gathering about the little blue-eyed Murdock. He had killed his wife, her lover and three children. Then he had run into the street and quite wantonly shot two men, innocently passing the house. He sat talking quietly and all the police of the city, and all the reporters for the other newspapers, were looking for him. There he sat talking, nervously telling his story. There wasn't much to the story. "I did it. I just did it. I guess I was off my nut," he kept saying.

"Well, the story will have to be stretched out." The cub reporter who has brought him in walks about the office proudly. "I've done it! I've done it! I've proven myself the greatest newspaper man in the city." The older men are laughing. "The fool! It's fool's luck. If he hadn't been a fool he would never have done it. Why he walked right up. 'Are you Murdock?' He had gone about all over town, into saloons, asking men, 'Are you Murdock?' God is good to fools and drunkards!"

My friend told the story to me ten, twelve, fifteen times, and did not know it had grown to be an old story. When he had reproduced the scene in the newspaper office he made always the same comment. "It's a good yarn, eh. Well it's the truth. I was there. Someone ought to write it up for one of the magazines."

I looked at him, watched him closely as he told the story and as I grew older and kept hearing the murderer's story and certain others, he also told regularly without knowing he had told them before, an idea came to me. "He is a tale-teller who has had no audience," I thought. "He is a stream dammed up. He is full of stories that whirl and circle about within him. Well, he is not a stream dammed up, he is a stream overfull." As I walked beside him and heard again the story of the cub reporter and the murderer I remembered a creek back of my father's house in an Ohio town. In the spring the water overflowed a field near our house and the brown muddy water ran round and round in crazy circles. One threw a stick into the water and it was carried far away but, after a time, it came whirling back to where one stood on a piece of high ground, watching.

What interested me was that the untold stories, or rather the uncompleted stories of my friend's mind, did not seem to run in circles. When a story had attained form it had to be told about every so often, but the unformed fragments were satisfied to peep out at one and then retire, never to reappear.

It was a spring evening and he and I had gone for a walk in Jackson Park. We went on a street-car and when we were alighting the car started suddenly and my awkward friend was thrown to the ground and rolled over and over in the dusty street. The motorman, the conductor and several of the men passengers alighted and gathered about. No, he was not hurt and would not give his name and address to the anxious conductor. "I'm not hurt. I'm not going to sue the company. Damn it, man, I defy you to make me give my name and address if I do not care to do so."

He assumed a look of outraged dignity. "Just suppose now that I happen to be some great man, traveling about the country—in foreign parts, incognito, as it were. Let us suppose I am a great prince or a dignitary of some sort. Look how big I am." He pointed to his huge round paunch. "If I told who I was cheers might break forth. I do not care for that. With me, you see, it is different than with yourselves. I have had too much of that sort of thing already. I'm sick of it. If it happens that, in the process of my study of the customs of your charming country, I chose to fall off a street-car that is my own affair. I did not fall on anyone."

We walked away leaving the conductor, the motorman and passengers somewhat mystified. "Ah, he's a nut," I heard one of the passengers say to another.

As for the fall, it had shaken something out of my friend. When later we were seated on a bench in the park one of the fragments, the little illuminating bits of his personal history, that sometimes came from him and that were his chief charm for me, seemed to have been shaken loose and fell from him as a ripe apple falls from a tree in a wind.

He began talking, a little hesitatingly, as though feeling his way in the darkness along the hallway of a strange house at night. It had happened I had never seen him with a woman and he seldom spoke of women, except with a witty and half scornful gesture, but now he began speaking of an experience with a woman.

The tale concerned an adventure of his young manhood and occurred after his mother had died and after his father married again, in fact after he had left home, not to return.

The enmity, that seemed always to have existed between himself and his father became while he continued living at home, more and more pronounced, but on the part of the son, my friend, it was never expressed in words and his dislike of his father took the form of contempt that he had made so bad a second marriage. The new woman in the house seemed such a poor stick. The house was always dirty and the children, some other man's children, were always about under foot. When the two men who had been working in the fields came into the house to eat, the food was badly cooked.

The father's desire to have God make him, in some mysterious way a Methodist minister continued and, as he grew older, the son had difficulty keeping back certain sharp comments upon life in the house, that wanted to be expressed. "What was a Methodist minister after all?" The son was filled with the intolerance of youth. His father was a laborer, a man who had never been to school. Did he think that God could suddenly make him something else and that without effort on his own part, by this interminable praying? If he had really wanted to be a minister why had he not prepared himself? He had chased off and got married and when his first wife died he could hardly wait until she was buried before making another marriage. And what a poor stick of a woman he had got.

The son looked across the table at his step-mother who was afraid of him. Their eyes met and the woman's hands began to tremble. "Do you want anything?" she asked anxiously. "No," he replied and began eating in silence.

One day in the spring, when he was working in the field with his father, he decided to start out into the world. He and his father were planting corn. They had no corn-planter and the father had marked out the rows with a home-made marker and now he was going along in his bare feet, dropping the grains of corn and the son, with a hoe in his hand, was following. The son drew earth over the corn and then patted the spot with the back of the hoe. That was to make the ground solid above so that the crows would not come down and find the corn before it had time to take root.

All morning the two worked in silence, and then at noon and when they came to the end of a row, they stopped to rest. The father went into a fence corner.

The son was nervous. He sat down and then got up and walked about. He did not want to look into the fence corner, where his father was no doubt kneeling and praying—he was always doing that at odd moments—but presently he did. Dread crept over him. His father was kneeling and praying in silence and the son could see again the bottoms of his two bare feet, sticking out from among low-growing bushes. Tom shuddered. Again he saw the heels and the cushions of the feet, the two ball-like cushions below the toes. They were black but the instep of each foot was white with an odd whiteness—not unlike the whiteness of the belly of a fish.

The reader will understand what was in Tom's mind—a memory.

Without a word to his father or to his father's wife, he walked across the fields to the house, packed a few belongings and left, saying good-bye to no one. The woman of the house saw him go but said nothing and after he had disappeared, about a bend in the road, she ran across the fields to her husband, who was still at his prayers, oblivious to what had happened. His wife also saw the bare feet sticking out of the bushes and ran toward them screaming. When her husband arose she began to cry hysterically. "I thought something dreadful had happened, Oh, I thought something dreadful had happened," she sobbed.

"Why, what's the matter,—what's the matter?" asked her husband but she did not answer but ran and threw herself into his arms, and as the two stood thus, like two grotesque bags of grain, embracing in a black newly-plowed field under a grey sky, the son, who had stopped in a small clump of trees, saw them. He walked to the edge of a wood and stood for a moment and then went off along the road. Afterward he never saw or heard from them again.

About Tom's woman adventure—he told it as I have told you the story of his departure from home, that is to say in a fragmentary way. The story, like the one I have just tried to tell, or rather perhaps give you a sense of, was told in broken sentences, dropped between long silences. As my friend talked I sat looking at him and I will admit I sometimes found myself thinking he must be the greatest man I would ever know. "He has felt more things, has by his capacity for silently feeling things, penetrated further into human life than any other man I am likely ever to know, perhaps than any other man who lives in my day," I thought—deeply stirred.

And so he was on the road now and working his way slowly along afoot through Southern Ohio. He intended to make his way to some city and begin educating himself. In the winter, during boyhood, he had attended a country school, but there were certain things he wanted he could not find in the country, books, for one thing. "I knew then, as I know now, something of the importance of books, that is to say real books. There are only a few such books in the world and it takes a long time to find them out. Hardly anyone knows what they are and one of the reasons I have never married is because I did not want some woman coming between me and the search for the books that really have something to say," he explained. He was forever breaking the thread of his stories with little comments of this kind.

All during that summer he worked on the farms, staying sometimes for two or three weeks and then moving on and in June he had got to a place, some twenty miles west of

Cincinnati, where he went to work on the farm of a German, and where the adventure happened that he told me about that night on the park bench.

The farm on which he was at work belonged to a tall, solidly-built German of fifty, who had come to America twenty years before, and who, by hard work, had prospered and had acquired much land. Three years before he had made up his mind he had better marry and had written to a friend in Germany about getting him a wife. "I do not want one of these American girls, and I would like a young woman, not an old one," he wrote. He explained that the American girls all had the idea in their heads that they could run their husbands and that most of them succeeded. "It's getting so all they want is to ride around all dressed up or trot off to town," he said. Even the older American women he employed as housekeepers were the same way; none of them would take hold, help about the farm, feed the stock and do things the wife of a European farmer expected to do. When he employed a housekeeper she did the housework and that was all.

Then she went to sit on the front porch, to sew or read a book. "What nonsense! You get me a good German girl, strong and pretty good-looking. I'll send the money and she can come over here and be my wife," he wrote.

The letter had been sent to a friend of his young manhood, now a small merchant in a German town and after talking the matter over with his wife the merchant decided to send his daughter, a woman of twenty-four. She had been engaged to marry a man who was taken sick and had died while he was serving his term in the army and her father decided she had been mooning about long enough. The merchant called the daughter into a room where he and his wife sat and told her of his decision and, for a long time she sat looking at the floor. Was she about to make a fuss? A prosperous American husband who owned a big farm was not to be sneezed at. The daughter put up her hand and fumbled with her black hair—there was a great mass of it. After all she was a big strong woman. Her husband wouldn't be cheated. "Yes, I'll go," she said quietly, and getting up walked out of the room.

In America the woman had turned out all right but her husband thought her a little too silent. Even though the main purpose in life be to do the work of a house and farm, feed the stock and keep a man's clothes in order, so that he is not always having to buy new ones, still there are times when something else is in order. As he worked in his fields the farmer sometimes muttered to himself. "Everything in its place. For everything there is a time and a place," he told himself. One worked and then the time came when one played a little too. Now and then it was nice to have a few friends about, drink beer, eat a good deal of heavy food and then have some fun, in a kind of way. One did not go too far but if there were women in the party someone tickled one of them and she giggled. One made a remark about legs—nothing out of the way. "Legs is legs. On horses or women legs count a good deal." Everyone laughed. One had a jolly evening, one had some fun.

Often, after his woman came, the farmer, working in his fields, tried to think what was the matter with her. She worked all the time and the house was in order. Well, she fed the stock so that he did not have to bother about that. What a good cook she was. She even made beer, in the old-fashioned German way, at home—and that was fine too.

The whole trouble lay in the fact that she was silent, too silent. When one spoke to her she answered nicely but she herself made no conversation and at night she lay in the bed silently. The German wondered if she would be showing signs of having a child pretty soon. "That might make a difference," he thought. He stopped working and looked across the fields to where there was a meadow. His cattle were there feeding quietly. "Even cows, and surely cows were quiet and silent enough things, even cows had times. Sometimes the very devil got into a cow. You were leading her along a road or a lane and suddenly she went half insane. If one weren't careful she would jam her head through fences, knock a man over, do almost anything. She wanted something insanely, with a riotous hunger. Even a cow wasn't always just passive and quiet." The German felt cheated. He thought of the friend in Germany who had sent his daughter. "Ugh, the deuce, he might have sent a livelier one," he thought.

It was June when Tom came to the farm and the harvest was on. The German had planted several large fields to wheat and the yield was good. Another man had been employed to work on the farm all summer but Tom could be used too. He would have to sleep on the hay in the barn but that he did not mind. He went to work at once.

And anyone knowing Tom, and seeing his huge and rather ungainly body, must realize that, in his youth, he might have been unusually strong. For one thing he had not done so much thinking as he must have done later, nor had he been for years seated at a desk. He worked in the fields with the other two men and at the meal time came into the house with them to eat. He and the German's wife must have been a good deal alike. Tom had in his mind certain things—thoughts concerning his boyhood—and he was thinking a good deal of the future. Well, there he was working his way westward and making a little money all the time as he went, and every cent he made he kept. He had not yet been into an American city, had purposely avoided such places as Springfield, Dayton and Cincinnatti and had kept to the smaller places and the farms.

After a time he would have an accumulation of money and would go into cities, study, read books, live. He had then a kind of illusion about American cities. "A city was a great gathering of people who had grown tired of loneliness and isolation. They had come to realize that only by working together could they have the better things of life. Many hands working together might build wonderfully, many minds working together might think clearly, many impulses working together might channel all lives into an expression of something rather fine."

I am making a mistake if I give you the impression that Tom, the boy from the Ohio farm, had any such definite notions. He had a feeling—of a sort. There was a dumb kind of hope in him. He had even then, I am quite sure, something else, that he later always retained, a kind of almost holy inner modesty. It was his chief attraction as a man but perhaps it stood in the way of his ever achieving the kind of outstanding and assertive manhood we Americans all seem to think we value so highly.

At any rate there he was, and there was that woman, the silent one, now twenty-seven years old. The three men sat at table eating and she waited on them. They ate in the farm kitchen, a large old-fashioned one, and she stood by the stove or went silently about putting more food on the table as it was consumed.

At night the men did not eat until late and sometimes darkness came as they sat at table and then she brought lighted lamps for them. Great winged insects flew violently against the screen door and a few moths, that had managed to get into the house, flew about the lamps. When the men had finished eating they sat at the table drinking beer and the woman washed the dishes.

The farm hand, employed for the summer, was a man of thirty-five, a large bony man with a drooping mustache. He and the German talked. Well, it was good, the German thought, to have the silence of his house broken. The two men spoke of the coming threshing time and of the hay harvest just completed. One of the cows would be calving next week. Her time was almost here. The man with the mustache took a drink of beer and wiped his mustache with the back of his hand, that was covered with long black hair.

Tom had drawn his chair back against the wall and sat in silence and, when the German was deeply engaged in conversation, he looked at the woman, who sometimes turned from her dish-washing to look at him.

There was something, a certain feeling he had sometimes— she, it might be, also had—but of the two men in the room that could not be said. It was too bad she spoke no English. Perhaps, however even though she spoke his language, he could not speak to her of the things he meant. But, pshaw, there wasn't anything in his mind, nothing that could be said in words. Now and then her husband spoke to her in German and she replied quietly, and then the conversation between the two men was resumed in English. More beer was brought. The German felt expansive. How good to have talk in the house. He urged beer upon Tom who took it and drank. "You're another close-mouthed one, eh?" he said laughing.

Tom's adventure happened during the second week of his stay. All the people about the place had gone to sleep for the night but, as he could not sleep, he arose silently and came down out of the hay loft carrying his blanket. It was a silent

hot soft night without a moon and he went to where there was
a small grass plot that came down to the barn and spreading
his blanket sat with his back to the wall of the barn.

That he could not sleep did not matter. He was young and
strong. "If I do not sleep tonight I will sleep tomorrow night,"
he thought. There was something in the air that he thought
concerned only himself, and that made him want to be thus
awake, sitting out of doors and looking at the dim distant trees
in the apple orchard near the barn, at the stars in the sky, at the
farm house, faintly seen some few hundred feet away. Now
that he was out of doors he no longer felt restless. Perhaps it
was only that he was nearer something that was like himself at
the moment, just the night perhaps.

He became aware of something, of something moving, restlessly in the darkness. There was a fence between the farm yard
and the orchard, with berry bushes growing beside it, and
something was moving in the darkness along the berry bushes.
Was it a cow that had got out of the stable or were the bushes
moved by a wind? He did a trick known to country boys.
Thrusting a finger into his mouth he stood up and put the wet
finger out before him. A wind would dry one side of the warm
wet finger quickly and that side would turn cold. Thus one
told oneself something, not only of the strength of a wind but
its direction. Well, there was no wind strong enough to move
berry bushes—there was no wind at all. He had come down
out of the barn loft in his bare feet and in moving about had
made no sound and now he went and stood silently on the
blanket with his back against the wall of the barn.

The movement among the bushes was growing more distinct but it wasn't in the bushes. Something was moving along
the fence, between him and the orchard. There was a place
along the fence, an old rail one, where no bushes grew and
now the silent moving thing was passing the open space.

It was the woman of the house, the German's wife. What
was up? Was she also trying dumbly to draw nearer something
that was like herself, that she could understand, a little? Thoughts
flitted through Tom's head and a dumb kind of desire arose
within him. He began hoping vaguely that the woman was in
search of himself.

Later, when he told me of the happenings of that night, he

was quite sure that the feeling that then possessed him was not physical desire for a woman. His own mother had died several years before and the woman his father had later married had seemed to him just a thing about the house, a not very competent thing, bones, a hank of hair, a body that did not do very well what one's body was supposed to do. "I was intolerant as the devil, about all women. Maybe I always have been but then —I'm sure I was a queer kind of country bumpkin aristocrat. I thought myself something, a special thing in the world, and that woman, any women I had ever seen or known, the wives of a few neighbors as poor as my father, a few country girls—I had thought them all beneath my contempt, dirt under my feet.

"About that German's wife I had not felt that way. I don't know why. Perhaps because she had a habit of keeping her mouth shut as I did just at that time, a habit I have since lost."

And so Tom stood there—waiting. The woman came slowly along the fence, keeping in the shadow of the bushes and then crossed an open space toward the barn.

Now she was walking slowly along the barn wall, directly toward the young man who stood in the heavy shadows holding his breath and waiting for her coming.

Afterwards, when he thought of what had happened, he could never quite make up his mind whether she was walking in sleep or was awake as she came slowly toward him. They did not speak the same language and they never saw each other after that night. Perhaps she had only been restless and had got out of the bed beside her husband and made her way out of the house, without any conscious knowledge of what she was doing.

She became conscious when she came to where he was standing however, conscious and frightened. He stepped out toward her and she stopped. Their faces were very close together and her eyes were large with alarm. "The pupils dilated," he said in speaking of that moment. He insisted upon the eyes. "There was a fluttering something in them. I am sure I do not exaggerate when I say that at the moment I saw everything as clearly as though we had been standing together in the broad daylight. Perhaps something had happened to my own eyes, eh? That might be possible. I could not speak to her, reassure

her—I could not say, 'Do not be frightened, woman.' I couldn't
say anything. My eyes I suppose had to do all the saying."

Evidently there was something to be said. At any rate there
my friend stood, on that remarkable night of his youth, and his
face and the woman's face drew nearer each other. Then their
lips met and he took her into his arms and held her for a
moment.

That was all. They stood together, the woman of twenty-
seven and the young man of nineteen and he was a country
boy and was afraid. That may be the explanation of the fact
that nothing else happened.

I do not know as to that but in telling this tale I have an
advantage you who read cannot have. I heard the tale told,
brokenly, by the man—who had the experience I am trying
to describe. Story-tellers of old times, who went from place to
place telling their wonder tales, had an advantage we, who
have come in the age of the printed word, do not have. They
were both story tellers and actors. As they talked they modu-
lated their voices, made gestures with their hands. Often they
carried conviction simply by the power of their own conviction. All of our modern fussing with style in writing is an attempt to do the same thing.

And what I am trying to express now is a sense I had that
night, as my friend talked to me in the park, of a union of two
people that took place in the heavy shadows by a barn in Ohio,
a union of two people that was not personal, that concerned
their two bodies and at the same time did not concern their
bodies. The thing has to be felt, not understood with the
thinking mind.

Anyway they stood for a few minutes, five minutes perhaps,
with their bodies pressed against the wall of the barn and their
hands together, clasped together tightly. Now and then one of
them stepped away from the barn and stood for a moment directly facing the other. One might say it was Europe facing
America in the darkness by a barn. One might grow fancy and
learned and say almost anything but all I am saying is that they
stood as I am describing them, and oddly enough with their
faces to the barn wall—instinctively turning from the house I
presume—and that now and then one of them stepped out

and stood for a moment facing the other. Their lips did not meet after the first moment.

The next step was taken. The German awoke in the house and began calling, and then he appeared at the kitchen door with a lantern in his hand. It was the lantern, his carrying of the lantern, that saved the situation for the wife and my friend. It made a little circle of light outside of which he could see nothing, but he kept calling his wife, whose name was Katherine, in a distracted frightened way. "Oh, Katherine. Where are you? Oh, Katherine," he called.

My friend acted at once. Taking hold of the woman's hand he ran—making no sound—along the shadows of the barn and across the open space between the barn and the fence. The two people were two dim shadows flitting along the dark wall of the barn, nothing more and at the place in the fence where there were no bushes he lifted her over and climbed over after her. Then he ran through the orchard and into the road before the house and putting his two hands on her shoulders shook her. As though understanding his wish, she answered her husband's call and as the lantern came swinging down toward them my friend dodged back into the orchard.

The man and wife went toward the house, the German talking vigorously and the woman answering quietly, as she had always answered him. Tom was puzzled. Everything that happened to him that night puzzled him then and long afterward when he told me of it. Later he worked out a kind of explanation of it—as all men will do in such cases—but that is another story and the time to tell it is not now.

The point is that my friend had, at the moment, the feeling of having completely possessed the woman, and with that knowledge came also the knowledge that her husband would never possess her, could never by any chance possess her. A great tenderness swept over him and he had but one desire, to protect the woman, not to by any chance make the life she had yet to live any harder.

And so he ran quickly to the barn, secured the blanket and climbed silently up into the loft.

The farm hand with the drooping mustache was sleeping quietly on the hay and Tom lay down beside him and closed his eyes. As he expected the German came, almost at once, to the loft and flashed the lantern, not into the face of the older man but into Tom's face. Then he went away and Tom lay awake smiling happily. He was young then and there was something proud and revengeful in him—in his attitude toward the German, at the moment. "Her husband knew, but at the same time did not know, that I had taken his woman from him," he said to me when he told of the incident long afterward. "I don't know why that made me so happy then, but it did. At the moment I thought I was happy only because we had both managed to escape, but now I know that wasn't it."

And it is quite sure my friend did have a sense of something. On the next morning when he went into the house the breakfast was on the table but the woman was not on hand to serve it. The food was on the table and the coffee on the stove and the three men ate in silence. And then Tom and the German stepped out of the house together, stepped, as by a prearranged plan into the barnyard. The German knew nothing—his wife had grown restless in the night and had got out of bed and walked out into the road and both the other men were asleep in the barn. He had never had any reason for suspecting her of anything at all and she was just the kind of woman he had wanted, never went traipsing off to town, didn't spend a lot of money on clothes, was willing to do any kind of work, made no trouble. He wondered why he had taken such a sudden and violent dislike for his young employee.

Tom spoke first. "I think I'll quit. I think I'd better be on my way," he said. It was obvious his going, at just that time, would upset the plans the German had made for getting the work done at the rush time but he made no objection to Tom's going and at once. Tom had arranged to work by the week and the German counted back to the Saturday before and tried to cheat a little. "I owe you for only one week, eh?" he said. One might as well get two days extra work out of the man without pay—if it were possible.

But Tom did not intend being defeated. "A week and four days," he replied, purposely adding an extra day. "If you do not want to pay for the four days I'll stay out the week."

The German went into the house and got the money and Tom set off along the road.

When he had walked for two or three miles he stopped and went into a wood where he stayed all that day thinking of what had happened.

Perhaps he did not do much thinking. What he said, when he told the story that night in the Chicago park, was that all day there were certain figures marching through his mind and that he just sat down on a log and let them march. Did he have some notion that an impulse toward life in himself had come, and that it would not come again?

As he sat on the log there were the figures of his father and his dead mother and of several other people who had lived about the Ohio countryside where he had spent his boyhood. They kept doing things, saying things. It will be quite clear to my readers that I think my friend a story teller who for some reason has never been able to get his stories outside himself, as one might say, and that might of course explain the day in the wood. He himself thought he was in a sort of comatose state. He had not slept during the night before and, although he did not say as much, there was something a bit mysterious in the thing that had happened to him.

There was one thing he told me concerning that day of dreams that is curious. There appeared in his fancy, over and over again, the figure of a woman he had never seen in the flesh and has never seen since. At any rate it wasn't the German's wife, he declared.

"The figure was that of a woman but I could not tell her age," he said. "She was walking away from me and was clad in a blue dress covered with black dots. Her figure was slender and looked strong but broken. That's it. She was walking in a path in a country such as I had then never seen, have never seen, a country of very low hills and without trees. There was no grass either but only low bushes that came up to her knees. One might have thought it an Arctic country, where there is summer but for a few weeks each year. She had her sleeves rolled to her shoulders so that her slender arms showed, and had buried her face in the crook of her right arm. Her left arm hung like a broken thing, her legs were like broken things, her body was a broken thing.

"And yet, you see, she kept walking and walking, in the path, among the low bushes, over the barren little hills. She walked vigorously too. It seems impossible and a foolish thing to tell about but all day I sat in the woods on the stump and every time I closed my eyes I saw that woman walking thus, fairly rushing along, and yet, you see, she was all broken to pieces."

The Man Who Became a Woman

My father was a retail druggist in our town, out in Nebraska, which was so much like a thousand other towns I've been in since that there's no use fooling around and taking up your time and mine trying to describe it.

Anyway I became a drug clerk and after father's death the store was sold and mother took the money and went west, to her sister in California, giving me four hundred dollars with which to make my start in the world. I was only nineteen years old then.

I came to Chicago, where I worked as a drug clerk for a time, and then, as my health suddenly went back on me, perhaps because I was so sick of my lonely life in the city and of the sight and smell of the drug store, I decided to set out on what seemed to me then the great adventure and became for a time a tramp, working now and then, when I had no money, but spending all the time I could loafing around out of doors or riding up and down the land on freight trains and trying to see the world. I even did some stealing in lonely towns at night— once a pretty good suit of clothes that someone had left hanging out on a clothesline, and once some shoes out of a box in a freight car—but I was in constant terror of being caught and put into jail so realized that success as a thief was not for me.

The most delightful experience of that period of my life was when I once worked as a groom, or swipe, with race horses and it was during that time I met a young fellow of about my own age who has since become a writer of some prominence.

The young man of whom I now speak had gone into race track work as a groom, to bring a kind of flourish, a high spot, he used to say, into his life.

He was then unmarried and had not been successful as a writer. What I mean is he was free and I guess, with him as with me, there was something he liked about the people who hang about a race track, the touts, swipes, drivers, niggers and gamblers. You know what a gaudy undependable lot they are —if you've ever been around the tracks much—about the best liars I've ever seen, and not saving money or thinking about morals, like most druggists, dry-goods merchants and the others who used to be my father's friends in our Nebraska town—and not bending the knee much either, or kowtowing to people, they thought must be grander or richer or more powerful than themselves.

What I mean is, they were an independent, go-to-the-devil, come-have-a-drink-of-whisky, kind of a crew and when one of them won a bet, "knocked 'em off," we called it, his money was just dirt to him while it lasted. No king or president or soap manufacturer—gone on a trip with his family to Europe —could throw on more dog than one of them, with his big diamond rings and the diamond horse-shoe stuck in his neck-tie and all.

I liked the whole blamed lot pretty well and he did too.

He was groom temporarily for a pacing gelding named Lumpy Joe owned by a tall black-mustached man named Al-fred Kreymborg and trying the best he could to make the bluff to himself he was a real one. It happened that we were on the same circuit, doing the West Pennsylvania county fairs all that fall, and on fine evenings we spent a good deal of time walking and talking together.

Let us suppose it to be a Monday or Tuesday evening and our horses had been put away for the night. The racing didn't start until later in the week, maybe Wednesday, usually. There was always a little place called a dining-hall, run mostly by the Woman's Christian Temperance Associations of the towns, and we would go there to eat where we could get a pretty good meal for twenty-five cents. At least then we thought it pretty good.

I would manage it so that I sat beside this fellow, whose name was Tom Means and when we had got through eating we would go look at our two horses again and when we got there Lumpy Joe would be eating his hay in his box stall and Alfred Kreymborg would be standing there, pulling his mus-tache and looking as sad as a sick crane.

But he wasn't really sad. "You two boys want to go down town to see the girls. I'm an old duffer and way past that my-self. You go on along. I'll be setting here anyway, and I'll keep an eye on both the horses for you," he would say.

So we would set off, going, not into the town to try to get

in with some of the town girls, who might have taken up with us because we were strangers and race track fellows, but out into the country. Sometimes we got into a hilly country and there was a moon. The leaves were falling off the trees and lay in the road so that we kicked them up with the dust as we went along.

To tell the truth I suppose I got to love Tom Means, who was five years older than me, although I wouldn't have dared say so, then. Americans are shy and timid about saying things like that and a man here don't dare own up he loves another man, I've found out, and they are afraid to admit such feelings to themselves even. I guess they're afraid it may be taken to mean something it don't need to at all.

Anyway we walked along and some of the trees were already bare and looked like people standing solemnly beside the road and listening to what we had to say. Only I didn't say much. Tom Means did most of the talking.

Sometimes we came back to the race track and it was late and the moon had gone down and it was dark. Then we often walked round and round the track, sometimes a dozen times, before we crawled into the hay to go to bed.

Tom talked always on two subjects, writing and race horses, but mostly about race horses. The quiet sounds about the race tracks and the smells of horses, and the things that go with horses, seemed to get him all excited. "Oh, hell, Herman Dudley," he would burst out suddenly, "don't go talking to me. I know what I think. I've been around more than you have and I've seen a world of people. There isn't any man or woman, not even a fellow's own mother, as fine as a horse, that is to say a thoroughbred horse."

Sometimes he would go on like that a long time, speaking of people he had seen and their characteristics. He wanted to be a writer later and what he said was that when he came to be one he wanted to write the way a well bred horse runs or trots or paces. Whether he ever did it or not I can't say. He has written a lot, but I'm not too good a judge of such things. Anyway I don't think he has.

But when he got on the subject of horses he certainly was a darby. I would never have felt the way I finally got to feel about horses or enjoyed my stay among them half so much if it hadn't been for him. Often he would go on talking for an hour maybe, speaking of horses' bodies and of their minds and wills as though they were human beings. "Lord help us, Herman," he would say, grabbing hold of my arm, "don't it get you up in the throat? I say now, when a good one, like that Lumpy Joe I'm swiping, flattens himself at the head of the stretch and he's coming, and you know he's coming, and you know his heart's sound, and he's game, and you know he isn't going to let himself get licked—don't it get you Herman, don't it get you like the old Harry?"

That's the way he would talk, and then later, sometimes, he'd talk about writing and get himself all het up about that too. He had some notions about writing I've never got myself around to thinking much about but just the same maybe his talk, working in me, has led me to want to begin to write this story myself.

There was one experience of that time on the tracks that I am forced, by some feeling inside myself, to tell.

Well, I don't know why but I've just got to. It will be kind of like confession is, I suppose, to a good Catholic, or maybe, better yet, like cleaning up the room you live in, if you are a bachelor, like I was for so long. The room gets pretty mussy and the bed not made some days and clothes and things thrown on the closet floor and maybe under the bed. And then you clean all up and put on new sheets, and then you take off all your clothes and get down on your hands and knees, and scrub the floor so clean you could eat bread off it, and then take a walk and come home after a while and your room smells sweet and you feel sweetened-up and better inside yourself too.

What I mean is, this story has been on my chest, and I've often dreamed about the happenings in it, even after I married Jessie and was happy. Sometimes I even screamed out at night and so I said to myself, "I'll write the dang story," and here goes.

Fall had come on and in the mornings now when we crept out of our blankets, spread out on the hay in the tiny lofts above the horse stalls, and put our heads out to look around, there was a white rime of frost on the ground. When we woke the horses woke too. You know how it is at the tracks—the little barn-like stalls with the tiny lofts above are all set along in a row and there are two doors to each stall, one coming up to a horse's breast and then a top one, that is only closed at night and in bad weather.

In the mornings the upper door is swung open and fastened back and the horses put their heads out. There is the white rime on the grass over inside the grey oval the track makes. Usually there is some outfit that has six, ten or even twelve horses, and perhaps they have a negro cook who does his cooking at an open fire in the clear space before the row of stalls and he is at work now and the horses with their big fine eyes are looking about and whinnying, and a stallion looks out at the door of one of the stalls and sees a sweet-eyed mare looking at him and sends up his trumpet-call, and a man's voice laughs, and there are no women anywhere in sight or no sign of one anywhere, and everyone feels like laughing and usually does.

It's pretty fine but I didn't know how fine it was until I got to know Tom Means and heard him talk about it all.

At the time the thing happened of which I am trying to tell now Tom was no longer with me. A week before his owner, Alfred Kreymborg, had taken his horse Lumpy Joe over into the Ohio Fair Circuit and I saw no more of Tom at the tracks.

There was a story going about the stalls that Lumpy Joe, a big rangy brown gelding, wasn't really named Lumpy Joe at all, that he was a ringer who had made a fast record out in Iowa and up through the northwest country the year before, and that Kreymborg had picked him up and had kept him under wraps all winter and had brought him over into the Pennsylvania country under this new name and made a clean-up in the books.

I know nothing about that and never talked to Tom about it but anyway he, Lumpy Joe and Kreymborg were all gone now.

I suppose I'll always remember those days, and Tom's talk at night, and before that in the early September evenings how we sat around in front of the stalls, and Kreymborg sitting on an upturned feed box and pulling at his long black mustache and some times humming a little ditty one couldn't catch the words of. It was something about a deep well and a little grey squirrel crawling up the sides of it, and he never laughed or smiled much but there was something in his solemn grey eyes, not quite a twinkle, something more delicate than that.

The others talked in low tones and Tom and I sat in silence. He never did his best talking except when he and I were alone.

For his sake—if he ever sees my story—I should mention that at the only big track we ever visited, at Readville, Pennsylvania, we saw old Pop Geers, the great racing driver, himself. His horses were at a place far away across the tracks from where we were stabled. I suppose a man like him was likely to get the choice of all the good places for his horses.

We went over there one evening and stood about and there was Geers himself, sitting before one of the stalls on a box tapping the ground with a riding whip. They called him, around the tracks, "The silent man from Tennessee" and he was silent—that night anyway. All we did was to stand and look at him for maybe a half hour and then we went away and that night Tom talked better than I had ever heard him. He said that the ambition of his life was to wait until Pop Geers died and then write a book about him, and to show in the book that there was at least one American who never went nutty about getting rich or owning a big factory or being any other kind of a hell of a fellow. "He's satisfied I think to sit around like that and wait until the big moments of his life come, when he heads a fast one into the stretch and then, darn his soul, he can give all of himself to the thing right in front of him," Tom said, and then he was so worked up he began to blubber. We were walking along the fence on the inside of the tracks and it was dusk and, in some trees nearby, some birds, just sparrows maybe, were making a chirping sound, and you could hear insects singing and, where there was a little light, off to the west between some trees, motes were dancing in the air. Tom said that about Pop Geers, although I think he was thinking most about something he wanted to be himself and wasn't, and then he went and stood by the fence and sort of blubbered and I began to blubber too, although I didn't know what about.

But perhaps I did know, after all. I suppose Tom wanted to feel, when he became a writer, like he thought old Pop must feel when his horse swung around the upper turn, and there lay the stretch before him, and if he was going to get his horse home in front he had to do it right then. What Tom said was that any man had something in him that understands about a thing like that but that no woman ever did except up in her brain. He often got off things like that about women but I notice he later married one of them just the same.

But to get back to my knitting. After Tom had left, the stable I was with kept drifting along through nice little Pennsylvania county seat towns. My owner, a strange excitable kind of a man from over in Ohio, who had lost a lot of money on horses but was always thinking he would maybe get it all back in some big killing, had been playing in pretty good luck that year. The horse I had, a tough little gelding, a five year old, had been getting home in front pretty regular and so he took some of his winnings and bought a three years old black pacing stallion named "O, My Man." My gelding was called "Pick-it-boy" because when he was in a race and had got into the stretch my owner always got half wild with excitement and shouted so you could hear him a mile and a half. "Go, pick it boy, pick it boy, pick it boy," he kept shouting and so when he had got hold of this good little gelding he had named him that.

The gelding was a fast one, all right. As the boys at the tracks used to say, he "picked 'em up sharp and set 'em down clean," and he was what we called a natural race horse, right up to all the speed he had, and didn't require much training. "All you got to do is to drop him down on the track and he'll go," was what my owner was always saying to other men, when he was bragging about his horse.

And so you see, after Tom left, I hadn't much to do evenings and then the new stallion, the three year old, came on with a negro swipe named Burt.

I liked him fine and he liked me but not the same as Tom and me. We got to be friends all right and I suppose Burt would have done things for me, and maybe me for him, that Tom and me wouldn't have done for each other.

But with a negro you couldn't be close friends like you can with another white man. There's some reason you can't understand but it's true. There's been too much talk about the difference between whites and blacks and you're both shy, and anyway no use trying and I suppose Burt and I both knew it and so I was pretty lonesome.

Something happened to me that happened several times, when I was a young fellow, that I have never exactly understood. Sometimes now I think it was all because I had got to be almost a man and had never been with a woman. I don't know what's the matter with me. I can't ask a woman. I've tried it a good many times in my life but every time I've tried the same thing happened.

Of course, with Jessie now, it's different, but at the time of which I'm speaking Jessie was a long ways off and a good many things were to happen to me before I got to her.

Around a race track, as you may suppose, the fellows who are swipes and drivers and strangers in the towns do not go without women. They don't have to. In any town there are always some fly girls will come around a place like that. I suppose they think they are fooling with men who lead romantic lives. Such girls will come along by the front of the stalls where the race horses are and, if you look all right to them, they will stop and make a fuss over your horse. They rub their little hands over the horse's nose and then is the time for you—if you aren't a fellow like me who can't get up the nerve—then is the time for you to smile and say, "Hello, kid," and make a date with one of them for that evening up town after supper. I couldn't do that, although the Lord knows I tried hard enough, often enough. A girl would come along alone, and she would be a little thing and give me the eye, and I would try and try but couldn't say anything. Both Tom, and Burt afterwards, used to laugh at me about it sometimes but what I think is that, had I been able to speak up to one of them and had managed to make a date with her, nothing would have come of it. We would probably have walked around the town and got off together in the dark somewhere, where the town came to an end, and then she would have had to knock me over with a club before it got any further.

And so there I was, having got used to Tom and our talks together, and Burt of course had his own friends among the black men. I got lazy and mopey and had a hard time doing my work.

It was like this. Sometimes I would be sitting, perhaps under a tree in the late afternoon when the races were over for the day and the crowds had gone away. There were always a lot of other men and boys who hadn't any horses in the races that day and they would be standing or sitting about in front of the stalls and talking.

I would listen for a time to their talk and then their voices would seem to go far away. The things I was looking at would go far away too. Perhaps there would be a tree, not more than a hundred yards away, and it would just come out of the ground and float away like a thistle. It would get smaller and smaller, away off there in the sky, and then suddenly—bang, it would be back where it belonged, in the ground, and I would begin hearing the voices of the men talking again.

When Tom was with me that summer the nights were splendid. We usually walked about and talked until pretty late and then I crawled up into my hole and went to sleep. Always out of Tom's talk I got something that stayed in my mind, after I was off by myself, curled up in my blanket. I suppose he had a way of making pictures as he talked and the pictures stayed by me as Burt was always saying pork chops did by him. "Give me the old pork chops, they stick to the ribs," Burt was always saying and with the imagination it was always that way about Tom's talks. He started something inside you that went on and on, and your mind played with it like walking about in a strange town and seeing the sights, and you slipped off to sleep and had splendid dreams and woke up in the morning feeling fine.

And then he was gone and it wasn't that way any more and I got into the fix I have described. At night I kept seeing women's bodies and women's lips and things in my dreams, and woke up in the morning feeling like the old Harry.

Burt was pretty good to me. He always helped me cool Pick-it-boy out after a race and he did the things himself that take the most skill and quickness, like getting the bandages on a horse's leg smooth, and seeing that every strap is setting just right, and every buckle drawn up to just the right hole, before your horse goes out on the track for a heat.

Burt knew there was something wrong with me and put himself out not to let the boss know. When the boss was around he was always bragging about me. "The brightest kid I've ever worked with around the tracks," he would say and grin, and that at a time when I wasn't worth my salt.

When you go out with the horses there is one job that always takes a lot of time. In the late afternoon, after your horse has been in a race and after you have washed him and rubbed him out, he has to be walked slowly, sometimes for hours and hours, so he'll cool out slowly and won't get muscle-bound. I got so I did that job for both our horses and Burt did the more important things. It left him free to go talk or shoot dice with the other niggers and I didn't mind. I rather liked it and after a hard race even the stallion, O My Man, was tame enough, even when there were mares about.

You walk and walk and walk, around a little circle, and your horse's head is right by your shoulder, and all around you the life of the place you are in is going on, and in a queer way you get so you aren't really a part of it at all. Perhaps no one ever gets as I was then, except boys that aren't quite men yet and who like me have never been with girls or women—to really be with them, up to the hilt, I mean. I used to wonder if young girls got that way too before they married or did what we used to call "go on the town."

If I remember it right though, I didn't do much thinking then. Often I would have forgotten supper if Burt hadn't shouted at me and reminded me, and sometimes he forgot and went off to town with one of the other niggers and I did forget.

There I was with the horse, going slow slow slow, around a circle that way. The people were leaving the fair grounds now, some afoot, some driving away to the farms in wagons and fords. Clouds of dust floated in the air and over to the west, where the town was, maybe the sun was going down, a red ball of fire through the dust. Only a few hours before the crowd had been all filled with excitement and everyone shouting. Let us suppose my horse had been in a race that afternoon and I had stood in front of the grandstand with my horse blanket over my shoulder, alongside of Burt perhaps, and when they came into the stretch my owner began to call, in that queer high voice of his that seemed to float over the top of all the shouting up in the grandstand. And his voice was saying over and over, "Go, pick it boy, pick it boy, pick it boy," the way he always did, and my heart was thumping so I could hardly breathe, and Burt was leaning over and snapping his fingers and muttering, "Come, little sweet. Come on home. Your Mama wants you. Come get your 'lasses and bread, little Pick-it-boy."

Well, all that was over now and the voices of the people left around were all low. And Pick-it-boy—I was leading him slowly around the little ring, to cool him out slowly, as I've said,—he was different too. Maybe he had pretty nearly broken his heart trying to get down to the wire in front, or getting down there in front, and now everything inside him was quiet and tired, as it was nearly all the time those days in me, except in me tired but not quiet.

You remember I've told you we always walked in a circle, round and round and round. I guess something inside me got to going round and round and round too. The sun did sometimes and the trees and the clouds of dust. I had to think sometimes about putting down my feet so they went down in the right place and I didn't get to staggering like a drunken man.

And a funny feeling came that it is going to be hard to describe. It had something to do with the life in the horse and in me. Sometimes, these late years, I've thought maybe negroes would understand what I'm trying to talk about now better than any white man ever will. I mean something about men and animals, something between them, something that can perhaps only happen to a white man when he has slipped off his base a little, as I suppose I had then. I think maybe a lot of horsey people feel it sometimes though. It's something like this, maybe—do you suppose it could be that something we whites have got, and think such a lot of, and are so proud about, isn't much of any good after all?

It's something in us that wants to be big and grand and important maybe and won't let us just be, like a horse or a dog or a bird can. Let's say Pick-it-boy had won his race that day. He did that pretty often that summer. Well, he was neither proud, like I would have been in his place, or mean in one part of the inside of him either. He was just himself, doing something with a kind of simplicity. That's what Pick-it-boy was like and I got to feeling it in him as I walked with him slowly in the gathering darkness. I got inside him in some way I can't explain and he got inside me. Often we would stop walking for no cause and he would put his nose up against my face.

I wished he was a girl sometimes or that I was a girl and he was a man. It's an odd thing to say but it's a fact. Being with him that way, so long, and in such a quiet way, cured something in me a little. Often after an evening like that I slept all right and did not have the kind of dreams I've spoken about.

But I wasn't cured for very long and couldn't get cured. My body seemed all right and just as good as ever but there wasn't no pep in me.

Then the fall got later and later and we came to the last town we were going to make before my owner laid his horses up for the winter, in his home town over across the State line in Ohio, and the track was up on a hill, or rather in a kind of high plain above the town.

It wasn't much of a place and the sheds were rather rickety and the track bad, especially at the turns. As soon as we got to the place and got stabled it began to rain and kept it up all week so the fair had to be put off.

As the purses weren't very large a lot of the owners shipped right out but our owner stayed. The fair owners guaranteed expenses, whether the races were held the next week or not.

And all week there wasn't much of anything for Burt and me to do but clean manure out of the stalls in the morning, watch for a chance when the rain let up a little to jog the horses around the track in the mud and then clean them off, blanket them and stick them back in their stalls.

It was the hardest time of all for me. Burt wasn't so bad off as there were a dozen or two blacks around and in the evening they went off to town, got liquored up a little and came home late, singing and talking, even in the cold rain.

And then one night I got mixed up in the thing I'm trying to tell you about.

It was a Saturday evening and when I look back at it now it seems to me everyone had left the tracks but just me. In the early evening swipe after swipe came over to my stall and asked me if I was going to stick around. When I said I was he would ask me to keep an eye out for him, that nothing happened to his horse. "Just take a stroll down that way now and then, eh, kid," one of them would say, "I just want to run up to town for an hour or two."

I would say "yes" to be sure, and so pretty soon it was dark as pitch up there in that little ruined fairground and nothing living anywhere around but the horses and me.

I stood it as long as I could, walking here and there in the mud and rain, and thinking all the time I wished I was someone else and not myself. "If I were someone else," I thought, "I wouldn't be here but down there in town with the others." I saw myself going into saloons and having drinks and later going off to a house maybe and getting myself a woman.

I got to thinking so much that, as I went stumbling around up there in the darkness, it was as though what was in my mind was actually happening.

Only I wasn't with some cheap woman, such as I would have found had I had the nerve to do what I wanted but with such a woman as I thought then I should never find in this world. She was slender and like a flower and with something in her like a race horse too, something in her like Pick-it-boy in the stretch, I guess.

And I thought about her and thought about her until I couldn't stand thinking any more. "I'll do something anyway," I said to myself.

So, although I had told all the swipes I would stay and watch their horses, I went out of the fair grounds and down the hill a ways. I went down until I came to a little low saloon, not in the main part of the town itself but half way up the hillside. The saloon had once been a residence, a farmhouse perhaps, but if it was ever a farmhouse I'm sure the farmer who lived there and worked the land on that hillside hadn't made out very well. The country didn't look like a farming country, such as one sees all about the other county-seat towns we had been visiting all through the late summer and fall. Everywhere you looked there were stones sticking out of the ground and the trees mostly of the stubby, stunted kind. It looked wild and untidy and ragged, that's what I mean. On the flat plain, up above, where the fairground was, there were a few fields and pastures, and there were some sheep raised and in the field right next to the tracks, on the furtherest side from town, on the back stretch side, there had once been a slaughter-house, the ruins of which were still standing. It hadn't been used for quite some time but there were bones of animals lying all about in the field, and there was a smell coming out of the old building that would curl your hair.

The horses hated the place, just as we swipes did, and in the morning when we were jogging them around the track in the mud, to keep them in racing condition, Pick-it-boy and O My Man both raised old Ned every time we headed them up the back stretch and got near to where the old slaughter-house stood. They would rear and fight at the bit, and go off their stride and run until they got clear of the rotten smells, and neither Burt nor I could make them stop it. "It's a hell of a town down there and this is a hell of a track for racing," Burt kept saying. "If they ever have their danged old fair someone's going to get spilled and maybe killed back here." Whether they did or not I don't know as I didn't stay for the fair, for reasons I'll tell you pretty soon, but Burt was speaking sense all right. A race horse isn't like a human being. He won't stand for it to have to do his work in any rotten ugly kind of a dump the way a man will, and he won't stand for the smells a man will either.

But to get back to my story again. There I was, going down the hillside in the darkness and the cold soaking rain and breaking my word to all the others about staying up above and watching the horses. When I got to the little saloon I decided to stop and have a drink or two. I'd found out long before that about two drinks upset me so I was two-thirds piped and couldn't walk straight, but on that night I didn't care a tinker's dam.

So I went up a kind of path, out of the road, toward the front door of the saloon. It was in what must have been the parlor of the place when it was a farmhouse and there was a little front porch.

I stopped before I opened the door and looked about a little. From where I stood I could look right down into the main street of the town, like being in a big city, like New York or Chicago, and looking down out of the fifteenth floor of an office building into the street.

The hillside was mighty steep and the road up had to wind

and wind or no one could ever have come up out of the town to their plagued old fair at all.

It wasn't much of a town I saw—a main street with a lot of saloons and a few stores, one or two dinky moving-picture places, a few fords, hardly any women or girls in sight and a raft of men. I tried to think of the girl I had been dreaming about, as I walked around in the mud and darkness up at the fair ground, living in the place but I couldn't make it. It was like trying to think of Pick-it-boy getting himself worked up to the state I was in then, and going into the ugly dump I was going into. It couldn't be done.

All the same I knew the town wasn't all right there in sight. There must have been a good many of the kinds of houses Pennsylvania miners live in back in the hills, or around a turn in the valley in which the main street stood.

What I suppose is that, it being Saturday night and raining, the women and kids had all stayed at home and only the men were out, intending to get themselves liquored up. I've been in some other mining towns since and if I was a miner and had to live in one of them, or in one of the houses they live in with their women and kids, I'd get out and liquor myself up too.

So there I stood looking, and as sick as a dog inside myself, and as wet and cold as a rat in a sewer pipe. I could see the mass of dark figures moving about down below, and beyond the main street there was a river that made a sound you could hear distinctly, even up where I was, and over beyond the river were some railroad tracks with switch engines going up and down. I suppose they had something to do with the mines in which the men of the town worked. Anyway, as I stood watching and listening there was, now and then, a sound like thunder rolling down the sky, and I suppose that was a lot of coal, maybe a whole carload, being let down plunk into a coal car.

And then besides there was, on the side of a hill far away, a long row of coke ovens. They had little doors, through which the light from the fire within leaked out and as they were set closely, side by side, they looked like the teeth of some big man-eating giant lying and waiting over there in the hills.

The sight of it all, even the sight of the kind of hellholes men are satisfied to go on living in, gave me the fantods and the shivers right down in my liver, and on that night I guess I had in me a kind of contempt for all men, including myself, that I've never had so thoroughly since. Come right down to it, I suppose women aren't so much to blame as men. They aren't running the show.

Then I pushed open the door and went into the saloon. There were about a dozen men, miners I suppose, playing cards at tables in a little long dirty room, with a bar at one side of it, and with a big red-faced man with a mustache standing back of the bar.

The place smelled, as such places do where men hang around who have worked and sweated in their clothes and perhaps slept in them too, and have never had them washed but have just kept on wearing them. I guess you know what I mean if you've ever been in a city. You smell that smell in a city, in street cars on rainy nights when a lot of factory hands get on. I got pretty used to that smell when I was a tramp and pretty sick of it too.

And so I was in the place now, with a glass of whisky in my hand, and I thought all the miners were staring at me, which they weren't at all, but I thought they were and so I felt just the same as though they had been. And then I looked up and saw my own face in the old cracked looking-glass back of the bar. If the miners had been staring, or laughing at me, I wouldn't have wondered when I saw what I looked like.

It—I mean my own face—was white and pasty-looking, and for some reason, I can't tell exactly why, it wasn't my own face at all. It's a funny business I'm trying to tell you about and I know what you may be thinking of me as well as you do, so you needn't suppose I'm innocent or ashamed. I'm only wondering. I've thought about it a lot since and I can't make it out. I know I was never that way before that night and I know I've never been that way since. Maybe it was lonesomeness, just lonesomeness, gone on in me too long. I've often wondered if women generally are lonesomer than men.

The point is that the face I saw in the looking-glass back of that bar, when I looked up from my glass of whisky that evening, wasn't my own face at all but the face of a woman. It was a girl's face, that's what I mean. That's what it was. It was a girl's face, and a lonesome and scared girl too. She was just a kid at that.

When I saw that the glass of whisky came pretty near falling out of my hand but I gulped it down, put a dollar on the bar, and called for another. "I've got to be careful here—I'm up against something new," I said to myself. "If any of these men in here get on to me there's going to be trouble." When I had got the second drink in me I called for a third and I thought, "When I get this third drink down I'll get out of here and back up the hill to the fair ground before I make a fool of myself and begin to get drunk."

And then, while I was thinking and drinking my third glass of whisky, the men in the room began to laugh and of course I thought they were laughing at me. But they weren't. No one in the place had really paid any attention to me.

What they were laughing at was a man who had just come in at the door. I'd never seen such a fellow. He was a huge big man, with red hair, that stuck straight up like bristles out of his head, and he had a red-haired kid in his arms. The kid was just like himself, big, I mean, for his age, and with the same kind of stiff red hair.

He came and set the kid up on the bar, close beside me, and called for a glass of whisky for himself and all the men in the room began to shout and laugh at him and his kid. Only they didn't shout and laugh when he was looking, so he could tell which ones did it, but did all their shouting and laughing when his head was turned the other way. They kept calling him "cracked." "The crack is getting wider in the old tin pan," someone sang and then they all laughed.

I'm puzzled you see, just how to make you feel as I felt that night. I suppose, having undertaken to write this story, that's what I'm up against, trying to do that. I'm not claiming to be able to inform you or to do you any good. I'm just trying to make you understand some things about me, as I would like to understand some things about you, or anyone, if I had the chance. Anyway the whole blamed thing, the thing that went on I mean in that little saloon on that rainy Saturday night, wasn't like anything quite real. I've already told you how I had looked into the glass back of the bar and had seen there, not my own face but the face of a scared young girl. Well, the men, the miners, sitting at the tables in the half dark room, the red-faced bartender, the unholy looking big man who had come in and his queer-looking kid, now sitting on the bar—all of them were like characters in some play, not like real people at all.

There was myself, that wasn't myself—and I'm not any fairy. Anyone who has ever known me knows better than that.

And then there was the man who had come in. There was a feeling came out of him that wasn't like the feeling you get from a man at all. It was more like the feeling you get maybe from a horse, only his eyes weren't like a horse's eyes. Horses' eyes have a kind of calm something in them and his hadn't. If you've ever carried a lantern through a wood at night, going along a path, and then suddenly you felt something funny in the air and stopped, and there ahead of you somewhere were the eyes of some little animal, gleaming out at you from a dead wall of darkness—The eyes shine big and quiet but there is a point right in the centre of each, where there is something dancing and wavering. You aren't afraid the little animal will jump at you, you are afraid the little eyes will jump at you—that's what's the matter with you.

Only of course a horse, when you go into his stall at night, or a little animal you had disturbed in a wood that way, wouldn't be talking and the big man who had come in there with his kid was talking. He kept talking all the time, saying something under his breath, as they say, and I could only un-derstand now and then a few words. It was his talking made him kind of terrible. His eyes said one thing and his lips an-other. They didn't seem to get together, as though they be-longed to the same person.

For one thing the man was too big. There was about him an unnatural bigness. It was in his hands, his arms, his shoulders, his body, his head, a bigness like you might see in trees and bushes in a tropical country perhaps. I've never been in a tropi-cal country but I've seen pictures. Only his eyes were small. In his big head they looked like the eyes of a bird. And I remem-ber that his lips were thick, like negroes' lips.

He paid no attention to me or to the others in the room but kept on muttering to himself, or to the kid sitting on the bar —I couldn't tell to which.

First he had one drink and then, quick, another. I stood staring at him and thinking—a jumble of thoughts, I suppose.

What I must have been thinking was something like this. "Well he's one of the kind you are always seeing about towns," I thought. I meant he was one of the cracked kind. In almost any small town you go to you will find one, and sometimes two or three cracked people, walking around. They go through the street, muttering to themselves and people generally are cruel to them. Their own folks make a bluff at being kind, but they aren't really, and the others in the town, men and boys, like to tease them. They send such a fellow, the mild silly kind, on some fool errand after a round square or a dozen post-holes or tie cards on his back saying "Kick me," or something like that, and then carry on and laugh as though they had done something funny.

And so there was this cracked one in that saloon and I could see the men in there wanted to have some fun putting up some kind of horseplay on him, but they didn't quite dare. He wasn't one of the mild kind, that was a cinch. I kept looking at the man and at his kid, and then up at that strange unreal reflection of myself in the cracked looking-glass back of the bar. "Rats, rats, digging in the ground—miners are rats, little jack-rabbit," I heard him say to his solemn-faced kid. I guess, after all, maybe he wasn't so cracked.

The kid sitting on the bar kept blinking at his father, like an owl caught out in the daylight, and now the father was having another glass of whisky. He drank six glasses, one right after the other, and it was cheap ten-cent stuff. He must have had cast-iron insides all right.

Of the men in the room there were two or three (maybe they were really more scared than the others so had to put up a bluff of bravery by showing off) who kept laughing and making funny cracks about the big man and his kid and there was one fellow was the worst of the bunch. I'll never forget that fellow because of his looks and what happened to him afterwards.

He was one of the showing-off kind all right, and he was the one that had started the song about the crack getting bigger in the old tin pan. He sang it two or three times, and then he grew bolder and got up and began walking up and down the room singing it over and over. He was a showy kind of man with a fancy vest, on which there were brown tobacco spots, and he wore glasses. Every time he made some crack he thought was funny, he winked at the others as though to say, "You see me. I'm not afraid of this big fellow," and then the others laughed.

The proprietor of the place must have known what was going on, and the danger in it, because he kept leaning over the bar and saying, "Shush, now quit it," to the showy-off man, but it didn't do any good. The fellow kept prancing like a turkey-cock and he put his hat on one side of his head and stopped right back of the big man and sang that song about the crack in the old tin pan. He was one of the kind you can't shush until they get their blocks knocked off, and it didn't take him long to come to it that time anyhow.

Because the big fellow just kept on muttering to his kid and drinking his whisky, as though he hadn't heard anything, and then suddenly he turned and his big hand flashed out and he grabbed, not the fellow who had been showing off, but me. With just a sweep of his arm he brought me up against his big body. Then he shoved me over with my breast jammed against the bar and looking right into his kid's face and he said, "Now you watch him, and if you let him fall I'll kill you," in just quiet ordinary tones as though he was saying "good morning" to some neighbor.

Then the kid leaned over and threw his arms around my head, and in spite of that I did manage to screw my head around enough to see what happened.

It was a sight I'll never forget. The big fellow had whirled around, and he had the showy-off man by the shoulder now, and the fellow's face was a sight. The big man must have had some reputation as a bad man in the town, even though he was cracked for the man with the fancy vest had his mouth open now, and his hat had fallen off his head, and he was silent and scared. Once, when I was a tramp, I saw a kid killed by a train. The kid was walking on the rail and showing off before some other kids, by letting them see how close he could let an engine come to him before he got out of the way. And the engine was whistling and a woman, over on the porch of a house nearby, was jumping up and down and screaming, and the kid let the engine get nearer and nearer, wanting more and more to show off, and then he stumbled and fell. God, I'll never forget the look on his face, in just the second before he got hit and killed, and now, there in that saloon, was the same terrible look on another face.

I closed my eyes for a moment and was sick all through me and then, when I opened my eyes, the big man's fist was just coming down in the other man's face. The one blow knocked him cold and he fell down like a beast hit with an axe.

And then the most terrible thing of all happened. The big man had on heavy boots, and he raised one of them and brought it down on the other man's shoulder, as he lay white and groaning on the floor. I could hear the bones crunch and it made me so sick I could hardly stand up, but I had to stand up and hold on to that kid or I knew it would be my turn next.

Because the big fellow didn't seem excited or anything, but kept on muttering to himself as he had been doing when he was standing peacefully by the bar drinking his whisky, and now he had raised his foot again, and maybe this time he would bring it down in the other man's face and, "just eliminate his map for keeps," as sports and prize-fighters sometimes say. I trembled, like I was having a chill, but thank God at that moment the kid, who had his arms around me and one hand clinging to my nose, so that there were the marks of his fingernails on it the next morning, at that moment the kid, thank God, began to howl, and his father didn't bother any more with the man on the floor but turned around, knocked me aside, and taking the kid in his arms tramped out of that place, muttering to himself as he had been doing ever since he came in.

I went out too but I didn't prance out with any dignity, I'll tell you that. I slunk out like a thief or a coward, which perhaps I am, partly anyhow.

And so there I was, outside there in the darkness, and it was as cold and wet and black and Godforsaken a night as any man ever saw. I was so sick at the thought of human beings that night I could have vomited to think of them at all. For a while I just stumbled along in the mud of the road, going up the hill, back to the fair ground, and then, almost before I knew where I was, I found myself in the stall with Pick-it-boy.

That was one of the best and sweetest feelings I've ever had in my whole life, being in that warm stall alone with that horse

that night. I had told the other swipes that I would go up and
down the row of stalls now and then and have an eye on the
other horses, but I had altogether forgotten my promise now.
I went and stood with my back against the side of the stall,
thinking how mean and low and all balled-up and twisted-up
human beings can become, and how the best of them are likely
to get that way any time, just because they are human beings
and not simple and clear in their minds, and inside themselves,
as animals are, maybe.

Perhaps you know how a person feels at such a moment.
There are things you think of, odd little things you had thought
you had forgotten. Once, when you were a kid, you were with
your father, and he was all dressed up, as for a funeral or
Fourth of July, and was walking along a street holding your
hand. And you were going past a railroad station, and there
was a woman standing. She was a stranger in your town and
was dressed as you had never seen a woman dressed before,
and never thought you would see one, looking so nice. Long
afterwards you knew that was because she had lovely taste in
clothes, such as so few women have really, but then you
thought she must be a queen. You had read about queens in
fairy stories and the thoughts of them thrilled you. What lovely
eyes the strange lady had and what beautiful rings she wore on
her fingers.

Then your father came out, from being in the railroad station, maybe to set his watch by the station clock, and took you
by the hand and he and the woman smiled at each other, in an
embarrassed kind of way, and you kept looking longingly back
at her, and when you were out of her hearing you asked your
father if she really were a queen. And it may be that your father
was one who wasn't so very hot on democracy and a free country and talked-up bunk about a free citizenry, and he said he
hoped she was a queen, and maybe, for all he knew, she was.

Or maybe, when you get jammed up as I was that night, and
can't get things clear about yourself or other people and why
you are alive, or for that matter why anyone you can think
about is alive, you think, not of people at all but of other things
you have seen and felt—like walking along a road in the snow
in the winter, perhaps out in Iowa, and hearing soft warm
sounds in a barn close to the road, or of another time when

you were on a hill and the sun was going down and the sky suddenly became a great soft-colored bowl, all glowing like a jewel-handled bowl, a great queen in some far away mighty kingdom might have put on a vast table out under the tree, once a year, when she invited all her loyal and loving subjects to come and dine with her.

I can't, of course, figure out what you try to think about when you are as desolate as I was that night. Maybe you are like me and inclined to think of women, and maybe you are like a man I met once, on the road, who told me that when he was up against it he never thought of anything but grub and a big nice clean warm bed to sleep in. "I don't care about anything else and I don't ever let myself think of anything else," he said. "If I was like you and went to thinking about women some-time I'd find myself hooked up to some skirt, and she'd have the old double cross on me, and the rest of my life maybe I'd be working in some factory for her and her kids."

As I say, there I was anyway, up there alone with that horse in that warm stall in that dark lonesome fair ground and I had that feeling about being sick at the thought of human beings and what they could be like.

Well, suddenly I got again the queer feeling I'd had about him once or twice before, I mean the feeling about our under-standing each other in some way I can't explain.

So having it again I went over to where he stood and began running my hands all over his body, just because I loved the feel of him and as sometimes, to tell the plain truth, I've felt about touching with my hands the body of a woman I've seen and who I thought was lovely too. I ran my hands over his head and neck and then down over his hard firm round body and then over his flanks and down his legs. His flanks quivered a little I remember and once he turned his head and stuck his cold nose down along my neck and nipped my shoulder a little, in a soft playful way. It hurt a little but I didn't care.

So then I crawled up through a hole into the loft above thinking that night was over anyway and glad of it, but it wasn't, not by a long sight.

As my clothes were all soaking wet and as we race track swipes didn't own any such things as night-gowns or pajamas I had to go to bed naked, of course.

But we had plenty of horse blankets and so I tucked myself in between a pile of them and tried not to think any more that night. The being with Pick-it-boy and having him close right under me that way made me feel a little better.

Then I was sound asleep and dreaming and—bang like being hit with a club by someone who has sneaked up behind you—I got another wallop.

What I suppose is that, being upset the way I was, I had forgotten to bolt the door to Pick-it-boy's stall down below and two negro men had come in there, thinking they were in their own place, and had climbed up through the hole where I was. They were half lit up but not what you might call dead drunk, and I suppose they were up against something a couple of white swipes, who had some money in their pockets, wouldn't have been up against.

What I mean is that a couple of white swipes, having li-quored themselves up and being down there in the town on a bat, if they wanted a woman or a couple of women would have been able to find them. There is always a few women of that kind can be found around any town I've ever seen or heard of, and of course a bar tender would have given them the tip where to go.

But a negro, up there in that country, where there aren't any, or anyway mighty few negro women, wouldn't know what to do when he felt that way and would be up against it.

It's so always. Burt and several other negroes I've known pretty well have talked to me about it, lots of times. You take now a young negro man—not a race track swipe or a tramp or any other low-down kind of a fellow—but, let us say, one who has been to college, and has behaved himself and tried to be a good man, the best he could, and be clean, as they say. He isn't any better off, is he? If he has made himself some money and wants to go sit in a swell restaurant, or go to hear some good music, or see a good play at the theatre, he gets what we used to call on the tracks, "the messy end of the dung fork," doesn't he?

And even in such a low-down place as what people call a "bad house" it's the same way. The white swipes and others can go into a place where they have negro women fast enough, and they do it too, but you let a negro swipe try it the other way around and see how he comes out.

You see, I can think this whole thing out fairly now, sitting here in my own house and writing, and with my wife Jessie in the kitchen making a pie or something, and I can show just how the two negro men who came into that loft, where I was asleep, were justified in what they did, and I can preach about how the negroes are up against it in this country, like a daisy, but I tell you what, I didn't think things out that way that night.

For, you understand, what they thought, they being half liquored-up, and when one of them had jerked the blankets off me, was that I was a woman. One of them carried a lantern but it was smoky and dirty and didn't give out much light. So they must have figured it out—my body being pretty white and slender then, like a young girl's body I suppose—that some white swipe had brought me up there. The kind of girls around a town that will come with a swipe to a race track on a rainy night aren't very fancy females but you'll find that kind in the towns all right. I've seen many a one in my day.

And so, I figure, these two big buck niggers, being piped that way, just made up their minds they would snatch me away from the white swipe who had brought me out there, and who had left me lying carelessly around.

"Jes' you lie still honey. We ain't gwine hurt you none," one of them said, with a little chuckling laugh that had something in it besides a laugh, too. It was the kind of laugh that gives you the shivers.

The devil of it was I couldn't say anything, not even a word. Why I couldn't yell out and say "What the hell," and just kid them a little and shoo them out of there I don't know, but I couldn't. I tried and tried so that my throat hurt but I didn't say a word. I just lay there staring at them.

It was a mixed-up night. I've never gone through another night like it.

Was I scared? Lord Almighty, I'll tell you what, I was scared.

Because the two big black faces were leaning right over me now, and I could feel their liquored-up breaths on my cheeks, and their eyes were shining in the dim light from that smoky lantern, and right in the centre of their eyes was that dancing flickering light I've told you about your seeing in the eyes of wild animals, when you were carrying a lantern through the woods at night.

It was a puzzler! All my life, you see—me never having had any sisters, and at that time never having had a sweetheart either—I had been dreaming and thinking about women, and I suppose I'd always been dreaming about a pure innocent one, for myself, made for me by God, maybe. Men are that way. No matter how big they talk about "let the women go hang," they've always got that notion tucked away inside themselves, somewhere. It's a kind of chesty man's notion, I suppose, but they've got it and the kind of up-and-coming women we have nowdays who are always saying, "I'm as good as a man and will do what the men do," are on the wrong trail if they really ever want to, what you might say "hog-tie" a fellow of their own.

So I had invented a kind of princess, with black hair and a slender willowy body to dream about. And I thought of her as being shy and afraid to ever tell anything she really felt to anyone but just me. I suppose I fancied that if I ever found such a woman in the flesh I would be the strong sure one and she the timid shrinking one.

And now I was that woman, or something like her, myself.

I gave a kind of wriggle, like a fish, you have just taken off the hook. What I did next wasn't a thought-out thing. I was caught and I squirmed, that's all.

The two niggers both jumped at me but somehow—the lantern having been kicked over and having gone out the first move they made—well in some way, when they both lunged at me they missed.

As good luck would have it my feet found the hole, where you put hay down to the horse in the stall below, and through which we crawled up when it was time to go to bed in our blankets up in the hay, and down I slid, not bothering to try to find the ladder with my feet but just letting myself go.

In less than a second I was out of doors in the dark and the rain and the two blacks were down the hole and out the door of the stall after me.

How long or how far they really followed me I suppose I'll never know. It was black dark and raining hard now and a roaring wind had begun to blow. Of course, my body being white, it must have made some kind of a faint streak in the darkness as

I ran, and anyway I thought they could see me and I knew I couldn't see them and that made my terror ten times worse. Every minute I thought they would grab me.

You know how it is when a person is all upset and full of terror as I was. I suppose maybe the two niggers followed me for a while, running across the muddy race track and into the grove of trees that grew in the oval inside the track, but likely enough, after just a few minutes, they gave up the chase and went back, found their own place and went to sleep. They were liquored-up, as I've said, and maybe partly funning too.

But I didn't know that, if they were. As I ran I kept hearing sounds, sounds made by the rain coming down through the dead old leaves left on the trees and by the wind blowing, and it may be that the sound that scared me most of all was my own bare feet stepping on a dead branch and breaking it or something like that.

There was something strange and scary, a steady sound, like a heavy man running and breathing hard, right at my shoulder. It may have been my own breath, coming quick and fast. And I thought I heard that chuckling laugh I'd heard up in the loft, the laugh that sent the shivers right down through me. Of course every tree I came close to looked like a man standing there, ready to grab me, and I kept dodging and going—bang —into other trees. My shoulders kept knocking against trees in that way and the skin was all knocked off, and every time it happened I thought a big black hand had come down and clutched at me and was tearing my flesh.

How long it went on I don't know, maybe an hour, maybe five minutes. But anyway the darkness didn't let up, and the terror didn't let up, and I couldn't, to save my life, scream or make any sound.

Just why I couldn't I don't know. Could it be because at the time I was a woman, while at the same time I wasn't a woman? It may be that I was too ashamed of having turned into a girl and being afraid of a man to make any sound. I don't know about that. It's over my head.

But anyway I couldn't make a sound. I tried and tried and my throat hurt from trying and no sound came.

And then, after a long time, or what seemed like a long time,

I got out from among the trees inside the track and was on the track itself again. I thought the two black men were still after me, you understand, and I ran like a madman.

Of course, running along the track that way, it must have been up the back stretch, I came after a time to where the old slaughter-house stood, in that field, beside the track. I knew it by its ungodly smell, scared as I was. Then, in some way, I managed to get over the high old fairground fence and was in the field, where the slaughter-house was.

All the time I was trying to yell or scream, or be sensible and tell those two black men that I was a man and not a woman, but I couldn't make it. And then I heard a sound like a board cracking or breaking in the fence and thought they were still after me.

So I kept on running like a crazy man, in the field, and just then I stumbled and fell over something. I've told you how the old slaughter-house field was filled with bones, that had been lying there a long time and had all been washed white. There were heads of sheep and cows and all kinds of things.

And when I fell and pitched forward I fell right into the midst of something, still and cold and white.

It was probably the skeleton of a horse lying there. In small towns like that, they take an old worn-out horse, that has died, and haul him off to some field outside of town and skin him for the hide, that they can sell for a dollar or two. It doesn't make any difference what the horse has been, that's the way he usually ends up. Maybe even Pick-it-boy, or O My Man, or a lot of other good fast ones I've seen and known have ended that way by this time.

And so I think it was the bones of a horse lying there and he must have been lying on his back. The birds and wild animals had picked all his flesh away and the rain had washed his bones clean.

Anyway I fell and pitched forward and my side got cut pretty deep and my hands clutched at something. I had fallen right in between the ribs of the horse and they seemed to wrap themselves around me close. And my hands, clutching upwards, had got hold of the cheeks of that dead horse and the bones of his cheeks were cold as ice with the rain washing over them. White bones wrapped around me and white bones in my hands.

There was a new terror now that seemed to go down to the very bottom of me, to the bottom of the inside of me, I mean. It shook me like I have seen a rat in a barn shaken by a dog. It was a terror like a big wave that hits you when you are walking on a seashore, maybe. You see it coming and you try to run and get away but when you start to run inshore there is a stone cliff you can't climb. So the wave comes high as a mountain, and there it is, right in front of you and nothing in all this world can stop it. And now it had knocked you down and rolled and tumbled you over and over and washed you clean, clean, but dead maybe.

And that's the way I felt—I seemed to myself dead with blind terror. It was a feeling like the finger of God running down your back and burning you clean, I mean.

It burned all that silly nonsense about being a girl right out of me.

I screamed at last and the spell that was on me was broken. I'll bet the scream I let out of me could have been heard a mile and a half.

Right away I felt better and crawled out from among the pile of bones, and then I stood on my own feet again and I wasn't a woman, or a young girl any more but a man and my own self, and as far as I know I've been that way ever since. Even the black night seemed warm and alive now, like a mother might be to a kid in the dark.

Only I couldn't go back to the race track because I was blubbering and crying and was ashamed of myself and of what a fool I had made of myself. Someone might see me and I couldn't stand that, not at that moment.

So I went across the field, walking now, not running like a crazy man, and pretty soon I came to a fence and crawled over and got into another field, in which there was a straw stack, I just happened to find in the pitch darkness.

The straw stack had been there a long time and some sheep had nibbled away at it until they had made a pretty deep hole, like a cave, in the side of it. I found the hole and crawled in and there were some sheep in there, about a dozen of them.

When I came in, creeping on my hands and knees, they didn't make much fuss, just stirred around a little and then settled down.

So I settled down amongst them too. They were warm and gentle and kind, like Pick-it-boy, and being in there with them made me feel better than I would have felt being with any human person I knew at that time.

So I settled down and slept after a while, and when I woke up it was daylight and not very cold and the rain was over. The clouds were breaking away from the sky now and maybe there would be a fair the next week but if there was I knew I wouldn't be there to see it.

Because what I expected to happen did happen. I had to go back across the fields and the fairground to the place where my clothes were, right in the broad daylight, and me stark naked, and of course I knew someone would be up and would raise a shout, and every swipe and every driver would stick his head out and would whoop with laughter.

And there would be a thousand questions asked, and I would be too mad and too ashamed to answer, and would perhaps begin to blubber, and that would make me more ashamed than ever.

It all turned out just as I expected, except that when the noise and the shouts of laughter were going it the loudest, Burt came out of the stall where O My Man was kept, and when he saw me he didn't know what was the matter but he knew something was up that wasn't on the square and for which I wasn't to blame.

So he got so all-fired mad he couldn't speak for a minute, and then he grabbed a pitchfork and began prancing up and down before the other stalls, giving that gang of swipes and drivers such a royal old dressing-down as you never heard. You should have heard him sling language. It was grand to hear.

And while he was doing it I sneaked up into the loft, blubbering because I was so pleased and happy to hear him swear that way, and I got my wet clothes on quick and got down, and gave Pick-it-boy a goodbye kiss on the cheek and lit out.

The last I saw of all that part of my life was Burt, still going it, and yelling out for the man who had put up a trick on me to come out and get what was coming to him. He had the pitchfork in his hand and was swinging it around, and every now and then he would make a kind of lunge at a tree or something, he was so mad through, and there was no one else in sight at all. And Burt didn't even see me cutting out along the fence through a gate and down the hill and out of the race-horse and the tramp life for the rest of my days.

Milk Bottles

I LIVED, during that summer, in a large room on the top floor of an old house on the North Side in Chicago. It was August and the night was hot. Until after midnight I sat—the sweat trickling down my back—under a lamp, laboring to feel my way into the lives of the fanciful people who were trying also to live in the tale on which I was at work.

It was a hopeless affair.

I became involved in the efforts of the shadowy people and they in turn became involved in the fact of the hot uncomfortable room, in the fact that, although it was what the farmers of the Middle West call "good corn-growing weather" it was plain hell to be alive in Chicago. Hand in hand the shadowy people of my fanciful world and myself groped our way through a forest in which the leaves had all been burned off the trees. The hot ground burned the shoes off our feet. We were striving to make our way through the forest and into some cool beautiful city. The fact is, as you will clearly understand, I was a little off my head.

When I gave up the struggle and got to my feet the chairs in the room danced about. They also were running aimlessly through a burning land and striving to reach some mythical city. "I'd better get out of here and go for a walk or go jump into the lake and cool myself off," I thought.

I went down out of my room and into the street. On a lower floor of the house lived two burlesque actresses who had just come in from their evening's work and who now sat in their room talking. As I reached the street something heavy whirled past my head and broke on the stone pavement. A white liquid spurted over my clothes and the voice of one of the actresses could be heard coming from the one lighted room of the house. "Oh, hell! We live such damned lives, we do, and we work in such a town! A dog is better off! And now they are going to take booze away from us too! I come home from working in that hot theatre on a hot night like this and what do I see—a half-filled bottle of spoiled milk standing on a window sill!

"I won't stand it! I got to smash everything!" she cried.

I walked eastward from my house. From the northwestern end of the city great hordes of men women and children had come to spend the night out of doors, by the shore of the lake. It was stifling hot there too and the air was heavy with a sense of struggle. On a few hundred acres of flat land, that had formerly been a swamp, some two million people were fighting for the peace and quiet of sleep and not getting it. Out of the half darkness, beyond the little strip of park land at the water's edge, the huge empty houses of Chicago's fashionable folk made a greyish-blue blot against the sky. "Thank the gods," I thought, "there are some people who can get out of here, who can go to the mountains or the seashore or to Europe." I stumbled in the half darkness over the legs of a woman who was lying and trying to sleep on the grass. A baby lay beside her and when she sat up it began to cry. I muttered an apology and stepped aside and as I did so my foot struck a half-filled milk bottle and I knocked it over, the milk running out on the grass. "Oh, I'm sorry. Please forgive me," I cried. "Never mind," the woman answered, "the milk is sour."

He is a tall stoop-shouldered man with prematurely greyed hair and works as a copy writer in an advertising agency in Chicago—an agency where I also have sometimes been employed—and on that night in August I met him, walking with quick eager strides along the shore of the lake and past the tired petulant people. He did not see me at first and I wondered at the evidence of life in him when everyone else seemed half dead; but a street lamp hanging over a nearby roadway threw its light down upon my face and he pounced. "Here you, come up to my place," he cried sharply. "I've got something to show you. I was on my way down to see you. That's where I was going," he lied as he hurried me along.

We went to his apartment on a street leading back from the lake and the park. German, Polish, Italian and Jewish families, equipped with soiled blankets and the ever-present half-filled bottles of milk, had come prepared to spend the night out of doors; but the American families in the crowd were giving up the struggle to find a cool spot and a little stream of them trickled along the sidewalks, going back to hot beds in the hot houses.

It was past one o'clock and my friend's apartment was disorderly as well as hot. He explained that his wife, with their two children, had gone home to visit her mother on a farm near Springfield, Illinois.

We took off our coats and sat down. My friend's thin cheeks were flushed and his eyes shone. "You know—well—you see," he began and then hesitated and laughed like an embarrassed schoolboy. "Well now," he began again, "I've long been wanting to write something real, something besides advertisements. I suppose I'm silly but that's the way I am. It's been my dream to write something stirring and big. I suppose it's the dream of a lot of advertising writers, eh? Now look here—don't you go laughing. I think I've done it."

He explained that he had written something concerning Chicago, the capital and heart, as he said, of the whole Central West. He grew angry. "People come here from the East or from farms, or from little holes of towns like I came from and they think it smart to run Chicago into the ground," he declared. "I thought I'd show 'em up," he added, jumping up and walking nervously about the room.

He handed me many sheets of paper covered with hastily scrawled words, but I protested and asked him to read it aloud. He did, standing with his face turned away from me. There was a quiver in his voice. The thing he had written concerned some mythical town I had never seen. He called it Chicago, but in the same breath spoke of great streets flaming with color, ghostlike buildings flung up into night skies and a river, running down a path of gold into the boundless West. It was the city, I told myself, I and the people of my story had been trying to find earlier on that same evening, when because of the heat I went a little off my head and could not work any more. The people of the city, he had written about, were a cool-headed, brave people, marching forward to some spiritual triumph, the promise of which was inherent in the physical aspects of the town.

Now I am one who, by the careful cultivation of certain traits in my character, have succeeded in building up the more brutal side of my nature, but I cannot knock women and children down in order to get aboard Chicago street-cars, nor can I tell an author to his face that I think his work is rotten.

"You're all right, Ed. You're great. You've knocked out a

regular soc-dolager of a masterpiece here. Why you sound as good as Henry Mencken writing about Chicago as the literary centre of America, and you've lived in Chicago and he never did. The only thing I can see you've missed is a little something about the stockyards, and you can put that in later," I added and prepared to depart.

"What's this?" I asked, picking up a half-dozen sheets of paper that lay on the floor by my chair. I read it eagerly. And when I had finished reading it he stammered and apologized and then, stepping across the room, jerked the sheets out of my hand and threw them out at an open window. "I wish you hadn't seen that. It's something else I wrote about Chicago," he explained. He was flustered.

"You see the night was so hot, and, down at the office, I had to write a condensed-milk advertisement, just as I was sneaking away to come home and work on this other thing, and the street-car was so crowded and the people stank so, and when I finally got home here—the wife being gone—the place was a mess. Well, I couldn't write and I was sore. It's been my chance, you see, the wife and kids being gone and the house being quiet. I went for a walk. I think I went a little off my head. Then I came home and wrote that stuff I've just thrown out of the window."

He grew cheerful again. "Oh, well—it's all right. Writing that fool thing stirred me up and enabled me to write this other stuff, this real stuff I showed you first, about Chicago."

And so I went home and to bed, having in this odd way stumbled upon another bit of the kind of writing that is—for better or worse—really presenting the lives of the people of these towns and cities—sometimes in prose, sometimes in stirring colorful song. It was the kind of thing Mr. Sandburg or Mr. Masters might have done after an evening's walk on a hot night in, say West Congress Street in Chicago.

The thing I had read of Ed's, centred about a half-filled bottle of spoiled milk standing dim in the moonlight on a window sill. There had been a moon earlier on that August evening, a new moon, a thin crescent golden streak in the sky. What had happened to my friend, the advertising writer, was something like this—I figured it all out as I lay sleepless in bed after our talk.

I am sure I do not know whether or not it is true that all advertising writers and newspaper men, want to do other kinds of writing, but Ed did all right. The August day that had preceded the hot night had been a hard one for him to get through. All day he had been wanting to be at home in his quiet apartment producing literature, rather than sitting in an office and writing advertisements. In the late afternoon, when he had thought his desk cleared for the day, the boss of the copy writers came and ordered him to write a page advertisement for the magazines on the subject of condensed milk. "We got a chance to get a new account if we can knock out some crackerjack stuff in a hurry," he said. "I'm sorry to have to put it up to you on such a rotten hot day, Ed, but we're up against it. Let's see if you've got some of the old pep in you. Get down to hardpan now and knock out something snappy and unusual before you go home."

Ed had tried. He put away the thoughts he had been having about the city beautiful—the glowing city of the plains—and got right down to business. He thought about milk, milk for little children, the Chicagoans of the future, milk that would produce a little cream to put in the coffee of advertising writers in the morning, sweet fresh milk to keep all his brother and sister Chicagoans robust and strong. What Ed really wanted was a long cool drink of something with a kick in it, but he tried to make himself think he wanted a drink of milk. He gave himself over to thoughts of milk, milk condensed and yellow, milk warm from the cows his father owned when he was a boy —his mind launched a little boat and he set out on a sea of milk.

Out of it all he got what is called an original advertisement. The sea of milk on which he sailed became a mountain of cans of condensed milk, and out of that fancy he got his idea. He made a crude sketch for a picture showing wide rolling green fields with white farm houses. Cows grazed on the green hills and at one side of the picture a barefooted boy was driving a herd of Jersey cows out of the sweet fair land and down a lane into a kind of funnel at the small end of which was a tin of the condensed milk. Over the picture he put a heading: "The health and freshness of a whole countryside is condensed into one can of Whitney-Wells Condensed Milk." The head copy writer said it was a humdinger.

And then Ed went home. He wanted to begin writing about the city beautiful at once and so didn't go out to dinner, but fished about in the ice chest and found some cold meat out of which he made himself a sandwich. Also, he poured himself a glass of milk, but it was sour. "Oh, damn!" he said and poured it into the kitchen sink.

As Ed explained to me later, he sat down and tried to begin writing his real stuff at once, but he couldn't seem to get into it. The last hour in the office, the trip home in the hot smelly car, and the taste of the sour milk in his mouth had jangled his nerves. The truth is that Ed has a rather sensitive, finely balanced nature, and it had got mussed up.

He took a walk and tried to think, but his mind wouldn't stay where he wanted it to. Ed is now a man of nearly forty and on that night his mind ran back to his young manhood in the city,—and stayed there. Like other boys who had become grown men in Chicago, he had come to the city from a farm at the edge of a prairie town, and like all such town and farm boys, he had come filled with vague dreams.

What things he had hungered to do and be in Chicago! What he had done you can fancy. For one thing he had got himself married and now lived in the apartment on the North Side. To give a real picture of his life during the twelve or fifteen years that had slipped away since he was a young man would involve writing a novel, and that is not my purpose.

Anyway, there he was in his room—come home from his walk—and it was hot and quiet and he could not manage to get into his masterpiece. How still it was in the apartment with the wife and children away! His mind stayed on the subject of his youth in the city.

He remembered a night of his young manhood when he had gone out to walk, just as he did on that August evening. Then his life wasn't complicated by the fact of the wife and children and he lived alone in his room; but something had got on his nerves then, too. On that evening long ago he grew restless in his room and went out to walk. It was summer and first he went down by the river where ships were being loaded and then to a crowded park where girls and young fellows walked about.

He grew bold and spoke to a woman who sat alone on a park bench. She let him sit beside her and, because it was dark and she was silent, he began to talk. The night had made him sentimental. "Human beings are such hard things to get at. I wish I could get close to someone," he said. "Oh, you go on! What you doing? You ain't trying to kid someone?" asked the woman.

Ed jumped up and walked away. He went into a long street lined with dark silent buildings and then stopped and looked about. What he wanted was to believe that in the apartment buildings were people who lived intense eager lives, who had great dreams, who were capable of great adventures. "They are really only separated from me by the brick walls," was what he told himself on that night.

It was then that the milk bottle theme first got hold of him. He went into an alleyway to look at the backs of the apartment buildings and, on that evening also, there was a moon. Its light fell upon a long row of half-filled bottles standing on window sills.

Something within him went a little sick and he hurried out of the alleyway and into the street. A man and woman walked past him and stopped before the entrance to one of the buildings. Hoping they might be lovers, he concealed himself in the entrance to another building to listen to their conversation.

The couple turned out to be a man and wife and they were quarreling. Ed heard the woman's voice saying: "You come in here. You can't put that over on me. You say you just want to take a walk, but I know you. You want to go out and blow in some money. What I'd like to know is why you don't loosen up a little for me."

That is the story of what happened to Ed, when, as a young man, he went to walk in the city in the evening, and when he had become a man of forty and went out of his house wanting to dream and to think of a city beautiful, much the same sort of thing happened again. Perhaps the writing of the condensed milk advertisement and the taste of the sour milk he had got out of the ice box had something to do with his mood; but, anyway, milk bottles, like a refrain in a song, got into his brain. They seemed to sit and mock at him from the windows of all the buildings in all the streets, and when he turned to look at people, he met the crowds from the West and the Northwest Sides going to the park and the lake. At the head of each little group of people marched a woman who carried a milk bottle in her hand.

And so, on that August night, Ed went home angry and disturbed, and in anger wrote of his city. Like the burlesque actress in my own house he wanted to smash something, and, as milk bottles were in his mind, he wanted to smash milk bottles. "I could grasp the neck of a milk bottle. It fits the hand so neatly. I could kill a man or woman with such a thing," he thought desperately.

He wrote, you see, the five or six sheets I had read in that mood and then felt better. And after that he wrote about the ghostlike buildings flung into the sky by the hands of a brave adventurous people and about the river that runs down a path of gold, and into the boundless West.

As you have already concluded, the city he described in his masterpiece was lifeless, but the city he, in a queer way, expressed in what he wrote about the milk bottle could not be forgotten. It frightened you a little but there it was and in spite of his anger or perhaps because of it, a lovely singing quality had got into the thing. In those few scrawled pages the miracle had been worked. I was a fool not to have put the sheets into my pocket. When I went down out of his apartment that evening I did look for them in a dark alleyway, but they had become lost in a sea of rubbish that had leaked over the tops of a long row of tin ash cans that stood at the foot of a stairway leading from the back doors of the apartments above.

The Sad Horn Blowers

IT had been a disastrous year in Will's family. The Appletons lived on one of the outlying streets of Bidwell and Will's father was a house painter. In early February, when there was deep snow on the ground, and a cold bitter wind blew about the houses, Will's mother suddenly died. He was seventeen years old then, and rather a big fellow for his age.

The mother's death happened abruptly, without warning, as a sleepy man kills a fly with the hand in a warm room on a summer day. On one February day there she was coming in at the kitchen door of the Appleton's house, from hanging the wash out on the line in the back yard, and warming her long hands, covered with blue veins, by holding them over the kitchen stove—and then looking about at the children with that half-hidden, shy smile of hers—there she was like that, as the three children had always known her, and then, but a week later, she was cold in death and lying in her coffin in the place vaguely spoken of in the family as "the other room."

After that, and when summer came and the family was trying hard to adjust itself to the new conditions, there came another disaster. Up to the very moment when it happened it looked as though Tom Appleton, the house painter, was in for a prosperous season. The two boys, Fred and Will, were to be his assistants that year.

To be sure Fred was only fifteen, but he was one to lend a quick alert hand at almost any undertaking. For example, when there was a job of paper hanging to be done, he was the fellow to spread on the paste, helped by an occasional sharp word from his father.

Down off his step ladder Tom Appleton hopped and ran to the long board where the paper was spread out. He liked this business of having two assistants about. Well, you see, one had the feeling of being at the head of something, of managing affairs. He grabbed the paste brush out of Fred's hand. "Don't spare the paste," he shouted. "Slap her on like this. Spread her out—so. Do be sure to catch all the edges."

It was all very warm, and comfortable, and nice, working at

paper-hanging jobs in the houses on the March and April days. When it was cold or rainy outside, stoves were set up in the new houses being built, and in houses already inhabited the folks moved out of the rooms to be papered, spread newspapers on the floors over the carpets and put sheets over the furniture left in the rooms. Outside it rained or snowed, but inside it was warm and cosy.

To the Appletons it seemed, at the time, as though the death of the mother had drawn them closer together. Both Will and Fred felt it, perhaps Will the more consciously. The family was rather in the hole financially—the mother's funeral had cost a good deal of money, and Fred was being allowed to stay out of school. That pleased him. When they worked in a house where there were other children, they came home from school in the late afternoon and looked in through the door to where Fred was spreading paste over the sheets of wall paper. He made a slapping sound with the brush, but did not look at them. "Ah, go on, you kids," he thought. This was a man's business he was up to. Will and his father were on the step ladders, putting the sheets carefully into place on the ceilings and walls. "Does she match down there?" the father asked sharply. "Oh-kay, go ahead," Will replied. When the sheet was in place Fred ran and rolled out the laps with a little wooden roller. How jealous the kids of the house were. It would be a long time before any of them could stay out of school and do a man's work, as Fred was doing.

And then in the evening, walking homeward, it was nice, too. Will and Fred had been provided with suits of white overalls that were now covered with dried paste and spots of paint and looked really professional. They kept them on and drew their overcoats on over them. Their hands were stiff with paste, too. On Main Street the lights were lighted, and other men passing called to Tom Appleton. He was called Tony in the town. "Hello, Tony!" some storekeeper shouted. It was rather too bad, Will thought that his father hadn't more dignity. He was too boyish. Young boys growing up and merging into manhood do not fancy fathers being too boyish. Tom Appleton played a cornet in the Bidwell Silver Cornet Band and didn't do the job very well—rather made a mess of it, when there was a bit of solo work to be done—but was so well liked by the other members of the band that no one said anything. And then he talked so grandly about music, and about the lip of a cornet player, that everyone thought he must be all right. "He has an education. I tell you what, Tony Appleton knows a lot. He's a smart one," the other members of the band were always saying to each other.

"Well, the devil! A man should grow up after a time, perhaps. When a man's wife had died but such a short time before, it was just as well to walk through Main Street with more dignity—for the time being, anyway."

Tom Appleton had a way of winking at men he passed in the street, as though to say, "Well, now I've got my kids with me, and we won't say anything, but didn't you and I have the very hell of a time last Wednesday night, eh? Mum's the word, old pal. Keep everything quiet. There are gay times ahead for you and me. We'll cut loose, you bet, when you and me are out together next time."

Will grew a little angry about something he couldn't exactly understand. His father stopped in front of Jake Mann's meat market. "You kids go along home. Tell Kate I am bringing a steak. I'll be right on your heels," he said.

He would get the steak and then he would go into Alf Geiger's saloon and get a good, stiff drink of whisky. There would be no one now to bother about smelling it on his breath when he got home later. Not that his wife had ever said anything when he wanted a drink—but you know how a man feels when there's a woman in the house. "Why, hello, Bildad Smith—how's the old game leg? Come on, have a little nip with me. Were you on Main Street last band meeting night and did you hear us do that new gallop? It's a humdinger. Turkey White did that trombone solo simply grand."

Will and Fred had got beyond Main Street now, and Will took a small pipe with a curved stem out of his overcoat pocket and lighted it. "I'll bet I could hang a ceiling without father there at all, if only some one would give me a chance," he said. Now that his father was no longer present to embarrass him with his lack of dignity, he felt comfortable and happy. Also, it was something to be able to smoke a pipe without discomfiture. When mother was alive she was always kissing a fellow when he came home at night, and then one had to be mighty careful about smoking. Now it was different. One had become a man and one accepted manhood with its responsibilities. "Don't it make you sick at all?" Fred asked. "Huh, naw!" Will answered contemptuously.

The new disaster to the family came late in August, just when the fall work was all ahead, and the prospects good too. A. P. Wrigley, the jeweler, had just built a big, new house and barn on a farm he had bought the year before. It was a mile out of town on the Turner pike.

That would be a job to set the Appletons up for the winter. The house was to have three coats outside, with all the work inside, and the barn was to have two coats—and the two boys were to work with their father and were to have regular wages.

And just to think of the work to be done inside that house made Tom Appleton's mouth water. He talked of it all the time, and in the evenings liked to sit in a chair in the Appleton's front yard, get some neighbor over, and then go on about it. How he slung house-painter's lingo about! The doors and cupboards were to be grained in imitation of weathered oak, the front door was to be curly maple, and there was to be black walnut, too. Well, there wasn't another painter in the town could imitate all the various kinds of wood as Tom could. Just show him the wood, or tell him—you didn't have to show him anything. Name what you wanted—that was enough. To be sure a man had to have the right tools, but give him the tools and then just go off and leave everything to him. What the devil! When A. P. Wrigley gave him this new house to do, he showed he was a man who knew what he was doing.

As for the practical side of the matter, everyone in the family knew that the Wrigley job meant a safe winter. There wasn't any speculation, as when taking work on the contract plan. All work was to be paid for by the day, and the boys were to have their wages, too. It meant new suits for the boys, a new dress and maybe a hat for Kate, the house rent paid all winter, pota-toes in the cellar. It meant safety—that was the truth.

In the evenings, sometimes, Tom got out his tools and looked at them. Brushes and graining tools were spread out on the kitchen table, and Kate and the boys gathered about. It was Fred's job to see that all brushes were kept clean and, one by one, Tom ran his fingers over them, and then worked them back and forth over the palm of his hand. "This is a camel's hair," he said, picking a soft fine-haired brush up and handing it to Will. "I paid four dollars and eighty cents for that." Will also worked it back and forth over the palm of his hand, just as his father had done and then Kate picked it up and did the same thing. "It's as soft as the cat's back," she said. Will thought that rather silly. He looked forward to the day when he would have brushes ladders and pots of his own, and could show them off before people and through his mind went words he had picked up from his father's talk. One spoke of the "heel" and "toe" of a brush. The way to put on varnish was to "flow" it on. Will knew all the words of his trade now and didn't have to talk like one of the kind of muts who just does, now and then, a jack job of house painting.

On the fatal evening a surprise party was held for Mr. and Mrs. Bardshare, who lived just across the road from the Appletons on Piety Hill. That was a chance for Tom Appleton. In any such affair he liked to have a hand in the arrangements. "Come on now, we'll make her go with a bang. They'll be setting in the house after supper, and Bill Bardshare will be in his stocking feet, and Ma Bardshare washing the dishes. They won't be expecting nothing, and we'll slip up, all dressed in our Sunday clothes, and let out a whoop. I'll bring my cornet and let out a blast on that too. 'What in Sam Hill is that?' Say, I can just see Bill Bardshare jumping up and beginning to swear, thinking we're a gang of kids come to bother him, like Hallowe'en, or something like that. You just get the grub, and I'll make the coffee over to my house and bring it over hot. I'll get ahold of two big pots and make a whooping lot of it."

In the Appleton house all was in a flurry. Tom, Will and Fred were painting a barn, three miles out of town, but they knocked off work at four and Tom got the farmer's son to drive them to town. He himself had to wash up, take a bath in a tub in the woodshed, shave and everything—just like Sunday. He looked more like a boy than a man when he got all dogged up.

And then the family had to have supper, over and done with, a little after six, and Tom didn't dare go outside the house until dark. It wouldn't do to have the Bardshares see him so fixed up. It was their wedding anniversary, and they might suspect something. He kept trotting about the house, and occasionally looked out of the front window toward the Bardshare house. "You kid, you," Kate said, laughing. Sometimes she talked up to him like that, and after she said it he went upstairs, and getting out his cornet blew on it, so softly, you could hardly hear him downstairs. When he did that you couldn't tell how badly he played, as when the band was going it on Main Street and he had to carry a passage right through alone. He sat in the room upstairs thinking. When Kate laughed at him it was like having his wife back, alive. There was the same shy sarcastic gleam in her eyes.

Well, it was the first time he had been out anywhere since his wife had died, and there might be some people think it would be better if he stayed at home now—look better, that is. When he had shaved he had cut his chin, and the blood had come. After a time he went downstairs and stood before the looking glass, hung above the kitchen sink, and dabbed at the spot with the wet end of a towel.

Will and Fred stood about.

Will's mind was working—perhaps Kate's, too. "Was there—could it be?—well, at such a party—only older people invited —there were always two or three widow women thrown in for good measure, as it were."

Kate didn't want any woman fooling around her kitchen. She was twenty years old.

"And it was just as well not to have any monkeyshine talk about motherless children," such as Tom might indulge in. Even Fred thought that. There was a little wave of resentment against Tom in the house. It was a wave that didn't make much noise, just crept, as it were softly, up a low sandy beach.

"Widow women went to such places, and then of course, people were always going home in couples." Both Kate and Will had the same picture in mind. It was late at night and in fancy they were both peeking out at front upper windows of the Appleton house. There were all the people coming out at the front door of the Bardshare house, and Bill Bardshare was standing there and holding the door open. He had managed to sneak away during the evening, and got his Sunday clothes on all right.

And the couples were coming out. "There was that woman

now, that widow, Mrs. Childers." She had been married twice, both husbands dead now, and she lived away over Maumee Pike way. "What makes a woman of her age want to act silly like that? It is the very devil how a woman can keep looking young and handsome after she has buried two men. There are some who say that, even when her last husband was alive—"

"But whether that's true or not, what makes her want to act and talk silly that way?" Now her face is turned to the light and she is saying to old Bill Bardshare, "Sleep light, sleep tight, sweet dreams to you tonight."

"It's only what one may expect when one's father lacks a sense of dignity. There is that old fool Tom now, hopping out of the Bardshare house like a kid, and running right up to Mrs. Childers. 'May I see you home?' he is saying, while all the others are laughing and smiling knowingly. It makes one's blood run cold to see such a thing."

"Well, fill up the pots. Let's get the old coffee pots started, Kate. The gang'll be creeping along up the street pretty soon now," Tom shouted self-consciously, skipping busily about and breaking the little circle of thoughts in the house.

What happened was that—just as darkness came and when all the people were in the front yard before the Appleton house —Tom went and got it into his head to try to carry his cornet and two big coffee pots at the same time. Why didn't he leave the coffee until later? There the people were in the dusk outside the house, and there was that kind of low whispering and tittering that always goes on at such a time—and then Tom stuck his head out at the door and shouted, "Let her go!"

And then he must have gone quite crazy, for he ran back into the kitchen and grabbed both of the big coffee pots, hanging on to his cornet at the same time. Of course he stumbled in the darkness in the road outside and fell, and of course all of that boiling hot coffee had to spill right over him.

It was terrible. The flood of boiling hot coffee made steam under his thick clothes, and there he lay screaming with the pain of it. What a confusion! He just writhed and screamed, and the people ran 'round and 'round in the half darkness like crazy things. Was it some kind of joke the crazy fellow was up to at the last minute! Tom always was such a devil to think up things. "You should see him down at Alf Geigers, sometimes on Saturday nights, imitating the way Joe Douglas got out on a limb, and then sawed it off between himself and the tree, and the look on Joe's face when the limb began to crack. It would make you laugh until you screamed to see him imitate that."

"But what now? My God!" There was Kate Appleton trying to tear her father's clothes off, and crying and whimpering, and young Will Appleton knocking people aside. "Say, the man's hurt! What's happened? My God! Run for the doctor, someone. He's burnt, something awful!"

Early in October Will Appleton sat in the smoking car of a day train that runs between Cleveland and Buffalo. His destination was Erie, Pennsylvania, and he had got on the passenger train at Ashtabula, Ohio. Just why his destination was Erie he couldn't very easily have explained. He was going there anyway, going to get a job in a factory or on the docks there. Perhaps it was just a quirk of the mind that had made him decide upon Erie. It wasn't as big as Cleveland or Buffalo or Toledo or Chicago, or any one of a lot of other cities to which he might have gone, looking for work.

At Ashtabula he came into the car and slid into a seat beside a little old man. His own clothes were wet and wrinkled, and his hair, eyebrows and ears were black with coal dust.

At the moment, there was in him a kind of bitter dislike of his native town, Bidwell. "Sakes alive, a man couldn't get any work there—not in the winter." After the accident to his father, and the spoiling of all the family plans, he had managed to find employment during September on the farms. He worked for a time with a threshing crew, and then got work cutting corn. It was all right. "A man made a dollar a day and board, and as he wore overalls all the time, he didn't wear out no clothes. Still and all, the time when a fellow could make any money in Bidwell was past now, and the burns on his father's body had gone pretty deep, and he might be laid up for months."

Will had just made up his mind one day, after he had tramped about all morning from farm to farm without finding work, and then he had gone home and told Kate. "Dang it all," he hadn't intended lighting out right away—had thought he would stay about for a week or two, maybe. Well, he would go up town in the evening, dressed up in his best clothes, and stand around. "Hello, Harry, what you going to do this winter? I thought I would run over to Erie, Pennsylvania. I got an offer in a factory over there. Well, so long—if I don't see you again."

Kate hadn't seemed to understand, had seemed in an almighty hurry about getting him off. It was a shame she couldn't have a little more heart. Still, Kate was all right—worried a good deal no doubt. After their talk she had just said, "Yes, I think that's best, you had better go," and had gone to change the bandages on Tom's legs and back. The father was sitting among pillows in a rocking chair in the front room.

Will went up stairs and put his things, overalls and a few shirts, into a bundle. Then he went down stairs and took a walk—went out along a road that led into the country, and stopped on a bridge. It was near a place where he and other kids used to come swimming on summer afternoons. A thought had come into his head. There was a young fellow worked in Pawsey's jewelry store came to see Kate sometimes on Sunday evenings and they went off to walk together. "Did Kate want to get married?" If she did his going away now might be for good. He hadn't thought about that before. On that after-noon, and quite suddenly, all the world outside of Bidwell seemed huge and terrible to him and a few secret tears came into his eyes, but he managed to choke them back. For just a moment his mouth opened and closed queerly, like the mouth of a fish, when you take it out of the water and hold it in your hand.

When he returned to the house at supper time things were better. He had left his bundle on a chair in the kitchen and Kate had wrapped it more carefully, and had put in a number of things he had forgotten. His father called him into the front room. "It's all right, Will. Every young fellow ought to take a whirl out in the world. I did it myself, at about your age," Tom had said, a little pompously.

Then supper was served, and there was apple pie. That was a luxury the Appletons had perhaps better not have indulged in at that time, but Will knew Kate had baked it during the after-noon,—it might be as a way of showing him how she felt. Eating two large slices had rather set him up.

And then, before he realized how the time was slipping

away, ten o'clock had come, and it was time for him to go. He was going to beat his way out of town on a freight train, and there was a local going toward Cleveland at ten o'clock. Fred had gone off to bed, and his father was asleep in the rocking chair in the front room. He had picked up his bundle, and Kate had put on her hat. "I'm going to see you off," she had said.

Will and Kate had walked in silence along the streets to where he was to wait, in the shadow of Whaley's Warehouse, until the freight came along. Later when he thought back over that evening he was glad, that although she was three years older, he was taller than Kate.

How vividly everything that happened later stayed in his mind. After the train came, and he had crawled into an empty coal car, he sat hunched up in a corner. Overhead he could see the sky, and when the train stopped at towns there was always the chance the car in which he was concealed would be shoved into a siding, and left. The brakemen walked along the tracks beside the car shouting to each other and their lanterns made little splashes of light in the darkness.

"How black the sky!" After a time it began to rain. "His suit would be in a pretty mess. After all a fellow couldn't come right out and ask his sister if she intended to marry. If Kate married, then his father would also marry again. It was all right for a young woman like Kate, but for a man of forty to think of marriage—the devil! Why didn't Tom Appleton have more dignity? After all, Fred was only a kid and a new woman coming in, to be his mother—that might be all right for a kid."

All during that night on the freight train Will had thought a good deal about marriage—rather vague thoughts—coming and going like birds flying in and out of a bush. It was all a matter —this business of man and woman—that did not touch him very closely—not yet. The matter of having a home—that was something else. A home was something at a fellow's back. When one went off to work all week at some farm, and at night maybe went into a strange room to sleep, there was always the Appleton house—floating as it were, like a picture at the back of the mind—the Appleton house, and Kate moving about. She had been up town, and now had come home and was going up the stairs. Tom Appleton was fussing about in the

kitchen. He liked a bite before he went off to bed for the night
but presently he would go up stairs and into his own room. He
liked to smoke his pipe before he slept and sometimes he got
out his cornet and blew two or three soft sad notes.

At Cleveland Will had crawled off of the freight train and had
gone across the city in a street car. Workingmen were just
going to the factories and he passed among them unnoticed. If
his clothes were crumpled and soiled, their clothes weren't so
fine. The workingmen were all silent, looking at the car floor,
or out at the car windows. Long rows of factories stood along
the streets through which the car moved.

  He had been lucky, and had caught another freight out of a
place called Collinswood at eight, but at Ashtabula had made
up his mind it would be better to drop off the freight and take
a passenger train. If he was to live in Erie it would be just as
well to arrive looking more like a gentleman and having paid
his fare.

As he sat in the smoking car of the train he did not feel much
like a gentleman. The coal dust had got into his hair and the
rain had washed it in long dirty streaks down over his face. His
clothes were badly soiled and wanted cleaning and brushing
and the paper package, in which his overalls and shirts were
tied, had become torn and dirty.

  Outside the train window the sky was grey, and no doubt
the night was going to turn cold. Perhaps there would be a
cold rain.

  It was an odd thing about the towns through which the
train kept passing—all of the houses in all the towns looked
cold and forbidding. "Dang it all." In Bidwell, before the night
when his father got so badly burned being such a fool about
old Bill Bardshare's party—all the houses had always seemed
warm cozy places. When one was alone, one walked along the
streets whistling. At night warm lights shone through the windows of the houses. "John Wyatt, the drayman, lives in that
house. His wife has a wen on her neck. In that barn over there
old Doctor Musgrave keeps his bony old white horse. The
horse looks like the devil, but you bet he can go."

Will squirmed about on the car seat. The old man who sat beside him was small, almost as small as Fred, and he wore a queer looking suit. The pants were brown, and the coat checked, grey and black. There was a small leather case on the floor at his feet.

Long before the man spoke Will knew what would happen. It was bound to turn out that such a fellow played a cornet. He was a man, old in years, but there was no dignity in him. Will remembered his father's marchings through the main street of Bidwell with the band. It was some great day, Fourth of July, perhaps, and all the people were assembled and there was Tony Appleton, making a show of blowing his cornet at a great rate. Did all the people along the street know how badly he played and was there a kind of conspiracy, that kept grown men from laughing at each other? In spite of the seriousness of his own situation a smile crept over Will's face.

The little man at his side smiled in return.

"Well," he began, not stopping for anything but plunging headlong into a tale concerning some dissatisfaction he felt with life, "well, you see before you a man who is up against it, young fellow." The old man tried to laugh at his own words, but did not make much of a success of it. His lip trembled. "I got to go home like a dog, with my tail 'twixt my legs," he declared abruptly.

The old man balanced back and forth between two impulses. He had met a young man on a train, and hungered for companionship and one got oneself in with others by being jolly, a little gay perhaps. When one met a stranger on a train one told a story—"By the way, Mister, I heard a new one the other day—perhaps you haven't heard it? It's about the miner up in Alaska who hadn't seen a woman for years." One began in that way, and then later perhaps, spoke of oneself, and one's affairs.

But the old man wanted to plunge at once into his own story. He talked, saying sad discouraged words, while his eyes kept smiling with a peculiar appealing little smile. "If the words uttered by my lips annoy or bore you, do not pay any attention to them. I am really a jolly fellow although I am an old man, and not of much use any more," the eyes were saying. The eyes were pale blue and watery. How strange to see them set in the head of an old man. They belonged in the head of a lost dog.

The smile was not really a smile. "Don't kick me, young fellow. If you can't give me anything to eat, scratch my head. At least show you are a fellow of good intentions. I've been kicked about quite enough." It was so very evident the eyes were speaking a language of their own.

Will found himself smiling sympathetically. It was true there was something dog-like in the little old man and Will was pleased with himself for having so quickly caught the sense of him. "One who can see things with his eyes will perhaps get along all right in the world, after all," he thought. His thoughts wandered away from the old man. In Bidwell there was an old woman lived alone and owned a shepherd dog. Every summer she decided to cut away the dog's coat, and then—at the last moment and after she had in fact started the job—she changed her mind. Well, she grasped a long pair of scissors firmly in her hand and started on the dog's flanks. Her hand trembled a little. "Shall I go ahead, or shall I stop?" After two minutes she gave up the job. "It makes him look too ugly," she thought, justifying her timidity.

Later the hot days came, the dog went about with his tongue hanging out and again the old woman took the scissors in her hand. The dog stood patiently waiting but, when she had cut a long wide furrow through the thick hair of his back, she stopped again. In a sense, and to her way of looking at the matter, cutting away his splendid coat was like cutting away a part of himself. She couldn't go on. "Now there—that made him look worse than ever," she declared to herself. With a determined air she put the scissors away, and all summer the dog went about looking a little puzzled and ashamed.

Will kept smiling and thinking of the old woman's dog and then looked again at his companion of the train. The variegated suit the old man wore gave him something of the air of the half-sheared shepherd dog. Both had the same puzzled, ashamed air.

Now Will had begun using the old man for his own ends. There was something inside himself that wanted facing, he didn't want to face—not yet. Ever since he had left home, in fact ever since that day when he had come home from the country and had told Kate of his intention to set out into the world, he had been dodging something. If one thought of the little old man, and of the half-sheared dog, one did not have to think of oneself.

One thought of Bidwell on a summer afternoon. There was the old woman, who owned the dog, standing on the porch of her house, and the dog had run down to the gate. In the winter, when his coat had again fully grown, the dog would bark and make a great fuss about a boy passing in the street but now he started to bark and growl, and then stopped. "I look like the devil, and I'm attracting unnecessary attention to myself," the dog seemed to have decided suddenly. He ran furiously down to the gate, opened his mouth to bark, and then, quite abruptly, changed his mind and trotted back to the house with his tail between his legs.

Will kept smiling at his own thoughts. For the first time since he had left Bidwell he felt quite cheerful.

And now the old man was telling a story of himself and his life, but Will wasn't listening. Within the young man a cross-current of impulses had been set up and he was like one standing silently in the hallway of a house, and listening to two voices, talking at a distance. The voices came from two widely separated rooms of the house and one couldn't make up one's mind to which voice to listen.

To be sure the old man was another cornet player like his father—he was a horn blower. That was his horn in the little worn leather case on the car floor.

And after he had reached middle age, and after his first wife had died, he had married again. He had a little property then and, in a foolish moment, went and made it all over to his second wife, who was fifteen years younger than himself. She took the money and bought a large house in the factory district of Erie, and then began taking in boarders.

There was the old man, feeling lost, of no account in his own house. It just came about. One had to think of the boarders —their wants had to be satisfied. His wife had two sons, almost fully grown now, both of whom worked in a factory.

Well, it was all right—everything on the square—the sons paid board all right. Their wants had to be thought of, too. He liked blowing his cornet a while in the evenings, before he went to bed, but it might disturb the others in the house. One got rather desperate going about saying nothing, keeping out of the way and he had tried getting work in a factory himself, but they wouldn't have him. His grey hairs stood in his way, and so one night he had just got out, had gone to Cleveland, where he had hoped to get a job in a band, in a movie theatre perhaps. Anyway it hadn't turned out and now he was going back to Erie and to his wife. He had written and she had told him to come on home.

"They didn't turn me down back there in Cleveland because I'm old. It's because my lip is no good any more," he explained. His shrunken old lip trembled a little.

Will kept thinking of the old woman's dog. In spite of himself, and when the old man's lip trembled, his lip also trembled.

What was the matter with him?

He stood in the hallway of a house hearing two voices. Was he trying to close his ears to one of them? Did the second voice, the one he had been trying all day, and all the night before, not to hear, did that have something to do with the end of his life in the Appleton house at Bidwell? Was the voice trying to taunt him, trying to tell him that now he was a thing swinging in air, that there was no place to put down his feet? Was he afraid? Of what was he afraid? He had wanted so much to be a man, to stand on his own feet and now what was the matter with him? Was he afraid of manhood?

He was fighting desperately now. There were tears in the old man's eyes, and Will also began crying silently and that was the one thing he felt he must not do.

The old man talked on and on, telling the tale of his troubles, but Will could not hear his words. The struggle within was becoming more and more definite. His mind clung to the life of his boyhood, to the life in the Appleton house in Bidwell.

There was Fred, standing in the field of his fancy now, with just the triumphant look in his eyes that came when other boys saw him doing a man's work. A whole series of pictures floated up before Will's mind. He and his father and Fred were painting a barn and two farmer boys had come along a road and stood looking at Fred, who was on a ladder, putting on paint. They shouted, but Fred wouldn't answer. There was a certain air Fred had—he slapped on the paint, and then turning his head, spat on the ground. Tom Appleton's eyes looked into Will's and there was a smile playing about the corners of the father's eyes and the son's eyes too. The father and his oldest son were like two men, two workmen, having a delicious little secret between them. They were both looking lovingly at Fred. "Bless him! He thinks he's a man already."

And now Tom Appleton was standing in the kitchen of his house, and his brushes were laid out on the kitchen table. Kate was rubbing a brush back and forth over the palm of her hand. "It's as soft as the cat's back," she was saying.

Something gripped at Will's throat. As in a dream, he saw his sister Kate walking off along the street on Sunday evening with that young fellow who clerked in the jewelry store. They were going to church. Her being with him meant—well, it perhaps meant the beginning of a new home—it meant the end of the Appleton home.

Will started to climb out of the seat beside the old man in the smoking car of the train. It had grown almost dark in the car. The old man was still talking, telling his tale over and over. "I might as well not have any home at all," he was saying. Was Will about to begin crying aloud on a train, in a strange place, before many strange men. He tried to speak, to make some commonplace remark, but his mouth only opened and closed like the mouth of a fish taken out of the water.

And now the train had run into a train shed, and it was quite dark. Will's hand clutched convulsively into the darkness and alighted upon the old man's shoulder.

Then suddenly, the train had stopped, and the two stood half embracing each other. The tears were quite evident in Will's eyes, when a brakeman lighted the overhead lamps in the car, but the luckiest thing in the world had happened. The old man, who had seen Will's tears, thought they were tears of sympathy for his own unfortunate position in life and a look of gratitude came into his blue watery eyes. Well, this was something new in life for him, too. In one of the pauses, when he had first begun telling his tale, Will had said he was going to Erie to try to get work in some factory and now, as they got off the train, the old man clung to Will's arm. "You might as well come live at our house," he said. A look of hope flared up in the old man's eyes. If he could bring home with him, to his young wife, a new boarder, the gloom of his own home-coming would be somewhat lightened. "You come on. That's the best thing to do. You just come on with me to our house," he plead, clinging to Will.

Two weeks had passed and Will had, outwardly, and to the eyes of the people about him, settled into his new life as a factory hand at Erie, Pennsylvania.

Then suddenly, on a Saturday evening, the thing happened that he had unconsciously been expecting and dreading ever since the moment when he climbed aboard the freight train in the shadow of Whaley's Warehouse at Bidwell. A letter, containing great news, had come from Kate.

At the moment of their parting, and before he settled himself down out of sight in a corner of the empty coal car, on that night of his leaving, he had leaned out for a last look at his sister. She had been standing silently in the shadows of the warehouse, but just as the train was about to start, stepped toward him and a light from a distant street lamp fell on her face.

Well, the face did not jump toward Will, but remained dimly outlined in the uncertain light.

Did her lips open and close, as though in an effort to say something to him, or was that an effect produced by the distant, uncertain and wavering light? In the families of working people the dramatic and vital moments of life are passed over in silence. Even in the moments of death and birth, little is said. A child is born to a laborer's wife and he goes into the room. She is in bed with the little red bundle of new life beside her and her husband stands a moment, fumblingly, beside the bed. Neither he or his wife can look directly into each other's eyes. "Take care of yourself, Ma. Have a good rest," he says, and hurries out of the room.

In the darkness by the warehouse at Bidwell Kate had taken two or three steps toward Will, and then had stopped. There was a little strip of grass between the warehouse and the tracks, and she stood upon it. Was there a more final farewell trembling on her lips at the moment? A kind of dread had swept over Will, and no doubt Kate had felt the same thing. At the moment she had become altogether the mother, in the presence of her child, and the thing within that wanted utterance became submerged. There was a word to be said that she could not say. Her form seemed to sway a little in the darkness and, to Will's eyes, she became a slender indistinct thing. "Good-bye," he had whispered into the darkness, and perhaps her lips had formed the same words. Outwardly there had been only the silence, and in the silence she had stood as the train rumbled away.

And now, on the Saturday evening, Will had come home from the factory and had found Kate saying in the letter what she had been unable to say on the night of his departure. The factory closed at five on Saturday and he came home in his overalls and went to his room. He had found the letter on a little broken table under a spluttering oil lamp, by the front door, and had climbed the stairs carrying it in his hand. He read the letter anxiously, waiting as for a hand to come out of the blank wall of the room and strike.

His father was getting better. The deep burns that had taken such a long time to heal, were really healing now and the doctor had said the danger of infection had passed. Kate had found a new and soothing remedy. One took slippery elm and let it lie in milk until it became soft. This applied to the burns enabled Tom to sleep better at night.

As for Fred, Kate and her father had decided he might as well go back to school. It was really too bad for a young boy to miss the chance to get an education, and anyway there was no work to be had. Perhaps he could get a job, helping in some store on Saturday afternoons.

A woman from the Woman's Relief Corps had had the nerve to come to the Appleton house and ask Kate if the family needed help. Well, Kate had managed to hold herself back, and had been polite but, had the woman known what was in her mind, her ears would have been itching for a month. The idea!

It had been fine of Will to send a postcard, as soon as he had got to Erie and got a job. As for his sending money home—of course the family would be glad to have anything he could spare—but he wasn't to go depriving himself. "We've got good credit at the stores. We'll get along all right," Kate had said stoutly.

And then it was she had added the line, had said the thing she could not say that night when he was leaving. It concerned herself and her future plans. "That night when you were going away I wanted to tell you something, but I thought it was silly, talking too soon." After all though, Will might as well know she was planning to be married in the spring. What she wanted was for Fred to come and live with her and her husband. He could keep on going to school, and perhaps they could manage so that he could go to college. Some one in the family ought to have a decent education. Now that Will had made his start in life, there was no point in waiting longer before making her own.

Will sat, in his tiny room at the top of the huge frame house, owned now by the wife of the old cornet player of the train, and held the letter in his hand. The room was on the third floor, under the roof, in a wing of the house, and beside it was another small room, occupied by the old man himself. Will had taken the room because it was to be had at a low price and he could manage the room and his meals, get his washing done, send three dollars a week to Kate, and still have left a dollar a week to spend. One could get a little tobacco, and now and then see a movie.

"Ugh!" Will's lips made a little grunting noise as he read Kate's words. He was sitting in a chair, in his oily overalls, and where his fingers gripped the white sheets of the letter there was a little oily smudge. Also his hand trembled a little. He got up, poured water out of a pitcher into a white bowl, and began washing his face and hands.

When he had partly dressed a visitor came. There was the shuffling sound of weary feet along a hallway, and the cornet player put his head timidly in at the door. The dog-like appealing look Will had noted on the train was still in his eyes. Now he was planning something, a kind of gentle revolt against his wife's power in the house, and he wanted Will's moral support.

For a week he had been coming for talk to Will's room almost every evening. There were two things he wanted. In the evening sometimes, as he sat in his room, he wanted to blow upon his cornet, and he wanted a little money to jingle in his pockets.

And there was a sense in which Will, the newcomer in the house, was his property, did not belong to his wife. Often in the evenings he had talked to the weary and sleepy young workman, until Will's eyes had closed and he snored gently. The old

man sat on the one chair in the room, and Will sat on the edge
of the bed, while old lips told the tale of a lost youth, boasted
a little. When Will's body had slumped down upon the bed the
old man got to his feet and moved with cat-like steps about the
room. One mustn't raise the voice too loudly after all. Had
Will gone to sleep? The cornet player threw his shoulders back
and bold words came, in a half-whisper, from his lips. To tell
the truth, he had been a fool about the money he had made
over to his wife and, if his wife had taken advantage of him, it
wasn't her fault. For his present position in life he had no one to
blame but himself. What from the very beginning he had most
lacked was boldness. It was a man's duty to be a man and, for a
long time, he had been thinking—well, the boarding-house no
doubt made a profit and he should have his share. His wife was
a good girl all right, but when one came right down to it, all
women seemed to lack a sense of a man's position in life.

"I'll have to speak to her—yes siree, I'm going to speak right
up to her. I may have to be a little harsh but it's my money
runs this house, and I want my share of the profits. No foolishness now. Shell out, I tell you," the old man whispered, peering
out of the corners of his blue, watery eyes at the sleeping form
of the young man on the bed.

And now again the old man stood at the door of the room,
looking anxiously in. A bell called insistently, announcing that
the evening meal was ready to be served, and they went below,
Will leading the way. At a long table in the dining room several
men had already gathered, and there was the sound of more
footsteps on the stairs.

Two long rows of young workmen eating silently. Saturday
night and two long rows of young workmen eating in silence.

After the eating, and on this particular night, there would be
a swift flight of all these young men down into the town, down
into the lighted parts of the town.

Will sat at his place gripping the sides of his chair.

There were things men did on Saturday nights. Work was at
an end for the week and money jingled in pockets. Young
workmen ate in silence and hurried away, one by one, down
into the town.

Will's sister Kate was going to be married in the spring. Her

walking about with the young clerk from the jewelry store, in
the streets of Bidwell, had come to something.

Young workmen employed in factories in Erie, Pennsylvania,
dressed themselves in their best clothes and walked about in
the lighted streets of Erie on Saturday evenings. They went
into parks. Some stood talking to girls while others walked
with girls through the streets. And there were still others who
went into saloons and had drinks. Men stood talking together
at a bar. "Dang that foreman of mine! I'll bust him in the jaw
if he gives me any of his lip."

There was a young man from Bidwell, sitting at a table in a
boarding house at Erie, Pennsylvania, and before him on a
plate was a great pile of meat and potatoes. The room was not
very well lighted. It was dark and gloomy, and there were black
streaks on the grey wall paper. Shadows played on the walls.
On all sides of the young man sat other young men—eating
silently, hurriedly.

Will got abruptly up from the table and started for the door
that led into the street but the others paid no attention to him.
If he did not want to eat his meat and potatoes, it made no
difference to them. The mistress of the house, the wife of the
old cornet player, waited on table when the men ate, but now
she had gone away to the kitchen. She was a silent grim-looking
woman, dressed always in a black dress.

To the others in the room—except only the old cornet
player—Will's going or staying meant nothing at all. He was a
young workman, and at such places young workmen were always going and coming.

A man with broad shoulders and a black mustache, a little
older than most of the others, did glance up from his business
of eating. He nudged his neighbor, and then made a jerky
movement with his thumb over his shoulder. "The new guy
has hooked up quickly, eh?" he said, smiling. "He can't even
wait to eat. Lordy, he's got an early date—some skirt waiting
for him."

At his place, opposite where Will had been seated, the cornet
player saw Will go, and his eyes followed, filled with alarm. He
had counted on an evening of talk, of speaking to Will about
his youth, boasting a little in his gentle hesitating way. Now
Will had reached the door that led to the street, and in the old

man's eyes tears began to gather. Again his lip trembled. Tears were always gathering in the man's eyes, and his lips trembled at the slightest provocation. It was no wonder he could no longer blow a cornet in a band.

And now Will was outside the house in the darkness and, for the cornet player, the evening was spoiled, the house a deserted empty place. He had intended being very plain in his evening's talk with Will, and wanted particularly to speak of a new attitude, he hoped to assume toward his wife, in the matter of money. Talking the whole matter out with Will would give him new courage, make him bolder. Well, if his money had bought the house, that was now a boarding house, he should have some share in its profits. There must be profits. Why run a boarding house without profits? The woman he had married was no fool.

Even though a man were old he needed a little money in his pockets. Well, an old man, like himself, has a friend, a young fellow, and now and then he wanted to be able to say to his friend, "Come on friend, let's have a glass of beer. I know a good place. Let's have a glass of beer and go to the movies. This is on me."

The cornet player could not eat his meat and potatoes. For a time he stared over the heads of the others, and then got up to go to his room. His wife followed into the little hallway at the foot of the stairs. "What's the matter, dearie—are you sick?" she asked.

"No," he answered, "I just didn't want any supper." He did not look at her, but tramped slowly and heavily up the stairs.

Will was walking hurriedly through streets but did not go down into the brightly lighted sections of town. The boarding house stood on a factory street and, turning northward, he crossed several railroad tracks and went toward the docks, along the shore of Lake Erie. There was something to be settled with himself, something to be faced. Could he manage the matter?

He walked along, hurriedly at first, and then more slowly. It was getting into late October now and there was a sharpness like frost in the air. The spaces between street lamps were long, and he plunged in and out of areas of darkness. Why was it that everything about him seemed suddenly strange and un-real? He had forgotten to bring his overcoat from Bidwell and would have to write Kate to send it.

Now he had almost reached the docks. Not only the night but his own body, the pavements under his feet, and the stars far away in the sky—even the solid factory buildings he was now passing—seemed strange and unreal. It was almost as though one could thrust out an arm and push a hand through the walls, as one might push his hand into a fog or a cloud of smoke. All the people Will passed seemed strange, and acted in a strange way. Dark figures surged toward him out of the darkness. By a factory wall there was a man standing—perfectly still, motionless. There was something almost unbelievable about the actions of such men and the strangeness of such hours as the one through which he was now passing. He walked within a few inches of the motionless man. Was it a man or a shadow on the wall? The life Will was now to lead alone, had become a strange, a vast terrifying thing. Perhaps all life was like that, a vastness and emptiness.

He came out into a place where ships were made fast to a dock and stood for a time, facing the high wall-like side of a vessel. It looked dark and deserted. When he turned his head he became aware of a man and a woman passing along a road-way. Their feet made no sound in the thick dust of the roadway, and he could not see or hear them, but knew they were there. Some part of a woman's dress—something white—flashed faintly into view and the man's figure was a dark mass against the dark mass of the night. "Oh, come on, don't be afraid," the man whispered, hoarsely. "There won't anything happen to you."

"Do shut up," a woman's voice answered, and there was a quick outburst of laughter. The figures fluttered away. "You don't know what you are talking about," the woman's voice said again.

Now that he had got Kate's letter, Will was no longer a boy. A boy is, quite naturally, and without his having anything to do with the matter, connected with something—and now that connection had been cut. He had been pushed out of the nest and that fact, the pushing of himself off the nest's rim, was some-thing accomplished. The difficulty was that, while he was no longer a boy, he had not yet become a man. He was a thing swinging in space. There was no place to put down his feet.

He stood in the darkness under the shadow of the ship making queer little wriggling motions with his shoulders, that had become now almost the shoulders of a man. No need now to think of evenings at the Appleton house with Kate and Fred standing about, and his father, Tom Appleton, spreading his paint brushes on the kitchen table, no need of thinking of the sound of Kate's feet going up a stairway of the Appleton house, late at night when she had been out walking with her clerk. What was the good of trying to amuse oneself by thinking of a shepherd dog in an Ohio town, a dog made ridiculous by the trembling hand of a timid old woman?

One stood face to face with manhood now—one stood alone. If only one could get one's feet down upon something, could get over this feeling of falling through space, through a vast emptiness.

"Manhood"—the word had a queer sound in the head. What did it mean?

Will tried to think of himself as a man, doing a man's work in a factory. There was nothing in the factory, where he was now employed, upon which he could put down his feet. All day he stood at a machine and bored holes in pieces of iron. A boy brought to him the little, short, meaningless pieces of iron in a box-like truck and, one by one, he picked them up and placed them under the point of a drill. He pulled a lever and the drill came down and bit into the piece of iron. A little, smoke-like vapor arose, and then he squirted oil on the spot where the drill was working. Then the lever was thrown up again. The hole was drilled and now the meaningless pieces of iron was thrown into another box-like truck. It had nothing to do with him. He had nothing to do with it.

At the noon hour, at the factory, one moved about a bit, stepped outside the factory door to stand for a moment in the sun. Inside, men were sitting along benches eating lunches out of dinner pails and some had washed their hands while others had not bothered about such a trivial matter. They were eating in silence. A tall man spat on the floor and then drew his foot across the spot. Nights came and one went home from the factory to eat, sitting with other silent men, and later a boastful old man came into one's room to talk. One lay on a bed and tried to listen, but presently fell asleep. Men were like the pieces of iron in which holes had been bored—one pitched them aside into a box-like truck. One had nothing really to do with them. They had nothing to do with oneself. Life became a procession of days and perhaps all life was just like that—just a procession of days.

"Manhood."

Did one go out of one place and into another? Were youth and manhood two houses, in which one lived during different periods in life? It was evident something of importance must be about to happen to his sister Kate. First, she had been a young woman, having two brothers and a father, living with them in a house at Bidwell, Ohio.

And then a day was to come when she became something else. She married and went to live in another house and had a husband. Perhaps children would be born to her. It was evident Kate had got hold of something, that her hands had reached out and had grasped something definite. Kate had swung herself off the rim of the home nest and, right away, her feet had landed on another limb of the tree of life— womanhood.

As he stood in the darkness something caught at Will's throat. He was fighting again but what was he fighting? A fellow like himself did not move out of one house and into another. There was a house in which one lived, and then suddenly and unexpectedly, it fell apart. One stood on the rim of the nest and looked about, and a hand reached out from the warmth of the nest and pushed one off into space. There was no place for a fellow to put down his feet. He was one swinging in space.

What—a great fellow, nearly six feet tall now, and crying in the darkness, in the shadow of a ship, like a child! He walked, filled with determination, out of the darkness, along many streets of factories and came into a street of houses. He passed a store where groceries were sold and looking in saw, by a clock on the wall, that it was already ten o'clock. Two drunken men came out at the door of a house and stood on a little porch. One of them clung to a railing about the porch, and the other pulled at his arm. "Let me alone. It's settled. I want you to let me alone," grumbled the man clinging to the railing.

Will went to his boarding house and climbed the stairs wearily. The devil—one might face anything if one but knew what was to be faced!

He turned on a light and sat down in his room on the edge of the bed, and the old cornet player pounced upon him, pounced like a little animal, lying under a bush along a path in a forest, and waiting for food. He came into Will's room carrying his cornet, and there was an almost bold look in his eyes. Standing firmly on his old legs in the centre of the room, he made a declaration. "I'm going to play it. I don't care what she says, I'm going to play it," he said.

He put the cornet to his lips and blew two or three notes—so softly that even Will, sitting so closely, could barely hear. Then his eyes wavered. "My lip's no good," he said. He thrust the cornet at Will. "You blow it," he said.

Will sat on the edge of the bed and smiled. There was a notion floating in his mind now. Was there something, a thought in which one could find comfort. There was now, before him, standing before him in the room, a man who was after all not a man. He was a child as Will was too really, had always been such a child, would always be such a child. One need not be too afraid. Children were all about, everywhere. If one were a child and lost in a vast, empty space, one could at least talk to some other child. One could have conversations, understand perhaps something of the eternal childishness of oneself and others.

Will's thoughts were not very definite. He only felt suddenly warm and comfortable in the little room at the top of the boarding house.

And now the man was again explaining himself. He wanted to assert his manhood. "I stay up here," he explained, "and don't go down there, to sleep in the room with my wife because I don't want to. That's the only reason. I could if I wanted to. She has the bronchitis—but don't tell anyone. Women hate to have anyone told. She isn't so bad. I can do what I please."

He kept urging Will to put the cornet to his lips and blow. There was in him an intense eagerness. "You can't really make any music—you don't know how—but that don't make any difference," he said. "The thing to do is to make a noise, make a deuce of a racket, blow like the devil."

Again Will felt like crying but the sense of vastness and loneliness, that had been in him since he got aboard the train that night at Bidwell, had gone. "Well, I can't go on forever being a baby. Kate has a right to get married," he thought, putting the cornet to his lips. He blew two or three notes, softly.

"No, I tell you, no! That isn't the way! Blow on it! Don't be afraid! I tell you I want you to do it. Make a deuce of a racket! I tell you what, I own this house. We don't need to be afraid. We can do what we please. Go ahead! Make a deuce of a racket!" the old man kept pleading.

The Man's Story

DURING his trial for murder and later, after he had been cleared through the confession of that queer little bald chap with the nervous hands, I watched him, fascinated by his continued effort to make something understood.

He was persistently interested in something, having nothing to do with the charge that he had murdered the woman. The matter of whether or not, and by due process of law, he was to be convicted of murder and hanged by the neck until he was dead didn't seem to interest him. The law was something outside his life and he declined to have anything to do with the killing as one might decline a cigarette. "I thank you, I am not smoking at present. I made a bet with a fellow that I could go along without smoking cigarettes for a month."

That is the sort of thing I mean. It was puzzling. Really, had he been guilty and trying to save his neck he couldn't have taken a better line. You see, at first, everyone thought he had done the killing; we were all convinced of it, and then, just because of that magnificent air of indifference, everyone began wanting to save him. When news came of the confession of the crazy little stage-hand everyone broke out into cheers.

He was clear of the law after that but his manner in no way changed. There was, somewhere, a man or a woman who would understand just what he understood and it was important to find that person and talk things over. There was a time, during the trial and immediately afterward, when I saw a good deal of him, and I had this sharp sense of him, feeling about in the darkness trying to find something like a needle or a pin lost on the floor. Well, he was like an old man who cannot find his glasses. He feels in all his pockets and looks helplessly about.

There was a question in my own mind too, in everyone's mind—"Can a man be wholly casual and brutal, in every outward way, at a moment when the one nearest and dearest to him is dying, and at the same time, and with quite another part of himself, be altogether tender and sensitive?"

Anyway it's a story, and once in a while a man likes to tell a
story straight out, without putting in any newspaper jargon
about beautiful heiresses, cold-blooded murderers and all that
sort of tommyrot.

As I picked the story up the sense of it was something like
this—

The man's name was Wilson,—Edgar Wilson—and he had
come to Chicago from some place to the westward, perhaps
from the mountains. He might once have been a sheep herder
or something of the sort in the far west, as he had the peculiar
abstract air, acquired only by being a good deal alone. About
himself and his past he told a good many conflicting stories
and so, after being with him for a time, one instinctively dis-
carded the past.

"The devil—it doesn't matter—the man can't tell the truth
in that direction.—Let it go," one said to oneself. What was
known was that he had come to Chicago from a town in Kansas and that he had run away from the Kansas town with another man's wife.

As to her story, I knew little enough of it. She had been at
one time, I imagine, a rather handsome thing, in a big strong
upstanding sort of way, but her life, until she met Wilson, had
been rather messy. In those dead flat Kansas towns lives have a
way of getting ugly and messy without anything very definite
having happened to make them so. One can't imagine the
reasons— Let it go. It just is so and one can't at all believe the
writers of Western tales about the life out there.

To be a little more definite about this particular woman—in
her young girlhood her father had got into trouble. He had
been some sort of a small official, a travelling agent or something of the sort for an express company, and got arrested in
connection with the disappearance of some money. And then,
when he was in jail and before his trial, he shot and killed himself. The girl's mother was already dead.

Within a year or two she married a man, an honest enough
fellow but from all accounts rather uninteresting. He was a
drug clerk and a frugal man and after a short time managed to
buy a drug store of his own.

The woman, as I have said, had been strong and well-built
but now grew thin and nervous. Still she carried herself well

with a sort of air, as it were, and there was something about her that appealed strongly to men. Several men of the seedy little town were smitten by her and wrote her letters, trying to get her to creep out with them at night. You know how such things are done. The letters were unsigned. "You go to such and such a place on Friday evening. If you are willing to talk things over with me carry a book in your hand."

Then the woman made a mistake and told her husband about the receipt of one of the letters and he grew angry and tramped off to the trysting place at night with a shotgun in his hand. When no one appeared he came home and fussed about. He said little mean tentative things. "You must have looked—in a certain way—at the man when he passed you on the street. A man don't grow so bold with a married woman unless an opening has been given him."

The man talked and talked after that, and life in the house must have been gay. She grew habitually silent, and when she was silent the house was silent. They had no children.

Then the man Edgar Wilson came along, going eastward, and stopped over in the town for two or three days. He had at that time a little money and stayed at a small workingmen's boarding-house, near the railroad station. One day he saw the woman walking in the street and followed her to her home and the neighbors saw them standing and talking together for an hour by the front gate and on the next day he came again.

That time they talked for two hours and then she went into the house; got a few belongings and walked to the railroad station with him. They took a train for Chicago and lived there together, apparently very happy, until she died—in a way I am about to try to tell you about. They of course could not be married and during the three years they lived in Chicago he did nothing toward earning their common living. As he had a very small amount of money when they came, barely enough to get them here from the Kansas town, they were miserably poor.

They lived, when I knew about them, over on the North side, in that section of old three- and four-story brick residences that were once the homes of what we call our nice people, but that had afterward gone to the bad. The section is having a kind of rebirth now but for a good many years it rather went to seed. There were these old residences, made into boarding-houses, and with unbelievably dirty lace curtains at the windows, and now and then an utterly disreputable old tumble-down frame house—in one of which Wilson lived with his woman.

The place is a sight! Someone owns it, I suppose, who is shrewd enough to know that in a big city like Chicago no section gets neglected always. Such a fellow must have said to himself, "Well, I'll let the place go. The ground on which the house stands will some day be very valuable but the house is worth nothing. I'll let it go at a low rental and do nothing to fix it up. Perhaps I will get enough out of it to pay my taxes until prices come up."

And so the house had stood there unpainted for years and the windows were out of line and the shingles nearly all off the roof. The second floor was reached by an outside stairway with a handrail that had become just the peculiar grey greasy black that wood can become in a soft-coal-burning city like Chicago or Pittsburgh. One's hand became black when the railing was touched; and the rooms above were altogether cold and cheerless.

At the front there was a large room with a fireplace, from which many bricks had fallen, and back of that were two small sleeping rooms.

Wilson and his woman lived in the place, at the time when the thing happened I am to tell you about, and as they had taken it in May I presume they did not too much mind the cold barrenness of the large front room in which they lived. There was a sagging wooden bed with a leg broken off—the woman had tried to repair it with sticks from a packing box—a kitchen table, that was also used by Wilson as a writing desk, and two or three cheap kitchen chairs.

The woman had managed to get a place as wardrobe woman in a theatre in Randolph Street and they lived on her earnings. It was said she had got the job because some man connected with the theatre, or a company playing there, had a passion for her but one can always pick up stories of that sort about any woman who works about the theatre—from the scrubwoman to the star.

Anyway she worked there and had a reputation in the theatre of being quiet and efficient.

As for Wilson, he wrote poetry of a sort I've never seen before, although, like most newspaper men, I've taken a turn at verse making myself now and then—both of the rhymed kind and the newfangled vers libre sort. I rather go in for the classical stuff myself.

About Wilson's verse—it was Greek to me. Well now, to get right down to hardpan in this matter, it was and it wasn't.

The stuff made me feel just a little bit woozy when I took a whole sheaf of it and sat alone in my room reading it at night. It was all about walls, and deep wells, and great bowls with young trees standing erect in them—and trying to find their way to the light and air over the rim of the bowl.

Queer crazy stuff, every line of it, but fascinating too—in a way. One got into a new world with new values, which after all is I suppose what poetry is all about. There was the world of fact—we all know or think we know—the world of flat buildings and middle-western farms with wire fences about the fields and fordson tractors running up and down, and towns with high schools and advertising billboards, and everything that makes up life—or that we think makes up life.

There was this world, we all walk about in, and then there was this other world, that I have come to think of as Wilson's world—a dim place to me at least—of far-away near places—things taking new and strange shapes, the insides of people coming out, the eyes seeing new things, the fingers feeling new and strange things.

It was a place of walls mainly. I got hold of the whole lot of Wilson's verse by a piece of luck. It happened that I was the first newspaper man who got into the place on the night when the woman's body was found, and there was all his stuff, carefully written out in a sort of child's copy book, and two or three stupid policemen standing about. I just shoved the book under my coat, when they weren't looking, and later, during Wilson's trial, we published some of the more intelligible ones in the paper. It made pretty good newspaper stuff—the poet who killed his mistress,

> "He did not wear his purple coat,
> For blood and wine are red"—

and all that. Chicago loved it.

To get back to the poetry itself for a moment. I just wanted to explain that all through the book there ran this notion, that men had erected walls about themselves and that all men were perhaps destined to stand forever behind the walls—on which they constantly beat with their fists, or with whatever tools they could get hold of. Wanted to break through to something, you understand. One couldn't quite make out whether there was just one great wall or many little individual walls. Sometimes Wilson put it one way, sometimes another. Men had themselves built the walls and now stood behind them, knowing dimly that beyond the walls there was warmth, light, air, beauty, life in fact—while at the same time, and because of a kind of madness in themselves, the walls were constantly being built higher and stronger.

The notion gives you the fantods a little, doesn't it? Anyway it does me.

And then there was that notion about deep wells, men everywhere constantly digging and digging themselves down deeper and deeper into deep wells. They not wanting to do it, you understand, and no one wanting them to do it, but all the time the thing going on just the same, that is to say the wells getting constantly deeper and deeper, and the voices growing dimmer and dimmer in the distance—and again the light and the warmth of life going away and going away, because of a kind of blind refusal of people to try to understand each other, I suppose.

It was all very strange to me—Wilson's poetry, I mean—when I came to it. Here is one of his things. It is not directly concerned with the walls, the bowl or the deep well theme, as you will see, but it is one we ran in the paper during the trial and a lot of folks rather liked it—as I'll admit I do myself. Maybe putting it in here will give a kind of point to my story, by giving you some sense of the strangeness of the man who is the story's hero. In the book it was called merely "Number Ninety-seven," and it went as follows:

> The firm grip of my fingers on the thin paper of this cigarette is a sign that I am very quiet now. Sometimes it is not so. When I am unquiet I am weak but when I am quiet, as I am now, I am very strong.

Just now I went along one of the streets of my city and in at a door and came up here, where I am now, lying on a bed and looking out at a window. Very suddenly and completely the knowledge has come to me that I could grip the sides of tall buildings as freely and as easily as I now grip this cigarette. I could hold the building between my fingers, put it to my lips and blow smoke through it. I could blow confusion away. I could blow a thousand people out through the roof of one tall building into the sky, into the unknown. Building after building I could consume, as I consume the cigarettes in this box. I could throw the burning ends of cities over my shoulder and out through a window.

It is not often I get in the state I am now in—so quiet and sure of myself. When the feeling comes over me there is a directness and simplicity in me that makes me love myself. To myself at such times I say strong sweet words.

I am on a couch by this window and I could ask a woman to come here to lie with me, or a man either for that matter.

I could take a row of houses standing on a street, tip them over, empty the people out of them, squeeze and compress all the people into one person and love that person.

Do you see this hand? Suppose it held a knife that could cut down through all the falseness in you. Suppose it could cut down through the sides of buildings and houses where thousands of people now lie asleep.

It would be something worth thinking about if the fingers of this hand gripped a knife that could cut and rip through all the ugly husks in which millions of lives are enclosed.

Well, there is the idea you see, a kind of power that could be tender too. I will quote you just one more of his things, a more gentle one. It is called in the book, "Number Eighty-three."

I am a tree that grows beside the wall. I have been thrusting up and up. My body is covered with scars. My body is old but still I thrust upward, creeping toward the top of the wall.

It is my desire to drop blossoms and fruit over the wall.

I would moisten dry lips.

I would drop blossoms on the heads of children, over the top of the wall.

I would caress with falling blossoms the bodies of those who live on the further side of the wall.

My branches are creeping upward and new sap comes into me out of the dark ground under the wall.

My fruit shall not be my fruit until it drops from my arms, into the arms of the others, over the top of the wall.

And now as to the life led by the man and woman in the large upper room in that old frame house. By a stroke of luck I have recently got rather a line on that by a discovery I have made.

After they had moved into the house—it was only last spring—the theatre in which the woman was employed was dark for a long time and they were more than usually hard up, so the woman tried to pick up a little extra money—to help pay the rent I suppose—by sub-letting the two little back rooms of that place of theirs.

Various people lived in the dark tiny holes, just how I can't make out as there was no furniture. Still there are places in Chicago called "flops" where one may sleep on the floor for five or ten cents and they are more patronized than respectable people know anything about.

What I did discover was a little woman—she wasn't so young but she was hunchbacked and small and it is hard not to think of her as a girl—who once lived in one of the rooms for several weeks. She had a job as ironer in a small hand-laundry in the neighborhood and someone had given her a cheap folding cot. She was a curiously sentimental creature, with the kind of hurt eyes deformed people often have, and I have a fancy she had herself a romantic attachment of a sort for the man Wilson. Anyway I managed to find out a lot from her.

After the other woman's death and after Wilson had been cleared on the murder charge, by the confession of the stage hand, I used to go over to the house where he had lived, sometimes in the late afternoon after our paper had been put to bed for the day. Ours is an afternoon paper and after two o'clock most of us are free.

I found the hunchback girl standing in front of the house one day and began talking with her. She was a gold mine.

There was that look in her eyes I've told you of, the hurt sensitive look. I just spoke to her and we began talking of Wilson. She had lived in one of the rooms at the back. She told me of that at once.

On some days she found herself unable to work at the laundry because her strength suddenly gave out and so, on such days, she stayed in the room, lying on the cot. Blinding headaches came that lasted for hours during which she was almost entirely unconscious of everything going on about her. Then afterward she was quite conscious but for a long time very weak. She wasn't one who is destined to live very long I suppose and I presume she didn't much care.

Anyway, there she was in the room, in that weak state after the times of illness, and she grew curious about the two people in the front room, so she used to get off her cot and go softly in her stockinged feet to the door between the rooms and peek through the keyhole. She had to kneel on the dusty floor to do it.

The life in the room fascinated her from the beginning. Sometimes the man was in there alone, sitting at the kitchen table and writing the stuff he afterward put into the book I collared, and from which I have quoted; sometimes the woman was with him, and again sometimes he was in there alone but wasn't writing. Then he was always walking and walking up and down.

When both people were in the room, and when the man was writing, the woman seldom moved but sat in a chair by one of the windows with her hands crossed. He would write a few lines and then walk up and down talking to himself or to her. When he spoke she did not answer except with her eyes, the crippled girl said. What I gathered of all this from her talk with me, and what is the product of my own imaginings, I confess I do not quite know.

Anyway what I got and what I am trying, in my own way, to transmit to you is a sense of a kind of strangeness in the relationship of the two. It wasn't just a domestic household, a little down on its luck, by any means. He was trying to do something very difficult—with his poetry I presume—and she in her own way was trying to help him.

And of course, as I have no doubt you have gathered from what I have quoted of Wilson's verse, the matter had something to do with the relationships between people—not necessarily between the particular man and woman who happened to be there in that room, but between all peoples.

The fellow had some half-mystic conception of all such things, and before he found his own woman had been going aimlessly about the world looking for a mate. Then he had found the woman in the Kansas town and—he at least thought —things had cleared, for him.

Well, he had the notion that no one in the world could think or feel anything alone, and that people only got into trouble and walled themselves in by trying it, or something of the sort. There was a discord. Things were jangled. Someone, it seems, had to strike a pitch that all voices could take up before the real song of life could begin. Mind you I'm not putting forth any notions of my own. What I am trying to do is to give you a sense of something I got from having read Wilson's stuff, from having known him a little, and from having seen something of the effect of his personality upon others.

He felt, quite definitely, that no one in the world could feel or even think alone. And then there was the notion, that if one tried to think with the mind without taking the body into account, one got all balled-up. True conscious life built itself up like a pyramid. First the body and mind of a beloved one must come into one's thinking and feeling and then, in some mystic way, the bodies and minds of all the other people in the world must come in, must come sweeping in like a great wind—or something of the sort.

Is all this a little tangled up to you, who read my story of Wilson? It may not be. It may be that your minds are more clear than my own and that what I take to be so difficult will be very simple to you.

However, I have to bring up to you just what I can find, after diving down into this sea of motives and impulses—I admit I don't rightly understand.

The hunchback girl felt (or is it my own fancy coloring what she said?)—it doesn't really matter. The thing to get at is what the man Edgar Wilson felt.

He felt, I fancy, that in the field of poetry he had something to express that could never be expressed until he had found a woman who could, in a peculiar and absolute way, give herself in the world of the flesh—and that then there was to be a marriage out of which beauty would come for all people. He had to find the woman who had that power, and the power had to be untainted by self-interest, I fancy. A profound egotist, you see—and he thought he had found what he needed in the wife of the Kansas druggist.

He had found her and had done something to her. What it was I can't quite make out, except that she was absolutely and wholly happy with him, in a strangely inexpressive sort of way.

Trying to speak of him and his influence on others is rather like trying to walk on a tightrope stretched between two tall buildings above a crowded street. A cry from below, a laugh, the honk of an automobile horn, and down one goes into nothingness. One simply becomes ridiculous.

He wanted, it seems, to condense the flesh and the spirit of himself and his woman into his poems. You will remember that in one of the things of his I have quoted he speaks of condensing, of squeezing all the people of a city into one person and of loving that person.

One might think of him as a powerful person, almost hideously powerful. You will see, as you read, how he has got me in his power and is making me serve his purpose.

And he had caught and was holding the woman in his grip. He had wanted her—quite absolutely, and had taken her—as all men, perhaps, want to do with their women, and don't quite dare. Perhaps too she was in her own way greedy and he was making actual love to her always day and night, when they were together and when they were apart.

I'll admit I am confused about the whole matter myself. I am trying to express something I have felt, not in myself, nor in the words that came to me from the lips of the hunchback girl whom, you will remember, I left kneeling on the floor in that back room and peeking through a keyhole.

There she was, you see, the hunchback, and in the room before her were the man and woman and the hunchback girl also had fallen under the power of the man Wilson. She also was in love with him—there can be no doubt of that. The room in which she knelt was dark and dusty. There must have been a thick accumulation of dust on the floor.

What she said—or if she did not say the words what she made me feel was that the man Wilson worked in the room, or walked up and down in there before his woman, and that, while he did that, his woman sat in the chair, and that there was in her face, in her eyes, a look—

He was all the time making love to her, and his making love to her in just that abstract way, was a kind of love-making with all people? and that was possible because the woman was as purely physical as he was something else. If all this is meaningless to you, at least it wasn't to the hunchback girl—who certainly was uneducated and never would have set herself up as having any special powers of understanding. She knelt in the dust, listening, and looking in at the keyhole, and in the end she came to feel that the man, in whose presence she had never been and whose person had never in any way touched her person, had made love to her also.

She had felt that and it had gratified her entire nature. One might say it had satisfied her. She was what she was and it had made life worth living for her.

Minor things happened in the room and one may speak of them.

For example, there was a day in June, a dark warm rainy day. The hunchback girl was in her room, kneeling on the floor, and Wilson and his woman were in their room.

Wilson's woman had been doing a family washing, and as it could not be dried outdoors she had stretched ropes across the room and had hung the clothes inside.

When the clothes were all hung Wilson came from walking outside in the rain and going to the desk sat down and began to write.

He wrote for a few minutes and then got up and went about the room, and in a walking a wet garment brushed against his face.

He kept right on walking and talking to the woman but as he walked and talked he gathered all the clothes in his arms and going to the little landing at the head of the stairs outside, threw them down into the muddy yard below. He did that and the woman sat without moving or saying anything until he had gone back to his desk, then she went down the stairs, got the clothes and washed them again—and it was only after she had done that and when she was again hanging them in the room above that he appeared to know what he had done.

While the clothes were being rewashed he went for another walk and when she heard his footsteps on the stairs the hunchback girl ran to the keyhole. As she knelt there, and as he came into the room, she could look directly into his face. "He was like a puzzled child for a moment and then, although he said nothing, the tears began to run down his cheeks," she said. That happened and then the woman, who was at the moment re-hanging the clothes, turned and saw him. She had her arm filled with clothes but dropped them on the floor and ran to him. She half knelt, the hunchback girl said, and putting her arms about his body and looking up into his face pleaded with him. "Don't. Don't be hurt. Believe me I know everything. Please don't be hurt," was what she said.

And now as to the story of the woman's death. It happened in the fall of that year.

In the place where she was sometimes employed—that is to say in the theatre—there was this other man, the little half-crazed stage-hand who shot her.

He had fallen in love with her and, like the men in the Kansas town from which she came, had written her several silly notes of which she said nothing to Wilson. The letters weren't very nice and some of them, the most unpleasant ones, were by some twist of the fellow's mind, signed with Wilson's name. Two of them were afterwards found on her person and were brought in as evidence against Wilson during his trial.

And so the woman worked in the theatre and the summer had passed and on an evening in the fall there was to be a dress rehearsal at the theatre and the woman went there, taking Wilson with her. It was a fall day, such as we sometimes have in Chicago, cold and wet and with a heavy fog lying over the city.

The dress rehearsal did not come off. The star was ill, or something of the sort happened, and Wilson and his woman sat about, in the cold empty theatre, for an hour or two and then the woman was told she could go for the night.

She and Wilson walked across the city, stopping to get something to eat at a small restaurant. He was in one of the abstract silent moods common to him. No doubt he was thinking of the things he wanted to express in the poetry I have tried to tell you about. He went along, not seeing the woman beside him, not seeing the people drifting up to them and passing them in the streets. He went along in that way and she—

She was no doubt then as she always was in his presence— silent and satisfied with the fact that she was with him. There was nothing he could think or feel that did not take her into account. The very blood flowing up through his body was her blood too. He had made her feel that, and she was silent and satisfied as he went along, his body walking beside her but his fancy groping its way through the land of high walls and deep wells.

They had walked from the restaurant, in the Loop District, over a bridge to the North Side, and still no words passed between them.

When they had almost reached their own place the stage-hand, the small man with the nervous hands who had written the notes, appeared out of the fog, as though out of nowhere, and shot the woman.

That was all there was to it. It was as simple as that.

They were walking, as I have described them, when a head flashed up before the woman in the midst of the fog, a hand shot out, there was the quick abrupt sound of a pistol shot and then the absurd little stage-hand, he with the wrinkled impotent little old woman's face—then he turned and ran away.

All that happened, just as I have written it and it made no impression at all on the mind of Wilson. He walked along as though nothing had happened and the woman, after half falling, gathered herself together and managed to continue walking beside him, still saying nothing.

They went thus, for perhaps two blocks, and had reached the foot of the outer stairs that led up to their place when a policeman came running, and the woman told him a lie. She told him some story about a struggle between two drunken men, and after a moment of talk the policeman went away, sent away by the woman in a direction opposite to the one taken by the fleeing stage-hand.

They were in the darkness and the fog now and the woman took her man's arm while they climbed the stairs. He was as yet—as far as I will ever be able to explain logically—unaware of the shot, and of the fact that she was dying, although he had seen and heard everything. What the doctors said, who were put on the case afterwards, was that a cord or muscle, or something of the sort that controls the action of the heart, had been practically severed by the shot.

She was dead and alive at the same time, I should say.

Anyway the two people marched up the stairs, and into the room above, and then a really dramatic and lovely thing happened. One wishes that the scene, with just all its connotations, could be played out on a stage instead of having to be put down in words.

The two came into the room, the one dead but not ready to acknowledge death without a flash of something individual and lovely, that is to say, the one dead while still alive and the other alive but at the moment dead to what was going on.

The room into which they went was dark but, with the sure instinct of an animal, the woman walked across the room to the fireplace, while the man stopped and stood some ten feet from the door—thinking and thinking in his peculiarly abstract way. The fireplace was filled with an accumulation of waste matter, cigarette ends—the man was a hard smoker—bits of paper on which he had scribbled—the rubbishy accumulation that gathers about all such fellows as Wilson. There was all of this quickly combustible material, stuffed into the fireplace, on this—the first cold evening of the fall.

And so the woman went to it, and found a match somewhere in the darkness, and touched the pile off.

There is a picture that will remain with me always—just that —the barren room and the blind unseeing man standing there, and the woman kneeling and making a little flare of beauty at the last. Little flames leaped up. Lights crept and danced over the walls. Below, on the floor of the room, there was a deep well of darkness in which the man, blind with his own purpose, was standing.

The pile of burning papers must have made, for a moment,

quite a glare of light in the room and the woman stood for a moment, beside the fireplace, just outside the glare of light.

And then, pale and wavering, she walked across the light, as across a lighted stage, going softly and silently toward him. Had she also something to say? No one will ever know. What happened was that she said nothing.

She walked across to him and, at the moment she reached him, fell down on the floor and died at his feet, and at the same moment the little fire of papers died. If she struggled before she died, there on the floor, she struggled in silence. There was no sound. She had fallen and lay between him and the door that led out to the stairway and to the street.

It was then Wilson became altogether inhuman—too much so for my understanding.

The fire had died and the woman he had loved had died.

And there he stood looking into nothingness, thinking— God knows—perhaps of nothingness.

He stood a minute, five minutes, perhaps ten. He was a man who, before he found the woman, had been sunk far down into a deep sea of doubt and questionings. Before he found the woman no expression had ever come from him. He had per-haps just wandered from place to place, looking at people's faces, wondering about people, wanting to come close to others and not knowing how. The woman had been able to lift him up to the surface of the sea of life for a time, and with her he had floated on the surface of the sea, under the sky, in the sunlight. The woman's warm body—given to him in love—had been as a boat in which he had floated on the surface of the sea, and now the boat had been wrecked and he was sinking again, back into the sea.

All of this had happened and he did not know—that is to say he did not know, and at the same time he did know.

He was a poet, I presume, and perhaps at the moment a new poem was forming itself in his mind.

At any rate he stood for a time, as I have said, and then he must have had a feeling that he should make some move, that he should if possible save himself from some disaster about to overtake him.

He had an impulse to go to the door, and by way of the

stairway, to go down stairs and into the street.—but the body of the woman was between him and the door.

What he did and what, when he later told of it, sounded so terribly cruel to others, was to treat the woman's dead body as one might treat a fallen tree in the darkness in a forest. First he tried to push the body aside with his foot and then as that seemed impossible, he stepped awkwardly over it.

He stepped directly on the woman's arm. The discolored mark where his heel landed was afterward found on the body.

He almost fell, and then his body righted itself and he went walking, marched down the rickety stairs and went walking in the streets.

By chance the night had cleared. It had grown colder and a cold wind had driven the fog away. He walked along, very nonchalantly, for several blocks. He walked along as calmly as you, the reader, might walk, after having had lunch with a friend.

As a matter of fact he even stopped to make a purchase at a store. I remember that the place was called "The Whip." He went in, bought himself a package of cigarettes, lighted one and stood a moment, apparently listening to a conversation going on among several idlers in the place.

And then he strolled again, going along smoking the cigarette and thinking of his poem no doubt. Then he came to a moving picture theatre.

That perhaps touched him off. He also was an old fireplace, stuffed with old thoughts, scraps of unwritten poems—God knows what rubbish! Often he had gone at night to the theatre, where the woman was employed, to walk home with her, and now the people were coming out of a small moving-picture house. They had been in there seeing a play called "The Light of the World."

Wilson walked into the midst of the crowd, lost himself in the crowd, smoking his cigarette, and then he took off his hat, looked anxiously about for a moment, and suddenly began shouting in a loud voice.

He stood there, shouting and trying to tell the story of what had happened in a loud voice, and with the uncertain air of one trying to remember a dream. He did that for a moment and then, after running a little way along the pavement, stopped and began his story again. It was only after he had gone thus, in short rushes, back along the street to the house and up the rickety stairway to where the woman was lying— the crowd following curiously at his heels—that a policeman came up and arrested him.

He seemed excited at first but was quiet afterwards and he laughed at the notion of insanity, when the lawyer who had been retained for him, tried to set up the plea in court.

As I have said his action, during his trial, was confusing to us all, as he seemed wholly uninterested in the murder and in his own fate. After the confession of the man who had fired the shot he seemed to feel no resentment toward him either. There was something he wanted, having nothing to do with what had happened.

There he had been, you see, before he found the woman, wandering about in the world, digging himself deeper and deeper into the deep wells he talked about in his poetry, building the wall between himself and all us others constantly higher and higher.

He knew what he was doing but he could not stop. That's what he kept talking about, pleading with people about. The man had come up out of the sea of doubt, had grasped for a time the hand of the woman, and with her hand in his had floated for a time upon the surface of life—but now he felt himself again sinking down into the sea.

His talking and talking, stopping people in the street and talking, going into people's houses and talking, was I presume but an effort, he was always afterward making, not to sink back forever into the sea, it was the struggle of a drowning man I dare say.

At any rate I have told you the man's story—have been compelled to try to tell you his story. There was a kind of power in him, and the power has been exerted over me as it was exerted over the woman from Kansas and the unknown hunchback girl, kneeling on the floor in the dust and peering through a keyhole.

Ever since the woman died we have all been trying and trying to drag the man Wilson back out of the sea of doubt and dumbness into which we feel him sinking deeper and deeper— and to no avail.

It may be I have been impelled to tell his story in the hope that by writing of him I may myself understand. Is there not a possibility that with understanding would come also the strength to thrust an arm down into the sea and drag the man Wilson back to the surface again?

An Ohio Pagan

TOM EDWARDS was a Welshman, born in Northern Ohio, and a descendant of that Thomas Edwards, the Welsh poet, who was called, in his own time and country, Twn O'r Nant—which in our own tongue means "Tom of the dingle or vale."

The first Thomas Edwards was a gigantic figure in the history of the spiritual life of the Welsh. Not only did he write many stirring interludes concerning life, death, earth, fire and water but as a man he was a true brother to the elements and to all the passions of his sturdy and musical race. He sang beautifully but he also played stoutly and beautifully the part of a man. There is a wonderful tale, told in Wales and written into a book by the poet himself, of how he, with a team of horses, once moved a great ship out of the land into the sea, after three hundred Welshmen had failed at the task. Also he taught Welsh woodsmen the secret of the crane and pulley for lifting great logs in the forests, and once he fought to the point of death the bully of the countryside, a man known over a great part of Wales as The Cruel Fighter. Tom Edwards, the descendant of this man was born in Ohio near my own native town of Bidwell. His name was not Edwards, but as his father was dead when he was born, his mother gave him the old poet's name out of pride in having such blood in her veins. Then when the boy was six his mother died also and the man for whom both his mother and father had worked, a sporting farmer named Harry Whitehead, took the boy into his own house to live.

They were gigantic people, the Whiteheads. Harry himself weighed two hundred and seventy pounds and his wife twenty pounds more. About the time he took young Tom to live with him the farmer became interested in the racing of horses, moved off his farms, of which he had three, and came to live in our town.

In the town of Bidwell there was an old frame building, that had once been a factory for the making of barrel staves but that had stood for years vacant, staring with windowless eyes into the streets, and Harry bought it at a low price and transformed it into a splendid stable with a board floor and two long rows of box stalls. At a sale of blooded horses held in the city of Cleveland he bought twenty young colts, all of the trotting strain, and set up as a trainer of race horses.

Among the colts thus brought to our town was one great black fellow named Bucephalus. Harry got the name from John Telfer, our town poetry lover. "It was the name of the mighty horse of a mighty man," Telfer said, and that satisfied Harry.

Young Tom was told off to be the special guardian and caretaker of Bucephalus, and the black stallion, who had in him the mighty blood of the Tennessee Patchens, quickly became the pride of the stables. He was in his nature a great ugly-tempered beast, as given to whims and notions as an opera star, and from the very first began to make trouble. Within a year no one but Harry Whitehead himself and the boy Tom dared go into his stall. The methods of the two people with the great horse were entirely different but equally effective. Once big Harry turned the stallion loose on the floor of the stable, closed all the doors, and with a cruel long whip in his hand, went in to conquer or to be conquered. He came out victorious and ever after the horse behaved when he was about.

The boy's method was different. He loved Bucephalus and the wicked animal loved him. Tom slept on a cot in the barn and day or night, even when there were mares about, walked into Bucephalus' box-stall without fear. When the stallion was in a temper he sometimes turned at the boy's entrance and with a snort sent his iron-shod heels banging against the sides of the stall, but Tom laughed and putting a simple rope halter over the horse's head led him forth to be cleaned or hitched to a cart for his morning's jog on our town's half-mile race track. A sight it was to see the boy with the blood of Twn O'r Nant in his veins leading by the nose Bucephalus of the royal blood of the Patchens.

When he was six years old the horse Bucephalus went forth

to race and conquer at the great spring race meeting at Columbus, Ohio. He won two heats of the trotting free-for-all—the great race of the meeting—with heavy Harry in the sulky and then faltered. A gelding named "Light o' the Orient" beat him in the next heat. Tom, then a lad of sixteen, was put into the sulky and the two of them, horse and boy, fought out a royal battle with the gelding and a little bay mare, that hadn't been heard from before but that suddenly developed a whirl-wind burst of speed.

The big stallion and the slender boy won. From amid a mob of cursing, shouting, whip-slashing men a black horse shot out and a pale boy, leaning far forward, called and murmured to him. "Go on, boy! Go boy! Go boy!" the lad's voice had called over and over all through the race. Bucephalus got a record of 2.06 1/4 and Tom Edwards became a newspaper hero. His picture was in the Cleveland *Leader* and the Cincinnati *Enquirer*, and when he came back to Bidwell we other boys fairly wept in our envy of him.

Then it was however that Tom Edwards fell down from his high place. There he was, a tall boy, almost of man's stature and, except for a few months during the winters when he lived on the Whitehead farms, and between his sixth and thirteenth years, when he had attended a country school and had learned to read and write and do sums, he was without education. And now, during that very fall of the year of his triumph at Columbus, the Bidwell truant officer, a thin man with white hair, who was also superintendent of the Baptist Sunday School, came one afternoon to the Whitehead stables and told him that if he did not begin going to school both he and his employer would get into serious trouble.

Harry Whitehead was furious and so was Tom. There he was, a great tall slender fellow who had been with race horses to the fairs all over Northern Ohio and Indiana, during that very fall, and who had just come home from the journey during which he had driven the winner in the free-for-all trot at a Grand Circuit meeting and had given Bucephalus a mark of 2.06 1/4.

Was such a fellow to go sit in a schoolroom, with a silly school book in his hand, reading of the affairs of the men who dealt in butter, eggs, potatoes and apples, and whose unnecessarily complicated business life the children were asked to unravel,—was such a fellow to go sit in a room, under the eyes of a woman teacher, and in the company of boys half his age and with none of his wide experience of life?

It was a hard thought and Tom took it hard. The law was all right, Harry Whitehead said, and was intended to keep no-account kids off the streets but what it had to do with himself Tom couldn't make out. When the truant officer had gone and Tom was left alone in the stable with his employer the man and boy stood for a long time glumly staring at each other. It was all right to be educated but Tom felt he had book education enough. He could read, write and do sums, and what other book-training did a horseman need? As for books, they were all right for rainy evenings when there were no men sitting by the stable door and talking of horses and races. And also when one went to the races in a strange town and arrived, perhaps on Sunday, and the races did not begin until the following Wednesday—it was all right then to have a book in the chest with the horse blankets. When the weather was fine and the work was all done on a fine fall afternoon, and the other swipes, both niggers and whites, had gone off to town, one could take a book out under a tree and read of life in far away places that was as strange and almost as fascinating as one's own life. Tom had read "Robinson Crusoe," "Uncle Tom's Cabin" and "Tales from the Bible," all of which he had found in the Whitehead house and Jacob Friedman, the school superintendent at Bidwell, who had a fancy for horses, had loaned him other books that he intended reading during the coming winter. They were in his chest—one called "Gulliver's Travels" and the other "Moll Flanders."

And now the law said he must give up being a horseman and go every day to a school and do little foolish sums, he who had already proven himself a man. What other schoolboy knew what he did about life? Had he not seen and spoken to several of the greatest men of this world, men who had driven horses to beat world records, and did they not respect him? When he became a driver of race horses such men as Pop Geers, Walter Cox, John Splan, Murphy and the others would not ask him what books he had read, or how many feet make a rod and how many rods in a mile. In the race at Columbus, where he had won his spurs as a driver, he had already proven that life had given him the kind of education he needed. The driver of the gelding "Light o' the Orient" had tried to bluff him in that third heat and had not succeeded. He was a big man with a black mustache and had lost one eye so that he looked fierce and ugly, and when the two horses were fighting it out, neck and neck, up the back stretch, and when Tom was tooling Bucephalus smoothly and surely to the front, the older man turned in his sulky to glare at him. "You damned little whipper-snapper," he yelled, "I'll knock you out of your sulky if you don't take back."

He had yelled that at Tom and then had struck at the boy with the butt of his whip—not intending actually to hit him perhaps but just missing the boy's head, and Tom had kept his eyes steadily on his own horse, had held him smoothly in his stride and at the upper turn, at just the right moment, had begun to pull out in front.

Later he hadn't even told Harry Whitehead of the incident, and that fact too, he felt vaguely, had something to do with his qualifications as a man.

And now they were going to put him into a school with the kids. He was at work on the stable floor, rubbing the legs of a trim-looking colt, and Bucephalus was in his stall waiting to be taken to a late fall meeting at Indianapolis on the following Monday, when the blow fell. Harry Whitehead walked back and forth swearing at the two men who were loafing in chairs at the stable door. "Do you call that law, eh, robbing a kid of the chance Tom's got?" he asked, shaking a riding whip under their noses. "I never see such a law. What I say is Dod blast such a law."

Tom took the colt back to its place and went into Bucephalus' box-stall. The stallion was in one of his gentle moods and turned to have his nose rubbed, but Tom went and buried his face against the great black neck and for a long time stood thus, trembling. He had thought perhaps Harry would let him drive Bucephalus in all his races another season and now that was all to come to an end and he was to be pitched back into childhood, to be made just a kid in school. "I won't do it," he decided suddenly and a dogged light came into his eyes. His future as a driver of race horses might have to be sacrificed but that didn't matter so much as the humiliation of this other, and he decided he would say nothing to Harry Whitehead or his wife but would make his own move.

"I'll get out of here. Before they get me into that school I'll skip out of town," he told himself as his hand crept up and fondled the soft nose of Bucephalus, the son royal of the Patchens.

Tom left Bidwell during the night, going east on a freight train, and no one there ever saw him again. During that winter he lived in the city of Cleveland, where he got work driving a milk wagon in a district where factory workers lived.

Then spring came again and with it the memory of other springs—of thunder-showers rolling over fields of wheat, just appearing, green and vivid, out of the black ground—of the sweet smell of new plowed fields, and most of all the smell and sound of animals about barns at the Whitehead farms north of Bidwell. How sharply he remembered those days on the farms and the days later when he lived in Bidwell, slept in the stables and went each morning to jog race horses and young colts round and round the half-mile race track at the fair grounds at Bidwell.

That was a life! Round and round the track they went, young colthood and young manhood together, not thinking but carrying life very keenly within themselves and feeling tremendously. The colt's legs were to be hardened and their wind made sound and for the boy long hours were to be spent in a kind of dream world, and life lived in the company of something fine, courageous, filled with a terrible, waiting surge of life. At the fair ground, away at the town's edge, tall grass grew in the enclosure inside the track and there were trees from which came the voices of squirrels, chattering and scolding, accompanied by the call of nesting birds and, down below on the ground, by the song of bees visiting early blossoms and of insects hidden away in the grass.

How different the life of the city streets in the springtime! To Tom it was in a way fetid and foul. For months he had been living in a boarding house with some six, and often eight or ten, other young fellows, in narrow rooms above a foul street. The young fellows were unmarried and made good wages, and on the winter evenings and on Sundays they dressed in good

clothes and went forth, to return later, half drunk, to sit for
long hours boasting and talking loudly in the rooms. Because
he was shy, often lonely and sometimes startled and frightened
by what he saw and heard in the city, the others would have
nothing to do with Tom. They felt a kind of contempt for him,
looked upon him as a "rube" and in the late afternoon when
his work was done he often went for long walks alone in grim
streets of workingmen's houses, breathing the smoke-laden air
and listening to the roar and clatter of machinery in great factories. At other times and immediately after the evening meal
he went off to his room and to bed, half sick with fear and with
some strange nameless dread of the life about him.

And so in the early summer of his seventeenth year Tom left
the city and going back into his own Northern Ohio lake
country found work with a man name John Bottsford who
owned a threshing outfit and worked among the farmers of
Erie County, Ohio. The slender boy, who had urged Bucephalus to his greatest victory and had driven him the fastest mile
of his career, had become a tall strong fellow with heavy features, brown eyes, and big nerveless hands—but in spite of his
apparent heaviness there was something tremendously alive in
him. He now drove a team of plodding grey farm horses and it
was his job to keep the threshing engine supplied with water
and fuel and to haul the threshed grain out of the fields and
into farmers' barns.

The thresherman Bottsford was a broad-shouldered, powerful old man of sixty and had, besides Tom, three grown sons in
his employ. He had been a farmer, working on rented land, all
his life and had saved some money, with which he had bought
the threshing outfit, and all day the five men worked like
driven slaves and at night slept in the hay in the farmers' barns.
It was rainy that season in the lake country and at the beginning of the time of threshing things did not go very well for
Bottsford.

The old thresherman was worried. The threshing venture
had taken all of his money and he had a dread of going into
debt and, as he was a deeply religious man, at night when he
thought the others asleep, he crawled out of the hayloft and
went down onto the barn floor to pray.

Something happened to Tom and for the first time in his life he began to think about life and its meaning. He was in the country, that he loved, in the yellow sunwashed fields, far from the dreaded noises and dirt of city life, and here was a man, of his own type, in some deep way a brother to himself, who was continuously crying out to some power outside himself, some power that was in the sun, in the clouds, in the roaring thunder that accompanied the summer rains—that was in these things and that at the same time controlled all these things.

The young threshing apprentice was impressed. Throughout the rainy days, when no work could be done, he wandered about and waited for night, and then, when they all had gone into the barn loft and the others prepared to sleep, he stayed awake to think and listen. He thought of God and of the possibilities of God's part in the affairs of men. The thresherman's youngest son, a fat jolly fellow, lay beside him and, for a time after they had crawled into the hay, the two boys whispered and laughed together. The fat boy's skin was sensitive and the dry broken ends of grass stalks crept down under his clothes and tickled him. He giggled and twisted about, wriggling and kicking and Tom looked at him and laughed also. The thoughts of God went out of his mind.

In the barn all became quiet and when it rained a low drumming sound went on overhead. Tom could hear the horses and cattle, down below, moving about. The smells were all delicious smells. The smell of the cows in particular awoke something heady in him. It was as though he had been drinking strong wine. Every part of his body seemed alive. The two older boys, who like their father had serious natures, lay with their feet buried in the hay. They lay very still and a warm musty smell arose from their clothes, that were full of the sweat of toil. Presently the bearded old thresherman, who slept off by himself, arose cautiously and walked across the hay in his stockinged feet. He went down a ladder to the floor below, and Tom listened eagerly. The fat boy snored but he was quite sure that the older boys were awake like himself. Every sound from below was magnified. He heard a horse stamp on the barn floor and a cow rub her horns against a feed box. The old thresherman prayed fervently, calling on the name of Jesus to help him out of his difficulty. Tom could not hear all his words but some of them came to him quite clearly and one group of words ran like a refrain through the thresherman's prayer. "Gentle Jesus," he cried, "send the good days. Let the good days come quickly. Look out over the land. Send us the fair warm days."

Came the warm fair days and Tom wondered. Late every morning, after the sun had marched far up into the sky and after the machines were set by a great pile of wheat bundles he drove his tank wagon off to be filled at some distant creek or at a pond. Sometimes he was compelled to drive two or three miles to the lake. Dust gathered in the roads and the horses plodded along. He passed through a grove of trees and went down a lane and into a small valley where there was a spring and he thought of the old man's words, uttered in the silence and the darkness of the barns. He made himself a figure of Jesus as a young god walking about over the land. The young god went through the lanes and through the shaded covered places. The feet of the horses came down with a thump in the dust of the road and there was an echoing thump far away in the wood. Tom leaned forward and listened and his cheeks became a little pale. He was no longer the growing man but had become again the fine and sensitive boy who had driven Bucephalus through a mob of angry, determined men to victory. For the first time the blood of the old poet Twn O'r Nat awoke in him.

The water boy for the threshing crew rode the horse Pegasus down through the lanes back of the farm houses in Erie County, Ohio, to the creeks where the threshing tanks must be filled. Beside him on the soft earth in the forest walked the young god Jesus. At the creek Pegasus, born of the springs of Ocean, stamped on the ground. The plodding farm horses stopped. With a dazed look in his eyes Tom Edwards arose from the wagon seat and prepared his hose and pump for filling the tank. The god Jesus walked away over the land, and with a wave of his hand summoned the smiling days.

A light came into Tom Edwards' eyes and grace seemed to come also into his heavy maturing body. New impulses came to him. As the threshing crew went about, over the roads and through the villages from farm to farm, women and young girls looked at the young man and smiled. Sometimes as he came from the fields to a farmer's barn, with a load of wheat in bags on his wagon, the daughter of the farmer stepped out of the farm house and stood looking at him. Tom looked at the woman and hunger crept into his heart and, in the evenings while the thresherman and his sons sat on the ground by the barns and talked of their affairs, he walked nervously about. Making a motion to the fat boy, who was not really interested in the talk of his father and brothers, the two younger men went to walk in the nearby fields and on the roads. Sometimes they stumbled along a country road in the dusk of the evening and came into the lighted streets of a town. Under the store-lights young girls walked about. The two boys stood in the shadows by a building and watched and later, as they went homeward in the darkness, the fat boy expressed what they both felt. They passed through a dark place where the road wound through a wood. In silence the frogs croaked, and birds roosting in the trees were disturbed by their presence and fluttered about. The fat boy wore heavy overalls and his fat legs rubbed against each other. The rough cloth made a queer creaking sound. He spoke passionately. "I would like to hold a woman, tight, tight, tight," he said.

One Sunday the thresherman took his entire crew with him to a church. They had been working near a village called Castalia, but did not go into the town but to a small white frame church that stood amid trees and by a stream at the side of a road, a mile north of the village. They went on Tom's water wagon, from which they had lifted the tank and placed boards for seats. The boy drove the horses.

Many teams were tied in the shade under the trees in a little grove near the church, and strange men—farmers and their sons—stood about in little groups and talked of the season's crops. Although it was hot, a breeze played among the leaves of the trees under which they stood, and back of the church and the grove the stream ran over stones and made a persistent soft murmuring noise that arose above the hum of voices.

In the church Tom sat beside the fat boy who stared at the country girls as they came in and who, after the sermon began, went to sleep while Tom listened eagerly to the sermon. The minister, an old man with a beard and a strong sturdy body, looked, he thought not unlike his employer Bottsford the thresherman.

The minister in the country church talked of that time when

Mary Magdalene, the woman who had been taken in adultery, was being stoned by the crowd of men who had forgotten their own sins and when, in the tale the minister told, Jesus approached and rescued the woman Tom's heart thumped with excitement. Then later the minister talked of how Jesus was tempted by the devil, as he stood on a high place in the mountain, but the boy did not listen. He leaned forward and looked out through a window across fields and the minister's words came to him but in broken sentences. Tom took what was said concerning the temptation on the mountain to mean that Mary had followed Jesus and had offered her body to him, and that afternoon, when he had returned with the others to the farm where they were to begin threshing on the next morning, he called the fat boy aside and asked his opinion.

The two boys walked across a field of wheat-stubble and sat down on a log in a grove of trees. It had never occurred to Tom that a man could be tempted by a woman. It had always seemed to him that it must be the other way, that women must always be tempted by men. "I thought men always asked," he said, "and now it seems that women sometimes do the asking. That would be a fine thing if it could happen to us. Don't you think so?"

The two boys arose and walked under the trees and dark shadows began to form on the ground underfoot. Tom burst into words and continually asked questions and the fat boy, who had been often to church and for whom the figure of Jesus had lost most of its reality, felt a little embarrassed. He did not think the subject should be thus freely discussed and when Tom's mind kept playing with the notion of Jesus, pursued and tempted by a woman, he grunted his disapproval. "Do you think he really refused?" Tom asked over and over. The fat boy tried to explain. "He had twelve disciples," he said. "It couldn't have happened. They were always about. Well, you see, she wouldn't ever have had no chance. Wherever he went they went with him. They were men he was teaching to preach. One of them later betrayed him to soldiers who killed him."

Tom wondered. "How did that come about? How could a man like that be betrayed?" he asked. "By a kiss," the fat boy replied.

On the evening of the day when Tom Edwards—for the first

and last time in his life—went into a church, there was a light shower, the only one that fell upon John Bottsford's threshing crew during the last three months the Welsh boy was with them and the shower in no way interfered with their work. The shower came up suddenly and a few minutes was gone. As it was Sunday and as there was no work the men had all gathered in the barn and were looking out through the open barn doors. Two or three men from the farm house came and sat with them on boxes and barrels on the barn floor and, as is customary with country people, very little was said. The men took knives out of their pockets and finding little sticks among the rubbish on the barn floor began to whittle, while the old thresherman went restlessly about with his hands in his trouser pockets. Tom who sat near the door, where an occasional drop of rain was blown against his cheek, alternately looked from his employer to the open country where the rain played over the fields. One of the farmers remarked that a rainy time had come on and that there would be no good threshing weather for several days and, while the thresherman did not answer, Tom saw his lips move and his grey beard bob up and down. He thought the thresherman was protesting but did not want to protest in words.

As they had gone about the country many rains had passed to the north, south and east of the threshing crew and on some days the clouds hung over them all day, but no rain fell and when they had got to a new place they were told it had rained there three days before. Sometimes when they left a farm Tom stood up on the seat of his water wagon and looked back. He looked across fields to where they had been at work and then looked up into the sky. "The rain may come now. The threshing is done and the wheat is all in the barn. The rain can now do no harm to our labor," he thought.

On the Sunday evening when he sat with the men on the floor of the barn Tom was sure that the shower that had now come would be but a passing affair. He thought his employer must be very close to Jesus, who controlled the affairs of the heavens, and that a long rain would not come because the thresherman did not want it. He fell into a deep reverie and John Bottsford came and stood close beside him. The thresherman put his hand against the door jamb and looked out and

Tom could still see the grey beard moving. The man was praying and was so close to himself that his trouser leg touched
Tom's hand. Into the boy's mind came the remembrance of
how John Bottsford had prayed at night on the barn floor. On
that very morning he had prayed. It was just as daylight came
and the boy was awakened because, as he crept across the hay
to descend the ladder, the old man's foot had touched his hand.

As always Tom had been excited and wanted to hear every
word said in the older man's prayers. He lay tense, listening to
every sound that came up from below. A faint glow of light
came into the hayloft, through a crack in the side of the barn,
a rooster crowed and some pigs, housed in a pen near the
barn, grunted loudly. They had heard the thresherman moving about and wanted to be fed and their grunting, and the
occasional restless movement of a horse or a cow in the stable
below, prevented Tom's hearing very distinctly. He, however,
made out that his employer was thanking Jesus for the fine
weather that had attended them and was protesting that he did
not want to be selfish in asking it to continue. "Jesus," he said,
"send, if you wish, a little shower on this day when, because of
our love for you, we do not work in the fields. Let it be fine
tomorrow but today, after we have come back from the house
of worship, let a shower freshen the land."

As Tom sat on a box near the door of the barn and saw how
aptly the words of his employer had been answered by Jesus he
knew that the rain would not last. The man for whom he
worked seemed to him so close to the throne of God that
he raised the hand, that had been touched by John Bottsford's
trouser leg to his lips and secretly kissed it—and when he looked
again out over the fields the clouds were being blown away by
a wind and the evening sun was coming out. It seemed to him
that the young and beautiful god Jesus must be right at hand,
within hearing of his voice. "He is," Tom told himself, "standing behind a tree in the orchard." The rain stopped and he
went silently out of the barn, towards a small apple orchard
that lay beside the farm house, but when he came to a fence
and was about to climb over he stopped. "If Jesus is there he
will not want me to find him," he thought. As he turned again
toward the barn he could see, across a field, a low grass-covered
hill. He decided that Jesus was not after all in the orchard. The

long slanting rays of the evening sun fell on the crest of the hill and touched with light the grass stalks, heavy with drops of rain and for a moment the hill was crowned as with a crown of jewels. A million tiny drops of water, reflecting the light, made the hilltop sparkle as though set with gems. "Jesus is there," muttered the boy. "He lies on his belly in the grass. He is looking at me over the edge of the hill."

CHAPTER II

JOHN BOTTSFORD went with his threshing crew to work for a large farmer named Barton near the town of Sandusky. The threshing season was drawing near an end and the days remained clear, cool and beautiful. The country into which he now came made a deep impression on Tom's mind and he never forgot the thoughts and experiences that came to him during the last weeks of that summer on the Barton farms.

The traction engine, puffing forth smoke and attracting the excited attention of dogs and children as it rumbled along and pulled the heavy red grain separator, had trailed slowly over miles of road and had come down almost to Lake Erie. Tom, with the fat Bottsford boy sitting beside him on the water wagon, followed the rumbling puffing engine, and when they came to the new place, where they were to stay for several days, he could see, from the wagon seat, the smoke of the factories in the town of Sandusky rising into the clear morning air.

The man for whom John Bottsford was threshing owned three farms, one on an island in the bay, where he lived, and two on the mainland, and the larger of the mainland farms had great stacks of wheat standing in a field near the barns. The farm was in a wide basin of land, very fertile, through which a creek flowed northward into Sandusky Bay and, besides the stacks of wheat in the basin, other stacks had been made in the upland fields beyond the creek, where a country of low hills began. From these latter fields the waters of the bay could be seen glistening in the bright fall sunlight and steamers went from Sandusky to a pleasure resort called Cedar Point. When the wind blew from the north or west and when the threshing machinery had been stopped at the noon hour the men, resting with their backs against a straw-stack, could hear a band playing on one of the steamers.

Fall came on early that year and the leaves on the trees in the forests that grew along the roads that ran down through the low creek bottom lands began to turn yellow and red. In the afternoons when Tom went to the creek for water he walked beside his horses and the dry leaves crackled and snapped underfoot.

As the season had been a prosperous one Bottsford decided that his youngest son should attend school in town during the fall and winter. He had bought himself a machine for cutting firewood and with his two older sons intended to take up that work. "The logs will have to be hauled out of the wood lots to where we set up the saws," he said to Tom. "You can come with us if you wish."

The thresherman began to talk to Tom of the value of learning. "You'd better go to some town yourself this winter. It would be better for you to get into a school," he said sharply. He grew excited and walked up and down beside the water wagon, on the seat of which Tom sat listening and said that God had given men both minds and bodies and it was wicked to let either decay because of neglect. "I have watched you," he said. "You don't talk very much but you do plenty of thinking, I guess. Go into the schools. Find out what the books have to say. You don't have to believe when they say things that are lies."

The Bottsford family lived in a rented house facing a stone road near the town of Bellevue, and the fat boy was to go to that town—a distance of some eighteen miles from where the men were at work—afoot, and on the evening before he set out he and Tom went out of the barns intending to have a last walk and talk together on the roads.

They went along in the dusk of the fall evening, each thinking his own thoughts, and coming to a bridge that led over the creek in the valley sat on the bridge rail. Tom had little to say but his companion wanted to talk about women and, when darkness came on, the embarrassment he felt regarding the subject went quite away and he talked boldly and freely. He said that in the town of Bellevue, where he was to live and attend school during the coming winter, he would be sure to get in with a woman. "I'm not going to be cheated out of that chance," he declared. He explained that as his father would be away from home when he moved into town he would be free to pick his own place to board.

The fat boy's imagination became inflamed and he told Tom his plans. "I won't try to get in with any young girl," he declared shrewdly. "That only gets a fellow in a fix. He might have to marry her. I'll go live in a house with a widow, that's what I'll do. And in the evening the two of us will be there alone. We'll begin to talk and I'll keep touching her with my hands. That will get her excited."

The fat boy jumped to his feet and walked back and forth on the bridge. He was nervous and a little ashamed and wanted to justify what he had said. The thing for which he hungered had he thought become a possibility—an act half achieved. Coming to stand before Tom he put a hand on his shoulder. "I'll go into her room at night," he declared. "I'll not tell her I'm coming, but will creep in when she is asleep. Then I'll get down on my knees by her bed and I'll kiss her, hard, hard. I'll hold her tight, so she can't get away and I'll kiss her mouth till she wants what I want. Then I'll stay in her house all winter. No one will know. Even if she won't have me I'll only have to move, I'm sure to be safe. No one will believe what she says, if she tells on me. I'm not going to be like a boy any more, I'll tell you what—I'm as big as a man and I'm going to do like men do, that's what I am."

The two young men went back to the barn where they were to sleep on the hay. The rich farmer for whom they were now at work had a large house and provided beds for the thresherman and his two older sons but the two younger men slept in the barn loft and on the night before had lain under one blanket. After the talk by the bridge however, Tom did not feel very comfortable and that stout exponent of manhood, the younger Bottsford, was also embarrassed. In the road the young man, whose name was Paul, walked a little ahead of his companion and when they got to the barn each sought a separate place in the loft. Each wanted to have thoughts into which he did not want the presence of the other to intrude.

For the first time Tom's body burned with eager desire for a female. He lay where he could see out through a crack, in the side of the barn, and at first his thoughts were all about animals. He had brought a horse blanket up from the stable below and crawling under it lay on his side with his eyes close to the crack and thought about the love-making of horses and cattle. Things he had seen in the stables when he worked for Whitehead, the racing man, came back to his mind and a queer animal hunger ran through him so that his legs stiffened. He rolled restlessly about on the hay and for some reason, he did not understand, his lust took the form of anger and he hated the fat boy. He thought he would like to crawl over the hay and pound his companion's face with his fists. Although he had not seen Paul Bottsford's face, when he talked of the widow, he had sensed in him a flavor of triumph. "He thinks he has got the better of me," young Edwards thought.

He rolled again to the crack and stared out into the night. There was a new moon and the fields were dimly outlined and clumps of trees, along the road that led into the town of Sandusky, looked like black clouds that had settled down over the land. For some reason the sight of the land, lying dim and quiet under the moon, took all of his anger away and he began to think, not of Paul Bottsford, with hot eager lust in his eyes, creeping into the room of the widow at Bellevue, but of the god Jesus, going up into a mountain with his woman, Mary.

His companion's notion of going into a room where a woman lay sleeping and taking her, as it were unawares, now seemed to him entirely mean and the hot jealous feeling that had turned into anger and hatred went entirely away. He tried to think what the god, who had brought the beautiful days for the threshing, would do with a woman.

Tom's body still burned with desire and his mind wanted to think lascivious thoughts. The moon that had been hidden behind clouds emerged and a wind began to blow. It was still early evening and in the town of Sandusky pleasure seekers were taking the boat to the resort over the bay and the wind brought to Tom's ears the sound of music, blown over the waters of the bay and down the creek basin. In a grove near the barn the wind swayed gently the branches of young trees and black shadows ran here and there on the ground.

The younger Bottsford had gone to sleep in a distant part of the barn loft, and now began to snore loudly. The tenseness went out of Tom's legs and he prepared to sleep but before sleeping he muttered, half timidly, certain words, that were half a prayer, half an appeal to some spirit of the night. "Jesus, bring me a woman," he whispered.

Outside the barn, in the fields, the wind, becoming a little stronger, picked up bits of straw and blew them about among the hard up-standing stubble and there was a low gentle whispering sound as though the gods were answering his appeal.

Tom went to sleep with his arm under his head and with his eye close to the crack that gave him a view of the moonlit fields, and in his dream the cry from within repeated itself over and over. The mysterious god Jesus had heard and answered the needs of his employer John Bottsford and his own need would, he was quite sure, be understood and attended to. "Bring me a woman. I need her. Jesus, bring me a woman," he kept whispering into the night, as consciousness left him and he slipped away into dreams.

After the youngest of the Bottsfords had departed a change took place in the nature of Tom's work. The threshing crew had got now into a country of large farms where the wheat had all been brought in from the fields and stacked near the barns and where there was always plenty of water near at hand. Everything was simplified. The separator was pulled in close by the barn door and the threshed grain was carried directly to the bins from the separator. As it was not a part of Tom's work to feed the bundles of grain into the whirling teeth of the separator—this work being done by John Bottsford's two elder sons—there was little for the crew's teamster to do. Sometimes John Bottsford, who was the engineer, departed, going to make arrangements for the next stop, and was gone for a half day, and at such times Tom, who had picked up some knowledge of the art, ran the engine.

On other days however there was nothing at all for him to do and his mind, unoccupied for long hours, began to play him tricks. In the morning, after his team had been fed and cleaned until the grey coats of the old farm horses shone like racers, he went out of the barn and into an orchard. Filling his pockets with ripe apples he went to a fence and leaned over. In a field young colts played about. As he held the apples and called softly they came timidly forward, stopping in alarm and then running a little forward, until one of them, bolder than the others, ate one of the apples out of his hand.

All through those bright warm clear fall days a restless feeling, it seemed to Tom, ran through everything in nature. In the clumps of woodland still standing on the farms flaming red spread itself out along the limbs of trees and there was one grove of young maple trees, near a barn, that was like a troop of girls, young girls who had walked together down a sloping field, to stop in alarm at seeing the men at work in the barnyard. Tom stood looking at the trees. A slight breeze made them sway gently from side to side. Two horses standing among the trees drew near each other. One nipped the other's neck. They rubbed their heads together.

The crew stopped at another large farm and it was to be their last stop for the season. "When we have finished this job we'll go home and get our own fall work done," Bottsford said. Saturday evening came and the thresherman and his sons took the horses and drove away, going to their own home for the Sunday, and leaving Tom alone. "We'll be back early, on Monday morning," the thresherman said as they drove away. Sunday alone among the strange farm people brought a sharp experience to Tom and when it had passed he decided he would not wait for the end of the threshing season but a few days off now—but would quit his job and go into the city and surrender to the schools. He remembered his employer's words, "Find out what the books have to say. You don't have to believe, when they say things that are lies."

As he walked in lanes, across meadows and upon the hillsides of the farm, also on the shores of Sandusky Bay, that Sunday morning Tom thought almost constantly of his friend the fat fellow, young Paul Bottsford, who had gone to spend the fall and winter at Bellevue, and wondered what his life there might be like. He had himself lived in such a town, in Bidwell, but had rarely left Harry Whitehead's stable. What went on in such a town? What happened at night in the houses of the towns? He remembered Paul's plan for getting into a house alone with a widow and how he was to creep into her room at night, holding her tightly in his arms until she wanted what he wanted. "I wonder if he will have the nerve. Gee, I wonder if he will have the nerve," he muttered.

For a long time, ever since Paul had gone away and he had no one with whom he could talk, things had taken on a new aspect in Tom's mind. The rustle of dry leaves underfoot, as he walked in a forest—the playing of shadows over the open face of a field—the murmuring song of insects in the dry grass beside the fences in the lanes—and at night the hushed contented sounds made by the animals in the barns, were no longer so sweet to him. For him no more did the young god Jesus walk beside him, just out of sight behind low hills, or down the dry beds of streams. Something within himself, that had been sleeping was now awakening. When he returned from walking in the fields on the fall evenings and, thinking of Paul Bottsford alone in the house with the widow at Bellevue, half wishing he were in the same position, he felt ashamed in the presence of the gentle old thresherman, and afterward did not lie awake listening to the older man's prayers. The men who had come from nearby farms to help with the threshing laughed and shouted to each other as they pitched the straw into great stacks or carried the filled bags of grain to the bins, and they had wives and daughters who had come with them and who were now at work in the farmhouse kitchen, from which also laughter came. Girls and women kept coming out at the kitchen door into the barnyard, tall awkward girls, plump red-cheeked girls, women with worn thin faces and sagging breasts. All men and women seemed made for each other.

They all laughed and talked together, understood one another. Only he was alone. He only had no one to whom he could feel warm and close, to whom he could draw close.

On the Sunday when the Bottsfords had all gone away Tom came in from walking all morning in the fields and ate his dinner with many other people in a big farmhouse dining room. In preparation for the threshing days ahead, and the feeding of many people, several women had come to spend the day and to help in preparing food. The farmer's daughter, who was married and lived in Sandusky, came with her husband, and three other women, neighbors, came from farms in the neighborhood. Tom did not look at them but ate his dinner in silence and as soon as he could manage got out of the house and went to the barns. Going into a long shed he sat on the tongue of a wagon, that from long disuse was covered with dust. Swallows flew back and forth among the rafters overhead and, in an upper corner of the shed where they evidently had a nest, wasps buzzed in the semi-darkness.

The daughter of the farmer, who had come from town, came from the house with a babe in her arms. It was nursing time, and she wanted to escape from the crowded house and, without having seen Tom, she sat on a box near the shed door and opened her dress. Embarrassed and at the same time fascinated by the sight of a woman's breasts, seen through cracks of the wagon box, Tom drew his legs up and his head down and remained concealed until the woman had gone back to the house. Then he went again to the fields and did not go back to the house for the evening meal.

As he walked on that Sunday afternoon the grandson of the Welsh poet experienced many new sensations. In a way he came to understand that the things Paul had talked of doing and that had, but a short time before, filled him with disgust were now possible to himself also. In the past when he had thought about women there had always been something healthy and animal-like in his lusts but now they took a new form. The passion that could not find expression through his body went up into his mind and he began to see visions. Women became to him something different than anything else in nature, more desirable than anything else in nature, and at the same time everything in nature became woman. The trees, in the apple orchard by the barn, were like the arms of women. The apples on the trees were round like the breasts of women. They were the breasts of women—and when he had got on to a low hill the contour of the fences that marked the confines of the fields fell into the forms of women's bodies. Even the clouds in the sky did the same thing.

He walked down along a lane to a stream and crossed the stream by a wooden bridge. Then he climbed another hill, the highest place in all that part of the country, and there the fever that possessed him became more active. An odd lassitude crept over him and he lay down in the grass on the hilltop and closed his eyes. For a long time he remained in a hushed, half-sleeping, dreamless state and then opened his eyes again.

Again the forms of women floated before him. To his left the bay was ruffled by a gentle breeze and far over towards the city of Sandusky two sailboats were apparently engaged in a race. The masts of the boats were fully dressed but on the great stretch of water they seemed to stand still. The bay itself, in Tom's eyes, had taken on the form and shape of a woman's head and body and the two sailboats were the woman's eyes looking at him.

The bay was a woman with her head lying where lay the city of Sandusky. Smoke arose from the stacks of steamers docked at the city's wharves and the smoke formed itself into masses of black hair. Through the farm, where he had come to thresh, ran a stream. It swept down past the foot of the hill on which he lay. The stream was the arm of the woman. Her hand was thrust into the land and the lower part of her body was lost— far down to the north, where the bay became a part of Lake Erie—but her other arm could be seen. It was outlined in the further shore of the bay. Her other arm was drawn up and her hand was pressing against her face. Her form was distorted by pain but at the same time the giant woman smiled at the boy on the hill. There was something in the smile that was like the smile that had come unconsciously to the lips of the woman who had nursed her child in the shed.

Turning his face away from the bay Tom looked at the sky. A great white cloud that lay along the southern horizon formed itself into the giant head of a man. Tom watched as the cloud crept slowly across the sky. There was something noble and quieting about the giant's face and his hair, pure white and as thick as wheat in a rich field in June, added to its nobility. Only the face appeared. Below the shoulders there was just a white shapeless mass of clouds.

And then this formless mass began also to change. The face of a giant woman appeared. It pressed upward toward the face of the man. Two arms formed themselves on the man's shoulders and pressed the woman closely. The two faces merged. Something seemed to snap in Tom's brain.

He sat upright and looked neither at the bay nor at the sky. Evening was coming on and soft shadows began to play over the land. Below him lay the farm with its barns and houses and in the field, below the hill on which he was lying, there were two smaller hills that became at once in his eyes the two full breasts of a woman. Two white sheep appeared and stood nibbling the grass on the woman's breasts. They were like babes being suckled. The trees in the orchards near the barns were the woman's hair. An arm of the stream that ran down to the bay, the stream he had crossed on the wooden bridge when he came to the hill, cut across a meadow beyond the two low hills. It widened into a pond and the pond made a mouth for the woman. Her eyes were two black hollows—low spots in a field where hogs had rooted the grass away, looking for roots. Black puddles of water lay in the hollows and they seemed eyes shining invitingly up at him.

This woman also smiled and her smile was now an invitation. Tom got to his feet and hurried away down the hill and going stealthily past the barns and the house got into a road. All night he walked under the stars thinking new thoughts. "I am obsessed with this idea of having a woman. I'd better go to the city and go to school and see if I can make myself fit to have a woman of my own," he thought. "I won't sleep tonight but will wait until tomorrow when Bottsford comes back and then I'll quit and go into the city." He walked, trying to make plans. Even a good man like John Bottsford, had a woman for himself. Could he do that?

The thought was exciting. At the moment it seemed to him that he had only to go into the city, and go to the schools for a time, to become beautiful and to have beautiful women love him. In his half ecstatic state he forgot the winter months he had spent in the city of Cleveland, and forgot also the grim streets, the long rows of dark prison-like factories and the loneliness of his life in the city. For the moment and as he walked in the dusty roads under the moon, he thought of American towns and cities as places for beautifully satisfying adventures, for all such fellows as himself.

DEATH IN THE WOODS

AND OTHER STORIES

TO MY FRIEND
FERDINAND SCHEVILL

CONTENTS

Death in the Woods

S HE was an old woman and lived on a farm near the town in which I lived. All country and small-town people have seen such old women, but no one knows much about them. Such an old woman comes into town driving an old worn-out horse or she comes afoot carrying a basket. She may own a few hens and have eggs to sell. She brings them in a basket and takes them to a grocer. There she trades them in. She gets some salt pork and some beans. Then she gets a pound or two of sugar and some flour.

Afterwards she goes to the butcher's and asks for some dog-meat. She may spend ten or fifteen cents, but when she does she asks for something. Formerly the butchers gave liver to any one who wanted to carry it away. In our family we were always having it. Once one of my brothers got a whole cow's liver at the slaughter-house near the fairgrounds in our town. We had it until we were sick of it. It never cost a cent. I have hated the thought of it ever since.

The old farm woman got some liver and a soup-bone. She never visited with any one, and as soon as she got what she wanted she lit out for home. It made quite a load for such an old body. No one gave her a lift. People drive right down a road and never notice an old woman like that.

There was such an old woman who used to come into town past our house one Summer and Fall when I was a young boy and was sick with what was called inflammatory rheumatism. She went home later carrying a heavy pack on her back. Two or three large gaunt-looking dogs followed at her heels.

The old woman was nothing special. She was one of the nameless ones that hardly any one knows, but she got into my thoughts. I have just suddenly now, after all these years, re-membered her and what happened. It is a story. Her name was Grimes, and she lived with her husband and son in a small unpainted house on the bank of a small creek four miles from town.

The husband and son were a tough lot. Although the son was but twenty-one, he had already served a term in jail. It was whispered about that the woman's husband stole horses and ran them off to some other county. Now and then, when a horse turned up missing, the man had also disappeared. No one ever caught him. Once, when I was loafing at Tom White-head's livery-barn, the man came there and sat on the bench in front. Two or three other men were there, but no one spoke to him. He sat for a few minutes and then got up and went away. When he was leaving he turned around and stared at the men. There was a look of defiance in his eyes. "Well, I have tried to be friendly. You don't want to talk to me. It has been so wherever I have gone in this town. If, some day, one of your fine horses turns up missing, well, then what?" He did not say anything actually. "I'd like to bust one of you on the jaw," was about what his eyes said. I remember how the look in his eyes made me shiver.

The old man belonged to a family that had had money once. His name was Jake Grimes. It all comes back clearly now. His father, John Grimes, had owned a sawmill when the country was new, and had made money. Then he got to drinking and running after women. When he died there wasn't much left.

Jake blew in the rest. Pretty soon there wasn't any more lumber to cut and his land was nearly all gone.

He got his wife off a German farmer, for whom he went to work one June day in the wheat harvest. She was a young thing then and scared to death. You see, the farmer was up to something with the girl—she was, I think, a bound girl and his wife had her suspicions. She took it out on the girl when the man wasn't around. Then, when the wife had to go off to town for supplies, the farmer got after her. She told young Jake that nothing really ever happened, but he didn't know whether to believe it or not.

He got her pretty easy himself, the first time he was out with her. He wouldn't have married her if the German farmer hadn't tried to tell him where to get off. He got her to go riding with him in his buggy one night when he was threshing on the place, and then he came for her the next Sunday night.

She managed to get out of the house without her employer's seeing, but when she was getting into the buggy he showed up. It was almost dark, and he just popped up suddenly at the horse's head. He grabbed the horse by the bridle and Jake got out his buggy-whip.

They had it out all right! The German was a tough one. Maybe he didn't care whether his wife knew or not. Jake hit him over the face and shoulders with the buggy-whip, but the horse got to acting up and he had to get out.

Then the two men went for it. The girl didn't see it. The horse started to run away and went nearly a mile down the road before the girl got him stopped. Then she managed to tie him to a tree beside the road. (I wonder how I know all this. It must have stuck in my mind from small-town tales when I was a boy.) Jake found her there after he got through with the German. She was huddled up in the buggy seat, crying, scared to death. She told Jake a lot of stuff, how the German had tried to get her, how he chased her once into the barn, how another time, when they happened to be alone in the house together, he tore her dress open clear down the front. The German, she said, might have got her that time if he hadn't heard his old woman drive in at the gate. She had been off to town for supplies. Well, she would be putting the horse in the barn. The German managed to sneak off to the fields without his wife seeing. He told the girl he would kill her if she told. What could she do? She told a lie about ripping her dress in the barn when she was feeding the stock. I remember now that she was a bound girl and did not know where her father and mother were. Maybe she did not have any father. You know what I mean.

Such bound children were often enough cruelly treated. They were children who had no parents, slaves really. There were very few orphan homes then. They were legally bound into some home. It was a matter of pure luck how it came out.

II

She married Jake and had a son and daughter, but the daughter died.

Then she settled down to feed stock. That was her job. At the German's place she had cooked the food for the German and his wife. The wife was a strong woman with big hips and

worked most of the time in the fields with her husband. She
fed them and fed the cows in the barn, fed the pigs, the horses
and the chickens. Every moment of every day, as a young girl,
was spent feeding something.

Then she married Jake Grimes and he had to be fed. She was
a slight thing, and when she had been married for three or four
years, and after the two children were born, her slender shoulders became stooped.

Jake always had a lot of big dogs around the house, that
stood near the unused sawmill near the creek. He was always
trading horses when he wasn't stealing something and had a
lot of poor bony ones about. Also he kept three or four pigs
and a cow. They were all pastured in the few acres left of the
Grimes place and Jake did little enough work.

He went into debt for a threshing outfit and ran it for several
years, but it did not pay. People did not trust him. They were
afraid he would steal the grain at night. He had to go a long
way off to get work and it cost too much to get there. In the
Winter he hunted and cut a little firewood, to be sold in some
nearby town. When the son grew up he was just like the father.
They got drunk together. If there wasn't anything to eat in the
house when they came home the old man gave his old woman
a cut over the head. She had a few chickens of her own and had
to kill one of them in a hurry. When they were all killed she
wouldn't have any eggs to sell when she went to town, and
then what would she do?

She had to scheme all her life about getting things fed, getting the pigs fed so they would grow fat and could be butchered in the Fall. When they were butchered her husband took
most of the meat off to town and sold it. If he did not do it
first the boy did. They fought sometimes and when they fought
the old woman stood aside trembling.

She had got the habit of silence anyway—that was fixed.
Sometimes, when she began to look old—she wasn't forty yet
—and when the husband and son were both off, trading horses
or drinking or hunting or stealing, she went around the house
and the barnyard muttering to herself.

How was she going to get everything fed?—that was her
problem. The dogs had to be fed. There wasn't enough hay in
the barn for the horses and the cow. If she didn't feed the

chickens how could they lay eggs? Without eggs to sell how could she get things in town, things she had to have to keep the life of the farm going? Thank heaven, she did not have to feed her husband—in a certain way. That hadn't lasted long after their marriage and after the babies came. Where he went on his long trips she did not know. Sometimes he was gone from home for weeks, and after the boy grew up they went off together.

They left everything at home for her to manage and she had no money. She knew no one. No one ever talked to her in town. When it was Winter she had to gather sticks of wood for her fire, had to try to keep the stock fed with very little grain.

The stock in the barn cried to her hungrily, the dogs followed her about. In the Winter the hens laid few enough eggs. They huddled in the corners of the barn and she kept watching them. If a hen lays an egg in the barn in the Winter and you do not find it, it freezes and breaks.

One day in Winter the old woman went off to town with a few eggs and the dogs followed her. She did not get started until nearly three o'clock and the snow was heavy. She hadn't been feeling very well for several days and so she went muttering along, scantily clad, her shoulders stooped. She had an old grain bag in which she carried her eggs, tucked away down in the bottom. There weren't many of them, but in Winter the price of eggs is up. She would get a little meat in exchange for the eggs, some salt pork, a little sugar, and some coffee perhaps. It might be the butcher would give her a piece of liver.

When she had got to town and was trading in her eggs the dogs lay by the door outside. She did pretty well, got the things she needed, more than she had hoped. Then she went to the butcher and he gave her some liver and some dog-meat.

It was the first time any one had spoken to her in a friendly way for a long time. The butcher was alone in his shop when she came in and was annoyed by the thought of such a sick-looking old woman out on such a day. It was bitter cold and the snow, that had let up during the afternoon, was falling again. The butcher said something about her husband and her son, swore at them, and the old woman stared at him, a look of mild surprise in her eyes as he talked. He said that if either the husband or the son were going to get any of the liver or the heavy bones with scraps of meat hanging to them that he had put into the grain bag, he'd see him starve first.

Starve, eh? Well, things had to be fed. Men had to be fed, and the horses that weren't any good but maybe could be traded off, and the poor thin cow that hadn't given any milk for three months.

Horses, cows, pigs, dogs, men.

III

The old woman had to get back before darkness came if she could. The dogs followed at her heels, sniffing at the heavy grain bag she had fastened on her back. When she got to the edge of town she stopped by a fence and tied the bag on her back with a piece of rope she had carried in her dress-pocket for just that purpose. That was an easier way to carry it. Her arms ached. It was hard when she had to crawl over fences and once she fell over and landed in the snow. The dogs went frisking about. She had to struggle to get to her feet again, but she made it. The point of climbing over the fences was that there was a short cut over a hill and through a woods. She might have gone around by the road, but it was a mile farther that way. She was afraid she couldn't make it. And then, besides, the stock had to be fed. There was a little hay left and a little corn. Perhaps her husband and son would bring some home when they came. They had driven off in the only buggy the Grimes family had, a rickety thing, a rickety horse hitched to the buggy, two other rickety horses led by halters. They were going to trade horses, get a little money if they could. They might come home drunk. It would be well to have something in the house when they came back.

The son had an affair on with a woman at the county seat, fifteen miles away. She was a rough enough woman, a tough one. Once, in the Summer, the son had brought her to the house. Both she and the son had been drinking. Jake Grimes was away and the son and his woman ordered the old woman about like a servant. She didn't mind much; she was used to it. Whatever happened she never said anything. That was her way of getting along. She had managed that way when she was a young girl at the German's and ever since she had married

Jake. That time her son brought his woman to the house they stayed all night, sleeping together just as though they were married. It hadn't shocked the old woman, not much. She had got past being shocked early in life.

With the pack on her back she went painfully along across an open field, wading in the deep snow, and got into the woods.

There was a path, but it was hard to follow. Just beyond the top of the hill, where the woods was thickest, there was a small clearing. Had some one once thought of building a house there? The clearing was as large as a building lot in town, large enough for a house and a garden. The path ran along the side of the clearing, and when she got there the old woman sat down to rest at the foot of a tree.

It was a foolish thing to do. When she got herself placed, the pack against the tree's trunk, it was nice, but what about getting up again? She worried about that for a moment and then quietly closed her eyes.

She must have slept for a time. When you are about so cold you can't get any colder. The afternoon grew a little warmer and the snow came thicker than ever. Then after a time the weather cleared. The moon even came out.

There were four Grimes dogs that had followed Mrs. Grimes into town, all tall gaunt fellows. Such men as Jake Grimes and his son always keep just such dogs. They kick and abuse them, but they stay. The Grimes dogs, in order to keep from starving, had to do a lot of foraging for themselves, and they had been at it while the old woman slept with her back to the tree at the side of the clearing. They had been chasing rabbits in the woods and in adjoining fields and in their ranging had picked up three other farm dogs.

After a time all the dogs came back to the clearing. They were excited about something. Such nights, cold and clear and with a moon, do things to dogs. It may be that some old instinct, come down from the time when they were wolves and ranged the woods in packs on Winter nights, comes back into them.

The dogs in the clearing, before the old woman, had caught two or three rabbits and their immediate hunger had been satisfied. They began to play, running in circles in the clearing. Round and round they ran, each dog's nose at the tail of the next dog. In the clearing, under the snow-laden trees and under the wintry moon they made a strange picture, running thus silently, in a circle their running had beaten in the soft snow. The dogs made no sound. They ran around and around in the circle.

It may have been that the old woman saw them doing that before she died. She may have awakened once or twice and looked at the strange sight with dim old eyes.

She wouldn't be very cold now, just drowsy. Life hangs on a long time. Perhaps the old woman was out of her head. She may have dreamed of her girlhood, at the German's, and before that, when she was a child and before her mother lit out and left her.

Her dreams couldn't have been very pleasant. Not many pleasant things had happened to her. Now and then one of the Grimes dogs left the running circle and came to stand before her. The dog thrust his face close to her face. His red tongue was hanging out.

The running of the dogs may have been a kind of death ceremony. It may have been that the primitive instinct of the wolf, having been aroused in the dogs by the night and the running, made them somehow afraid.

"Now we are no longer wolves. We are dogs, the servants of men. Keep alive, man! When man dies we becomes wolves again."

When one of the dogs came to where the old woman sat with her back against the tree and thrust his nose close to her face he seemed satisfied and went back to run with the pack. All the Grimes dogs did it at some time during the evening, before she died. I knew all about it afterward, when I grew to be a man, because once in a woods in Illinois, on another Winter night, I saw a pack of dogs act just like that. The dogs were waiting for me to die as they had waited for the old woman that night when I was a child, but when it happened to me I was a young man and had no intention whatever of dying.

The old woman died softly and quietly. When she was dead and when one of the Grimes dogs had come to her and had found her dead all the dogs stopped running.

They gathered about her.

Well, she was dead now. She had fed the Grimes dogs when she was alive, what about now?

There was the pack on her back, the grain bag containing the piece of salt pork, the liver the butcher had given her, the dog-meat, the soup bones. The butcher in town, having been suddenly overcome with a feeling of pity, had loaded her grain bag heavily. It had been a big haul for the old woman.

It was a big haul for the dogs now.

IV

One of the Grimes dogs sprang suddenly out from among the others and began worrying the pack on the old woman's back. Had the dogs really been wolves that one would have been the leader of the pack. What he did, all the others did.

All of them sank their teeth into the grain bag the old woman had fastened with ropes to her back.

They dragged the old woman's body out into the open clearing. The worn-out dress was quickly torn from her shoulders. When she was found, a day or two later, the dress had been torn from her body clear to the hips, but the dogs had not touched her body. They had got the meat out of the grain bag, that was all. Her body was frozen stiff when it was found, and the shoulders were so narrow and the body so slight that in death it looked like the body of some charming young girl.

Such things happened in towns of the Middle West, on farms near town, when I was a boy. A hunter out after rabbits found the old woman's body and did not touch it. Something, the beaten round path in the little snow-covered clearing, the silence of the place, the place where the dogs had worried the body trying to pull the grain bag away or tear it open—something startled the man and he hurried off to town.

I was in Main street with one of my brothers who was town newsboy and who was taking the afternoon papers to the stores. It was almost night.

The hunter came into a grocery and told his story. Then he went to a hardware-shop and into a drugstore. Men began to gather on the sidewalks. Then they started out along the road to the place in the woods.

My brother should have gone on about his business of distributing papers but he didn't. Every one was going to the woods. The undertaker went and the town marshal. Several men got on a dray and rode out to where the path left the road and went into the woods, but the horses weren't very sharply shod and slid about on the slippery roads. They made no better time than those of us who walked.

The town marshal was a large man whose leg had been injured in the Civil War. He carried a heavy cane and limped rapidly along the road. My brother and I followed at his heels, and as we went other men and boys joined the crowd.

It had grown dark by the time we got to where the old woman had left the road but the moon had come out. The marshal was thinking there might have been a murder. He kept asking the hunter questions. The hunter went along with his gun across his shoulders, a dog following at his heels. It isn't often a rabbit hunter has a chance to be so conspicuous. He was taking full advantage of it, leading the procession with the town marshal. "I didn't see any wounds. She was a beautiful young girl. Her face was buried in the snow. No, I didn't know her." As a matter of fact, the hunter had not looked closely at the body. He had been frightened. She might have been murdered and some one might spring out from behind a tree and murder him. In a woods, in the late afternoon, when the trees are all bare and there is white snow on the ground, when all is silent, something creepy steals over the mind and body. If something strange or uncanny has happened in the neighborhood all you think about is getting away from there as fast as you can.

The crowd of men and boys had got to where the old woman had crossed the field and went, following the marshal and the hunter, up the slight incline and into the woods.

My brother and I were silent. He had his bundle of papers in a bag slung across his shoulder. When he got back to town he would have to go on distributing his papers before he went home to supper. If I went along, as he had no doubt already determined I should, we would both be late. Either mother or our older sister would have to warm our supper.

Well, we would have something to tell. A boy did not get

such a chance very often. It was lucky we just happened to go into the grocery when the hunter came in. The hunter was a country fellow. Neither of us had ever seen him before.

Now the crowd of men and boys had got to the clearing. Darkness comes quickly on such Winter nights, but the full moon made everything clear. My brother and I stood near the tree, beneath which the old woman had died.

She did not look old, lying there in that light, frozen and still. One of the men turned her over in the snow and I saw everything. My body trembled with some strange mystical feeling and so did my brother's. It might have been the cold.

Neither of us had ever seen a woman's body before. It may have been the snow, clinging to the frozen flesh, that made it look so white and lovely, so like marble. No woman had come with the party from town; but one of the men, he was the town blacksmith, took off his overcoat and spread it over her. Then he gathered her into his arms and started off to town, all the others following silently. At that time no one knew who she was.

V

I had seen everything, had seen the oval in the snow, like a miniature race-track, where the dogs had run, had seen how the men were mystified, had seen the white bare young-looking shoulders, had heard the whispered comments of the men.

The men were simply mystified. They took the body to the undertaker's, and when the blacksmith, the hunter, the marshal and several others had got inside they closed the door. If father had been there perhaps he could have got in, but we boys couldn't.

I went with my brother to distribute the rest of his papers and when we got home it was my brother who told the story.

I kept silent and went to bed early. It may have been I was not satisfied with the way he told it.

Later, in the town, I must have heard other fragments of the old woman's story. She was recognized the next day and there was an investigation.

The husband and son were found somewhere and brought

to town and there was an attempt to connect them with the woman's death, but it did not work. They had perfect enough alibis.

However, the town was against them. They had to get out. Where they went I never heard.

I remember only the picture there in the forest, the men standing about, the naked girlish-looking figure, face down in the snow, the tracks made by the running dogs and the clear cold Winter sky above. White fragments of clouds were drifting across the sky. They went racing across the little open space among the trees.

The scene in the forest had become for me, without my knowing it, the foundation for the real story I am now trying to tell. The fragments, you see, had to be picked up slowly, long afterwards.

Things happened. When I was a young man I worked on the farm of a German. The hired-girl was afraid of her employer. The farmer's wife hated her.

I saw things at that place. Once later, I had a half-uncanny, mystical adventure with dogs in an Illinois forest on a clear, moon-lit Winter night. When I was a schoolboy, and on a Summer day, I went with a boy friend out along a creek some miles from town and came to the house where the old woman had lived. No one had lived in the house since her death. The doors were broken from the hinges; the window lights were all broken. As the boy and I stood in the road outside, two dogs, just roving farm dogs no doubt, came running around the corner of the house. The dogs were tall, gaunt fellows and came down to the fence and glared through at us, standing in the road.

The whole thing, the story of the old woman's death, was to me as I grew older like music heard from far off. The notes had to be picked up slowly one at a time. Something had to be understood.

The woman who died was one destined to feed animal life. Anyway, that is all she ever did. She was feeding animal life before she was born, as a child, as a young woman working on the farm of the German, after she married, when she grew old and when she died. She fed animal life in cows, in chickens, in pigs, in horses, in dogs, in men. Her daughter had died in childhood and with her one son she had no articulate relations. On the night when she died she was hurrying homeward, bearing on her body food for animal life.

She died in the clearing in the woods and even after her death continued feeding animal life.

You see it is likely that, when my brother told the story, that night when we got home and my mother and sister sat listening, I did not think he got the point. He was too young and so was I. A thing so complete has its own beauty.

I shall not try to emphasize the point. I am only explaining why I was dissatisfied then and have been ever since. I speak of that only that you may understand why I have been impelled to try to tell the simple story over again.

The Return

E IGHTEEN years. Well, he was driving a good car, an expensive roadster. He was well clad, a rather solid, fine-looking man, not too heavy. When he had left the Middle-Western town to go live in New York City he was twenty-two and now, on his way back, he was forty. He drove toward the town from the east, stopping for lunch at another town ten miles away.

When he went away from Caxton, after his mother died, he used to write letters to friends at home, but after several months the replies began to come with less and less frequency. On the day when he sat eating his lunch at a small hotel in the town ten miles east of Caxton he suddenly thought of the reason, and was ashamed. "Am I going back there on this visit for the same reason I wrote the letters?" he asked himself. For a moment he thought he might not go on. There was still time to turn back.

Outside, in the principal business street of the neighboring town, people were walking about. The sun shone warmly. Although he has lived for so many years in New York, he had always kept, buried away in him somewhere, a hankering for his own country. All the day before he had been driving through the Eastern Ohio country, crossing many small streams, running down through small valleys, seeing the white farmhouses set back from the road, and the big red barns.

The elders were still in bloom along the fences, boys were swimming in a creek, the wheat had been cut, and now the corn was shoulder-high. Everywhere the drone of bees; in patches of woodland along the road, a heavy, mysterious silence.

Now, however, he began thinking of something else. Shame crept over him. "When I first left Caxton, I wrote letters back to my boyhood friends there, but I wrote always of myself. When I had written a letter telling what I was doing in the city, what friends I was making, what my prospects were, I put, at the very end of the letter, perhaps, a little inquiry: 'I hope you are well. How are things going with you?' Something of that sort."

The returning native—his name was John Holden—had grown very uneasy. After eighteen years it seemed to him he could see, lying before him, one of the letters written eighteen years before, when he had first come into the strange Eastern city. His mother's brother, a successful architect in the city, had given him such and such an opportunity: he had been at the theater to see Mansfield as Brutus; he had taken the night boat up-river to Albany with his aunt; there were two very handsome girls on the boat.

Everything must have been in the same tone. His uncle had given him a rare opportunity, and he had taken advantage of it. In time he had also become a successful architect. In New York City there were certain great buildings, two or three skyscrapers, several huge industrial plants, any number of handsome and expensive residences, that were the products of his brain.

When it came down to scratch, John Holden had to admit that his uncle had not been excessively fond of him. It had just happened that his aunt and uncle had no children of their own. He did his work in the office well and carefully, had developed a certain rather striking knack for design. The aunt had liked him better. She had always tried to think of him as her own son, had treated him as a son. Sometimes she called him son. Once or twice, after his uncle died, he had a notion. His aunt was a good woman, but sometimes he thought she would rather have enjoyed having him, John Holden, go in a bit more for wickedness, go a little on the loose, now and then. He never did anything she had to forgive him for. Perhaps she hungered for the opportunity to forgive.

Odd thoughts, eh? Well, what was a fellow to do? You had but the one life to live. You had to think of yourself.

Botheration! John Holden had rather counted on the trip back to Caxton, had really counted on it more than he realized. It was a bright Summer day. He had been driving over the mountains of Pennsylvania, through New York State, through Eastern Ohio. Gertrude, his wife, had died during the Summer before, and his one son, a lad of twelve, had gone away for the Summer to a boys' camp in Vermont.

The idea had just come to him. "I'll drive the car along slowly through the country, drinking it in. I need a rest, time to think. What I really need is to renew old acquaintances. I'll go back to Caxton and stay several days. I'll see Herman and Frank and Joe. Then I'll go call on Lillian and Kate. What a lot of fun, really!" It might just be that when he got to Caxton, the Caxton ball team would be playing a game, say with a team from Yerington. Lillian might go to the game with him. It was in his mind faintly that Lillian had never married. How did he know that? He had heard nothing from Caxton for many years. The ball game would be in Heffler's field, and he and Lillian would go out there, walking under the maple trees along Turner Street, past the old stave factory, then in the dust of the road, past where the sawmill used to stand, and on into the field itself. He would be carrying a sunshade over Lillian's head, and Bob French would be standing at the gate where you went into the field and charging the people twenty-five cents to see the game.

Well, it would not be Bob; his son, perhaps. There would be something very nice in the notion of Lillian's going off to a ball game that way with an old sweetheart. A crowd of boys, women and men, going through a cattle gate into Heffler's field, tramping through the dust, young men with their sweethearts, a few gray-haired women, mothers of boys who belonged to the team, Lillian and he sitting in the rickety grandstand in the hot sun.

Once it had been—how they had felt, he and Lillian, sitting there together! It had been rather hard to keep the attention centered on the players in the field. One couldn't ask a neighbor, "Who's ahead now, Caxton or Yerington?" Lillian's hands lay in her lap. What white, delicate, expressive hands they were! Once—that was just before he went away to live in the city with his uncle and but a month after his mother died—he and Lillian went to the ball field together at night. His father had died when he was a young lad, and he had no relatives left in the town. Going off to the ball field at night was maybe a risky thing for Lillian to do—risky for her reputation if any one found it out—but she had seemed willing enough. You know how small-town girls of that age are.

Her father owned a retail shoe store in Caxton, and was a good, respectable man; but the Holdens—John's father had been a lawyer.

After they got back from the ball field that night—it must

have been after midnight—they went to sit on the front porch before her father's house. He must have known. A daughter cavorting about half the night with a young man that way! They had clung to each other with a sort of queer, desperate feeling neither understood. She did not go into the house until after three o'clock, and went then only because he insisted. He hadn't wanted to ruin her reputation. Why, he might have . . . She was like a little frightened child at the thought of his going away. He was twenty-two then, and she must have been about eighteen.

Eighteen and twenty-two make forty. John Holden was forty on the day when he sat at lunch at the hotel in the town ten miles from Caxton.

Now, he thought, he might be able to walk through the streets of Caxton to the ball park with Lillian with a certain effect. You know how it is. One has to accept the fact that youth is gone. If there should turn out to be such a ball game and Lillian would go with him, he would leave the car in the garage and ask her to walk. One saw pictures of that sort of thing in the movies—a man coming back to his native village after twenty years; a new beauty taking the place of the beauty of youth—something like that. In the Spring the leaves on maple trees are lovely, but they are even more lovely in the Fall—a flame of color—manhood and womanhood.

After he had finished his lunch John did not feel very comfortable. The road to Caxton—it used to take nearly three hours to travel the distance with a horse and buggy, but now, and without any effort, the distance might be made in twenty minutes.

He lit a cigar and went for a walk, not in the streets of Caxton, but in the streets of the town ten miles away. If he got to Caxton in the evening, just at dusk, say, now . . .

With an inward pang John realized that he wanted darkness, the kindliness of soft evening lights. Lillian, Joe, Herman and the rest. It had been eighteen years for the others as well as for himself. Now he had succeeded, a little, in twisting his fear of Caxton into fear for the others, and it made him feel somewhat better; but at once he realized what he was doing and again felt uncomfortable. One had to look out for changes, new people, new buildings, middle-aged people grown old, youth grown middle-aged. At any rate, he was thinking of the other now. He wasn't, as when he wrote letters home eighteen years before, thinking only of himself. "Am I?" It *was* a question.

An absurd situation, really. He had sailed along so gayly through upper New York State, through Western Pennsylvania, through Eastern Ohio. Men were at work in the fields and in the towns, farmers drove into towns in their cars, clouds of dust rose on some distant road, seen across a valley. Once he had stopped his car near a bridge and had gone for a walk along the banks of a creek where it wound through a wood.

He was liking people. Well, he had never before given much time to people, to thinking of them and their affairs. "I hadn't time," he told himself. He had always realized that, while he was a good enough architect, things move fast in America. New men were coming on. He couldn't take chances of going on forever on his uncle's reputation. A man had to be always on the alert. Fortunately, his marriage had been a help. It had made valuable connections for him.

Twice he had picked up people on the road. There was a lad of sixteen from some town of Eastern Pennsylvania, working his way westward toward the Pacific Coast by picking up rides in cars—a Summer's adventure. John had carried him all of one day and had listened to his talk with keen pleasure. And so this was the younger generation. The boy had nice eyes and an eager, friendly manner. He smoked cigarettes, and once, when they had a puncture, he was very quick and eager about changing the tire. "Now, don't you soil your hands, Mister, I can do it like a flash," he said, and he did. The boy said he intended working his way overland to the Pacific Coast, where he would try to get a job of some kind on an ocean freighter, and that, if he did, he would go on around the world. "But do you speak any foreign languages?" The boy did not. Across John Holden's mind flashed pictures of hot Eastern deserts, crowded Asiatic towns, wild half-savage mountain countries. As a young architect, and before his uncle died, he had spent two years in foreign travel, studying buildings in many countries; but he said nothing of this thought to the boy. Vast plans entered into with eager, boyish abandon, a world tour undertaken as he, when a young man, might have undertaken to find his way from his uncle's house in East Eighty-first Street downtown to the Battery. "How do I know—perhaps he will do it?" John thought. The day in company with the boy had been very pleasant, and he had been on the alert to pick him up again the next morning; but the boy had gone on his way, had caught a ride with some earlier riser. Why hadn't John invited him to his hotel for the night? The notion hadn't come to him until too late.

Youth, rather wild and undisciplined, running wild, eh? I wonder why I never did it, never wanted to do it.

If he had been a bit wilder, more reckless—that night, that time when he and Lillian . . . "It's all right being reckless with yourself, but when some one else is involved, a young girl in a small town, you yourself lighting out . . ." He remembered sharply that on the night, long before, as he sat with Lillian on the porch before her father's house, his hand . . . It had seemed as though Lillian, on that evening, might not have objected to anything he wanted to do. He had thought— well, he had thought of the consequences. Women must be protected by men, all that sort of thing. Lillian had seemed rather stunned when he walked away, even though it was three o'clock in the morning. She had been rather like a person waiting at a railroad station for the coming of a train. There is a blackboard, and a strange man comes out and writes on it, "Train Number 287 has been discontinued"—something like that.

Well, it had been all right.

Later, four years later, he had married a New York woman of good family. Even in a city like New York, where there are so many people, her family had been well known. They had connections.

After marriage, sometimes, it is true, he had wondered. Gertrude used to look at him sometimes with an odd light in her eyes. That boy he picked up in the road—once during the day when he said something to the boy, the same queer look came into his eyes. It would be rather upsetting if you knew that the boy had purposely avoided you next morning. There had been Gertrude's cousin. Once after his marriage, John heard a rumor that Gertrude had wanted to marry that cousin, but of course he had said nothing to her. Why should he have? She was his wife. There had been, he had heard, a good deal of family objection to the cousin. He was reputed to be wild, a gambler and drinker.

Once the cousin came to the Holden apartment at two in the morning, drunk and demanding that he be allowed to see Gertrude, and she slipped on a dressing-gown and went down to him. That was in the hallway of the apartment, downstairs, where almost any one might have come in and seen her. As a matter of fact, the elevator boy and janitor did see her. She had stood in the hallway below talking for nearly an hour. What about? He had never asked Gertrude directly, and she had never told him anything. When she came upstairs again and had got into her bed, he lay in his own bed trembling, but remained silent. He had been afraid that if he spoke he might say something rude; better keep still. The cousin had disappeared. John had a suspicion that Gertrude later supplied him with money. He went out West somewhere.

Now Gertrude was dead. She had always seemed very well, but suddenly she was attacked by a baffling kind of slow fever that lasted nearly a year. Sometimes she seemed about to get better, and then suddenly the fever grew worse. It might be that she did not want to live. What a notion! John had been at the bedside with the doctor when she died. There was something of the same feeling he had that night of his youth when he went with Lillian to the ball field, an odd sense of inadequacy. There was no doubt that in some subtle way both women had accused him.

Of what? There had always been, in some vague, indefinable way, a kind of accusation in the attitude toward him of his uncle, the architect, and of his aunt. They had left him their money, but . . . It was as though the uncle had said, as though Lillian during that night long ago had said . . .

Had they all said the same thing, and was Gertrude his wife saying it as she lay dying? A smile. "You have always taken such good care of yourself, haven't you, John dear? You have observed the rules. You have taken no chances for yourself or the others." She had actually said something of that sort to him once in a moment of anger.

II

In the small town ten miles from Caxton there wasn't any park to which a man could go to sit. If one stayed about the hotel, some one from Caxton might come in. "Hello, what are you doing here?"

It would be inconvenient to explain. He had wanted the kindliness of soft evening light, both for himself and the old friends he was to see again.

He began thinking of his son, now a boy of twelve. "Well," he said to himself, "his character has not begun to form yet." There was, as yet, in the son, an unconsciousness of other people, a rather casual selfishness, an unawareness of others, an unhealthy sharpness about getting the best of others. It was a thing that should be corrected in him and at once. John Holden had got himself into a small panic. "I must write him a letter at once. Such a habit gets fixed in a boy and then in the man, and it cannot later be shaken off. There are such a lot of people living in the world! Every man and woman has his own point of view. To be civilized, really, is to be aware of the others, their hopes, their gladnesses, their illusions about life."

John Holden was now walking along a residence street of a small Ohio town, composing in fancy a letter to his son in the boys' camp in Vermont. He was a man who wrote to his son every day. "I think a man should," he told himself. "He should remember that now the boy has no mother."

He had come to an outlying railroad station. It was neat with grass and flowers growing in a round bed in the very center of a lawn. Some man, the station agent and telegraph operator perhaps, passed him and went inside the station. John followed him in. On the wall of the waiting-room there was a framed copy of the time-table, and he stood studying it. A train went to Caxton at five. Another train came from Caxton and passed through the town he was now in at seven forty-three, the seven-nineteen out of Caxton. The man in the small business section of the station opened a sliding-panel and looked at him. The two men just stared at each other without speaking, and then the panel was slid shut again.

John looked at his watch. Two twenty-eight. At about six he could drive over to Caxton and dine at the hotel there. After

he had dined, it would be evening and people would be coming into the main street. The seven-nineteen would come in.
When John was a lad, sometimes, he, Joe, Herman, and often
several other lads had climbed on the front of the baggage or
mail car and had stolen a ride to the very town he was now in.
What a thrill, crouched down in the gathering darkness on the
platform as the train ran the ten miles, the car rocking from
side to side! When it got a little dark, in the Fall or Spring, the
fields beside the track were lighted up when the fireman
opened his fire box to throw in coal. Once John saw a rabbit
running along in the glare of light beside the track. He could
have reached down and caught it with his hand. In the neighboring town the boys went into saloons and played pool and
drank beer. They could depend upon catching a ride back
home on the local freight that got to Caxton at about ten
thirty. On one of the adventures John and Herman got drunk
and Joe had to help them into an empty coal car and later get
them out at Caxton. Herman got sick, and when they were
getting off the freight at Caxton, he stumbled and came very
near falling under the wheels of the moving train. John wasn't
as drunk as Herman. When the others weren't looking, he had
poured several of the glasses of beer into a spittoon. In Caxton
he and Joe had to walk about with Herman for several hours
and when John finally got home, his mother was still awake
and was worried. He had to lie to her. "I drove out into the
country with Herman, and a wheel broke. We had to walk
home." The reason Joe could carry his beer so well was because
he was German. His father owned the town meat market and
the family had beer on the table at home. No wonder it did
not knock him out as it did Herman and John.

There was a bench at the side of the railroad station, in the
shade, and John sat there for a long time—two hours, three
hours. Why hadn't he brought a book? In fancy he composed
a letter to his son and in it he spoke of the fields lying beside
the road outside the town of Caxton, of his greeting old
friends there, of things that had happened when he was a boy.
He even spoke of his former sweetheart, of Lillian. If he now
thought out just what he was going to say in the letter, he
could write it in his room at the hotel over in Caxton in a few
minutes without having to stop and think what he was going

to say. You can't always be too fussy about what you say to a young boy. Really, sometimes, you should take him into your confidence, into your life, make him a part of your life.

It was six twenty when John drove into Caxton and went to the hotel, where he registered, and was shown to a room. On the streets as he drove into town he saw Billy Baker, who, when he was a young man, had a paralyzed leg that dragged along the sidewalk when he walked. Now he was getting old; his face seemed wrinkled and faded, like a dried lemon, and his clothes had spots down the front. People, even sick people, live a long time in small Ohio towns. It is surprising how they hang on.

John had put his car, of a rather expensive make, into a garage beside the hotel. Formerly, in his day, the building had been used as a livery barn. There used to be pictures of famous trotting and pacing horses on the walls of the little office at the front. Old Dave Grey, who owned race horses of his own, ran the livery barn then, and John occasionally hired a rig there. He hired a rig and took Lillian for a ride into the country, along moonlit roads. By a lonely farmhouse a dog barked. Sometimes they drove along a little dirt road lined with elders and stopped the horse. How still everything was! What a queer feeling they had! They couldn't talk. Sometimes they sat in silence thus, very near each other, for a long, long time. Once they got out of the buggy, having tied the horse to the fence, and walked in a newly cut hay field. The cut hay lay all about in little cocks. John wanted to lie on one of the haycocks with Lillian, but did not dare suggest it.

At the hotel John ate his dinner in silence. There wasn't even a traveling salesman in the dining-room, and presently the proprietor's wife came and stood by his table to talk with him. The hotel had a good many tourists, but this just happened to be a quiet day. Dull days came that way in the hotel business. The woman's husband was a traveling man and had bought the hotel to give his wife something to keep her interested while he was on the road. He was away from home so much! They had come to Caxton from Pittsburgh.

After he had dined, John went up to his room, and presently the woman followed. The door leading into the hall had been left open, and she came and stood in the doorway. Really, she

was rather handsome. She only wanted to be sure that everything was all right, that he had towels and soap and everything
he needed.

For a time she lingered by the door talking of the town.

"It's a good little town. General Hurst is buried here. You
should drive out to the cemetery and see the statue." He wondered who General Hurst was. In what war had he fought.
Odd that he hadn't remembered about him. The town had a
piano factory, and there was a watch company from Cincinnati
talking of putting up a plant. "They figure there is less chance
of labor trouble in a small town like this."

The woman went reluctantly away. As she was going along
the hallway she stopped once and looked back. There was
something a little queer. They were both self-conscious. "I
hope you'll be comfortable," she said. At forty a man did not
come home to his own home town to start . . . A traveling
man's wife, eh? Well! Well!

At seven forty-five John went out for a walk on Main Street
and almost at once he met Tom Ballard, who at once recognized him, a fact that pleased Tom. He bragged about it.
"Once I see a face, I never forget. Well! Well!" When John was
twenty-two, Tom must have been about fifteen. His father was
the leading doctor of the town. He took John in tow, walked
back with him toward the hotel. He kept exclaiming: "I knew
you at once. You haven't changed much, really."

Tom was in his turn a doctor, and there was about him something . . . Right away John guessed what it was. They went
up into John's room, and John, having in his bag a bottle of
whisky, poured Tom a drink, which he took somewhat too
eagerly, John thought. There was talk. After Tom had taken
the drink he sat on the edge of the bed, still holding the bottle
John had passed to him. Herman was running a dray now. He
had married Kit Small and had five kids. Joe was working for
the International Harvester Company. "I don't know whether
he's in town now or not. He's a trouble-shooter, a swell mechanic, a good fellow," Tom said. He drank again.

As for Lillian, mentioned with an air of being casual by
John, he, John, knew of course that she had been married and
divorced. There was some sort of trouble about another man.
Her husband married again later, and now she lived with her

mother, her father, the shoe merchant, having died. Tom spoke somewhat guardedly, as though protecting a friend.

"I guess she's all right now, going straight and all. Good thing she never had any kids. She's a little nervous and queer; has lost her looks a good deal."

The two men went downstairs and, walking along Main Street, got into a car belonging to the doctor.

"I'll take you for a little ride," Tom said; but as he was about to pull away from the curb where the car had been parked, he turned and smiled at his passenger. "We ought to celebrate a little, account of your coming back here," he said. "What do you say to a quart?"

John handed him a ten-dollar bill, and he disappeared into a nearby drug store. When he came back he laughed.

"I used your name, all right. They didn't recognize it. In the prescription I wrote out I said you had a general breakdown, that you needed to be built up. I recommended that you take a teaspoonful three times a day. Lord! my prescription book is getting almost empty." The drug store belonged to a man named Will Bennett. "You remember him, maybe. He's Ed Bennett's son; married Carrie Wyatt." The names were but dim things in John's mind. "This man is going to get drunk. He is going to try to get me drunk, too," he thought.

When they had turned out of Main Street and into Walnut Street they stopped midway between two street lights and had another drink, John holding the bottle to his lips, but putting his tongue over the opening. He remembered the evenings with Joe and Herman when he had secretly poured his beer into a spittoon. He felt cold and lonely. Walnut Street was one along which he used to walk, coming home late at night from Lillian's house. He remembered people who then lived along the street, and a list of names began running through his head. Often the names remained, but did not call up images of people. They were just names. He hoped the doctor would not turn the car into the street in which the Holdens had lived. Lillian had lived over in another part of town, in what was called "The Red House District." Just why it had been called that John did not know.

III

They drove silently along, up a small hill, and came to the edge of town, going south. Stopping before a house that had evidently been built since John's time, Tom sounded his horn.

"Didn't the fair grounds used to stand about here?" John asked. The doctor turned and nodded his head.

"Yes, just here," he said. He kept on sounding his horn, and a man and woman came out of the house and stood in the road beside the car.

"Let's get Maud and Alf and all go over to Lylse's Point," Tom said. John had indeed been taken into tow. For a time he wondered if he was to be introduced. "We got some hooch. Meet John Holden; used to live here years ago." At the fair grounds, when John was a lad, Dave Grey, the livery man, used to work out his race horses in the early morning. Herman, who was a horse enthusiast, dreaming of some day becoming a horseman, came often to John's house in the early morning and the two boys went off to the fair grounds without breakfast. Herman had got some sandwiches made of slices of bread and cold meat out of his mother's pantry. They went 'cross-lots, climbing fences and eating the sandwiches. In a meadow they had to cross there was heavy dew on the grass, and meadow larks flew up before them. Herman had at least come somewhere near expressing in his life his youthful passion: he still lived about horses; he owned a dray. With a little inward qualm John wondered. Perhaps Herman ran a motortruck.

The man and woman got into the car, the woman on the back seat with John, the husband in front with Tom, and they drove away to another house. John could not keep track of the streets they passed through. Occasionally he asked the woman, "What street are we in now?" They were joined by Maud and Alf, who also crowded into the back seat. Maud was a slender woman of twenty-eight or thirty, with yellow hair and blue eyes, and at once she seemed determined to make up to John. "I don't take more than an inch of room," she said, laughing and squeezing herself in between John and the first woman, whose name he could not later remember.

He had rather liked Maud. When the car had been driven

some eighteen miles along a gravel road, they came to Lylse's farmhouse, which had been converted into a road-house, and got out. Maud had been silent most of the way, but she sat very close to John and as he felt cold and lonely, he was grateful for the warmth of her slender body. Occasionally she spoke to him in a half-whisper: "Ain't the night swell! Gee! I like it out in the dark this way."

Lylse's Point was at a bend of the Samson River, a small stream to which John as a lad had occasionally gone on fishing excursions with his father. Later he went out there several times with crowds of young fellows and their girls. They drove out then in Grey's old bus, and the trip out and back took several hours. On the way home at night they had great fun singing at the top of their voices and waking the sleeping farmers along the road. Occasionally some of the party got out and walked for a way. It was a chance for a fellow to kiss his girl when the others could not see. By hurrying a little, they could easily enough catch up with the bus.

A rather heavy-faced Italian named Francisco owned Lylse's, and it had a dance hall and dining-room. Drinks could be had if you knew the ropes, and it was evident the doctor and his friends were old acquaintances. At once they declared John should not buy anything, the declaration, in fact, being made before he had offered. "You're our guest now; don't you forget that. When we come sometime to your town, then it will be all right," Tom said. He laughed. "And that makes me think. I forgot your change," he said, handing John a five-dollar bill. The whisky got at the drug-store had been consumed on the way out, all except John and Maud drinking heartily. "I don't like the stuff. Do you, Mr. Holden?" Maud said and giggled. Twice during the trip out her fingers had crept over and touched lightly his fingers, and each time she had apologized. "Oh, do excuse me!" she said. John felt a little as he had felt earlier in the evening when the woman of the hotel had come to stand at the door of his room and had seemed reluctant about going away.

After they got out of the car at Lylse's, he felt uncomfortably old and queer. "What am I doing here with these people?" he kept asking himself. When they had got into the light, he stole a look at his watch. It was not yet nine o'clock. Several

other cars, most of them, the doctor explained, from Yerington, stood before the door, and when they had taken several
drinks of rather mild Italian red wine, all of the party except
Maud and John went into the dance hall to dance. The doctor
took John aside and whispered to him: "Lay off Maud," he
said. He explained hurriedly that Alf and Maud had been having a row and that for several days they had not spoken to each
other, although they lived in the same house, ate at the same
table, and slept in the same bed. "He thinks she gets too gay
with men," Tom explained. "You better look out a little."

The woman and man sat on a bench under a tree on the
lawn before the house, and when the others had danced, they
came out, bringing more drinks. Tom had got some more
whisky. "It's moon, but pretty good stuff," he declared. In the
clear sky overhead stars were shining, and when the others
were dancing, John turned his head and saw across the road
and between the trees that lined its banks the stars reflected in
the waters of the Samson. A light from the house fell on Maud's
face, a strikingly lovely face in that light, but when looked at
closely, rather petulant. "A good deal of the spoiled child in
her," John thought.

She began asking him about life in the city of New York.

"I was there once, but for only three days. It was when I
went to school in the East. A girl I knew lived there. She married a lawyer named Trigan, or something like that. You didn't
know him, I guess."

And now there was a hungry, dissatisfied look on her face.

"God! I'd like to live in a place like that, not in this hole!
There hadn't no man better tempt me." When she said that she
giggled again. Once during the evening they walked across the
dusty road and stood for a time by the river's edge, but got
back to the bench before the others finished their dance. Maud
persistently refused to dance.

At ten thirty, all of the others having got a little drunk, they
drove back to town, Maud again sitting beside John. On the
drive Alf went to sleep. Maud pressed her slender body against
John's, and after two or three futile moves to which he made
no special response, she boldly put her hand into his. The second woman and her husband talked with Tom of people they

had seen at Lylse's. "Do you think there's anything up between Fanny and Joe? No; I think she's on the square."

They got to John's hotel at eleven thirty, and, bidding them all good night, he went upstairs. Alf had awakened. When they were parting, he leaned out of the car and looked closely at John. "What did you say your name was?" he asked.

John went up a dark stairway and sat on the bed in his room. Lillian had lost her looks. She had married, and her husband had divorced her. Joe was a trouble-shooter. He worked for the International Harvester Company, a swell mechanic. Herman was a drayman. He had five kids.

Three men in a room next to John's were playing poker. They laughed and talked, and their voices came clearly to John. "You think so, do you? Well, I'll prove you're wrong." A mild quarrel began. As it was Summer, the windows of John's room were open, and he went to one to stand, looking out. A moon had come up, and he could see down into an alleyway. Two men came out of a street and stood in the alleyway, whispering. After they left, two cats crept along a roof and began a love-making scene. The game in the next room broke up. John could hear voices in the hallway.

"Now, forget it. I tell you, you're both wrong." John thought of his son at the camp up in Vermont. "I haven't written him a letter today." He felt guilty.

Opening his bag, he took out paper and sat down to write; but after two or three attempts gave it up and put the paper away again. How fine the night had been as he sat on the bench beside the woman at Lylse's! Now the woman was in bed with her husband. They were not speaking to each other.

"Could I do it?" John asked himself, and then, for the first time that evening, a smile came to his lips.

"Why not?" he asked himself.

With his bag in his hand he went down the dark hallway and into the hotel office and began pounding on a desk. A fat old man with thin red hair and sleep-heavy eyes appeared from somewhere. John explained.

"I can't sleep. I think I'll drive on. I want to get to Pittsburgh and as I can't sleep, I might as well be driving." He paid his bill.

Then he asked the clerk to go and arouse the man in the garage, and gave him an extra dollar. "If I need gas, is there any place open?" he asked, but evidently the man did not hear. Perhaps he thought the question absurd.

He stood in the moonlight on the sidewalk before the door of the hotel and heard the clerk pounding on a door. Presently voices were heard, and the headlights of his car shone. The car appeared, driven by a boy. He seemed very alive and alert.

"I saw you out to Lylse's," he said, and, without being asked, went to look at the tank. "You're all right; you got 'most eight gallons," he assured John, who had climbed into the driver's seat.

How friendly the car, how friendly the night! John was not one who enjoyed fast driving, but he went out of the town at very high speed. "You go down two blocks, turn to your right, and go three. There you hit the cement. Go right straight to the east. You can't miss it."

John was taking the turns at racing speed. At the edge of town some one shouted to him from the darkness, but he did not stop. He hungered to get into the road going east.

"I'll let her out," he thought. "Lord! It will be fun! I'll let her out."

There She is—She is Taking Her Bath

ANOTHER day when I have done no work. It is maddening. I went to the office this morning as usual and tonight came home at the regular time. My wife and I live in an apartment in the Bronx, here in New York City, and we have no children. I am ten years older than she. Our apartment is on the second floor and there is a little hallway downstairs used by all the people in the building.

If I could only decide whether or not I am a fool, a man turned suddenly a little mad or a man whose honor has really been tampered with, I should be quite all right. Tonight I went home, after something most unusual had happened at the office, determined to tell everything to my wife. "I will tell her and then watch her face. If she blanches, then I will know all I suspect is true," I said to myself. Within the last two weeks everything about me has changed. I am no longer the same man. For example, I never in my life before used the word "blanched." What does it mean? How am I to tell whether my wife blanches or not when I do not know what the word means? It must be a word I saw in a book when I was a boy, perhaps a book of detective stories. But wait, I know how that happened to pop into my head.

But that is not what I started to tell you about. Tonight, as I have already said, I came home and climbed the stairs to our apartment.

When I got inside the house I spoke in a loud voice to my wife. "My dear, what are you doing?" I asked. My voice sounded strange.

"I am taking a bath," my wife answered.

And so you see she was at home taking a bath. There she was.

She is always pretending she loves me, but look at her now. Am I in her thoughts? Is there a tender look in her eyes? Is she dreaming of me as she walks along the streets?

You see she is smiling. There is a young man who has just passed her. He is a tall fellow with a little mustache and is smoking a cigarette. Now I ask you—is he one of the men who, like myself, does, in a way, keep the world going?

Once I knew a man who was president of a whist club. Well, he was something. People wanted to know how to play whist. They wrote to him. "If it turns out that after three cards are played the man to my right still has three cards while I have only two, etc., etc."

My friend, the man of whom I am now speaking, looks the matter up. "In rule four hundred and six you will see, etc., etc.," he writes.

My point is that he is of some account in the world. He helps keep things going and I respect him. Often we used to have lunch together.

But I am a little off the point. The fellows of whom I am now thinking, these young squirts who go through the streets ogling women—what do they do? They twirl their mustaches. They carry canes. Some honest man is supporting them too. Some fool is their father.

And such a fellow is walking in the street. He meets a woman like my wife, an honest woman without too much experience of life. He smiles. A tender look comes into his eyes. Such deceit. Such callow nonsense.

And how are the women to know? They are children. They know nothing. There is a man, working somewhere in an office, keeping things moving, but do they think of him?

The truth is the woman is flattered. A tender look, that should be saved and bestowed only upon her husband, is thrown away. One never knows what will happen.

But pshaw, if I am to tell you the story, let me begin. There are men everywhere who talk and talk, saying nothing. I am afraid I am becoming one of that kind. As I have already told you, I have come home from the office at evening and am standing in the hallway of our apartment, just inside the door. I have asked my wife what she is doing and she has told me she is taking a bath.

Very well, I am then a fool. I shall go out for a walk in the park. There is no use my not facing everything frankly. By facing everything frankly one gets everything quite cleared up.

Aha! The very devil has got into me now. I said I would remain cool and collected, but I am not cool. The truth is I am growing angry.

I am a small man but I tell you that, once aroused, I will fight. Once when I was a boy I fought another boy in the school yard. He gave me a black eye but I loosened one of his teeth. "There, take that and that. Now I have got you against a wall. I will muss your mustache. Give me that cane. I will break it over your head. I do not intend to kill you, young man. I intend to vindicate my honor. No, I will not let you go. Take that and that. When next you see a respectable married woman on the street, going to the store, behaving herself, do not look at her with a tender light in your eyes. What you had better do is to go to work. Get a job in a bank. Work your way up. You said I was an old goat but I will show you an old goat can butt. Take that and that."

Very well, you, who read, also think me a fool. You laugh. You smile. Look at me. You are walking along here in the park. You are leading a dog.

Where is your wife? What is she doing?

Well, suppose she is at home taking a bath. What is she thinking? If she is dreaming, as she takes her bath, of whom is she dreaming?

I will tell you what, you who go along leading that dog, you may have no reason to suspect your wife, but you are in the same position as myself.

She was at home taking a bath and all day I had been sitting at my desk and thinking such thoughts. Under the circumstances I would never have had the temerity to go calmly off and take a bath. I admire my wife. Ha, ha. If she is innocent I admire her, of course, as a husband should, and if she is guilty I admire her even more. What nerve, what insouciance. There is something noble, something almost heroic in her attitude toward me, just at this time.

With me this day is like every day now. Well, you see, I have been sitting all day with my head in my hand thinking and thinking and while I have been doing that she has been going about, leading her regular life.

She has got up in the morning and has had her breakfast sitting opposite her husband; that is, myself. Her husband has gone off to his office. Now she is speaking to our maid. She is going to the stores. She is sewing, perhaps making new curtains for the windows of our apartment.

There is the woman for you. Nero fiddled while Rome was burning. There was something of the woman in him.

A wife has been unfaithful to her husband. She has gone gayly off, let us say on the arm of a young blade. Who is he? He dances. He smokes cigarettes. When he is with his companions, his own kind of fellows, he laughs. "I have got me a woman," he says. "She is not very young but she is terrifically in love with me. It is very convenient." I have heard such fellows talk, in the smoking cars, on trains and in other places.

And there is the husband, a fellow like myself. Is he calm? Is he collected? Is he cool? His honor is perhaps being tampered with. He sits at his desk. He smokes a cigar. People come and go. He is thinking, thinking.

And what are his thoughts? They concern her. "Now she is still at home, in our apartment," he thinks. "Now she is walking along a street." What do you know of the secret life led by your wife? What do you know of her thoughts? Well, hello! You smoke a pipe. You put your hands in your pockets. For you, your life is all very well. You are gay and happy. "What does it matter, my wife is at home taking a bath," you are telling yourself. In your daily life you are, let us say, a useful man. You publish books, you run a store, you write advertisements. Sometimes you say to yourself, "I am lifting the burden off the shoulders of others." That makes you feel good. I sympathize with you. If you let me, or rather I should say, if we had met in the formal transactions of our regular occupations, I dare say we would be great friends. Well, we would have lunch together, not too often, but now and then. I would tell you of some real-estate deal and you would tell me what you had been doing. "I am glad we met! Call me up. Before you go away, have a cigar."

With me it is quite different. All today, for example, I have been in my office, but I have not worked. A man came in, a Mr. Albright. "Well, are you going to let that property go or are you going to hold on?" he said.

What property did he mean? What was he talking about?

You can see for yourself what a state I am in.

And now I must be going home. My wife will have finished taking her bath. We will sit down to dinner. Nothing of all this I have been speaking about will be mentioned at all. "John, what is the matter with you?" "Aha. There is nothing the matter. I am worried about business a little. A Mr. Albright came in. Shall I sell or shall I hold on?" The real thing that is on my mind shall not be mentioned at all. I will grow a little nervous. The coffee will be spilled on the table-cloth or I will upset my dessert.

"John, what is the matter with you?" What coolness. As I have already said, what insouciance.

What is the matter? Matter enough.

A week, two weeks, to be exact, just seventeen days ago, I was a happy man. I went about my affairs. In the morning I rode to my office in the subway, but, had I wished to do so, I could long ago have bought an automobile.

But no, long ago, my wife and I had agreed there should be no such silly extravagance. To tell the truth, just ten years ago I failed in business and had to put some property in my wife's name. I bring the papers home to her and she signs. That is the way it is done.

"Well, John," said my wife, "we will not get us any automobile." That was before the thing happened that so upset me. We were walking together in the park. "Mabel, shall we get us an automobile?" I asked. "No," she said, "we will not get us an automobile." "Our money," she has said, more than a thousand times, "will be a comfort to us later."

A comfort indeed. What can be a comfort now that this thing has happened?

It was just two weeks, more than that, just seventeen days ago, that I went home from the office just as I came home to-night. Well, I walked in the same streets, passed the same stores.

I am puzzled as to what that Mr. Albright meant when he asked me if I intended to sell the property or hold on to it. I answered in a noncommittal way. "We'll see," I said. To what property did he refer? We must have had some previous conversation regarding the matter. A mere acquaintance does not come into your office and speak of property in that careless, one might say, familiar way, without having previous conversation on the same subject.

As you see I am still a little confused. Even though I am facing things now, I am still, as you have guessed, somewhat confused. This morning I was in the bathroom, shaving as usual. I always shave in the morning, not in the evening, unless my wife and I are going out. I was shaving and my shaving brush dropped to the floor. I stooped to pick it up and struck my head on the bath-tub. I only tell you this to show what a state I am in. It made a large bump on my head. My wife heard me groan and asked me what was the matter. "I struck my head," I said. Of course, one quite in control of his faculties does not hit his head on a bath-tub when he knows it is there, and what man does not know where the bath-tub stands in his own house?

But now I am thinking again of what happened, of what has upset me this way. I was going home on that evening, just seventeen days ago. Well, I walked along, thinking nothing. When I reached our apartment building I went in, and there, lying on the floor in the little hallway, in front, was a pink envelope with my wife's name, Mabel Smith, written on it. I picked it up thinking, "This is strange." It had perfume on it and there was no address, just the name Mabel Smith, written in a bold man's hand.

I quite automatically opened it and read.

Since I first met her, twelve years ago at a party at Mr. Westley's house, there have never been any secrets between me and my wife; at least, until that moment in the hallway seventeen days ago this evening, I had never thought there were any secrets between us. I have always opened her letters and she had always opened mine. I think it should be that way between a man and his wife. I know there are some who do not agree with me but what I have always argued is I am right.

I went to the party with Harry Selfridge and afterward took my wife home. I offered to get a cab. "Shall we have a cab?" I asked her. "No," she said, "let's walk." She was the daughter of a man in the furniture business and he has died since. Every one thought he would leave her some money but he didn't. It turned out he owed almost all he was worth to a firm in Grand Rapids. Some would have been upset, but I wasn't. "I married you for love, my dear," I said to her on the night when her father died. We were walking home from his house, also in the

Bronx, and it was raining a little, but we did not get very wet. "I married you for love," I said, and I meant what I said.

But to return to the note. "Dear Mabel," it said, "come to the park on Wednesday when the old goat has gone away. Wait for me on the bench near the animal cages where I met you before."

It was signed Bill. I put it in my pocket and went upstairs.

When I got into my apartment, I heard a man's voice. The voice was urging something upon my wife. Did the voice change when I came in? I walked boldly into our front room where my wife sat facing a young man who sat in another chair. He was tall and had a little mustache.

The man was pretending to be trying to sell my wife a patent carpet-sweeper, but just the same, when I sat down in a chair in the corner and remained there, keeping silent, they both became self-conscious. My wife, in fact, became positively excited. She got up out of her chair and said in a loud voice, "I tell you I do not want any carpet-sweeper."

The young man got up and went to the door and I followed. "Well, I had better be getting out of here," he was saying to himself. And so he had been intending to leave a note telling my wife to meet him in the park on Wednesday but at the last moment he had decided to take the risk of coming to our house. What he had probably thought was something like this: "Her husband may come and get the note out of the mail box." Then he decided to come and see her and had quite accidentally dropped the note in the hallway. Now he was frightened. One could see that. Such men as myself are small but we will fight sometimes.

He hurried to the door and I followed him into the hallway. There was another young man coming from the floor above, also with a carpet-sweeper in his hand. It is a pretty slick scheme, this carrying carpet-sweepers with them, the young men of this generation have worked out, but we older men are not to have the wool pulled over our eyes. I saw through everything at once. The second young man was a confederate and had been concealed in the hallway in order to warn the first young man of my approach. When I got upstairs, of course, the first young man was pretending to sell my wife a carpet-sweeper. Perhaps the second young man had tapped with the handle of the carpet-sweeper on the floor above. Now that I think of that I remember there was a tapping sound.

At the time, however, I did not think everything out as I have since done. I stood in the hallway with my back against the wall and watched them go down the stairs. One of them turned and laughed at me, but I did not say anything. I suppose I might have gone down the stairs after them and challenged them both to fight but what I thought was, "I won't."

And sure enough, just as I suspected from the first, it was the young man pretending to sell carpet-sweepers I had found sitting in my apartment with my wife, who had lost the note. When they got down to the hallway at the front of the house the man I had caught with my wife began to feel in his pocket. Then, as I leaned over the railing above, I saw him looking about the hallway. He laughed. "Say, Tom, I had a note to Mabel in my pocket. I intended to get a stamp at the postoffice and mail it. I had forgotten the street number. 'Oh, well,' I thought, 'I'll go see her!' I didn't want to bump into that old goat, her husband."

"You have bumped into him," I said to myself; "now we will see who will come out victorious."

I went into our apartment and closed the door.

For a long time, perhaps for ten minutes, I stood just inside the door of our apartment thinking and thinking, just as I have been doing ever since. Two or three times I tried to speak, to call out to my wife, to question her and find out the bitter truth at once but my voice failed me.

What was I to do? Was I to go to her, seize her by the wrists, force her down into a chair, make her confess at the risk of personal violence? I asked myself that question.

"No," I said to myself, "I will not do that. I will use finesse."

For a long time I stood there thinking. My world had tumbled down about my ears. When I tried to speak, the words would not come out of my mouth.

At last I did speak, quite calmly. There is something of the man of the world about me. When I am compelled to meet a situation I do it. "What are you doing?" I said to my wife, speaking in a calm voice. "I am taking a bath," she answered.

And so I left the house and came out here to the park to think, just as I have done tonight. On that night, and just as I came out at our front door, I did something I have not done since I was a boy. I am a deeply religious man but I swore. My wife and I have had a good many arguments as to whether or not a man in business should have dealings with those who do such things; that is to say, with men who swear. "I cannot refuse to sell a man a piece of property because he swears," I have always said. "Yes, you can," my wife says.

It only shows how little women know about business. What I have always maintained is I am right.

And I maintain too that we men must protect the integrity of our homes and our firesides. On that first night I walked about until dinner time and then went home. I had decided not to say anything for the present but to remain quiet and use finesse, but at dinner my hand trembled and I spilled the dessert on the table-cloth.

And a week later I went to see a detective.

But first something else happened. On Wednesday—I had found the note on Monday evening—I could not bear sitting in my office and thinking perhaps that that young squirt was meeting my wife in the park, so I went to the park myself.

Sure enough there was my wife sitting on a bench near the animal cages and knitting a sweater.

At first I thought I would conceal myself in some bushes but instead I went to where she was seated and sat down beside her. "How nice! What brings you here?" my wife said smiling. She looked at me with surprise in her eyes.

Was I to tell her or was I not to tell her? It was a moot question with me. "No," I said to myself. "I will not. I will go see a detective. My honor has no doubt already been tampered with and I shall find out." My naturally quick wits came to my rescue. Looking directly into my wife's eyes I said: "There was a paper to be signed and I had my own reasons for thinking you might be here, in the park."

As soon as I had spoken I could have torn out my tongue. However, she had noticed nothing and I took a paper out of my pocket and, handing her my fountain pen, asked her to sign; and when she had done so I hurried away. At first I thought perhaps I would linger about, in the distance, that is to say, but no, I decided not to do that. He will no doubt have his confederate on the watchout for me, I told myself.

And so on the next afternoon, I went to the office of the detective. He was a large man, and when I told him what I wanted he smiled. "I understand," he said, "we have many such cases. We'll track the guy down."

And so, you see, there it was. Everything was arranged. It was to cost me a pretty penny but my house was to be watched and I was to have a report on everything. To tell the truth, when everything was arranged I felt ashamed of myself. The man in the detective place—there were several men standing about—followed me to the door and put his hand on my shoulder. For some reason I don't understand, that made me mad. He kept patting me on the shoulder as though I were a little boy. "Don't worry. We'll manage everything," was what he said. It was all right. Business is business but for some reason I wanted to bang him in the face with my fist.

That's the way I am, you see. I can't make myself out. "Am I a fool, or am I a man among men?" I keep asking myself, and I can't get an answer.

After I had arranged with the detective I went home and didn't sleep all night long.

To tell the truth I began to wish I had never found that note. I suppose that is wrong of me. It makes me less a man, perhaps, but it's the truth.

Well, you see, I couldn't sleep. "No matter what my wife was up to I could sleep now if I hadn't found that note," was what I said to myself. It was dreadful. I was ashamed of what I had done and at the same time ashamed of myself for being ashamed. I had done what any American man, who is a man at all, would have done, and there I was. I couldn't sleep. Every time I came home in the evening I kept thinking: "There is that man standing over there by a tree—I'll bet he is a detective." I kept thinking of the fellow who had patted me on the shoulders in the detective office, and every time I thought of him I grew madder and madder. Pretty soon I hated him more than I did the young man who had pretended to sell the carpet-sweeper to Mabel.

And then I did the most foolish thing of all. One afternoon —it was just a week ago—I thought of something. When I had been in the detective office I had seen several men standing about but had not been introduced to any of them. "And so," I thought, "I'll go there pretending to get my reports. If the man I engaged is not there I'll engage some one else."

So I did it. I went to the detective office, and sure enough my man was out. There was another fellow sitting by a desk and I made a sign to him. We went into an inner office. "Look here," I whispered; you see I had made up my mind to pretend I was the man who was ruining my own fireside, wrecking my own honor. "Do I make clear what I mean?"

It was like this, you see—well, I had to have some sleep, didn't I? Only the night before my wife had said to me, "John, I think you had better run away for a little vacation. Run away by yourself for a time and forget about business."

At another time her saying that would have been nice, you see, but now it only upset me worse than ever. "She wants me out of the way," I thought, and for just a moment I felt like jumping up and telling her everything I knew. Still I didn't. "I'll just keep quiet. I'll use finesse," I thought.

A pretty kind of finesse. There I was in that detective office again hiring a second detective. I came right out and pretended I was my wife's paramour. The man kept nodding his head and I kept whispering like a fool. Well, I told him that a man named Smith had hired a detective from that office to watch his wife. "I have my own reasons for wanting him to get a report that his wife is all right," I said, pushing some money across a table toward him. I had become utterly reckless about money. "Here is fifty dollars and when he gets such a report from your office you come to me and you may have two hundred more," I said.

I had thought everything out. I told the second man my name was Jones and that I worked in the same office with Smith. "I'm in business with him," I said, "a silent partner, you see."

Then I went out and, of course, he, like the first one, followed me to the door and patted me on the shoulder. That was the hardest thing of all to stand, but I stood it. A man has to have sleep.

And, of course, today both men had to come to my office within five minutes of each other. The first one came, of course, and told me my wife was innocent. "She is as innocent as a little lamb," he said. "I congratulate you upon having such an innocent wife."

Then I paid him, backing away so he couldn't pat me on the shoulders, and he had only just closed the door when in came the other man, asking for Jones.

And I had to see him too and give him two hundred dollars.

Then I decided to come on home, and I did, walking along the same street I have walked on every afternoon since my wife and I married. I went home and climbed the stairs to our apartment just as I described everything to you a little while ago. I could not decide whether I was a fool, a man who has gone a little mad, or a man whose honor has been tampered with, but anyway I knew there would be no detectives about.

What I thought was that I would go home and have everything out with my wife, tell her of my suspicions and then watch her face. As I have said before, I intended to watch her face and see if she blanched when I told her of the note I had found in the hallway downstairs. The word "blanched" got into my mind because I once read it in a detective story when I was a boy and I had been dealing with detectives.

And so I intended to face my wife down, force a confession from her, but you see how it turned out. When I got home the apartment was silent and at first I thought it was empty. "Has she run away with him?" I asked myself, and maybe my own face blanched a little.

"Where are you, dear, what are you doing?" I shouted in a loud voice and she told me she was taking a bath.

And so I came out here in the park.

But now I must be going home. Dinner will be waiting. I am wondering what property that Mr. Albright had in his mind. When I sit at dinner with my wife my hands will shake. I will spill the dessert. A man does not come in and speak of property in that offhand manner unless there has been conversation about it before.

The Lost Novel

H E said it was all like a dream. A man like that, a writer. Well, he works for months and, perhaps, years, on a book, and there is not a word put down. What I mean is that his mind is working. What is to be the book builds itself up and is destroyed.

In his fancy, figures are moving back and forth.

But there is something I neglected to say. I am talking of a certain English novelist who has got some fame, of a thing that once happened to him.

He told me about it one day in London when we were walking together. We had been together for hours. I remember that we were on the Thames Embankment when he told me about his lost novel.

He had come to see me early in the evening at my hotel. He spoke of certain stories of my own. "You almost get at something, sometimes," he said.

We agreed that no man ever quite got at—the thing.

If some one once got at it, if he really put the ball over the plate, you know, if he hit the bull's-eye.

What would be the sense of anyone trying to do anything after that?

I'll tell you what, some of the old fellows have come pretty near.

Keats, eh? And Shakespeare. And George Borrow and DeFoe.

We spent a half hour going over names.

We went off to dine together and later walked. He was a little, black, nervous man with ragged locks of hair sticking out from under his hat.

I began talking of his first book.

But here is a brief outline of his history. He came from a poor farming family in some English village. He was like all writers. From the very beginning he wanted to write.

He had no education. At twenty he got married.

She must have been a very respectable, nice girl. If I remember rightly she was the daughter of a priest of the Established English Church.

Just the kind he should not have married. But who shall say whom anyone shall love—or marry? She was above him in station. She had been to a woman's college; she was well educated.

I have no doubt she thought him an ignorant man.

"She thought me a sweet man, too. The hell with that," he said, speaking of it. "I am not sweet. I hate sweetness."

We had got to that sort of intimacy, walking in the London night, going now and then into a pub to get a drink.

I remember that we each got a bottle, fearing the pubs would close before we got through talking.

What I told him about myself and my own adventures I can't remember.

The point is he wanted to make some kind of a pagan out of his woman, and the possibilities weren't in her.

They had two kids.

Then suddenly he did begin to burst out writing—that is to say, really writing.

You know a man like that. When he writes he writes. He had some kind of a job in his English town. I believe he was a clerk.

Because he was writing, he, of course, neglected his job, his wife, his kids.

He used to walk about the fields at night. His wife scolded. Of course, she was all broken up—would be. No woman can quite bear the absolute way in which a man who has been her lover can sometimes drop her when he is at work.

I mean an artist, of course. They can be first-class lovers. It may be they are the only lovers.

And they are absolutely ruthless about throwing direct personal love aside.

You can imagine that household. The man told me there was a little bedroom upstairs in the house where they were living at that time. This was while he was still in the English town.

The man used to come home from his job and go upstairs. Upstairs he went and locked his door. Often he did not stop to eat, and sometimes he did not even speak to his wife.

He wrote and wrote and wrote and threw away.

Then he lost his job. "The hell," he said, when he spoke of it. He didn't care, of course. What is a job?

What is a wife or child? There must be a few ruthless people in this world.

Pretty soon there was practically no food in the house.

He was upstairs in that room behind the door, writing. The house was small and the children cried. "The little brats," he said, speaking of them. He did not mean that, of course. I understand what he meant. His wife used to come and sit on the stairs outside the door, back of which he was at work. She cried audibly and the child she had in her arms cried.

"A patient soul, eh?" the English novelist said to me when he told me of it. "And a good soul, too," he said. "To hell with her," he also said.

You see, he had begun writing about her. She was what his novel was about, his first one. In time it may prove to be his best one.

Such tenderness of understanding—of her difficulties and her limitations, and such a casual, brutal way of treating her, personally.

Well, if we have a soul, that is worth something, eh?

It got so they were never together a moment without quarreling.

And then one night he struck her. He had forgotten to fasten the door of the room in which he worked. She came bursting in.

And just as he was getting at something about her, some understanding of the reality of her. Any writer will understand the difficulty of his position. In a fury he rushed at her, struck her and knocked her down.

And then, well, she quit him then. Why not? However, he finished the book. It was a real book.

But about his lost novel. He said he came up to London after his wife left him and began living alone. He thought he would write another novel.

You understand that he had got recognition, had been acclaimed.

And the second novel was just as difficult to write as the first. It may be that he was a good deal exhausted.

And, of course, he was ashamed. He was ashamed of the way in which he had treated his wife. He tried to write another novel so that he wouldn't always be thinking. He told me that, for the next year or two, the words he wrote on the paper were all wooden. Nothing was alive.

Months and months of that sort of thing. He withdrew from people. Well, what about his children? He sent money to his wife and went to see her once.

He said she was living with her father's people, and he went to her father's house and got her. They went to walk in the fields. "We couldn't talk," he said. "She began to cry and called me a crazy man. Then I glared at her, as I had once done that time I struck her, and she turned and ran away from me back to her father's house, and I came away."

Having written one splendid novel, he wanted, of course, to write some more. He said there were all sorts of characters and situations in his head. He used to sit at his desk for hours writing and then go out in the streets and walk as he and I walked together that night.

Nothing would come right for him.

He had got some sort of theory about himself. He said that the second novel was inside him like an unborn child. His conscience was hurting him about his wife and children. He said he loved them all right but did not want to see them again.

Sometimes he thought he hated them. One evening, he said, after he had been struggling like that, and long after he had quit seeing people, he wrote his second novel. It happened like this.

All morning he had been sitting in his room. It was a small room he had rented in a poor part of London. He had got out of bed early, and without eating any breakfast had begun to write. And everything he wrote that morning was also no good.

About three o'clock in the afternoon, as he had been in the habit of doing, he went out to walk. He took a lot of writing-paper with him.

"I had an idea I might begin to write at any time," he said.

He went walking in Hyde Park. He said it was a clear, bright day, and people were walking about together. He sat on a bench.

He hadn't eaten anything since the night before. As he sat there he tried a trick. Later I heard that a group of young poets in Paris took up that sort of thing and were profoundly serious about it.

The Englishman tried what is called "automatic writing."

He just put his pencil on the paper and let the pencil make what words it would.

Of course the pencil made a queer jumble of absurd words. He quit doing that.

There he sat on the bench staring at the people walking past.

He was tired, like a man who has been in love for a long time with some woman he cannot get.

Let us say there are difficulties. He is married or she is. They look at each other with promises in their eyes and nothing happens.

Wait and wait. Most people's lives are spent waiting.

And then suddenly, he said, he began writing his novel. The theme, of course, was men and women—lovers. What other theme is there for such a man? He told me that he must have been thinking a great deal of his wife and of his cruelty to her. He wrote and wrote. The evening passed and night came. Fortunately, there was a moon. He kept on writing. He said it was the most intense writing he ever did or ever hoped to do. Hours and hours passed. He sat there on that bench writing like a crazy man.

He wrote a novel at one sitting. Then he went home to his room.

He said he never was so happy and satisfied with himself in his life.

"I thought that I had done justice to my wife and to my children, to everyone and everything," he said. If they did not know it, never would know—what difference would that make?

He said that all the love he had in his being went into the novel.

He took it home and laid it on his desk.

What a sweet feeling of satisfaction to have done—the thing.

Then he went out of his room and found an all-night place where he could get something to eat.

After he got food he walked around the town. How long he walked he didn't know.

Then he went home and slept. It was daylight by this time. He slept all through the next day.

He said that when he woke up he thought he would look at his novel. "I really knew all the time it wasn't there," he said. "On the desk, of course, there was nothing but blank empty sheets of paper.

"Anyway," he said, "this I know. I never will write such a beautiful novel as that one was."

When he said it he laughed.

I do not believe there are too many people in the world who will know exactly what he was laughing about.

But why be so arbitrary? There may be even a dozen.

The Fight

THE man—the guest—came up out of the garden to the porch of the house. He had a flat even voice. He was rather bulky. Immediately he began to talk.

The man of the house—his name was John Wilder—had to make a special effort to seem attentive. "Now I shall have to listen to some more of his gabble. He is trying to be polite."

What the guest had to say amounted to nothing. He spoke of the sunset. The porch of the house faced the west. Yes, yes, there was a sunset. There was a gray stone wall at the end of the garden and, beyond, a hill. On the side of the hill were a few apple trees.

The guest was also named Wilder—Alfred Wilder. He was John Wilder's cousin.

They were both substantial-looking men. John Wilder was a lawyer, his cousin a scientist who did some sort of experimental work for a large manufacturing company in another city.

The two cousins had not seen each other for several years. Alfred Wilder's wife was in Europe with his daughter. They were spending the Summer over there.

For years there had been no correspondence between the two men. They were both born in the same Middle-Western American small town. When they were boys they lived on the same street.

There had always been something wrong with their relationship. When they were small boys they always wanted to fight.

They never did. There were other children in both families. The cousins always played together. At Christmas time they gave each other presents. It was presumed they had for each other a cousinly feeling. Some one was always presuming that. The fools!

There was a combined Christmas celebration held by the two families. John had to buy a present for Alfred and Alfred had to buy one for John.

That day at John Wilder's house, when both men were nearly fifty years old and when Alfred was speaking of the sunset, John was thinking of a Christmas of his youth.

There had been another boy on the street who had a dog with several small puppies. The boy—a special friend—had given one to John. He had been delighted and had taken it home.

But his mother did not like dogs. She would not let him keep it. He stood in tears holding the puppy in his arms. He had been commanded to take it back where he got it, but at the last moment he had an idea.

John's mother knew his cousin Alfred wanted a dog. John would keep it for a time but give it to his cousin as a Christmas present. It was such a sweet idea. It had just popped into his head. He had never intended to do it.

He would keep the puppy around. His mother would grow fond of it. When he said he would give it to his cousin he was being like the master of a vessel in a storm. He was putting into the nearest port, taking certain chances to save a vessel—or a pup.

He had got the pup in the late Fall. He kept it in the barn back of the house.

He went to see it twenty times a day. At night sometimes he crept out of bed and went to visit the pup.

His mother paid no attention. The pup had made no progress with her. John had another idea. He would so win the affection of the pup that when he gave it to his cousin and his cousin took it home, it would not stay.

The pup would keep on coming back and back. In the end his mother would surrender.

John had heard many stories about the affection of dogs. You win the affection of a dog once and he will never desert you. If you die he will come and howl over your grave.

John had felt like dying when he thought of Alfred owning the pup. He had wanted to die.

If he were dead it would pay his mother out—well, a dead boy buried in the snow. Snow on his grave, a dead pup lying across the grave. It had died of grief. Tears came into John's eyes when he thought of the scene.

As has been suggested John had got the puppy in the Fall. At Christmas time he had to give it to his cousin and Alfred had given him a cheap watch with a chain. It wasn't really his gift. His father had to put up the money.

Alfred took the pup home and John waited. It did not come back. He began to hate the pup.

He decided that Alfred had locked it up and went to see. When he got to his cousin's house his cousin wasn't at home. He had gone skating.

However, the pup was in the yard. John called but the pup would not come. He just stood wagging his tail. Then he barked as though John were some stranger.

John went away hating the dog. His hatred of his cousin had always been an unreasonable thing in him and he was often ashamed of it.

The pup grew into doghood. It was a shepherd dog.

One day John was in a field near the town. He was sixteen then. He had a gun, his father's gun, and was out hunting rabbits.

He was in a small wood and suddenly, in a nearby field, he saw the dog. He was a big shaggy fellow now, an ugly-looking dog, John thought. There were sheep in the field. The dog was creeping along a fence toward the sheep.

John had heard of sheep-killing dogs. Just at that time there had been several sheep killed one night in a field near the town.

John went along the fence toward the dog. Of course the dog knew him. He was called "Shep." When he saw John he began wagging his tail.

Undoubtedly there was a guilty look in the dog's face. John became stern. It is every good citizen's duty to kill at sight a sheep-killing dog. John had never thought of the obligation involved in citizenship until that moment. Suddenly he became filled with it. He shot the dog. He had to fire both barrels of a double-barreled gun. The first shot crippled the dog and he howled with pain, but the second shot finished him off.

It was an oddly satisfactory feeling to see him die. John was ashamed of the feeling.

He was ashamed and at the same time glad. How pleasant that he had the excuse of thinking the dog was about to attack the sheep. Of course he could not be quite sure. No one knew he had killed the dog. He told no one. It was discovered later lying dead in the field. There were sheep pastured in the field. . . . Well, Alfred had become attached to the dog and was all broken up.

It wasn't however because Alfred was particularly affectionate
—John knew that. He was just rubbing it in.

He was fond of the dog because he knew in his heart John
had not wanted to give it to him. He was that kind.

John wasn't like that. He remembered Alfred's present. It
was really his uncle's present. John had lost the watch right
away. It slipped out of his pocket. The chain wasn't fastened.
Well, it was a cheap watch.

He might have kept the watch and taken it out of his pocket
from time to time when Alfred was about. Neither boy wanted
to give the other a present. They had to. Their parents made
them.

Taking the watch out of his pocket in that way would have
plagued Alfred.

John had felt that, in losing the watch, he had been in some
obscure way generous. However, he never boasted of his generosity.

He just knew that Alfred wasn't generous. After John had
given him the pup at Christmas it got sick. It might have died
but that Alfred took extra good care of it. He even took it to a
veterinary. "It just shows how some people are," John said to
himself.

The two boys had grown up in a small town never having a
fight. They left the town and went to different colleges. When
they struck out into life they went to different cities.

Their hatred of each other continued. When they grew older
and had to communicate with each other—for family reasons
—they were always elaborately polite.

When John advanced a little in life—for example, when he
served a term in Congress—Alfred wrote to congratulate him.
John did the same thing when something good happened to
Alfred. Both men got married, but in each case the other
found it impossible to go to the wedding.

It happened that both men were a little ill just at that time.
It was a coincidence. John was always glad it happened to him
first. He used to tell himself that, had he married first and had
Alfred been ill, when it came Alfred's time to marry he would
have been there if he had had to get up out of his death bed.

"I would never have let him know how ill I was. Or, at least
I would have thought up some other excuse."

That was just the trouble. Neither man had ever let the other know how he felt.

When they grew older it was more difficult. For years they never corresponded.

And then Alfred came to visit John. John's house was in a suburb in Chicago and Alfred had some business in the city.

He had merely intended coming to John's house for a casual call but John had urged him to stay.

The more he hated Alfred the more he kept urging him. That was because he felt guilty. He hated himself for being such a fool.

It had happened also that John's wife had taken a liking to his cousin Alfred. Sometimes the two sat together for hours. They were both interested in music. John wasn't. His wife played the piano. Sometimes she played for Alfred all evening. She played a while and then she and Alfred talked. When Alfred's wife came back from Europe, John's wife said, they would have to come for a long visit. They would have to bring their daughter.

John and his wife had no children.

When he heard his wife ask the whole family to visit his house, John cringed. He was quite sure Alfred's daughter must be a fast, vulgar girl.

John sat in a chair reading a book and Alfred was with his wife in another room. John doubled his fists. His hatred of Alfred amused him sometimes. There was no reason for it. "It's just silly," he told himself.

On the evening when the two men were alone together on the porch of the house, John's wife was not at home. They had dined an hour earlier. Alfred's visit was almost over. He was leaving in two or three days.

He had said something about the beauty of the sunset and John had nodded his head.

Then both grew silent. The silence lasted a long time. It got rather heavy.

"Let's go for a walk," Alfred said.

John did not want to go. He did not know what else to do. His wife had gone to some kind of a women's club meeting. She would be gone all evening. He hated women's clubs.

John's house stood on a bluff that led down to a lake.

Beyond a garden wall there was a stairway going down to the beach.

The two men climbed down. It was a Summer night and some young men and women were in bathing.

John and Alfred did not speak to each other going down, and on the beach the silence between them continued. Minutes seemed to become hours.

Well, it wasn't unbearable. Both men were standing it.

It was all they could stand. They walked a little way along the beach and sat on the sand.

Time passed. Each man was telling himself the same thing. "I am utterly foolish. Here is my cousin. He is all right. What is the matter with him? I had better say, 'What is the matter with me.'"

They really wanted to fight. It was an absurd idea. They should have done it when they were boys. They were men of fifty, respectable men. Presently the young people on the beach went away. They were alone together.

John got to his feet and Alfred also started to rise. The sand may have been somewhat slippery. He fell against John.

John pushed him violently, sent him sprawling. He had not intended to. He just did it. His hand wouldn't behave.

Of course, Alfred did not know that John's act was not premeditated. He hadn't judgment enough to think things out. A scientist doesn't have to use judgment as a lawyer does. He just fools around with a lot of chemicals and things.

A man's hand slips and there you are. It is so easy to misunderstand. As John told himself afterward, Alfred was that kind of a man. He had no understanding.

At bottom that was what was the matter with him. That was why John hated him.

Alfred jumped up from the sand and struck at John. Of course John struck back. A fight started on the beach in the dark.

Both men were past the fighting age. They grunted a great deal. John got a black and blue eye. He made Alfred's nose bleed. Also he tore Alfred's clothes.

It was a good thing there was no one about. Both men belonged to athletic clubs in their respective cities. They had seen prize fights. They both tried to be scientific. Afterward each man had to laugh at the spectacle the other made of himself.

They couldn't keep it up. Pretty soon they both had to stop because they were short-winded.

They were just where they were before the fight. Nothing had changed. The fight had settled nothing.

They went back up the stairs to John's house, neither man speaking. Then Alfred went to his room and changed his clothes. He packed his bags and went to the phone and called a cab.

He tried to appear calm. John thought he was just acting.

John was in a bathroom nursing his eye when Alfred came downstairs. He was putting cold water on his eye. When Alfred called he had to come. Both men had to smile.

However, they continued hating each other. Each man was laughing at the other.

Alfred made a suggestion. "You tell your wife," he said, "that I got a telegram and had to leave in a hurry."

The way he said "your wife" made John furious. She was just as good as any wife Alfred could get. And he had pretended to like John's wife. The skunk.

And then, almost at once, the cab came and Alfred was gone.

The house felt fine. Of course, John would have to make up a story to explain about his eye. When his wife came in he said that he and Alfred—his cousin—had been down on the beach. When they were coming up he fell and hurt his eye. "I should say you did," his wife said.

And then Alfred had got the telegram and had to leave. He had just time to catch a train.

John's wife was rather broken up. She said she had become very fond of Alfred. "I wish I had a cousin," she said.

She said that when Alfred's wife and daughter returned from Europe it would be nice to have them all for a long visit.

"Yes," John said. In spite of the inflamed eye he was so happy he would have agreed to anything. He got out of his wife's presence as soon as he could and took a walk about the house.

He thought the air of the house felt better in his lungs now that Alfred was gone.

As for the fight he was pretty sure he had got the best of it. Of course, Alfred hadn't a black eye but John had got in some good body punches.

"He'll be pretty sore in the morning," he thought, with satisfaction. As for the visit. Well, if it had to happen it wouldn't be for a long time. Alfred might have sense enough not to come.

And yet, John was a little in doubt. Alfred might bring his wife and daughter just to get even.

His wife might take a shine to John's wife.

John himself might like Alfred's daughter. He was fond of young girls. That thought made him miserable again.

"That would be a pretty mess, now wouldn't it?"

It would be just like Alfred to have an attractive wife and daughter. It would be a way of showing off, making believe he was himself nice.

John thought his cousin Alfred never had been very nice. He hoped the punches he had got in on Alfred's body would make him so sore that in the morning on the train he would be unable to get out of his berth.

Like a Queen

THERE is a great deal of talk made about beauty but no one defines it. It clings to some people.

Among women, now . . . the figure is something, of course, the face, the lips, the eyes.

The way the head sits on the shoulders.

The way a woman walks across the room may mean everything.

I myself have seen beauty in the most unexpected places. What has happened to me has happened also to a great many other men.

I remember a friend I had formerly in Chicago. He had something like a nervous breakdown and went down into Missouri —to the Ozark Mountains, I think.

One day he was walking on a mountain road and passed a cabin. It was a poor place with lean dogs in the yard.

There were a great many dirty children, a slovenly woman and one young girl. The young girl had gone from the cabin to a wood-pile in the yard. She had gathered an armful of wood and was walking toward the house.

There in the road was my friend. He looked up and saw her.

There must have been something—the time, the place, the mood of the man. Ten years later he was still speaking of that woman, of her extraordinary beauty.

And there was another man. He was from Central Illinois and was raised on a farm. Later he went to Chicago and became a successful lawyer out there. He was the father of a large family.

The most beautiful woman he ever saw was with some horse traders that passed the farm where he lived as a boy. When he was in his cups one night he told me that all of his night dreams, the kind men have and that are concerned with women, were always concerned with her. He said he thought it was the way she walked. The odd part of it was she had a bruised eye. Perhaps, he said, she was the wife or the mistress of one of the horse traders.

It was a cold day and she was barefooted. The road was

muddy. The horse traders, with their wagon, followed by a lot of bony horses, passed the field where the young man was at work. They did not speak to him. You know how such people stare.

And there she came along the road alone.

It may just have been another case of a rare moment for that man.

He had some sort of tool in his hand, a corn-cutting knife, he said. The woman looked at him. The horse traders looked back. They laughed. The corn-cutting knife dropped from his hand. Women must know when they register like that.

And thirty years later she was still registering.

All of which brings me to Alice.

Alice used to say the whole problem of life lay in getting past what she called the "times between."

I wonder where Alice is. She was a stout woman who had once been a singer. Then she lost her voice.

When I knew her she had blue veins spread over her red cheeks and short gray hair. She was the kind of woman who can never keep her stockings up. They were always falling down over her shoes.

She had stout legs and broad shoulders and had grown mannish as she grew older.

Such women can manage. Being a singer, of some fame once, she had made a great deal of money. She spent money freely.

For one thing, she knew a good many very rich men, bankers and others.

They took her advice about their daughters and sons. A son of such a man got into trouble. Well, he got mixed up with some woman, a waitress or a servant. The man sent for Alice. The son was resentful and determined.

The girl might be all right and then again . . .

Alice took the girl's part. "Now, you look here," she said to the banker. "You know nothing about people. Those who are interested in people do not get as rich as you have.

"And you do not understand your son either. This affair he has got into. His finest feelings may be involved in this matter."

Alice simply swept the banker, and perhaps his wife, out of the picture. "You people." She laughed when she said that.

Of course, the son was immature. Alice did really seem to know a lot about people. She took the boy in hand—went to see the girl.

She had been through dozens of such experiences. For one thing, the boy wasn't made to feel a fool. Sons of rich men, when they have anything worth while in them, go through periods of desperation, like other young men. They go to college and read books.

Life in such men's houses is something pretty bad. Alice knew about all that. The rich man may go off and get himself a mistress—the boy's mother a lover. Such things happen.

Still the people are not so bad. There are all sorts of rich men, just as there are of poor and middle-class men.

After we became friends Alice used to explain a lot of things to me. At that time I was always worried about money. She laughed at me. "You take money too seriously," she said.

"Money is simply a way of expressing power," she said. "Men who get rich understand that. They get money, a lot of it, because they aren't afraid of it.

"The poor man or the middle-class man goes to a banker timidly. That will never do.

"If you have your own kind of power, show your hand. Make the man fear you in your own field. For example, you can write. Your rich man cannot do that. It is quite all right to exercise your own power. Have faith in yourself. If it is necessary to make him a little afraid, do so. The fact that you can do so, that you can express yourself makes you seem strange to him. Suppose you uncovered his life. The average rich man has got his rotten side and his weak side.

"And for Heaven's sake do not forget that he has his good side.

"You may go at trying to understand such a one like a fool if you want to—I mean with all sorts of preconceived notions. You could show just his rottenness, a distorted picture, ruin his vanity.

"Your poor man, or your small merchant or lawyer. Such men haven't the temptations as regards women, for example, that rich men have. There are plenty of women grafters about—some of them are physically beautiful, too.

"The poor man or the middle-class man goes about

condemning the rich man for the rotten side of his life, but what rottenness is there in him?

"What secret desires has he, what greeds, buried under a placid, commonplace face?"

In the matter of the rich man's son and the woman he had got involved with, Alice in some way did manage to get at the bottom of things.

I gathered that in such affairs she took it for granted people were on the whole better than others thought them or than they thought themselves. She made the idea seem more reasonable than you would ever have thought possible.

It may be that Alice really had brains. I have met few enough people I thought had.

Most people are so one-sided, so specialized. They can make money, or fight prize-fights or paint pictures, or they are men who are physically attractive and can get women who are physically beautiful, women who can tie men up in knots.

Or they are just plain dubs. There are plenty of dubs everywhere.

Alice swept dubs aside; she did not bother with them. She could be as cruel as a cold wind.

She got money when she wanted it. She lived around in fine houses.

Once she got a thousand dollars for me. I was in New York and broke. One day I was walking on Fifth Avenue. You know how a writer is when he cannot write. Months of that for me. My money gone. Everything I wrote was dead.

I had grown a little shabby. My hair was long and I was thin.

Lots of times I have thought of suicide when I cannot write. Every writer has such times.

Alice took me to a man in an office building. "You give this man a thousand dollars."

"What the devil, Alice? What for?"

"Because I say so. He can write, just as you can make money. He has talent. He is discouraged now, is on his uppers. He has lost his pride in life, in himself. Look at the poor fool's lips trembling."

It was quite true. I was in a bad state.

In me a great surge of love for Alice. Such a woman! She became beautiful to me.

She was talking to the man.

"The only value I can be to you is now and then when I do something like this."

"Like what?"

"When I tell you where and how you can use a thousand dollars and use it sensibly.

"To give it to a man who is as good as yourself, who is better. When he is down—when his pride is low."

Alice came from the mountains of East Tennessee. You would not believe it. When she was twenty-four, at the height of her power as a singer, she had seemed tall. The reason I speak of it was that when I knew her she appeared short—and thick.

Once I saw a photograph of her when she was young.

She was half vulgar, half lovely.

She was a mountain woman who could sing. An older man, who had been her lover, told me that at twenty-four and until she was thirty, she was like a queen.

"She walked like a queen," he said. To see her walk across a room or across the stage was something not to be forgotten.

She had lovers, a dozen of them in her time.

Then she had a bad period—for two years she drank and gambled.

Her life had apparently become useless to her and she tried to throw it away.

But people who believe in themselves make others believe. Men who had been lovers of Alice never forgot her. They never went back on her.

They said she gave them something. She was sixty when I knew her.

Once she took me up to the Adirondack Mountains. We went together in a big car with a Negro driver to a house that was half a palace. It took us two days to get there.

The whole outfit belonged to some rich man.

It was the time when Alice said she was flat. "I got you something once when you were flat, now you come with me," she had said when she saw me in New York.

She did not mean flat as regards money. She was spiritually flat.

So we went and stayed alone together in a big house. There were servants there. They had been provided for. I don't know how.

We had been there for a week and Alice had been silent. One evening we went to walk.

This was a wild country. There was a lake before the house and a mountain at the back.

It was a chilly night with a clear sky and a moon and we walked in a country road.

Then we began to climb the mountains. I can remember Alice's thick legs and her stockings coming down.

She was short-winded too. She kept stopping to puff and blow.

We plowed on silently like that. Alice, when herself, was seldom silent.

We got clear to the top of the mountain before she spoke.

She talked about what flatness is, how it hits people—floors them. Houses gone all flat, people all flat, life flat. "You think I am courageous," she said. "The hell with that. I haven't the courage of a mouse."

We sat down on a stone and she began to tell me of her life. It was an odd complex story, told in that way, in little jerks by an old woman.

There it was, the whole thing. She had come down out of the Tennessee mountains as a young girl to the city of Nashville, in Tennessee.

She got in with a singing master there who knew she could sing. "Well, I took him as a lover. He wasn't so bad."

The man spent money on her; he interested some Nashville rich man.

That man also may have been her lover. Alice did not say. There were plenty of others.

One of them—he must have amounted to less than any of the others—she had loved.

She said he was a young poet. There was something crooked in him. He did sneaking things.

That was when she was past thirty and he was twenty-five. She lost her head, she said, and of course lost him.

It was then she went to drinking, gambled, went broke. She declared she lost him because she loved him too much.

"But why wasn't he any good? Why did you have to love that sort?"

She did not know why. It had happened.

It must have been the experience that had tempered her.

But I was speaking of beauty in people, what an odd thing it is, how it appears, disappears and reappears.

I got a glimpse of it in Alice that night.

It was when we were coming back to the house, from the mountain, down the road.

We were on a hillside and stout Alice in front. There was a muddy stretch of road and then a woods and then an open space.

The moonlight was in the open space and I was in the woods, in the darkness of the woods, but a few steps behind.

She crossed the open space ahead of me and there it was.

The thing lasted but a fleeting second. I think that all of the rich powerful men Alice had known, who had given her money, helped her when she needed help, and who have got so much from her, must have seen what I saw then. It was what the man saw in the woman by the mountain cabin and what the other man saw in the horse trader's woman in the road.

Alice when she said she was flat wasn't flat. Alice trying to shake off the memory of an unsuccessful love.

She was walking across the open moonlit stretch of road like a queen, as that man who was once her lover said she used to walk across a room or across a stage.

The mountains out of which she came as a child must have been in her at the moment, and the moon and the night.

Myself in love with her, madly, for a moment.

Is anyone in love longer than that?

Alice shaking her head slightly. There may have been a trick of the light. Her stride lengthened and she became tall, and young. I remember stopping in the woods and staring. I was like the two other men of whom I have spoken. I had a cane in my hand and it fell to the ground. I was like the man in the road and the other man in the field.

That Sophistication

LONGMAN was a man I met in Paris some six or eight years ago. With his wife he had an apartment in the Boulevard Raspail. You climbed up to it with difficulty. There was no elevator.

I am not just sure where I first met him. It might have been in the studio of Madam T. Madam T. was an American woman. She came from Indianapolis. Or was it Dayton?

Anyway, she was said to have been the mistress of the Spanish poet, Sarasen. A dozen people had told me about that. It was when Sarasen was an old man.

But who was Sarasen? I had never heard of him before. I told Mabel Cathers about that. Mabel is from Chicago. She was indignant. "How should you?" she asked. "You do not know Spanish."

It was quite true. I didn't.

I suspected that Madam T. had a goiter. She wore a yellow ribbon about her neck. I was frivolous all that Summer. Being with Mabel made me so. When I was in Madam T.'s studio, I was always thinking of a song we used to sing in our Ohio town when I was a boy:

> "Around her neck, she wore a yellow ribbon,
>   She wore it all the night and she wore it all the day.
>   When they asked her why in the hell she wore it,
>   She wore it for her lover who was far, far away."

It is all right even to have a goiter if you have as much money as Madam T. She wore exquisite gowns.

Someone said that when Sarasen was an old man she took tender and loving care of him. The old giant of literature in his dotage. I wished I could get me one like that. I told Mabel so. We were living at the same little hotel. I presume Mabel's husband was at home, in Chicago. "But you are no giant and never will be," she said smiling. She smiled so nicely I didn't mind what she said.

There was another song also in my head a lot, just at that time. It went like this:

> *"There's where she stays all day.*
> *I wonder where she stays all night."*

That was all I knew of the song.

No chance of keeping track of Mabel. She ran all around Paris, day and night. And she had no French. She was getting culture, sophistication. That was her purpose. She told me so herself. I liked Mabel.

But be that as it may, we will say that I did meet Harry Long-man in the studio of Madam T. The house was on the Left Bank. I have forgotten the name of the street. French names never would stick in my head. There was a court, such as you see in old houses in New Orleans. In New Orleans they call them "patios." The studio occupied all the ground floor. Ralph Cook took me there the first time. But you do not know Ralph. Well, never mind.

Madam T. had bought any number of pictures by European painters, the kind that cost a lot of money. Cezannes, Von Goghs, etc. She had a lot of Monets, I remember.

Cook also had some Monets. He was the son of an American rich man.

Cook had been at Oxford, as a student, taking his degree there I think. He brought a young Englishman back with him.

The Englishman was of the healthy rosy-cheeked sort. He laughed all the time. Life was one grand show for him. He was the son of an English lord and had a title of his own but kept it out of sight. "For God's sake don't tell anybody that," he said to me, when I found it out.

He delighted in Americans. He, Cook, Mabel, and I went to Madam T.'s together. In the large room downstairs, with the pictures on the wall, many people were gathered. They were, for the most part, mannish women and womanly men. It was to be an afternoon of poetry.

Through an open window we could see into a little court outside. In a corner there was a small structure built of stone. A stone dove perched on it. Someone told us it was a temple of love.

The Englishman liked that. The idea delighted him. He said he would like to get Cook and Mabel to go with him and wor-ship out there. "Come on," he whispered. "Let's go and fall on

our knees together. Everyone will see us. We will declare love
has just come to us."

Mabel said it wasn't a subject to be dealt with lightly like
that. She did not like the Englishman and told me so afterwards. "He's too frivolous about sacred things," she said. I
suspected Mabel would have liked being a Madam T. herself.
She hadn't the money.

"Love of what?" growled Cook. He was a big, broad-
shouldered young man from somewhere in Texas. At Oxford
he had made a record.

The young Englishman was a scholar, too. He seemed to
me too light-minded for that, but Cook told me he was all
right. "His mind sometimes lights up the whole lecture room
over there at Oxford," Cook said.

On the afternoon when we went to Madam T.'s there was
some sort of ceremony going on. A woman got up and read a
poem. There was a great deal said about the dove and I did
not exactly understand the symbolism. "What do doves do?" I
asked Mabel, but she did not know. I think she was ashamed,
not being better informed. There was, Cook told me afterwards, a good deal of that sort of talk going on among the
English upper classes. "Well, it's sophistication, isn't it? That's
what you're after, isn't it?" I asked Mabel. She treated my inquiry with scorn.

The young Englishman, Cook had got in with, had told him
a good deal about it. He said that at Oxford, after he and Cook
got acquainted, they used to walk about and speak of it.

The young Englishman had told Cook he thought such
ideas came from living too long at one place—the English living too long in England, the French in France, the Germans in
Germany. "The Russians and the Americans are still primitive
peoples," he said. That made Mabel sore. It seemed, to Mabel
and me, a kind of slur on our native land, the way Cook explained it.

Europeans are too tired, the Englishman had told Cook. He
had a notion people are like this—well, they have apparently to
believe that if they move to a new place life will go better with
them. A horde of people had come out of Europe to America
feeling that way. Americans were still always moving about. It
was certainly true of people like Mabel and myself.

The Russians too were great wanderers. They believed in the possibility of the salvation of their race through new forms of government—"all that sort of rot," the Englishman had said when he talked to Cook. You understand that Mabel and I got all this from Cook, who had certainly learned a lot since he left Texas.

The young Englishman thought the Americans an altogether primitive people. They could still believe in government. They looked toward Heaven as another and more successful America, he thought. They believed in such things as Prohibition, for example.

And it wasn't, as it sometimes seemed on the surface, merely a matter of a passion for interfering in the lives of others. There was a deep-seated and rather childish belief that all people could be saved.

But what did they mean by "being saved"?

"They meant just what they said when they used the words. They thought vaguely that a good and powerful leader would be found to lead them out of the wilderness of this life."

"Something as Moses led the Children of Israel out of Egypt, eh?"

"But he is not speaking about Jews," Mabel said. Afterwards she spoke several times about what an intellectual afternoon it was. She said she thought it was swell. Just the same there was a lot of—shall I say Krafft-Ebing—talk that got over my head and that I know Mabel didn't get. We had both missed something, not having been enough among the world-weary, I guess.

But I have got a long way from Henry Longman. Now I will come to him.

He came from Cleveland, Ohio. We saw him first, at least I did, that afternoon at Madam T.'s. He was a strange figure there. For one thing he had his wife with him. That, in that place, was strange in itself.

It seemed Cook and the young Englishman had pounced on him. I have already said that he lived in a studio apartment, on the Boulevard Raspail, on the top floor.

It was a six-storied building, six flights of stairs to climb.

Henry's wife was a big blonde and he was a big man with a fat, red face. Cook had in some way got the low-down on him.

He came from Cleveland where he had got his wife. His father was a candy manufacturer out there.

And his wife's father was also rich.

The two fathers had been hard-working young men and had got on, in the American world. They both got rich.

Then their son and daughter had got the culture hunger. Their fathers might have been half proud of them, half ashamed. The woman, when she was in college, won a poetry prize. An American magazine, of the better class, published the poem.

Then she married the young man, the son of her father's friend. They went to live in Paris. They were conducting a salon.

They had taken that top floor, in the old building without an elevator, because it seemed to them artistic.

Their effort was to get the French to come to their place, and they did come, of course. Why not? There was food and drink, an abundance of both.

Longman and his wife spoke little French, about as much as Mabel and I. They couldn't get the hang of it.

Longman wanted us to think him an Englishman of the upper classes.

He hinted vaguely of an English family, of good blood, ruined, I gathered. "How could that be—his having all of that money?" the young Englishman asked Mabel. He, the young Englishman, had taken a fancy to Mabel. "He thinks you primitive and interesting," I kept telling her. I knew how to be nasty too. Longman's father sent him a lot of money and his wife's father sent her some money and—having all of that money—they fancied the idea of seeming poor. "We are dreadfully in debt," Longman's wife was always saying.

As she said it, we sat drinking the most expensive wines to be had in France.

They had a crowd always about—feeding people as they did, wining them.

The wine was brought in. It was opened and a glass poured for the blonde wife. She always made a wry face at the first taste. "Henry," she said sharply to her husband, "I think the wine is slightly corked." Mabel thought it was grand technique. It was a word the blonde had got hold of. When she said it her husband ran to her. We were in a large studio room, built for a painter. There was a glass roof. In the corner there was a cheap sink, such as you see in American small hotels. The husband, with a look of horror on his face, ran and poured the wine down the sink.

Expensive wine going off like that. I could see Mabel shiver. "I'll bet Mabel is a good economical housewife at home," Cook whispered to me.

Longman began to talk. He liked to give the impression that he was in Paris on some important mission, say, for the British government—for Downing Street, say. He didn't exactly say so.

And he referred to a book—one, you were to understand he was writing or had written. I couldn't get that clear. He did not say, "My Life of Napoleon" or "My Secrets of Downing Street." Just how did he get it across? There was the distinct impression left that he had written several important works. He was like an author, too modest really to refer directly to his work.

We got all that, going on day after day, month after month.

The Americans from Cleveland pretending to themselves they were important people, the guests pretending they were important.

They, the guests, pretending they had important reasons for being in Paris. A little string of lies, each telling the other a lie.

Why not? I went there on several occasions with Cook, Mabel and the young Englishman. Every evening the same thing happened.

Mabel, Cook and I got a little tired of the young Englishman sometimes, and Mabel let him know it. It was a little hard on him and Cook. Cook had to decide whether he wanted to stick to the Englishman or to us. He stuck to us—on account of Mabel, of course.

He said it was a fair sight to see the way Mabel could cut people out of our herd. We did make up a small herd, the crowd of us at our cheap Left Bank hotel. Cook came to live there and we got three or four more—males, you may be sure.

We all used to go to Longman's a lot. There was good food and good wine and we all liked to hear Longman's wife say the wine was corked. She always said it at the first taste of the first bottle after we arrived. When someone else came in, she said it again. Mabel said she was sorry we had Prohibition in America. She would have liked, she said, to spring it on the folks at home, but it would cost too much.

She said she had come to Europe, as we all had, to get sophistication and that she thought she was getting it. Cook and I and several others tried to give her some.

She said the trouble was that the more sophistication she got the more she felt like Chicago. She said it was almost like being in Chicago, the sophistication she picked up after four or five other Americans, all of them men, began living with us at our hotel.

"I might have saved my husband all this money and got all this sophistication I'm getting, or anyway all I needed, right in Chicago," she declared several times during that Summer.

In a Strange Town

A MORNING in a country town in a strange place. Everything is quiet. No, there are sounds. Sounds assert themselves. A boy whistles. I can hear the sound here, where I stand, at a railroad station. I have come away from home. I am in a strange place. There is no such thing as silence. Once I was in the country. I was at the house of a friend. "You see, there is not a sound here. It is absolutely silent." My friend said that because he was used to the little sounds of the place, the humming of insects, the sound of falling water—far-off—the faint clattering sound of a man with a machine in the distance, cutting hay. He was accustomed to the sounds and did not hear them. Here, where I am now, I hear a beating sound. Some one has hung a carpet on a clothesline and is beating it. Another boy shouts, far off—"A-ho, a-ho."

It is good to go and come. You arrive in a strange place. There is a street facing a railroad track. You get off a train with your bags. Two porters fight for possession of you and the bags as you have seen porters do with strangers in your own town.

As you stand at the station there are things to be seen. You see the open doors of the stores on the street that faces the station. People go in and out. An old man stops and looks. "Why, there is the morning train," his mind is saying to him.

The mind is always saying such things to people. "Look, be aware," it says. The fancy wants to float free of the body. We put a stop to that.

Most of us live our lives like toads, sitting perfectly still, under a plantain leaf. We are waiting for a fly to come our way. When it comes out darts the tongue. We nab it.

That is all. We eat it.

But how many questions to be asked that are never asked. Whence came the fly? Where was he going?

The fly might have been going to meet his sweetheart. He was stopped; a spider ate him.

The train on which I have been riding, a slow one, pauses for a time. All right, I'll go to the Empire House. As though I cared.

673

It is a small town—this one—to which I have come. In any event I'll be uncomfortable here. There will be the same kind of cheap brass beds as at the last place to which I went unexpectedly like this—with bugs in the bed perhaps. A traveling salesman will talk in a loud voice in the next room. He will be talking to a friend, another traveling salesman. "Trade is bad," one of them will say. "Yes, it's rotten."

There will be confidences about women picked up—some words heard, others missed. That is always annoying.

But why did I get off the train here at this particular town? I remember that I had been told there was a lake here—that there was fishing. I thought I would go fishing.

Perhaps I expected to swim. I remember now.

"Porter, where is the Empire House? Oh, the brick one. All right, go ahead. I'll be along pretty soon. You tell the clerk to save me a room, with a bath, if they have one."

I remember what I was thinking about. All my life, since that happened, I have gone off on adventures like this. A man likes to be alone sometimes.

Being alone doesn't mean being where there are no people. It means being where people are all strangers to you.

There is a woman crying there. She is getting old, that woman. Well, I am myself no longer young. See how tired her eyes are. There is a younger woman with her. In time that younger woman will look exactly like her mother.

She will have the same patient, resigned look. The skin will sag on her cheeks that are plump now. The mother has a large nose and so has the daughter.

There is a man with them. He is fat and has red veins in his face. For some reason I think he must be a butcher.

He has that kind of hands, that kind of eyes.

I am pretty sure he is the woman's brother. Her husband is dead. They are putting a coffin on the train.

They are people of no importance. People pass them casually. No one has come to the station to be with them in their hour of trouble. I wonder if they live here. Yes, of course they do. They live somewhere, in a rather mean little house, at the edge of town, or perhaps outside the town. You see the brother is not going away with the mother and daughter. He has just come down to see them off.

They are going, with the body, to another town where the husband, who is dead, formerly lived.

The butcher-like man has taken his sister's arm. That is a gesture of tenderness. Such people make such gestures only when someone in the family is dead.

The sun shines. The conductor of the train is walking along the station platform and talking to the station-master. They have been laughing loudly, having their little joke.

That conductor is one of the jolly sort. His eyes twinkle, as the saying is. He has his little joke with every station-master, every telegraph operator, baggage man, express man, along the way. There are all kinds of conductors of passenger trains.

There, you see, they are passing the woman whose husband has died and is being taken away somewhere to be buried. They drop their jokes, their laughter. They become silent.

A little path of silence made by that woman in black and her daughter and the fat brother. The little path of silence has started with them at their house, has gone with them along streets to the railroad station, will be with them on the train and in the town to which they are going. They are people of no importance, but they have suddenly become important.

They are symbols of Death. Death is an important, a majestic thing, eh?

How easily you can comprehend a whole life, when you are in a place like this, in a strange place, among strange people. Everything is so much like other towns you have been in. Lives are made up of little series of circumstances. They repeat themselves, over and over, in towns everywhere, in cities, in all countries.

They are of infinite variety. In Paris, when I was there last year, I went into the Louvre. There were men and women there, making copies of the works of the old masters that were hung on the walls. They were professional copyists.

They worked painstakingly, were trained to do just that kind of work, very exactly.

And yet no one of them could make a copy. There were no copies made.

The little circumstances of no two lives anywhere in the world are just alike.

You see I have come over into a hotel room now, in this strange town. It is a country-town hotel. There are flies in here. A fly has just alighted on this paper on which I have been writing these impressions. I stopped writing and looked at the fly. There must be billions of flies in the world and yet, I dare say, no two of them are alike.

The circumstances of their lives are not just alike.

I think I must come away from my own place on trips, such as I am on now, for a specific reason.

At home I live in a certain house. There is my own household, the servants, the people of my household. I am a professor of philosophy in a college in my town, hold a certain definite position there, in the town life and in the college life.

Conversations in the evening, music, people coming into our house.

Myself going to a certain office, then to a class room where I lecture, seeing people there.

I know some things about these people. That is the trouble with me perhaps. I know something but not enough.

My mind, my fancy, becomes dulled looking at them.

I know too much and not enough.

It is like a house in the street in which I live. There is a particular house in that street—in my home town—I was formerly very curious about. For some reason the people who lived in it were recluses. They seldom came out of their house and hardly ever out of the yard, into the street.

Well, what of all that?

My curiosity was aroused. That is all.

I used to walk past the house with something strangely alive in me. I had figured out this much. An old man with a beard and a white-faced woman lived there. There was a tall hedge and once I looked through. I saw the man walking nervously up and down, on a bit of lawn, under a tree. He was clasping and unclasping his hands and muttering words. The doors and shutters of the mysterious house were all closed. As I looked, the old woman with the white face opened the door a little and looked out at the man. Then the door closed again. She said nothing to him. Did she look at him with love or with fear in her eyes? How do I know? I could not see.

Another time I heard a young woman's voice, although I never saw a young woman about the place. It was evening and the woman was singing—a rather sweet young woman's voice it was.

There you are. That is all. Life is more like that than people suppose. Little odd fragmentary ends of things. That is about all we get. I used to walk past that place all alive, curious. I enjoyed it. My heart thumped a little.

I heard sounds more distinctly, felt more.

I was curious enough to ask my friends along the street about the people.

"They're queer," people said.

Well, who is not queer?

The point is that my curiosity gradually died. I accepted the queerness of the life of that house. It became a part of the life of my street. I became dulled to it.

I have become dulled to the life of my own house, or my street, to the lives of my pupils.

"Where am I? Who am I? Whence came I?" Who asks himself these questions any more?

There is that woman I saw taking her dead husband away on the train. I saw her only for a moment before I walked over to this hotel and came up to this room (an entirely commonplace hotel room it is) but here I sit, thinking of her. I reconstruct her life, go on living the rest of her life with her.

Often I do things like this, come off alone to a strange place like this. "Where are you going?" my wife says to me. "I am going to take a bath," I say.

My wife thinks I am a bit queer too, but she has grown used to me. Thank God, she is a patient and a good-natured woman.

"I am going to bathe myself in the lives of people about whom I know nothing."

I will sit in this hotel until I am tired of it and then I will walk in strange streets, see strange houses, strange faces. People will see me.

Who is he?

He is a stranger.

That is nice. I like that. To be a stranger sometimes, going about in a strange place, having no business there, just walking, thinking, bathing myself.

To give others, the people here in this strange place, a little jump at the heart too—because I am something strange.

Once, when I was a young man I would have tried to pick up a girl. Being in a strange place, I would have tried to get my jump at the heart out of trying to be with her.

Now I do not do that. It is not because I am especially faithful —as the saying goes—to my wife, or that I am not interested in strange and attractive women.

It is because of something else. It may be that I am a bit dirty with life and have come here, to this strange place, to bathe myself in strange life and get clean and fresh again.

And so I walk in such a strange place. I dream. I let myself have fancies. Already I have been out into the street, into several streets of this town and have walked about. I have aroused in myself a little stream of fresh fancies, clustered about strange lives, and as I walked, being a stranger, going along slowly, carrying a cane, stopping to look into stores, stopping to look into the windows of houses and into gardens, I have, you see, aroused in others something of the same feeling that has been in me.

I have liked that. Tonight, in the houses of this town, there will be something to speak of.

"There was a strange man about. He acted queerly. I wonder who he was."

"What did he look like?"

An attempt to delve into me too, to describe me. Pictures being made in other minds. A little current of thoughts, fancies, started in others, in me too.

I sit here in this room in this strange town, in this hotel, feeling oddly refreshed. Already I have slept here. My sleep was sweet. Now it is morning and everything is still. I dare say that, some time today, I shall get on another train and go home.

But now I am remembering things.

Yesterday, in this town, I was in a barber shop. I got my hair cut. I hate getting my hair cut.

"I am in a strange town, with nothing to do, so I'll get my hair cut," I said to myself as I went in.

A man cut my hair. "It rained a week ago," he said. "Yes," I said. That is all the conversation there was between us.

However, there was other talk in that barber shop, plenty of it.

A man had been here in this town and had passed some bad checks. One of them was for ten dollars and was made out in the name of one of the barbers in the shop.

The man who passed the checks was a stranger, like myself. There was talk of that.

A man came in who looked like President Coolidge and had his hair cut.

Then there was another man who came for a shave. He was an old man with sunken cheeks and for some reason looked like a sailor. I dare say he was just a farmer. This town is not by the sea.

There was talk enough in there, a whirl of talk.

I came out thinking.

Well, with me it is like this. A while ago I was speaking of a habit I have formed of going suddenly off like this to some strange place. "I have been doing it ever since it happened," I said. I used the expression "it happened."

Well, what happened?

Not so very much.

A girl got killed. She was struck by an automobile. She was a girl in one of my classes.

She was nothing special to me. She was just a girl—a woman, really—in one of my classes. When she was killed I was already married.

She used to come into my room, into my office. We used to sit in there and talk.

We used to sit and talk about something I had said in my lecture.

"Did you mean this?"

"No, that is not exactly it. It is rather like this."

I suppose you know how we philosophers talk. We have almost a language of our own. Sometimes I think it is largely nonsense.

I would begin talking to that girl—that woman—and on and on I would go. She had gray eyes. There was a sweet serious look on her face.

Do you know, sometimes, when I talked to her like that (it is, I am pretty sure, all nonsense), well, I thought . . .

Her eyes seemed to me sometimes to grow a little larger as I talked to her. I had a notion she did not hear what I said.

I did not care much.

I talked so that I would have something to say.

Sometimes, when we were together that way, in my office in the college building, there would come odd times of silence.

No, it was not silence. There were sounds.

There was a man walking in a hallway, in the college building outside my door. Once when this happened I counted the man's footsteps. Twenty-six, twenty-seven, twenty-eight.

I was looking at the girl—the woman—and she was looking at me.

You see I was an older man. I was married.

I am not such an attractive man. I did, however, think she was very beautiful. There were plenty of young fellows about.

I remember now that when she had been with me like that— after she had left—I used to sit sometimes for hours alone in my office, as I have been sitting here, in this hotel room, in a strange town.

I sat thinking of nothing. Sounds came in to me. I remembered things of my boyhood.

I remembered things about my courtship and marriage. I sat like that dumbly, a long time.

I was dumb, but I was at the same time more aware than I had ever been in my life.

It was at that time I got the reputation with my wife of being a little queer. I used to go home, after sitting dumbly like that, with that girl, that woman, and I was even more dumb and silent when I got home.

"Why don't you talk?" my wife said.

"I'm thinking," I said.

I wanted her to believe that I was thinking of my work, my studies. Perhaps I was.

Well, the girl, the woman, was killed. An automobile struck her when she was crossing a street. They said she was absent-minded—that she walked right in front of a car. I was in my office, sitting there, when a man, another professor, came in and told me. "She is quite dead, was quite dead when they picked her up," he said.

"Yes." I dare say he thought I was pretty cold and unsympathetic—a scholar, eh, having no heart.

"It was not the driver's fault. He was quite blameless."

"She walked right out in front of the car?"

"Yes."

I remember that at the moment I was fingering a pencil. I did not move. I must have been sitting like that for two or three hours.

I got out and walked. I was walking when I saw a train. So I got on.

Afterward I telephoned to my wife. I don't remember what I told her at that time.

It was all right with her. I made some excuse. She is a patient and a good-natured woman. We have four children. I dare say she is absorbed in the children.

I came to a strange town and I walked about there. I forced myself to observe the little details of life. That time I stayed three or four days and then I went home.

At intervals I have been doing the same thing ever since. It is because at home I grow dull to little things. Being in a strange place like this makes me more aware. I like it. It makes me more alive.

So you see, it is morning and I have been in a strange town, where I know no one and where no one knows me.

As it was yesterday morning, when I came here, to this hotel room, there are sounds. A boy whistles in the street. Another boy, far off, shouts "A-ho."

There are voices in the street, below my window, strange voices. Some one, somewhere in this town, is beating a carpet. I hear the sound of the arrival of a train. The sun is shining.

I may stay here in this town another day or I may go on to another town. No one knows where I am. I am taking this bath in life, as you see, and when I have had enough of it I shall go home feeling refreshed.

These Mountaineers

HEN I had lived in the Southwest Virginia mountains for
some time, people of the North, when I went up there,
used to ask me many questions about the mountain people.
They did it whenever I went to the city. You know how people
are. They like to have everything ticketed.

The rich are so and so, the poor are so and so, the politi-
cians, the people of the Western Coast. As though you could
draw one figure and say—"there it is. That's it."

The men and women of the mountains were what they
were. They were people. They were poor whites. That certainly
meant that they were white and poor. Also they were mountaineers.

After the factories began to come down into this country,
into Virginia, Tennessee and North Carolina, a lot of them went,
with their families, to work in the factories and to live in mill
towns. For a time all was peace and quiet, and then strikes
broke out. Every one who reads newspapers knows about that.
There was a lot of writing in newspapers about these mountain
people. Some of it was pretty keen.

But there had been a lot of romancing about them before
that. That sort of thing never did any one much good.

So I was walking alone in the mountains and had got down
into what in the mountain country is called "a hollow." I was
lost. I had been fishing for trout in mountain streams and was
tired and hungry. There was a road of a sort I had got into. It
would have been difficult to get a car over that road. "This
ought to be a good whisky-making country," I thought.

In the hollow along which the road went I came to a little
town. Well, now, you would hardly call it a town. There were
six or eight little unpainted frame houses and, at a cross roads,
a general store.

The mountains stretched away, above the poor little houses.
On both sides of the road were the magnificent hills. You understand, when you have been down there, why they are called the
"Blue Ridge." They are always blue, a glorious blue. What a
country it must have been before the lumber men came! Over

near my place in the mountains men were always talking of the
spruce forests of former days. Many of them worked in the
lumber camps. They speak of soft moss into which a man sank
almost to the knees, the silence of the forest, the great trees.

The great forest is gone now, but the young trees are growing. Much of the country will grow nothing but timber.

The store before which I stood that day was closed, but an
old man sat on a little porch in front. He said that the storekeeper also carried the mail and was out on his route but that
he would be back and open his store in an hour or two.

I had thought I might at least get some cheese and crackers
or a can of sardines.

The man on the porch was old. He was an evil-looking old
man. He had gray hair and a gray beard and might have been
seventy, but I could see that he was a tough-bodied old fellow.

I asked my way back over the mountain to the main road
and had started to move off up the hollow when he called to
me. "Are you the man who has moved in here from the North
and has built a house in here?"

There is no use my trying to reproduce the mountain
speech. I am not skilled at it.

The old man invited me to his house to eat. "You don't
mind eating beans, do you?" he asked.

I was hungry and would be glad to have beans. I would have
eaten anything at the moment. He said he hadn't any woman,
that his old woman was dead. "Come on," he said, "I think I
can fix you up."

We went up a path, over a half mountain and into another
hollow, perhaps a mile away. It was amazing. The man was old.
The skin on his face and neck was wrinkled like an old man's
skin and his legs and body were thin, but he walked at such a
pace that to follow him kept me panting.

It was a hot, still day in the hills. Not a breath of air stirred.
That old man was the only being I saw that day in that town.
If any one else lived there he had kept out of sight.

The old man's house was on the bank of another mountain
stream. That afternoon, after eating with him, I got some fine
trout out of the stream.

But this isn't a fishing story. We went to his house.

It was dirty and small and seemed about to fall down. The

old man was dirty. There were layers of dirt on his old hands and on his wrinkled neck. When we were in the house, which had but one room on the ground floor, he went to a small stove. "The fire is out," he said. "Do you care if the beans are cold?"

"No," I said. By this time I did not want any beans and wished I had not come. There was something evil about this old mountain man. Surely the romancers could not have made much out of him.

Unless they played on the Southern hospitality chord. He had invited me there. I had been hungry. The beans were all he had.

He put some of them on a plate and put them on a table before me. The table was a home-made one covered with a red oil cloth, now quite worn. There were large holes in it. Dirt and grease clung about the edges of the holes. He had wiped the plate, on which he had put the beans, on the sleeve of his coat.

But perhaps you have not eaten beans prepared in the mountains, in the mountain way. They are the staff of life down there. Without beans there would be no life in some of the hills. The beans are, when prepared by a mountain woman and served hot, often delicious. I do not know what they put in them or how they cook them, but they are unlike any beans you will find anywhere else in the world.

As Smithfield ham, when it is real Smithfield ham, is unlike any other ham.

But beans cold, beans dirty, beans served on a plate wiped on the sleeve of that coat . . .

I sat looking about. There was a dirty bed in the room in which we sat and an open stairway, leading up to the room above.

Some one moved up there. Some one walked barefooted across the floor. There was silence for a time and then it happened again.

You must get the picture of a very hot still place between hills. It was June. The old man had become silent. He was watching me. Perhaps he wanted to see whether or not I was going to scorn his hospitality. I began eating the beans with a dirty spoon. I was many miles away from any place I had ever been before.

And then there was that sound again. I had got the impression that the old man had told me his wife was dead, that he lived alone.

How did I know it was a woman upstairs? I did know.

"Have you got a woman up there?" I asked. He grinned, a toothless malicious grin, as though to say, "Oh, you're curious, eh?"

And then he laughed, a queer cackle.

"She ain't mine," he said.

We sat in silence after that and then there was the sound again. I heard bare feet walking across a plank floor.

Now the feet were descending the crude open stairs. Two legs appeared, two thin, young girl's legs.

She didn't look to be over twelve or thirteen.

She came down, almost to the foot of the stairs, and then stopped and sat down.

How dirty she was, how thin, what a wild look she had! I have never seen a wilder-looking creature. Her eyes were bright. They were like the eyes of a wild animal.

And, at that, there was something about her face. In many of these young mountain faces there is a look it is difficult to explain—it is a look of breeding, of aristocracy. I know no other word for the look.

And she had it.

And now the two were sitting there, and I was trying to eat. Suppose I rose and threw the dirty beans out at the open door. I might have said, "Thank you, I have enough." I didn't dare.

But perhaps they weren't thinking of the beans. The old man began to speak of the girl, sitting ten feet from him, as though she were not there.

"She ain't mine," he said. "She came here. Her pop died. She ain't got any one."

I am making a bad job of trying to reproduce his speech.

He was giggling now, a toothless old man's giggle. "Ha, she won't eat.

"She's a hell cat," he said.

He reached over and touched me on the arm. "You know what. She's a hell cat. You couldn't satisfy her. She had to have her a man.

"And she got one too."

"Is she married?" I asked, half whispering the words, not wanting her to hear.

He laughed at the idea. "Ha. Married, eh?"

He said it was a young man from farther down the hollow. "He lives here with us," the old man said laughing, and as he said it the girl rose and started back up the stairs. She had said nothing, but her young eyes had looked at us, filled with hatred. As she went up the stairs the old man kept laughing at her, his queer, high-pitched, old man's laugh. It was really a giggle. "Ha, she can't eat. When she tries to eat she can't keep it down. She thinks I don't know why. She's a hell cat. She would have a man and now she's got one.

"Now she can't eat."

I fished in the creek in the hollow during the afternoon and toward evening began to get trout. They were fine ones. I got fourteen of them and got back over a mountain and into the main road before dark.

What took me back into the hollow I don't know. The face of the girl possessed me.

And then there was good trout fishing there. That stream at least had not been fished out.

When I went back I put a twenty-dollar bill in my pocket. "Well," I thought—I hardly know what I did think. There were notions in my head, of course.

The girl was very, very young.

"She might have been kept there by that old man," I thought, "and by some young mountain rough. There might be a chance for her."

I thought I would give her the twenty dollars. "If she wants to get out perhaps she can," I thought. Twenty dollars is a lot of money in the hills.

It was just another hot day when I got in there again and the old man was not at home. At first I thought there was no one there. The house stood alone by a hardly discernible road and near the creek. The creek was clear and had a swift current. It made a chattering sound.

I stood on the bank of the creek before the house and tried to think.

"If I interfere . . ."

Well, let's admit it. I was a bit afraid. I thought I had been a fool to come back.

And then the girl suddenly came out of the house and came toward me. There was no doubt about it. She was that way. And unmarried, of course.

At least my money, if I could give it to her, would serve to buy her some clothes. The ones she had on were very ragged and dirty. Her feet and legs were bare. It would be winter by the time the child was born.

A man came out of the house. He was a tall young mountain man. He looked rough. "That's him," I thought. He said nothing.

He was dirty and unkempt as the old man had been and as the child was.

At any rate she was not afraid of me. "Hello, you are back here," she said. Her voice was clear.

Just the same I saw the hatred in her eyes. I asked about the fishing. "Are the trout biting?" I asked. She had come nearer me now, and the young man had slouched back into the house.

Again I am at a loss about how to reproduce her mountain speech. It is peculiar. So much is in the voice.

Hers was cold and clear and filled with hatred.

"How should I know? He" (indicating with a gesture of her hand the tall slouching figure who had gone into the house) "is too damn' lazy to fish.

"He's too damn' lazy for anything on earth."

She was glaring at me.

"Well," I thought, "I will at least try to give her the money." I took the bill in my hand and held it toward her. "You will need some clothes," I said. "Take it and buy yourself some clothes."

It may have been that I had touched her mountain pride. How am I to know? The look of hatred in her eyes seemed to grow more intense.

"You go to hell," she said. "You get out of here. And don't you come back in here again."

She was looking hard at me when she said this. If you have never known such people, who live like that, "on the outer fringe of life," as we writers say (you may see them sometimes in the tenement districts of cities as well as in the lonely and lovely hills)—such a queer look of maturity in the eyes of a child. . . .

It sends a shiver through you. Such a child knows too much and not enough. Before she went back into the house she turned and spoke to me again. It was about my money.

She told me to put it somewhere, I won't say where. The most modern of modern writers has to use some discretion.

Then she went into the house. That was all. I left. What was I to do? After all, a man looks after his hide. In spite of the trout I did not go fishing in that hollow again.

A Sentimental Journey

My friend David, with his wife, Mildred, came to live in the hills. She was a delicate little woman. I used to go often to the cabin they had rented. Although David is a scholar, he and a mountain man, named Joe, a man much older than David, became friends. I sat in their cabin one evening, after I had first met David, while he told me the story. Joe was not there and Mildred was in the kitchen at work.

Joe is a thin mountain man of forty with the straight wiry figure of a young boy. David spoke of the first time he ever saw the man. He said: "I remember that he frightened me. It was a day last Fall, when we had first come in here, and I was on the gray horse riding the hills.

"I was a little nervous. You know how it is. Romantic tales of mountain men shooting strangers from behind trees or from wooded mountain-sides floated through my mind. Suddenly, out of an old timber road, barely discernible, leading off up into the hills, he emerged.

"He was mounted on a beautifully gaited but bony bay horse, and while I admired the horse's gait I feared the rider.

"What a fierce-looking man! Stories of men taken for Federal agents and killed by such fellows on lonely roads became suddenly real. His face was long and lean and he had a huge nose. His thin cheeks had not been shaved for weeks. He had on, I remember, an old wide-brimmed black hat, pulled well down over his eyes, and the eyes were cold and gray. The eyes stared at me. They were as cold as the gray sky overhead.

"Out of the thick golden-brown trees, well up the side of the mountain down which Joe had just come, I saw a thin column of smoke floating up into the sky. 'He has a still up there,' I thought. I felt myself in a dangerous position.

"Joe rode past me without speaking. My horse stood motionless in the road. I did not dare take my eyes off the man. 'He will shoot me in the back,' I thought. What a silly notion! My hands were trembling. 'Well,' I thought. 'Howdy,' said Joe.

"Stopping the bay horse he waited for me and we rode together down the mountain-side. He was curious about me. As to whether he had a still concealed in the woods I do not now know and I haven't asked. No doubt he had.

"And so Joe the mountain-man rode with me to my house here. (It was a log cabin built on the bank of a creek.) Mildred was inside cooking dinner. When we got to the little bridge that crosses the creek I looked at the man who had ridden beside me for half an hour without speaking and he looked at me. ''Light,' I said, 'and come in and eat.' We walked across the bridge toward the house. The night was turning cold. Before we entered the house he touched my arm gently with his long bony hand. He made a motion for me to stop and took a bottle from his coat pocket. I took a sip, but it was raw new stuff and burned my throat. It seemed to me that Joe took a half pint in one great gulp. 'It's new, he'll get drunk,' I thought, 'he'll raise hell in the house.' I was afraid for Mildred. She had been ill. That was the reason we had come up here, into this country.

"We were sitting here in the house by the fireplace here and could look through that open door. While we ate Mildred was nervous and kept looking at Joe with frightened eyes. There was the open door there, and Joe looked through it and into his hills. Darkness was coming on fast and in the hills a strong wind blew, but it did not come down into this valley. The air above was filled with floating yellow and red leaves. The room here was heavy with late Fall smells and the smell of moon whisky. That was Joe's breath.

"He was curious about my typewriter and the row of books on the shelves up there along the wall, but the fact that we were living in this old log house put him at his ease. We were not too grand. Mountain men are, as a rule, as you know, uncommunicative, but it turned out that Joe is a talker. He wanted to talk. He said that he had been wanting to come and see us for a long time. Someone had told him we were from distant parts, that we had seen the ocean and foreign lands. He had himself always wanted to go wandering in the big world but had been afraid. The idea of his being frightened of anything seemed absurd. I glanced at Mildred and we both smiled. We were feeling easier.

"And now Joe began to talk to us of his one attempt to go out of these mountains and into the outside world. It hadn't been successful. He was a hill man and could not escape the hills, had been raised in the hills and had never learned to read or write. He got up and fingered one of my books cautiously and then sat down again. 'Oh, Lord,' I thought, 'the man is lucky.' I had just read the book he had touched and after the glowing blurb on the jacket it had been a bitter disappointment.

"He told us that he had got married when he was sixteen and suggested vaguely that there was a reason. There often is, I guess, among these mountain people. Although he is yet a young man he is the father of fourteen children. Back in the hills somewhere he owned a little strip of land, some twenty acres, on which he raised corn. Most of the corn, I fancy, goes into whisky. A man who has fourteen children and but twenty acres of land has to scratch hard to live. I imagined that the coming of Prohibition and the rise in the price of moon has been a big help to him.

"That first evening his being with us started his mind reaching out into the world. He began talking of the journey he had once taken—that time he tried to escape from the hills.

"It was when he had been married but a short time and had but six children. Suddenly he decided to go out of the hills and into the broad world. Leaving his wife and five of the children at home in his mountain cabin, he set out—taking with him the oldest, a boy of seven.

"He said he did it because his corn crop had failed and his two hogs had died. It was an excuse. He really wanted to travel. He had a bony horse, and taking the boy on behind him he set out over the hills. I gathered that he had taken the boy because he was afraid he would be too lonely in the big world without some of his family. It was late Fall and the boy had no shoes.

"They went through the hills and down into a plain and then on into other hills and came at last to a coal-mining town where there were also factories. It was a large town. Joe got a job in the mines at once and he got good wages. It must have been a good year. He had never made so much money before. He told us, as though it were a breath-taking statement, that he made four dollars a day.

"It did not cost him much to live. He and the boy slept on the floor in a miner's cabin. The house in which they slept must have belonged to an Italian. Joe spoke of the people with whom he lived as 'Tallies.'

"And there was Joe, the mountain man, in the big world and he was afraid. There were the noises in the house at night. Joe and the boy were accustomed to the silence of the hills. In another room, during the evenings, men gathered and sat talking. They drank and began to sing. Sometimes they fought. They seemed as strange and terrible to Joe and his son as these mountain people had seemed at first to Mildred and myself. At night he came home from the mine, having bought some food at a store, and then he and the boy sat on a bench and ate. There were tears of loneliness in the boy's eyes. Joe hadn't put him in school. None of his children ever went to school. He was ashamed. He was only staying in the mining country to make money. His curiosity about the outside world was quite gone. How sweet these distant hills now seemed to him!

"On the streets of the mining town crowds of men were going along. There was a huge factory with grim-looking walls. What a noise it made! It kept going night and day. The air was filled with black smoke. Freight trains were always switching up and down a siding near the house where Joe and the boy lay on the floor, under the patched quilts they had brought with them from the hills.

"And then winter came. It snowed and froze and then snowed again. In the hills now the snow would be ten feet deep in places. Joe was hungry for its whiteness. He was working in the mines but he said he did not know how to get his money at the week's end. He was shy about asking. You had to go to a certain office where they had your name on a book. Joe said he did not know where it was.

"At last he found out. What a lot of money he had! Clutching it in his hand he went to the miner's house and got the boy. They had left the horse with a small farmer across the plain at the place where the hills began.

"They went there that evening, wading through the deep snow. It was bitter cold. I asked Joe if he had got shoes for the boy and he said 'no.' He said that by the time he got ready to start back into the hills it was night and the stores were closed. He figured he had enough money to buy a hog and some corn. He could go back to making whisky, back to these hills. Both he and the boy were half insane with desire.

"He cut up one of the quilts and made a covering for the boy's feet. Sitting in our house here, as the darkness came, he described the journey.

"It was an oddly dramatic recital. Joe had the gift. There was really no necessity for his starting off in such a rush. He might have waited until the roads were broken after the great snow.

"The only explanation he could give us was that he could not wait and the boy was sick with loneliness.

"And so, since he had been a boy, Joe had wanted to see the outside world, and now, having seen it, he wanted back his hills. He spoke of the happiness of himself and the boy trudging in the darkness in the deep snow.

"There was his woman in his cabin some eighty miles away in the hills. What of her? No one in the family could read or write. She might be getting out of wood. It was absurd. Such mountain women can fell trees as well as a man.

"It was all sentimentality on Joe's part. He knew that. At midnight he and the boy reached the cabin where they had left the horse and getting on the horse rode all of that night. When they were afraid they would freeze they got off the horse and struggled forward afoot. Joe said it warmed them up.

"They kept it up like that all the way home. Occasionally they came to a mountain cabin where there was a fire.

"Joe said the trip took three days and three nights and that he lost his way but he had no desire to sleep. The boy and the horse had, however, to have rest. At one place, while the boy slept on the floor of a mountain house before a fire and the horse ate and rested in a stable, Joe sat up with another mountain man and played cards from after midnight until four in the morning. He said he won two dollars.

"All the people in the mountain cabins on the way welcomed him and there was but one house where he had trouble. Looking at Mildred and myself, Joe smiled when he spoke of that night. It was when he had lost his way and had got down out of the hills and into a valley. The people of that house were outsiders. They were not hill people. I fancy they were afraid of Joe, as Mildred and I had been afraid, and that being afraid they had wanted to close the door on him and the boy.

"When he stopped at the house and called from the road a man put his head out at a window and told him to go away. The boy was almost frozen. Joe laughed. It was two in the morning.

"What he did was to take the boy in his arms and walk to the front door. Then he put his shoulder to the door and pushed. He got in. There was a little fireplace in a large front room and he went through the house to the back door and got wood.

"The man and his wife, dressed, Joe said, like city folks—that is to say, evidently in night clothes, pajamas perhaps—came to the door of a bedroom and looked at him. What he looked like, standing there in the firelight with the old hat pulled down over his face—the long lean face and the cold eyes—you may imagine.

"He stayed in the house three hours, warming himself and the boy. He went into a stable and fed the horse. The people in the house never showed themselves again. They had taken the one look at Joe and then going quickly back into the bedroom had closed and locked the door.

"Joe was curious. He said it was a grand house. I gathered it was much grander than my place. The whole inside of the house, he said, was like one big grand piece of furniture. Joe went into the kitchen but would not touch the food he found. He said he reckoned the people of the house were higher toned than we were. They were, he said, so high and mighty that he would not touch their food. What they were doing with such a house in that country he did not know. In some places, in the valleys among the hills, he said high-toned people like us were now coming in. He looked at Mildred and smiled when he said that.

"And, anyway, as Joe said, the people of the grand house evidently did not have any better food than he sometimes had at home. He had been curious and had gone into the kitchen and the pantry to look. I looked at Mildred. I was glad he had seemed to like our food.

"And so Joe and the boy were warmed and the horse was fed and they left the house as they had found it, the two strange people, who might also have heard or read tales of the dangerous character of mountain people, trembling in the room in which they had locked themselves.

"They got, Joe said, to their own house late on the next evening and they were almost starved. The snow had grown deeper. After the first heavy snow there had been a rain followed by sleet and then came more snow. In some of the mountain passes he and the boy had to go ahead of the horse, breaking the way.

"They got home at last and Joe did nothing but sleep for two days. He said the boy was all right. He also slept. Joe tried to explain to us that he had taken the desperate trip out of the mining country back into his own hills in such a hurry because he was afraid his wife, back in her cabin in the hills, would be out of firewood, but when he said it he had to smile.

" 'Pshaw,' he said, grinning sheepishly, 'there was plenty of wood in the house.' "

A Jury Case

THEY had a still up in the mountains. There were three of them. They were all tough.

What I mean is they were not men to fool with—at least two of them weren't.

First of all, there was Harvey Groves. Old man Groves had come into the mountain country thirty years before, and had bought a lot of mountain land.

He hadn't a cent and had only made a small payment on the land.

Right away he began to make moon whisky. He was one of the kind that can make pretty fair whisky out of anything. They make whisky out of potatoes, buckwheat, rye, corn or whatever they can get—the ones who really know how. One of that kind from here was sent to prison. He made whisky out of the prunes they served the prisoners for breakfast—anyway, he called it whisky. Old man Groves used to sell his whisky down at the lumber mills. There was a big cutting going on over on Briar Top Mountain.

They brought the lumber down the mountain to a town called Lumberville.

Old Groves sold his whisky to the lumberjacks and the manager of the mill got sore. He had old Groves into his office and tried to tell him what was what.

Instead, old Groves told him something. The manager said he would turn old Groves up. What he meant was that he would send the Federal men up the mountains after him, and old Groves told the manager that if a Federal man showed up in his hills he would burn the lumber stacked high about the mills at Lumberville.

He said it and he meant it and the mill manager knew he meant it.

The old man got away with that. He stayed up in his hills and raised a large family. Those at home were all boys. Every one about here speaks of the Groves girls, but what became of them I've never heard. They are not here now.

Harvey Groves was a tall, raw-boned young man with one

eye. He lost the other one in a fight. He began drinking and raising the devil all over the hills when he was little more than a boy and after the old man died of a cancer, and the old woman died and the land was divided among the sons and sold, and he got his share, he blew it in gambling and drinking.

He went moonshining when he was twenty-five. Cal Long and George Small went in with him. They all chipped in to buy the still.

Nowadays you can make moon whisky in a small still—it's called "over-night stuff"—about fourteen gallons to the run, and you make a run in one night.

You can sell it fast. There are plenty of men to buy and run it into the coal mining country over east of here. It's pretty raw stuff.

Cal Long, who went in with Harvey, is a big man with a beard. He is as strong as an ox. They don't make them any meaner. He seems a peaceful enough man, when he isn't drinking, but when he starts to drink, look out. He usually carries a long knife and he has cut several men pretty badly. He has been in jail three times.

The third man in the party was George Small. He used to come by our house—lived out our way for a time. He is a small nervous-looking young man who worked, until last Summer, on the farm of old man Barclay. One day last Fall, when I was over on the Barclay road and was sitting under a bridge, fishing, George came along the road.

What was the matter with him that time I've never found out.

I was sitting in silence under the bridge and he came along the road making queer movements with his hands. He was giving them a dry wash. His lips were moving. The road makes a turn right beyond the bridge and I could see him coming for almost a half mile before he got to the bridge. I was under the bridge and could see him without his seeing me. When he got close I heard his words. "Oh, my God, don't let me do it," he said. He kept saying it over and over. He had got married the Spring before. He might have had some trouble with his wife. I remember her as a small, red-haired woman. I saw the pair together once. George was carrying their baby in his arms and we stopped to talk. The woman moved a little away. She was shy as most mountain women are. George showed me the baby—not more than two weeks old—and it had a wrinkled little old face. It looked ages older than the father and mother but George was fairly bursting with pride while I stood looking at it.

How he happened to go in with men like Harvey Groves and Cal Long is a wonder to me, and why they wanted him is another wonder.

I had always thought of George as a country neurotic—the kind you often see in cities. He always seemed to me out of place among the men of these hills.

He might have fallen under the influence of Cal Long. A man like Cal likes to bully people physically. Cal liked to bully them spiritually too.

Luther Ford told me a tale about Cal and George. He said that one night in the Winter Cal went to George Small's house —it is a tumble-down little shack up in the hills—and called George out. The two men went off together to town and got drunk. They came back about two o'clock in the morning and stood in the road before George's house. I have already told you something about the wife. Luther said that at that time she was sick. She was going to have another baby. A neighbor had told Luther Ford. It was a queer performance, one of the kind of things that happen in the country and that give you the creeps.

He said the two men stood in the road before the house cursing the sick woman inside.

Little nervous George Small walking up and down the road in the snow, cursing his wife—Cal Long egging him on. George strutting like a little rooster. It must have been a sight to see and to make you a little sick seeing. Luther Ford said just hearing about it gave him a queer feeling in the pit of his stomach.

This Spring early these three men went in together, making whisky.

Between Cal and Harvey Groves it was a case of dog eat dog. They had bought the still together, each putting in a third of its cost, and then, one night after they had made and sold two runs, Harvey stole the still from the other two.

Of course Cal set out to get him for that.

There wasn't any law he and George Small could evoke—or whatever it is you do with a law when you use it to get some man.

It took Cal a week to find out where Harvey had hidden, and was operating, the still, and then he went to find George.

He wanted to get Harvey, but he wanted to get the still too.

He went to George Small's house and tramped in. George was sitting there and when he saw Cal was frightened stiff. His wife, thinner than ever since her second child was born and half sick, was lying on a bed. In these little mountain cabins there is often but one room and they cook, eat and sleep in it—often a big family.

When she saw Cal, George's wife began to cry and, very likely, George wanted to cry too.

Cal sat down in a chair and took a bottle out of his pocket. George's wife says he had been drinking. He gave George a drink, staring at him hard when he offered it, and George had to take it.

George took four or five stiff drinks, not looking again at Cal or at his wife, who lay on the bed moaning and crying, and Cal never said a word.

Then suddenly George jumped up—his hands not doing the dry wash now—and began swearing at his wife.

"You keep quiet, God damn you!" he yelled.

Then he did an odd thing. There were only two chairs in the cabin and Cal Long had been sitting on one and George on the other. When Cal got up George took the chairs, one at a time, and going outside smashed them to splinters against a corner of the cabin.

Cal Long laughed at that. Then he told George to get his shotgun.

George did get it. It was hanging on a hook in the house and was loaded, I presume, and the two went away together into the woods.

Harvey Groves had got bold. He must have thought he had Cal Long bluffed. That's the weakness of these tough men. They never think any one else is as tough as they are.

Harvey had set the still up in a tiny, half-broken-down old house, on what had once been his father's land, and was making a daylight run.

He had two guns up there but never got a chance to use either of them.

Cal and George must have just crept up pretty close to the house in the long grass and weeds.

They got up close, George with the gun in his hands, and then Harvey came to the door of the house. He may have heard them. Some of these mountain men, who have been law-breakers since they were small boys, have sharp ears and eyes.

There must have been a terrific moment. I've talked with Luther Ford and several others about it. We are all, of course, sorry for George.

Luther, who is something of a dramatist, likes to describe the scene. His version is, to be sure, all a matter of fancy. When he tells the story he kneels in the grass with a stick in his hand. He begins to tremble and the end of the stick wobbles about. He has taken a distant tree for the figure of Harvey Groves, now dead. When he tells of the scene in that way, all of us standing about and, in spite of the ridiculous figure Luther cuts, a little breathless, he goes on for perhaps five seconds, wobbling the stick about, apparently utterly helpless and fright-ened and then his figure suddenly seems to stiffen and harden.

Luther could do it better if he wasn't built as he is—long and loose-jointed, whereas George Small, whose part in the tragedy he is playing, is small, and, as I have said, nervous and rather jerky.

But Luther does what he can, saying in low voice to us others standing and looking, "Now, Cal Long has touched me on the shoulder."

The idea, you understand, is that the two men have crept up to the lonely little mountain house in the late afternoon, George Small creeping ahead with the heavily loaded shotgun in his hands, really being driven forward by Cal Long, creeping at his heels, a man, Luther explains, simply too strong for him, and that, at the fatal moment, when they faced Harvey Groves, and I presume had to shoot or be shot, and George weakened, Cal Long just touched George on the shoulder.

The touch, you see, according to Luther's notion, was a command.

It said, "Shoot!" and George's body stiffened, and he shot.

He shot straight, too.

There was a piece of sheet-iron lying by the door of the house. What it was doing there I don't know. It may have been some part of the stolen still. In the fraction of a second that Harvey Groves had to live he snatched it up and tried to hold it up before his body.

The shot tore right through the metal and through Harvey Groves' head and through a board back of his head. The gun may not have been loaded when George Small brought it from his house. Cal Long may have loaded it.

Anyway Harvey Groves is dead. He died, Luther says, like a rat, in a hole—just pitched forward and flopped around a little and died. How a rat in a hole, when he dies, can do much flopping around I don't know.

After the killing, of course, Cal and George ran, but before they did any running Cal took the gun out of George Small's hands and threw it in the grass.

That, Luther says, was to show just whose gun did the killing.

They ran and, of course, they hid themselves.

There wasn't any special hurry. They had shot Harvey Groves in that lonely place and he might not have been found for days but that George Small's wife, being sick and nervous, just as he is, ran down into town, after Cal and George had left their place, and went around to the stores crying and wringing her hands like a little fool, telling every one that her husband and Cal Long were going to kill some one.

Of course, that stirred every one up.

There must have been people in town who knew that Cal and George and Harvey had been in together and what they had been up to.

They found the body the next morning—the shooting had happened about four in the afternoon—and they got George Small that next afternoon.

Cal Long had stayed with him until he got tired of it and then had left him to shift for himself. They haven't got Cal yet. A lot of people think they never will get him. "He's too smart," Luther Ford says.

They got George sitting beside a road over on the other side of the mountains. He says Cal Long stopped an automobile driving past, a Ford, stopped the driver with a revolver he had in his pocket all the time.

They haven't even found the man who drove the Ford. It may be he was some one who knows Cal and is afraid.

Anyway, they have got George Small in jail over at the county seat and he tells every one he did the killing and sits and moans and rubs his funny little hands together and keeps saying over and over, "God, don't let me do it," just as he did that day when he crossed the bridge, long before he got into this trouble, and I was under the bridge fishing and saw and heard him. I presume they'll hang him, or electrocute him—whichever it is they do in this State—when the time for his trial comes.

And his wife is down with a high fever, and, Luther says, has gone clear off her nut.

But Luther, who acts the whole thing out so dramatically whenever he can get an audience, and who is something of a prophet, says that if they have to get a jury from this county to try George Small, even though the evidence is all against him, he thinks the jury will just go it blind and bring in a verdict of not guilty.

He says, anyway, that is what he would do, and others, who see him acting the thing out and who know Cal Long and Harvey Groves and George Small better than I do, having lived longer in this county and having known them all since they were boys, say the same thing.

It may be true. As for myself—being what I am, hearing and seeing all this . . .

How do I know what I think?

It's a matter, of course, the jury will have to decide.

Another Wife

HE thought himself compelled to say something special to her—knowing her—loving her—wanting her. What he thought was that perhaps she wanted him too, or she wouldn't have spent so much time with him. He wasn't exactly modest.

After all, he was modest enough. He was quite sure several men must have loved her and thought it not unlikely she had experimented with at least a few of them. It was all imagined. Seeing her about had started his mind—his thoughts—racing. "Modern women, of her class, used to luxuries, sensitive, are not going to miss anything, even though they don't take the final plunge into matrimony as I did when I was younger," he thought. The notion of sin had, for him, more or less been taken out of that sort of thing. "What you try to do, if you are a modern woman with any class to you, is to try to use your head," he thought.

He was forty-seven and she ten years younger. His wife had been dead two years.

For the last month she had been in the habit of coming down from her mother's country house to his cabin two or three evenings a week. She might have invited him up the hill to the house—would have invited him oftener—but that she preferred having him, his society, in his own cabin. The family, her family, had simply left the whole matter to her, let her manage it. She lived in her mother's country house, with the mother and two younger sisters—both unmarried. They were delightful people to be with. It was the first summer he had been up in that country and he had met them after he took the cabin. He ate at a hotel nearly a half mile away. Dinner was served early. By getting right back he could be sure of being at home if she decided to stroll down his way.

Being with her, at her mother's house with the others, was fun, of course, but some one was always dropping in. He thought the sisters liked to tease her and him by arranging things that would tie them down.

It was all pure fancy, just a notion. Why should they be concerned about him?

What a whirlpool of notions were stirred up in him that Summer by the woman! He thought about her all the time, having really nothing else to do. Well, he had come to the country to rest. His one son was at a Summer school.

"It's like this—here I am, practically alone. What am I letting myself in for? If she, if any of the women of that family, were of the marrying sort, she would have made a marriage with a much more likely man long ago." Her younger sisters were so considerate in their attitude toward her. There was something tender, respectful, teasing, too, about the way they acted when he and she were together.

Little thoughts kept running through his head. He had come to the country because something inside him had let down. It might have been his forty-seven years. A man like himself, who had begun life as a poor boy, worked himself up in his profession, who had become a physician of some note— well, a man dreams his dreams, he wants a lot.

At forty-seven he is likely, at any moment, to run into a slump.

You won't get half, a third of what you wanted, in your work, in life. What's the use going on? These older men who keep on striving like young men, what about them? They are a little childlike, immature, really.

A great man might go on like that, to the bitter end, to the brink of the grave, but who, having any sense, any head, wants to be a great man? What is called a great man may be just an illusion in people's minds. Who wants to be an illusion?

Thoughts like that, driving him out of the city—to rest. God knows it would have been a mistake if she hadn't been there. Before he met her and before she got into the unwomanly habit of coming to see him in his own cabin during the long Summer evenings, the country, the quiet of the country, was dreadful.

"It may be she only comes down here to me because she is bored. A woman like that, who has known many men, brilliant men, who has been loved by men of note. Still, why does she come? I'm not so gay. It's sure she doesn't think me witty or brilliant."

She was thirty-seven, a bit inclined to extremes in dress, plump, to say the least. Life didn't seem to have quieted her much.

When she came down to his cabin, at the edge of the stream facing the country road, she dropped onto a couch by the door and lit a cigarette. She had lovely ankles. Really, they were beautiful ankles.

The door was open and he sat by a chair near a table. He burned an oil-lamp. The cabin door was left open. Country people went past.

"The trouble with all this silly business about resting is that a man thinks too much. A physician in practice—people coming in, other people's troubles—hasn't time."

Women had come to him a good deal—married and unmarried women. One woman—she was married—wrote him a long letter after he had been treating her for three years. She had gone with her husband to California. "Now that I am away from you, will not see you again, I tell you frankly I love you."

What an idea!

"You have been patient with me for these three years, have let me talk to you. I have told you all the intimate things of my life. You have been always a little aloof and wise."

What nonsense! How could he have stopped the woman's talking intimately? There was more of that sort of thing in the letter. The doctor did not feel he had been specially wise with the woman patient. He had really been afraid of her. What she had thought was aloofness was really fright.

Still, he had kept the letter—for a time. He destroyed it finally because he did not want it to fall accidentally into his wife's hands.

A man likes to feel he has been of some account to some one.

The doctor, say, in the cabin, the new woman near him. She was smoking a cigarette. It was Saturday evening. People—men, women and children—were going along the country road toward a mountain town. Presently the country women and children would be coming back without the men. On Saturday evenings nearly all the mountain-men got drunk.

You come from the city and, because the hills are green, the water in mountain streams clear, you think the people of the hills must be at the bottom clear and sweet.

Now the country people in the road were turning to stare into the cabin at the woman and the doctor. On a previous

Saturday evening, after midnight, the doctor had been awakened by a noisy drunken conversation carried on in the road. It
had made him tremble with wrath. He had wanted to rush out
into the road and fight the drunken country men, but a man
of forty-seven . . . The men in the road were sturdy young
fellows.

One of the men was telling the others in a loud voice that
the woman now on the couch near the doctor—that she was
really a loose city woman. He had used a very distasteful word
and had sworn to the others that, before the Summer was
over, he intended having her himself.

It was just crude drunken talk. The fellow had laughed
when he said it, and the others had laughed. It was a drunken
man trying to be funny.

If the woman with the doctor had known—if he told her? She
would only have smiled.

How many thoughts about her in the doctor's head! He felt
sure she had never cared much what others thought. They had
been sitting like that, she smoking her after-dinner cigarette,
he thinking, but a few minutes. In her presence, thoughts came
quickly, dancing through his head. He wasn't used to such a
multitude of thoughts. When he was in town—in practice—
there were plenty of things to think of other than women,
being in love with some woman.

With his wife it had never been like that. She had never excited him, except at first physically. After that he had just accepted her. "There are many women. She is my woman. She is
rather nice, does her share of the job"—that sort of an attitude.

When she had died it had left a gaping hole in his life.

"That may be what is the matter with me."

"This other woman is a different sort surely. The way she dresses;
her ease with people. Such people, having money always, from
the first, a secure position in life—they just go along, quite
sure of themselves, never afraid."

His early poverty had, the doctor thought, taught him a
good many things he was glad to know. It had taught him
other things not so good to know. Both he and his wife had
always been a little afraid of people—of what people might

think—of his standing in his profession. He had married a woman who also came from a poor family. She was a nurse before she married him. The woman now in the room with him got up from the couch and threw the end of her cigarette into the fireplace. "Let's walk," she said.

When they got out into the road and had turned away from the town and her mother's house, standing on a hill between his cabin and town, another person on the road behind might have thought him the distinguished one. She was a bit too plump—not tall enough—while he had a tall, rather slender figure and walked with a free, easy carriage. He carried his hat in his hand. His thick graying hairs added to his air of distinction.

The road grew more uneven and they walked close to each other. She was trying to tell him something. There had been something he had determined to tell her—on this very evening. What was it?

Something of what the woman in California had tried to tell him in that foolish letter—not doing very well at it— something to the effect that she—this new woman—met while he was off guard, resting—was aloof from himself— unattainable—but that he found himself in love with her.

If she found, by any odd chance, that she wanted him, then he would try to tell her.

After all, it was foolish. More thoughts in the doctor's head. "I can't be very ardent. This being in the country—resting— away from my practice—is all foolishness. My practice is in the hands of another man. There are cases a new man can't understand.

"My wife who died—she didn't expect much. She had been a nurse, was brought up in a poor family, had always had to work, while this new woman . . ."

There had been some kind of nonsense the doctor had thought he might try to put into words. Then he would get back to town, back to his work. "I'd much better light out now, saying nothing."

She was telling him something about herself. It was about a man she had known and loved, perhaps.

Where had he got the notion she had had several lovers? He had merely thought—well, that sort of woman—always plenty of money—being always with clever people.

When she was younger she had thought for a time she would be a painter, had studied in New York and Paris.

She was telling him about an Englishman—a novelist.

The devil—how had she known his thoughts?

She was scolding him. What had he said?

She was talking about such people as himself, simple, straight, good people, she called them, people who go ahead in life, doing their work, not asking much.

She, then, had illusions as he had.

"Such people as you get such ideas in your heads—silly notions."

Now she was talking about herself again.

"I tried to be a painter. I had such ideas about the so-called big men in the arts. You, being a doctor, without a great reputation—I have no doubt you have all sorts of ideas about so-called great doctors, great surgeons."

Now she was telling what happened to her. There had been an English novelist she had met in Paris. He had an established reputation. When he seemed attracted to her she had been much excited.

The novelist had written a love story and she had read it. It had just a certain tone. She had always thought that above everything in life she wanted a love affair in just that tone. She had tried it with the writer of the story and it had turned out nothing of the sort.

It was growing dark in the road. Laurels and elders grew on a hillside. In the half-darkness he could see faintly the little hurt shrug of her shoulders.

Had all the lovers he had imagined for her, the brilliant, witty men of the great world, been like that? He felt suddenly as he had felt when the drunken country men talked in the road. He wanted to hit someone with his fist, in particular he wanted to hit a novelist—preferably an English novelist—or a painter or musician.

He had never known any such people. There weren't any about. He smiled at himself, thinking: "When that country man talked I sat still and let him." His practice had been with well-to-do merchants, lawyers, manufacturers, their wives and families.

Now his body was trembling. They had come to a small bridge over a stream, and suddenly, without premeditation, he put his arm about her.

There had been something he had planned to tell her. What was it? It was something about himself. "I am no longer young. What I could have to offer you would not be much. I cannot offer it to such a one as yourself, to one who has known great people, been loved by witty, brilliant men."

There had no doubt been something of the sort he had foolishly thought of saying. Now she was in his arms in the darkness on the bridge. The air was heavy with Summer perfumes. She was a little heavy—a real armful. Evidently she liked having him hold her thus. He had thought, really, she might like him but have at the same time a kind of contempt for him.

Now he had kissed her. She liked that too. She moved closer and returned the kiss. He leaned over the bridge. It was a good thing there was a support of some sort. She was sturdily built. His first wife, after thirty, had been fairly plump, but this new woman weighed more.

And now they were again walking in the road. It was the most amazing thing. There was something quite taken for granted. It was that he wanted her to marry him.

Did he? They walked along the road toward his cabin and there was in him the half-foolish, half-joyful mood a boy feels walking in the darkness the first time, alone with a girl.

A quick rush of memories, evenings as a boy and as a young man remembered.

Does a man ever get too old for that? A man like himself, a physician, should know more about things. He was smiling at himself in the darkness—feeling foolish, feeling frightened, glad. Nothing definite had been said.

It was better at the cabin. How nice it had been of her to have no foolish, conventional fears about coming to see him! She was a nice person. Sitting alone with her in the darkness of the cabin he realized that they were at any rate both mature— grown up enough to know what they were doing.

Did they?

When they had returned to the cabin it was quite dark and he lighted an oil-lamp. It all got very definite very rapidly. She had another cigarette and sat as before, looking at him. Her eyes were gray. They were gray, wise eyes.

She was realizing perfectly his discomfiture. The eyes were smiling—being old eyes. The eyes were saying: "A man is a man and a woman is a woman. You can never tell how or when it will happen. You are a man and, although you think yourself a practical, unimaginative man, you are a good deal of a boy. There is a way in which any woman is older than any man and that is the reason I know."

Never mind what her eyes were saying. The doctor was plainly fussed. There had been a kind of speech he had intended making. It may have been he had known, from the first, that he was caught.

"O Lord, I won't get it in now."

He tried, haltingly, to say something about the life of a physician's wife. That he had assumed she might marry him, without asking her directly, seemed a bit rash. He was assuming it without intending anything of the sort. Everything was muddled.

The life of a physician's wife—a man like himself—in general practice—wasn't such a pleasant one. When he had started out as a physician he had really thought, some time, he might get into a great position, be some kind of a specialist.

But now—

Her eyes kept on smiling. If he was muddled she evidently wasn't. "There is something definite and solid about some women. They seem to know just what they want," he thought.

She wanted him.

What she said wasn't much. "Don't be so foolish. I've waited a long time for just you."

That was all. It was final, absolute—terribly disconcerting too. He went and kissed her, awkwardly. Now she had the air that had from the first disconcerted him, the air of worldliness. It might not be anything but her way of smoking a cigarette—an undoubtedly good, although rather bold, taste in clothes.

His other wife never seemed to think about clothes. She hadn't the knack.

Well, he had managed again to get her out of his cabin. It might be she had managed. His first wife had been a nurse before he married her. It might be that women who have been nurses should not marry physicians. They have too much respect for physicians, are taught to have too much respect. This one, he was quite sure, would never have too much respect.

It was all, when the doctor let it sink in, rather nice. He had taken the great leap and seemed suddenly to feel solid ground under his feet. How easy it had been!

They were walking along the road toward her mother's house. It was dark and he could not see her eyes.

He was thinking—

"Four women in her family. A new woman to be the mother of my son." Her mother was old and quiet and had sharp gray eyes. One of the younger sisters was a bit boyish. The other one—she was the handsome one of the family—sang Negro songs.

They had plenty of money. When it came to that his own income was quite adequate.

It would be nice, being a kind of older brother to the sisters, a son to her mother. O Lord!

They got to the gate before her mother's house and she let him kiss her again. Her lips were warm, her breath fragrant. He stood, still embarrassed, while she went up a path to the door. There was a light on the porch.

There was no doubt she was plump, solidly built. What absurd notions he had had!

Well, it was time to go on back to his cabin. He felt foolishly young, silly, afraid, glad.

"O Lord—I've got me a wife, another wife, a new one," he said to himself as he went along the road in the darkness. How glad and foolish and frightened he still felt! Would he get over it after a time?

A Meeting South

H E told me the story of his ill fortune—a crack-up in an airplane—with a very gentlemanly little smile on his very sensitive, rather thin, lips. Such things happened. He might well have been speaking of another. I liked his tone and I liked him.

This happened in New Orleans, where I had gone to live. When he came, my friend, Fred, for whom he was looking, had gone away, but immediately I felt a strong desire to know him better and so suggested we spend the evening together. When we went down the stairs from my apartment I noticed that he was a cripple. The slight limp, the look of pain that occasionally drifted across his face, the little laugh that was intended to be jolly, but did not quite achieve its purpose, all these things began at once to tell me the story I have now set myself to write.

"I shall take him to see Aunt Sally," I thought. One does not take every caller to Aunt Sally. However, when she is in fine feather, when she has taken a fancy to her visitor, there is no one like her. Although she has lived in New Orleans for thirty years, Aunt Sally is Middle Western, born and bred.

However I am plunging a bit too abruptly into my story.

First of all I must speak more of my guest, and for convenience's sake I shall call him David. I felt at once that he would be wanting a drink and, in New Orleans—dear city of Latins and hot nights—even in Prohibition times such things can be managed. We achieved several and my own head became somewhat shaky but I could see that what we had taken had not affected him. Evening was coming, the abrupt waning of the day and the quick smoky soft-footed coming of night, characteristic of the semi-tropic city, when he produced a bottle from his hip pocket. It was so large that I was amazed. How had it happened that the carrying of so large a bottle had not made him look deformed? His body was very small and delicately built. "Perhaps, like the kangaroo, his body has developed some kind of a natural pouch for taking care of supplies," I thought. Really he walked as one might fancy a kangaroo

713

would walk when out for a quiet evening stroll. I went along thinking of Darwin and the marvels of Prohibition. "We are a wonderful people, we Americans," I thought. We were both in fine humor and had begun to like each other immensely.

He explained the bottle. The stuff, he said, was made by a Negro man on his father's plantation somewhere over in Alabama. We sat on the steps of a vacant house deep down in the old French Quarter of New Orleans—the Vieux Carré—while he explained that his father had no intention of breaking the law—that is to say, in so far as the law remained reasonable. "Our nigger just makes whisky for us," he said. "We keep him for that purpose. He doesn't have anything else to do, just makes the family whisky, that's all. If he went selling any, we'd raise hell with him. I dare say Dad would shoot him if he caught him up to any such unlawful trick, and you bet, Jim, our nigger, I'm telling you of, knows it too.

"He's a good whisky-maker, though, don't you think?" David added. He talked of Jim in a warm friendly way. "Lord, he's been with us always, was born with us. His wife cooks for us and Jim makes our whisky. It's a race to see which is best at his job, but I think Jim will win. He's getting a little better all the time and all of our family—well, I reckon we just like and need our whisky more than we do our food."

Do you know New Orleans? Have you lived there in the Summer when it is hot, in the Winter when it rains, and through the glorious late Fall days? Some of its own, more progressive, people scorn it now. In New Orleans there is a sense of shame because the city is not more like Chicago or Pittsburgh.

It, however, suited David and me. We walked slowly, on account of his bad leg, through many streets of the Old Town, Negro women laughing all around us in the dusk, shadows playing over old buildings, children with their shrill cries dodging in and out of old hallways. The old city was once almost altogether French, but now it is becoming more and more Italian. It however remains Latin. People live out of doors. Families were sitting down to dinner within full sight of the street—all doors and windows open. A man and his wife quarreled in Italian. In a patio back of an old building a Negress sang a French song.

We came out of the narrow little streets and had a drink in front of the dark cathedral and another in a little square in front. There is a statue of General Jackson, always taking off his hat to Northern tourists who in Winter come down to see the city. At his horse's feet an inscription—"The Union must and will be preserved." We drank solemnly to that declaration and the general seemed to bow a bit lower. "He was sure a proud man," David said, as we went over toward the docks to sit in the darkness and look at the Mississippi. All good New Orleanians go to look at the Mississippi at least once a day. At night it is like creeping into a dark bedroom to look at a sleeping child—something of that sort—gives you the same warm nice feeling, I mean. David is a poet and so in the darkness by the river we spoke of Keats and Shelley, the two English poets all good Southern men love.

All of this, you are to understand, was before I took him to see Aunt Sally.

Both Aunt Sally and myself are Middle Westerners. We are but guests down here, but perhaps we both in some queer way belong to this city. Something of the sort is in the wind. I don't quite know how it has happened.

A great many Northern men and women come down our way and, when they go back North, write things about the South. The trick is to write nigger stories. The North likes them. They are so amusing. One of the best-known writers of nigger stories was down here recently and a man I know, a Southern man, went to call on him. The writer seemed a bit nervous. "I don't know much about the South or Southerners," he said. "But you have your reputation," my friend said. "You are so widely known as a writer about the South and about Negro life." The writer had a notion he was being made sport of. "Now look here," he said, "I don't claim to be a highbrow. I'm a business man myself. At home, up North, I associate mostly with business men and when I am not at work I go out to the country club. I want you to understand I am not setting myself up as a highbrow.

"I give them what they want," he said. My friend said he appeared angry. "About what now, do you fancy?" he asked innocently.

However, I am not thinking of the Northern writer of

Negro stories. I am thinking of the Southern poet, with the bottle clasped firmly in his hands, sitting in the darkness beside me on the docks facing the Mississippi.

He spoke at some length of his gift for drinking. "I didn't always have it. It is a thing built up," he said. The story of how he chanced to be a cripple came out slowly. You are to remember that my own head was a bit unsteady. In the darkness the river, very deep and very powerful off New Orleans, was creeping away to the gulf. The whole river seemed to move away from us and then to slip noiselessly into the darkness like a vast moving sidewalk.

When he had first come to me, in the late afternoon, and when we had started for our walk together I had noticed that one of his legs dragged as we went along and that he kept putting a thin hand to an equally thin cheek.

Sitting over by the river he explained, as a boy would explain when he has stubbed his toe running down a hill.

When the World War broke out he went over to England and managed to get himself enrolled as an aviator, very much, I gathered, in the spirit in which a countryman, in a city for a night, might take in a show.

The English had been glad enough to take him on. He was one more man. They were glad enough to take any one on just then. He was small and delicately built but after he got in he turned out to be a first-rate flyer, serving all through the War with a British flying squadron, but at the last got into a crash and fell.

Both legs were broken, one of them in three places, the scalp was badly torn and some of the bones of the face had been splintered.

They had put him into a field hospital and had patched him up. "It was my fault if the job was rather bungled," he said. "You see it was a field hospital, a hell of a place. Men were torn all to pieces, groaning and dying. Then they moved me back to a base hospital and it wasn't much better. The fellow who had the bed next to mine had shot himself in the foot to avoid going into a battle. A lot of them did that, but why they picked on their own feet that way is beyond me. It's a nasty place, full of small bones. If you're ever going to shoot yourself don't pick on a spot like that. Don't pick on your feet. I tell you it's a bad idea.

"Anyway, the man in the hospital was always making a fuss and I got sick of him and the place too. When I got better I faked, said the nerves of my leg didn't hurt. It was a lie, of course. The nerves of my leg and of my face have never quit hurting. I reckon maybe, if I had told the truth, they might have fixed me up all right."

I got it. No wonder he carried his drinks so well. When I understood, I wanted to keep on drinking with him, wanted to stay with him until he got tired of me as he had of the man who lay beside him in the base hospital over there somewhere in France.

The point was that he never slept, could not sleep, except when he was a little drunk. "I'm a nut," he said smiling.

It was after we got over to Aunt Sally's that he talked most. Aunt Sally had gone to bed when we got there, but she got up when we rang the bell and we all went to sit together in the little patio back of her house. She is a large woman with great arms and rather a paunch, and she had put on nothing but a light flowered dressing-gown over a thin, ridiculously girlish, nightgown. By this time the moon had come up and, outside, in the narrow street of the Vieux Carré, three drunken sailors from a ship in the river were sitting on a curb and singing a song,

> "*I've got to get it,*
> *You've got to get it,*
> *We've all got to get it*
> *In our own good time.*"

They had rather nice boyish voices and every time they sang a verse and had done the chorus they all laughed together heartily.

In Aunt Sally's patio there are many broad-leafed banana plants and a Chinaberry tree throwing its soft purple shadows on a brick floor.

As for Aunt Sally, she is as strange to me as he was. When we came and when we were all seated at a little table in the patio, she ran into her house and presently came back with a bottle of whisky. She, it seemed, had understood him at once, had understood without unnecessary words that the little Southern man lived always in the black house of pain, that whisky was good to him, that it quieted his throbbing nerves, temporarily at least. "Everything is temporary, when you come to that," I can fancy Aunt Sally saying.

We sat for a time in silence, David having shifted his allegiance and taken two drinks out of Aunt Sally's bottle. Presently he rose and walked up and down the patio floor, crossing and re-crossing the network of delicately outlined shadows on the bricks. "It's really all right, the leg," he said, "something just presses on the nerves, that's all." In me there was a self-satisfied feeling. I had done the right thing. I had brought him to Aunt Sally. "I have brought him to a mother." She has always made me feel that way since I have known her.

And now I shall have to explain her a little. It will not be so easy. That whole neighborhood in New Orleans is alive with tales concerning her.

Aunt Sally came to New Orleans in the old days, when the town was wild, in the wide-open days. What she had been before she came no one knew, but anyway she opened a place. That was very, very long ago when I was myself but a lad, up in Ohio. As I have already said Aunt Sally came from somewhere up in the Middle-Western country. In some obscure subtle way it would flatter me to think she came from my State.

The house she had opened was one of the older places in the French Quarter down here, and when she had got her hands on it, Aunt Sally had a hunch. Instead of making the place modern, cutting it up into small rooms, all that sort of thing, she left it just as it was and spent her money rebuilding falling old walls, mending winding broad old stairways, repairing dim high-ceilinged old rooms, soft-colored old marble mantels. After all, we do seem attached to sin and there are so many people busy making sin unattractive. It is good to find someone who takes the other road. It would have been so very much to Aunt Sally's advantage to have made the place modern, that is to say, in the business she was in at that time. If a few old rooms, wide old stairways, old cooking ovens built into the walls, if all these things did not facilitate the stealing in of couples on dark nights, they at least did something else. She had opened a gambling and drinking house, but one can have no doubt about the ladies stealing in. "I was on the make all right," Aunt Sally told me once.

She ran the place and took in money, and the money she

spent on the place itself. A falling wall was made to stand up straight and fine again, the banana plants were made to grow in the patio, the Chinaberry tree got started and was helped through the years of adolescence. On the wall the lovely Rose of Montana bloomed madly. The fragrant Lantana grew in a dense mass at a corner of the wall.

When the Chinaberry tree, planted at the very center of the patio, began to get up into the light it filled the whole neighborhood with fragrance in the Spring.

Fifteen, twenty years of that, with Mississippi River gamblers and race-horse men sitting at tables by windows in the huge rooms upstairs in the house that had once, no doubt, been the town house of some rich planter's family—in the boom days of the Forties. Women stealing in, too, in the dusk of evenings. Drinks being sold. Aunt Sally raking down the kitty from the game, raking in her share, quite ruthlessly.

At night, getting a good price too from the lovers. No questions asked, a good price for drinks. Moll Flanders might have lived with Aunt Sally. What a pair they would have made! The Chinaberry tree beginning to be lusty. The Lantana blossoming —in the Fall the Rose of Montana.

Aunt Sally getting hers. Using the money to keep the old house in fine shape. Salting some away all the time.

A motherly soul, good, sensible Middle-Western woman, eh? Once a race-horse man left twenty-four thousand dollars with her and disappeared. No one knew she had it. There was a report the man was dead. He had killed a gambler in a place down by the French Market and while they were looking for him he managed to slip in to Aunt Sally's and leave his swag. Some time later a body was found floating in the river and it was identified as the horseman but in reality he had been picked up in a wire-tapping haul in New York City and did not get out of his Northern prison for six years.

When he did get out, naturally, he skipped for New Orleans. No doubt he was somewhat shaky. She had him. If he squealed there was a murder charge to be brought up and held over his head. It was night when he arrived and Aunt Sally went at once to an old brick oven built into the wall of the kitchen and took out a bag. "There it is," she said. The whole affair was part of the day's work for her in those days.

Gamblers at the tables in some of the rooms upstairs, lurking couples, from the old patio below the fragrance of growing things.

When she was fifty, Aunt Sally had got enough and had put them all out. She did not stay in the way of sin too long and she never went in too deep, like that Moll Flanders, and so she was all right and sitting pretty. "They wanted to gamble and drink and play with the ladies. The ladies liked it all right. I never saw none of them come in protesting too much. The worst was in the morning when they went away. They looked so sheepish and guilty. If they felt that way, what made them come? If I took a man, you bet I'd want him and no monkey-business or nothing doing.

"I got a little tired of all of them, that's the truth." Aunt Sally laughed. "But that wasn't until I had got what I went after. Oh, pshaw, they took up too much of my time, after I got enough to be safe."

Aunt Sally is now sixty-five. If you like her and she likes you she will let you sit with her in her patio gossiping of the old times, of the old river days. Perhaps—well, you see there is still something of the French influence at work in New Orleans, a sort of matter-of-factness about life—what I started to say is that if you know Aunt Sally and she likes you, and if, by chance, your lady likes the smell of flowers growing in a patio at night—really, I am going a bit too far. I only meant to suggest that Aunt Sally at sixty-five is not harsh. She is a motherly soul.

We sat in the garden talking, the little Southern poet, Aunt Sally and myself—or rather they talked and I listened. The Southerner's great-grandfather was English, a younger son, and he came over here to make his fortune as a planter, and did it. Once he and his sons owned several great plantations with slaves, but now his father had but a few hundred acres left, about one of the old houses—somewhere over in Alabama. The land is heavily mortgaged and most of it has not been under cultivation for years. Negro labor is growing more and more expensive and unsatisfactory since so many Negroes have run off to Chicago, and the poet's father and the one brother at home are not much good at working the land. "We aren't strong enough and we don't know how," the poet said.

The Southerner had come to New Orleans to see Fred, to

talk with Fred about poetry, but Fred was out of town. I could only walk about with him, help him drink his home-made whisky. Already I had taken nearly a dozen drinks. In the morning I would have a headache.

I drew within myself, listening while David and Aunt Sally talked. The Chinaberry tree had been so and so many years growing—she spoke of it as she might have spoken of a daughter. "It had a lot of different sicknesses when it was young, but it pulled through." Some one had built a high wall on one side of her patio so that the climbing plants did not get as much sunlight as they needed. The banana plants, however, did very well and now the Chinaberry tree was big and strong enough to take care of itself. She kept giving David drinks of whisky and he talked.

He told her of the place in his leg where something, a bone perhaps, pressed on the nerve, and of the place on his left cheek. A silver plate had been set under the skin. She touched the spot with her fat old fingers. The moonlight fell softly down on the patio floor. "I can't sleep except somewhere out of doors," David said.

He explained how that, at home on his father's plantation, he had to be thinking all day whether or not he would be able to sleep at night.

"I go to bed and then I get up. There is always a bottle of whisky on the table downstairs and I take three or four drinks. Then I go out doors." Often very nice things happened.

"In the Fall it's best," he said. "You see the niggers are making molasses." Every Negro cabin on the place had a little clump of ground back of it where cane grew and in the Fall the Negroes were making their 'lasses. "I take the bottle in my hand and go into the fields, unseen by the niggers. Having the bottle with me, that way, I drink a good deal and then lie down on the ground. The mosquitoes bite me some, but I don't mind much. I reckon I get drunk enough not to mind. The little pain makes a kind of rhythm for the great pain—like poetry.

"In a kind of shed the niggers are making the 'lasses, that is to say, pressing the juice out of the cane and boiling it down. They keep singing as they work. In a few years now I reckon our family won't have any land. The banks could take it now if they wanted it. They don't want it. It would be too much trouble for them to manage, I reckon.

"In the Fall, at night, the niggers are pressing the cane. Our niggers live pretty much on 'lasses and grits.

"They like working at night and I'm glad they do. There is an old mule going round and round in a circle and beside the press a pile of the dry cane. Niggers come, men and women, old and young. They build a fire outside the shed. The old mule goes round and round.

"The niggers sing. They laugh and shout. Sometimes the young niggers with their gals make love on the dry cane pile. I can hear it rattle.

"I have come out of the big house, me and my bottle, and I creep along, low on the ground, 'til I get up close. There I lie. I'm a little drunk. It all makes me happy. I can sleep some, on the ground like that, when the niggers are singing, when no one knows I'm there.

"I could sleep here, on these bricks here," David said, pointing to where the shadows cast by the broad leaves of the banana plants were broadest and deepest.

He got up from his chair and went limping, dragging one foot after the other, across the patio and lay down on the bricks.

For a long time Aunt Sally and I sat looking at each other, saying nothing, and presently she made a sign with her fat finger and we crept away into the house. "I'll let you out at the front door. You let him sleep, right where he is," she said. In spite of her huge bulk and her age she walked across the patio floor as softly as a kitten. Beside her I felt awkward and uncertain. When we had got inside she whispered to me. She had some champagne left from the old days, hidden away somewhere in the old house. "I'm going to send a magnum up to his dad when he goes home," she explained.

She, it seemed, was very happy, having him there, drunk and asleep on the brick floor of the patio. "We used to have some good men come here in the old days too," she said. As we went into the house through the kitchen door I had looked back at David, asleep now in the heavy shadows at a corner of the wall. There was no doubt he also was happy, had been happy ever since I had brought him into the presence of Aunt Sally. What a small huddled figure of a man he looked, lying thus on the brick, under the night sky, in the deep shadows of the banana plants.

I went into the house and out at the front door and into a dark narrow street, thinking. Well, I was, after all, a Northern man. It was possible Aunt Sally had become completely Southern, being down here so long.

I remembered that it was the chief boast of her life that once she had shaken hands with John L. Sullivan and that she had known P. T. Barnum.

"I knew Dave Gears. You mean to tell me you don't know who Dave Gears was? Why, he was one of the biggest gamblers we ever had in this city."

As for David and his poetry—it is in the manner of Shelley. "If I could write like Shelley I would be happy. I wouldn't care what happened to me," he had said during our walk of the early part of the evening.

I went along enjoying my thoughts. The street was dark and occasionally I laughed. A notion had come to me. It kept dancing in my head and I thought it very delicious. It had something to do with aristocrats, with such people as Aunt Sally and David. "Lordy," I thought, "maybe I do understand them a little. I'm from the Middle West myself and it seems we can produce our aristocrats too." I kept thinking of Aunt Sally and of my native State, Ohio. "Lordy, I hope she comes from up there, but I don't think I had better inquire too closely into her past," I said to myself, as I went smiling away into the soft smoky night.

The Flood

IT came about while he was trying to do a very difficult thing. He was a college professor and was trying to write a book on the subject of values.

A good many men had written on the subject, but now he was trying his hand.

He had read, he said, everything he could find that had been written on the subject.

There had been books consumed, months spent sitting and reading books.

The man had a house of his own at the edge of the town where stood the college in which he taught, but he was not teaching that year. It was his sabbatical year. There was a whole year to be spent just on his book.

"I thought," he said, "I would go to Europe." He thought of some quiet place, say in a little Normandy town. He remembered such a town he had once visited.

It would have to be very quiet, a place where no one would know him, where he would be undisturbed.

He had got a world of notes down into little books, piled neatly on a long work table in his room. He was a small alert almost bald man and had been married, but his wife was dead. He told me that for years he had been a very lonely man.

He had lived alone in his house for several years, having no children. There was an old housekeeper. There was a walled garden.

The old housekeeper did not sleep in the house. She came there early in the morning and went to her own home at night.

Nothing had happened to the man for months at a time, through several years, he said.

He had been lonely, had felt his loneliness a good deal. He hadn't much of a way with people.

He had, I gathered, before that Summer, been rather hungry for people. "My wife was a cheerful soul, when she was here," he said, speaking of his loneliness. I got from him and others—I had never known his wife—the sense of her as a rather frivolous-seeming woman.

She had been a light-hearted little woman, fond of frills, one of the kind whose blond hair is always flying in the wind. They are always chattering, that kind. They love everyone. My friend, the scholar, had adored his wife.

And then she had died, and there he was. He was one of the sort who hurry along through streets, with books under their arms. You are always seeing such men about college towns. They go along staring at people with their impersonal eyes. If you speak to such a one he answers you absent-mindedly. "Don't bother me, please," he seems to be saying, while all the time, within himself, he is cursing himself that he cannot be more outgoing toward people.

He told me that, when his wife was alive and he was in his study, absorbed in his books, taking notes, lost in thought as one might say, preparing to write his book on values that was to be his magnum opus, she used to come in there.

She would come in, put one arm about his neck, lean over him, kiss him, and with the other hand would punch him in the stomach.

He said she used to drag him out and make him play croquet on the lawn or help with the garden. It was her money, he said, that had built the house.

He said she always called him an old stick.

"Come on, you old stick, kiss me, make love to me," she said to him sometimes. "You aren't much good to me or anyone, but you're all I've got." She would have people in, worlds of people, just anyone. When the house was full of people and the scholar, that little wide-eyed man, was standing about among them, rather confused, trying, in the midst of the hubbub, to hang onto his thoughts on the subject of values, remembering the far dim reaches of thought that occasionally came to him when he was alone . . . In him a feeling that all of man's notions of values, particularly in America, had got distorted, "perverted," he said, and that, when he was alone, when his wife and the people she was always dragging into the house did not disturb him—he had a feeling sometimes, at moments, when he was undisturbed thus, that persistent mind of his reaching out, himself impersonal, untouched . . . "I almost thought sometimes," he said, "that I had got something."

"There was," he said, "a kind of divine balance to all values to be found."

You got, to be sure, the crude sense of values that every one understands, values in land, money, possessions.

Then you got more subtle values, feeling coming in.

You got a painting, let us say by Rembrandt, selling to a rich man for fifty thousand dollars.

That is enough money to raise a dozen poor families, add some fifty or sixty citizens to the State.

The citizens being, let us say, all worthy men and women, without question of value to the State, producers, let us say.

Then you got the Rembrandt painting, hanging on a wall, say in some rich man's house, he having people into his house. He would stand before the painting.

He would brag about it as though he had himself painted it.

"I was pretty shrewd to get it at all," he would say. He would tell how he got it. Another rich man had been after it.

He talked about it as he might have talked about getting control of some industry by a skillful maneuver in the stock market.

Just the same it, the painting, was, in some way, adding a kind of value to that rich man's life.

It, the painting, was hanging on his wall, producing by hanging there nothing he could put his fingers on, producing no food, no clothes, nothing at all in the material world.

He himself being essentially a man of the material world. He had got rich being that.

Just the same . . .

My acquaintance, the scholar, wanted to be very just. No, that wasn't it. He said he wanted truth.

His mind reached out. He got hold of things a little sometimes, or thought he did. He took notes, he prepared to write his book.

He adored his wife and sometimes, often, he said he hated her. She used to laugh at him. "Your old values," she said. It seems he had been on that subject for years. He used to read papers before philosophical societies and afterward they were printed in little pamphlets by the societies. No one understood them, not even perhaps his fellow-philosophers, but he read them aloud to his wife.

"Kiss me, kiss me hard," she would say. "Do it now. Don't wait."

He wanted to kill her sometimes, he said. He said he adored her.

She died. He was alone. He was bitterly lonely sometimes.

People, remembering his wife, came for a time to see him, but he was cold with them. It was because he was absorbed in thought. They talked to him and he replied absent-mindedly. "Yes, that's so. Perhaps you're right." Remarks of that kind.

Wanting them just the same, he said.

Then, he said, the flood came. He said you couldn't account for floods.

"What's the use talking of balance?" he asked. "There is no balance."

He couldn't account for what happened during the Summer of that sabbatical year. He had a theory about life. I had heard it before.

"Everything in life comes in surges, floods, really. There is a whole city, thousands, even millions of people in it," he said.

"They are all, let us say, dull; they are all stupid; they are coarse and crude.

"All of them have become bored with life; they are full of hatreds for each other.

"It is not only cities. Whole nations are like that sometimes.

"How else are you to account for wars?

"And then there are other times when whole neighborhoods, whole cities, whole nations become something else. They are all irreligious, and then suddenly, without any cause any one has ever understood, ever perhaps can understand, they become religious. They are proud and they become humble, full of hatred and then suddenly filled with love.

"The individual, trying to assert himself against the mass, always without success, is drowned in a flood.

"There is a lifetime of work and thought washed away thus.

"There are these little tragedies. Are they tragedies or are they merely amusing?"

He, my friend the scholar, was seeking, as I have said, a kind of impersonal delicate balance on the subject of values.

That, in solitude, to be transcribed into words. His book, that was to be his magnum opus, the work of a lifetime justified.

There was no wife to bother him now by dragging people into the house.

There was no wife to say, "Come on, old stick, kiss me quick, now, while I want your kisses.

"Get this, get what I have to offer you while I have it to offer."

That sort of thing, of course, pitching him down off his mountain top of thought, thump.

He having to struggle for days afterwards, trying to get back up there again.

In his thinking he had, alone that Summer in his house, almost achieved the thing, the perfect balance of thought.

He said he struggled all through the Winter, Spring and early Summer. For years no one had come to see him.

Then suddenly his wife's sister, a younger sister, came. She hadn't even written him for a year, and then she telegraphed she was coming that way. It seems she was driving in a car, going to some place; he couldn't remember where.

She brought a young woman, a cousin, with her. The cousin, like his wife's sister, was another frivolous one.

And then the scholar's brother came. He was a big boastful youngish man who was in business.

He only came to stay a day or two, but, like the scholar, he had lost his wife. He was attracted to the two young women.

He stayed on and on because of them. They may have stayed on and on because of him.

He was a man who had a big car. He brought other men into the house.

Suddenly the scholar's house was filled with men and women. There was a good deal of gin-drinking.

There was a flood of people. The scholar's brother brought in a phonograph and wanted to install a radio.

There were dances in the evening.

Even the old housekeeper caught it. She had always been

rather quiet, a staid, sad old woman. One evening the scholar said, after a day, during the afternoon of which he had struggled and struggled, alone in his room, the door shut, sound coming in nevertheless, coarse sounds, he said, sound of women's laughter, men's voices.

He said the two young women who had come there and who he believed had stayed because of his brother—he having stayed because of them—the two had met other people of the town. They filled his house with people.

He had, however, almost got something he was after in spite of them.

"I swear I almost had it."

"Had what?"

"Why, my definition of values. There had to be something, you see, at the very core of my book."

"Yes, of course."

"I mean one place in my book where everything was defined. In simple words, so that everyone could understand."

"Of course."

I shall never forget the scholar when he was telling me all this, the puzzled, half-hurt, look in his eyes.

He said they had even got his housekeeper going. "What do you think of it—she also drinking gin?"

There was a crash of sounds that afternoon in his house.

He was alone in his room upstairs in his house, in his study.

They had got the sad, staid old housekeeper going. He said his brother was very efficient. They had her dancing to the music of the phonograph. The scholar's brother, that big blustering bragging man—he was a manufacturer of some sort—was dancing with the housekeeper—with that staid, sad old woman.

The others had got into a circle.

The phonograph was going.

What happened was that the wife's sister—just, I imagine from all he said and from what others afterward said of her, a miniature edition, a new printing one might say, of his dead wife . . .

She, it seems, came running upstairs and burst into his room, her blond hair flying. She was laughing.

"I had almost got it," he said.

"What? Oh, yes. Your definition."

"Yes, just the definition I had been after for years."

"I was about to write it down. It embraced all, everything I had to say."

She burst in.

I gather the sister must have been at least a little in love with the man and that he, after all, did not want the bragging, blustering brother to have her. He admitted that.

She rushed in.

"Come on, you old stick," she said to him.

He said he tried to explain to her. "I made a fight," he said.

He got up from his desk and tried to reason with her. She had fairly taken possession of his house.

He tried to tell her what he was up to. He spoke of standing there, beside his desk, where he sat when he told me all this, trying to explain all this to her.

I thought the scholar got a bit vulgar when he told me of that moment.

"There was nothing doing," he said. He had got that expression from the young woman, his wife's sister.

She was laughing at him as his wife had formerly done; she wouldn't have kissed him.

She wouldn't have said, "Kiss me quick, you old stick, while I feel that way."

I gathered she merely dragged him downstairs. He said he went with her, couldn't help himself, couldn't, of course, be rude to her, his wife's sister.

He went with her and saw his staid, sad old housekeeper acting like that.

The housekeeper didn't seem to care whether he saw or not. She had broken loose. The whole house had broken loose.

And so, in the end, my acquaintance, the scholar, didn't care either.

"I was in the flood," he said. "What was the use?"

He was a little afraid that, if he didn't do something about it, his bragging brother, or some man like him, might get his wife's sister.

He didn't quite want that to happen. So that evening, when he was alone with her, he proposed to her.

He said she called him an old stick. "It must have been a family expression," he said. Something of the scholar came back into him when he said that.

He had been caught in a flood. He had let go.

He had proposed to his wife's sister, in the garden back of his house, under an apple tree, near the croquet grounds, and she had said . . .

He didn't tell me what she said. I imagine she said, "Yes, you old stick."

"Kiss me quick while I feel that way," she said.

That, at least, gets a certain balance to my tale.

The scholar, however, says there is no balance.

"There are only floods, one flood following another," he says. When I talked to him of all this he was a bit discouraged.

However, he seemed cheerful enough.

Why They Got Married

PEOPLE keep on getting married. Evidently hope is eternal in the human breast. Every one laughs about it. You cannot go to a show but that some comedian takes a shot at the institution of marriage—and gets a laugh. It is amusing to watch the faces of married couples at such moments.

But I had intended to speak about Will. Will is a painter. I had intended to tell you about a conversation that took place in Will's apartment one night. Every man or woman who marries must wonder sometimes how it happened to be just that other one he or she married.

"You have to live so close to the other when you are married," said Will.

"Yes, you do," said Helen, his wife.

"I get awfully tired of it sometimes," Will said.

"And don't I?" said Helen.

"It is worse for me than it is for you."

"No, I think it is worse for me."

"Well, gracious sakes, I would like to know how you figure that out."

"I was in New York, was a student there," said Will. It was evident that he had risen above the little choppy matrimonial sea in which he had been swimming with Helen—conversational swimming—he was ready to tell how it happened. That is always an interesting moment.

"Well," said Will, "as I said, there I was, in New York. I was a young bachelor. I was going to school. Then I got through school. I got a job. It wasn't much of a job. I got thirty dollars a week. I was making advertising drawings. So I met a fellow named Bob. He was getting his seventy-five dollars a week. Think of that, Helen. Why didn't you get that one?"

"But, Will, dear, you are now making more than he will ever make," Helen said. "But it wasn't only that. Will is such a sweet, gentle man. You can see that by just looking at him." She walked across the room and took her husband's hands.

"You can't tell about that gentle-looking kind sometimes," I said.

"I know it," Helen said, smiling.

She was surely a very lovely thing at that moment. She had big gray eyes and was very slender and graceful.

Will said that the man Bob, he had met, had some relatives living over near Philadelphia. He was, Helen said, a large, rather mushy-looking man with white hands.

So they began going over there for week-ends. Will and Bob. Will's own people lived in Kansas.

At the place where Bob had the relatives—it was in a suburb of Philadelphia—there were two girls. They were cousins of Bob's.

Will said the girls were all right, and when he said it Helen smiled. He said their father was an advertising man. "They made us welcome at their house. They gave us grand beds to sleep in." Will had got launched into his tale.

"We would get over there about five o'clock of a Saturday afternoon. The father's name was J. G. Small. He had a swell-looking car.

"So he would be at home and he would take a look at us, the way an older man does look at two young fellows making up to the young women folks in his house. At first he looks at you as much as to say, 'Hello, I envy you your youth, etc.,' and then he takes another look and his eyes say, 'What are you hanging around here for, you young squirt?'

"After dinner, of a Saturday night, we got the car, or rather the girls did. I sat on the back seat with one of them. Her name was Cynthia.

"She was a tall, heavy-looking girl with dark eyes. She embarrassed me. I don't know why."

Will went a bit aside from his subject to speak of men's embarrassment with such women. "There is a certain kind that just get your goat," he said, speaking a bit inelegantly, I thought, for a painter. "They feel they ought to be up to their business, getting themselves a man, but maybe they have thought too much about it. They are self-conscious and, of course, they make you feel that way.

"Naturally, we made love. It seemed to be expected. Bob

was at it with her sister on the front seat. Everybody does it nowadays, and I was glad enough for the chance. Just the same I kept wishing it came a little more natural with me—with that one I mean."

When Will was saying all this to me he was sitting on a couch in his apartment in New York. I had dined with him and his wife. She was sitting on the couch beside him. When he spoke about the other woman, she crept a little nearer to him. She remarked casually that it was only a chance that she, instead of the woman Cynthia, got Will. When she said that, it was very hard to believe her. I doubt whether she wanted me to believe.

Will said that, with Cynthia, it was very hard indeed to get close. He said she never really did, what he called "melt." The fellow on the front seat, that is to say his friend Bob, was usually in a playful mood during these drives. Of the two girls, his cousins, he always seemed to prefer, not the one named Cynthia, but a smaller, darker, livelier one named Grace. He used to stop the car sometimes, on a dark road in that country somewhere outside Philadelphia, and he and Grace would make up to each other.

It was simply amazing how the girl named Grace could talk. Will said she used to swear at Bob and that when he got, what she called "too gay," she hit him. Sometimes Bob stopped the car and he and Grace got out and took a walk. They would be gone quite a long time. Will sat in the back seat with Cynthia. He said her hands were like men's hands. "They looked like competent hands," he thought. She was older than her sister Grace, and had taken a job in the city.

Apparently she was not very competent in love making; Will thought Grace and Bob would never come back. He was trying to think up things to say to Cynthia. One night they all went together to a dance. It was at a road-house, somewhere near Philadelphia.

It must have been a rather tough place. Will said it was, but when he said so, his wife, Helen, laughed. "What the devil were you doing there anyway?" Will suddenly said, turning and glaring at her as though it were the first time he had thought of asking the question.

"I was after a man and I got one, too. I got you," she said.

She had gone to the dance with a young man of the same suburb in which Bob's cousins lived. Her father was a doctor. Helen took the tale right out of Will's hands. She explained that when Will and Bob and the two girls, Grace and Cynthia, came into the dance hall she spotted Will at once. "That one's mine," she said to herself and almost before they had got inside the door she had been introduced to Will. They danced together at once.

There must really have been some tough people in the road-house that night. When Will and Helen were dancing together there was a big, low-browed, tough-looking fellow who kept trying to "make" Helen, Will said. He had started to tell me about it and then got an idea. "Say, you look here, Helen," he said, turning to look at his wife, "didn't you have something to do with that? Had you given that low-browed man the eye? Were you egging him on?"

"Sure," she said.

She explained that when a woman, like herself, was at work, when she really was laying herself out to get a man, the right thing to do was to have a rival in the field. "You have to work with what material you have at hand, don't you? You are an artist. You are always talking about art. You ought to understand that."

There came very near being a row. Will had taken Helen to a table where Bob sat with Grace and Cynthia. The young tough swaggered up—he was a little high—and demanded a dance with Helen.

Helen got indignant. She looked frightened and Will felt it was up to him, and he isn't the kind that is good at that sort of thing. Will is the kind that in such an emergency grows rather helpless.

Such a man begins to tremble. His back hurts. He dreams of being cool and determined, but is so helpless that very likely he shouts, makes the situation much worse, goes too far. What happened was that Helen settled the matter. She had already become a little tender about Will.

"What did you do?" I asked. "I understood you had become indignant."

"I had," she said, "but I managed. I got up and danced with him. I liked it. He was a good dancer."

Helen, like Grace and Cynthia, had got her father's car for the evening. When they left that tough place the young man who had come with her was on the back seat of the other car with Cynthia, and Will was in the car with her. That did not much please Cynthia, but it seemed Cynthia had very little to do with it.

So they had got started in that way. Afterward, Will continued going to Philadelphia with Bob for the week-ends, but things were different at the cousin's house. "It was not so warm and cheerful there," Will said. Helen was always dropping in. Soon the two young men began stopping at a hotel in Philadelphia. Bob had also got interested in Helen. They stopped at a cheap hotel, not having much money, and Helen came to see them. Will said she came right up into the hotel bedroom. As he began thinking of what went on during that time, Will looked at Helen with a kind of wonder in his eyes. "I guess you could have had either of us," he said, with a note of awe in his voice. It was obvious he admired his wife.

"I was not so sure about Bob," Helen said.

She wrote letters to both of the men during the week, when they were in New York at work, and when they arrived in Philadelphia, there she was. She always managed to get her father's car. She went home to her suburb late on Saturday nights and came back again early on Sundays. Saturday nights they all went together to a dance.

One day her father grew alarmed and angry, and followed her. He saw her go to the two men, right into their room, in the cheap hotel.

She had to decide the matter. She had made up her mind to marry one of the men, was tired of living at home. Things, I gathered, were getting rather warm at home. She was an only child. She said her mother was crying all the time and her father was furious. "I had to be hard-boiled with them for the time," she explained. She was rather like a surgeon about to perform an operation on a frightened patient. She cajoled and bullied them. When her father tried to put his foot down she issued an ultimatum. "I'm twenty-one," she said. "If you interfere with me I shall leave home."

"But how will you live?"

"Don't be silly, Father, a woman can always live."

She went right out to the garage, got her father's car and drove to Philadelphia. In the room in the hotel she was studying the two men. She got Will to go down to the car with her. "Get in," she said. They drove away from the hotel. "I didn't know where we were going," Will said.

They drove and drove. Will spoke of her mood that night. He was in love. When I heard this tale he was still very much in love. "It was a soft clear night with stars." Speaking of it, he took hold of his wife's hands.

"Let's get married," she said to Will that night. "But when?" he asked. She thought they had better do it at once. "But think of my salary," Will said. "I am thinking about it. It isn't much, is it?" The meagerness of his salary didn't seem to alter her determination. "I can't wait any longer," was what she said. She said they would drive around all night and get married early the next morning.

And so they did. Her people, the doctor and his wife, were in a panic.

Will and his wife went to them the next day. "How were you received?" I asked. "Fine," Will said. He said that the doctor and his wife would have been happy no matter whom she had married. "You see, I had arranged for that," Helen said. "I had got them into a state where marriage sure seemed like salvation to them."

Brother Death

THERE were the two oak stumps, knee high to a not-too-tall man and cut quite squarely across. They became to the two children objects of wonder. They had seen the two trees cut but had run away just as the trees fell. They hadn't thought of the two stumps, to be left standing there; hadn't even looked at them. Afterwards Ted said to his sister Mary, speaking of the stumps: "I wonder if they bled, like legs, when a surgeon cuts a man's leg off." He had been hearing war stories. A man came to the farm one day to visit one of the farm-hands, a man who had been in the World War and had lost an arm. He stood in one of the barns talking. When Ted said that Mary spoke up at once. She hadn't been lucky enough to be at the barn when the one-armed man was there talking, and was jealous. "Why not a woman or a girl's leg?" she said, but Ted said the idea was silly. "Women and girls don't get their legs and arms off," he declared. "Why not? I'd just like to know why not?" Mary kept saying.

It would have been something if they had stayed, that day the trees were cut. "We might have gone and touched the places," Ted said. He meant the stumps. Would they have been warm? Would they have bled? They did go and touch the places afterwards, but it was a cold day and the stumps were cold. Ted stuck to his point that only men's arms and legs were cut off, but Mary thought of automobile accidents. "You can't think just about wars. There might be an automobile accident," she declared, but Ted wouldn't be convinced.

They were both children, but something had made them both in an odd way old. Mary was fourteen and Ted eleven, but Ted wasn't strong and that rather evened things up. They were the children of a well-to-do Virginia farmer named John Grey in the Blue Ridge country in Southwestern Virginia. There was a wide valley called the "Rich Valley," with a railroad and a small river running through it and high mountains in sight, to the north and south. Ted had some kind of heart disease, a lesion, something of the sort, the result of a severe attack of diphtheria when he was a child of eight. He was thin and not strong but curiously alive. The doctor said he might die at any moment, might just drop down dead. The fact had drawn him peculiarly close to his sister Mary. It had awakened a strong and determined maternalism in her.

The whole family, the neighbors, on neighboring farms in the valley, and even the other children at the schoolhouse where they went to school recognized something as existing between the two children. "Look at them going along there," people said. "They do seem to have good times together, but they are so serious. For such young children they are too serious. Still, I suppose, under the circumstances, it's natural." Of course, everyone knew about Ted. It had done something to Mary. At fourteen she was both a child and a grown woman. The woman side of her kept popping out at unexpected moments.

She had sensed something concerning her brother Ted. It was because he was as he was, having that kind of a heart, a heart likely at any moment to stop beating, leaving him dead, cut down like a young tree. The others in the Grey family, that is to say, the older ones, the mother and father and an older brother, Don, who was eighteen now, recognized something as belonging to the two children, being, as it were, between them, but the recognition wasn't very definite. People in your own family are likely at any moment to do strange, sometimes hurtful things to you. You have to watch them. Ted and Mary had both found that out.

The brother Don was like the father, already at eighteen almost a grown man. He was that sort, the kind people speak of, saying: "He's a good man. He'll make a good solid dependable man." The father, when he was a young man, never drank, never went chasing the girls, was never wild. There had been enough wild young ones in the Rich Valley when he was a lad. Some of them had inherited big farms and had lost them, gambling, drinking, fooling with fast horses and chasing after the women. It had been almost a Virginia tradition, but John Grey was a land man. All the Greys were. There were other large cattle farms owned by Greys up and down the valley.

John Grey, every one said, was a natural cattle man. He knew beef cattle, of the big so-called export type, how to pick and feed them to make beef. He knew how and where to get the right kind of young stock to turn into his fields. It was blue-grass country. Big beef cattle went directly off the pastures to market. The Grey farm contained over twelve hundred acres, most of it in blue grass.

The father was a land man, land hungry. He had begun, as a cattle farmer, with a small place, inherited from his father, some two hundred acres, lying next to what was then the big Aspinwahl place and, after he began, he never stopped getting more land. He kept cutting in on the Aspinwahls who were a rather horsey, fast lot. They thought of themselves as Virginia aristocrats, having, as they weren't so modest about pointing out, a family going back and back, family tradition, guests always being entertained, fast horses kept, money being bet on fast horses. John Grey getting their land, now twenty acres, then thirty, then fifty, until at last he got the old Aspinwahl house, with one of the Aspinwahl girls, not a young one, not one of the best-looking ones, as wife. The Aspinwahl place was down, by that time, to less than a hundred acres, but he went on, year after year, always being careful and shrewd, making every penny count, never wasting a cent, adding and adding to what was now the Grey place. The former Aspinwahl house was a large old brick house with fireplaces in all the rooms and was very comfortable.

People wondered why Louise Aspinwahl had married John Grey, but when they were wondering they smiled. The Aspinwahl girls were all well educated, had all been away to college, but Louise wasn't so pretty. She got nicer after marriage, suddenly almost beautiful. The Aspinwahls were, as every one knew, naturally sensitive, really first class but the men couldn't hang onto land and the Greys could. In all that section of Virginia, people gave John Grey credit for being what he was. They respected him. "He's on the level," they said, "as honest as a horse. He has cattle sense, that's it." He could run his big hand down over the flank of a steer and say, almost to the pound, what he would weigh on the scales or he could look at a calf or a yearling and say, "He'll do," and he would do. A steer is a steer. He isn't supposed to do anything but make beef.

There was Don, the oldest son of the Grey family. He was so evidently destined to be a Grey, to be another like his father. He had long been a star in the 4H Club of the Virginia county and, even as a lad of nine and ten, had won prizes at steer judging. At twelve he had produced, no one helping him, doing all the work himself, more bushels of corn on an acre of land than any other boy in the State.

It was all a little amazing, even a bit queer to Mary Grey, being as she was a girl peculiarly conscious, so old and young, so aware. There was Don, the older brother, big and strong of body, like the father, and there was the young brother Ted. Ordinarily, in the ordinary course of life, she being what she was—female—it would have been quite natural and right for her to have given her young girl's admiration to Don but she didn't. For some reason, Don barely existed for her. He was outside, not in it, while for her Ted, the seemingly weak one of the family, was everything.

Still there Don was, so big of body, so quiet, so apparently sure of himself. The father had begun, as a young cattle man, with the two hundred acres, and now he had the twelve hundred. What would Don Grey do when he started? Already he knew, although he didn't say anything, that he wanted to start. He wanted to run things, be his own boss. His father had offered to send him away to college, to an agricultural college, but he wouldn't go. "No. I can learn more here," he said.

Already there was a contest, always kept under the surface, between the father and son. It concerned ways of doing things, decisions to be made. As yet the son always surrendered.

It is like that in a family, little isolated groups formed within the larger group, jealousies, concealed hatreds, silent battles secretly going on—among the Greys, Mary and Ted, Don and his father, the mother and the two younger children, Gladys, a girl child of six now, who adored her brother Don, and Harry, a boy child of two.

As for Mary and Ted, they lived within their own world, but their own world had not been established without a struggle. The point was that Ted, having the heart that might at any moment stop beating, was always being treated tenderly by the others. Only Mary understood that—how it infuriated and hurt him.

"No, Ted, I wouldn't do that.

"Now, Ted, do be careful."

Sometimes Ted went white and trembling with anger, Don, the father, the mother, all keeping at him like that. It didn't matter what he wanted to do, learn to drive one of the two family cars, climb a tree to find a bird's nest, run a race with Mary. Naturally, being on a farm, he wanted to try his hand at breaking a colt, beginning with him, getting a saddle on, having it out with him. "No, Ted. You can't." He had learned to swear, picking it up from the farm-hands and from boys at the country school. "Hell! Goddam!" he said to Mary. Only Mary understood how he felt, and she had not put the matter very definitely into words, not even to herself. It was one of the things that made her old when she was so young. It made her stand aside from the others of the family, aroused in her a curious determination. "They shall not." She caught herself saying the words to herself. "They shall not.

"If he is to have but a few years of life, they shall not spoil what he is to have. Why should they make him die, over and over, day after day?" The thoughts in her did not become so definite. She had resentment against the others. She was like a soldier, standing guard over Ted.

The two children drew more and more away, into their own world and only once did what Mary felt come to the surface. That was with the mother.

It was on an early Summer day and Ted and Mary were playing in the rain. They were on a side porch of the house, where the water came pouring down from the eaves. At a corner of the porch there was a great stream, and first Ted and then Mary dashed through it, returning to the porch with clothes soaked and water running in streams from soaked hair. There was something joyous, the feel of the cold water on the body, under clothes, and they were shrieking with laughter when the mother came to the door. She looked at Ted. There was fear and anxiety in her voice. "Oh, Ted, you know you mustn't, you mustn't." Just that. All the rest implied. Nothing said to Mary. There it was. "Oh, Ted, you mustn't. You mustn't run hard, climb trees, ride horses. The least shock to you may do it." It was the old story again, and, of course, Ted understood. He went white and trembled. Why couldn't the rest understand that was a hundred times worse for him? On that day, without answering his mother, he ran off the porch and through the rain toward the barns. He wanted to go hide himself from every one. Mary knew how he felt.

She got suddenly very old and very angry. The mother and

daughter stood looking at each other, the woman nearing fifty and the child of fourteen. It was getting everything in the family reversed. Mary felt that but felt she had to do something. "You should have more sense, Mother," she said seriously. She also had gone white. Her lips trembled. "You mustn't do it any more. Don't you ever do it again."

"What, child?" There was astonishment and half anger in the mother's voice. "Always making him think of it," Mary said. She wanted to cry but didn't.

The mother understood. There was a queer tense moment before Mary also walked off, toward the barns, in the rain. It wasn't all so clear. The mother wanted to fly at the child, perhaps shake her for daring to be so impudent. A child like that to decide things—to dare to reprove her mother. There was so much implied—even that Ted be allowed to die, quickly, suddenly, rather than that death, danger of sudden death, be brought again and again to his attention. There were values in life, implied by a child's words: "Life, what is it worth? Is death the most terrible thing?" The mother turned and went silently into the house while Mary, going to the barns, presently found Ted. He was in an empty horse stall, standing with his back to the wall, staring. There were no explanations. "Well," Ted said presently, and, "Come on, Ted," Mary replied. It was necessary to do something, even perhaps more risky than playing in the rain. The rain was already passing. "Let's take off our shoes," Mary said. Going barefoot was one of the things forbidden Ted. They took their shoes off and, leaving them in the barn, went into an orchard. There was a small creek below the orchard, a creek that went down to the river and now it would be in flood. They went into it and once Mary got swept off her feet so that Ted had to pull her out. She spoke then. "I told Mother," she said, looking serious.

"What?" Ted said. "Gee, I guess maybe I saved you from drowning," he added.

"Sure you did," said Mary. "I told her to let you alone." She grew suddenly fierce. "They've all got to—they've got to let you alone," she said.

There was a bond. Ted did his share. He was imaginative and could think of plenty of risky things to do. Perhaps the mother spoke to the father and to Don, the older brother. There was a new inclination in the family to keep hands off the pair, and the fact seemed to give the two children new room in life. Something seemed to open out. There was a little inner world created, always, every day, being re-created, and in it there was a kind of new security. It seemed to the two children—they could not have put their feeling into words—that, being in their own created world, feeling a new security there, they could suddenly look out at the outside world and see, in a new way, what was going on out there in the world that belonged also to others.

It was a world to be thought about, looked at, a world of drama too, the drama of human relations, outside their own world, in a family, on a farm, in a farmhouse. . . . On a farm, calves and yearling steers arriving to be fattened, great heavy steers going off to market, colts being broken to work or to saddle, lambs born in the late Winter. The human side of life was more difficult, to a child often incomprehensible, but after the speech to the mother, on the porch of the house that day when it rained, it seemed to Mary almost as though she and Ted had set up a new family. Everything about the farm, the house and the barns got nicer. There was a new freedom. The two children walked along a country road, returning to the farm from school in the late afternoon. There were other children in the road but they managed to fall behind or they got ahead. There were plans made. "I'm going to be a nurse when I grow up," Mary said. She may have remembered dimly the woman nurse, from the county-seat town, who had come to stay in the house when Ted was so ill. Ted said that as soon as he could—it would be when he was younger yet than Don was now—he intended to leave and go out West . . . far out, he said. He wanted to be a cowboy or a bronco-buster or something, and, that failing, he thought he would be a railroad engineer. The railroad that went down through the Rich Valley crossed a corner of the Grey farm, and, from the road in the afternoon, they could sometimes see trains, quite far away, the smoke rolling up. There was a faint rumbling noise, and, on clear days they could see the flying piston rods of the engines.

As for the two stumps in the field near the house, they were what was left of two oak trees. The children had known the trees. They were cut one day in the early Fall.

There was a back porch to the Grey house—the house that had once been the seat of the Aspinwahl family—and from the porch steps a path led down to a stone spring house. A spring came out of the ground just there, and there was a tiny stream that went along the edge of a field, past two large barns and out across a meadow to a creek—called a "branch" in Virginia, and the two trees stood close together beyond the spring house and the fence.

They were lusty trees, their roots down in the rich, always damp soil, and one of them had a great limb that came down near the ground, so that Ted and Mary could climb into it and out another limb into its brother tree, and in the Fall, when other trees, at the front and side of the house, had shed their leaves, blood-red leaves still clung to the two oaks. They were like dry blood on gray days, but on other days, when the sun came out, the trees flamed against distant hills. The leaves clung, whispering and talking when the wind blew, so that the trees themselves seemed carrying on a conversation.

John Grey had decided he would have the trees cut. At first it was not a very definite decision. "I think I'll have them cut," he announced.

"But why?" his wife asked. The trees meant a good deal to her. They had been planted, just in that spot, by her grandfather, she said, having in mind just a certain effect. "You see how, in the Fall, when you stand on the back porch, they are so nice against the hills." She spoke of the trees, already quite large, having been brought from a distant woods. Her mother had often spoken of it. The man, her grandfather, had a special feeling for trees. "An Aspinwahl would do that," John Grey said. "There is enough yard, here about the house, and enough trees. They do not shade the house or the yard. An Aspinwahl would go to all that trouble for trees and then plant them where grass might be growing." He had suddenly determined, a half-formed determination in him suddenly hardening. He had perhaps heard too much of the Aspinwahls and their ways. The conversation regarding the trees took place at the table, at the noon hour, and Mary and Ted heard it all.

It began at the table and was carried on afterwards out of doors, in the yard back of the house. The wife had followed her husband out. He always left the table suddenly and silently, getting quickly up and going out heavily, shutting doors with a bang as he went. "Don't, John," the wife said, standing on the porch and calling to her husband. It was a cold day but the sun was out and the trees were like great bonfires against gray distant fields and hills. The older son of the family, young Don, the one so physically like the father and apparently so like him in every way, had come out of the house with the mother, followed by the two children, Ted and Mary, and at first Don said nothing, but, when the father did not answer the mother's protest but started toward the barn, he also spoke. What he said was obviously the determining thing, hardening the father.

To the two other children—they had walked a little aside and stood together watching and listening—there was something. There was their own child's world. "Let us alone and we'll let you alone." It wasn't as definite as that. Most of the definite thoughts about what happened in the yard that afternoon came to Mary Grey long afterwards, when she was a grown woman. At the moment there was merely a sudden sharpening of the feeling of isolation, a wall between herself and Ted and the others. The father, even then perhaps, seen in a new light, Don and the mother seen in a new light.

There was something, a driving destructive thing in life, in all relationships between people. All of this felt dimly that day —she always believed both by herself and Ted—but only thought out long afterwards, after Ted was dead. There was the farm her father had won from the Aspinwahls—greater persistence, greater shrewdness. In a family, little remarks dropped from time to time, an impression slowly built up. The father, John Grey, was a successful man. He had acquired. He owned. He was the commander, the one having power to do his will. And the power had run out and covered, not only other human lives, impulses in others, wishes, hungers in others . . . he himself might not have, might not even understand . . . but it went far out beyond that. It was, curiously, the power also of life and death. Did Mary Grey think such thoughts at that moment? . . . ? She couldn't have. . . . Still there was her own peculiar situation, her relationship with her brother Ted, who was to die.

Ownership that gave curious rights, dominances—fathers over children, men and women over lands, houses, factories in cities, fields. "I will have the trees in that orchard cut. They produce apples but not of the right sort. There is no money in apples of that sort any more."

"But, Sir . . . you see . . . look . . . the trees there against that hill, against the sky."

"Nonsense. Sentimentality."

Confusion.

It would have been such nonsense to think of the father of Mary Grey as a man without feeling. He had struggled hard all his life, perhaps, as a young man, gone without things wanted, deeply hungered for. Some one has to manage things in this life. Possessions mean power, the right to say, "do this" or "do that." If you struggle long and hard for a thing it becomes infinitely sweet to you.

Was there a kind of hatred between the father and the older son of the Grey family? "You are one also who has this thing— the impulse to power, so like my own. Now you are young and I am growing old." Admiration mixed with fear. If you would retain power it will not do to admit fear.

The young Don was so curiously like the father. There were the same lines about the jaws, the same eyes. They were both heavy men. Already the young man walked like the father, slammed doors as did the father. There was the same curious lack of delicacy of thought and touch—the heaviness that plows through, gets things done. When John Grey had married Louise Aspinwahl he was already a mature man, on his way to success. Such men do not marry young and recklessly. Now he was nearing sixty and there was the son—so like himself, having the same kind of strength.

Both land lovers, possession lovers. "It is my farm, my house, my horses, cattle, sheep." Soon now, another ten years, fifteen at the most, and the father would be ready for death. "See, already my hand slips a little. All of this to go out of my grasp." He, John Grey, had not got all of these possessions so easily. It had taken much patience, much persistence. No one but himself would ever quite know. Five, ten, fifteen years of work and saving, getting the Aspinwahl farm piece by piece. "The fools!" They had liked to think of themselves as aristocrats, throwing the land away, now twenty acres, now thirty, now fifty.

Raising horses that could never plow an acre of land.

And they had robbed the land too, had never put anything back, doing nothing to enrich it, build it up. Such a one thinking: "I'm an Aspinwahl, a gentleman. I do not soil my hands at the plow.

"Fools who do not know the meaning of land owned, possessions, money—responsibility. It is they who are second-rate men."

He had got an Aspinwahl for a wife and, as it had turned out, she was the best, the smartest and, in the end, the best-looking one of the lot.

And now there was his son, standing at the moment near the mother. They had both come down off the porch. It would be natural and right for this one—he being what he already was, what he would become—for him, in his turn, to come into possession, to take command.

There would be, of course, the rights of the other children. If you have the stuff in you (John Grey felt that his son Don had) there is a way to manage. You buy the others out, make arrangements. There was Ted—he wouldn't be alive—and Mary and the two younger children. "The better for you if you have to struggle."

All of this, the implication of the moment of sudden struggle between a father and son, coming slowly afterwards to the man's daughter, as yet little more than a child. Does the drama take place when the seed is put into the ground or afterwards when the plant has pushed out of the ground and the bud breaks open, or still later, when the fruit ripens? There were the Greys with their ability—slow, saving, able, determined, patient. Why had they superseded the Aspinwahls in the Rich Valley? Aspinwahl blood also in the two children, Mary and Ted.

There was an Aspinwahl man—called "Uncle Fred," a brother to Louise Grey—who came sometimes to the farm. He was a rather striking-looking, tall old man with a gray Vandyke beard and a mustache, somewhat shabbily dressed but always with an indefinable air of class. He came from the county-seat town, where he lived now with a daughter who had married a merchant, a polite courtly old man who always froze into a queer silence in the presence of his sister's husband.

The son Don was standing near the mother on the day in the Fall, and the two children, Mary and Ted, stood apart.

"Don't, John," Louise Grey said again. The father, who had started away toward the barns, stopped.

"Well, I guess I will."

"No, you won't," said young Don, speaking suddenly. There was a queer fixed look in his eyes. It had flashed into life— something that was between the two men: "I possess" . . . "I will possess." The father wheeled and looked sharply at the son and then ignored him.

For a moment the mother continued pleading.

"But why, why?"

"They make too much shade. The grass does not grow."

"But there is so much grass, so many acres of grass."

John Grey was answering his wife, but now again he looked at his son. There were unspoken words flying back and forth.

"I possess. I am in command here. What do you mean by telling me that I won't?"

"Ha! So! You possess now but soon I will possess."

"I'll see you in hell first."

"You fool! Not yet! Not yet!"

None of the words, set down above, was spoken at the moment, and afterwards the daughter Mary never did remember the exact words that had passed between the two men. There was a sudden quick flash of determination in Don—even perhaps sudden determination to stand by the mother—even perhaps something else—a feeling in the young Don out of the Aspinwahl blood in him—for the moment tree love superseding grass love—grass that would fatten steers. . . .

Winner of 4H Club prizes, champion young corn-raiser, judge of steers, land lover, possession lover.

"You won't," Don said again.

"Won't what?"

"Won't cut those trees."

The father said nothing more at the moment but walked away from the little group toward the barns. The sun was still shining brightly. There was a sharp cold little wind. The two trees were like bonfires lighted against distant hills.

It was the noon hour and there were two men, both young,

employees on the farm, who lived in a small tenant house beyond the barns. One of them, a man with a harelip, was married and the other, a rather handsome silent young man,
boarded with him. They had just come from the midday meal
and were going toward one of the barns. It was the beginning
of the Fall corn-cutting time and they would be going together
to a distant field to cut corn.

The father went to the barn and returned with the two men.
They brought axes and a long crosscut saw. "I want you to cut
those two trees." There was something, a blind, even stupid
determination in the man, John Grey. And at that moment his
wife, the mother of his children . . . There was no way any of
the children could ever know how many moments of the sort
she had been through. She had married John Grey. He was her
man.

"If you do, Father . . ." Don Grey said coldly.

"Do as I tell you! Cut those two trees!" This addressed to
the two workmen. The one who had a harelip laughed. His
laughter was like the bray of a donkey.

"Don't," said Louise Grey, but she was not addressing her
husband this time. She stepped to her son and put a hand on
his arm.

"Don't.

"Don't cross him. Don't cross my man." Could a child like
Mary Grey comprehend? It takes time to understand things
that happen in life. Life unfolds slowly to the mind. Mary was
standing with Ted, whose young face was white and tense.
Death at his elbow. At any moment. At any moment.

"I have been through this a hundred times. That is the way
this man I married has succeeded. Nothing stops him. I married him; I have had my children by him.

"We women choose to submit.

"This is my affair, more than yours, Don, my son."

A woman hanging onto her thing—the family, created about
her.

The son not seeing things with her eyes. He shook off his
mother's hand, lying on his arm. Louise Grey was younger
than her husband, but, if he was now nearing sixty, she was
drawing near fifty. At the moment she looked very delicate and
fragile. There was something, at the moment, in her bearing.

. . . Was there, after all, something in blood, the Aspinwahl blood?

In a dim way perhaps, at the moment, the child Mary did comprehend. Women and their men. For her then, at that time, there was but one male, the child Ted. Afterwards she remembered how he looked at that moment, the curiously serious old look on his young face. There was even, she thought later, a kind of contempt for both the father and brother, as though he might have been saying to himself—he couldn't really have been saying it—he was too young: "Well, we'll see. This is something. These foolish ones—my father and my brother. I myself haven't long to live. I'll see what I can, while I do live."

The brother Don stepped over near to where his father stood.

"If you do, Father . . ." he said again.

"Well?"

"I'll walk off this farm and I'll never come back."

"All right. Go then."

The father began directing the two men who had begun cutting the trees, each man taking a tree. The young man with the harelip kept laughing, the laughter like the bray of a donkey. "Stop that," the father said sharply, and the sound ceased abruptly. The son Don walked away, going rather aimlessly toward the barn. He approached one of the barns and then stopped. The mother, white now, half ran into the house.

The son returned toward the house, passing the two younger children without looking at them, but did not enter. The father did not look at him. He went hesitatingly along a path at the front of the house and through a gate and into a road. The road ran for several miles down through the valley and then, turning, went over a mountain to the county-seat town.

As it happened, only Mary saw the son Don when he returned to the farm. There were three or four tense days. Perhaps, all the time, the mother and son had been secretly in touch. There was a telephone in the house. The father stayed all day in the fields, and when he was in the house was silent.

Mary was in one of the barns on the day when Don came back and when the father and son met. It was an odd meeting.

The son came, Mary always afterwards thought, rather sheepishly. The father came out of a horse's stall. He had been
throwing corn to work horses. Neither the father nor son saw
Mary. There was a car parked in the barn and she had crawled
into the driver's seat, her hands on the steering wheel, pretending she was driving.

"Well," the father said. If he felt triumphant, he did not
show his feeling.

"Well," said the son, "I have come back."

"Yes, I see," the father said. "They are cutting corn." He
walked toward the barn door and then stopped. "It will be
yours soon now," he said. "You can be boss then."

He said no more and both men went away, the father toward
the distant fields and the son toward the house. Mary was afterwards quite sure that nothing more was ever said.

What had the father meant?

"When it is yours you can be boss." It was too much for the
child. Knowledge comes slowly. It meant:

"You will be in command, and for you, in your turn, it will
be necessary to assert.

"Such men as we are cannot fool with delicate stuff. Some
men are meant to command and others must obey. You can
make them obey in your turn.

"There is a kind of death.

"Something in you must die before you can possess and
command."

There was, so obviously, more than one kind of death. For
Don Grey one kind and for the younger brother Ted, soon
now perhaps, another.

Mary ran out of the barn that day, wanting eagerly to get
out into the light, and afterwards, for a long time, she did not
try to think her way through what had happened. She and her
brother Ted did, however, afterwards, before he died, discuss
quite often the two trees. They went on a cold day and put
their fingers on the stumps, but the stumps were cold. Ted
kept asserting that only men got their legs and arms cut off,
and she protested. They continued doing things that had been
forbidden Ted to do, but no one protested, and, a year or two
later, when he died, he died during the night in his bed.

But while he lived, there was always, Mary afterwards

thought, a curious sense of freedom, something that belonged to him that made it good, a great happiness, to be with him. It was, she finally thought, because having to die his kind of death, he never had to make the surrender his brother had made—to be sure of possessions, success, his time to command —would never have to face the more subtle and terrible death that had come to his older brother.

UNCOLLECTED STORIES

Sister

THE young artist is a woman, and at evening she comes to talk to me in my room. She is my sister, but long ago she has forgotten that and I have forgotten.

Neither my sister nor I live in our father's house, and among all my brothers and sisters I am conscious only of her. The others have positions in the city and in the evening go home to the house where my sister and I once lived. My father is old and his hands tremble. He is not concerned about me, but my sister who lives alone in a room in a house on North Dearborn Street has caused him much unhappiness.

Into my room in the evening comes my sister and sits upon a low couch by the door. She sits cross-legged and smokes cigarettes. When she comes it is always the same—she is embarrassed and I am embarrassed.

Since she has been a small girl my sister has always been very strange. When she was quite young she was awkward and boyish and tore her clothes climbing trees. It was after that her strangeness began to be noticed. Day after day she would slip away from the house and go to walk in the streets. She became a devout student and made such rapid strides in her classes that my mother—who to tell the truth is fat and uninteresting—spent the days worrying. My sister, she declared, would end by having brain fever.

When my sister was fifteen years old she announced to the family that she was about to take a lover. I was away from home at the time, on one of the wandering trips that have always been a passion with me.

My sister came into the house, where the family were seated at the table, and, standing by the door, said she had decided to spend the night with a boy of sixteen who was the son of a neighbor.

The neighbor boy knew nothing of my sister's intentions. He was at home from college, a tall, quiet, blue-eyed fellow, with his mind set upon foot-ball. To my family my sister explained that she would go to the boy and tell him of her desires. Her eyes flashed and she stamped with her foot upon the floor.

My father whipped my sister. Taking her by the arm he led her into the stable at the back of the house. He whipped her with a long black whip that always stood upright in the whip-socket of the carriage in which, on Sundays, my mother and father drove about the streets of our suburb. After the whipping my father was ill.

I am wondering how I know so intimately all the details of the whipping of my sister. Neither my father nor my sister have told me of it. Perhaps sometime, as I sat dreaming in a chair, my mother gossiped of the whipping. It would be like her to do that, and it is a trick of my mind never to remember her figure in connection with the things she has told me.

After the whipping in the stable my sister was quite changed. The family sat tense and quiet at the table and when she came into the house she laughed and went upstairs to her own room. She was very quiet and well-behaved for several years and when she was twenty-one inherited some money and went to live alone in the house on North Dearborn Street. I have a feeling that the walls of our house told me the story of the whipping. I could never live in the house afterwards and came away at once to this room where I am now and where my sister comes to visit me.

And so there is my sister in my room and we are embarrassed. I do not look at her but turn my back and begin writing furiously. Presently she is on the arm of my chair with her arm about my neck.

I am the world and my sister is the young artist in the world. I am afraid the world will destroy her. So furious is my love of her that the touch of her hand makes me tremble.

My sister would not write as I am now writing. How strange it would seem to see her engaged in anything of the kind. She would never give the slightest bit of advice to any one. If you were dying and her advice would save you she would say nothing.

My sister is the most wonderful artist in the world, but when she is with me I do not remember that. When she has talked of her adventures, up from the chair I spring and go ranting about the room. I am half blind with anger, thinking perhaps that strange, furtive looking youth, with whom I saw her walking yesterday in the streets, has had her in his arms. The flesh of my sister is sacred to me. If anything were to happen to her body I think I should kill myself in sheer madness.

In the evening after my sister is gone I do not try to work any more. I pull my couch to the opening by the window and lie down. It is then a little that I begin to understand my sister. She is the artist right to adventure in the world, to be destroyed in the adventure, if that be necessary, and I, on my couch, am the worker in the world, blinking up at the stars that can be seen from my window when my couch is properly arranged.

The White Streak

I

HE IS old now and looks old, but when this story begins he was a man of twenty-five. His father, a commission merchant dealing in poultry, butter and eggs, had an office in South Water Street in the City of Chicago.

He was married to the daughter of a respectable merchant and had bought a white frame house in a suburb. He went into his father's business and for a time things went well with him. Then something happened. He grew weary of the selling of butter and eggs and of living in a suburb. Something like a revolution went on in his soul. His boyish blue eyes were clouded and as he went up and down in the noisy, crowded street where he was employed and heard men higgling and quarreling over the price to be paid for a shipment of butter, he trembled with anger. He began to hate the other men in the office, and in a fury of hatred ran out of the narrow, dirty street filled with wagons piled high with food stuffs. Running around the corner he stood under the elevated railroad at Lake and State Streets. His body trembled and he looked about with wild eyes. In State Street he saw thousands of men, women and children going into stores to buy clothes.

"The world is mad," he muttered to himself. "If people are not thinking of the clothes they wear they are thinking and talking of food. Am I to spend my life in the silly business of seeing that people are fed?"

The young man, whose name was Bushnell, could not understand what had happened to him. He tried to discuss the matter with his wife but wasn't very clear, and his wife did not know what he was talking about. Like thousands of other young people who live in respectable suburbs, Bushnell and his wife had been married because of a situation founded on emotional hunger. They had met at a dinner party given at the house of a mutual friend and had wanted each other. When the hunger within became too persistent to be quieted, the young man blurted out a proposal. For months before their marriage

they spent their evenings together, sitting in silence, each tremendously conscious of the other. After marriage they found
they had little to say to each other.

It was during the third summer after his marriage that the
revolution took place in the soul of young Bushnell. In the
evening when he went home from the office in the elevated
train he put his head out of the car window and tried to reason
with himself.

"Everyone has to work," he thought. "It does not make any
difference what a man does."

He looked at the long rows of grim brick buildings past
which the train hurried and thought of the millions who, like
himself, must be employed in dark ugly places.

"It is what life is like," he muttered to himself. "It cannot be
helped."

The whole city was, he thought, given over to ugliness and
the people who rode with him on the trains were ugly in the
dreary sameness of their lives and their thoughts. The men and
women sitting in the car homeward bound from the city talked
of their affairs. It seemed to young Bushnell that the women
talked always of clothes and the men of the buying and selling
of foods. He dreaded the thought of going into his own house
and sitting at table. His wife, he was afraid, would talk of the
buying and cooking of food. The street in which his house
stood was lined with shade trees and he liked to walk under
the trees, but he decided he did not like the people who lived
in the houses.

The suburb in which young Bushnell lived was called Evanston. There were many newly married young people living in
white houses on tree lined streets in Evanston, and the Bush-
nells became part of a group of young people who spent their
evenings together. There was a man who lived across the street
and who made his living in the advertising business. He was
forever planning to put on the market some new kind of food-
stuff. He specialized in that. When he went into a new project
he asked young Bushnell's advice.

"You are connected with the selling of foods. Give me the
dope," he begged. "You know better than I what people think
about foods."

Young Bushnell hated the advertising man and he hated also

the retail merchant, the lawyer and the man who dealt in real estate who helped to make up the neighboring group. On the evenings when they with their wives came to his house he wanted to cry out against them, to tell them to go away and never come back. He said nothing of the sort because he could think of no possible excuse for so unexpected and unexplainable an outburst.

The summer during which all this occurred was unusually hot. Young Bushnell was tired. All the time he wanted to fight or to cry. His wife had a guest at the house, a young woman cousin who taught school in some town in the East. When she came the young man paid no attention to her, but after she had been at the house for two or three weeks he noted that she was habitually silent. He began to be attracted to her.

In the evening, when people of the neighborhood came to sit and talk with him and his wife on the front porch of their house, he remained silent and looked at the school teacher. He thought the talk and the laughter of all the men and women sitting about sounded like the croaking of frogs in a pond late at night. He looked over their heads and shuddered. Then he looked at the school teacher clad in a white dress and persistently silent. He wondered what she was thinking about.

One evening when it seemed to him that the talk of his wife and his friends had become utterly meaningless, he arose from his chair and went unobserved into the house. On an impulse he crept upstairs and went stealthily into the room occupied by his wife's guest. Standing in the darkness he tried to think what he wanted to do. Then going to a closet door he opened it and saw hanging there one of the white dresses worn by the woman. It made a white streak in the darkness, just as the silent white-clad woman made a white streak in the darkness of his mind. Dropping to his knees he laid his cheek against the soft cloth of the dress. Tears came into his eyes. Although he had never given the subject of marriage much thought, he was sure that his wife, because of her marriage to him, would not have understood what he was doing. The thought made him blindly resentful. In the darkness he muttered words concerning the matter. Holding the white dress tightly against his cheek he declared his love for the silent woman who had worn it and would wear it again.

"She's beautiful because she has kept herself to herself," he declared. "She has let herself stand alone and far off. She has dignity and does not talk of food and of clothes. It is wonderful to have her here and not know what she is thinking about."

II

The man who went into his father's commission business in South Water Street is now at the head of the firm. He is sixty years old and has prospered. His father is dead. On the whole he is happy enough. When he and his wife had been married for a long time she gave birth to a daughter who is now a young woman at school in the East. The feeling he once had in regard to the buying and selling of foods has gone quite away. He is a prominent member of a church in Evanston and stands very well in that respectable suburb.

As for the school teacher who is his wife's cousin and who once came to visit at his house, he has forgotten her name. He only thinks of her once in a long time.

Sometimes when business is unusually heavy he works over his books in the office at night. He has dinner at one of the big restaurants in the city and then hurries away to the office. Although he has prospered, his office, like most of the offices in South Water Street in Chicago, is a small dirty affair upstairs over a storeroom. At the back of the office there is a window that looks out over the Chicago River.

As Bushnell walks at night through the dark silent streets he is reminded of the feeling he once had in regard to the buying and selling of foods. As he is now an old man he stumbles a little. He is bald and a nervous disease had twisted his head to one side. As he hurries along he peers into the darkness and shudders.

During the day South Water Street, where rations for millions of people are handed about, is the busiest place in Chicago, but at night it is dark, lonely and dreary. The roar of the voices of innumerable hucksters has drifted away and the multitude of wagons loaded with boxes and bales that all day blocked the roadway have disappeared into the darkness. In the dim light at the edge of the sidewalks huge iron cans are heaped high with half decayed fruit and vegetables. A sour pungent smell greets the nostrils. Decrepit old women wander about, creeping here and there in the darkness. In their arms they carry baskets which they fill with frozen potatoes and spoiled bananas, apples and oranges.

The merchant goes into his office and bends over his books. He tries not to think. On summer evenings when it is very hot he opens the window that looks out over the river. When his work is done and he has put on his coat he stands for a moment looking into the darkness. As when he was a young comely man he thinks of a life spent in the buying and selling of food with a shudder.

At night the Chicago River, a grey stream running under ugly bridges out of the lake into the land, is transformed. It becomes at times, when the night is clear and the surface of the river is stirred by night winds, utterly lovely. Looking down at it, a sense of mystery with dread creeps over the old merchant. He forgets his old wife and his daughter and feels suddenly young and alone in the world. On the river below a boat passes making a white streak in the darkness and he is reminded of the time long ago when a silent, white-clad woman sat among the chattering people on the porch of his house. He wants to put his cheek against the sides of the boat as he once put his cheek against the white gown that had been worn by the woman. For a moment his mind, that for years has been quite normal and sure of itself, is confused. He walks up and down in the office and opens and closes his fists. Although the river is close at hand and although it is within a stone's throw of the dark evil-smelling street, in which the horrible old women go up and down, it seems to him strangely remote and unreal.

"It stands alone and far off," he whispers.

He tries to reason with himself and tells himself that the stream is in reality a sewer, that it is not love at all.

"I am becoming a doddering old fool," he declares, and closing the window, hurries away.

In spite of himself the merchant remembers the school teacher. He decides that she is the most beautiful thing that ever came into his life. Overcome with emotion he wanders about muttering and talking aloud. He decides to do something desperate to find and to declare his love for the woman in white, but when he gets into a lighted street and sees his reflection in a store window, his desperate mood passes away. The figure he sees reflected in the window of the stores is old, twisted and worn. It is like the old women who salvage spoiled fruit in the street out of which he has come.

In the mind of the merchant, the school teacher, whom he has not seen for twenty-five years, will always remain young, silent and lovely. She is for him a white streak in the dark places of life, something far off and beautifully strange, something to dream of but not to be touched.

On summer evenings the merchant goes home to his suburb lost in reflection. He is depressed but on the streets of Evanston he meets men and women who speak to him with respect. The mood he was in when he came out of his office passes away. The reappearance of the white streak has no outward effect on his mind. However, for several days after a night in the office he is somewhat more tender and thoughtful in his attitude toward the fat, grey-haired old woman who is his wife and toward his daughter in school when she comes into his mind.

Certain Things Last

For a year now I have been thinking of writing a certain book. "Well, tomorrow I'll get at it," I've been saying to myself. Every night when I get into bed I think about the book. The people that are to be put between its covers dance before my eyes. I live in the city of Chicago and at night motor trucks go rumbling along the roadway outside my house. Not so very far away there is an elevated railroad and after twelve o'clock at night trains pass at pretty long intervals. Before it began I went to sleep during one of the quieter intervals but now that the idea of writing this book has got into me I lie awake and think.

For one thing it is hard to get the whole idea of the book fixed in the setting of the city I live in now. I wonder if you, who do not try to write books, perhaps will understand what I mean. Maybe you will, maybe you won't. It is a little hard to explain. You see, it's something like this. You as a reader will, some evening or some afternoon, be reading in my book and then you will grow tired of reading and put it down. You will go out of your house and into the street. The sun is shining and you meet people you know. There are certain facts of your life just the same as of mine. If you are a man, you go from your house to an office and sit at a desk where you pick up a telephone and begin to talk about some matter of business with a client or a customer of your house. If you are an honest housewife, the ice man has come or there drifts into your mind the thought that yesterday you forgot to remember some detail concerned with running your house. Little outside thoughts come and go in your mind, and it is so with me too. For example when I have written the above sentence, I wonder why I have written the words "honest housewife." A housewife I suppose can be as dishonest as I can. What I am trying to make clear is that, as a writer, I am up against the same things that confront you, as a reader.

What I want to do is to express in my book a sense of the strangeness that has gradually, since I was a boy, been creeping more and more into my feeling about everyday life. It would all be very simple if I could write of life in an interior city of China or in an African forest. A man I know has recently told me of another man who, wanting to write a book about Parisian life and having no money to go to Paris to study the life there, went instead to the city of New Orleans. He had heard that many people lived in New Orleans whose ancestors were French. "They will have retained enough of the flavor of Parisian life for me to get the feeling," he said to himself. The man told me that the book turned out to be very successful and that the city of Paris read with delight a translation of his work as a study of French life, and I am only sorry I can't find as simple a way out of my own job.

The whole point with me is that my wish to write this book springs from a somewhat different notion. "If I can write everything out plainly, perhaps I will myself understand better what has happened," I say to myself and smile. During these days I spend a good deal of time smiling at nothing. It bothers people. "What are you smiling about now?" they ask, and I am up against as hard a job trying to answer as I am trying to get underway with my book.

Sometimes in the morning I sit down at my desk and begin writing, taking as my subject a scene from my own boyhood. Very well, I am coming home from school. The town in which I was born and raised was a dreary, lonely little place in the far western section of the state of Nebraska, and I imagine myself walking along one of its streets. Sitting upon a curbing before a store is a sheep herder who has left his flock many miles away in the foothills at the base of the western mountains and has come into our town, for what purpose he himself does not seem to know. He is a bearded man without a hat and sits with his mouth slightly open, staring up and down the street. There is a half-wild uncertain look in his eyes and his eyes have awakened a creepy feeling in me. I hurry away with a kind of dread of some unknown thing eating at my vital organs. Old men are great talkers. It may be that only kids know the real terror of loneliness.

I have tried, you see, to start my book at that particular point in my own life. "If I can catch exactly the feeling of that afternoon of my boyhood, I can give the reader the key to my character," I tell myself.

The plan won't work. When I have written five, ten, fifteen hundred words, I stop writing and look out at my window. A man is driving a team of horses hitched to a wagon-load of coal along my street and is swearing at another man who drives a Ford. They have both stopped and are cursing each other. The coal wagon driver's face is black with coal dust but anger has reddened his cheeks and the red and black have produced a dusky brown like the skin of a Negro.

I have got up from my typewriter and walk up and down in my room smoking cigarettes. My fingers pick up little things on my desk and then put them down.

I am nervous like the race horses I used to be with at one period of my boyhood. Before a race and when they had been brought out on the tracks before all the people and before the race started, their legs quivered. Sometimes there was a horse got into such a state that when the race started he would do nothing. "Look at him. He can't untrack himself," we said.

Right now I am in that state about my book. I run to the typewriter, write for a time, and then walk nervously about. I smoke a whole package of cigarettes during the morning.

And then suddenly I have again torn up all I have written. "It won't do," I have told myself.

In this book I am not intending to try to give you the story of my life. "What of life, any man's life?—forked radishes running about, writing declarations of independence, telling themselves little lies, having dreams, getting puffed up now and then with what is called greatness. Life begins, runs its course and ends," a man I once knew told me one evening, and it is true. Even as I write these words a hearse is going through my street. Two young girls, who are going off with two young men to walk I suppose in the fields where the city ends, stop laughing for a moment and look up at the hearse. It will be a moment before they forget the passing hearse and begin laughing again.

"A life is like that, it passes like that," I say to myself as I tear up my sheets and begin again walking and smoking the cigarettes.

If you think I am sad, having these thoughts about the brevity and insignificance of a life, you are mistaken. In the state I am in such things do not matter. "Certain things last," I say to myself. "One might make things a little clear. One might even imagine a man, say a Negro, going along a city street and humming a song. It catches the ear of another man who repeats it on the next day. A thin strand of song, like a tiny stream far up in some hill, begins to flow down into the wide plains. It waters the fields. It freshens the air above a hot stuffy city."

Now I have got myself worked up into a state. I am always doing that these days. I write again and again tear up my words.

I go out of my room and walk about.

I have been with a woman I have found and who loves me. It has happened that I am a man who has not been loved by women and have all my life been awkward and a little mixed up when in their presence. Perhaps I have had too much respect for them, have wanted them too much. That may be. Anyway I am not so rattled in her presence.

She, I think, has a certain control over herself and that is helpful to me. When I am with her I keep smiling to myself and thinking, "It would be rather a joke all around if she found me out."

When she is looking in another direction I study her a little. That she should seem to like me so much surprises me and I am sore at my own surprise. I grow humble and do not like my humbleness either. "What is she up to? She is very lovely. Why is she wasting her time with me?"

I shall remember always certain hours when I have been with her. Late on a certain Sunday afternoon I remember I sat in a chair in a room in her apartment. I sat with my hand against my cheek, leaning a little forward. I had dressed myself carefully because I was going to see her, had put on my best suit of clothes. My hair was carefully combed and my glasses carefully balanced on my rather large nose.

And there I was, in her apartment in a certain city, in a chair in a rather dark corner, with my hand against my cheek, looking as solemn as an old owl. We had been walking about and had come into the house and she had gone away leaving me sitting there, as I have said. The apartment was in a part of the city where many foreign people live and from my chair I could, by turning my head a little, look down into a street filled with Italians.

It was growing dark outside and I could just see the people in the street. If I cannot remember facts about my own and other people's lives, I can always remember every feeling that has gone through me, or that I have thought went through anyone about me.

The men going along the street below the window all had dark swarthy faces and nearly all of them wore, somewhere about them, a spot of color. The younger men, who walked with a certain swagger, all had on flaming red ties. The street was dark but far down the street there was a spot where a streak of sunlight still managed to find its way in between two tall buildings and fell sharp against the face of a smaller red-brick building. It pleased my fancy to imagine the street had also put on a red necktie, perhaps because there would be lovemaking along the street before Monday morning.

Anyway I sat there looking and thinking such thoughts as came to me. The women who went along the street nearly all had dark colored shawls drawn up about their faces. The roadway was filled with children whose voices made a sharp tinkling sound.

My fancy went out of my body in a way of speaking, I suppose, and I began thinking of myself as being at that moment in a city in Italy. Americans like myself who have not traveled are always doing that. I suppose the people of another nation would not understand how doing it is almost necessity in our lives, but any American will understand. The American, particularly a middle-American, sits as I was doing at that moment, dreaming you understand, and suddenly he is in Italy or in a Spanish town where a dark-looking man is riding a bony horse along a street, or he is being driven over the Russian steppes in a sled by a man whose face is all covered with whiskers. It is an idea of the Russians got from looking at cartoons in newspapers but it answers the purpose. In the distance a pack of wolves are following the sled. A fellow I once knew told me that Americans are always up to such tricks because all of our old stories and dreams have come to us from over the sea and because we have no old stories and dreams of our own.

Of that I can't say. I am not putting myself forward as a thinker on the subject of the causes of the characteristics of the

American people or any other monstrous or important matter of that kind.

But anyway, there I was, sitting, as I have told you, in the Italian section of an American city and dreaming of myself being in Italy.

To be sure I wasn't alone. Such a fellow as myself never is alone in his dreams. And as I sat having my dream, the woman with whom I had been spending the afternoon, and with whom I am no doubt what is called "in love," passed between me and the window through which I had been looking. She had on a dress of some soft clinging stuff and her slender figure made a very lovely line across the light. Well, she was like a young tree you might see on a hill, in a windstorm perhaps.

What I did, as you may have supposed, was to take her with me into Italy.

The woman became at once, and in my dream, a very beautiful princess in a strange land I have never visited. It may be that when I was a boy in my western town some traveler came there to lecture on life in Italian cities before a club that met at the Presbyterian church and to which my mother belonged, or perhaps later I read some novel the name of which I can't remember.

And so my princess had come down to me along a path out of a green wooded hill where her castle was located. She had walked under blossoming trees in the uncertain evening light and some blossoms had fallen on her black hair. The perfume of Italian nights was in her hair. That notion came into my head. That's what I mean.

What really happened was that she saw me sitting there lost in my dream and, coming to me, rumpled my hair and upset the glasses perched on my big nose and, having done that, went laughing out of the room.

I speak of all this because later, on that same evening, I lost all notion of the book I am now writing and sat until three in the morning writing on another book, making the woman the central figure. "It will be a story of old times, filled with moons and stars and the fragrance of half-decayed trees in an old land," I told myself, but when I had written many pages I tore them up too.

"Something has happened to me or I should not be filled with the idea of writing this book at all," I told myself going to my window to look out at the night. "At a certain hour of a certain day and in a certain place, something happened that has changed the whole current of my life.

"The thing to be done," I then told myself, "is to begin writing my book by telling as clearly as I can the adventures of that certain moment."

Off Balance

ALONZO FUNKHOUSER was vice-president of the Griver-Wharton Company, advertising agents. He was a big man, some six feet two inches tall, and had got heavy. He wasn't fat, that is to say he hadn't a paunch, but he was big. He was a football star when he attended Harvard, and after he got into advertising that helped him, especially in Chicago and the Middle-Western cities where he had his clients. He was a Harvard man but didn't put on any side. He made his cleanup during the World War, when he was forty-eight.

He had the Calico Truck account and about ten others, and they all became suddenly good, but the Calico was a wow. They just wallowed in it, making trucks for the old Russian government, and all the orders that came in were underwritten, first by the British government and later by the U.S.A.

It was in the bag. They got what price they asked. You know how it was during the war. No wonder some people like wars. God, the cleanup! Better page Al Capone.

Later, to be sure, there was the income tax, but that wasn't as bad as it looked. You could put down as legitimate expenditure in running a business, to be deducted from profits, the money spent in advertising.

It was a cleanup, and a good many American boys got made nice and clean over there too. Alonzo Funkhouser lost a son.

He was a great man for making speeches, to associations of advertising men, associations of manufacturers, associations of publishers, etc. And for several years after his son got his head blown off, he never made a speech without referring to his son's death. "We who have suffered . . . the war has been brought home to us . . . my own son . . . right now, as I stand here before you today, I can see my boy . . .

"As though he stood over there . . . there in the far corner of this room [this said with a finger pointing] or over there, as though he had just stepped in at the door."

Billy Moore, of the copy department of Griver-Wharton, was a little black Irishman, also forty-eight, who had always had a hard time hanging on to a job because he was an alcoholic. He went out about once in three weeks and stayed out for three or four days. He was a Catholic, and had a big family of girls, and he could sling the ink, although he couldn't talk much. He couldn't have made a speech to get through purgatory. He had a strong sense of the dramatic, and should have been a playwright. He kept saying he intended to be one some day. It was pathetic—he being forty-eight and an alcoholic, always losing jobs and putting his family in a hole. During and just after the war, any kind of a copywriter could get a job, and Billy was good.

"I'm going to get out of this damn advertising racket and write at least one good play before I die," Billy said.

"What about, Billy?"

"Why, about this advertising racket. I'll show 'em up for once, anyway."

Billy wrote all of Alonzo Funkhouser's speeches after Alonzo became a big man, and Billy was the one who had worked out that pointing business, ". . . as though, at this minute, he were standing over there."

"You pause. Throw out your hand, so."

"Yes, I see."

"Then, when their heads are turned . . ."

Billy hated Alonzo Funkhouser with his whole soul, and Alonzo had the same kind of hatred for Billy.

Alonzo used to stand up like that, making one of his speeches written by Billy—he was a fine figure of a man—and he always ended with that bit about the boy killed in France. "The little bastard really was killed," Billy used to say sometimes, speaking to other copywriters employed by Griver-Wharton.

"The Huns blew his god damn little head off." He had never seen the boy.

When Alonzo got his speech off to a lot of businessmen, say at a banquet, it always went big.

"As I stand here, before you men, I can see my boy, just as I last saw him alive, as though he were standing over there back of you all, or coming in at that door . . . Look!" His arm shot out and a finger pointed. Billy had coached him on that.

"A clean, sweet, American boy." The businessmen, associa

tion of advertising men, association of publishers, association of manufacturers, were startled. They would all turn their heads to look.

"A curly-haired, clean, American boy."

A surprising number of the men at the banquets or other places where speeches are made were bald.

"That guy ought to get him a good hair-tonic account," Billy said. "Gee, he's a swell contact man."

During the war, the Calico Truck people made so much, it rolled in so fast, they just had to pour it out for advertising; otherwise the government would have got it to help pay the cost of the war. They used to call Alonzo Funkhouser on the long-distance telephone. They had been careless or he had.

"We're behind on our schedule," they said. "You got to spend three hundred thousand in the next ten days."

"Yes, but—"

"But what?"

"About copy, for newspaper spreads, et cetera—do you want to O.K. it?"

"Hell no. Shoot."

Billy Moore used to sit making calculations. He was jealous. He knew the deal Alonzo had with the Griver-Wharton people. It was fifty-fifty.

"Let's see. Fifteen per cent on three hundred thousand for that ten days on that one account—that's forty-five thousand, and a half of that . . ." He was schoolboyish about it, like some high-school kid figuring up how much Babe Ruth gets for every hour he is actually at work. The three hundred thousand was just an oversight. There was the regular flow, several accounts, and all good, the flow going on for three or four years.

"Well, say two hundred and fifty thousand a year, for Alonzo, while the bloody mess lasted over there." Billy didn't have any sons. He didn't lose anyone in the war.

Alonzo kept on pulling it, whenever he made a speech, for a long time.

"I can see my boy, standing over there now. We were pals." The businessmen all turned to look. When they turned their faces back to Alonzo, he was just putting his handkerchief away. What the businessmen liked about Alonzo was that he was so sincere. Alonzo said so, a little hesitatingly, to Billy. He had been during the summer on a visit to France, where his son was buried.

"How about some new stuff, Billy?" he said.

"What do you mean?" Billy inquired. He had just been on one of his bad ones, and his wife had been riding him pretty hard. Alonzo was shy about bringing the matter up, but he had become a big man in advertising, and he did love to make speeches.

"You know, I have been over there, where the boy is buried. I didn't let them bring his body home. 'Let it lie where it fell,' I wrote to our congressman."

"You mean?" Billy said. He was getting it. "Yes, I guess we ought to revamp the speech."

"Do you know, Billy," Alonzo said, "you made me feel that boy's death, what it meant to me, as I never would have felt it but for you."

"Yes?"

"Just the same, we should give it a new turn." Billy stood in Alonzo's office lost in deep thought.

"Do you know, Billy, what about—well now, something about the boy's grave, over there, at the edge of a battlefield, say at night?"

"Jesus, that's a thought!" Billy said. He stood there hating Alonzo. Sometimes he had the whimsical notion that he didn't hate him at all. He stood in the room beside Alonzo's big mahogany desk, muttering to himself, and Alonzo got up and came near to listen.

"Now you see—something about the French countryside at night—a summer night. It is pathetic and terrible—the ground all torn up, limbs of trees shot away," Billy was saying.

"Yes, yes," Alonzo said.

"Something strange takes possession of your soul."

"Since the American Legion has got into politics, the war itself isn't so good any more," Alonzo said. "You couldn't get production for a war play now if you wrote one, Billy."

"Still, there is always something. People like the idea of ghosts. How would this be? . . . You see, you got to a little

French town, at the edge of the battlefield, late at night. You found a little French hotel, but you couldn't sleep. A voice seemed to be calling you. The town was very quiet, but in fancy you could hear guns roaring. You got up and dressed, crept out of the house."

"Yes, yes," Alonzo said again.

"You got out where the ghostly trees were. There was that dim light. You saw it now here, now there. There was a voice that seemed to want to speak to you. It was saying, 'Tell them. Tell them.'"

"Yes, yes. Yes, yes. Yes, yes."

Billy was having a swell idea, a hunch, and what good advertising-copy man doesn't know what that means? The really snappy ideas don't come every day. Alonzo yes-yessing him as the idea grew. The wife may have been riding Billy extra hard after the drunk he had been on. Suddenly he plunked Alonzo Funkhouser, vice-president of Griver-Wharton, right on the jaw, just as he was opening his mouth to get off another "yes, yes." Billy never had any idea he could hit so hard. He knocked Alonzo over a chair and his head hit a corner of his desk. Afterward he bled like a stuck pig.

"I guess I caught him off his balance," Billy always afterward explained.

Everyone came running, stenographers, other copy men, contact men, other officials of the company, and of course Billy got fired. The president of the company, George B. Wharton, fired him on the spot, but later they took him back. Billy's wife came down to see Mr. Wharton, and Alonzo Funkhouser insisted.

"Look here," he said, "the man's got a family, and he had been drunk. I insist," he said. They kept arguing with him, saying that to take Billy back would break down the morale of the employees of the company, but Alonzo stood pat. The others thought he was being foolishly big-hearted, but he was a big man in the company, and he had his way. They sent word to Billy to come on back.

"I guess I caught him a little off balance," was all Billy had to say about that.

I Get So I Can't Go On

THE four advertising men went to dine at a place called Skully's. "It's just a hole," Little Gil said, "but we'll be quiet." Frank Blandin wondered what there was to be quiet about. This was in Chicago and Frank went with the others because he just happened to be coming out of the office and met the three men. "Come along," they said. He hadn't any plans for dining. It was a cold, sloppy night with a drizzle of rain and he was in a sour mood. "All right," he said and walked along beside Little Gil, a copywriter like himself, looking at Gil and at the two men ahead. "Jesus," he thought, "ain't people up to a lot? . . .

"Civilization," he thought. Being in a sour mood, he was thinking about the others and himself, how they lived, going along, getting advertising ideas . . . some making drawings, others writing words. Things had to be sold. That was the terribly important thing. If you wrote a book, what good was it unless it was sold? The same with magazines and newspapers, automobile tires, clothes, shoes, hats, food, everything. "Sell it. Sell it. Sell it."

"Jesus, I'd better be thinking of something else." Little Gil, the man he was walking with, didn't say anything. It was like it was sometimes when he went to bed. Frank wasn't married. He had been, but his wife had got a divorce. That might be the real point of being married . . . someone to lie with at night. You can get into a scrap with her or make love or something. You've got someone to blame things on.

If you lie alone you think too much. Perhaps you read a book. An old Jew in the ghetto. How he suffers! You get to thinking about him. You have stopped reading in the middle of a chapter, so you try to carry the story along. Anything to get away from yourself. That's what books are for, isn't it? That's what men write them for. How do you know that isn't the reason men and women get married? You let yourself dream you are an old Jew in the ghetto, in the Middle Ages, putting out money, "hiring money to men," as Cal Coolidge would have said. "They hired the money, didn't they? Make 'em pay up. Make 'em pay the interest. Squeeze 'em. Squeeze 'em. Get even!" Thinking of things like that. Thinking of anything to get to sleep. You wake up and start another day.

They got to Skully's. Why was it called Skully's? The man who ran the place was a short squat figure of a man with dark skin and short coarse black hair. He looked greasy but he had a rather handsome wife. She was a big one with soft eyes. The man in the party who had steered them to the place was Bud, a commercial artist. Very likely he thought, "I'd like to paint her." He had happened to drop into the place and had thought that, and so he had come back, bringing Gil, the copywriter, with him, and the two had talked—that is to say, Bud had talked. "Look, Gil. I'd like to paint her. What a body! What arms! What legs! What shoulders! You'd have to get into it just the feeling of flesh, strong and sweet, very still, waiting and waiting. You get the idea?" Gil wouldn't have been much interested. "Sure, Bud. It ought to be swell." He knew Bud would never do it. Bud had to make advertising designs.

So there the four men were, in the place, sitting at a table at the back, in a corner. The fourth man in the party was named Al and he was a fat man with red cheeks on which blue veins showed. He was well dressed and had a big loose mouth and thin hair. He ate and drank too much, but that night he wasn't talking. He was a salesman, a contact man they called them now in advertising agencies.

Except for Frank, they were all busy on a new account . . . women's shoes . . . women's shoes of fine quality . . . expensive shoes. Bud had pried the account away from some other advertising agency. Frank looked at him. That night Al was placid as a cow, or better yet, a steer, but Frank supposed that when he got after an account he woke up, got up on his toes. He'd have a shot or two and go to it. Talk. Talk. Talk. Women's shoes of fine quality, made in St. Louis, Missouri. Well, why not? What's the matter with St. Louis?

"But I dunno. I always thought of St. Louis . . . it's in my mind that way . . . you know, fat Germans with fat wives. Heat. The muddy Mississippi. Everybody always sweating."

After dining, the three men would be going back to the office to spend the evening making designs for advertisements and writing advertisements, Little Gil to get the ideas and write the copy and Bud to make the designs, the drawings. Frank looked across the table at Little Gil. He had his hands lying on the table, soft, rather meaningless little hands, like the hands of a girl child. He was self-conscious. When you looked at him he got nervous.

The men at the table were talking about the new account, what had to be expressed in the newspaper and magazine advertisements, the hook-up with shoe dealers—advertising men's talk. Bud said to Frank, "What's wrong with you, Frank? What makes you so quiet?" "Oh, I don't know," Frank said. "I'm that way," he said, and the others laughed, all except Al. They knew all right. They got that way themselves.

Al took a long, silver flask out of his hip pocket. It held a lot and he poured everyone a stiff drink. Frank looked at him and then at Al. "He's drinking too much," he thought. "What the hell do I care if he is?" Al called the proprietor's wife over to the table and asked her, "Have you got any lemons?" She hadn't any. "Well, can you get us some?"

The proprietor came in from the kitchen. The four men were the only diners in the place that night. The proprietor wore a little greasy white cap and a soiled white apron. The restaurant was on a side street in a wholesale district. Little Gil had said, "We can be quiet there," but Frank had thought, "What's to be quiet about?" Al gave the man a quarter and he went out for lemons, so they wouldn't have to drink straight grain alcohol, unflavored.

The woman, the proprietor's wife, might have been Italian, or a Greek or a Syrian. She was handsome, all right. . . . She and her husband both spoke brokenly. When the four men had given their orders she went a little away from them, to where there was a counter, near the front, and stood there. Pretty soon she got a chair and sat. From where she sat Frank was the only man of the four she could see, and she sat thus until they left. Her husband waited on the men. They all had the same thing—steak, that turned out to be pretty tough, French-fried potatoes, and peas out of a can. Then they all had some pie and coffee. . . . Anyway, a man's life goes like that. "I read too many books. I think too much," Frank thought. What was that line of Shakespeare's . . . "Perchance to dream . . . Ah, there's the rub. . . .

> "There's the rub-a-dub-dub
> There's the rub-a-dub-dub. . . ."

Frank decided he'd think about Little Gil, who sat across from him. "I'd better not look at him. It will make him self-conscious," he thought. Thinking about another man was like reading a book or being with a woman. It took you away from self. That was what you wanted. He began making a picture of Gil's life, for the rest of the evening.

He'd go back to the office with the other two, Bud and Al. Al wouldn't work. Why should he work? He was a salesman. Frank smiled. "You got to sell it. What good is it unless you sell it?" he thought. Al would sit around, smoke cigars, read his newspaper. In comes Little Gil. "What about this idea?" He shows it to Al. Well, Al's got to sell it. Al stretches, takes the cigar out of his mouth. "Pretty good, Gil." Gil is just making rough suggestions. If Al thinks they'll do, Bud will make quick drawings and then Gil will write the text. Talk. Al might go out to a show later. He was going to take the one A.M. train for St. Louis.

"You see, this is the idea, Al. . . ." Gil would be making layouts, shapely women's legs. That's an original idea. Show a woman's leg.

"Say, in this game the less original you are the better. Get that out of your noodle about being original. Who do you think reads the ads, a lot of highbrows?"

The woman's foot in the shoe might be resting on purple velvet. There's a thought. Purple velvet suggests royalty. "Royal American beauties are demanding, etc." Look, the shoes are like little boats, sailing out on a purple sea.

Little boats on purple seas, going adventuring. Say, little shoes, where are you taking those lovely feet, lovely young women's legs . . . hips, breasts, shoulders, arms? . . . Whoa! What you got in the package, little woman?

> Helen, Thy beauty is to me
> Like some Nicean bark of yore. . . .

Funny how a man reads books, walks about, sleeps, eats, remembers snatches of poetry and song . . . all the time wondering, what the hell for, where the hell to. . . .

Surely not just to be able to write shoe advertisements. One of the copywriters in Frank's firm, Griver-Wharton . . . Tower-top Building, Chicago . . . once said to Frank . . . "I get so I can't go on," he said.

"So? What do you do?"

"I read Ralph Waldo Emerson. An essay of his, called 'Self Reliance,' helps me most."

"Then you go back at it again, eh?"

"Sure."

That Little Gil—copywriter—Frank never had thought much about him. Gee, what a lot of people you see every day, touch elbows. . . . Ha, here we go! Forward, march! Here we go! You never really think about them. How can you? There are so many of them. . . . What happened to Frank that night he dined with Bud, Al and Gil was a matter of no importance. You read a lot of books, don't you, and never think about them again? Very likely the author has sweat blood, trying to write that book. All right. That's his funeral. Take it back to the three-cent-a-day. Get me another. It was just a rainy night and Frank didn't feel like going home to read. He just sat there in the res-taurant with the others. He was eating in silence and taking a good look at the woman, the wife of the proprietor of the place, the one Bud had thought he wanted to paint. She was sitting so none of the others could see her and she kept looking at Frank and he returned the compliment. She wasn't so young, maybe thirty-three or four, with dark soft skin and big dark eyes. Big breasts, big shoulders and strong shapely legs. The way she was sitting in the chair she spread her legs a little, and Frank thought . . . "Gates of Hercules," he thought,

> "When out of Palos came the gold
> To storm the gates of Hercules."
>
> *
>
> Tiger, tiger, burning bright
> In the forests of the night. . . .

There was a creeping smile, back somewhere, in Frank, and in the woman. Frank let his thoughts drift. He thought about Bud. Bud didn't want to be a commercial artist. He remem-bered what someone in the office had said that day . . .

"Bud's drinking too much. He's slipping. He isn't half the man he was a year ago. His drawings haven't any zip to them any more." The knockers! Bud had a flair for Frank. He thought Frank was wise, onto people, sophisticated. "That's the way to be," Bud said to himself, "don't expect anything. Trust no one." I am master of my fate. I am captain of my soul. "Rats," Frank thought. Still he thought Bud was O.K.

What was that line he had thought out, Bud talking to Gil. Oh, yes. "Look, Gil. What arms! What legs! What shoulders! Flesh, strong and sweet, very still, waiting and waiting." That is what Bud would have said to Gil.

I suppose that's the way it starts between a man and a woman, any man and any woman. What was it William James said about religion? . . . Music at the back of the mind—that's it. You don't always follow it up . . . not one time in ten. How can you? What's all this got to do with anything?

The point is that Frank found out that Gil was a fairy. How? How does a man find such things out—suddenly like that? You are sitting and don't know it and then you are sitting, and you do know.

You don't want to know. It hurts . . . not you, but him. That man's cork's out. What about pity? The poor guy.

Nothing happened that night when the four advertising men dined. They had steaks and French-frieds and peas that came out of a can. No, we haven't any other vegetable. Forty cents each. Al paid. He left another forty cents for the big woman who came to get the dishes and she took it smiling. Frank didn't talk. "A fellow ought to take a thing like this," he thought, "like reading a book." Title of book, "Rainy Night in Chicago" . . . "a mystery story." Nights in Chicago were just as mysterious and strange as, say, nights in Egypt, on the Nile—why not? Or Stanley in Africa . . . Stanley in darkest African jungles . . . rain, fever, sores on the legs, animals in the dense forests at night. . . .

> Tiger, tiger, burning bright
> In the forests of the night. . . .

The point was that Frank's eyes looked up suddenly from that embrace—you might call it that—with the eyes of that big dark-skinned woman and met the eyes of Little Gil. Her eyes had been saying it as a woman's eyes do say it to a man who has taken her fancy. Gee, wouldn't it be swell living in the world, if people could be honest? You, being a man, don't ever get one woman. . . . "There, that settles it—that's off my mind" . . . and a woman, a real woman, don't ever get that from any one man.

But Frank, looking around suddenly, had got it also from Little Gil's eyes.

What . . . you mean . . . from a man?

Well, yes. If Gil was a man.

That, to Frank, was the sudden hurtful thing that night he dined with the three men. It shocked and hurt him . . . that hungry waiting thing in Gil's eyes. There must have been something that gave Frank away, a shadow passing across his face. Something within him drew away and then, in a flash, he got it all. Once Little Gil had been ill at home and Frank went with Bud to see him. He remembered two sisters and an old mother. The mother was a gentle quiet white-haired old woman. In that family the father was dead and they all dependent on Little Gil. Sometimes you have moments of looking into the future. You are in the dark—in the dark tunnel of life, as it were—and you look ahead and see what is going to happen as you look along a tunnel to the opening at the far end. Gil was in business and dependent on men like Al, now sitting and talking to Bud. Suddenly Frank heard a conversation going on between Al and some other man, like Al, say five or ten years ahead.

"D'you remember that Little Gil who used to be at Griver-Wharton's?"

"Sure. Why?"

"Well, at Detroit . . . in a hotel lobby. The man knocked him down and he got thrown out of the hotel."

"Of course he lost his job?"

"Sure."

"Where the hell's he now?"

"How should I know? Say, I never could stand one of those guys. Once one of them spoke to me. I knocked hell out of him."

That sort of thing hadn't happened often to Frank and it gave him a queer feeling. Gil's hands and lips were trembling and he was blushing like a young girl. He looked quickly away, but Frank saw something. Terror came into Gil's eyes as he looked away. Al and Bud kept on talking. "Who was it took Christ down from the cross?" Frank thought. "I remember about their nailing him up. Who was it took him down? Oh, I remember now. It was Joseph, the rich young man."

Frank Blandin in the rain walking and walking . . . alone, after the dinner with the three men. He left them at the door of Skully's and they went back to the office of Griver-Wharton. The rain was cold. Frank didn't have a date and didn't feel like reading. He decided to walk home. He lived far out on the South Side. He walked. . . .

Through nigger streets. . . .

White streets. . . .

Swell streets. . . .

Poor streets. . . .

He passed street-car barns. He thought of something. "Remember those guys they called the street-car bandits. I wish someone would try to hold me up here, in this dark street. I'd like to punch someone."

Gil would be at work at the office of Griver-Wharton. When Frank had left the others at the door of Skully's, Gil had shrunk away. Now he would always be a little afraid of Frank. He'd be at work now, trying to think up ideas for advertisements for women's shoes. Bud would be there, making quick drawings.

Al would be waiting around. He might go out to a show. "Gil, don't you want another shot out of my flask?"

"No, thanks, Al."

"Those ideas you're getting are O.K. Go ahead." Bud was drinking too much. He got spiffed almost every night. If a guy like that wants to paint, why don't he just go ahead? Suppose he starves? What of it? You get to thinking about someone, like Bud or Little Gil, and it's like reading some queer book. You get to thinking about a city, like Chicago, or an advertising agency, or the members of a church, it's like a book . . . like fiction written by some crazy man.

Gil might be in his office, alone now for a moment. "Did I give myself away to him?" He knows he did. "I've tried. I've tried. I can't help it if I'm this way.

"I get so tired trying."

He'd put his little girlish face down in his little hands and cry a little. Frank walking in the rain. "Go on and cry, little thing. It'll do you good.

"But, they'll get you. They'll get you.

"They'll get onto you.

"They'll find out.

"They'll find out."

When Frank got home, pretty wet and tired, he mixed himself a shot. Then he took a hot bath. Gee, I got to find something to read. I got to get my mind off all this. . . . He found a new book beside his bed. Rackets and swindles. And the wiser birds, the bankers. . . . It was no use. He turned off the light. "There's Little Gil," he thought, again. "What about him? . . . Jesus, I better be thinking about something else."

Mr. Joe's Doctor

WHEN Mr. Joe first came down into our country we were all a little afraid of him. Some of us had read about him in the newspapers, his adventures, divorces, etc. Evidently he wanted to find a quiet place. He went out from town a few miles, and bought a farm. It was in the hills. When he built his house the workmen, some from town, others country fellows, all liked him.

You couldn't help liking him. He was so unpretentious. If I were to put down here his real name . . . a man like that . . . successful plays on Broadway . . . married to first this and then that successful actress . . . the marriages breaking up . . . anyway, there he was, a man you'd like.

He was a quiet man, walking around, never thrusting himself forward. He was always wanting to pay his workmen a little more than they asked.

It was Doctor Haggerty who took me to Mr. Joe's. Our country doctor is something rather special. He is a shy man, a bachelor who has been practicing in this one section since he came out of medical school. It is a section of poor farms and poor little towns. How the doctor has managed to live on us I don't know. It doesn't cost much to keep such a man going. Although he does all kinds of difficult and dangerous operations . . . in cabins in winter on lonely mountain roads . . . very likely the patient snowed in . . . and treats every kind of disease; he has nothing but his small, worn medicine case and the few surgeon's tools he must have had when he started his practice.

The doctor, a small, bald-headed man, with a little turned-up nose and quick, alive hands, has one passion. He loves to play croquet, and used to play every afternoon with old Judge Graves, also a bachelor. Then Judge Graves died, and Mr. Joe came in here, bought his mountain farm out on Swift Creek, and built his house.

Mr. Joe must have taken a fancy at once to Doctor Haggerty. Being a New Yorker, he couldn't have had a passion for croquet. But the croquet ground he built cost a lot. A hill was cut down, sod was brought in, and men worked for days,

watering and rolling. It was as though every blade of grass had
been touched by some man's hand. We all talked about it in
the drug store in town. "Say, it must be nice to be rich, be the
author of successful plays, have money rolling in like that."
The cashier of the bank told me about it. "The money comes
in gobs," he said.

It was something for our Doctor Haggerty, the little shy
one. There were the two shy men, he and Mr. Joe, together
almost every afternoon that summer . . . that is to say, when
the little doctor wasn't racing over the hills in his shabby,
wornout car, doing his operations sometimes—often, I dare
say, up all night. It didn't matter how busy he was, some time
during the day or night he would be at Mr. Joe's.

Sometimes they played their game at night. Mr. Joe had
built a high stone wall, shutting the croquet ground off from
the road. He had put up electric lights. Harry Thompson, a
farmer who lives out that way, told me that he got curious and
went over there two or three times at night to sit around
and watch, but that, when he did it, the game broke up. Mr.
Joe went into his house and to his typewriter, and our doctor
got into his old car and drove away.

I was glad they didn't mind me, sitting and watching. They
were like two kids at their game. Our little doctor is past sixty,
but when he played with Mr. Joe he became a kid. The two
men had something going on between them, a laughing kind
of thing. You see it sometimes between married couples that
really make a go of marriage.

But here is the point to my story: Last summer a famous surgeon from New York came to visit Mr. Joe. It is all a little odd.
Our own people are just people to us. Who would think of
Doctor Haggerty, living right here with us all these years, dressing rather shabbily, driving his rickety car, as anything special?

The city surgeon who came here to visit Mr. Joe had a big
foreign car and he had style. You could tell, looking at him a
mile away, that he was a successful man. He had the air. It was
in his clothes, in his walk.

And he also took at once to our little doctor. I was out there
when the city surgeon came. He planned to stay only the day,
but at once he and Doctor Haggerty began to talk . . . our

little doctor not at all shy before him, and pretty soon they drove off together, not in the big foreign car, but in Doc Haggerty's little shabby one.

They went up to look at a case our doctor had begun talking about, a Mrs. Friedman. She is a poor woman, a widow who lives with her son in a cabin on a poor farm back up in the hills. The big car never could have got up there. They were gone all afternoon and went again the next day.

And when you come to that, who would think that anything wrong with a woman like Mrs. Friedman would be of special interest to a big, successful city surgeon? It seems it was a matter of an operation. We haven't any hospitals in our country. They performed an operation on her; that is to say, our Doctor Haggerty did, the city man watching.

It was the city surgeon who told me about it. That was after he had been here four or five days. I was out at Mr. Joe's, and Doctor Haggerty and Mr. Joe were at one of their games and the city doctor and I were sitting on a low stone wall and watching. I am writing about this whole matter because it was an eye-opener to me. I had been rather afraid of the swank city man myself but had got over it a little.

He began to talk to me, speaking of our little country doctor, and there was a curious note of respect in his voice that puzzled me.

"There's a man," he said, indicating with a movement of his head that he meant our funny little doc. At the moment Doc was down on his hands and knees sighting across at Mr. Joe's ball. Then he spoke of something that puzzled me.

"I might have been O. K. myself if I had been given his opportunities," he said.

Gee, life gets you woozy. The city man got reflective.

"Do you know," he said to me, "I think maybe the little cuss has got an inferiority complex. Isn't it swell!" he said. "That may have saved him. He doesn't think he's anything special.

"Say," he said, "take a look. Look at his hands, so delicate, so alive.

"Gee, he's had a swell life," he said.

The city doc seemed to think that his own life, being what he was, having the kind of personality that would make success inevitable, was a pure waste. He amused me, that man did.

"Here I am," he said, "and what am I?" He sighed. "A fool specialist," he said.

He seemed to think he had pretty much wasted his life, being what he so evidently was, a successful big-city surgeon. I laughed. I didn't know what to say.

And anyway, afterward, on that same evening, I drove back to town with our own little doc. I can smell his old car as I write, I can hear it rattle. Our own little doc was very humble that night.

"I was ashamed," he said.

"About what?" I asked.

As I said, he had performed the operation on Mrs. Friedman in the presence of the city surgeon. He was ashamed of his equipment for the job. He had wanted the city man to do the operation, but the city man wouldn't. He had told our doc that he wanted to watch.

"He had the nerve to tell me that his own diagnosis of Mrs. Friedman's case was wrong and that mine was right," Doctor Haggerty said. Evidently our little doc didn't believe it. "I guess he was trying to let me down easy," he said.

"And about this Mrs. Friedman," I asked; "did you operate? Was it a difficult case? Will she live?"

"Yes," he said. He had that curious doctor's tone, as though the patient didn't matter so much. I suppose it is inevitable. He was concerned with the other doctor. He looked at me with his funny little childlike eyes. "I was so ashamed before him," he said.

"You mean?" I asked. I was amused.

"I mean I haven't any equipment," he said.

The other doctor had spoken of him with such sincere admiration, even envy. "What that man can do with a pocketknife!" he had said.

"If I had only had the nerve, when I was younger," our own doctor said, "I should have gone off to the city, been a specialist. I might have learned something, got an education.

"I might have amounted to something, been something," Doctor Haggerty said to me that day, driving his rickety old car along the road and regretting, just as had the city man, the opportunities he had missed in his life.

The Corn Planting

THE farmers who come to our town to trade are a part of the town life. Saturday is the big day. Often the children come to the high school in town.

It is so with Hatch Hutchenson. Although his farm, some three miles from town, is small, it is known as one of the best-kept and best-worked places in all our section. Hatch is a little, gnarled old figure of a man. His place is on the Scratch Gravel Road, and there are plenty of poorly kept places out that way. Hatch's place stands out. The little frame house is always kept painted, the trees in his orchard are whitened with lime half-way up the trunks, the barn and the sheds are in repair, and his fields are always clean-looking.

Hatch is almost seventy. He got rather a late start in life. His father, who owned the same farm, was a Civil War man and came home so badly wounded that, although he lived a long time after the war, he couldn't work much. Hatch was the only son and stayed at home, working the place until his father died.

Then, when he was nearing fifty, he married a school-teacher of forty, and they had a son.

The school-teacher was a small one, like Hatch. After they married they both stuck close to the land. They seemed to fit into their farm life as certain people fit into the clothes they wear. I have noticed something about people who make a go of marriage. They grow more and more alike. They even grow to look alike.

Their one son, Will Hutchenson, was a small but remarkably strong boy. He came to our high school in town and pitched on our town baseball team. He was a fellow always cheerful, bright, and alert and a great favorite with all of us.

For one thing, he began as a young boy to make amusing little drawings. It was a talent. He made drawings of fish and pigs and cows, and they looked like people you knew. I never knew before that people could look so much like cows and horses and pigs and fish.

When he finished in the town high school Will Hutchenson went to Chicago, where his mother had a cousin living, and he became a student in the Art Institute out there. Another young fellow from our town was also in Chicago. He really went two years before Will did. His name is Hal Weyman and he was a student at the University of Chicago. After he graduated he came home and got a job as principal of our high school.

Hal and Will Hutchenson hadn't been close friends before, Hal being several years older than Will, but in Chicago they got together, spent a good many evenings together, went together to see plays, and, as Hal later told me, had a good many long talks.

I got it from Hal that in Chicago, as at home here when he was a young boy, Will was immediately popular. He was good-looking, so the girls in the art school liked him, and he had a straightforwardness that made him popular with all the young fellows.

Hal told me that Will was out to some party nearly every night, and right away he began to sell some of his amusing little drawings and to make money. The drawings were used in advertisements and he was well paid.

He even began to send some money home. You see, after Hal came back here, he used to go quite often out to the Hutchenson place to see Will's father and mother. He would walk or drive out there in the afternoon or on summer evenings and sit with them. The talk was always of Will.

Hal said it was touching how much the father and mother depended on their one son, how much they talked about him and dreamed of his future. They had never been people who went about much with the town folks or even with their neighbors. They were of the sort who work all the time, from early morning till late in the evening; and on moonlight nights, Hal said, and after the little old wife had got the supper, they often went out into the fields and worked again.

You see, by this time old Hatch was nearing seventy and his wife would have been ten years younger. Hal said that whenever he went out to the farm they quit work and came to sit with him. They might be in one of the fields, working together, but when they saw him in the road they came running. They had got a letter from Will. He wrote every week.

The little old mother would come running, following the father. "We got another letter, Mr. Weyman," Hatch would cry. And then his wife, quite breathless, would say the same thing: "Mr. Weyman, we got a letter."

The letter would be brought out at once and read aloud. Hal said the letters were always delicious. Will larded them with little sketches. There were humorous drawings of people he had seen or been with, rivers of automobiles on Michigan Avenue in Chicago, a policeman at a street crossing, young stenographers hurrying into office buildings. Neither of the old people had ever been to a city and they were curious and eager. They wanted the drawings explained, and Hal said they were like two children wanting to know every little detail Hal could remember about their son's life in the big city. He was always at them to come there on a visit, and they would spend hours talking of that.

"Of course," Hatch said, "we couldn't go. How could we?" he said.

He had been on that one little farm since he was a boy. When he was a young fellow his father was an invalid, and so Hatch had to run things. A farm, if you run it right, is very exacting. You have to fight weeds all the time. There are the farm animals to take care of.

"Who would milk our cows?" Hatch said.

The idea of anyone but him or his wife touching one of the Hutchenson cows seemed to hurt him. While he was alive he didn't want anyone else plowing one of his fields, tending his corn, looking after things about the barn. He felt that way about his farm. It was a thing you couldn't explain, Hal said. He seemed to understand the two old people. . . .

It was a spring night, past midnight, when Hal came to my house and told me the news. In our town we have a night telegraph operator at the railroad station and Hal had got a wire. It was really addressed to Hatch Hutchenson, but the operator brought it to Hal. Will Hutchenson was dead, had been killed. It turned out later that he was on a party with some other young fellows and there might have been some drinking. Anyway, the car was wrecked and Will Hutchenson was killed. The operator wanted Hal to go out and take the message to Hatch and his wife, and Hal wanted me to go along.

I offered to take my car but Hal said no. "Let's walk out," he said. He wanted to put off the moment, I could see that. So we did walk. It was early spring and I remember every moment of the silent walk we took, the little leaves just coming on the trees, the little streams we crossed, how the moonlight made the water seem alive. We loitered and loitered, not talking, hating to go on.

Then we got out there and Hal went to the front door of the farmhouse, while I stayed in the road. I heard a dog bark, away off somewhere. I heard a child crying in some distant house. I think that Hal, after he got to the front door of the house, must have stood there for ten minutes, hating to knock.

Then he did knock, and the sound his fist made on the door seemed terrible. It seemed like guns going off. Old Hatch came to the door and I heard Hal tell him. I know what happened. Hal had been trying, all the way out from town, to think up words to tell the old couple in some gentle way; but when it came to the scratch he couldn't. He blurted everything right out, right into old Hatch's face.

That was all. Old Hatch didn't say a word. The door was opened, he stood there in the moonlight, wearing a funny long white nightshirt. Hal told him, and the door went shut again with a bang and Hal was left standing there.

He stood for a time, and then came back out into the road to me. "Well," he said, and "Well," I said. We stood in the road looking and listening. There wasn't a sound from the house.

And then—it might have been ten minutes or it might have been a half-hour—we stood silently listening and watching, not knowing what to do; we couldn't go away. . . . "I guess they are trying to get so they can believe it," Hal whispered to me. I got his notion all right. The two old people must have thought of their son Will always only in terms of life, never of death.

We stood watching and listening, and then, suddenly, after a long time, Hal touched me on the arm. "Look," he whispered.

There were two white-clad figures going from the house to the barn. It turned out, you see, that old Hatch had been plowing that day. He had finished plowing and harrowing a field near the barn.

The two figures went into the barn and presently came out. They went into the field, and Hal and I crept across the farmyard to the barn, and got to where we could see what was going on without being seen.

It was an incredible thing. The old man had got a hand corn-planter out of the barn and his wife had got a bag of seed corn, and there, in the moonlight, that night, after they got that news, they were planting corn.

It was a thing to curl your hair—it was so ghostly. They were both in their night clothes. They would do a row across the field, coming quite close to us as we stood in the shadow of the barn, and then, at the end of each row, they would kneel side by side by the fence and stay silent for a time. The whole thing went on in silence.

It was the first time in my life I ever understood something, and I am far from sure now that I can put down what I understood and felt that night . . . I mean something about the connection between certain people and the earth—a kind of silent cry, down into the earth, of those two old people, putting corn down into the earth. It was as though they were putting death down into the ground that life might grow again, something like that.

They must have been asking something of the earth, too. But what's the use? What they were up to in connection with the life in their field and the lost life in their son is something you can't very well make clear in words. All I know is that Hal and I stood the sight as long as we could, and then we crept away and went back to town.

But Hatch Hutchenson and his wife must have got what they were after that night, because Hal told me that when he went out in the morning to see them and to make the arrangements for bringing their dead son home, they were both curiously quiet and, Hal thought, in command of themselves. Hal said he thought they had got something. "They have their farm and they have still got Will's letters to read," Hal said.

Feud

JOHN LAMPSON and Dave Rivers had been friends when they were boys and young men, but they got into a fight, and then later John Lampson died. Dave was ashamed because, after the fight he had with John, he didn't go to him and try to make it up. A long time afterwards, and just because he was ashamed, he took it out on John's son. There were really two fights between John and Dave. When they were both young men they went out of the hill country of eastern Tennessee to work together in the West Virginia coal mines.

They both had the same thing in mind. They didn't want to be coal miners. What they wanted was to make enough money in the mines to come back into the hills and buy farms. A good many hillmen do that. When they are young they go off to the mines or to a factory town. They work hard and save money, and then they come back. A hillman is a hillman. He doesn't want to live his life away from the hills.

You may know how miners work. Two men work together in a little room far down under the ground. It is dangerous work, and a man must have faith in his partner. Any little slip, a moment of carelessness on the part of one man, and both he and his partner may be killed.

So there are these friendships that spring up between miners. "Here I am, working with you, day after day. I am going around with your life held in the hollow of my hand." Such an experience makes two men feel close. Dave and John, both powerful men and both unmarried, had such a friendship.

And then John and Dave fought. They fought over a woman met in a West Virginia town, and I don't know much of that side of their story. They fought once underground and once on the main street of a mining town. As it happened, neither man got the woman. She married another miner and left the town in which they were working.

They fought twice, and Dave Rivers won both fights, and then they quit working together, but both stayed on in the same town.

I think later that when both men got home to the hills and

each man got his own little farm in the same neighborhood and had married—it happened that they married second cousins—I think that both men wanted to make it up but that neither man would make the first move. "He began it," Dave Rivers said to himself. "Well, he licked me," John Lampson said. The result was a growing resentment. The two wives kept at them and both men were stubborn. . . .

But this story is not concerned primarily with two men. It concerns John Lampson's son, Jim Lampson, and Dave Rivers' daughter, Elvira.

In the hill country girls often get married at sixteen, and at that age young men push out into the world. Jim Lampson is a sensitive, rather slender man and he began paying court to Dave's daughter, Elvira.

It happens that I know about the courtship, for two reasons. I am fond of taking long walks alone in the hills, and one night I saw the two walking together hand in hand on a mountain road. And then young Jim sometimes talks to me. He is ambitious. He wants an education, and sometimes comes to me to borrow books. It was young Jim who told me what had happened between himself and Dave Rivers. His voice shook when he told me the story.

Jim is in love with Elvira and he got bold. It was Sunday, and he went to Dave Rivers' house, and there was Dave all dressed up and sitting on the porch.

"What do you want?" Dave asked gruffly, addressing young Jim.

Jim said that Dave didn't even let him come into the yard. He stood at the gate. It has been only a year since Jim's father died. A wild colt he was trying to break bolted with him.

Young Jim stood in the road and told Dave Rivers that he wanted to come into the house and call on his daughter Elvira, and Elvira, a slim, lovely mountain girl, was standing in the house doorway back of her father. She stood listening. Dave got suddenly furious. He was, I am pretty sure now, really furious that he hadn't made it up with Jim's father before his old coal-mining partner got killed. He was furious at himself, and he took it out on young Jim.

He began to rave and swear at Jim. Then he ran into the

house and got his gun. He waved it about and kept on cursing: "You get out of here! You are the son of that skunk. You get out of here!"

It was all very absurd. I am sure that Dave Rivers' gun wasn't loaded.

But when he talked to me young Jim was furious. Jim isn't one of the noisy sort. That day, after standing for a moment in the road and listening to Dave Rivers curse him and his father, Jim went white and, turning, walked trembling away.

This happened late of a Sunday afternoon in the fall, and it also happened that on that same evening I went for a walk. It might have been ten at night, and there was a moon. I went along up hill and down. It was a fine night. I was listening to the night sounds, getting the night smell. Dave Rivers' house is just at the foot of a sharp hill and there is a wood above the house along the road. The edge of the wood is not more than a hundred yards from the house. Dave was sitting in the open doorway.

I moved into the wood by the fence and stood thinking of what Jim Lampson had told me that afternoon. "I'll go down and talk to him," I thought. I do not know Dave Rivers as I do young Jim, but Dave had said things about Jim's father I know he couldn't mean, and I had said so to young Jim. I had tried to quiet Jim.

"I'll go talk to Dave Rivers tomorrow," I had said to Jim; but, "I had better do it right now," I told myself as I stood that night above the house. I hesitated. There was a lamp burning in the room at Dave Rivers' back. The man was doing what I had been doing, enjoying the night. Was he thinking of what he had done to young Jim's father and of what he had on that day done to young Jim?

I stood hesitant. There is a man's natural inclination not to interfere in other men's quarrels. "I'm going to do it," I said to myself, and then it was too late. It may be that I heard a little sound or that some instinct told me to turn my head.

In the road, twenty feet away, was young Jim, who had come silently up, and he had a gun in his hands and it was aimed at Dave Rivers. Dave was a fair target, down there in the light from the lamp.

It was a thing to give you the shivers down to your toes. Why I didn't shout or run to young Jim I don't know. I stood frozen and silent. Of what does a man think at such moments? Did I see all that was about to happen—Dave Rivers shot by young Jim—my own position, a witness—Jim, a boy I liked—myself running afterwards to report it all to the sheriff? And then later the trial in the courtroom in town—my words sending young Jim to his death on the gallows.

But, thank heaven, it did not happen. Young Jim stood like that, his hand on the trigger of his gun, myself hidden from sight in the shadow of a tree, Dave Rivers sitting down there, smoking his pipe and unaware of it all; and then young Jim lowered his gun. After standing for a moment he turned and walked away. . . .

And so that happened, and you can see how I felt. "I'll go down to Dave Rivers and talk to him now," I told myself.

"No, I won't do that. I'll go back up the road to young Jim."

Jim lives with his mother on a farm three miles back in the hills. He is his mother's only child, but Dave Rivers has the daughter Elvira and two younger sons.

And so I stood in the road, hesitating again, and, as is usual with me, again I did nothing. "Tomorrow," I said to myself. I went on home, but I did not sleep, and on the next day I went to Dave's house.

I went to the house in the late afternoon of a fall day, and there was Dave at work in the barnyard back of the house.

It was the time for the fall pig-killing, and Dave was at it alone.

It had turned cold during the night and there was the promise of snow in the air. There was a creek near the barn, and along it red sumac grew. Dave's wife, his daughter Elvira, and the two younger children were standing and watching. Dave looked up and grunted at me.

There was a fire still blazing under a kettle but Dave had the hog in the scalding barrel filled with the boiling water. I remember the hill beyond where Dave stood, the fall colors of the trees, the bare black trunks of trees beginning to show through, the two children dancing about. And Elvira, and her slim girlishness.

"It will snow before the day is over," I thought.

How was I to begin on Dave? What would he think of my trying to interfere in one of his quarrels? Dave is a gruff one. He isn't easy to handle.

"Hello," he said, looking up and growling at me. He had the hog by the legs and was turning it about in the barrel of hot water. A hog, when ready for killing, is heavy. . . .

And then . . . it happened again.

Young Jim came from among the sumac bushes with his gun in his hand. He had come up along the creek, beyond the barn, and he walked directly to Dave. His face was white. He had made up his mind to kill Dave openly there in the daytime.

He went directly to Dave, and Dave stood for a moment, staring at him. I saw Elvira put her two hands over her eyes, and a little cry came from her lips. The wife ran toward Dave. Jim brought the gun to his shoulder.

"Now! *Now!*" I said to myself. It was a kind of inner cry. I did not speak. The hands of Death were gripping my throat.

But Death didn't get Dave. I saw his big shoulders heave and, with a quick movement of his arms, he had the hog out of the barrel, but in doing so he fell. He and the hog were in a sprawling heap on the ground.

So there he was. In falling he had upset the barrel of boiling water, and it came flooding over his body. He was on the ground, writhing in pain.

All of this had happened more quickly than thought. The wife had been running toward her husband. She was still running. I saw Elvira take her hands from her eyes. Young Jim had thrown his gun to one side and had got his knife out of his pocket. I still stood helpless.

"No, no," I said to myself. For just a moment I thought, "He is going to kill the man with the knife," but in the next moment I saw my mistake.

Jim was on his knees beside Dave and was working furiously. He was cutting Dave's clothes away, and Dave, who had been rolling on the ground and crying with pain, was now very quiet. I saw his eyes as they were watching the boy.

And so Dave let the boy handle him like a child, and when

we had got him into the house I rode Dave's horse off to town for a doctor. I yelled with delight. I was beating the horse over the flanks with my hat. I had seen the look in Dave's eyes as he lay on the ground, letting young Jim cut his clothing away, and I knew that the feud, that had begun between Dave and Jim's father and that Jim had taken up in his turn, was over at last.

Harry Breaks Through

WHEN the depression came to America in 1929, Harry was ready for it. He might be pounding the pavements in Chicago, trying to get hooked on, as an advertising writer, but he didn't do much mourning. His son Jim kept slipping him twenties and seemed to have the gift of knowing when his father was down to his last dollar. Harry didn't have to ask his son. He had two sons and three daughters, and once he said to Frank Blandin—he liked Frank but was doubtful about him— "You haven't had your change of life yet, have you, Frank?" he said. Frank liked Harry and admired him but didn't understand. Harry tried to explain. It was his notion that there was something peculiar about American life and American men. Harry worked for another advertising agency but used to come to Frank's office to sit talking—this in the boom days in advertising, before the great depression. When he came, he was usually half spiffed. He was a fat, curiously awkward man, always knocking against the side of the door frame as he came in. When he went to sit in a chair, you were afraid he might miss it and fall to the floor.

Harry was a great reader. He explained to Frank. "What else is there to do on the evenings when I am at home?" He was a married man and lived in a very respectable suburb. Early in life he had married a woman several years older than himself who was a devout Methodist. He had always stayed, outwardly, well hooked into the upper middle class and supported a pew for his family in a suburban church. Such a man had to spend at least three or four evenings a week at home. "What else is there to do but read, if you don't want to go to the movies or listen in on the radio?" His life as an advertising writer had rather spoiled the radio for him. "I can see what we are coming to," he said. "Pretty soon they'll have all the novelists, all the poets, actors, etc.,—to say nothing of the United States Senators—putting on evening talks, sponsored by somebody's face cream or an automobile tire company, and we guys will have to write their speeches and the introductory spiels for them. 'Senator Cowhide was a poor boy and has risen to his present great position in American life by his own efforts. Now he is chairman of the important Cucumber Committee of the United States Senate. The Senator is an extremely modest man. He says the opportunities of American life, not any special merit in himself, should be given credit for his rise to fame. He comes to you tonight through the courtesy of Soilless Wash Cloths. B-U-N-K talking from Chicago—the voice of the Future on the Air.'"

Harry said to Frank, "Frank, you ought to read more of these books that explain American life." He said there are a lot of good ones coming out. "It seems," he continued, "that we Americans have been, from the beginning, a nation of dreamers. We got that way, according to these guys, because this was such a swell, big, rich continent when it first got opened up. So we all got the dream that we were all going to be rich. Ain't that swell, Frank? The rich you and I have known are such great guys. They're all so happy, too, eh? So we got this dream and it's busted, but we can't get over it and that makes us all children. Do you know what we've got, Frank? We've got a cultural lag."

"The hell we have," said Frank.

"Yes we have, and a lot of other things too. I've been reading them all up in these books—you know, nights at home. What the hell is a man to talk about to his wife, if she's a Methodist and everything?

"Yes, we go around like children, expecting we can all be happy or rich or gorgeously wicked, like some movie king or queen, or something, and when we get older we stay the same and so the country gets filled up with old boys—not with men. You see, Frank? . . .

"We got to have a change of life, see? I've had mine."

Frank didn't understand. He was a long time getting Harry's slant. Sometimes the man would come in and get off something about his wife. Her name was Sue and Frank Blandin had never seen her. "Sue's down with a bad cold," Harry would say. "I'm fifty and she's fifty-seven. She's been a good Methodist now for fifty years and is sure of Heaven. Ain't it nice, Frank? It won't be long for the old girl now."

Harry told Frank that all of his children were respectable and good upstanding members of society except his one son

Jim. Jim had studied law, and when he got into practice had managed to catch on as attorney for one of the Chicago gangs. It had feathered his nest, and as he hadn't married—all the rest of Harry's children had—the nest was the same one Harry lived in. "Ma," said Harry, "ain't onto Jim, but I am, and Jim knows I am, and it makes it more comfortable for us both at home."

There had been a time, Frank gathered from Harry's talk, when the man had been all cut up about his son Jim. There were always shootings and killings going on between the various gangs in Chicago, and Jim was always in court and his name was always getting into the papers,—not that he ever did anything illegal—Jim was slick, they couldn't pin anything on him—justice is justice—even the blackest criminal has a right to be heard.

Just the same, his name was always being hooked up with such people. Jim could always square it with his mother. She said she knew her son would never do anything wrong, or against Christianity, but Harry . . . At that time he was still prosperous. Once, he asked his son to quit it, and later he told Frank about that. "Come on. Quit it, Jim. Start to build up a real practice—say among business men. I can let you have any money you need. You got the brains, Jim. Why, you could be another Charles Evans Hughes." But Jim had only given his father the laugh. "Don't get into the deep water, Dad," he said, "you might sink."

So Harry—he was forty-seven when it happened—passed through what he called his change of life. He decided to commit suicide. Later he told Frank about that. He didn't tell everything. A part of it he just hinted at. There was a stenographer, a tall red-haired woman, Frank gathered. "O Love! O Romance!" he said. "She couldn't see it and was my secretary, and I didn't know whether to fire her or go jump in the lake." So he went to walk, he said, all afternoon in the rain, over on the West Side—on Halstead Street—he said, and was silly and cried.

It was in the early fall and the night was rainy. He had bought a big revolver and went home to his surburb and had dinner with his wife. His son Jim wasn't at home.

Then after dinner he slipped out, the revolver, all loaded, in his raincoat pocket.

He said his suburb, where he had a big frame house—one of the best on one of the best streets—was pretty far out and you could get out into open prairie. He did. He said he floundered about, going across some cornfields in the mud, slipping and falling now and then. Frank understood about that. He thought Harry about the most awkward fat man he had ever seen.

He had to climb over some barbed wire fences. He was trying to make for a creek, on the banks of which he was in the habit of walking alone, sometimes on Sunday afternoons, when he had got fed up on being at home alone, just with the wife, and that night he had got the notion into his head that if he walked in the paved roads, someone driving past in a car would suddenly stop, jump out of the car, take the loaded revolver away from him and perhaps even overpower him and take him back home or to jail.

There would be an absurd article in the newspapers—"Harry Wells, a prominent Chicago advertising man, attempts suicide," —something like that.

So he floundered around in the mud, in the fields, always near paved roads, with cars going up and down, and got at last to the creek. It didn't take long. The place to which he had got was near a big cement bridge, where a highway crossed the creek, and the bridge was only some fifty yards away from the spot where he came down to the creek. There was a sloping grassy bank there, all wet now. He sat down on the bank in the rain.

His scheme, he told Frank Blandin, was to shoot himself in the head, at a moment when there were no cars in sight, and then, he figured, his body being round as it was, would roll down the slick, grassy bank into the creek, swollen now by the fall rains. The body would be found on the next day somewhere down stream, and there would be the bullet hole in the head. "Another gang murder. Harry Wells, the father of James K. Wells, well known as an attorney for the Smearcase Gang, meets a sudden and violent death." It would set Jim to thinking and perhaps put his feet back onto the straight and narrow path.

"It wasn't that raw," Harry said, telling about it; "no evangelical stuff, but you get the idea.

"And I was wrong, too. Jim would only have shrugged his shoulders. He would have thought I had been reading novels or going to the movies and had got softened up." You gathered, hearing Harry talk, that he was rather strong, at bottom, for his son Jim.

As for that night, on the creek bank in the rain, near the bridge, he got all set and felt in his raincoat pocket for the revolver and it was gone. He had dropped it somewhere, perhaps in struggling through or over a barbed wire fence.

So he sat and thought. He said he always did have a horror of cold water, and besides, that stuff about a gang killing would be all off if there were no evidence of violence.

He decided to go on home, and perhaps try again some other night; but he couldn't. He was sitting on the wet sloping bank and now he began to feel himself slipping. Fortunately, there were two small trees near by, trees with trunks about the size of fish poles, and as his raincoat was slick and he was every moment slipping more and more, he dropped flat on his back and threw out his hands. Luckily, his right hand got hold of the trunk of one of the little trees, and presently his left hand found the other.

And there he was. The rain was pouring down—icy cold rain too, he said. Even if he had called out, the people driving by in cars might not have heard; but he didn't call. He tried hauling himself up the bank, and then tried getting to his feet as he was but he couldn't do it.

"So I did some more thinking," he said. He decided to turn over on his belly, and after a struggle, managed it, but even then he wasn't clear. Every time he tried to creep up the bank, to get on his hands and knees and thus rise, his feet slipped or got tangled up in the tails of his raincoat. "I'd get part way up, you know—to my hands and knees, or maybe part way erect even—and then—thump! down I'd come, hitting on my belly. You see what it's like—my belly, I mean. Every time, it knocked the wind out of me."

He said it happened to him a dozen times, and then, lying there like that—trying to get his breath back—the rain pouring down on him—respectable, solid people, very likely from his own suburb, scooting by him so nice and comfortable in their closed cars, going maybe to a restaurant for dinner or into town to the theatre, belonging maybe to the same church he and his wife did, so near him and yet so far away—

He was pretty sure that presently, his fat, not overstrong hands—that had written so much advertising copy, "helping," he said in telling about it, "thus to build up modern civilization,"— he was pretty sure that presently his hands would slip and down the bank into the creek he would go, like a fat pig into the scalding barrel. He said he couldn't swim a stroke.

He began to laugh. "It was my change of life," he told Frank Blandin. "There's where it happened, there on that creek bank, in the rain that night." He said he did finally manage to get up the bank when his strength was about gone, and that then he marched straight down the broad highway home—mud and all, not giving a damn.

He said his wife had a headache and had gone to her room upstairs and that he got on some dry clothes and went into the hallway to the door of her room and shouted through the door telling her he had got a long distance call and had to get into town and take a night train to Detroit.

"But what are you laughing about, Harry?" she asked, but he didn't answer. He got a train into town and went to a hotel and sent for some whiskey. "When you get your change of life fast like that, you got to have you a bracer," he said. So he got one from a bell boy. He had put into his bag one of the books about American civilization, and what is wrong with it and why, and so he lay in the bed and had a good time drinking and reading and laughing.

And after the depression came, he was still all right. He lost his job but there was Jim. Jim had an instinct for knowing when his Dad was close up to the wind, and slipped him a twenty, or maybe two or three. "For civilization, eh, Dad?" Jim would say, and he'd laugh and Harry would laugh.

Harry kept trying, after the depression came, to get a job, but not too hard. Every day he went into town and walked around, and if there was an advertising men's dinner, or something of that sort, there he was. He said that being among advertising men and hearing them talk and make speeches had got to be one of the great joys of his life.

Or if he was on the street and some man, more down and out than he was, stopped him, saying "What about a piece of change, Mister?" he stopped and looked at the man and shook his head and laughed. "Not from me," he said. "I'm not giving out the kind of change you need. What you need," he said to the panhandlers on the Chicago streets, "is not the kind of change you're talking about, but a change of life."

And then he had himself another laugh. He thought the laughs were coming to him, he having been a serious advertising man as long as he had.

Mrs. Wife

THE doctor told the story. He got very quiet, very serious in speaking of it. I knew him well, knew his wife and his daughter. He said that I must know of course that in his practice he came into intimate contact with a good many women. We had been speaking of the relations of men and women. He had been living through an experience that must come to a great many men.

In the first place I should say, in speaking of the doctor, that he is a rather large, very strong and very handsome man. He had always lived in the country where I knew him. He was a doctor and his father had been a doctor in that country before him. I spent only one summer there but we became great friends. I went with him in his car to visit his patients, living here and there over a wide countryside, valleys, hills and plains. We were both fond of fishing and there were good trout streams in that country.

And then besides there was something else we had in common. The doctor was a great reader and, as with all true book lovers, there were certain books, certain tales, he read over and over.

"Do you know," he said laughing, "I one time thought seriously of trying to become a writer. I couldn't make it, found that when I took pen in hand I became dumb and self-conscious. I knew that Chekhov the Russian was a doctor." He looked at me smiling. He had steady grey eyes and a big head on which grew thick curly hair, now turning a little grey.

"You see, we doctors find out a good many things." That I, of course, knew. What writer does not envy these country doctors the opportunity they have to enter houses, hear stories, stand with people in times of trouble? Oh the stories buried away in the houses, in lonely farm houses, in the houses of town people, the rich, the well-to-do, the poor, tales of love, of sacrifice and of envy, hatred too. There is, however, this consolation: the problem is never to find and know a little the people whose stories are interesting. There are too many stories. The great difficulty is to tell them.

"When I got my pen in hand I became dumb." How foolish. After I had left the country the doctor used to write me long letters. He still does it sometimes, but not often enough. The letters are wonderful little stories of the doctor's moods on certain days as he drives about in the country, descriptions of days, of fall days and spring days . . . how full of true feeling the man is . . . what a deep and true culture he has . . . little tales of people, his patients. He has forgotten he is writing. The letters are like his talk.

But I must say something of the doctor's wife and of his daughter. The daughter was a cripple, like President Roosevelt a victim of infantile paralysis, moving about with great difficulty. She would have been, but for this misfortune, a very beautiful woman. She died some four years after the summer when her father and I were so much together. And there was the wife. Her name was, I remember, Martha.

I did not know well either the wife or the daughter. Sometimes there are such friendships formed between two men. "Now you look here . . . I have a certain life inside my own house. I have, let me say, a certain loyalty to that life but it is not the whole of my life. It isn't that I don't want to share that intimate life with you but . . . I am sure you will understand . . . we have chanced upon each other . . . you are in one field of work and I in another."

There is a life that goes on between men too . . . something almost like love can be born and grow steadily . . . what an absurd word that "love" . . . it does not at all describe what I mean.

Common experience, feelings a man sometimes has, his own kind of male flights of fancy as it were . . . we men you see . . . I wonder if it is peculiarly true of Americans? I often think so. We men here, I often think, depend too much upon women. It is due to our intense hunger, half shy, for each other.

I wonder if two men, in the whole history of man, were ever much together that they did not begin to speak presently of their experiences with women. I dare say that the same thing goes on between women and women. Not that the doctor ever spoke much of his wife. She was rather small and dark, a woman very beautiful in her own way . . . the way I should say of a good deal of suffering.

In the first place, the doctor, that man, so very male, virile, was naturally quick and even affectionate in all his relations with people and particularly with women. He was a man needing more than one outlet for his feelings. He needed dozens. If he had let himself go in that direction he could have had his office always full of women patients of the neurotic sort. There are that sort, plenty of them, on farms and in country towns as well as in the cities. He could not stand them. "I won't have it, will not be that sort of doctor." They were the only sort of people he ever treated rudely. "Now you get out of here and don't come back. There is nothing wrong with you that I can cure."

I knew from little tales he told of what a struggle it had been. Some of the women were very persistent, were determined not to be put off. It happened that his practice was in a hill country to which in the summer a good many city people came. There would be wives without husbands, the husbands coming from a distant city for the weekend or for a short vacation in the hot months . . . women with money, with husbands who had money. There was one such woman with a husband who was an insurance man in a city some two hundred miles away. I think he was president of the company, a small rather mouse-like man but with eyes that were like the eyes of a ferret, sharp, quick-moving little eyes, missing nothing. The woman, his wife, had money, plenty of it from him, and she had inherited money.

She wanted the doctor to come to the city. "You could be a great success. You could get rich." When he would not see her in his office she wrote him letters and every day sent flowers for his office, to the office of a country doctor. "I don't mind selling her out to you," he said. "There are women and women." There were roses ordered for him from the city. They came in big boxes and he used to throw them out of his office window and into an alleyway. "The whole town, including my wife, knew of it. You can't conceal anything of this sort in a small town. At any rate my wife has a head. She knew well enough I was not to be caught by one of that sort."

He showed me a letter she had written him. It may sound fantastic but she actually offered, in the letter, to place at his disposal a hundred thousand dollars. She said she did not feel disloyal to her husband in making the offer. It was her own money. She said she was sure he had in him the making of a great doctor. Her husband need know nothing at all of the transaction. She did not ask him to give himself to her, to be her lover. There was but one string to the offer, intended to give him the great opportunity, to move to the city, set up offices in a fashionable quarter, become a doctor to rich women. He was to take her as a patient, see her daily.

"The hell," he said. "I am in no way a student and never have been. By much practice I have become a fairly good country doctor. It is what I am."

"There is but one other thing I ask. If you are not to be my lover, you must promise that you will not become the lover of some other woman." He was, I gathered, to keep himself, as she said, pure.

The doctor had very little money. His daughter was the only living child of his marriage. There had been two sons born but they had both died in the outbreak of infantile paralysis that had crippled the daughter.

The daughter, then a young woman of seventeen, had to spend most of her life in a wheel chair. It was possible that, with plenty of money to send her off to some famous physician, perhaps to Europe . . . the woman in her letter suggested something of the sort . . . she might be cured.

"Oho!" The doctor was one of the men who throw money about, cannot save it, cannot accumulate. He was very careless about sending bills. His wife had undertaken that job but there were many calls he did not report to her. He forgot them, often purposely.

"My husband need know nothing of all this."

"Is that so? What, that little ferret-eyed man? Why, he has never missed a money bet in his life."

The doctor took the letter to his wife who read it and smiled. I have already said that his wife was in her own way beautiful. Her beauty was certainly not very obvious. She had been through too much, had been too badly hurt in the loss of her sons. She had grown thin and, in repose, there was a seeming hardness about her mouth and about her eyes that were of a curious greenish grey. The great beauty of the doctor's wife only came to life when she smiled. There was then a curious, a quite wonderful transformation. "By this woman, hard or soft, hurt or unhurt, I will stand until I die.

"It is not always, however, so easy," said the doctor. He spoke of something. We had gone for an afternoon fishing and were sitting and resting on a flat rock, under a small tree by a mountain brook. We had brought some beer packed in ice in a hamper. "It is not a story you may care to use." I have already said that the doctor is a great reader. "Nowadays, it seems there is not much interest in human relations. Human relations are out of style. You must write now of the capitalists and of the proletariat. You must give things an economic slant. Hurrah for economics! Economics forever!"

I have spoken of his wife's smile. The doctor seldom smiled. He laughed heartily, with a great roar of laughter that could frighten the trout for a mile along a stream. His big body and his big head shook. He enjoyed his own laughter.

"And so it shall be an old fashioned story of love, eh, what?"

Another woman had come to him. It had all happened some two or three years before the summer when I knew him and when I spent so much time in his company. There was a well-to-do family, he said, that came into that country for the summer and they had an only child, a daughter, crippled as was his own daughter. They were not, he said, extremely rich but they had money enough or at first he thought they had. He said that the father, the head of that family, was some sort of manufacturer. "I never saw him but twice and then we did not have much talk, although I think we liked each other. He let me know that he was very busy and I saw that he was a little worried. It was because things at his factory were not going so well.

"There was the man's wife and daughter and a servant and they had brought for the daughter a nurse. She was a very strong woman, a Pole. They engaged me to come on my regular rounds to their house. They had taken a house in the country, some three miles out of town. There were certain instructions from their city doctor. There was the wish to have within call a doctor, to be at hand in case of an emergency.

"And so I went there." I have already spoken of sitting with the doctor at the end of an afternoon's fishing. Moments and hours with such people as the doctor are always afterward remembered. There is something . . . shall I call it inner laughter . . . to speak in the terms of fighters, "They can take it." They have something . . . it may be knowledge, or better yet maturity . . . surely a rare enough quality, that last, that maturity. You get the feeling from all sorts of people.

There is a little farmer who has worked for years. For no fault of his own . . . as everyone knows, nature can be very whimsical and cruel . . . long droughts coming, corn withering, hail in the young crops, or sudden pests of insects coming suddenly, destroying all. And so everything goes. You imagine such a one, struggling on into late middle life, trying, let us say, to get money to educate his children, to give them a chance he did not have, a man not afraid of work, an upstanding straight-going man.

And so all is gone. Let us think of him thus, say on a fall day. His little place, fields he has learned to love, as all real workers love the materials in which they work, to be sold over his head. You imagine him, the sun shining. He takes a walk alone over the fields. His old wife, who has also worked as he has, with rough hands and careworn face . . . she is in the house, has been trying to brace him up. "Never mind, John. We'll start over again. We'll make it yet." The children with solemn faces. The wife would really like to go alone into a room and cry. "We'll make it yet, eh."

"The hell we will. Not us."

He says nothing of the sort. He walks across his fields, goes into a wood. He stands for a while there, perhaps at the edge of the wood, looking over the fields.

And then the laughter, down inside him . . . laughter not bitter. "It has happened to others. I am not alone in this. All over the world men are getting it in the neck as I am now . . . men are being forced into wars in which they do not believe . . . there is a Jew, an upright man, cultured, a man of fine feeling, suddenly insulted in a hotel or in the street . . . the bitter necessity of standing and taking it . . . a Negro scholar spat upon by some ignorant white.

"Well, men, here we are. Life is like this.

"But I do not go back on life. I have learned to laugh, not loudly, boisterously, bitterly, because it happens that I, by some strange chance, have been picked upon by fate. I laugh quietly.

"Why?

"Why, because I laugh."

There must be thousands of men and women . . . they may be the finest flowers of humanity . . . who will understand the above. It is the secret of America's veneration for Abraham Lincoln. He was that sort of man.

"And so.

"So I went to that house." It was my friend, the country doctor, telling his tale. "There was the woman, the mother of the crippled girl, a very gentle-looking woman, in some odd way like my wife. I have told you that I had a talk with the girl's father, the manufacturer.

"There was the crippled girl herself, destined perhaps to spend her life in bed, or going laboriously about in a wheel chair. Surely she had done nothing, this girl, that God, or nature, call it what you will, should have done this to her. Would it not be wonderful to have some of these cock-sure people explain the mystery of such things in the world? There is a job for your thinker, eh what?"

And then there was the woman, the Polish woman. The doctor, with a queer smile, began to speak of something that often happens suddenly to men and women. He was a man at that time forty-seven years old and the Polish woman . . . he never told me her name . . . might have been thirty. I have already said that the doctor was physically very strong, have tried to give the suggestion of a fine animal. There are men like that who are sometimes subject to very direct and powerful sex calls. The calls descend on them as storms descend on peaceful fields. It happened to him with the Polish woman the moment he saw her and as it turned out it also happened to her.

He said that she was in the room with the crippled girl when he went in. She was sitting in a chair near the bed. She arose and they faced each other. It all happened, I gather, at once. "I am the doctor."

"Yes," she said. There was something slightly foreign in her pronunciation of even the one simple English word, a slight shade of something he thought colored the word, made it extraordinarily nice. For a moment he just stood, looking at her as she did at him. She was a rather large woman, strong in the shoulders, big breasted, in every way, he said, physically full and rich. She had, he said, something very full and strong about her head. He spoke particularly of the upper part of her face, the way the eyes were set in the head, the broad white forehead, the shape of the head. "It is odd," he said, "now that she is gone, that I do not remember the lower part of her face." He began to speak of woman's beauty. "All this nonsense you writers write, concerning beauty in women," he said. "You know yourself that the extraordinary beauty of my own wife is not in the color of her eyes, the shape of her mouth . . . this rosebud mouth business, Cupid's bow, eyes of blue, or, damn it man, of red or pink or lavender for that matter." I remember thinking, as the man talked, that he might have made a fine sculptor. He was emphasizing form, what he felt in the Polish woman as great beauty of line. "In my wife beauty comes at rare intervals but then how glorious it is. It comes, as I think you may have noted, with her rare and significant smile."

He was standing in that room, with the little crippled girl and the Polish woman.

"For a time, I do not know how long, I couldn't move, could not take my eyes from her.

"My God, how crazy it now seems," the doctor said.

"There she was. Voices I had never heard before were calling in me and, as I later found out, in her also. The strangeness of it. 'Why there you are, at last, at last, there you are.'

"You have to keep it all in mind," said the doctor, "my love of my wife, what my wife and I had been through, our suffering together over the loss of our two sons, our one child, our daughter, a cripple as you know.

"And then our daily life together for years. My wife had done something very fine for me. You know how I am. But for her I might have starved. I could not remember to send bills, was always getting into debt, spending too freely. She had taken my affairs in hand. She attended to everything for me.

"And there I was, you see, suddenly stricken like that . . . by love, ha! What does any sensible man know of this love?

"Why, it was pure lust in me and nothing else. I did not know that woman, had never seen her until that moment, did not know her name. As it was with me so it turned out it was with her. In some way I knew that. Afterwards she told me, and I believed her, that, as the Bible likes to put it, she had never known man.

"I stood there, you understand, looking at her and she at me." He spoke of all this happening, as he presently realized, when with an effort he got himself in hand, in the presence of the little crippled girl in her bed. "It was almost as though I had, in that moment, in the child's presence, actually taken the woman. It seemed to me that she was something I had all of my life been wanting with a kind of terrible force, you understand, with my entire being."

The doctor's mind went off at a tangent. The reader is not to think that he told me all this in a high excited voice. Quite the contrary. His voice was very low and quiet and I remember the scene before us as we sat on the flat rock above the mountain stream . . . we had driven a hundred miles to get to that stream . . . the soft hills in the distance beyond the stream, which just there went dashing down over the rocks, the deepening light over distant hills and distant forests. Later we got some very nice trout out of a pool below the rapids above which we sat.

It may have been the stream that sent him off into a side tale of a fishing trip taken alone, on a moonlight night, in a very wild mountain stream, on the night after he had buried his second son, the strangeness of that night, himself wading in a rushing stream, feeling his way sometimes in the half darkness, touches of moonlight on occasional pools, the casts made into such pools, often dark forests coming down to the stream's edge, the cast and, now and then, the strike, himself standing in the swift running water.

Himself fighting, all that night, not to be overcome by the loss of the second and last of his sons, the utter strangeness of what seemed to him that night a perfectly primitive world. "As though," he said, "I had stepped off into a world never before known to man, untouched by any man."

And then the strike, perhaps of a fine big trout . . . the

sudden sharp feeling of life out there at the end of a slender cord running between it and him . . . the fight for life out there and, at the other end of the cord, in him.

The fight to save himself from despair.

Was it the same thing between him and the Polish woman? He said he did manage at last to free himself from the immediate thing. The city doctor had written him a letter. "I am told you have yourself a daughter, a sufferer from infantile paralysis." My friend had thought of the city doctor. "He must have been a man of sense."

"We know so very little," the city doctor had said. "There is perhaps nothing we can do. I do not quite know why it is but the foolish people seem to like to have one of us about, within call." My friend, the country doctor, made on that day of his first visit a passing examination of the child and went on his way.

"So she is the nurse they have brought here," he thought that time when he first saw her. He said he had a terrible week, a time of intense jealousy. "Would you believe it, it did not seem possible to me that any man could resist that woman," he said. He suspected the child's father. "That man, that manufacturer . . . he is her lover. It cannot be otherwise." The doctor laughed. "As for my wife, she was, for the time, utterly out of my life.

"Why, I do not mean to say I did not respect her. What a word, eh, that respect. I even told myself that I loved her. For the rest of the week I was in a muddle, could not remember what patients needed my services. I kept missing calls, and of course my wife, who, as I have told you, attends to all the details of my life, was disturbed.

"And, at that, she may well have been deeply aware. I do not think that people ever successfully lie to each other."

It was during that week he saw and talked briefly to the manufacturer from the city, the father of the crippled child, going there, to that house, he said, hoping again to see the woman. He did not see her and as for the man . . . "I had been having such silly suspicions . . . I wonder yet whether or not, at the time, I knew how silly they were.

"The manufacturer was a man in terrible trouble. Afterwards I learned that at just that time his affairs were going to pieces.

He stood to lose all he had gained by a lifetime of work. He was thinking of his wife and of his crippled daughter. He might have to begin life again, perhaps as a workman, with a workman's pay. His daughter would perhaps, all her life, be needing the care of physicians."

I gathered that the city man had tried to take the country doctor into his confidence. They had gone into the yard of the country house and had stood together, the doctor's heart beating heavily. "I am near her. She is there in the house. If I were a real man I would go to her at once, tell her how I feel. In some way I know that this terrible hunger in me is in her also." The man, the manufacturer, was trying to tell him.

"Yes, yes, of course, it is all right."

There were certain words said. The man in trouble was trying to explain to him.

"Doctor, I will be very grateful if you can feel that you can come here, that we can depend upon you. I am a stranger to you. It may be you will get no pay for your trouble."

"Aha! What, in God's name, could keep me away?"

He did not say the words. "It is all right. I understand. It is all right."

The doctor waited a few days and then he went again. He said he was asleep in his own house, or rather was lying in his bed. Of a sudden he determined upon something. He arose. To leave the house he had to pass through his wife's room. "It is," he said, "a great mistake for a man and wife to give up sleeping together. There is something in the perfectly natural and healthy fact of being nightly so close physically to the other, your sworn companion in life. It should not be given up." The doctor and his wife had, however, I gathered, given it up. He went through her room and she was awake. "It is you, Harry?" she asked.

Yes, it was he.

"And you are going out? I have not heard any call. I have been wide awake."

It was a white moonlit night, just such a night as the one when he went in his desperation over the loss of his second son to wade in the mountain stream.

It was a moonlit night and the moonlight was streaming into his wife's room and fell upon her face. It was one of the times when she was, for some perverse reason, most beautiful to him.

"And I had got out of bed to go to that woman, had thought out a plan."

He would go to that house, would arouse and speak to the mistress of the house. "There has been an accident. I need a nurse for the night. There is no one available."

He would get the Polish woman into his car.

"I was sure . . . I don't know why . . . that she felt as I did. As I had been lying so profoundly disturbed in my bed, so she in her bed had been lying."

She was almost a stranger to him. "She wants me. I know she does."

He had got into his wife's room. "Well, you see, when at night I had to go out, to answer a call, it was my custom to go to her, to kiss her before I left. It was a simple enough thing. I could not do it.

"I know that the Polish woman is waiting for me, that she also aches, that she hungers for me. I will take her into my car. We will turn into a wood, and there, in the moonlight . . .

"A man cannot help what he is. When I have been with her this one time it may be that things will get clear."

He was hurrying thus through his wife's room.

"No, my dear, I have had no call.

"There is a feeling has come to me," he said. "It is that girl, the crippled one, crippled as is our Katie." Katie was the name of his daughter. "I have told you of her. It is, my dear, as though a voice has been calling me.

"And what a lie, what a terrible lie, and to that woman, my own wife.

"All right. I accepted that. There was a voice calling to me. It was the voice of that strange woman, the woman I scarcely knew, who had never spoken but the one word to me."

The doctor was hurrying through his wife's room. There was a stairway that led directly down out of the room. His crippled daughter slept in another room on the same floor and a servant, a colored woman who had been in the household for years, slept in the daughter's room on a cot. The doctor had got through his wife's room and was on the stairs when his wife spoke to him.

"But Harry!" she said. "You have forgotten something. You have not kissed me."

"Why, of course," he said. His feet were on the stairs but he came back up into her room. She was lying there, wide awake. "I am going to that woman. I do not know what will happen. I must, I must. She will surrender.

"It may all end in some sort of a scandal. I do not know but I cannot help doing what I am about to do. There are times when a man is in the grip of forces stronger than himself.

"What is this thing about women, about men? Why does all of this thing, this force, so powerful, so little understood, why with the male does it all become suddenly directed upon one woman and not upon another? Why is it sometimes true also of the female?

"There is this force, so powerful. I have suddenly, at forty-seven, a man established in life, fallen into its grip. I am powerless.

"There is this woman, my wife, in bed here, in this room. The moonlight is falling upon her upturned face. How beautiful she is. I do not want her, do not want to kiss her. She is looking up expectantly at me." The doctor was by his wife's bed. He leaned over her.

"I am going to this woman. I am going. I am going."

He was leaning over his wife, about to kiss her, but suddenly turned away.

"Martha," he said, "I cannot explain. This is a strange night for me. I will perhaps explain it all later. I cannot kiss you now."

"Wait. Wait."

He was hurrying away from her down the stairs. He got into his car. He went to that house. He got the woman, the Polish woman. "When I explained to her she was quite willing." He thought afterwards that she had been on the whole rather fine, telling him quite plainly that as he had felt when he saw her so she had felt.

She was definite enough. "I am not a weak woman. Although I am thirty I am still a virgin. However I am in no way virginal."

She had been, the doctor said, half a mystic, saying that she had always known that the man who would answer some powerful call in her would some day come. "He has come. It is you."

They went, I gathered, to walk. She told him that since she

had first seen him she had made some inquiries. She had found out about the loss of his two sons, about his crippled daughter, about his wife. "I do not want you to be unfaithful to her."

All this, the doctor explained, said to him by the woman, as, having left his car by the roadside, they walked in country roads. It was a very beautiful night and they had got into a road lined with trees. There were splashes of moonlight falling down through the leaves in the road before them as they walked. For an hour, two hours, they walked, not, as it turned out, ever touching each other. Sometimes they stopped and stood for long silent times. He said that several times he put out his hand to touch her but each time he drew it back.

"Why?"

It was the doctor himself who asked the question. He tried to explain. "There she was. She was mine to possess." He said that he thought she was to him the most beautiful woman he had ever known or ever would know.

"But that is not true," he said. "It is both true and untrue.

"It may be that if I had touched her, even with my finger ends, there would have been quite a different story to tell. She was beautiful, with her own beauty, so appealing, oh so very appealing to me, but there was also, at home, lying as I knew awake in her bed, my own wife."

He said that in the end, after he had been with the Polish woman for perhaps an hour, she understood. He thought she must have been extremely intelligent. They had stopped in the road and she turned to him and again, as in the room with the cripple, there was a long silence. "You are not going to take me," she said.

"I am a woman of thirty and have never been taken by a man. I had never wanted to be until I saw you.

"It may be that now I never shall be."

The doctor said he did not answer. What was to be said? "I couldn't," he explained. He thought that it was the great moment of his life. He used the word I have also used in speaking of him. "I think, a little, I have been, since that moment, a mature man."

The doctor had stopped talking but I could not resist questioning him.

"And you ended by not touching her?" I asked.

"Yes. I took her back to her place and when I next went there to see the crippled girl she was gone and another woman had taken her place.

"I think that man, that manufacturer, did not fail after all."

There was another time of silence. "After all," I thought, "this man has, from his own impulse, told me this tale. I have not asked for it. There is a question I think now that I may dare ask." I ventured. "And your wife?" There was that laugh that I so liked. It is my theory that it can come only from the men and women who have got their maturity.

"I returned to her. I gave her the kiss I had denied earlier that night."

I was of course not satisfied. "But," I said. Again the laugh. "If I had not wanted to tell you I should not have begun this tale," he said. We got up from the flat stone on which we had been sitting and prepared for the great moment of trout fishing, as every trout fisherman knows, the quivering time, so short a time between the last of the day and the beginning of the night. The doctor preceded me down across a flat sloping rock to the pool where we each got two fine trout. "I was in love with her as I had never really been with the Polish woman and in the same way. In a way until after that time I never had been.

"And there was all the rest, our life together, what we had gone through together."

The doctor stopped talking but did not look at me. He was selecting a fly. "You know my wife's name is Martha.

"When I returned to her that night and when I had kissed her, she for a moment held my face in her hands. She said something. "We have been through it again, haven't we?" she said. She took her hands away and turned her face from me. "I have been thinking for the last week or two that we had lost each other," she said. "I do not know why," she added and then she laughed. "It was the nicest laugh I ever heard from her lips. It seemed to come from so far down inside. I guess all men and women who have got something know that it might be easily lost," the doctor said as he finished his tale. He had hooked a trout and was absorbed in playing his fish.

Two Lovers

John Wescott, the father of Rudolph and Fred Wescott, was a small man with a little mustache. Life had always been difficult for him, but the difficulties he had to face had developed in him a kind of shrewdness. He got along. He went, stuttering painfully, with a little insinuating smile, through life. There was in him a kind of basic humbleness and sweetness that made other men like him. The other men in his office and the Chicago business men who were his acquaintances often smiled, thinking of the little stuttering man, but in the end he often had his own way with them. He had come up in the world financially without the help of a formal education and after his success came and until a sudden attack of appendicitis took him off . . . this in the somewhat distracted year after his wife's sudden death . . . he had always the feeling that he had missed something very important. He wasn't a man who would have spoken of the good life. He wouldn't have put it that way.

"I'll tell you what, education is the thing," he would have said.

It may be that he had got this feeling about education from association with his wife Clara. Being as he was, small and certainly never a distinguished looking man, it had always been a source of wonder to him that a talented woman like his wife had married him at all. He thought his wife beautiful. He always thought so. She had been to college. She had a master's degree. She had traveled in Europe. She could speak and read, it is true with some difficulty, both French and German. She read books he never would have thought of tackling. He spoke about it sometimes to his business associates.

"What books she reads," he said. "Occasionally I pick one of them up. I can't for the life of me make out what the man is talking about."

The fact that his wife had been willing and even perhaps anxious to marry him, was always to John Wescott a source of wonder. There was an evening, after his wife's death, when he spoke of it all to a friend. It was the first time he had ever done such a thing. The truth was that John Wescott was, all his life and in spite of the fact that the business he was in made it necessary for him to be constantly meeting and talking to people, much like the younger of his two sons. He was always a shy man.

He had however found out something. Although John Wescott never became what would be called a hard drinking man he had become, in secret, a tippler. He kept a bottle in a locked drawer in his desk at his office. He did not drink regularly, but took what he thought of as an occasional bracer. He did it because he had found out that, when he had to talk to some one, a real estate prospect, sometimes a man much higher up in the business and financial world than himself, some man he instinctively looked up to, he lost his nerve.

He made a discovery. He had found out that, in such a situation, or if it were a real important man he had to meet, a drink set him up. On rare occasions he took two. His shyness went away and there was even an improvement in his speech.

And there had been occasions, even before his wife's death and always in the summer . . . this after he had begun to be somewhat prosperous on his own, no longer so dependent upon the favor of his father-in-law . . . when his wife with the two sons, then both small, mere children, had gone away to a certain summer resort, there were occasions when John even became a bit spiffed.

He did it always with the same man, his one intimate friend. The man was a rather large, fat man with a round and baby-like face, who was at the head of an advertising agency.

The two had become friends through the medium of a real estate deal. John had sold, to his friend, whose name was A. P. Grubb, a lot on which to build a house, in a fashionable suburb of the city, and while the two men were negotiating something had happened. The man Grubb was known to all his associates as "A. P." John Wescott never knew any other name for him. It was one of the occasions when John, realizing that he had to meet and talk with a man who was the president of a rather large and prosperous business, had taken two drinks. He went to A. P.'s office. There was some talk of the deal about to be made, John speaking with a good deal of difficulty, and A. P. reached across his desk and poked the real estate man on the chest with a fat finger. A. P. was always that way. He was a warm friendly fellow.

"Look here, Wescott," he said. "I am about ready to close this deal. I have talked it over with the little woman but, you see, I can't think straight unless I have a couple of drinks under my belt."

The two men went from A. P.'s office in one of the Chicago skyscrapers, to a neighboring bar, where they had drinks. They each took two, A. P. setting them up and then John Wescott insisted that they have another. It was a time when John, with four straight drinks taken within an hour, had to make a struggle to keep his head but he did manage. The deal was closed and A. P. never knew that John was a little over the line. It was a rule of John's that when he had to see a prospect and had taken one, or two, to brace himself, to go and get a bag of salted peanuts. He had heard another man speak of it. The man had said that a bag of peanuts was the best thing he had found to sweeten his breath after he had taken a drink.

John Wescott and A. P. Grubb became close friends. A. P. was the only man to whom John ever spoke in any intimate way of his wife. On a certain occasion, on a summer night, the two men being together, A. P.'s wife having gone to the country, they were sitting together in a bar. They had taken several and, as often happens with men on such occasions, there was talk of women and of a man's relations with women.

A. P. did most of the talking. There was always in A. P. and in spite of John's fondness for him, something that a little shocked the real estate man. He was a little shocked but at the same time got a rather pleasant thrill out of his friend's boldness. After his marriage, to his employer's daughter, John had never even thought of anything that could be called an approach to intimacy with another woman, but with A. P. it was different.

On the summer evening the two men, having dined together, were sitting together in the back room of a saloon in South Dearborn Street in Chicago. It was a rather small and even perhaps a tough little place. They had been walking together on Michigan Boulevard and had crossed to Dearborn. A. P. was talking and was absorbed. He had unconsciously been looking for a bar and seeing the one, on South Dearborn Street, had suggested that they drop in.

They had passed into a little room at the back and as they sat, preparing to order a drink, two women came along a little hallway past the open door. There was a burlesque show playing on South State Street and the two women were from the show. They had dropped in between acts to get a drink.

One of them put her head in at the open door.

"Hello, boys," she said to the two middle-aged men sitting at a little table.

Nothing more happened. One of the women looked at A. P. and laughed. A. P. had a perfectly bald head. The woman who had laughed spoke of it as a radish. She took a step into the room where the two men sat and put out a hand to A. P.

"Do you mind if I touch the radish?" she said. She started to approach A. P. who sat smiling at her, but the other woman grabbed her arm. "Oh, come on, Mag," she said.

The incident may have been the cause of the drift taken by the conversation between the two men.

"A couple of hot babies, eh," said A. P. "I'll tell you how it is with me about women." It was A. P. talking. "With me it is like this. . . ." He hesitated and smiled. He sometimes felt a little awkward in the presence of John Wescott.

"I wonder how far you can go with this bird," he thought.

"At any rate," he thought, "he'll never be an advertiser." There was little danger that the man Wescott would ever become a client of his advertising agency. There was no need being too cautious.

"I wouldn't want you to think," A. P. said, "that I am a woman chaser." John Wescott assured him that such a thought had never entered his head. "Why, what an idea," he said.

A. P. spoke of his wife, now gone away to the country.

"I wouldn't ever do the little woman any dirt, not really. I'll tell you what, Wescott, I have always been faithful to her, that is to say . . . well you know." He winked.

He was, however, mistaken. John Wescott didn't know.

"I mean," A. P. added. He hesitated. "To tell you the truth, Wescott, there have been times, three or four times, since I have been married. . . ."

Again he hesitated.

"Oh, you know how it is. I dare say it has been the same with you. It has always happened when I have been a little high."

John Wescott didn't know what to say. For just a moment he half wished that he had himself been a more adventurous man. He kept nodding his head.

"This is what I mean," A. P. said. He leaned forward and lowered his voice. They could hear men's voices at the bar outside the little room and a woman laughed. John Wescott felt that in being with A. P. in such a place, he was getting a peep into real life.

"I mean . . . to tell the truth . . . this is just between us two . . . I guess, in the real estate game, you fellows don't have the temptations we advertising men have."

He didn't at the moment continue the explanation of what he had meant. He began speaking of John Wescott's business, of the buying and selling of real estate, of houses and lots.

"You are in this real estate game. You sell some fellow a lot on which to build a house, like you did to me. He is going to build himself a house, a home. He is a bird who is going to build himself a nest."

A. P. was often like that. He was inclined to slip off into something like poetry.

"You see the man is thinking of that, of the little woman, of his children. He is thinking of a happy home life, sitting by the fire on winter nights, eh . . . the little wife there beside him. She is knitting. The children are playing on the floor."

John Wescott was thinking of what a wonderful advertising man A. P. must be.

"What marvelous copy he must write," he thought.

His own firm, called Caldwell and Wescott, occasionally ran advertisements in the Chicago daily newspapers. Caldwell had been his wife's father but now Caldwell was dead and he was himself in control of the firm. He had taken in a young assistant, having made up his mind that neither of his two sons would become a real estate man.

He didn't really care about that, did not want them to be real estate men. He thought, he hoped sometime, that they might both become notable men in some other field, as scholars perhaps, or even as artists. It was something he felt his wife had wanted and that he also had come to want. He sat with his friend thinking.

"Here is A. P." he thought. "He and I have become friends. We are chums, buddies. Now that my wife is dead and his wife has gone to the country with his children, we occasionally go about together like this."

He was half wondering if he dare ask A. P. to do him a favor. It would be a rather delicate matter to bring up.

"Look here, A. P. . . . what you have just said . . . it would make wonderful advertising copy for my firm . . . would you mind writing it out for me? I could use it, you see, in an ad."

He decided he couldn't do it. It would be, he thought, too much like asking a doctor, who happened to be your friend . . . "Say Doc, what about it . . . look me over, eh?"

He couldn't. He didn't run many advertisements in the newspapers and they were usually small ones. He could not hope to become one of A. P.'s clients. It wouldn't be worth A. P.'s time.

"I'll tell you what, A. P. is a big man. He's smart. He can make words fairly sing."

John Wescott had often said something like that to his wife. As he was having this thought A. P. was still talking. He was still on the subject of house building, of nest building. He had got a little drunk with words.

"You take a fellow like that now . . . hell, of what is he thinking? He is thinking of what I just said. You Wescott, have sold him a lot, on which he is going to build a house, a little home, or you have sold him a house already built.

"So he is thinking of where, and how, he will have to change the house. You know how it is, Wescott, a new coat of paint, new wallpaper in the living room, eh. He may have to put in a new bathroom. There is one, but he wants two. He likes to sit in the morning having his morning cigarette and reading his morning paper. At my house every morning I demand a cup of coffee. I take it in there. I read the paper. I light a cigarette. I sip my coffee. The cup of coffee is perched on the edge of the bath tub. Mine has a flat edge.

"You do not take the saucer in there. You spill a little coffee in the saucer and what have you? When you take a sip, after a puff of your cigarette, it drips down on you. The coffee sets you up for the day. I have the maid get up early at my house and bring it to me. Sometimes my wife calls to me.

" 'Well, A. P., are you going to stay all day? It is much better to have two bathrooms."

A. P. paused.

"And so," he said, "such a man comes to you, a man who is going to build a home. His mind is full of things, such as I have described. But with me now. . . ." The two were interrupted by the two burlesque women who had come back along the hallway from the bar. One of the women again put her head in at the door of the room. To John Wescott there was something a little odd, and even thrilling, that two men, such as himself and A. P. had got into that sort of bar in that part of the town. It was a kind of adventure that, when his wife was alive, he wouldn't have dared tell her about. There had never been many things he could tell his wife. He had got into a little habit. He imagined a kind of warm intimacy existing between himself and his wife that never had been a reality. As he seldom conversed with her he imagined conversations. He was doing it as he sat in the room with A. P.

"I must tell you about it, my dear," he imagined himself saying, not to his wife, now dead, but to an imagined wife, he had himself now created.

"You see we were in there, my dear, having a drink, A. P. and myself, and this woman kept putting her head in at the door. She was all painted. To tell you the truth, my dear, she looked to me like a regular huzzy."

"Huzzy" was a word that John Wescott would never have thought of using in a conversation with his wife Clara. It was, however, he imagined, the sort of thing A. P. might have been able to do. A. P. was the kind of man you couldn't upset.

"Hello, baby," he now said to the woman who had put her head in at the door. A. P. was like that, quick on the trigger. The woman laughed and went on her way.

A. P. continued his talk.

"Now, with me," he said, "when it comes to one of my clients. . . ."

He hesitated. He lit a cigar. He seemed lost in thought. There was a look of something like sadness on his face.

"Often," he said, "I begin thinking, I began life as a poor boy . . . I was a farm boy and then I was a clerk in a small store in a small town.

"I came away from there. I came here to the city."

A. P. began relating to John Wescott his early experiences in the city. He had, he said, traveled a rough road. He was a big man, now grown fat and soft, but John Wescott could see that he had once been strong. He had been a common laborer, a soldier, a traveling salesman. He began writing advertisements for a firm he was with, doing it at first for fun, but right away it developed that he had a talent.

"It was a thing," he said, "he never even suspected in himself." Sometimes he regretted that he had not become a writer. In the advertising business he had gone straight up but, sometimes, when he was a little tired, or when one of his clients, now that he was at the head of a big advertising agency, became what he might call a little ugly or disagreeable, he often wished . . . he broke off again.

"I might have become a writer or a newspaper reporter, or, better yet, I might have stayed at home. I might have been just a farmer . . . you know, Wescott, tilling my own field, milking my own cows, hoeing my own corn, watching the wind, on a June morning, as it played in my ripe wheat.

"You have seen the wind, on a June morning playing in the ripe wheat, haven't you, Wescott?"

John Wescott said he had.

"A free man," said A. P. Again he began to throw words about and John Wescott was filled with admiration.

"So you see," he said, "I am on my own land. It is not a big farm. It is a small one.

"There is a creek running through my farm," he said. "At night I lie in my bed. I can hear the purling of the creek. I am tired, from honest labor in my own fields, and I am lying with my wife. She is a sturdy country girl, the daughter of a neighbor. I am a man who makes two blades of grass grow where but one grew before.

"So, you see, Wescott, I am lying there. I am an honest man.

I am upright. I reach out my hand and touch the body of my wife. I have the right, as you will understand, Wescott, to think of myself as one of God's true men, one of God's real men. There is my wife, lying now quietly asleep beside me in the bed and she is mine as the earth is mine."

It was evident that A. P. was deeply touched by his own words. He became silent and sat fingering his drink. He and John Wescott were having an "old fashioned." John Wescott was so touched that he felt like crying.

"It is so beautiful to hear him talk," he thought.

He had often tried to say something of the kind to his wife when she was alive. He began speaking to her in his half-frightened, stuttering way.

"I was out again with A. P."

He did not tell his wife of the drinking the two men did.

"When I go out with him there is always something said that I remember. He talks so beautifully."

He thought sometimes that A. P.'s talk gave him at least a hint of what he wanted for his two sons, that they be, at least in ability to express themselves, like A. P., not like himself. It was A. P. who had given him an inkling of what his wife had meant when she spoke of culture, and sometimes, when he was speaking of his friend to his wife, she questioned him.

"Well, what is it he says? You say he has these wonderful ideas, that he says these wonderful things. What are they?"

It had been a kind of tragedy in John Wescott's life that he had been unable to tell her.

"It is because I am so dumb. It is because I have no ability in words, no education, that I cannot make her understand how marvelous he sometimes is."

It was the source of never-ending wonder that A. P. kept on wanting to have him as friend. In the little room at the back of the saloon A. P. got up from the table and put his head out at the door. He called to the bartender.

"Hey," he called, "two more of the same."

When the two drinks had come he began talking again. He spoke now of the clients of his advertising agency. They were for the most part, he explained, manufacturers.

Or there might be a patent medicine man. He came from some city, perhaps in the middle west.

"Let's say Freeport, Illinois," he said.

Such a fellow came into his office. A. P. began to expand again.

"It is in the early morning. These fellows always get up early. Perhaps he has come in on the night train."

John Wescott felt a little guilty. He was himself a man, likely to get out of bed at six o'clock in the morning. When his wife was alive she stayed in her bed until ten. He got out of bed and walked about the garden surrounding his house. He sprinkled his lawn. He had always had a secret notion that people who could sleep until ten or eleven o'clock were sophisticated people. A. P. was explaining the relationship he had with his clients.

"So there the fellow is," he said. "He is in the office early, sometimes even before the stenographers have come. Later he talks things over with the boys and then, of course, he wants to see and talk to the head of the house. There are advertisements that have been gone over and o.k.'d. When all is done, I say to him . . . it is necessary, you see . . . what about dinner with me?

"And well enough I know what it means," said A. P. He sighed softly.

He went on with his explanation.

"We go out," he said. "Let us say that the man is from Columbus, Ohio. He is, we'll say, more or less, you understand, a big man out there."

"I understand," said John Wescott.

He wasn't at all sure that he did understand as yet, just what A. P. was driving at.

"At home he is what he is. He goes regularly to church. He is a man with a wife and children. It may be that he sings in the choir in his church. Let us say that he manufactures and sells a cure for rheumatism. It is an ointment that you rub on. It is going all right.

"At home, you see, day after day it is the same.

"You see, Wescott, I know how he feels. In his office he has a lot of stenographers, young things you understand, some pretty good-lookers. We will say that his wife is getting a little fat." A. P. was fingering his drink. He was in the act of creating an imaginary figure. He was pleased with himself.

"You understand, Wescott, that a man like that, no matter

what thoughts may sometimes be in his mind, has to be careful. He is well-known in Columbus. He is a good business man and a good business man does not get gay with the help in his office.

"And now you see he is in Chicago. He is unknown here. He is dining with me. We go to a place where there are girls, to a cabaret. We have a few drinks and, with our dinner, a bottle of wine.

"He is feeling safe. He is excited. I know what he wants. Let's say that the girls, in the cabaret, when they sing, come down and walk among the tables. I'll tell you what, Wescott . . . you take one of that kind . . . she knows her biz.

"She can pick them out. You understand, she doesn't get gay with me. 'Hello, Columbus,' she says to him. To tell the truth I have sent a note by a waiter. She sings to him. It may be that she leans over close. Her breath is on his cheek. 'Ain't it rotten I have to work,' she says to him. Very likely she whispers something like that in his ear, giving him the impression, you see, that her heart, in a way of speaking, has been pierced by the arrow of love, that she would like to chuck her job and go with him. I'll tell you what by this time" (A. P. winked at John Wescott).

"Boy, I'll say he is pretty hot."

The expression on A. P.'s face had changed. A shadow seemed to pass over his face.

"So," he said, "I take him to a show, a musical show."

A. P. leaned forward and lowered his voice.

"You can't come right out with a fellow like that," he explained. "What you say to him is that you know a couple of girls.

"But first, after the show you go and have a few more drinks. You make him feel, you understand, that whatever happens, it is o.k. with you.

"You have told him about the girls so you go and call one of them up. You tell him 'they are something special.' So you give him the guff. They have an apartment out south, not so far from the University. You tell him that they are university students."

A. P. sighed.

"Well, there you are, Wescott. Of course, by this time, I am myself a little high. I want to make him feel it is all right. I'll tell you, Wescott, there is something, however, I have never done."

There was a look of sadness and resignation in the presence of fate, on A. P.'s face.

"Anyway, Wescott, no matter how far I may have gone with one of them, you understand, when I am a little drunk, I have never kissed one of them on the lips," he said.

A. P. had finished his tale. To John Wescott it was a revelation. For the moment he was rather ashamed of the comparative purity of his own life. He felt he ought to say something, tell some story of his own adventure. He began to tell A. P. about his relations with his own wife.

"I have never," he said hesitatingly, "that is to say, you understand, with any one but my wife."

He hung his head. He did not look at A. P.

"It may be that I haven't the nerve."

He plunged rather desperately into the story of how his own marriage had come about.

"You see, A. P., there I was."

He told how he had begun working in the real estate office of his father-in-law and how his employer's daughter sometimes came in. He did not look at A. P. as he told his tale. It was, he felt, after all, something a little not so nice, to speak thus, to another man, of the woman he had married. He explained how when she came into the office, and he was alone in there, he got up out of his chair and they shook hands. And then, one evening . . . he said that it had been a thing, at the moment very difficult for him to believe . . . it had seemed to him that, for just a moment, her hand had clung to his.

John Wescott hesitated in telling his story. He began to stammer. There was a drink set on the table before him and he swallowed it nervously.

There was a certain evening in the fall of the year. He had been working a little late in the office and it was growing dark. He had got up from his desk and was about to go home to his room when she came in.

"She said she was looking for her father but he had been gone for two hours."

"We went together down the elevator and into the street."

He explained to A. P. that he had wanted to ask her to have dinner with him at some restaurant but he didn't dare. "I can't express myself like you can, A. P., I have always wished that I could." He had walked along with her that evening, this in the Chicago Loop, and they got over into Michigan Boulevard. There were all sorts of people walking along in the street, some of them well-dressed men and women, very evidently strolling about in the warm summer evening, and others were hurrying to the Illinois Central suburban train. To get to her home the woman he was with also had to take the Illinois Central but, he told A. P., when he was so frightened that he could barely speak, she had got suddenly almost bold. There was a little park over beyond the railroad tracks, to be reached by an overhead bridge and she had proposed that they go there and stand by the lake.

They did go. He tried to tell A. P. about it all.

"It was better out there," he said. Pretty soon darkness came. As he talked he grew more like A. P. Words came to him more freely. He said that the waves were beating against some piling. "I don't know why it was, but just looking at the waves, made me feel a little bolder," he explained.

"I had never in my life kissed any woman but my mother," he said. It was an explanation forced out of him. He told A. P. that he had been reared in a family where they never did kiss very much. "I never saw my father kiss my mother," he said.

He spoke a little of his father and mother, telling A. P. that his mother had died when he was little more than a kid and that he had been raised by an uncle, a man who kept a small retail grocery store on a street over on the west side of Chicago.

"I was out there in the dark with her," he explained, to A. P. "I never did know how it all happened. Suddenly I found myself holding her hand.

"And then we kissed and I asked her to be my wife." His voice dropped to a half whisper.

"You wouldn't marry me," I found myself saying to her, and when she said she would, I was overcome.

"I just couldn't speak. I couldn't believe it."

He said that, after a time . . . he didn't know how long he stayed out there with her that evening . . . they came out of the little park and were again in the street. They were once more on Michigan Boulevard and he told A. P. that the streets were full of cars. People were going to the theatre, he thought.

"Of course," he said, "there were, at that time, carriages too."

He had got his eye fixed on a certain car. He told A. P. that it was standing near the curb and that it was, he thought that night, the grandest, the most beautiful car he had ever seen.

"It was so shiny and nice, and, oh the upholstery," he said.

He said there was a man sitting in the car. He was trying to tell A. P. of how he had felt.

"I don't know how to tell you how I felt. I haven't your gift of words. I have always been so dumb. It was as though, as if that man . . . as if he had suddenly got out of the car and walked over to me . . . as if he had said, 'Do you want this car? You can have it. Take it away.'

"As if . . . just like that . . . he had given it to me. I felt like that about her saying she would be my wife."

John Wescott stopped talking and there was an embarrassing silence between the two men. It was A. P. who finally broke it. He got up from his chair and went and put his head out at the door. He called to the bartender.

"Hey," he called. "Come on, a little service here. Give us two more of the same."

White Spot

I AM quite sure that some of the women I had during this period never became real to me. I do not remember the names. They exist for me as a kind of fragrance as Ruth, Prudence, Genevieve, Holly, etc., etc. There was the very brutal looking very sensual woman seen one night in a low dive in Chicago. I would have been with certain business men on a spree. The business men were better when drunk. The shrewdness was gone. They became sometimes terrible, sometimes rather sweet children.

For example there was Albert, short, fat, baby faced. He was the president of a certain manufacturing concern for which I wrote advertisements. We got drunk together.

He had a wife who was rather literary and already I had published a few stories. Albert had bragged to her about me and once he took me to his house, in an Illinois town, to dine.

She would have talked only of books, as such women do talk. They can never by any chance be right about anything in the world of the arts. Better if they would keep still. They never do.

Albert being much pleased. "The little wife. You see, Sherwood, in our house also we have a highbrow." He was proud of her, wanted to be loyal. As woman, in bed with her man, she wouldn't have been much.

Albert knowing that and wanting in the flesh. He had got himself a little warm thing, bought her fur coats, sent her money. He could never go to her except when he had been drinking.

He explained to me, when we were drunk together. "I am faithful to my wife, Sherwood." He had his code. "To be sure I sleep with my Mable but I have been faithful. I never kissed her on the lips." His reserving that as his own rock on which to stand. I thought it as good as most rocks upon which men stand.

But I was speaking of women, certain women, who touched me vitally in the flesh, left something with me, it all very strange sometimes. I have just thought of that rather big, thick lipped woman seen in a cheap restaurant, half dive in South State Street. There was a little burlesque show a few doors up the street.

Business men, perhaps clients of the firm for which I worked, explaining to me. The president of our company would have been deacon in some suburban church. "Take these men out and entertain them. You do not need to make an itemized account of expenses.

"I would not want company money spent for anything evil." Oh thou fraud.

I would have been blowing money. The burlesque women came down along a dirty alleyway from the stage door of the cheap show and into the restaurant, half dive. They may have got a percentage on the cost of the drinks bought for them.

And there was that big one, with the thick lips, sitting and staring at me. "I want you," and myself wanting her.

Now! Now!

The evil smell of the terrible little place, street women's pimps sitting about, the business men with me. One of them made a remark. "God, look at that one." She had one eye gone, torn out perhaps in a fight with some other woman over some man, and there was the scar from a cut on her low forehead.

Above the cut her shining blue-black hair, very thick, very beautiful. I wanted my hands in it.

She knew. She felt as I felt but I was ashamed. I didn't want the business men with me to know.

What?

That I was a brute. That I was also gentle, modest, that I possessed also a subtle mind.

The women would have been going and coming in at a back door of the place, as the act they did, a kind of weird almost naked dance before yokels, was due to be repeated. I went out into the alleyway and waited and she came.

There were no preliminaries. Now or never. There were some boxes piled up and we got in behind them. What evil smells back in there. I got my two hands buried deep in her beautiful hair.

And afterwards, her saying when I asked her the question, "Do you want money?" "A little," she said. Her voice was soft. There were drunken men going up and down. There was the loud rasping sound from a phonograph, playing over and over some dance tune in the burlesque place.

Can a man retain something? I had no feeling of anything unclean. She laughed softly. "Give me something, fifty cents. I don't like the foolish feeling of giving it away."

"O.K."

Myself hurrying back to the business men, not wanting them to suspect.

"You were a long time."

"Yes." I would have made up some quick lie.

That other one, met on a train, when the train was delayed because something went wrong with the engine. Is there a sense in which the natural man loves all women? The train stopping by a wood and that woman and I giving into the mood to gather flowers.

Again. "Now. Now. You will be gone. We may never meet again."

And then our coming back to the train. She going to sit with an older woman, perhaps her mother, taking her the flowers we had got.

It was Sally, the quiet one, who saw the white spot. It was in a room in a hotel in Chicago, one of that sort. You go in without luggage. You register. "Mr. and Mrs. John James, Buffalo, New York." I remember a friend, who was a women's man, telling me that he always used my name.

We were lying in there in the dark at night, in that rabbit warren of a place. For all I knew the place was full of other such couples. We were in the half sleep that follows, lying in black darkness, a moment ago so close, now so far apart.

Sound of trains rattling along a nearby elevated railroad. This may have been on an election night. There was the sound of men cheering and a band played.

We are human, a male and a female. How lonely we are.

It may be that we only come close in art.

No. Wait.

There is something grown evil in men's minds about contacts.

How we want, want, want. How little we dare take.

It is very silent, here in the darkness. The sounds of the city, of life going on, city life, out there in the street.

A woman cry of animal gratification from a neighboring room.

We exist in infinite dirt, in infinite cleanliness.

Waters of life wash us.

The mind and fancy reaching out.

Now, for an hour, two, three hours, the puzzling lust of the flesh is gone. The mind, the fancy, is free.

It may have been that fancy, the always busy imagination of the artist man she wanted.

She began to talk softly of the white spot. "It floats in the darkness," she said softly and I think I did understand, almost at once, her need.

After the flesh the spirit. Minds, fancy, draw close now.

It was a wavering white spot, like a tiny snow white cloud in the darkness of a close little room in a Chicago bad house.

"You not wanting what our civilization has made of us.

"It is you men, males, always making the world ugly.

"You have made the dirt. It is you. It is you."

"Yes. I understand."

"But do you see the white spot?"

"Yes. It floats there, under the ceiling. Now it descends and floats along the floor.

"It is the thing lost. It eludes us.

"It belongs to us. It is our whiteness."

A moment of real closeness, with that strange thing to the male, a woman.

I had a thought I remember. It was a game played with my brother Earl when I was a lad and he not much more than a babe. We slept together for a time and I invented a game. With our minds we stripped the walls of a room in a little yellow house quite away. We swept the ceiling of our room and the floors away. Our bed floated in space. Perhaps I had picked up a line from some poem. "We are between worlds. Earth is far far beneath us. We float over earth."

All this on a hot August night but we could feel the coolness of outer space. I explained the game to the woman in the room and we played it, following on our floating bed the white drifting spot her fancy had found in that space.

How strange afterwards, going down into the street. It might have been midnight but the street was still crowded with people.

"And so we did float. We did see and follow the white spot and we are here. You make your living writing advertisements and I have a job in an office where they sell patent medicine.

"I am a woman of twenty-eight and unmarried. I live with my sister who is married."

The cheap little hotel room for such couples as we were had its office on the second floor. There was a little desk with a hotel register. What rows of Jones, Smiths, and, yes, Andersons. That friend of mine might have been in that place. He might have put my real name down there.

I would have gone down the stairs first, looked up and down the street. "O.K." The pair of us dodging out. "You'd better take a taxi home. Let me pay."

"But can you? It is such a long way out. It will cost so much."

"Yes. Here."

Who was it invented money? There it lies, the dirty green bill in her hand. The taxi man looking, perhaps listening.

"But, but, does anything of beauty cling to me? Is it to be remembered?"

"Yes. You are very beautiful. Good night." A lie. There was no beauty. The night, the street, the city was the night, the street, the city.

Nobody Laughed

I⟶T wasn't, more than others of its size, a dull town. Buzz McCleary got drunk regularly once a month and got arrested, and for two summers there was a semi-professional baseball team. Sol Grey managed the promoting of the ball team. He went about town to the druggist, the banker, the local Standard Oil manager and others, and got them to put up money. Some of the players were hired outright. They were college boys having a little fun during their vacation time, getting board and cigarette money, playing under assumed names, not to hurt their amateur standing. Then there were two fellows from the coal mining country a hundred miles to the north in a neighboring state. The handle factory gave these men jobs. Bugs Calloway was one of these. He was a home run hitter and afterwards got into one of the big leagues. That made the town pretty proud. "It puts us on the map," Sol Grey said.

However, the baseball team couldn't carry on. It had been in a small league and the league went to pieces. Things got dull after that. In such an emergency the town had to give attention to Hallie and Pinhead Perry.

The Perrys had been in Greenhope since the town was very small. Greenhope was a town of the upper South, and there had been Perrys there ever since long before the Civil War. There were rich Perrys, well-to-do Perrys, a Perry who was a preacher, and one who had been a brigadier general in the Northern army in the Civil War. That didn't go so well with the other well-to-do Perrys. They liked to keep reminding people that the Perrys were of the old South. "The Perrys are one of the oldest and best families of the old South," they said. They kept pretty quiet about Brigadier General Perry who went over to the damned Yanks.

As for Pinhead Perry, he, to be sure, belonged to the no-account branch of the Perrys. The tree of even the best Southern family must have some such branches. Look at the Pinametters. But let's not drag in names.

Pinhead Perry was poor. He was born poor, and he was

simpleminded. He was undersized. A girl named Mag Hunter got into trouble with a Perry named Robert, also of the no-account Perrys, and Mag's father went over to Robert's father's house one night with a shotgun. After Robert married Mag he lit out. No one knew where he went, but everyone said he went over into a neighboring state, into the coal mining country. He was a big man with a big nose and hard fists. "What the hell'd I want a wife for? Why keep a cow when milk's so cheap?" he said before he went away.

They called his son Pinhead, began calling him that when he was a little thing. His mother worked in the kitchen of several well-to-do families in Greenhope but it was a little hard for her to get a job, what with Negro help so cheap and her having Pinhead. Pinhead was a little off in the head from the first, but not so much.

His father was a big man but the only thing big about Pinhead was his nose. It was gigantic. It was a mountain of a nose. It was very red. It looked very strange, even grotesque, sticking on Pinhead. He was such a little scrawny thing, sitting often for a half day at a time on the kitchen step at the back of the house of some well-to-do citizen. He was a very quiet child and his mother, in spite of the rather hard life she had, always dressed him neatly. Other kitchen help, the white kitchen help, what there was of it in Greenhope, wouldn't have much to do with Mag Perry, and all the other Perrys were indignant at the very idea of her calling herself a Perry. It was confusing, they said. The other white kitchen help whispered. "She was only married to Bob Perry a month when the kid was born," they said. They avoided Mag.

There was a philosopher in the town, a sharp-tongued lawyer who hadn't much practice. He explained. "The sex morals of America have to be upheld by the working classes," he said. "The financial morals are in the hands of the middle-class.

"That keeps them busy," he said.

Pinhead Perry grew up and his mother Mag died and Pinhead got married. He married one of the Albright girls . . . her name was Hallie . . . from out by Albright's Creek. She was the youngest one of eight children and was a cripple. She was a little pale thing and had a twisted foot. "It oughten to be allowed," people said. They said such bad blood ought not to be allowed to breed. They said, "Look at them Albrights." The Albrights were always getting into jail. They were horse traders and chicken thieves. They were moon-liquor makers.

But just the same the Albrights were a proud and a defiant lot. Old Will Albright, the father, had land of his own. And he had money. If it came to paying a fine to get one of his boys out of jail, he could do it. He was the kind of man who, although he had less than a hundred acres of land . . . most of it hillside land and not much good, and a big family, mostly boys . . . always getting drunk, always fighting, always getting into jail for chicken stealing or liquor making, in spite, as they said in Greenhope, of hell and high water . . . in spite of everything as, you see, he had money. He didn't put it in a bank. He carried it. "Old Will's always got a roll," people in town said. "It's big enough to choke a cow," they said. The town people were impressed. It gave Will Albright a kind of distinction. That family also had big noses and old Will had a big walrus mustache.

They were rather a dirty and a disorderly lot, the Albrights, and they were sometimes sullen and defiant, but just the same, like the Perrys and other big families of that country, they had family pride. They stuck together. Suppose you had a few drinks in town on a Saturday night, and you felt a little quarrelsome and not averse to a fight yourself, and you met one of the Albright boys, say down in the lower end of town, down by the Greek restaurant, and he got gay and gave you a little of his lip, and you said to him, "Come on, you big stiff, let's see what you've got."

And you got ready to sock him.

Better not to do that. God only knows how many other Albrights you'd have on your hands. They'd be like Stonewall Jackson at the battle of Chancellorsville. They came down on you suddenly, seemingly out of nowhere, out of the woods, as it were.

"Now, you take one of that crew. You can't trust 'em. One of them'll stick a knife into you. That's what he'll do."

And think of it, little, quiet Pinhead Perry, marrying into that crew. He had grown up. But that's no way to put it. He was still small and rather sick looking. God knows how he had lived since his mother died.

He had become a beggar. That was it. He'd stand before one of the grocery stores when people were coming out with packages in their hands. "Hello!" He called all the other Perrys "cousin" and that was bad. "Hello, Cousin John," or "Cousin Mary," or Kate or Harry. He smiled in that rather nice little way he had. His mouth looked very tiny under his big nose and his teeth had got black. He was crazy about bananas. "Hello, Cousin Kate. Give me a dime please. I got to get me some bananas."

And there were men, the smart-alecks of the town, taking up with him too, men who should have known better, encouraging him.

That lawyer . . . his father was a Yank from Ohio . . . the philosophic one, always making wisecracks about decent people . . . getting Pinhead to sweep out his office . . . he let him sleep up there . . . and Burt McHugh, the plumber, and Ed Cabe, who ran the poolroom down by the tracks.

"Pinhead, I think you'd better go up and see your Cousin Tom. He was asking for you. I think he'll give you a quarter." Cousin Tom Perry was cashier of the biggest bank in town. One of those fellows, damn smart-alecks, had seen Judge Buchanan . . . the Perrys and the Buchanans were the two big families of the county . . . they'd seen Judge Buchanan go into the bank. He was a director. There was going to be a directors' meeting. There were other men going in. You could depend on Pinhead walking right into the directors' room where they had the big mahogany table and the mahogany chairs. The Buchanans sure liked to take down the Perrys.

"You go in there, Pinhead. Cousin Tom has been asking for you. He wants to give you a quarter."

"Lordy," said Burt McHugh, the plumber, "Cousin Tom give him a quarter, eh? Why, he'd as soon give him an automobile."

Pinhead took up with the Albrights. They liked him. He'd go out there and stay for weeks. The Albright place was three miles out of town. On a Saturday night, and sometimes all day on Sundays, there'd be a party out there.

There'd be moon whiskey, plenty of that, and sometimes some of the men from town, even sometimes men who should have known better, men like Ed Cabe and that smarty lawyer, or even maybe Willy Buchanan, the judge's youngest son, the one who drank so hard and they said had a cancer.

And all kinds of rough people.

There were two older Albright girls, unmarried, Sally and Katherine, and it was said they were "putting out."

Drinking and sometimes dancing and singing and general hell-raising and maybe a fight or two.

"What the hell?" old Will Albright said . . . his wife was dead and Sally and Katherine did the housework . . . "What the hell? It's my farm. It's my house. A man's king in his own house, ain't he?"

Pinhead grew fond of the little crippled Albright girl, little twisted-footed Hallie, and he'd sit out there in that house, dancing and all that kind of a jamboree going on . . . in a corner of the big untidy bare room at the front of the house, two of the Albright boys playing guitars and singing rough songs at the tops of their voices.

If the Albright boys were sullen and looking for a fight when they came to town, they weren't so much like that at home. They'd be singing some song like "Hand Me Down My Bottle of Moon" and that one about the warden and the prisoners in the prison, you know, on a Christmas morning, the warden trying to be Santa Claus to the boys and what the old hard-boiled prisoner said to him, the two older Albright girls dancing maybe with a couple of the men from town—old Will Albright . . . he was sure boss in his own family . . . sitting over near the fireplace, chewing tobacco and keeping time with his feet. He'd spit clean and sharp right through his walrus mustache and never leave a trace. That lawyer said he could keep perfect time with his feet and his jaws. "Look at it," he said, "there ain't another man in the state can spit like old Will."

Pinhead sitting quietly over in a corner with his Hallie. They both smiled softly. Pinhead didn't drink. He wouldn't. "You let him alone," Will Albright said to his boys. Pinhead and Hallie got married one Saturday night and there was a big party, everyone howling drunk. Two of the guests wrecked a car trying to get back to town and one of them, Henry Haem . . . a

nice young fellow, a clerk in Williamson's drygoods store . . .
you wouldn't think he'd want to associate with such people . . .
he got his arm broke. Will Albright gave Pinhead and Hallie
ten acres of land . . . good enough land . . . not too good
. . . down by the creek at the foot of a hill and he and the
boys built them a house. It wasn't much of a house but you
could live in it if you were hardy enough.

Neither Pinhead nor Hallie was so very hardy.

They lived. They had children. People said there had been ten
of the children. Pinhead and Hallie were getting pretty old. It
was after the Albrights were all gone. Pinhead was nearly seventy and Hallie was even older. Women in town said, "How
could she ever have had all of those children?

"I'd like to know," they said.

The children were nearly all gone. Some had died. An officer
had descended on the family and four of the children had been
carried off to a state institution.

There were left only Pinhead and Hallie and one daughter.
They had managed to cling to her and the little strip of land
given them by Will Albright, but the house, a mere shed in the
beginning, was now in ruins. Every day the three people struck
out for town where now, the philosophic lawyer being dead, a
new one had taken his place. There will always be at least one
such smarty in every town. This one was a tall, slender young
man who had inherited money and was fond of race horses.

He was also passionately fond of practical jokes.

The plumber, Burt McHugh, was also gone, but there were
new men, Ed Hollman the sheriff, Frank Collins, another young
lawyer, Joe Walker, who owned the hotel, and Bob Cairn, who
ran the weekly newspaper in Greenhope.

These were the men who with Sol Grey and others had
helped organize the baseball team. They went to every game.
When the team disbanded they were heartbroken.

And there was Pinhead coming into town followed by Hallie
and the one daughter. Mabel was her name. Mabel was tall and
gaunt and cross-eyed. She was habitually silent and had an odd
habit. Let some man or woman stop on the sidewalk and look
steadily at her for a moment and she would begin to cry. When
she did it, Pinhead and Hallie both ran to her. She was so tall

that they had to stand on tiptoes and reach up, but they both began patting her thin cheeks and her gaunt shoulders. "There, there," they said. It didn't turn out so badly. When someone had made Mabel cry, it usually ended by Pinhead collecting a nickel or a dime. He went up to the guilty one and smiled softly. "Give her a little something and she'll quit," he said. "She wants a banana."

He had kept to his plea for bananas. It was the best way to get money. He, Hallie and Mabel always walked into town single-file, Pinhead walking in front . . . although he was old now, he was still very alive . . . then came Hallie . . . her hair hanging down in strings about her pinched face . . . and then Mabel, very tall and in the summer barelegged. Summer or winter she wore the same dress.

It had been black. It had been given her by a widow. There was a little black hat that perched oddly on her head. The dress had been black but it had been patched with cloth of many colors. The colors blended. There was a good deal of discussion of the dress in town. No two people agreed as to its color. Everything depended on the angle at which she approached you.

These people came into town every day to beg. They begged food at the back doors of houses. The town had grown and many new people had come in. Formerly the Perrys came into town along a dirt road, passing town people who, when there had been a shower and the road was not too dusty, were out for a drive in buggies and phaetons, but now the road was paved and they, the Perrys, passed automobiles. It was too bad for the other Perrys. The family was still prosperous and had increased in numbers and standing. None of the other Perrys took their afternoon drives out of town by that road.

It was the lack of a baseball team. It was because of a dull summer. It was Sol Grey, the man who had the notion of organizing the baseball team, who got the big idea.

He told the others. He told the two young lawyers and Ed Hollman the sheriff. He told Joe Walker the hotel man and Bob Cairn who was editor of the newspaper. He explained. He said that he was standing in front of a store.

"I was in front of Herd's grocery," he said. He had just been standing there when the three Perrys had come along. He thought that Pinhead had intended to ask him for a nickel or a dime. Anyway Pinhead had stopped before Sol and then Hallie and Mabel had stopped. Sol thought he must have been thinking of something else. Perhaps he was trying to think of some new way to break the monotony of life in Greenhope that summer. He found himself staring hard and long, not at Mabel but at Hallie Perry.

He did it unconsciously like that and didn't know how long he had kept it up, but suddenly there had come a queer change over Pinhead.

"Why, you all know Pinhead," Sol said. The men were all gathered that day before Doc Foreman's drugstore. Sol kept bending over and slapping his knees with his hands as he told of what had happened. He had been staring at Hallie that way, not thinking of what he was doing, and Pinhead had got suddenly and furiously jealous.

Pinhead had no doubt intended to ask Sol for a nickel or a dime to buy bananas. Up to that moment no one in town had ever seen Pinhead angry.

"Well, did he get sore," Sol Grey cried. He shook with laughter. Pinhead had begun to berate him. "You let my woman alone!"

"What do you mean staring at my woman?

"I won't have any man fooling with my woman."

It was pretty rich. Pinhead had got the idea into his head that Sol . . . he was a lumber and coal dealer . . . a man who took pride in his clothes . . . a married man . . . the crazy loon had thought Sol was trying to make up to Pinhead's wife.

It was something gaudy. It was something to talk and to laugh about. It was something to work on. Sol said that Pinhead had offered to fight him. "My God," cried Joe Walker. Pinhead Perry was past seventy by that time and there was Hallie with her lame foot and her goiter—

And all three of the Perrys so hopelessly dirty.

"My God! Oh my Lord! He thinks she's beautiful," Joe Walker cried.

"Swell," said Bob Cairn. The newspaper man, who was always looking for ideas, had one at once.

It sure had innumerable funny angles and all the men went to work. They began stopping Pinhead on the street. He would be coming along followed by the two women, but the man who had stopped the little procession would draw Pinhead aside. "It's like this," he'd say. He'd declare he hated to bring the matter up but he thought he should. "A man's a man," he'd say. "He can't have other men fooling around with his woman." It was so much fun to see the serious, baffled, hurt look in Pinhead's eyes.

There would be dark hints cast out.

The man who had taken Pinhead aside spoke of an evening, a night in fact, of the past. He said he had been out at night and had come into town past Pinhead's house. There was no road out that way and Pinhead and his two women, when they made their daily trip into town, had to follow a cow path along Albright Creek to get into the main road, but the man did not bother to take that into account.

"I was going along the road past your house."

There had been various men of the town seen creeping away from the house at night.

No doubt Pinhead was asleep. Certain very respectable men of the town were named. There was Hal Pawsey. He kept the jewelry store in Greenhope and was a very shy modest man. Pinhead rushed into his store and began to shout. There was a woman, the wife of the Baptist minister, in the store at that time. She was seeing about getting her watch fixed. Hallie and Mabel were outside on the sidewalk and they were both crying. Pinhead began beating with his fists on the glass showcase in the store. He broke the case. He used such language that he frightened the Baptist minister's wife so that she ran out of the store.

That was one incident of the summer but there were many others. The hotel man, the newspaper man, the lawyer, Sol Grey, and several others kept busily at work.

They got Pinhead to tackle a stranger in town, a traveling man, coming out of a store with bags in his hand, and Pinhead got arrested and had to serve a term in jail. It was the first time he'd ever been in jail.

Then when he was let out, they began again. It was swell. It was great fun. There was a story going around town that

Pinhead had begun to beat his wife and that she took it stoi-
cally. Someone had seen him doing it on the road into town.
They said she just stood and took it and didn't cry much.

The men kept it going. It was a dull summer. One evening,
when the moon was shining and the corn was getting knee-
high, several of the men went in a car out to Pinhead's house.
They left the car in the road and crept through bushes until
they got quite near to the house. One of them had given Pinhead some money and had advised him to spend it to buy a
bag of flour. The men in the bushes could see into the open
door of the shack. "My God," said Joe Walker. "Look!" he
said. "He's got her tied to a chair."

"Ain't that rich?" he said.

Pinhead had Hallie sitting in the one chair of the one-
roomed house . . . the roof was almost gone and when it
rained the water poured in . . . and he was tying her to the
chair with a piece of rope. Someone of the men had told Pinhead that another man of the town had planned to visit the
house that night.

The men from town lay in the bushes watching. The tall
daughter Mabel was on the porch outside and she was crying.
Pinhead, having got his wife tied to the chair, began to scatter
flour on the floor of the room and on the porch outside. He
backed away from Hallie, scattering the flour, and she was crying. When he had got to the door and as he was backing across
the narrow rickety front porch, he scattered the flour thickly.
The idea was that if any one of Hallie's lovers came, he'd leave
his footprints in the flour.

He came out into a little yard at the front and got under a
bush. He sat on the ground under the bush. In the moonlight
the men from town could see him quite plainly. They said afterwards that he also began to cry. For some reason, even to
the men of Greenhope, who were trying as best they could to
get through a dull summer, the scene from the bushes before
Pinhead's house that night wasn't funny. When they had crept
out from under the bushes and had got back to their car and
into town, one of them went to the drugstore and told the
story, but nobody laughed.

A Landed Proprietor

WHEN I was a very young boy, one of several sons in a very poor family in an American middle western town, I was, for a time, the town newsboy and among my customers in the town, to whom I delivered daily the newspaper from our nearest big city, was a certain little old woman.

She, as I was later to find out, was also very poor. She must however have had a small income from some source unknown to us but her life in her house was a very lonely one. It was a narrow penny counting life. She was there, living alone in a little frame house, on a street of small houses, and beside her house was a vacant lot in which grew several gnarled old apple trees. Her own house was always very clean, very neatly kept but, during the winter months, she sat all day in her kitchen. She did it to save fuel. She heated only the one room in her house.

Such old women are often very wonderful. They grow old patiently, with quiet serenity, often a strange beauty in their wrinkled old faces. They attain a beauty that seldom comes to old men. Such an old woman may carry about a worn out body, may walk with difficulty, her body may be wracked with pain but a beautiful aliveness still shines out of her old eyes and it may be because women are less defeated by modern life. I have often thought that. They have been creators. Children have been born out of their bodies. There may be in them a feeling of accomplishment we men seldom get.

"See, I have done it. Now I am old and tired but there are these others, men and women, the seeds of whom I have carried in my body. They have gone away from me now but they are alive, somewhere in the world. Here I am. I have not just lived, I have given out life."

The particular old woman of whom I speak used to call me often into her house. On cold or rainy days she stood at her kitchen door waiting for my coming. She took an evening paper and at night, sometimes, the train from the city was late. She put a lamp in her kitchen window. She called to me.

"Come in, boy. Dry yourself a little. Warm yourself by my fire." She had baked a pie or had made cookies and she gave me some. She was quite small and, as I stood by her kitchen stove, she came and put a thin old arm about my shoulders. "It is good to be young, to have your life before you," she said. She smiled at me and lights danced in her old eyes. "I am sure you will be a fine man. I feel it. I am sure of it," she added and I drank in her words. When I left her house on winter nights I found myself running joyously along through the dark night streets of our little town and when I put my hand into my coat pocket I found that, while her arm was about my shoulder, she had slipped several more cookies into my pocket.

She died and she had put my name into her will. How proud I was. She had left her house and its furnishings to a son, a mechanic living in some distant city, but the vacant lot, beside her house, in which grew the gnarled old apple trees, she had left to me.

It was a gesture. It was because my daily visits to her house had broken her loneliness. It was because, after she was gone, she wanted me to remember and think of her. It was, to me, a matter of magnificent importance. There was this will, to be probated in our court. I had got the word "probated" from a lawyer of the town to whom I also delivered a daily newspaper. My name would be read out. I would be called upon to sign a paper. I walked about the streets with my chest thrown out.

And there was something else. I had become a land owner, a landed proprietor. I took some of my boy friends to see my lot. There was a particular boy, the son of a grocer. "You see, Herman, your father may own a store but what do you own?" It was fall and there were a few small gnarled apples on the old apple trees and scattered about among tall weeds. I grew generous. "Help yourself, Herman. Put some in your pocket. It's all right with me." I filled my own pockets and took my apples home, demanding that mother make me a pie, and, when it was made, I stood over it, handing out small wedges to my brothers and sisters. This was not a family affair. It was my pie, made from the apples of my own trees that grew on my own land. How gloriously generous I had become. To be thus generous with my own property was a new and sweet feeling to me.

I took my brothers with me to see my lot but they were scornful. "Ah, it is nothing," one of them said. "Such old, no-good trees.

"And look, at the back there, where it goes down to the creek. It is all wet back there. It is a swamp."

It was something I could not stand. One of my brothers and I fought. We stood under one of my apple trees and I pummelled him while a still younger brother, little more than a babe, stood on the sidewalk before my lot and cried.

It was better with my sister who was two years older than myself and, I thought, a very sensible person. She had understanding. She praised my lot. "What fine trees," she said. "Look, the ground must be very rich. How tall the weeds have grown."

In our family we had always been moving. We went from one small frame house in the town to another. There were six of us and no two of us had been born in the same house. Perhaps we moved whenever the rent became too much overdue. I can't be sure of that.

But now I had got this piece of land and, presently, I would build a house on it, such a magnificent house. What a joy it would be to our mother. My sister and I spent hours, walking up and down through tall weeds, making our plans. "You just wait, sister. You'll see. I shall grow rich." In a town some fifty miles away oil had recently been struck. "Who knows? There may be oil down here, under this very spot on which I stand."

In a stationery store of the town I had bought a magazine devoted to house plans and I took it home. To avoid my brothers, who continued scornful ("It is just pure jealousy," I told my sister), my sister and I went upstairs into a bedroom of our house. We sat on the edge of the bed.

What plans we made. Our house continued to grow and grow. Every day we added more rooms. My sister, from time to time, began to feel, I thought, too much a co-owner and I had to rebuke her a little. It was all right for her to make suggestions but all decisions were to be left to me. I made that quite clear to her.

And then it happened. The dream faded. It blew up.

It was the same small town lawyer who had given me the word "probate" who blew it up.

"You look here, kid," he one day said to me, "about that lot that old woman left you.

"I've been looking it up," he said. He explained to me that the unpaid taxes on my lot amounted to about four times what it was worth.

"I guess you don't want to prove up on it," he said but I could not answer him. I ran away. He had his office upstairs over a shoe store in our town and I ran quickly down the stairs and through an alleyway back of stores and along residence streets until I got out into the country.

It was in the spring, on a morning in the spring, when the lawyer gave me the dreadful news and I had my morning papers to distribute but, on that morning, I did not finish delivering the papers. At the edge of town I threw them angrily into a creek. I ran into a wood.

But who can understand the sadness of a boy? I was there in that wood, not far from our town. For a time I cried and then I grew angry. So there was a thing called "taxes." You had a vacant lot given you, a fine lot, I thought, with grand trees growing on it. You had it and then you had it not. Some mysterious force you didn't understand reached down and took it away from you. You had to pay these taxes. But where would you get the money for that?

I began to blame the town in which I lived. I would leave it, I decided. If I went home there would be my brothers and when they found out that the lot that had been mine wasn't really mine they would laugh at me.

I stayed in the wood all that day, did not go to school. I made plans. When night came I would go into town and get on a train. There was a local freight that passed through town in the early evening and I would crawl into a box car and, after a time, when the town realized that I was gone for good it would be sorry. I think that, at the time all this happened to me, I must have been reading *Huckleberry Finn*. For some obscure reason I decided I would go to Cairo, Illinois. I would be a bootblack on the streets there. Then I would become a steamboat captain, grow rich, return to my Ohio town a rich man, pay up the taxes on my lot, build on it a magnificent house.

I was very resolute, very determined but, in the late afternoon, it began to rain and I decided that, after all, I would put off fleeing from the town for a day or two. There were things I had to attend to. I had bought a bicycle and was paying for it on the installment plan and it was almost paid for. I would have to sell that, make myself a bootblacking outfit.

When night came I crept into town. I had begun a little to get my courage back. I went to the railroad station and there were my evening papers, in their bundle, lying against the closed door of the express office.

I had to think up an explanation of why some of my customers had not got their morning paper. That occupied my mind and also I had to think up things to say to my brothers. I ran along in the rain, distributing my papers, and when I had got into a dark residence street began talking aloud. I was making up speeches for my brothers.

"Ah, go on. Shut up. Anyway no one ever put your name in a will," I would say.

When I had got my papers delivered I could not resist going for a visit to my lot. I went and the street in which my lot stood was dark. The little frame house in which my old woman had lived was dark. Her son, the mechanic, had taken the furniture away. I stood for a time in the tall weeds, wet now by the rain, and was inclined to cry again and then, although I was frightened by the thought of the empty house, I went to the rear, to the kitchen door where, when she was alive, there had always been, on such rainy nights, a light in the window for me.

I did not stay there long. I ran away. For a time as I ran in a small town residence street in the rain I cried again and then I stopped crying. I remembered what I had planned to say to my brothers. It may be that just having said the words aloud had brought a dim realization of something that, as I grew older, would become more and more important to me. There was, after all, the fact that I had been mentioned in my old woman's will. Even after she had gone she had made the gesture of love and friendship to me.

The Persistent Liar

FRED said that he was fairly caught and for a moment did not know what to do.

"I came into the bedroom that night in my dressing gown and there was my wife standing by the little table and there, before her on the table, was the note from Mabel.

"I had put it down there an hour before, when I came in. How careless of me. I thought my wife had gone to the movies. Ann, our colored maid, said she had gone out.

"I had dined downtown. I had got Mabel's note at the office. We had quarreled and she wanted to make it up. It was one of those things a man does. I had reached the age of forty.

"You know, of course, that my wife Carrie and I have no children. You have been at our house.

"Did I ever tell you how we happened to marry? You see, we had spent a night together in a tree.

"Now do not laugh. It's a fact.

"That was when I was living in the town of Keokuk. I had a job there and had met the woman who became my wife.

"So on Sundays we used to stroll about. We were walking on a Sunday afternoon in a little grove. My wife Carrie had always been very strait-laced. She had always been very religious, very strict about any sort of moral stepping aside. Would you believe it, on the Sunday of which I am now speaking and when I had been courting her for months, I'd never even kissed her.

"I had tried three or four times but without success. She struggled, she fought me.

"'No, No,' she cried. 'I won't. I won't. I don't think it nice.'"

"As you may guess it was all terribly annoying to me. You know how I am. I am a man who must have women. Women are the very breath of my nostrils, that is to say, in a way of speaking. If I can't get one I go after another.

"For example just at that time, when I was going with my wife, she was pretty thin, really she was.

"You see she had been ill. There had been a good deal of

sickness. She is now, in secret, very sad that she has had no children.

"But I must tell you of the Sunday afternoon, in the grove of trees, near Keokuk. We were strolling along a path and there was a great tree. Some boys had built a little house in the tree.

"It was not quite built. They were building it. They had brought a ladder out there and it was leaning against the tree.

"They had got boxes and boards. You know how boys are. Once I myself, when I was a boy, helped build such a house in a tree.

"We were playing that we were robbers, something like that.

"Anyway there I was, with the woman who became my wife, and we were standing by the tree.

"'Let's go up,'" I said.

"I began daring her to go up the ladder.

"It was one of the times when I had been trying to kiss her and suddenly I grew angry.

"'I have found out what you are,' I said. 'You are a cold woman. You are pigheaded. Here I have been loving you for weeks, dreaming of you at night. My heart has fairly been torn out of my bosom,' I said.

"I kept calling her names and presently she was also angry.

"She was always a thin woman. Her pale thin lips grew paler and suddenly, I don't know why, I hadn't really meant it when I suggested she climb up the ladder to the box in the tree, but up she went.

"She went up like a squirrel and there she was.

"She was up there in that little house. It was like a big store box without a top. She was sitting in it and crying.

"And what was I to do? Of course I went up to her. I was a heavy man then as I am now and I have always been awkward.

"Anyway, up I went and when I had reached the top of the ladder and was trying to crawl into the box, down the ladder went.

"I'll tell you what, I almost fell. I had a struggle but I made it. I was in the box with her. There was just room for the two of us.

"When this happened it was late afternoon and then, after a time, it began to rain.

"There was water everywhere. You see she kept on crying. The tears were running down her cheeks and the rain was running over our bodies.

"We began to shout. We called until we were hoarse but no one answered and, after a time, darkness came.

"And what a night. She, you see, was thinly clad. She shivered. She cried. Oh how slowly the hours went by but, at any rate, she had to let me hug her. If I hadn't hugged her she would have been frozen.

"We were in the tree all night. We couldn't get down but, in the morning, let's say at seven . . . I can't be sure of that . . . it may have been eight o'clock when a man came through the grove.

"He was a working man of some sort. I remember that he carried a dinner pail. He may have been going to work in some factory in the town or on a nearby farm. How do I know?

"Anyway he got us down and I gave him a dollar. Carrie spoke of it later.

" 'Why did you give him a dollar?' she asked. This was after we married. She thought that twenty-five cents would have been enough.

"We had to walk through the streets to her house. Did I tell you that she was thinly clad? She was very wet and her dress was clinging to her body. Every sharp curve of her thin body could be seen by all the people we passed.

" 'Oh Fred,' she said, 'and what will I tell my mother?' She had grown quite affectionate, you see.

"As you can guess we had got quite well acquainted during the night.

" 'Oh tell her we are going to be married,' I said.

"So, we did marry and there we were. I had come to Chicago, had become quite a prosperous man.

"As for the other woman, that is to say Mabel, the one who wrote me the note, well, as I have suggested, it was one of those things.

"A man, you see, is near a woman every day and all day long. She is nice. She is quite pretty. She is his secretary.

"He intends nothing much. Well, he goes along. He is dictating letters and suddenly he stops and has a conversation with her.

"They are sitting quite close. He tells her about himself and she, in her turn, speaks of herself and, as you can see, a kind of intimacy begins to grow up.

"With some men, with perfectly honorable men. . . .

"But I do not pretend that I am that. I am not honorable. I am a man of impulse, a sensitive man. I am ashamed but I go ahead.

"I was in my house and there was a note from that Mabel. Had I told her that I loved her? Yes, I am afraid I had.

"I had been swept away. I was a ship without a rudder. To tell the truth, I had told her I loved her. I had even held her once, for a moment, in my arms.

"And then I had seen, clearly enough, how impossible it was.

" 'We can't go on,' I had said to her. After all, I was married to Carrie.

" 'You had better get another place,' I had said. I had promised to pay her wages while she was looking for another place and she had got angry.

"She had tramped out of my office, that was it. Whether or not the others in the office knew of what was going on I can't say.

"And then, after a week, or perhaps two weeks had passed, she had written me the note.

" 'I still love you,' it said.

"She had wanted me to meet her again. As it turned out, later when I did meet and talk with her for a moment, she had changed her mind about taking wages from me while she was looking for another place.

"I had put the note on the table in our bedroom. It was very careless of me. I had thought that Carrie had gone to the movies. Someone called me and I had gone downstairs.

"I had returned to our bedroom and had undressed for the night. I was in my bathrobe.

"And then Ann, our servant, called me again. It was something about the sink in the kitchen, it had got stopped up and she wanted me to fix it. It is a sink that is always getting out of order.

"So I did. I put some lye in. I fixed it and then I went back upstairs to our bedroom and there was Carrie, my wife. She was reading the note from Mabel. What a moment!

" 'Good God,' I thought.

" 'The fat is in the fire,' I thought.

"As it happens Mabel is a little fat but that has nothing to do with what I was thinking.

"I just stood by the door of the room and there, facing the little table on which lay the note from Mabel was my wife Carrie. She did not look at me. She turned her face away and then she walked across the room and stood by the window.

"I tried something on her. 'If a man lies and keeps on lying presently people will believe,' I have always thought. It is a theory of mine. 'Persistence does it,' I have always said to myself. 'This is my chance. I'll try out my theory,' I thought.

"I walked across the room, picking up the note as I passed the little table. I went into the bathroom and closed the door. I tore the note into bits and then I pulled the chain.

"There I was, you see, now there wasn't any note. I came out of the bathroom and there was a storm of tears. Oh, what tears were shed. It went on all night. It went on for several nights and then there was a long period of silence.

"She had decided not to speak to me.

" 'All right,' I said to myself. I had, you see, this theory. I was trying something out. Often enough I had said to myself, 'Persistence does it,' I had said.

" 'No matter how absurd the lie, tell it over and over and, in the end people will believe.' That was, you see, my faith.

"I was, you understand, trying it out on my wife, Carrie.

" 'No, there wasn't any note.' I had seen no note. I knew no one named Mabel.

"I said it quietly, firmly, over and over. During the time when she wouldn't speak to me I waited patiently. I said it when she was well and when she was ill.

"She tried something on me. She was ill and announced that she was about to die.

" 'Tell the truth. I will forgive you. I am about to die,' she said. But it didn't phase me. It had become, to me a kind of scientific experiment. I had, I may say, the attitude of a scientist.

"It took a year, nearly two years, but in the end I won.

"I saw doubt come into her eyes. I had, you understand, by this time, almost convinced myself.

"For long periods I really did convince myself and, of course, I convinced her.

"She broke down. She surrendered. I am quite sure that now, after several years of persistent lying to her, that she believes. She thinks there was some sort of hallucination. I have spoken from time to time of this, have told her of experiences of my own.

"And now, when I come to speak of all this, I am myself in a very strange state. I may be lying to you. I may just be amusing myself.

"At any rate, as I have always said to myself it is persistence that does it. There is nothing in the world so powerful as persistence."

CHRONOLOGY

NOTE ON THE TEXTS

ACKNOWLEDGMENTS

NOTES

Chronology

1876   Born Sherwood Berton Anderson on September 13, in
            Camden, Ohio, the third child of Irwin McClain Anderson
            (b. 1845) and Emma Anderson, née Smith (b. 1852). His
            father, a harness maker born near West Union, Ohio, had
            served in the Union Army during the Civil War and at-
            tended college for a year. His mother, a native of Oxford,
            Ohio, had worked as a housekeeper for a farm family. They
            married in March 1873 near Morning Sun, Ohio, and had
            a son, Karl James (b. 1874), and then a daughter, Stella
            (b. 1875), having moved in June 1874 to the nearby town
            of Camden.

1877–83   Moves with family to Independence (now Butler), Ohio,
            and then to Caledonia. Father's harness-making business
            gradually fails, and he begins—Anderson later remem-
            bers—"partaking of the bottle more frequently." Unable
            to support his children, now including Irwin (b. 1878) and
            Ray Maynard (b. 1883), father moves to a boardinghouse
            in nearby Mansfield, probably working in a machine fac-
            tory or another harness shop.

1884–87   In March 1884, moves with family to Clyde, Ohio, a farm
            town of about 2,400 inhabitants; father works for a local
            harness and saddle maker and mother takes in laundry.
            They rent a house at 147 Duane Street, the first of several
            they will occupy in Clyde. Enrolls in second grade; Earl
            (b. 1885) becomes the youngest child of six. By 1887, father
            has lost job and works intermittently as a house and sign
            painter; eldest brother Karl begins an apprenticeship at the
            harness and saddle maker's.

1888–90   Anderson works as newspaper delivery boy. Fern, last child
            of Irwin and Emma Anderson, born January 1890 (dies
            December 1891).

1891–92   Begins attending high school. As an adolescent, reads Scott,
            Balzac, Cooper, Mark Twain, Harriet Beecher Stowe, Wil-
            liam Dean Howells. Acts in amateur theatricals.

1893–94   Finishes high school, having attended only sporadically.

1895   Enlists in Ohio National Guard in March. Mother dies in May of lung disease. Anderson begins working in a bicycle factory.

1896–97   After bicycle factory closes in June, takes warehouse job in Erie, Pennsylvania. Moves to Chicago in 1897, where he lives with the Padens—a family from Clyde—and his brother Karl, an artist who had moved to Chicago several years earlier. Forms friendship with Clifton Paden. Works in a cold-storage warehouse. Takes evening classes in advanced arithmetic at the nearby Lewis Institute.

1898   In April, with the outbreak of the Spanish-American War, reenlists in the Ohio National Guard, later joining the 16th Regiment of the Ohio Volunteer Infantry. Serves at Camp Thomas (in Georgia) and Camp Poland (in Tennessee), and is promoted to corporal.

1899   Arrives in Cienfuegos, Cuba, with his regiment early in January; they are charged with guarding Spanish soldiers awaiting repatriation. Returns to Clyde, to a celebratory welcome, in May. During the summer works on a nearby farm and for a threshing company, travelling through rural Ohio. In September, begins college preparatory classes at the Wittenberg Academy in Springfield, Ohio, which he attends for three terms. Joins the Athenian Literary Society and participates in debate and oratory contests. Lives at "The Oaks," a boardinghouse, in exchange for lawn mowing, coal hauling, and other chores; his circle includes not only fellow students but older boarders working in publishing and academia.

1900   Receives praise for his June commencement address, "Zionism," and accepts a job in Chicago as advertising solicitor for the Crowell Publishing Company. Lives in Chicago with his sister Stella and younger brothers. Anderson's father leaves Clyde, and he remarries in March 1901; Anderson never sees him again.

1901   Starts a new job as a copywriter for Long-Crutchfield, publisher of *Agricultural Advertising*.

1902   Publishes essay "The Farmer Wears Clothes," his first appearance in print, in *Agricultural Advertising* in February. It is followed by "A Soliloquy" in April, "Writing it Down" in November, and "Not Knocking" in December.

1903   Writes regularly for *Agricultural Advertising*. Publishes
        first essay in a literary magazine, "A Business Man's Read-
        ing," in *The Reader*. Reads Shaw, Stevenson, Carlyle, and
        George Borrow (whom he later describes as "to me the
        great writer"). In May meets Cornelia Platt Lane (b. 1877),
        daughter of a wealthy Ohio businessman, on a business
        trip to Toledo, Ohio.

1904   Marries Cornelia Platt Lane on May 16. Keeps a "Honey-
        moon Journal" about their travels through Tennessee en
        route to the St. Louis World's Fair. Returning to Chicago,
        they rent an apartment on the South Side. Publishes a series
        of articles in *Agricultural Advertising* on "Business Types."

1905   In May delivers talk on "Making Good" at Long-Critch-
        field banquet. Visits Philadelphia at the expense of Cyrus
        Curtis, head of Curtis Publishing, to discuss a possible
        series of articles on American business life, but declines
        Curtis's proposal. *The Saturday Evening Post*, published by
        Curtis, solicits but ultimately rejects his fiction.

1906   Hoping to make more money, approaches one of his firm's
        clients, George Bottger of United Factories, a small mail
        order marketing firm, proposing he join their business. Is
        appointed president, and in September relocates to Cleve-
        land with his wife. Writes advertising copy and entertains
        manufacturers, hoping to market their products.

1907   Early in the year one of the products his firm has sold, a
        chicken incubator, is revealed to be fundamentally defec-
        tive; they lose thousands of dollars. (Later fictionalizes the
        episode in "The Egg.") His first child, Robert Lane, is
        born August 16. About the same time, suffers a nervous
        breakdown and is found "wandering around in the
        woods." Leaves United Factories, moving with wife to
        Elyria, Ohio, around September to start a new business.
        His "Anderson Manufacturing Company" buys a preserva-
        tive roofing paint in bulk, reselling it to individuals and
        hardware stores as "Roof-Fix."

1908   Joins the Elyria Country Club. Moves with wife and son
        and brother Earl into a new house. Begins selling house-
        hold items as well as paint. A second son, John Sherwood,
        is born December 31.

1909   Wins a local golf tournament. In August, buys a local paint
        manufacturer, renaming it the Anderson Paint Company.

Wife joins the Fortnightly Club, devoted to literary discussion. Late in the year, advertises a scheme he calls "Commercial Democracy," which would enable retailers to purchase shares in manufacturing profits.

1910   Spends an increasing amount of time writing stories, and begins a novel (eventually published as *Marching Men*). Publishes *Commercial Democracy*, a series of advertising pamphlets, to promote his profit-sharing plan. Anderson Manufacturing sponsors a float in the Elyria Fourth of July parade. With others in Elyria participates in a discussion group, the Round Table Club.

1911   Has his secretary type and submit for publication stories he has read into a Dictaphone. Addresses the Teachers' Club of Elyria on "Women in Business." In June, attends a rally of the Ohio Equal Suffrage Association with his wife. A daughter, Marion Anderson, is born October 29. In November, incorporates the American Merchants Company, which merges Anderson Manufacturing and Anderson Paint. Capitalized at $200,000, its shares are divided between Anderson ($25,000) and prominent local investors ($24,000), with the remainder to be sold to cooperating retailers.

1912   Secretary Frances Shute types early drafts of *Windy McPherson's Son* and *Marching Men*. Superintendent of Anderson Paint resigns and starts a rival firm. Business begins to fail. On Thanksgiving day, leaves office and walks toward Cleveland for four days, sleeping outdoors; sends his wife a disorganized seven-page letter describing his experiences; shows symptoms of amnesia. Is admitted to a Cleveland hospital, where he is visited by wife and secretary. On December 2, an Elyria newspaper recounts the episode and describes him as suffering from "nervous exhaustion."

1913   In February returns to Chicago to resume advertising work for Taylor-Critchfield; wife and children remain in Elyria, later relocating to Little Point Sable, Michigan. Lives in a cheap rooming house. Goes to Art Institute repeatedly to see Chicago version of the Armory Show, which had brought modernist art to America (and to which his brother Karl had contributed work). Becomes acquainted with the "Fifty-Seventh Street circle," community of writers and artists frequenting adjacent buildings near Jackson

Park, including Floyd Dell, Susan Glaspell, Ben Hecht, Carl Sandburg, Eunice Tietjens, Margaret Anderson, and Tennessee Mitchell. Forms friendship with Dell, who is impressed by the manuscript of *Windy McPherson's Son*. Dell leaves in October for New York, where Anderson visits him and enjoys Greenwich Village artistic milieu. In November goes with family to Hooker, Missouri, where they live together for around four months at isolated hunting lodge in Ozark Mountains; Anderson and wife agree to separate. Works on novels "Mary Cochran" and "Talbot Whittingham" (both completed but never published).

1914   Resumes job at Taylor-Critchfield in March. Contributes artistic statement ("The New Note") to first issue of Margaret Anderson's *The Little Review*. First published story, "The Rabbit-pen," appears in *Harper's* in July. Meets Marietta "Babs" Finley, a publisher's reader in Indianapolis, who becomes a close friend and frequent correspondent. Becomes increasingly involved with Tennessee Mitchell, artist and teacher of music and dance. Moves into rooming house at 735 Cass Street where he will live for the next several years. Reads Gertrude Stein's *Tender Buttons* with enthusiasm.

1915   Writes "Hands," first story of what will become *Winesburg, Ohio* (originally titled "The Book of the Grotesque"). Publishes stories in *The Masses*, whose literary editor is Floyd Dell.

1916   Travels with Tennessee in June to Camp Owlyout at Lake Chateaugay in upstate New York. Cornelia files for divorce, which becomes final on July 27; Anderson and Tennessee are married in Chateaugay on July 31, and spend the summer at Lake Chateaugay. Anderson forms close friendship with psychoanalyst Trigant Burrow. After returning to Chicago he and Tennessee continue to maintain separate apartments. *Windy McPherson's Son* is published in September by John Lane. Waldo Frank publishes an admiring review of it in *The Seven Arts* under the title "Emerging Greatness." Anderson works on novel "Immaturity" (subsequently abandoned).

1917   Visits New York in February; at *Seven Arts* office meets Waldo Frank and Van Wyck Brooks; subsequently meets *Seven Arts* associate Paul Rosenfeld. On return to Chicago, embarks on series of free-verse poems. Anderson spends summer at Lake Chateaugay, where he is visited by Waldo Frank; Tennessee joins him late in summer. Harriet Monroe publishes a sequence of Anderson's poems in *Poetry*. *Marching Men* published by John Lane in September, to generally unenthusiastic reviews. Essay "An Apology for Crudity" appears in *The Dial*.

1918   Corresponds with Van Wyck Brooks about Mark Twain, about whom Brooks is writing a book. *Mid-American Chants* published by John Lane in April. Travels in Kentucky and attends the Kentucky Derby. Clifton Paden, who has changed his name to John Emerson and married screenwriter Anita Loos, offers Anderson a job as publicist with their film production company Emerson-Loos Productions; Anderson resigns from Taylor-Critchfield and moves to New York in the summer, renting a room alone on West 22nd Street. Works desultorily as publicist while devoting himself chiefly to his own writing; writes a draft of novel *Poor White*. Forms friendship with French director Jacques Copeau, in residence in New York, and with Alfred Stieglitz and Georgia O'Keeffe. Manuscript of *Winesburg, Ohio* rejected by John Lane. Meets publisher B. W. Huebsch, who by the end of the year offers to publish *Winesburg, Ohio*. Tennessee spends September with him in New York. Suffers debilitating bout of Spanish influenza. Returns to Chicago in December; resumes working for Taylor-Critchfield.

1919   Works on a series of experimental pieces in quasi-biblical style (later forming part of *A New Testament*), of which thirteen appear in *The Little Review* between October 1919 and March 1921. *Winesburg, Ohio* published in May by B. W. Huebsch. Elicits enthusiastic response from many reviewers and readers, including H. L. Mencken, Floyd Dell, Heywood Broun, and Hart Crane, who writes: "America should read this book on her knees. It constitutes an important chapter in the Bible of her consciousness." Father dies in May. During the summer Anderson and Tennessee spend several weeks at a cabin near Ephraim, Wisconsin, with Waldo Frank and his wife Margaret. Opens private office in September for dealing with advertising clients. Heartened by Waldo Frank's praise of him in his book *Our America*. Is impressed by D. H. Lawrence's *Sons and Lovers* and by W. Somerset Maugham's *The Moon and Sixpence*, whose artist protagonist reminds him of himself.

1920   In February travels to Fairhope, Alabama, where (after spending some time in Mobile) he rents a beach cottage; becomes friendly with artist Wharton Esherick and his wife Letty. With great enthusiasm, takes up watercolor painting; visits the progressive School of Organic Education where Wharton teaches. Returns to Chicago briefly and convinces Tennessee, who has "gone to pieces nervously," to come to Alabama. There, she experiments with sculpture in clay, some of her portrait busts later to be photographed and included in *The Triumph of the Egg*. They take an excursion steamer trip up the Alabama River with the Eshericks. Anderson completes a draft of *Poor White*. Contemplates literary projects based on his observations of African American life: "a thing to be done as big as any of the great masters ever tackled." Begins novel *Many Marriages* and writes poetry. Visits New York, where he spends time with Rosenfeld, Stieglitz, and O'Keeffe. Spends summer with Tennessee in Ephraim, Wisconsin. Works on novel "Ohio Pagans" (never completed). Rents cottage in Palos Park, near Chicago, where he will be based for the next two years; befriends painter Felix Russman. Has a solo exhibition of his paintings at a bookstore in Chicago. *Poor White* published by Huebsch in October; it receives many strong reviews but sales are disappointing. Writes long story "Out of Nowhere into Nothing." Has Christmas dinner with his three children, now thirteen, eleven, and nine.

1921   Reads Lawrence's *Women in Love* with deep admiration. Meets Ernest Hemingway, who is working as an occasional copywriter and journalist. On a stopover in Baltimore, meets H. L. Mencken. In May, accompanied by Tennessee, sails to France with Paul Rosenfeld, who had invited him on the trip and paid his passage. Keeps a notebook of his stay, and spends much time studying Paris museums and architecture; dazzled by visit to Chartres ("poetry in stone . . . the last word in beauty"). Meets James Joyce and Sylvia Beach; forms friendship with Gertrude Stein, whose writing he has long admired. Travels to England in July and meets his new English publisher Jonathan Cape; returns to America in August. *The Triumph of the Egg* is published by Huebsch; the reviews are strong and in October he receives the first *Dial* award. Encourages Ernest Hemingway to go to Paris, which he does in November; Anderson writes letters of introduction to Stein, Joyce, and others.

1922   Uncomfortable with growing celebrity, moves alone to a room in New Orleans. Publishes in local literary magazine *The Double Dealer*; having abandoned "Ohio Pagans," works on *Many Marriages*. At Stein's request, writes preface to her *Geography and Plays*, published as "The Work of Gertrude Stein." Returns to Chicago in March. Obliged to vacate her own apartment, Tennessee moves in with him in Palos Park, but the reunion is uneasy; Anderson leaves Chicago for New York in July. Writes to Stein: "Have run away from all my friends, including friend wife." (He never sees Tennessee again.) Cuts ties with Taylor-Critchfield. Visits Hart Crane in Cleveland but occasion is spoiled by violent literary argument with Crane's friend Gorham Munson, who had recently attacked Anderson and Paul Rosenfeld in print. Enters agreement with Otto Liveright to serve as his literary agent. Decides to abandon advertising work permanently: "I shall quite separate myself from the advertising business . . . Enough is enough. I am forty-six next week." In New York takes a room on St. Luke's Place in Greenwich Village, next door to Theodore Dreiser, whom he meets on several occasions; meets F. Scott and Zelda Fitzgerald, John Dos Passos, and Edmund Wilson. Meets Elizabeth Prall, manager of Doubleday bookstore on Fifth Avenue, and falls in love with her. Visits New Orleans in November; writes to Jean Toomer after being impressed by a Toomer story in *The Double Dealer*.

1923   Sits for Alfred Stieglitz for series of photographic portraits. Has brief reunion with his children en route to Reno, Nevada, where he travels in February to obtain divorce from Tennessee (state law requires six-month residency); works on memoir later published as *A Story Teller's Story*. *Many Marriages* published in February. Elizabeth joins him in Reno in April for what turns out to be a process of more than a year as Tennessee seeks to delay the divorce. Story collection *Horses and Men* published in October. Works on novel "The Golden Circle" (never completed). Hires Clarence Darrow to handle his divorce suit, while Tennessee continues to raise difficulties. Writes to Jean Toomer in admiration of the just-published *Cane*.

1924   Gratified by letter of praise from Theodore Dreiser. Divorce becomes final in April. Anderson and Elizabeth marry in Martinez, California, on April 5. After a honeymoon trip to San Francisco they settle for a few months at her family's home in Berkeley. Works on "Father Abraham," uncompleted study of Lincoln. Approached by publisher Horace Liveright, who convinces him to change publishers. Joined in Berkeley by son Bob, who will stay with him for a year. Lectures at University of California on "Modern American Writing." In July Anderson moves to New Orleans; joined some weeks later by Elizabeth and Bob. William Faulkner, recently arrived in New Orleans and an admirer of Anderson's work, pays call on Anderson and the two become friends. Writes draft of novel *Dark Laughter* (originally titled "Love and War"). *A Story Teller's Story* appears in October, last book of Anderson's published by Huebsch. Signs with Leigh Lecture Bureau.

1925   Embarks on lecture tour of over a dozen cities from coast to coast. In New York at the end of January is guest of honor at literary luncheon organized by his publisher B. W. Huebsch and attended by Kenneth Burke, Waldo Frank, H. L. Mencken, Edmund Wilson, Mark Van Doren, and others. Enjoys a preview of the group show "Seven Americans" in which his newly married friends Georgia O'Keeffe and Alfred Stieglitz are participating; writes a poem for the exhibition catalog. Inspired by performance of *The Triumph of the Egg* at Provincetown Playhouse in Greenwich Village (adapted for the stage by Raymond O'Neil), becomes interested in writing for the theater. Returns to New Orleans in early March. With Elizabeth, finds a room in the French Quarter for Faulkner, who had worked on his first novel in Anderson's apartment during his absence. Begins work on a "Childhood book" (a fictionalized memoir later titled *Tar: A Midwest Childhood*) for serialization in *The Woman's Home Companion*. Buys house at 628–30 St. Ann Street (it will be sold, at a profit, later in the year). Charters a yacht for a Lake Pontchartrain cruise on March 14–15, in honor of visiting writer Anita Loos; at work on *Gentlemen Prefer Blondes*, she is unable to sail, but the cruise proceeds. (William Faulkner, one of those on board, will use it as the setting for his second novel, *Mosquitoes*). In April, signs a five-year, five-book contract with Boni & Liveright. Embarks on a two-week tugboat trip on the Mississippi. Anderson and Elizabeth travel in July to Troutdale, in the Blue Ridge Mountains near Marion, Virginia, where they settle into a cabin on the property of friends. Anderson purchases land on a hillside near Marion, where he will build first a cabin and then a four-bedroom house, to be called "Ripshin" after a creek running through the property. After recovering from serious bout of influenza, Anderson starts on two-and-a-half-month nationwide lecture tour. Novel *Dark Laughter* published by Boni & Liveright in September; the book is a bestseller, with eight printings within nine months. Spends Christmas in New Orleans. Reviews Dreiser's *An American Tragedy*, calling him "the most important American writing."

1926   Gives series of lectures on the west coast in January. Learns in February that his younger brother Earl, whom he had not seen in years, is critically ill in a New York hospital following a stroke; troubled to learn that Earl feels ill-treated by Anderson, he begins to correspond with him. Quarrels with Faulkner and their friendship cools thereafter. Publishes *Sherwood Anderson's Notebook*, a collection of earlier published pieces, in May. Ernest Hemingway's *The Torrents of Spring*, a parody of *Dark Laughter* and other works by Anderson, published by Scribner's in May. Anderson works in cabin at Ripshin while main house is under construction; works on novel "Another Man's House" and writes story "Death in the Woods." Depressed by inability to finish the novel on which he has been working. *Tar* appears in November. In December sails to Europe with Elizabeth, his son John, and daughter Mimi. Meets English novelists Frank Swinnerton and Arnold Bennett. Spends a week in London before going on to Paris. Celebrates Christmas with Gertrude Stein.

1927   Suffers from flu and continuing depression. Meets Hemingway on several occasions; does not attend party Stein gives in his honor; describes the trip to his son as "a dead, blank time." Sails to New York in March. On arriving learns of the death of his brother Earl; gives a lecture in Brooklyn, then with Karl accompanies Earl's body to Ohio for burial.

Returns to Ripshin in April; he and Elizabeth settle into country life. *A New Testament* published in June. Disturbed by *New Republic* review of the book that concludes: "The author of *Winesburg, Ohio* is dying before our eyes." Learns that two local Virginia newspapers—the *Smyth County News* and the *Marion Democrat*—are for sale and, with the help of a loan from advertising executive and bibliophile Burton Emmett, buys both in November and incorporates them as Marion Publishing Company. Declares his intention as editor-publisher to "give expression to . . . all of the everyday life of a typical American community." He and Elizabeth move to a hotel in Marion, staying at Ripshin on weekends.

1928 Immerses himself in the business of newspaper publishing while contributing columns and editorials. Establishes a lending library in the office of his print shop. Embarks on two-week lecture tour in November. Meets Eleanor Copenhaver, daughter of close friends from Marion, a social worker on the staff of the YWCA recently returned from an assignment in Europe. In December, at Anderson's suggestion, Elizabeth goes to California to visit her family; shortly after arrival, receives letter from him saying that he would prefer it if she did not return. They do not divorce for several years but marriage effectively ends.

1929 Anderson's son Bob moves in with him and assumes much responsibility for publishing newspapers. Anderson meets in Baltimore with writer V. F. Calverton, who hopes to become his biographer, but decides biographers should "wait till I am dead"; in March attends inauguration of Herbert Hoover. *Hello Towns!*, a collection of his newspaper writing, is published in April. Accompanies Eleanor to Elizabethton, Tennessee, where she has gone to observe labor unrest in the town's textile mills; publishes "Elizabethton, Tennessee" in *The Nation*. Continues to correspond steadily with Eleanor although they see each other only sporadically. Works on novel whose working titles include "Another Man's House" and "No God." Beginning in June, spends six weeks in a cottage in Dykemans, New York, owned by Charles Bockler, a painter friend, and his wife; has brief affair with Bockler's sister Mary Vernon Greer. Joins Theodore Dreiser, Waldo Frank, Fannie Hurst, and other writers on a committee supporting striking textile workers. Lectures at the University of Virginia. In November, reports that he has finished a draft of "No God." Back in Chicago in December, has several telephone conversations with Tennessee but does not respond to her invitations to come see her. Travels to St. Petersburg, Florida, for Christmas where he works on "No God" but decides to abandon the novel. Learns that Tennessee has been found dead of an overdose of sleeping pills, possibly a suicide; does not attend her funeral.

1930   Travels in January to Savannah, where Eleanor joins him. Visits mills elsewhere in Georgia and South Carolina, and writes stories and articles about factory conditions. Anderson and Eleanor become lovers. Anderson goes to New Orleans and visits further factories, including Ford auto plant. Moved by death in March of D. H. Lawrence, whom he will praise for "the bringing back into prose art of the sensual." Leaves New Orleans in April; has reunion with son John at Ripshin. Breaks with Otto Liveright and contracts with Anne Watkins as his new literary agent. Sees Eleanor as often as her peripatetic working life permits, in North Carolina, New Jersey, and (in October) at Ripshin. In Virginia in November, participates in public debate in Richmond on "Agrarianism versus Industrialism" and at mass meeting in Danville of striking cotton mill workers. Eleanor joins him in Marion for Christmas.

1931   Works on experimental "crazy book" that he soon abandons. Returns to Danville on January 13 to deliver speech to meeting of workers attempting to unionize; publishes account of his visit in The New Republic. Meets up as often as possible with Eleanor, whose work requires continual travel. Works on novel Beyond Desire. Lectures at Northwestern University and the University of Chicago in April. In New York in May sees Paul Rosenfeld, Alfred Stieglitz, and other friends; "deeply stirred" by Edmund Wilson's article "Detroit Motors" in The New Republic. Wilson visits him in Marion in June and at Anderson's request recommends books on Communism. Perhaps Women, a collection of stories and sketches centered on the varying effects of industrialism on men and women, published in September. Attends conference of southern writers at the University of Virginia in October; other participants include Ellen Glasgow, James Branch Cabell, Allen Tate, and

William Faulkner. Debates Bertrand Russell on issues of child rearing in New York in November. Addresses New York meeting of National Committee for the Defense of Political Prisoners in support of Theodore Dreiser, whom Kentucky officials have charged with criminal syndicalism.

1932   In January, hands over ownership of Marion Publishing Company to his son Bob. After lecturing in New York, works on *Beyond Desire* in Marion. Divorce from Elizabeth becomes final in February. Begins midwestern and western lecture tour in March; calls visit to San Joaquin Valley "the most delightful two days of my life." Along with John Dos Passos, Edmund Wilson, Waldo Frank, and others, signs manifesto calling for "a temporary dictatorship of the class-conscious workers"; supports William Z. Foster's presidential candidacy on the Communist ticket. As part of a delegation of writers also including Waldo Frank, attempts to see President Hoover to protest the calling out of armed forces to disperse marchers demanding army bonuses; meets with Hoover's press secretary, publishes open letter to Hoover in *The Nation*. Sails to Amsterdam in August as a delegate to the World Congress Against War. *Beyond Desire* appears in September. With Arthur Barton, an actor he meets in New York in the fall, works on dramatic adaptation of *Winesburg, Ohio*.

1933   Works on two novels in succession, abandoning both. *Death in the Woods and Other Stories* is published in April, last book with Boni & Liveright whose business has failed. Work with Barton on *Winesburg, Ohio* at Ripshin comes to an impasse, and Anderson, unimpressed by Barton's work, asks him to leave; continues revising script on his own. Marries Eleanor on July 6 at her parents' home in Marion. Approached by Maxwell Perkins on behalf of Scribner's, which becomes his publisher. Receives visit from Secretary of Agriculture Henry Wallace at Ripshin. Begins contributing political articles to *The American Spectator* and *Today*. Becomes enthusiastic supporter of Franklin D. Roosevelt. Travels to West Virginia to report on condition of coal miners for *Today*. Continues to work on memoir "I Build My House."

1934   Tours the South for *Today*, reporting on impact of New Deal programs. Dramatic adaptation of *Winesburg, Ohio*, revised by Jasper Deeter, opens in June at the Hedgerow Theatre, Deeter's community theater in Rose Valley,

Pennsylvania. In November and December makes motor tour with Eleanor through the Midwest to gather material for journalism; they have dinner on December 9 in St. Paul, Minnesota, with Gertrude Stein and Alice B. Toklas, who are touring America. *No Swank*, a short collection of articles including title profile of Henry Wallace, published in a limited edition by Centaur Press in December.

1935   Travels to Texas with Eleanor in January, making stops along the way in Vicksburg, Baton Rouge, and New Orleans; they stay in Corpus Christi and then Brownsville, making frequent visits across the Rio Grande to Matamoros, Mexico. Returns to New Orleans in February for reunion with Gertrude Stein, their last encounter. Works on novel "Brother Earl" (soon abandoned), based on his brother's life. *Puzzled America*, collection of *Today* articles, published by Scribner's in March. Accompanies Eleanor on trip through the South where she has a series of speaking engagements; they have brief visit with Eugene O'Neill in Sea Island, Georgia. Writes admiringly to Thomas Wolfe after reading *Of Time and the River*: "Some things I can write but you—you are a real novelist." In May travels to Roanoke, Virginia, to observe for a few days (at the request of Secretary of the Treasury Morgenthau) the conspiracy trial of members of a local bootlegging operation. Works on play *They Shall Be Free*. Returns to Roanoke for last days of trial and writes article on the case, published in *Liberty*; soon begins *Kit Brandon*, a novel on same subject. Reports on American Federation of Labor convention in Atlantic City in October. Immerses himself in the letters of Vincent van Gogh, which he says have become "a kind of Bible" to him.

1936   Lectures in Chicago in January. Drives with Eleanor and Mary Emmett, widow of friend Burton Emmett, on tour of the Southwest; Anderson and Eleanor have difficulty getting along with Mary and travel on without her. (The three will continue to be close, but with continuing frictions.) Anderson enjoys six-week stay in Tucson, Arizona. They drive back through Texas and arrive in New Orleans in late March for brief visit. Anderson works on play *Man Has Hands* and on autobiographical narrative "Rudolph's Book of Days" (which will become part of posthumously published *Sherwood Anderson's Memoirs*, edited by Paul

Rosenfeld). Spends a month with Eleanor in New York; sees many friends, including Paul Rosenfeld and Ben Hecht. *Kit Brandon* published; receives some strong reviews (including one by Alfred Kazin) but does not sell well. Visits Florida and North Carolina with Eleanor.

1937   Depressed and ill during January vacation in Texas; hospitalized with intestinal flu. Spends rest of winter at Ripshin. Writes radio play "Textiles," accepted for CBS series "Land of Plenty" but not broadcast because series is canceled. During trips to New York in April and May, meets Thomas Wolfe and James T. Farrell. Works on novel "How Green the Grass." Participates in writers' conference at the University of Colorado in August; others present include John Peale Bishop, Evelyn Scott, and John Crowe Ransom. Visited at Ripshin by Thomas Wolfe. *Plays: Winesburg and Others* published in September. Abandons novel and works on memoirs. Again in New York from October to December, sees Thomas Wolfe and meets young admirer Edward Dahlberg; meets with William Faulkner at the latter's request after Faulkner burns himself badly on a steampipe following heavy drinking. Friendship with Wolfe cools after Wolfe quarrels drunkenly with Eleanor at New York dinner party hosted by Anderson and then subsequently accosts Anderson with an angry tirade in a hotel lobby.

1938   Accompanies Eleanor to Chicago; when her work there is finished at the end of January, they travel south to Texas and then (with Mary Emmett and a friend) to Mexico. After some weeks in Mexico City, Anderson and Eleanor go off to Acapulco; they return to Brownsville, Texas, in mid-March and go back to Marion in mid-April. In July Eleanor accepts administrative job with YWCA that will necessitate living in New York; Anderson is deeply opposed but recognizes the financial necessity of accepting in view of the diminished sales of his books. Works on novel "A Late Spring" and becomes depressed when it fails to develop properly. Eleanor goes to New York to begin her new job at the beginning of October, and Anderson joins her there several weeks later.

1939   Travels to Olivet College, Michigan, as writer in residence for the winter term. Rejoins Eleanor for a month in New York, then travels alone to New Orleans for several weeks before returning to Marion. Spends spring in New York;

enjoys meeting Chilean writer María Luisa Bombal. Returns to Olivet in July for writers' conference also attended by Katherine Anne Porter and Padraic Colum. Attends Lexington Trots harness races in Kentucky and writes about them for *Esquire* ("Here They Come"). Delivers lecture on "Man and His Imagination" at Princeton in October. Accompanies Eleanor on business trip to the West and Southwest, October–December. Meets John Steinbeck in San Francisco, visits migrant labor camp near Fresno, and in Los Angeles sees Anita Loos and her guest Aldous Huxley. Works on memoirs.

1940   In Washington in January meets with representatives of Alliance Book Corporation and Farm Security Administration who ask him to write the text for *Home Town*, a book on small towns illustrated with FSA-commissioned photographs. Settles with Eleanor at the Royalton Hotel in New York for the winter. Suffers long bout of flu. Returns to Virginia in May. Works intensively on memoirs. Attends Olivet writers' conference where he meets Robert Penn Warren. *Home Town* published in October. Plans trip to South America.

1941   In New York City in January, works on his memoirs and practices his Spanish for planned South American trip with Eleanor. Travels home and then to Tampa, hoping without success to find a Spanish family willing to help him with his language skills. Returns to New York, ready for the voyage by way of Panama to Chile. Makes an agreement with Viking Press to purchase the rights to his works, except for *Winesburg, Ohio* and *A Story Teller's Story*, for just under $2,000. At a party on February 27, inadvertently swallows a toothpick, stuck in a cocktail olive. Sails the next day, and begins to suffer from abdominal pain. On March 5, is taken by ambulance to Colón Hospital in Colón, Panama. Dies on March 8 of peritonitis. Eleanor returns with his body to Marion, where he is buried on March 26 at Round Hill Cemetery, under a grave marker designed by Wharton Esherick, bearing the motto, chosen long before by Anderson: "Life not death is the great adventure."

Note on the Texts

This volume contains all of the story collections Sherwood Anderson published during his lifetime—*Winesburg, Ohio* (1919), *The Triumph of the Egg* (1921), *Horses and Men* (1923), and *Death in the Woods* (1933)—along with a selection of 15 stories he did not include in these books. The texts of Anderson's story collections have been taken from the first printings of the first editions, with the exception of the text of *Winesburg, Ohio*, which incorporates a handful of corrections made in later printings. The texts of Anderson's uncollected stories have been taken from a variety of sources, discussed below.

Winesburg, Ohio: A Group of Tales of Ohio Small Town Life. In his *Memoirs*—written late in life, and published posthumously—Anderson remembered finishing the interconnected stories of *Winesburg, Ohio* "in a few months, one following the other, a kind of joyous time for me, the words and ideas flowing freely, very little revision to be done." In fact, the composition of *Winesburg* was neither so rapid nor so effortless. Anderson's *Winesburg* manuscripts, now among his papers at the Newberry Library in Chicago, show considerable evidence of rewriting. He arranged and on more than one occasion rearranged the stories before submitting them for publication as a book. All told, he may have taken as long as two and a half years—from November 1915 to April 1918—to complete them.

Still, Anderson's recollection of an intensely creative "few months" only mildly exaggerates the pace at which *Winesburg* came into being. He began, very probably, in November 1915, with "The Book of the Grotesque"—an introductory reverie which gave him a working title for the collection and an outline of its final form—and the story "Hands." " 'Queer' " was probably finished in December 1915, because early in January Anderson learned that H. L. Mencken had decided not to publish it in *The Smart Set*. By November 1916, when Anderson wrote to Waldo Frank proposing that Frank publish some of the stories in *Seven Arts*, he reported he had written 15 of these "intensive studies of people in my home town, Clyde, Ohio," out of the 25 stories in the published *Winesburg* (counting the parts of "Godliness" separately).

The order in which each of the stories was written—"one following the other," as Anderson later remembered it—cannot be determined precisely. William L. Phillips, in "How Sherwood Anderson Wrote

Winesburg, Ohio" (*American Literature* 23.1 [March 1951]: 7–30), argues that the scrap paper on which Anderson drafted the stories offers substantial evidence toward an understanding of their composition history. Details within the stories provide additional evidence: "The Philosopher," "Death," "Sophistication," and "Departure" appear to have been among the last of the *Winesburg* stories to be written because they refer to scenes, incidents, and characters previously introduced.

Anderson began trying to publish stories from *Winesburg* in magazines almost immediately after he had begun the collection. Floyd Dell, coeditor of *The Masses*, was the first to print one, in February 1916, followed by Margaret Anderson at *The Little Review* and Waldo Frank at *Seven Arts*. The serial publication history of the stories in *Winesburg, Ohio* is given in more detail in the list below. Those stories that did not appear in magazines are marked with an asterisk (*):

The Book of the Grotesque: *Masses* 8 (February 1916): 17.
Hands: *Masses* 8 (March 1916): 5, 7.
Paper Pills: *Little Review* 3 (June–July 1916): 7–9 (as "The Philosopher").
Mother: *Seven Arts* 1 (March 1917): 452–61.
*The Philosopher
*Nobody Knows
*Godliness (Parts I and II)
*Surrender (Part III)
*Terror (Part IV)
A Man of Ideas: *Little Review* 5 (June 1918): 22–28 (as "The Man of Ideas").
*Adventure
*Respectability
The Thinker: *Seven Arts* 2 (September 1917): 584–97.
*Tandy
The Strength of God: *Masses* 8 (August 1916): 12–13.
*The Teacher
*Loneliness
An Awakening: *Little Review* 5 (December 1918): 13–21.
"Queer": *Seven Arts* 1 (December 1916): 97–108.
The Untold Lie: *Seven Arts* 1 (January 1917): 215–21.
*Drink
*Death
*Sophistication
*Departure

The magazine texts of the *Winesburg* stories differ, usually in minor ways, from both the surviving manuscripts and the published book

texts; "Hands" and "The Untold Lie" contain more substantial varia-
tion.

Anderson sent his publisher John Lane a copy of the collection in
May or June 1918, but sales of Anderson's previous books—*Windy
McPherson's Son* (1916), *Marching Men* (1917), and *Mid-American
Chants* (1918)—had been disappointing, and Lane reportedly found
the new work "too gloomy." Anderson traveled to New York to find
another publisher, and by December he had signed a contract with
B. W. Huebsch. (Francis Hackett, literary editor of *The New Republic*,
had done Anderson the favor of introducing the two.) Huebsch later
claimed that the collection had been presented to him without a title
and that he had suggested *Winesburg, Ohio*, but Anderson had referred to the book as *Winesburg* in his correspondence at least as early
as April 1918; he may also have circulated it among publishers as *The
Book of the Grotesque*. Huebsch suggested that Anderson work with
the illustrator Harald Toksvig to produce a sketch map of Winesburg
for the front endpaper.

Anderson read proofs of *Winesburg, Ohio* most probably in January
1919, and the book was published on May 8. It sold well enough
to warrant six additional printings: in December 1919, January and
December 1921, March 1922, March 1927 (as a Viking Press book,
Huebsch having merged with the larger firm), and June 1931. The
second of these printings contains nine corrections of typographical
errors, and there are two further corrections in the fifth. These corrections may have been made at Anderson's request: in August 1919,
he had sent Huebsch a list of errors found in the first printing. (His
list is not known to have survived.) Two other firms published *Winesburg, Ohio* during Anderson's lifetime, both in 1922: Jonathan Cape,
in London, and Boni & Liveright in New York (in their Modern
Library series). Both of these firms borrowed the Huebsch printing
plates rather than resetting the text. In 1925, a selection of stories from
Winesburg was published as *Hands, and Other Stories* by Haldeman-
Julius, in the Little Blue Book series, but Anderson was not involved
in the preparation of this edition.

Since Anderson's death several corrected or critical editions of *Winesburg* have appeared. In 1960, in a new text for the Viking Press,
Malcolm Cowley corrected "discrepancies in the spellings of proper
names" and made other changes—including the insertion of 37
commas—"needed to make Anderson's meaning clear." In 1997, Ray
Lewis White published an edition with Ohio University Press that
adopts a number of variant readings from Anderson's manuscripts,
emends "scores and scores of inconsistencies" in spelling and punctuation, and makes other changes intended to clarify Anderson's mean-
ings. In the present volume, the text of *Winesburg, Ohio* has been

taken from the corrected fifth printing of the first edition, published
by B. W. Huebsch in 1922.

*The Triumph of the Egg: A Book of Impressions from American Life in
Tales and Poems.* Anderson sent B. W. Huebsch a typescript of his
second collection of stories on March 24, 1921, but he was still unsure
what to title the book. In January, his friend Paul Rosenfeld had tried
to dissuade him from "Some Americans": "The Triumph of the Egg
was ever so much more colorful." Huebsch disliked "Unlighted
Lamps," another title Anderson proposed, because it sounded "too
much like O. Henry." But *The Triumph of the Egg*, Huebsch advo-
cated persuasively, "sounds like nothing else, and is a most arresting
title."

All but one of the stories in the collection had appeared in magazines or had been accepted for publication when Anderson submitted
his typescript. In early April, he sent "Unlighted Lamps"—the one
exception—to H. L. Mencken, who published it in *The Smart Set* in
July. Similarly, Anderson placed three of the previously unpublished
poems in the collection in the final issue of *Voices* (London), to appear
in the fall. The prior publication history of each of the parts of *The
Triumph of the Egg* is described in the list below:

[untitled opening poem]: *Voices* 5 (Autumn 1921): 107–9 (as "The
    Teller of Tales").
The Dumb Man: first published in *Triumph of the Egg* (1921).
I Want to Know Why: *Smart Set* 60 (November 1919): 35–40.
Seeds: *Little Review* 5 (July 1918): 24–31.
The Other Woman: *Little Review* 7 (May–June 1920): 37–44.
The Egg: *Dial* 68 (March 1920): 295–304 (as "The Triumph of the
    Egg").
Unlighted Lamps: *Smart Set* 65 (July 1921): 45–55.
Senility: *Little Review* 5 (September 1918): 37–39.
The Man in the Brown Coat: *Little Review* 7 (January–March
    1921): 18–21.
Brothers: *Bookman* 53 (April 1921): 110–15.
The Door of the Trap: *Dial* 68 (May 1920): 567–76.
The New Englander: *Dial* 70 (February 1921): 143–58.
War: *Little Review* 3 (May 1916): 7–10 (as "The Struggle").
Motherhood: *Voices* 5 (Autumn 1921): 107–9.
Out of Nowhere into Nothing: *Dial* 71 (July, August, September
    1921): 1–18, 153–69, 325–46.
The Man with the Trumpet: *Voices* 5 (Autumn 1921): 107–9 (as
    "The Tired Man").

Along with these stories and poems, Anderson arranged for the inclusion of "Impressions in Clay," a previously unpublished portfolio of photographs (by Eugene Hutchinson) of seven portrait busts by his wife Tennessee Mitchell.

Anderson urged Huebsch to provide him with a set of proofs by May 1, when he was scheduled to sail for Europe, so he could read them at sea and return them in time for publication early in the fall. As it happened, the typesetter sent an incomplete set of proofs, and publication was delayed until October 24, 1921. *The Triumph of the Egg* went through at least three additional printings (in December 1921, February 1922, and August 1924), and a British version was published by Jonathan Cape in 1922, but Anderson did not alter the text of his collection. The text of *The Triumph of the Egg* in the present volume has been taken from the first printing of the first edition.

Horses and Men: Tales, Long and Short, from Our American Life. On May 16, 1923, Anderson sent Huebsch "copy for the new book of tales—HORSES AND MEN." He had only just completed some of the longer stories in the collection—"'Unused'," "The Man Who Became a Woman," and "An Ohio Pagan"—and they were published in the forthcoming book for the first time. (Two of these—"'Unused'" and "An Ohio Pagan"—were drawn from *Ohio Pagans*, an unfinished novel.) The first part of the two-part story "A Chicago Hamlet" was previously unpublished as well; Anderson had published the second part separately in March, as "Broken," but revised it considerably for the new collection. The rest of the stories in the volume had appeared in magazines during the previous two years, as detailed in the list below. To these, he added a prefatory appreciation of Theodore Dreiser that had first appeared in 1916:

Dreiser: *Little Review* 3 (April 1916): 5.

I'm a Fool: *Dial* 72 (February 1922): 119–29.

The Triumph of a Modern: *New Republic* 33 (January 31, 1923): 245–47.

"Unused": first published in *Horses and Men* (1923).

A Chicago Hamlet: first published in *Horses and Men* (1923), revising and incorporating the story "Broken," *Century* 105 (March 1923): 643–56.

The Man Who Became a Woman: first publication in *Horses and Men* (1923).

Milk Bottles: *Vanity Fair* 16 (March 1921): 23–24 (as "Why There Must Be a Midwestern Literature").

The Sad Horn Blowers: *Harper's* 146 (February 1923): 273–89.
A Man's Story: *Dial* 75 (September 1923): 277–64. This story was
  begun as part of *Talbot Whittingham*, a novel Anderson
  would later abandon.
An Ohio Pagan: first published in *Horses and Men* (1923).

Anderson read proofs beginning in mid-July, returning a final set in
early August. Huebsch published *Horses and Men* on October 26,
1923. The collection was subsequently published in London by Jonathan Cape in 1924, and in London and New York by Jonathan Cape
and Harrison Smith in 1927, but Anderson is not known to have
corrected or altered his original text. In the present volume, the text
of *Horses and Men* has been taken from the 1923 Huebsch first printing.

Death in the Woods and Other Stories. Anderson sent a typescript of his
new collection *Death in the Woods* to Horace Liveright—his publisher
since 1925—at the beginning of 1933, having arranged its contents a
few months earlier. When the proofs arrived in February he found he
was dissatisfied with the book, however, and asked Liveright to make
significant changes: two stories were to be cut, and four to be added
("These Mountaineers," "A Meeting South," "The Flood," and
"Brother Death"). Liveright accommodated Anderson's requests, and
published *Death in the Woods* on April 8, 1933.
   The prior publication history of each story is given below:

Death in the Woods: *American Mercury* 9 (September 1926):
  7–13. See also *Tar: A Midwest Childhood* (New York: Boni &
  Liveright, 1926), pp. 231–33, and "Girl by the Stove," *Decision*
  1 (January 1941): 19–22, in which similar events are narrated.
The Return: *Century* 110 (May 1925): 3–14.
There She Is—She Is Taking Her Bath: first published in *Death in
  the Woods* (1933). Anderson had hoped to include this story in
  Horses and Men (1923), but was unable to because *Pictorial
  Review*, which had paid for first serial publication rights, did
  not print it in a timely fashion. They ultimately chose not to
  publish it at all, but allowed him to include it in the later
  collection.
The Lost Novel: *Scribner's* 84 (September 1928): 255–58; *Alice and
  The Lost Novel* (London: Elkin Mathews & Marrot, 1929),
  pp. 19–28.
The Fight: *Vanity Fair* 29 (October 1927): 72, 106, 108.
Like a Queen: *Harper's Bazaar* 63 (January 1929): 78–79, 118 (as
  "Beauty"); *Alice and The Lost Novel* (1929), pp. 3–15 (as
  "Alice").

That Sophistication: *Vanity Fair* 31 (December 1928): 68, 116.
In a Strange Town: *Scribner's* 87 (January 1930): 20–25.
These Mountaineers: *Vanity Fair* 33 (January 1930): 44–45, 94;
    This Quarter 3 (April–May–June 1931), 602–9.
A Sentimental Journey: *Vanity Fair* 29 (January 1928): 46, 118;
    Hello Towns! (New York: Horace Liveright, 1929), pp. 265–72.
A Jury Case: *American Mercury* 12 (December 1927): 431–34.
Another Wife: *Scribner's* 80 (December 1926): 587–94.
A Meeting South: *Dial* 78 (April 1925): 269–79; *Sherwood
    Anderson's Notebook* (New York: Boni & Liveright, 1926),
    pp. 103–21.
The Flood: first published in *Death in the Woods* (1933).
Why They Got Married: *Vanity Fair* 32 (March 1929): 74, 116.
Brother Death: first published in *Death in the Woods* (1933).
    Originally part of an unfinished novel, *Thanksgiving*.

Liveright went into bankruptcy soon after *Death in the Woods* was
published and only one printing of the collection appeared during
Anderson's lifetime. The text of *Death in the Woods* in the present
volume has been taken from that first printing.

Uncollected Stories. This volume concludes with a selection of 15 stories that Anderson did not gather in any of his books. They are presented in approximate chronological order of composition. Ten were
published in magazines during Anderson's lifetime and one in a
hardcover anthology; four remained unpublished. Two of the unpublished stories, "White Spot" and "A Landed Proprietor," have been
associated posthumously—in *Sherwood Anderson's Memoirs: A Critical Edition* (1969)—with a collection of autobiographical writings on
which Anderson was at work, along with other fiction and nonfiction,
toward the end of his life. Had Anderson lived, he might have published these stories as parts of such a collection rather than in a book
of stories: his final intentions remain ambiguous, and the line between
fiction and memoir is one he blurred or crossed often throughout his
career.
    The list below gives the source from which the text of each uncol-
lected story in the present volume has been taken and further information about their textual histories:

Sister: *The Little Review* 2 (December 1915): 3–4.
The White Streak: *The Smart Set* 55 (July 1918): 27–30.
Certain Things Last: *Certain Things Last: The Selected Short Stories
    of Sherwood Anderson*, Charles E. Modlin, ed. (New York:
    Four Walls Eight Windows, 1992), pp. 1–7. This story was
    probably written in the early 1920s but was not published

during Anderson's lifetime. The text in *Certain Things Last* was prepared from Anderson's untitled, annotated typescript, now at the Newberry Library; the title was supplied by Charles E. Modlin.

Off Balance: *The New Yorker* 9 (August 5, 1933): 12–14.

I Get So I Can't Go On: *Story* 3 (December 1933): 55–62.

Mr. Joe's Doctor: *American Magazine* 118 (August 1934): 81–82.

The Corn Planting: *American Magazine* 118 (November 1934): 47, 149–50.

Feud: *American Magazine* 119 (February 1935): 71, 112–14.

Harry Breaks Through: *The New Caravan*, Alfred Kreymborg, Lewis Mumford, Paul Rosenfeld, eds. (New York: W. W. Norton, 1936), pp. 84–89.

Mrs. Wife: *Certain Things Last*, pp. 271–87. This story was published during Anderson's lifetime as "A Moonlight Walk" (*Redbook* 70 [December 1937]: 43–45) in a version substantially revised by his mother-in-law, Laura Copenhaver, without his direct involvement. The text in *Certain Things Last* was prepared from an earlier typescript of the story, without Copenhaver's revisions.

Two Lovers: *Story* 14 (January–February 1939): 16–25.

White Spot: *Sherwood Anderson's Memoirs: A Critical Edition*, Ray Lewis White, ed. (Chapel Hill: University of North Carolina Press, 1969), pp. 230–34. This story, probably written in 1939, was first published posthumously in *The Sherwood Anderson Reader*, Paul Rosenfeld, ed. (Boston: Houghton Mifflin, 1947). The text in *Sherwood Anderson's Memoirs* was prepared from a Newberry Library manuscript, with some correction of punctuation and spelling and occasional emendation of "ambiguous sentences."

Nobody Laughed: *Certain Things Last*, pp. 307–17. Unpublished during Anderson's lifetime, this story went through several revisions in typescript, its title changing from "Playthings" to "The Town's Playthings" to "Nobody Laughed." It was first published, with revisions by Paul Rosenfeld, in *The Sherwood Anderson Reader* (1947). The text in *Certain Things Last* was prepared from the last of Anderson's typescripts (c. 1939).

A Landed Proprietor: *Sherwood Anderson's Memoirs: A Critical Edition*, pp. 57–62. First published in *The Rotarian* 58 (March 1941): 8–10. The text in *Sherwood Anderson's Memoirs* was prepared from a Newberry Library manuscript, with some correction of punctuation and spelling and occasional emendation of "ambiguous sentences."

The Persistent Liar: *Tomorrow* 6 (September 1946): 10–12.

This volume presents the texts of the editions chosen for inclusion here but does not attempt to reproduce every feature of their typographic design. The texts are reprinted without change, except for the correction of typographical errors. Spelling, punctuation, and capitalization are often expressive features, and they are not altered, even when inconsistent or irregular. The following is a list of typographical errors corrected, cited by page and line number: 7.9, carelessness; 9.6, has been; 20.1, Sinning's; 35.34, Winny's; 51.15, Aunt Sallie; 54.23, Hardy's; 68.25–26, Sinning's; 76.31, them Sometimes; 86.5, become; 92.15, track's; 99.36, than; 113.9, Winter's; 127.6, Nate; 134.33, Hanby; 143.2, Hearn's; 149.25, you-ve; 157.22, Wracker's; 173.37, Westley; 173.39 (and *passim*), Westley's; 180.16, Smallet; 180.18, over night; 206.25, Churchhill; 212.4, before its; 217.31, than; 222.2, superflous; 250.3, "You; 281.11, at dog.; 285.29, recah; 288.7, tinker it.; 297.13, still ,also; 305.6, bangs; 312.21, away..; 315.38, uncomforable; 332.4, the the; 338.25, on odd; 340.29, out hot; 345.10, women; 350.11, want her of; 382.22, trees,; 390.4, Lot's; 417.24, said she; 421.26, .lands; 426.4, Nickle; 433.7, hillock,—; 436.18, May had; 436.38, away."; 437.40, cloth s; 444.40, the house,"; 445.18, build; 447.35, Lets; 488.24, trapsing; 496.22, of being; 496.33, Gears,; 515.40, night,; 523.26, wonderd; 534.23, Sundey; 535.8, carrry; 535.28, resent; 540.16, arrive,; 565.17, her couch; 594.4, Tom ran; 660.36, undertand; 697.15, make; 729.34, scholar's sister; 782.36, But didn't; 802.37, "Senator; 803.8, Air."; 803.15, A'in't; 803.37, A'in't; 804.5, a'in't; 829.4, A.P.; 830.5, day'; 834.21, time (A. P.; 834.37–38, students.; 836.35, wife.'; 858.29, No,'"; 859.14, up,"; 860.26, mother. She.

Acknowledgments

From *Horses and Men*, "Foreword," "Dreiser," "Unused," "The Man Who Became a Woman," and "An Ohio Pagan" copyright © 1923 by B. W. Huebsch, Inc., copyright renewed © 1950 by Eleanor Copenhaver Anderson; "The Triumph of a Modern," copyright © 1923 by The Republic Publishing Co., copyright renewed © 1950 by Eleanor Copenhaver Anderson; "A Chicago Hamlet" copyright © 1923 by D. Appleton-Century Company, Inc., copyright renewed © 1950 by Eleanor Copenhaver Anderson; "The Sad Horn Blowers" copyright © 1923 by Harper & Brothers, copyright renewed © 1950 by Eleanor Copenhaver Anderson. Reprinted with permission of The Newberry Library.

Death in the Woods and Other Stories copyright © 1933 by Sherwood Anderson. Copyright renewed © 1960 by Eleanor Copenhaver Anderson. Reprinted with permission of The Newberry Library.

"Certain Things Last" copyright © 1992 by Charles E. Modlin, Hilbert H. Campbell, and Christopher R. Sergel, trustees of the Sherwood Anderson Literary Estate Trust; "Off Balance" copyright 1933 by F-R Pub. Corp., copyright renewed © 1960 by Eleanor Copenhaver Anderson; "I Get So I Can't Go On" copyright © 1933 by Story Magazine, Inc., copyright renewed © 1960 by Eleanor Copenhaver Anderson; "Mr. Joe's Doctor" copyright © 1934 by Crowell Pub. Co., copyright renewed © 1960 by Eleanor Copenhaver Anderson; "The Corn Planting" copyright © 1934 by Crowell Pub. Co., copyright renewed © 1961 by Eleanor Copenhaver Anderson; "Feud" copyright © 1935 by Crowell Pub. Co., copyright renewed © 1962 by Eleanor Copenhaver Anderson; "Mrs. Wife" copyright © 1937 by McCall Corp., copyright renewed © 1965 by Eleanor Copenhaver Anderson; "Two Lovers" copyright © 1938 by Story Magazine, copyright renewed © 1966 by Eleanor Copenhaver Anderson; "White Spot" and "Nobody Laughed," copyright © 1947 by Eleanor Anderson, copyright renewed © 1975 by Eleanor Anderson; "A Landed Proprietor" copyright © 1941 by Rotary International, copyright renewed © 1968 by Eleanor Copenhaver Anderson; "The Persistent Liar" copyright © 1946 by Creative Age Press, Inc., copyright renewed © 1974 by Eleanor Copenhaver Anderson. Reprinted with permission of The Newberry Library.

Notes

In the notes below, the reference numbers denote page and line of this volume (the line count includes titles and headings but not blank lines). No note is made for material included in standard desk-reference books. Biblical references are keyed to the King James version. For further information on Anderson's life and works, and references to other studies, see Hilbert H. Campbell, ed., *The Sherwood Anderson Diaries, 1936–1941* (Athens: University of Georgia Press, 1987); Hilbert H. Campbell and Charles E. Modlin, eds., *Sherwood Anderson: Centennial Studies* (Troy, NY: Whitston Publishing Company, 1976); Charles E. Modlin, ed., *Certain Things Last: The Selected Short Stories of Sherwood Anderson* (New York: Four Walls Eight Windows, 1992); Walter B. Rideout, *Sherwood Anderson: A Writer in America* (2 vols. Madison: University of Wisconsin Press, 2006–07); Kim Townsend, *Sherwood Anderson: A Biography* (Boston: Houghton Mifflin, 1987); Ray Lewis White, ed., *Sherwood Anderson's Winesburg, Ohio: With Variant Readings and Annotations* (Athens: Ohio University Press, 1997); Ray Lewis White, ed., *Sherwood Anderson's Memoirs: A Critical Edition* (Chapel Hill: University of North Carolina Press, 1969); and Ray Lewis White, ed., *Sherwood Anderson: Early Writings* (Kent: Kent State University Press, 1989).

WINESBURG, OHIO

5.15   Andersonville prison] Camp Sumter, Confederate prisoner-of-war camp in Macon County, Georgia, where nearly a third of some 45,000 Union prisoners died of disease, exposure, and other causes. Henry Wirz, the camp's commander, was executed for war crimes on November 10, 1865.

28.13   Doctor Cronin] Patrick Henry Cronin (1846–1889), an Irish-born physician and member of the secret Irish nationalist organization Clan-na-Gael, was expelled and assassinated on suspicion of being a British agent. His decomposing body was found in a Chicago sewer.

28.34   the Big Four] The Central Pacific Railroad, so called after its four principal executives: Leland Stanford (1824–1893), Collis P. Huntington (1821–1900), Mark Hopkins (1813–1878), and Charles Crocker (1822–1888).

41.20–21   another Jesse . . . old] Father of David, as recounted in 1 Samuel.

43.22   the old Bible story] See 1 Samuel 9–29.

68.10   Pop Geers]   Edward Franklin "Pop" Geers (1851–1924), Tennessee-born horse trainer and harness racer.

68.18   Pheidippides]   Courier (c. 530–490 BCE) who ran from Marathon to Sparta to announce the Greek victory over the Persians, and fell dead after having done so.

78.21–22   The Epworth League]   Fellowship organized in 1889 by the Methodist Episcopal Church in Cleveland, Ohio, to encourage and train young people in churchmanship and religious life.

90.25   McKinley and Mark Hanna]   Hanna (1837–1904), a millionaire businessman and U.S. senator, managed William McKinley's presidential campaigns in 1896 and 1900.

113.25   Charles Lamb]   English essayist (1775–1834) known chiefly for *Tales from Shakespeare* (1807) and *Essays of Elia* (1823).

113.33   Benvenuto Cellini]   Italian goldsmith and sculptor (1500–1571); his *Autobiography* was written between 1558 and 1563.

128.26   Cedar Point]   A Sandusky, Ohio, amusement park, which opened in 1870.

THE TRIUMPH OF THE EGG

181.5–11   In the fields . . . *Chants*]   From the poem "Chant To Dawn in a Factory Town," published in Anderson's *Mid-American Chants* (1918).

182.2–3   ROBERT AND JOHN ANDERSON]   Anderson's sons, born in 1907 and 1908.

185.3   *Tennessee Mitchell*]   Anderson's second wife (1874–1929).

185.4   EUGENE HUTCHINSON]   A Chicago portrait photographer (1880–1957).

203.18–19   waiting. // Upstairs]   Anderson may or may not have intended a new stanza here: in the only versions of "The Dumb Man" published during his lifetime, the line break coincides with a new page. The same is true at two other points within the poem, on page 204, lines 11–12 ("forward. / Her") and page 205, lines 3–4 ("story. // If") in the present volume.

215.2   a small man with a beard]   The main character of this story was based on a close friend of Anderson's, the psychoanalyst Trigant Burrow (1875–1950), author of *The Social Basis of Consciousness* (1927) and *The Structure of Insanity* (1932).

237.26–29   Christopher Columbus . . . stand on its end.]   In an anecdote dating at least to the 16th century, Columbus is said to have challenged fellow diners to make an egg stand on its head, a feat he then accomplished by cracking the shell slightly at the tip.

265.32 Cox] James M. Cox (1870–1957), governor of Ohio who ran for president on the Democratic ticket in 1920, with Franklin D. Roosevelt as his running mate, and was defeated by Warren Harding.

266.8–10 Chicago newspapers . . . with an actress.] Likely a reference to newspaper publisher William Randolph Hearst (1863–1951) and his affair with Marion Davies (1897–1961), with whom he lived openly after 1919.

266.22–24 Chicago newspapers . . . story of a murder] Anderson alludes to the case of Carl Otto Wanderer (1895–1921), who was executed for the murder of his wife Ruth Johnson in 1920. The case was investigated and solved by the journalist Ben Hecht, a close friend of Anderson.

HORSES AND MEN

368.2–3 *Heavy, heavy . . . or superfine?*] Phrases associated with forfeits, a children's game.

368.4 Theodore Dreiser is old] Dreiser (1871–1945) was fifty-two when *Horses and Men* was published.

368.19 *Delineator*] Dreiser was editor of the women's magazine *The Delineator* from 1907 to 1909.

373.14 swipe] Groom for horses at a racetrack.

374.22 Murphy and Walter Cox] Tommy Murphy and Walter Cox, well-known jockeys.

375.3 Deep River] An African-American spiritual.

375.36 skates] Nags; worn-out horses.

378.10 "About Ben Ahem"] The allusion is to Leigh Hunt's poem "Abou Ben Adhem" (1834).

382.9 tin horn] Cheap; of low quality.

383.23 Dan Patch] Stallion (1896–1916) famous as the champion harness horse of his day.

386.28–29 George Moore, Clive Bell, Paul Rosenfeld] George Moore (1852–1933), Irish novelist, poet, and art critic; Clive Bell (1881–1964), English art critic; Paul Rosenfeld (1890–1946), American music critic, a close friend of Anderson.

388.6 vorticist] Member of English modernist school of art and poetics led by Wyndham Lewis (1882–1957) and Ezra Pound (1885–1972).

406.20 Nickel Plate Railroad] The New York, Chicago, and St. Louis Railroad Company (1881–1964).

421.8–9 "The stone which the builders refused . . . of the corner."] See Psalms 1:22.

430.17–18   K of Ps]   Knights of Pythias, a fraternal organization founded in 1864.

460.32   Carl Sandburg]   Sandburg (1878–1967), a friend of Anderson, published his *Chicago Poems* in 1916. He was the regular movie critic for the *Chicago Daily News* from 1920 to 1928.

461.11   President McKinley . . . Mark Hanna]   See note 90.25.

461.31–32   Fitzsimmons . . . Australian]   The British-born boxer Bob Fitzsimmons (1863–1917) began his professional boxing career in Australia. He became world middleweight champion after defeating Jack Dempsey in 1891. He defeated Jim Corbett to win the heavyweight championship in 1897.

468.11   whippletree]   Bar-shaped device used in agriculture and elsewhere to equalize distribution of force.

469.10–14   A man came into . . . with her hair.]   See Luke 7:36–50.

485.5   bones, a hank of hair]   See Rudyard Kipling, "The Vampire" (1897), lines 1–3: "A fool there was and he made his prayer / (Even as you and I!) / To a rag, a bone, and a hank of hair."

492.16–17   Alfred Kreymborg]   The name alone recalls Anderson's friend the poet Alfred Kreymborg (1883–1966), to whose magazine *Broom* Anderson contributed work.

494.9–10   the old Harry]   Hell (as in, "raising the old Harry").

496.8   Pop Geers]   See note 68.10.

525.1   soc-dolager]   Or sockdolager; a beaut, a lulu, a humdinger.

525.2–3   Mencken . . . America]   H. L. Mencken (1880–1956) called Chicago "the literary capital of the United States" in his 1917 article "Civilized Chicago."

525.31–32   Mr. Sandburg . . . Mr. Masters]   Carl Sandburg (1878–1976) and Edgar Lee Masters (1868–1950), principal figures of the Chicago literary renaissance.

547.26   Woman's Relief Corps]   Patriotic organization founded in 1883, an auxiliary of the veterans' organization the Grand Army of the Republic.

561.18   fordson]   Brand name of tractors manufactured by Henry Ford & Son, Inc., and subsequently by Ford Motor Company.

561.37–38   "He did not wear . . . are red"]   See Oscar Wilde, "The Ballad of Reading Gaol" (1898), lines 1–2: "He did not wear his scarlet coat / For blood and wine are red."

573.31–32   "The Light of the World"]   Pierre Saisson's play of this title was produced in the United States in 1920. There is no known film version.

576.4–14   Thomas Edwards . . . wonderful tale]   Edwards (1739–1810) published an account of his life in *Y Greal* in 1805. Anderson's account follows that of George Borrow in his travel book *Wild Wales* (1862).

577.10   Bucephalus]   The horse of Alexander the Great.

579.38   John Splan]   Noted trotting horseman, author of *Life with the Trotters* (1889).

DEATH IN THE WOODS

600.2   FERDINAND SCHEVILL]   Schevill (1868–1954), a scholar of European history, taught at the University of Chicago from 1892 to 1937.

617.7   Mansfield as Brutus]   The English actor Richard Mansfield (1857–1907), known for his Shakespearean roles, performed frequently in the United States after 1882.

626.5   General Hurst]   Major General Samuel H. Hurst (1831–1908), who served with distinction in the Civil War, is buried in Chillicothe, Ohio.

645.25   George Borrow]   English author (1803–1881) whose novels *Lavengro* (1851) and *The Romany Rye* (1857) were among Anderson's favorite books.

662.18   dubs]   Fools; mediocrities (American slang).

669.25   Krafft-Ebing]   Richard von Krafft-Ebing (1840–1902), German psychiatrist, author of *Psychopathia Sexualis* (1886), pioneering study of sexual behavior.

713.24   David]   The character is a fictionalized portrait of William Faulkner, whom Anderson had just met.

715.3   a statue of General Jackson]   The statue of Andrew Jackson by Clark Mills was erected in 1856.

UNCOLLECTED STORIES

778.36–37   Coolidge . . . didn't they?]   Calvin Coolidge was alleged to have remarked, when rejecting the forgiveness of Allied war debts, "They hired the money, didn't they?" There is no evidence that he actually said it.

781.33–34   Helen, Thy beauty . . . bark of yore.]   The opening lines of Edgar Allan Poe's "To Helen" (1831).

782.30–31   "When out of Palos . . . Hercules."]   In *Sherwood Anderson's Memoirs* (1969), Anderson remembered these lines as "some verses Mike Carr had once recited to me"; Carr (1881–1929?) was an artist and friend of Anderson. The "gates of Hercules" refers to the Strait of Gibraltar, through which Christopher Columbus, departing from Palos, sailed in 1492.

782.32–33   Tiger, tiger . . . of the night.]   The opening lines of William Blake's "The Tyger," in *Songs of Experience* (1794).

783.6   I am master . . . of my soul.]   See William Ernest Henley's poem "Invictus" (1888), lines 15–16.

783.13–14   William James . . . back of the mind."]   William Ernest Hocking, discussing the notion of the existence of God in *The Christian Century* in 1933 (the year Anderson wrote this story), wrote: "William James once tried to express it, if my memory is not at fault, as a kind of quiet music playing in the back of the mind."

785.18   the street-car bandits]   Peter Niedermeyer, Gustav Marx, and Harvey Van Dine, implicated in seven murders, were executed in Chicago in 1904. The three were also known as the Car Barn Bandits and the Automatic Trio.

804.24   Charles Evans Hughes]   Hughes (1862–1948) served as governor of New York, secretary of state, and chief justice of the Supreme Court.

THE LIBRARY OF AMERICA SERIES

The Library of America fosters appreciation and pride in America's literary heritage by publishing, and keeping permanently in print, authoritative editions of America's best and most significant writing. An independent nonprofit organization, it was founded in 1979 with seed funding from the National Endowment for the Humanities and the Ford Foundation.

To subscribe to the series or to order individual copies, please visit www.loa.org or call (800) 964.5778.